The Soderberg Saga

The Soderberg Saga

In Search of Steenie Bergman
The Bishop's Horse Race
Brother Brigham's Gold
Seven Days for Ruby

BLAINE AND BRENTON
YORGASON

DESERET BOOK COMPANY
SALT LAKE CITY, UTAH

The books in this volume were originally published as follows:

This volume contains the complete and unabridged texts of the original editions.

Library of Congress Catalog Card Number 94-74867

ISBN 0-87579-957-4

Printed in the United States of America

10 9 8 7 6 5 4 3 2 1

Contents

In Search of Steenie Bergman

In Search of Steenie Bergman

Blaine M. Yorgason
Brenton G. Yorgason

Deseret Book Company
Salt Lake City, Utah

We express our gratitude to Rudolf Märkle, proprietor of the Hotel Spinne, in Grindelwald, Switzerland, who provided a wonderfully delightful setting for the creation of this book. We also acknowledge the contributions of Jack Schaefer and Will Henry, whose stirring writings launch so many of our own stories and tales.

For our great-grandfather, Jons Yorgason,
and Aunt Steenie, his first wife.

Foreword

Blaine and Brenton Yorgason have done it again! As in *Chester, I Love You*, they have worked a special kind of magic, providing a warm and touching story of people (amazingly like you or me or someone else we might know), their fascinating friendships with "lower" animals that possess a "higher" kind of love, and the indomitable spirits of both. The resulting human-animal team provides the framework for another masterpiece that you won't be able to put down until you have lived the experiences of the characters to the last word of the last page.

Add to this the Yorgasons' keen spiritual insight, and you have another classic that should be standard reading for anyone seeking a better understanding of such eternal principles as seeking, hearing, and acting upon the promptings of the Holy Spirit.

My whole family looks forward to each new work by the Yorgasons. Each book provides us with a great family adventure as we read together. More important, each touches our lives deeply and lastingly for good. *In Search of Steenie Bergman* is no exception. I am sure that at the conclusion of the book, you will say, as did my family and I, "We can hardly wait for the next one."

LYNN J. ANDERSON

CONSULTANT TO THE U.S. ARMY SURGEON GENERAL
ON HUMAN-ANIMAL BOND ISSUES AND
PRESIDENT OF DELTA SOCIETY INTERNATIONAL:
INTERACTIONS OF PEOPLE, ANIMALS, AND THE ENVIRONMENT

The king of France with twenty-thousand men,
Marched up a hill—and then marched down again.
—old nursery rhyme

Prologue

The young soldier of Company G of Colonel E. B. Alexander's Tenth Infantry leaned upon his musket on the vast sage plain of South Pass, the windy, level-lying spinal hump of the Rocky Mountains, and watched the slow progress of a train of teamsters. The column of heavy wagons of the firm of Russell, Majors, and Waddell was wending its way westward, carrying the copious supplies of the government's Utah Expedition. Around him more soldiers of the Tenth sprawled in repose, the ten-minute break in the march a welcome moment.

Ahead of him were other companies of the Tenth, and behind him, stretching for miles and miles and even days, were other companies of the Tenth and Fifth Infantries. There were also Phelps's and Reno's Batteries—artillery units with their wheeled cannons that would be used to blast the Mormons into submission.

But the resting soldier now watched the ponderous freight wagons and found himself wondering at them. These wagons were of the style called the J. Murphy Wagon, made in St. Louis especially for transporting goods across the plains. They were big and strongly built, with rear wheels over six feet high and ten inches across at the iron-tire. Their front wheels measured only slightly smaller, and each of these prairie behemoths could carry seven thousand pounds of freight.

The wagon boxes, he noticed, were exceptionally commodious, being about as large as the rooms in an ordinary house—

and were covered with two heavy canvas sheets stretched across high arching wooden bows designed to protect the enclosed merchandise from the weather.

The young soldier had been told that these particular wagons had been sent out from Leavenworth, each loaded with just six thousand pounds of freight so that they could travel faster. The Mormons in Utah were in rebellion, the nation had been informed, and the faster the army and its supplies got to Utah to quash the rebellion, the better off the United States would be. So each wagon was drawn by several yoke of oxen, selected for their endurance and pushed daily to their limits. Speed was truly of the essence if this war was to be fought and won before winter set in.

Each wagon and set of teams, the soldier knew, were in charge of one driver. And most trains, including the one he was watching, consisted of twenty-five wagons, all under the direction of a man known as the wagon-master.

The second in command was the assistant wagon-master; then came the extra hand. Next came the night herder, and, lastly, the cavayard driver, whose duty it was to drive the lame and loose cattle. That made thirty-one men, all told, in each train. The men, as did those in the soldier's company, took turns with their own cooking, being divided into messes of seven. One cooked, one hauled wood, another hauled water, and so on, each having a duty to perform. Besides, all were heavily armed with Colt's pistols and Mississippi yeagers, and every one of them had his weapons at the ready, so they boasted, to "use up" any enemy they might encounter as they pressed toward the valley.

The soldier grinned as he thought of the boastful bull-whackers, but then he saw one of them skillfully use his great long bull-whip, and he thought better of his smirk. The wagon-master was called the bull-wagon boss, and he was usually of the disposition of a teased tarantula. The teamsters were known as bull-whackers, and the whole train was called, by everybody involved, a bull outfit.

Squatting with his yeager or musket still held upright before him, the young trooper considered the train. He had been told that Russell, Majors, and Waddell were operating thirty-five hundred such wagons on the plains to Utah, being transported by forty thousand oxen and being driven by, or supported by, four thousand men. The youth could hardly imagine such numbers, but they didn't stagger him so much as the dollar figure he had also been told. That, the amount being invested to see that the army's goods reached Utah at the same time as the army, was over $2 million. He could not comprehend such a figure, and he felt inclined to doubt the truthfulness of the report, despite the fact that Captain Gove had confirmed it.

"Fall in!" ordered the booming voice of the sergeant of the day, and with a groan the young man forgot the lumbering oxen and wagons. Rising and swinging about, he quickly took up the order of march, a loose order on account of the terrain and sage, but an order that nevertheless covered up to twenty miles a day.

"Say, bunkie," the voice of his tent mate called from beside him, bringing the young man's attention back to the present, "what you reckon is in those wagons?"

"Food, I hope," the first soldier responded with a wry grin. "Either that or new boots. By gadfry, if I haven't worn these about out."

The fellow soldier nodded. "Me too. They say we're in Oregon now. You reckon we'll soon run into Mormons?"

The youth laughed. "Not hardly. According to Captain Gove, we still have a long way to go. The Mormons wouldn't be out this far. Besides, we're the army, and you can bet they'll be afraid to show when we're around."

"I don't know," the second soldier said, shaking his head. "Some of the boys have seen horsemen, way off on the ridges. Clay Purvis told me the captain thinks maybe they are Mormons."

"I wouldn't know," responded the first youth.

"Bunkie, you ever seen a Mormon?"

"Not that I know of. You?"

"No," the second youth replied, "but I've heard plenty, and

it gives me the jitters. I heard tell they have horns, little ones you can see in their hair if you look right careful. They say those Mormons can trance you, too, just with one look. That's how they get all those women to be their wives."

"You believe that?"

"About the horns or the women?"

The first soldier laughed. "The horns. Everybody alive knows the part about the women is true, else how could they get so many of them to join up with old Brigham and his boys and go west."

"Yeah, there is that. But tell you what – I'm looking forward to meeting me a bald-headed Mormon after we take the valley. The horns on a fellow like that ought to show up real pretty, that is if there are any."

Again the first soldier laughed. "If you catch one, call me quick. I'd like to take me a look myownself. I'll bet we find horns."

For a time the men marched in silence, the curses of the distant bull-whackers the only sound to break the monotonous tramping of dozens of pairs of number-10 army-issue boots. The ground sloped toward the west, but it was so gradual a slope that it could not be felt, and the men found no joy in marching downhill. Nor did they find joy in the wind, a frigid gale that whistled through the South Pass, carrying foot and hoof-raised dust that seeped through clothing and burned red and raw the soldiers' eyes and exposed necks and hands.

"You all right, men?" an officer asked as he drew his horse close to the tromping soldiers.

"Aye, Captain Gove, we're fine as can be expected."

"Good. Pacific Springs is only a few miles ahead, and we'll camp there for the night. There isn't much shelter, but the water is good, and I've been told that this brush burns hot."

"We'll make out," the first soldier replied. "Captain, how far do we have left to go?"

Captain Gove studied the horizon. "It's about sixty miles to the Green River and Fort Bridger. A man named Yates has a post we'll camp at near there. The Old Woman says we'll wait there for Colonel Albert Sidney Johnston. But I tell you, boys, the old man who leads us now is a doddering old fool! With a bit of a push, we'd be in the valley and feasting on Mormon beef by the time Colonel Johnston got up to us."

The two soldiers grinned, knowing that Gove was referring to Colonel Alexander. The man was indeed old and tediously careful, and he was notorious for not taking stern charge of his men. Instead he kept much to himself, and he preferred gentleness in his dealings with the soldiers. Hence he had been given the sobriquet "the Old Woman."

"Do you think the Mormons will fight?"

"Oh, but I hope so! If they do, boys, then we'll use them all up and winter in the Valley in style. According to some of the boys of the Fifth, they passed some Mormons the other day who were making their escape from Utah. They've been marching five weeks, hiding out much of the time to keep from being murdered by the Mormon scouts that are out searching after them."

"Do you think the Mormons really do that?" the second soldier asked. "I mean, I've heard that they kill all who oppose them, but my Pa met a fellow back on the Mississippi who had lived with the Mormons in Nauvoo for five years, and he says they are the most peaceable people alive. And he sure hadn't been killed when he refused to join their church."

"Well, he was likely a Mormon all along," the first soldier declared, "and just wouldn't admit it."

The second young man shook his head. "I don't think so. Besides that, I can't hardly imagine all the murders I hear tell these people committed. That doesn't make sense for folks to behave that way—no more sense than for them to have horns."

"Sense or not," Captain Gove declared, "I imagine that it is so, for fanaticism produces the worst sort of horrors imaginable. But boys, if the Mormons will only fight, then their days are numbered. We will sweep them from the face of the earth, and Mormonism in Utah will cease. Then our campaign will be at an end, and we can return to our homes and families."

The captain rode away, and the two soldiers walked in silence. A crow cried out from far above them, and then cried again. The wind continued to blow, the dust sifted into their eyes and down their necks, and both men readjusted their neckerchiefs over their mouths.

"You know, Bunkie, Captain Gove can't wait to return to his home and family, which is secure. I wonder how those Mormon folk feel, knowing that we're marching in to destroy *their* homes and families?"

The young soldier looked at his companion but said nothing, and for the rest of the afternoon the two marched in silence, hemmed in by their own thoughts of the impending war.

In spite of the cold wind, the mood around the cooking fires that night was lighthearted. The men sang and danced, and all felt glad that they had crossed the Great Divide and were getting close to the valley of the Mormons. In spite of the rapidly advancing season, there was still hope that with a grand push, they would have no trouble getting through the mountains. Even old Jim Bridger, the mountaineer guide, was hopeful, declaring to one and all that it didn't matter at all that the Mormons had blockaded Echo Canyon. He knew another route, up along the Bear River and down into the northern Utah valleys. It would be fifty miles or more longer, but it would take Brigham and his troops by surprise and would be well worth the little jaunt.

So the men of G and H Companies of the Tenth Infantry were enthusiastic, and as the young soldier stretched out in his bedroll and closed his eyes, he did his best to picture men with horns, glorious battles, and hordes of entranced women anxiously looking forward to the coming of their blue-coated deliverers.

Suddenly he sat bolt upright in bed. He had been asleep, but now his ears rang with the sound of gunfire and a cacophony of other noises, including screaming and the ringing of bells. There was also the thunder of hooves back and forth past his tent, and then the shout, "The mules are free and ours, Port! Let's send them home a'foggin'!"

"Soldiers turn out!" a voice screamed from a tent nearby. "We're attacked!"

The young soldier stared into the inky blackness of the inside of his tent, his heart hammering and his breath absolutely still.

The cry "Soldiers turn out!" rang again and again, and still he sat, terrified. At last, however, his tentmate's own frightened whisper pierced his frozen mind, and he started to snap out of his fear.

"Bunkie, you alive?"

"Yeah, I . . . I reckon."

"You think that was Indians?"

The young soldier shook his head, unmindful of the darkness.

"What? I can't hear you."

"Uh . . . no, I don't. Indians aren't on the warpath right now. It has to be Mormons, I reckon. Besides, I heard them talking English."

"Grief, Bunkie, I didn't think Mormons would fight."

"Well, now you know better. Come on, we've got to turn out."

The two young men scrambled from their tent and into the cold darkness, their pants and boots forgotten as they held their muskets and sought for direction to run or shoot.

"Over this way!" someone shouted, and they turned and stumbled forward, their feet taking great punishment from the rocks and prickly weeds of the high desert country.

"See anything?" the young soldier panted as he ran.

"Not much but dark on dark. Where're we going?"

The young man couldn't answer, so he stopped, then stumbled forward as his tentmate slammed into him from behind.

"Ummph!"

"Sorry, Bunkie."

"No worry. Say!" he then shouted. "Is anybody else out here?"

"Yeah." a quiet voice answered from directly behind them, "us Mormons are out here."

Spinning, the two young soldiers stared at the small group of men who had materialized out of the darkness. "Would you look at that?" one of the Mormons said. "Soldiers without britches."

The others laughed quietly.

"You . . . you going to kill us?" the young soldier stammered.

"Why? You want to die?"

"N . . . no, but . . . but—"

"We *could* kill you," another said, "mighty easy."

"So BANG," another added, and all broke into laughter again.

"All right, young fellers," the first speaker said, drawling his words considerably. "Consider yourselves 'killed.' And remember that us Mormon folks ain't so black as eastern fools would like to paint us. You boys ready to ride?"

"We're ready, Port."

"All right. Let's depart."

The Mormons slapped spurs to horses and were almost instantly swallowed by the night.

The two young men, their weapons forgotten in their hands, stared into the darkness, trying to understand what had just occurred. Then there was a faint halloo from back toward the camp, and finally someone lit a lantern. Using that as a beacon, the two soldiers picked their way through the sage and rocks and back to the tents.

"They got the mules," Captain Gove grumbled. "Those confounded Mormons got the mules."

"Anybody . . . hurt?" the second soldier asked.

Gove looked at him. "Yeah, one man, from Tracy's H Company. He had the heart disease, and it looks like he died of fright. It's a miracle the bloodthirsty devils didn't kill a dozen more of us."

"I like to have died of fright myself," the youth declared honestly. "When I first heard them, I thought the very demons of hell had been turned loose on the camp. For a minute I was too scared even to breathe—I was that slow getting out of my tent."

"Well, it wouldn't have done us much good to get out sooner," another man declared. "We couldn't have shot 'em."

"Oh, yeah?" a third man growled. "If I could have found my rifle . . ."

"I found mine," the second man said quietly, "and I got outside. But I couldn't fire."

"Why not?"

"Why? Because those Mormon fellers rode up and down between the rows of tents, close formation, hollering and shooting in the air. I seen them. And there was no way I could have shot at them, not without endangering the boys across the picket from me. It wouldn't have been any different for any of you. Those fellers had us boxed real good, and they knew it. But they weren't trying to use us up, either."

"They could have killed my bunkie and me, too," the second young soldier declared softly, "but they didn't. I . . . I'm with you, I don't think they were interested in killing us."

There was a long silence, and each of the men did his best to digest what he had just been told.

"Probably just afraid to," Captain Gove finally decided. "The murdering cowards. Well, boys, whether they could have killed us or not, now we're in a real pickle. We have no mules, and – "

"Captain," a man suddenly shouted from out in the darkness, "the bell mule is out here! His picket rope got caught in the sagebrush."

Captain Gove sighed with relief. "We're saved. The mules all follow that bell mule, so by morning we should have our animals back. Then we'll truly get after those black-hearted souls."

"Captain," the young soldier said then, "I heard one of the Mormons call another one by the name of Port. That mean anything to you?"

Jesse Gove sucked in his breath. "Yeah. It means that we are by-golly lucky, for that would be Orrin Porter Rockwell, the notorious Mormon outlaw and killer. I've heard that he never takes anyone alive. It is purely amazing that we aren't dead, every last one of us."

"I'm telling you," the second young soldier declared emphatically, "if he'd have wanted us to be dead, we would have been. He and his men had us clean to rights, Captain, and you know it. There was no luck involved. We're alive because the Mormons, including this Rockwell feller, chose to leave us that way."

There was a long silence, and then Jesse Gove spoke again. "You may be right, Soldier. But on the other hand, you might not be. So from now on, we'll be doubling the guard – no, tripling it – so that we have sentinels all around the camp. Anything suspicious, anything at all, and I want to be informed. Sergeant, see that tonight's guard, Cumming, is placed under arrest until we have an inquiry. Now, snap to it!"

He did, and before long the two young tent-mates were lying once again in the darkness.

"You know," the first young soldier finally said, his voice low and quiet, "I think you were right out there. If those Mormons had wanted, we would all be dead men right now."

"I know, Bunkie," the other replied with a sigh. "And I'm starting to wonder about those Mormon folks. Would I be so amazing charitable to soldier boys who were coming to burn me out and string up my leaders? I hope I would, but I don't know. I truly don't know."

And after that comment, the endless wind was all that was heard on the lonely plains of South Pass.

Chapter 1

When I first heard that Steenie had gone, I would not believe. Oh, it made sense, all right, that she would leave. It made all kinds of sense. The trouble was, it didn't *feel* right. There was just too much that had been happening between us for her to simply disappear.

"Ma," I said, looking up from where I sat at our newly constructed table, "Steenie didn't run. I *know* she didn't!"

My mother looked achingly at me, and then she glanced quickly out the window of our small log home. It was early fall, but already the days were getting shorter and the cottonwood grove where we lived was blue with evening shadow.

"Jons," she replied, her tongue struggling to form English words out of her still-Swedish thinking, "Brother Fordham says it iss so, und in spite of vhat ve know of Christena, I yust tink he must be right."

My three sisters looked at me in unison, but at my scowl they dropped their eyes back to their bowls of porridge. Elijah Fordham, our block teacher, had dropped by within the hour, telling us that the Crost family had pulled out during the night before, taking the trail east before Buchanan's Army could get here.

Of course, I had heard of *other* families who had become dissatisfied with our religion, or at least with the almost harsh conditions under which we were forced to live. And those folks had either picked up with a wagon train heading west or had returned to their homes in the east. But this was the first time I had ever known the people who had departed, and I truly struggled to understand.

"Ma," I argued, for once forgetting to be self-consciously proud that I had no such Swedish accent as had my mother and father, "Brother Fordham is wrong this time. He *must* be! I know Steenie too well, and running away is just not something she would do."

"Und how vould you know the girl so vell?" Pa shot back from where he had been silently judging the conversation. "Jons, ve have been only two veeks here in the Valley, und that iss not enough time for a boy to know a girl so vell."

Well, I colored up proper, for I knew that Pa was right. Most young men wouldn't have come to know a girl so well in such a short time. Nor would *I* have known a girl that well, had that girl been any other than Steenie Bergman. But she wasn't any other girl. She was Steenie, and that made Pa wrong.

Ma should have known that, too. She had come to know Steenie almost better than I did. But she remained silent—fearful, I suppose, for what Steenie's disappearance would do to me, her son.

But Steenie Bergman *was* someone special. From the day our dusty wagon had rolled into the area of the Salt Lake Valley known as South Cottonwood, having been released from Mathias Cowley's wagon company, I had known that. And I had known, for almost as long, that for the rest of forever she would be my one true love.

For a moment, I recalled the first time I had seen her—and in spite of myself and what I had just been told about her being gone, I smiled. I had been helping the folks unload what precious little we owned into our newly assigned cabin, when with great clumsiness I had dropped Ma's well-used wooden bread bowl.

Only seconds before, Ma had cautioned me to be careful with it, and teasingly I had told her to mind her own armful, for mine was secure. Instantly, then, the bowl, almost as if it had a life of its own, tumbled out of my arms and into the dirt.

Quickly, before Ma could turn and see the mishap, I stooped to pick the bowl up—and that was when I heard from behind me a low, throaty laugh that stopped me cold. Whirling around, I stared at the laugh's wondrous source. And just as instantly I felt my breath cut short—caught up tight in my chest.

Why, she was the loveliest Mormon girl who had ever stared back at a susceptible young convert from Sweden, and I was powerless to do anything but continue to stare.

A little thing less than shoulder high to me, she was creamy tan in complexion, with level blue-gray eyes and a rare dark hair that fired up mahogany-red when the sun shone directly behind it, as it did just then. Her features were regular and fine, and the gentle lines of her figure were scarcely damaged by the ill-fitting cling of her homespun dress and apron.

I continued to hold my breath.

"Look out!" she warned suddenly, and to my mortal shame and consternation, Ma's mixing bowl slipped and tumbled to the earth for the second time in just as many minutes.

Fighting frantically against the red blush that leaped up my neck and across my face, I looked away from her and stooped down, fumbling with my fingers as I again retrieved the wooden bowl. When next I looked, she was no longer standing before me. Instead, she had stepped to the wagon and taken up an armload of supplies.

"Hello," she said, almost in a whisper, as she again reached my side. "Welcome to South Cottonwood."

"Th-Thank you," I replied as I hastily fell into step beside her. "I . . . I am Jons Soderberg. How . . . are you called?"

Again she laughed, and I was becoming more aware by the minute of the musical tinkle that was hers. Glancing at her, I was also aware, and instantly, too, of the profile of her face—a profile more lovely than anything I had ever seen before.

Her forehead dropped almost straight from the soft curl of her hair, the saucy uptilt of her nose met it in the soft arch of dark eyebrow, her full lips had a look of pouting to them that her incredible smile gave the lie to. Her sparkling eyes were shaded by dark, curling lashes and framed by high cheekbones, and her chin, standing firm, dropped subtly and then led gently back and down to the splendor of her neck. From all angles she was beautiful, and I hardly noticed, as we walked, the gentle chiding she gave me for my grammar.

"In America, Jons Soderberg, we say, 'What is your name?' "

For a minute, I couldn't say anything. I had spent hours practicing English while wintering in Keokuk and helping my folks earn the means to cross the plains. Also, during my stay there and while crossing the plains, I had listened carefully to how Americans talked, and I had learned fast. Now most of the time I sounded as though I had been in America for years rather than months. But when I was nervous, I still occasionally allowed my Swedish heritage to seep into my speech.

Nor was I ashamed of my Swedish past. Not at all. But, along with many others, I had endured the hatred and persecution of many of Sweden's most prominent sons when my family and I had converted to Mormonism. And so with my parents, brothers, and sisters, I had put the land of my birth behind me and had set out, with all my heart and soul, to become a free son of America. And I would yet, I vowed daily, achieve that all-consuming goal.

"My name," she continued without a pause, "is Christena Bergman. But my friends call me Steenie."

"And am I your friend?" I asked bravely, still not taking my eyes from her face.

Her reply, given gently and almost in a whisper, thrilled me clear to the toes of the too-small, cast-off boots I was wearing.

"Oh, I hope so," she replied, sounding very sober, and looking once again directly up into my eyes. "I truly hope so."

We walked like that, side by side, up to our small cabin in the cottonwoods, and my mind reeled as I wondered at her words. I don't know how I knew it, I truly don't, for I was too young and inexperienced to discern such things by myself.

But still I knew!

This girl Steenie was saying something to me of loneliness, almost crying it out, and in that instant I added another vow to my one of Americanization. I vowed that I would not rest until

I could hold her close and help to ease the pain that somehow seemed to fill her tender heart.

"Bergman," I said, as I pushed Steenie in the big swing someone had hung south of our home, "that's Swedish, too—isn't it?"

We had been in Cottonwood for two days, and Pa had already been given work in the munitions factory that the Church had opened in the old sugar foundry in Sugarhouse. I had gone there as well, but the bishop who was managing the making of gunpowder for our coming war with the States had decided that he wanted only married men to do such dangerous work. So at the moment I was unemployed, and, frankly, I was enjoying every minute of it.

"It is Swedish," Steenie laughed as I pushed her higher, "though I've never been to Sweden."

"But then how—"

"My parents came to America before I was born and settled in Wisconsin. My mother died during my birth, and my father married again. A year ago, both he and my stepmother died quite suddenly of cholera, and I have been living ever since with my stepmother's brother and his wife and children. Their names are Ben and Maria Crost."

I pushed the swing again, thinking. "And how did you come to be a Latter-day Saint?" I finally asked.

"Two missionaries," she replied as she sailed back and forth on the end of the great ropes. "A good many of our Lutheran congregation accepted their message, were baptized, and emigrated to Zion. We came to the valley last year, and most of us went south past Nephi and into the Sanpete Valley. But my Uncle Ben wished to remain here near Church headquarters, and so here we are."

"Why did he do that?" I asked. "Not that I'm sad about his decision, mind you. Otherwise, I might not have met you."

Steenie smiled sweetly. I gave the swing another push, and again I felt a mighty urge to hold this beautiful girl close and protect her from the evil world we had been born into.

"I've thought of that as well," she told me then, "that is, how we might never have met each other if Ben had . . . had . . .

"Oh, Jons, I am *so* afraid of that man!"

"Who?" I asked, catching the swing and pulling it to a stop. For a moment Steenie made no move but sat staring silently at the ground. Then she stood and slowly walked away.

"My Uncle Ben," she then sighed, almost in a whisper. "He . . . he thought it would only be a short time until . . . Brother Brigham recognized his leadership abilities and made him a bishop or an . . . an apostle, or *something*. Now, a year later, that call has not been extended. In fact, Uncle Ben still has the calling of block teacher that the bishop gave him thirteen months past, and this rankles him severely. Regularly now he curses and rails upon Brother Brigham and the other Church leaders, and he cannot see that it is within *himself* that the fault lies, not within them.

"I have tried my best to talk with him, Jons—to encourage him to pray to feel the Spirit again that he felt when he was baptized. But he grows meaner by the day. Nor is his dear wife, Maria, any longer able to influence him for good. It is as though his mind has darkened and that he has set his heart against the kingdom of God. In fact, I'm reminded often of the phrases Nephi used to describe his two older brothers—hard-hearted and stiff-necked. There is much yelling and anger and cruelty in Uncle Ben's cabin now, and I can hardly bear being there with him."

With Steenie's words reeling in my mind, I found myself aware once again of the desire that was swelling inside me to rescue her—to get her away from the man that seemed to have such a hold on her life. But I said nothing. Instead we just walked—and before long I had taken her home and was working my way, thoughtfully, back through the willows to my own home. What could I do? How in the world could a boy like me help a wondrous person like her to be relieved of such great pain? I didn't know, but I knew I had to find a way—

"Oh, Jons, look how beautiful it is!"

I looked, and indeed the Valley was beautiful. It was early the following morning, and Steenie and I stood on a bluff south of Emigration Canyon, but just north of what I learned was Parley's Canyon. The chilly morning wind tugged at the blankets we had brought with us for warmth, and the first rays of the sun cast our shadows sternly before us, sending them tumbling helter-skelter down the rocky and brush-strewn slope. There they were lost, swallowed by the greater night-shadows that yet lingered below.

Off to the west, the Great Salt Lake glistened and sparkled like millions of acres of jewels, and the mountains that rose to the south of the lake, as well as those that formed islands to the north and west, receded in ever-diminishing hues of lavender and blue. Closer in, also to the northwest, the City of the Saints shown as an oasis of green amidst the all-encircling fields of fall-yellow and ochre, the colors of harvest time. It was an eye-catching view, and for long moments Steenie and I both stood spellbound by the sight of it.

Finally a lark trilled in the fields below us, and only then did I speak.

"Do you come here often?"

"Not as often as I would like to, Jons. There is so much work to be done that I have no time. But now that harvest is almost over, perhaps I will begin to enjoy a little more freedom."

"Have you put up much food?" I asked.

Steenie nodded vigorously. "Everything that we could bottle or dry, we have preserved. The Lord has blessed us immeasurably—folks say more than any other year since the Saints' arrival in the Valley ten years ago, and there will be little hunger this winter."

"Was the hunger bad in the past?" I asked.

"Oh, Jons, the sufferings I have seen are simply pitiful. Even last winter it was bad, and many days I spent from daylight till dark grubbing thistle roots from the frozen ground for our supper. For grain we often had nothing more than shorts with bran, and eating twice a day was a luxury that few could afford. Brother Brigham and the other Brethren constantly gave of their own supplies, the bishops distributed the food nearly every day, and still there did not seem ever to be enough."

"I've heard that there were crickets."

Steenie laughed. "Crickets? Jons, they are the most foul, ugly insects I have ever seen. They come in hordes, wave after wave of them, until the sky seems black and the earth is covered. To walk through them, feeling their bloated bodies crunching beneath our feet, is an experience I would rather never have again as long as I live! I fought them last spring, and that is enough for me, forever.

"And they were everywhere! They got into my hair and down my neck, they crawled up my skirts, they flew into my face and even into my mouth, and . . . Oh! I shudder to think about it."

"Sounds pretty bad," I agreed. "But what about the seagulls? Didn't they come and eat them?"

Again Steenie laughed. "Sometimes. They certainly came that first year in the Valley, and they are all that saved the Saints from starvation that year. But since then, well, our bishop says, when he mentions the work of the gulls against the crickets, that in his experience the birds come late and leave early. Most of the work is left to be done by the Saints."

I grinned. "I would say that the seagulls and I were cut from the same cloth. Or at least Ma would say that."

"I like your mother," Steenie smiled, looking off across the Valley. "I don't know your father very well, but I do like your mother. She seems so nice. Jons, please tell me what she is like."

Picking up a small rock, I tossed it over the edge of the bluff. "Ma is wonderful, Steenie, but I don't really know how to tell you what she is like. In Sweden her name was Karna Nilsdotter, but here she is called Caroline. Like you, she is just a bit of a thing, but she is tougher than old boot leather, as they say, and even my Pa, big man that he is, backs down from her once she gets riled.

"She's strong, too, and she can fool you with that. She hardly ever gets sick, and one day, before we left Sweden, when a cow came after one of my little sisters, Ma grabbed it by the horns and twisted its neck until that cow was on its side with her on top of it. I was amazed, but Pa said it didn't suprise him at all.

"The thing I like best about Ma, though, is her love. She loves every person she has ever known, and I truly can't think of an exception. When Elder Lars Nils Larsson was teaching my family and others the gospel back in Sweden, police came and arrested our neighbors, an aged couple name Matsson. They were taken to prison and forced to live sixteen days on bread and water, all because they had been baptized into Christ's church.

"For that entire sixteen days, Ma went to the prision every day and visited not only with our neighbors but with the police as well. She was so filled with love for the police that after the Mattsons were released, the offiers made no more arrests in Vallby province. Later one of the officers united with our faith, and he told my Pa that he had decided to embrace Mormonism because he had been able to feel Ma's love for him.

"Tell you the truth, Steenie, I've even heard Ma praying, the past few weeks, for President Buchanan—and for the officers and men of his army who are on their way this very hour to attack us."

"Praying *for* them?"

"That's right. Pa just shakes his head and, when it's his turn to offer family prayer, prays for the Brethren of the Church. But not Ma. She prays for our enemies, that their minds will be opened to the goodness of the Saints, that their families will be protected while they are away, that they will not be killed or seriously hurt when the Lord begins to assist us in our battles with them, and so forth."

"My goodness. I see what you mean about love. Truthfully though, I don't know if I could ever be that serious."

"Well, Ma isn't all serious, either. She sings all the time, she whistles until Pa calls her his Swedish canary, and she makes up silly rhyme songs about us children that are so awful they are funny. And she hardly ever stops teasing Pa, tickling him and flirting with him in front of the rest of us until he almost goes crazy with it. But we can tell he loves it, every minute of it—and there isn't anything on this earth that he wouldn't do for her.

"Sometimes Ma even takes over Pa's authority to call family prayer, doing if for him because his mind gets so befuddled with worry that he forgets. When I asked her about it once, she told me that it was as much her responsibility as it was his to see that our family got to the celestial kingdom. And she is bound and determined that we are going to get there together.

"She is truly an amazing woman, Steenie, and I am honored to call her my mother."

Steenie looked off across the valley, breathing deeply, trying to control her emotions. Finally, however, she spoke. "I never knew my mother, Jons, but I . . . I think she must have been a great deal like your mother. At least that is the feeling that my father used to give me, before he too passed away."

She paused, and in the silence the lark below us trilled again, a sweet, happy sound that somehow made me think of Steenie.

"Jons," she finally said, "do . . . do you think she . . . your mother, I mean . . . would mind if I tried to be like her? I mean, I have watched many women, but when I become a mother, if I could ever be like any single one of them, I would be most proud to be like *her*. Do . . . you think that she would mind?"

"Not hardly," I said, grinning.

"Then . . . uh . . . do you think she would mind," Steenie asked, her voice filled with apprehension, "if . . . if I were to spend time with her this winter, maybe helping out while I watched and learned?"

Well, I could hardly believe what Steenie was asking. If I had prayed about it, which truthfully I hadn't as yet, the Lord couldn't have answered my prayers more perfectly. Steenie would be getting close to my Ma, and at the same time she would be spending more time being close to me. For a gangly young Swedish convert, life was quickly assuming the glorious and hoped-for aspects of heaven on earth, and I was thrilled beyond words.

"She would truly love it," I declared as I reached out and

took Steenie's hand. "But no sense putting off until winter what you can do today. Let us be hurrying back, Christena Bergman, so that you might get about your task at once."

And so, with a giggling and lovely Steenie willingly in tow, I began my rapid descent of the mountain.

Chapter 2

"Could they use your services?" Steenie asked anxiously.

With a sense of great discouragement, I climbed onto the wagon bench beside her. I had already been in the Valley ten days, and other than being able to occasionally help some of our neighbors with the last of their harvests, which services were rewarded with grain and other produce for my family's table, I was still without work.

Of course, I had spent every possible moment of every day with Steenie, and that was pleasurable beyond words. The two of us had grown close in that time – laughing, teasing, walking, and riding about the valley, getting acquainted with it and with each other. And as we explored together, we engaged in long and earnest discussions that at the time seemed so important. And it wasn't all deep and thoughtful probing, either. We always seemed to end up chasing each other here and there among the trees in silly games of tag, or sitting on the creek bank playing jack slaps – generally acting in that tom-fool way that young folks can when they've nothing better to do than to be happy in each other's company.

And Steenie Bergman and I were happy, of that I can testify. In fact, through my entire life I could never remember being so completely consumed with joy.

Steenie had also managed to thoroughly captivate my mother's heart. And that was to prove significant, for in affairs of love, I was to learn, a young man can have no better ally than his own staunch and loyal mother.

Now Steenie and I were at Temple Square, where one of the buildings housing temple construction tools and materials had been converted to the manufacturing of weapons for the coming war with the States. Under Brother Jonathan Browning's able direction, the men were already making Colts' handguns, and equipment for manufacturing rifles had been ordered and was even then en route to Great Salt Lake City.

Elsewhere in the sprawling community, the shops were turning out canister bombs, bullets, and cannonballs, and of course at Pa's factory they were making gunpowder.

Old Buck, as most people called United States President James Buchanan, might be sending an army of Uncle Sam's finest to wipe out us "rebellious" Mormons. But the army wasn't going to get us without a fight, and a good one at that. The Mormons, with what seemed to be the whole world arrayed against them, were cheerfully readying themselves for war. Trouble was, with all that activity, no one anywhere seemed to have permanent use for me.

"They couldn't use me yet," I sighed, looking down into Steenie's captivating, dancing eyes. "Brother Browning told me, though, that in a week or so more men will be called to go into the mountains. He said I should tell my bishop I'm available, and then likely I'll be called to go with them."

Steenie looked at me. "But . . . but you just came from the mountains. Are you sure that you want to go back already?"

I smiled at her. "Steenie, that army is coming to attack our people, and I feel honor-bound to help keep them away. I've even heard the soldiers boast of what they intend to do when they get here, and it's enough to make a man's blood run cold. Many's the night the other fellows and I would sneak to their camps and listen to their ribald deviltry and evil plans."

"You did? *Truly?*"

"It was . . . sort of a game," I said, blushing a little, but at the same time feeling proud of the adoration on Steenie's face. "Our wagon train passed many of the government trains as we came to the valley, and after dark each night a few of us would make dares to see who could get the closest to their fires. Night after night, I've hidden in the grass and listened to soldiers and freighters boast of hanging Brigham Young and the other Mormon leaders; of dishonoring our wives, sisters, and daughters; and of plundering and pillaging our people. They even sang songs about it."

Steenie's expression was one of shock. "They . . . they did? Sing, I mean? I can hardly believe United States soldiers would behave so."

"They surely did, Steenie. One night I learned a verse of one of their songs that went something like this:

> The Mormons knew that Uncle Sam
> Had troops upon the route,
> And Brigham prayed the Holy Lamb
> Would help to keep them out.
> The distance then, one thousand miles,
> Me in the face did stare,
> For Brigham swore no damned gentiles
> Ere should winter there."

Steenie giggled. "You shouldn't use language like that," she said, wagging her finger at me.

"It's only a song," I countered, "and not my song at that. Besides, the army won't get into the Valley. Our people are innocent of the charges against them, and so Brother Brigham's prayers will surely be answered."

"Do . . . the soldiers *all* feel like that, Jons?"

I shook my head. "I don't know. One night I heard some of the troops say that General Harney—he's the leader of Buchanan's army—has fully determined that upon his arrival here, he will capture Brother Brigham and the twelve apostles, execute them, and then winter within the walls of our growing temple."

"Isn't he the one they call 'Squaw-killer' Harney?"

"Why, that's right," I agreed. "I heard one of the soldiers call him that, but I don't know how he got his name."

Steenie nodded. "I do. Aunt Maria says that he got it when

he killed all those Sioux men, women, and children under Little Thunder at Ash Hollow a couple of years ago. He was supposedly taking revenge for the Grattan Massacre, but he ended up perpetrating another massacre that was much worse. If Harney is leading the expedition, then the Saints truly have much to fear.

"Have you heard any of the songs our people sing about the army?"

"No," I said, surprised. "Do the Mormons have songs about them?"

Steenie laughed. "The Mormons have songs about most everything. Listen to this one. It's sung to the tune of Yankee Doodle Dandy:

When Uncle Sam he first set out,
His army to destroy us
Says he, "The Mormons we will route,
They will no more annoy us."

The force he sent was competent
To try and hang for treason,
That is, I mean, it would have been,
But don't you know the reason?

There's great commotion in the east
About the Mormon question,
The problem is, to say the least,
Too much for their digestion.

As they were going up the Platte
Singing many a lusty ditty
Saying we'll do this and we'll do that
When we get to the city,

And sure enough when they got there,
They made the Mormons stir, Sir.
That is, I mean they would have done,
But O they didn't get there."

"That's quite a song."

Steenie smiled. "I hear new verses all the time. I just wish the war wasn't really happening."

Slowly the horses drew the wagon east along Brigham Street, past Brigham Young's large home with the beehive symbol, and on toward the foothills. At Seventh East Street we turned south and followed the dusty road toward Cottonwood, and we had gone almost a mile when Steenie at last broke the silence.

"Jons," she said quietly, "why *is* the war happening? Why on earth has the American government decided to send an army to attack some poor religious colonists and their innocent wives and children?"

Feeling helplessly unable to answer her questions, I shook my head. "Steenie, I've been hearing that question argued and debated from both directions for most of the way across the plains, and at nearly every meal I've eaten or meeting I've attended since I came to the Valley. In that time I must have heard a hundred reasons, if not more. Truthfully, I don't hardly know which of them is correct."

"My Uncle Ben says that the government is right," Steenie then said with an air of sadness. "He says that Brother Brigham has got up a rebellion against Washington, and that he intends to be dictator of his own private empire out here in the mountains."

"That's nonsense," I declared. "My Ma says the coming war has to do with persecution, plain and simple. She says it's a common trial that all true Saints must endure. In her opinion, persecution must exist for the Saints of God no matter what age they live in or under what nation's flag they reside.

"Pa, though, looks at it a little differently, or at least more deeply. Some returning missionaries stayed a night with us out on the plains of Wyoming, and Pa spent nearly until morning talking with two of them. From what they said, Pa has decided that it's persecution, all right—but that it's all got up through Satan's usual method of selfishness and lies and ambition for power."

"What do you mean?"

Gently I urged the horses forward. "Steenie, I'm not hardly

the best one to say, for I wasn't here when all this happened. But Pa tells us, at night, what he learns at the powder factory—and from what he says, the same spirit rages in the hearts of eastern politicians and religionists today that raged when Brother Joseph and Hyrum were murdered. For whatever reasons, folks spread lies and falsehoods, other folks believe them, and innocent people suffer. I think—"

"Say, young folks, how about a ride?"

In surprise, Steenie and I spun around and examined the man who stood beside the road. Neither of us had even seen him approach, we had been so engrossed in our conversation. But now that Steenie looked at him, she gave a little cry of recognition.

"Brother Hanks! Why, we didn't see you. Please climb aboard and ride with us."

"Afternoon, Miss Steenie," the man said as he vaulted up onto the bench, "it's good to see you. And who might be this young buck sitting next to you?"

"Ephraim Hanks," Steenie replied, beaming radiantly, "this is Jons Soderberg, lately from Sweden."

"How do you do?" the man said, holding out his hand. I took it and felt a little shiver at the power I felt there. Brother Hanks was not overly tall. He wore a long, full beard, and he had a pleasant, peaceable look about him that I was later to learn could be quite deceptive. But for then I shook his hand and waited to see what might develop.

"How are your Uncle Ben and Aunt Maria?" Ephraim asked.

"They're . . . fine," Steenie said, dropping her eyes.

Ephraim Hanks looked straight ahead. "Then the Spirit of apostasy is still with Ben?"

Steenie nodded sorrowfully, and Brother Hanks gently patted her hand. "Keep exercising your faith, Christena. If the Lord could part the Red Sea, then he can surely change a man's heart. Say, what were the two of you discussing, that you didn't even see me waving at you?"

"We were talking about the army," Steenie said. "Jons, on

his way across the plains, crept to their fires at night and listened in on their plans."

Ephraim looked hard at me. "Is that so?" he asked gently. "What company did you come in with, Brother Soderberg?"

"Mathias Cowley's company, Sir."

"Ah! He told us that some of the young bucks had done a little scouting around, and he seemed right proud of their efforts. Did you scout the soldiers, or the teamsters?"

"Both, but mostly teamsters. They were out ahead of the regular troops."

"And what did you learn?"

This was feeling a bit like an inquisition, but I didn't know how to get out of it, so I went ahead and told him all I had told Steenie.

When I had finished, Ephraim Hanks shook his head. "Evil men—that's what a good many of them are. I find it passing strange that a corrupt government will send out evil, drunken adulterers and thieves to teach a moral, righteous people how to behave themselves. I suppose that's one reason why Brother Brigham has decided to declare martial law. Now we will go forth in the power of Zion's God to defend ourselves against their wicked assault."

"Martial law has been declared?" I asked, surprised.

"It has. I was in a meeting with the Church leaders only an hour ago, and Brother Brigham has signed the proclamation. Even as we speak it is being implemented."

"You . . . you were just with *Brigham Young?*" I asked, feeling awed to be talking to a man who had just spoken with the Prophet of the Lord.

"Certainly was."

"My goodness. I . . . I . . . "

Steenie, sensing what I was feeling, suddenly spoke. "Jons has never seen the Prophet, Brother Hanks. He's not used to being around him as we are."

Ephraim Hanks nodded with understanding. "Puts his trousers on one leg at a time, young man, just like the rest of us. And he has every other mortal problem and trial that the rest of us have, as well. Difference is, God has called *him* to be Prophet. The man Brigham is a great man, but it is the office he holds that I honor and serve."

I nodded, trying my best to understand what this unusual person was telling me.

"Brother Hanks," Steenie then asked, going back to what she and I had been discussing, "why *is* the army attacking us? What have the Mormons done that would get the government so upset?"

Ephraim Hanks grinned. "Do you want the short and simple answer or some rather lengthy explanations of it?"

"We'd like explanations, please."

"Well," he drawled, "since you're giving me a free ride, I'll pay with talk and tell you what I know as best I can. First, for background – as you know, Mormonism embraces all of Christ's gospel, and to most good Christian folk, that doesn't seem practical. Nor does it seem possible to them that, in our own enlightened age, a man would step forth and call himself a prophet. That such happened, and that such self-same prophet declared to folks that all their churches were false, truly grates on the self-righteous nerves of Christiandom. It was those same self-righteous people who saw to it that the Prophet Joseph Smith and his brother Hyrum were murdered, and it's the same ones who, today, have sent the army forth to slay us."

Steenie looked at him, and I wondered at the expression in her eyes. "Brother Hanks," she said, and her voice was full of admiration, "I . . . I've never heard it said quite like that. Now what the bishop and other folks say begins to make sense."

"Well," he said, looking a little uncomfortable because of her praise, "if a man has eyes to see, he sees. I'm just saying what I see.

"Another thing. As far as I've been able to tell, the political appointees chosen by Washington for our people have been pompous, self-serving, immoral, narrow-minded men who neither understand nor uphold the freedoms that America's constitution guarantees her people. Many of them can't see a united people without seeing treason, nor see a people enthusiastically following their prophet without seeing slavery and tyranny. Others decry our doctrine of the plurality of wives while living themselves in the midst of lust, adultery, and sin. And the list goes on.

"In fact, the most recent and wicked of these men, I'm afraid, is a judge who left here a year ago by the name of W. W. Drummond. He, more than anyone else, has brought this current crisis upon us.

"According to what the Brethren have learned, Drummond left a wife and family destitute in Illinois, and appeared here in the valley with a harlot whom he introduced as his wife. With her seated at his side on the judicial bench, that gambler and bully openly declared that he had come here to make money, and that money was his god. He then mocked our laws and institutions and took from the local courts all their powers. Then he struck at the heart of all our most sacred beliefs, rendering judicial decisions that would appall the devil himself.

"When Drummond's unpopularity finally forced him to quit the bench, he addressed his resignation and a letter to the attorney general in Washington, writing many lies and half-truths that were calculated to bring the wrath of the government down upon us. How well he succeeded, especially with that thimble-brained Buchanan, who hadn't the sense to examine the false allegations for himself, is evidenced by the army that even now is pounding on our eastern doors."

"Did Secretary of War Floyd have much to do with this?" Steenie asked.

"I reckon he did," Ephraim Hanks replied. "I don't know how much, but rumor has it that he's been a real force behind mobilizing the troops. Why do you ask?"

"I heard some men talking after meeting a few weeks ago," Steenie explained. "According to them, Secretary Floyd is an avowed secessionist, and the army coming here is part of his scheme to scatter and weaken U.S. forces. It frightens me that such selfish political ambitions are allowed to disrupt so many innocent lives."

"Well," I said, speaking for the first time, "President Buchanan certainly doesn't believe that we're innocent. One of the missionaries that Pa met with on the plains had Buchanan's message to Congress this year. Old Buck is convinced of Brother Brigham's despotism, our all-pervading fanaticism, and even our so-called illegal Indian policy. According to the president, all Mormons are in open rebellion against Washington, and we are all encouraging the Indians to fight the government with us. Why, my goodness, I've never even met an Indian, let alone incited one to war."

Steenie giggled. "Me neither."

"Well, I've met several more than somewhat," Ephraim Hanks declared. "Most of them are good people, too. Or were, that is, before they got corrupted by white men. I've not heard that we were encouraging them to fight, but if we decided to, I don't think it would take much to get them going. Most Americans have treated them shamefully."

"I've heard it said," Steenie then ventured, "that polygamy is the principle cause of this invasion. Colonel Fremont has called polygamy and slavery the 'twin relics of barbarianism,' and I've been told that Senator Stephen A. Douglas has said the same thing on the floor of Congress."

"That's so," Ephraim agreed. "There's no doubt that the doctrine of plurality of wives is the most bitter of all Mormon pills for the sectarian world to swallow.

"Well, young people," Ephraim Hanks concluded, "yonder is where I'm headed. Luck to the both of you, thank you for the ride . . . and Miss Steenie, give my best to Ben and Maria."

Steenie nodded. Ephraim Hanks vaulted from the wagon and strode down a lane that winded away from the road, and in another moment I had the horses moving again.

"He's an unusually good man," Steenie said quietly. "And a dear friend."

"Is he the same Ephraim Hanks who's been back and forth across the plains so many times on the mail routes and helping emigrants and so forth?"

"One and the same. Have you heard of him, Jons?"

"I'll say. Folks sit around the fire of a night and tell tales about him and Porter Rockwell. Some folks don't like them, but my Pa says to pay that no mind. He says that when an elephant walks through town, all the dogs bark."

Steenie giggled. "You do listen to your father, don't you."

I looked ahead, down the rutted road. "Pa's a fine man, Steenie, a deep thinker and a good listener. He and my ma were among the very first, in Sweden, to embrace the gospel. Pa said that from the first time he heard the missionaries, he could see the complete sense of it. The more I hear from him, the more sense he makes, too. So, yes—I try to listen."

Now Steenie looked away. "Jons . . . will your father . . . ever practice polygamy?"

"Pa?" I asked, startled. "Why, I don't hardly know. I don't think I've ever heard him talk about it, at least for himself. But I suppose that if Brother Brigham asked him . . . "

"Would *you* ever enter the principle?"

The question caught me unawares, and I looked hard at the girl by my side. She was still turned away, but I could tell by the smallness of her voice that she was serious, dead serious.

"Well," I said, slowly, carefully, "the young fellows in my wagon train used to talk about it nights, and all of us pretty much decided that, given the chance, we'd each have us a whole harem of pretty little wives."

"Jons—"

"Just trying to live the gospel," I said seriously. "And maybe build up the kingdom a mite, while I'm at it."

"Well, I declare . . . " Steenie sputtered furiously, and I could see that it was time to get out of this mess, and fast.

"Of course," I added, flicking the lines against the backs of the horses, "that was before I met you."

"What?" she asked as she looked quickly at me. "You mean . . . "

"I mean, now that I've met you and discovered what a real woman is like, I can see that a man would be in deep and serious trouble with several such wives hounding and pestering and questioning him from daylight to dark. Yes, ma'am, now that I've become better acquainted with you, I can see that one wife, if she was exactly like you, would be more than enough to keep a fellow hopping along the straight and narrow pathway forever."

"'A' fellow," she asked coyly, "or one particular fellow?"

"Only one," I replied, "unless you're planning on going into the principle yourself, with a whole harem full of husbands."

"Maybe I should," she mused. "But I'd want to start that harem with just the right sort of man . . . "

"Old, bald, plenty of middle to give him stability?"

"Exactly, Jons. Just the ticket for a good life."

"But not an exciting one?" I asked hopefully.

"Hardly exciting. But then, a woman must always give up something. For stability, most any woman I know would give up excitement, happiness, love . . . "

"Is there some particular man that could make you happy, Steenie?" I asked, feeling still more hopeful. "Say a scrawny sort of fellow who stands about six feet tall and has more than enough dark hair."

"Dark, wavy, beautiful hair," she added.

"Yes, I suppose. But a fellow who has nothing else that could recommend him except the aching deep feelings of his heart."

Embarrassed by my own boldness, I stopped speaking, and Steenie grew silent as well. The horses picked up their gait to a steady trot, and I was riding along beside her with my head in a cloud of happiness when her soft-spoken, husky-throated voice brought me down again, hard and fast.

"Jons?" she said, and again she was very serious and all a trembling.

"Yes ma'am?" I responded, and with her next statement, I felt certain that my whole world had exploded.

"My Uncle Ben wants me to be his second wife," she said tragically, desperately. "Here he doesn't even believe in the Church or the gospel, and he wants a second wife. He's even been to the bishop about it and says he was encouraged. Worse, he's getting mean because I keep fighting the idea, and I don't know what to do anymore to avoid his advances. Help me, Jons! Oh, please help me . . ."

I squatted on my haunches in the corner of our cabin, alone. Ma was off helping a neighbor woman stitch a quilt, my sisters were already enrolled in school, and Pa was up at the munitions plant in Sugarhouse. Before me on the floor, its lid open and back, was a small, musty wooden chest that held the total of my earthly treasures. Now, with a critical eye but with rapidly sinking heart, I examined them.

Inside were what was left of a set of Parker crayolas, two stubs of pencils with a mostly filled pad of sketches, a broken knife that one of Pa's younger brothers had given me before we had sailed from Sweden, assorted hard-fired clay marbles, an almost empty bottle of cinnamon oil, a bedraggled rabbit's foot, a compound-fractured measuring stick that I had found along the overland trail, a slightly burned candle, a single British halfpenney, and my once-treasured and forked-limbed slingshot.

Picking up the slingshot and sitting back on my haunches, I closed my eyes gloomily. Nothing. Nowhere in this silly horde of leftovers from my childhood was there a single treasure with which I might betroth, as my one and future love and wife, Miss Christena Bergman.

Even then she waited outside, sitting patiently on the wagon bench while I sought desperately within my mind to know what to do. But I didn't know, not how to ask her to marry me nor how to stop her Uncle Ben from pursuing what I frankly felt were his evil designs.

I could always just up and ask her to marry me, of course. But that made little sense, and I knew it. I was young for such a step—just eighteen, the same age as Steenie. But even worse, I had nothing to offer a wife. I had no job and no prospects for one, I had no home, and I had no skills with which I might earn a living. Of course, I had farmed since almost before I could walk, and I felt that I could do passibly well at it, given the chance. But to farm, a man needed land. And of land I had none.

No, I had nothing to offer Steenie that she deserved. Nor did I have any treasure to offer her by way of betrothal. But then, neither could I just stand by and see her forced into wedlock with a man she was already beginning to fear and loathe.

"You could just tell him no," I had said after I had digested the staggering news she had shared.

"But Jons," she had cried, "what if I'm *supposed* to marry him? What if I'm the one to turn his heart back to the Lord? What will I do if the Lord has chosen me for such a task, and I selfishly run from it? Ben tells me that, you know. Every day my step-uncle tells me that I will be his salvation after we are married, that the Lord has called me to be his wife, and . . . and . . . Oh, Jons, I don't know what to do!"

Steenie had wept then, and I had driven helplessly beside her. But at last I had understood the haunted look that came so often to her eyes, the anguish that crept with increasing urgency into her voice.

And so as we neared South Cottonwood, I had begun silently thinking, planning. I would marry her myself! Ben Crost could not be right about the Lord wanting Steenie to marry him—not when it produced such fear and loathing within her. They were no product of the Lord's work!

So, to stop him, I would ask her myself, and we would be married as soon as I could get something established. That would surely put a halt to her Uncle Ben's evil plans.

But now I stared helplessly. Now I could see that there was no reasonable or possible way I could ask Steenie to become my wife—

"Jons?"

Spinning, I gaped in surprise at Steenie, who was standing in the doorway behind me. I had not heard her come in, and the fact that she had been secretly watching startled me.

"Jons, what are you thinking?"

"Uh . . . about being foolish," I told her quietly, resignedly as I rose to my feet.

"What do you mean? I . . . I don't understand."

It was in my mind to say nothing, to just lead her back to the wagon and drive her home. I intended that, and I intended further to simply let circumstances after that day take their course, both for her and for my helpless self. Then we could both see what time brought us.

I intended that, all right. But to my surprise, I heard myself speaking. "I was looking for something," I said quietly, "something precious with which I could . . . troth you."

Steenie's eyes opened wide with surprise. "What?" she whispered. "You could *what?*" And my heart thrilled with the hope I could hear in her straining voice.

"I . . . I . . . wanted to ask you to marry me," I stammered, my boldness suddenly gone. "But I've nothing of value with which to troth you, nothing but this silly slingshot—"

In an instant the worn elm-fork slingshot was lifted from my grasp, and Steenie Bergman was straining against me, her arms lifted and pressed tightly around my neck. "Jons," she whispered, and once again tears were falling from the incredible depths of her blue-gray eyes, "did . . . you really mean that?"

"I . . . did," I replied while I awkwardly fumbled to put my arms about her waist.

"Then with all my heart I accept," she whispered as she buried her face against my pounding chest. "With this precious slingshot I accept thy troth and pledge thee my heart until such future day as we are sealed for eternity by one of God's mortal servants."

"And I'll see to it that you are the most well-taken-care-of woman in the West!" I replied, my eyes suddenly filling with moisture and with gladness.

And then, almost before I knew what was happening, our lips had come together, and I was clinging tightly, desperately, to my one and eternal love.

Chapter 3

I stood alone in the road before Steenie's cabin, gazing at the darkened windows. The log structure was empty, and now I knew that Brother Elijah Fordham had been right. Not only Steenie Bergman but also her Uncle Ben Crost's entire family were gone.

Bending over, I discovered the ruts the wagon had made as it left the yard. Though the only light came from the moon, they stretched plain before me, out into the road. There they turned directly toward the trail up Emigration Canyon. Truly had Ben Crost turned his back upon everything that he and the rest of us had given up so much to embrace.

What threw me, though, was Steenie. Why had she gone *with* him? What about our troth? Did the promises we had made to each other mean so little to her that she would pack up and leave for the wild mountains with winter coming on, just so she could throw herself on the mercy of the army? I couldn't see the reason of it, but neither could I argue with the evidence. Steenie was truly gone.

Numbly I walked to the door, pushed it aside, and stepped in. The cabin, one of the nicer in the area, was empty and clean, and I sensed that I was seeing the work not only of Maria but also of Steenie, both of whom had too much pride to leave the remnants of their living for others to clean up.

Of course, the table was still there, built into the wall, its one cracked leg leaning awkwardly. I looked at that leg, felt the knot that was still receding on the back of my head, and wondered.

Late the afternoon before, with Steenie fervently clutching my silly slingshot, I had brought her home. I had accompanied her inside, still excited but not expecting anything, and before I hardly knew what was happening, Steenie had announced our betrothal to her uncle and his wife.

Maria's face had been a study, so I couldn't tell what she was thinking. But Ben's face had been something else altogether. He had been angry, and he was mean enough to push his anger at me.

"*Betrothed?*" he had stormed as he rose to his feet. "Steenie betrothed to a foreign whelp like you? Over my dead body is she betrothed! Steenie, get to your room. I'll deal with you later. And you, Mister. Get out of here and don't ever let me see your face again!"

I had been stunned! I had never expected anything like that, and I didn't know how to react. I looked at Steenie, saw tears in her eyes, and was just turning back to face her uncle when he had hit me in the jaw, knocking me off my feet.

Astonished, I had gone down hard, my head snapping against the table leg as I fell, cracking the leg. Above me the table had collapsed. I had rolled to get out from under it, and Ben had kicked me hard in the ribs. I heard Steenie and Maria both cry out at that, but I was too stunned to respond. I hardly had enough air left to choke on, let alone to cry out with. But I strained and gasped, got a little wind, and pulled myself to my feet, all the time expecting another blow.

But none had come, and when my eyes had finally cleared enough that I could see, I understood why. Ben had shoved Steenie into her lean-to bedroom, and he was standing at the low doorway, yelling at her and at his wife, Maria.

"Mister . . . Brother Crost . . ." I gasped, "I . . ."

Whirling, the man had come at me like a mad dog, and involuntarily I had stepped backward. Then suddenly I had seen red, and doubling my fists I had prepared for battle. I was taller than he was, but he outweighed me considerably, and he had more experience. But I thought little of that, nor did I care how badly he might beat me. I wanted only to protect and preserve my love.

"Jons, no!" Blinking with loss of concentration, I looked aside at Steenie, wondering what I was doing wrong. I had felt Ben hit me then, felt myself going down the second time, and still my betrothed was all I could see. Her eyes were wide with horror, yet while I watched she stepped from the room and up to her Uncle Ben.

"Jons," she had pleaded with me as she clutched his arm, "don't . . . don't fight. You . . . go home, and we . . . we'll work this out."

Ben had kicked me again. I had staggered to my feet, and the man had shoved me out the door. And as I had reeled off toward the wagon, I had heard Steenie cry out, "I love you, Jons Soderberg! I love you!"

With Steenie's voice still ringing in my memory, haunting me with its agony, I stared down at the broken table. Moving quietly then, almost on tiptoe, I stepped past it and to the lean-to that had been Steenie's bedroom. I had never been inside the small room, and even now I felt nervous as I stepped past the threshold. But I needn't have, for it too was empty, stripped of every item that had been part of Steenie's personal life.

As I looked around the darkened room, lit only by the moonlight coming through the single window, I felt as though I would break apart inside. My stomach ached, my head began pounding, and sudden tears fell freely from my eyes.

What had I done? What could I possibly have done that would have made Steenie want to leave me? Had it been that I had acted the coward? Had she left because I had not fought Ben Crost for her? She had seemed so happy, so excited at the prospect of sharing her life with me. And she had seemed so determined that I would not fight him.

But now she was gone.

As I angrily wiped at my eyes and moved back through the low doorway, I caught a glimpse of something in the chinks between the logs above my head, something that seemed, even in the shadowy darkness, to be out of place. Reaching up, I touched what I had seen, felt its familiar smoothness, and with racing heart pulled from between the logs my old elm-crotch slingshot.

Staring at it, wondering that Steenie had not taken it with her, I wiped at my eyes again and finally became aware of the slip of paper tied around one of the forks. With anxious, fumbling fingers, I worked the string loose, and then I held the paper near the window.

There was writing, I could see that, but between the poor lighting and my difficulty in reading English, I could not make out what it said.

Stuffing the slingshot into my hip pocket, I clutched the paper and ran from the dwelling, intent upon finding someone who had a light, intent upon—

"Jons?"

Spinning to a halt in my headlong flight, I stared at the shadowy form. "Ma?" I asked. "Ma, is that you?"

"Ya," she replied as she walked toward me. "Und who did you tink it vould be?"

"I . . . I don't know," I stammered. "I was hoping it might be Steenie . . . Oh, Ma, what is happening?"

Gently she reached out and drew me down to her, and she held me tightly while I sobbed out my grief and despair. I hadn't needed my mother's arms so badly in years, hadn't supposed that I would ever need them again. But I learned that night that there are times, no matter how old a fellow gets, when the comfort of a mother's love is about all that can pull him through.

"Ma," I said when I had regained my composure, "Steenie left me a note. I found it in her cabin."

"Vhat does it say?"

"I don't know. There wasn't enough light to see."

"Ya," she said as she took my arm, "but there vill be plenty of light at home. Come, my boy, und ve vill see vhat the girl has to say."

Hurrying then, the two of us made our way along the darkened road, and a few moments later we arrived at our cabin.

"Soren," Ma said to Pa as we walked in, "Jons has found a message from young Christena. Perhaps it vill not be as ve have thought."

"So?" Pa said, smiling. "Don't you know from the message?"

Shaking my head, I unrolled the small strip of paper and stared at the writing. Steenie had written in pencil and had apparently been in a hurry, for the writing was light and I could hardly decipher the letters. But I finally did and felt my heart racing as I awkwardly concluded: "Jons, B won't let me stay. He'll hurt the others. Please come. I love you. S!"

Shaking, I read the note aloud to my folks.

"Vell," Ma concluded with finality, "that iss goot to hear."

"Yeah," I agreed, "But now what am I going to do?"

"Do?" Pa said as he turned back to his meal. "You vill do notting, my son. You are but a lad, und the girl iss part of another family. If the man who iss father of that family chooses to go, it iss none of our affair."

"But Pa—"

"Jons, I have spoken."

"Soren, dear?"

Pa looked up at Ma, warned by the sweet but determined tone of her voice.

"Ya?"

But Ma threw him a curve, and my poor father didn't even see it coming. "Brother Cole's young heifer," she said sweetly, "got mired yust before dark, und he vas asking if you might come und halp him."

Jumping to his feet, Pa grabbed his hat. "Voman, vhy didn't you tell me vhen I got here? I yust—"

Smiling sweetly, Ma took Pa's arm. "Soren, you do not need to go. There vill be others, und the calf might already be saved."

"Mother," Pa said as he took her hand from his arm, "I am a Soderberg, und if a neighbor needs a halping hand, day or night, then this Soderberg vill be there halping. Now I must be going."

Again Ma stopped him. "Soren, please listen to me."

"Voman, take your hand from my arm."

"There iss no young heifer," Ma stated then, leaning earnestly into Pa's big frame. "Not unless one considers poor little Christena Bergman. Und, my dear, iss she not more important than a cow?"

Pa looked hard at her, and I was having a difficult time not grinning.

"Iss not Jons also a Soderberg?" she continued tenderly. "Vould you want Jons to be less a man than you? Vould you vant that he should turn his back upon a cry for halp from such a sveet und innocent child as Christena Bergman?"

"Vell, no," Pa muttered, collapsing again into his chair. "But he iss too young—"

"Soren, Jons iss as old as your father vas vhen he married your mother und set off on his own. Besides, the lad iss not marrying Christena, yust halping her to come back to her people. The marriage vill come later, the good Lord villing. Now, my dear, vhy don't you halp me get a pack up for the lad. It vill be cold in the mountains, und I tink he could use your varm coat."

Pa grumbled but followed Ma's instructions, and hurriedly I headed out to the shed to get the chores done. My heart was singing again, for I was going after Steenie. And when I found her and brought her back, there would be a wedding. I knew it, for Ma had said so. And to tell the truth, I had never known Ma to be wrong.

Chapter 4

The sky was only just showing gray when I closed the door behind me and strode off toward Emigration Canyon. I truly had no idea of what it would take to find Steenie and bring her back, but ignorance is bliss, and I was feeling blissful as could be.

In my pack I carried Pa's warm coat and blanket, a large bait of food, a small knife, and some other odds and ends that Pa had called "get-along" stuff when he had given them to me. I also had my slingshot and Steenie's penciled note. And, finally, I had my Pa's blessing, pronounced upon my head, that the Lord would go with me and protect me and grant unto me success. With that, I knew I could not fail.

It was a Saturday morning in the latter part of September that I started out, and the day was bright and clear. By the time I topped the foothills the sun was rising, and ahead of me I saw the gathering dust of an incoming company of Saints. Stepping out, I soon reached the road, and there I learned from a returning missionary that the train was Captain William G. Young's company, containing the last of the season's emigrants.

The missionary, A. Milton Musser, was just returning home from a five-year mission to India and England, during which he had circumnavigated the globe, traveling, as he told me, "without purse or scrip." Yet he was anxious to see his family, so I let him go and sought someone else to question.

Unless you've seen an emigrant train on the move, you have

no idea of what it's truly like. In dry weather, first and last there is the dust, billowing clouds of it raised by churning wheels and plodding hooves and feet. It is promiscuous grit, seeping into and around and over everything in the train. Folks are forced to wear neckerchiefs over their noses and mouths just to keep from bogging down in their own mud.

And then there is the noise, a cacophony of sound that at times feels as though it will break the eardrums and render the brain useless. The sounds are made of the creaking and screeching of green wood on hard iron, of ungreased wheels on crooked and worn axle thimbles, the banging of iron-tires against rocky earth, the clatter of hundreds or thousands of hooves against stone, the thunderous bellowing and whinnying and bleating of cattle and horses and sheep, the chattering of many human languages being fused into one, and the shrieking of children's voices that all speak the same universal, and loud, language of childhood.

Next there is the smell, of smoke, dust, animals, and sweaty, unwashed bodies—and over all the pungent odor of crushed sage and cedar. The latter, while pleasant, hardly hides the first. Yet folks adjust, and most live with it for as long as there is need.

And last there are the faces, dozens upon dozens of faces, of men, women, and children. Each is an individual, each reflects through the dust and grime whatever he or she is feeling most strongly at the moment, and each suffers all the weaknesses and frailties that burden the rest of humanity. Yet somehow, over the course of the long trail to the valley, these faces all become fused, and it is almost as if they are a mighty, blood-related family.

That day, as I gazed upon the weary travelers, I saw mostly relief and joy, for the Valley had at last been reached, and the journey was nearly at an end. And even in the faces of those who reflected pain or anger or frustration, I sensed relief. These folks had come from all parts of America and Europe, had been traveling for months and sometimes years, and had each been driven by the urge to gather with the Saints of God in the valleys of the mountains of Zion. Now, at long last, it was accomplished.

"Hello," I called as I moved up the road past the laboring people. "Hello, and welcome to the Valley."

Some folks smiled and nodded in reply, some spoke, and a few ignored me, intent on dragging forward the complaining burdens of their own bodies. At length, however, I saw what I had been looking for, a man apart and alone. As I spied him sitting upon a rock, I thought he might have the time to tell me what I wanted to know.

I got closer and then realized with a start that he was old, real old. He sat still and quiet as a wrinkled lizard, ancient and craglike, weathered and withered to a thin angular shape of bent bones and stringy muscle. His hatchet face under his wide floppy hat brim had been whittled by age to dry leathery skin, and his white straggly whiskers showed thinning that must have reflected the growth on top of his head.

He sat alone, staring off over a herd of grazing cattle, and I wondered if he even saw me coming. Or if he saw anyone else. Or if they saw, or cared, about *him*. He gave the appearance of a decrepit old nuisance, a shiftless relic out of the past, and I nearly turned away before I saw his eyes.

The man, I knew instantly, wasn't as old as he looked, and I kept coming.

"Hello," I said loudly, fearing that he might be deaf.

"Howdy," he drawled in response, and I knew by the quiet tone of his voice that he could hear. I also knew, from the drawled "howdy" that he was a natural-bred American.

I stopped before him, and for a moment we regarded each other soberly. "Jons Soderberg," I finally said, thrusting my hand forward.

Slowly he reached up and took it in a surprisingly firm grip. "Gideon Monson," he replied. "Gideon Peabody Monson. If you figure on talking, call me Gideon."

Grinning, I nodded. "Monson. Are you Svenska?"

"Grandpap was Swedish," he replied. "Most of me, though, is Swiss. From Grindelwald under the Eiger, the Monch and the Jungfrau, up the river from Interlaken. Since Europe, I come by way of Tennessee."

"You a convert?" I asked.

"Who ain't?" the old man replied. "Hand a feller a Book of Mormon, and if he reads it in earnest, he's a convert. You a newspaper correspondent?"

"What?"

"All these tomfool questions can't be just out of general interest. So you're either a correspondent for some eastern paper, or a sheriff with a warrant for my arrest. You look too young to be a sheriff, so I reckon you're a correspondent."

For Gideon Monson that was a long speech, though at the time I didn't know him well enough to realize it. "Neither." I grinned. "I'm just a convert like yourself."

"Then why you heading the wrong way?"

"I'm looking for some folks who I think took the back trail a day ago. Maybe you saw them?"

Gideon stared ahead and did not respond. Above us the sun was sending streamers of pink and gold across the wide land. In a few hours it would be beating more directly down, building layers of late September heat. But right then, the night-cool of the canyon mouth lingered, fresh and sweet, and I took deep gulps of it, savoring the feel. Off to my left, a rock squirrel popped up, stared at us, and then disappeared into the waving grass. Then a high-bowed Conestoga creaked toward us, pulled by three span of oxen, and the noise of the complaining wheels was about all I could hear. Folks called those wagons prairie schooners, and from the way they loomed up like tall ships, it was easy to see why. Once the wagon had moved past, the old man spoke again.

"For six weeks I've been trying to get that idjut to grease his thimbles. Wouldn't do it, and now they're ruint. Serves him right! Why you looking?"

"It's a long story," I sighed. And then I described Ben Crost and his family, Steenie Bergman, Ben's wagon and team, and even the splayed left foot of Ben's riding horse. The last, I think, impressed Gideon Monson.

"For such a young pilgrim, friend, you take note of a good deal."

"I spent a year in Keokuk, farming and hunting meat for a butcher," I told him. "Then Captain Cowley had me on the scout a little, back on the plains. I'm no frontiersman, but I do try to see what I look at."

"Maybeso you do," Gideon grunted. "And I did see your wagon, yesterday about this time. They was beyond Henderson Spring on Little Mountain, going at a good clip. The girl was with 'em."

Gideon's statement was flat, unemotional—and served me instant notice that somehow he knew who I was really after.

"Did you speak with her?" I asked.

"Not hardly. But I looked at her, little wisp of a thing with the fire of a late sunset in her hair and a smile of sweet purity on her lips. She didn't look happy, though, and I wondered if her pa was taking her away from some young buck like yourself."

"He's not her pa. He's her uncle, or second uncle, maybe, and I think he took her against her will. She and I, we . . . well, we had a . . . an understanding of marriage, and I don't hardly think she'd cut and run."

"Never can tell," Gideon commented wisely.

"Maybe not," I groused, "but she left me a note of desperation, pleading for my help, and I won't stop until she's free."

"Luck," Gideon said as he reached down, took up a small stone, and flicked it at a straying crow. And with that, the conversation was over.

Adjusting my pack, I started out again, and as I walked I found myself feeling mighty grumpy about Gideon Monson's lack of confidence in Steenie and me. But the morning was fine, and it wasn't long before I stopped thinking of him and began to notice again the incoming Saints.

Every living soul of them had pain and weariness written on their faces. Many were barefoot, most wore rags and tatters, most were driving wagons or walking along beside them, and a few were in harness, pulling handcarts that contained a small heap of their remaining worldly goods.

Yet I hardly saw a soul who was not happy, and it put me in mind of one of the things Pa quoted from the Prophet Joseph. According to what Pa had been told, Joseph had said that a religion that didn't require the sacrifice of all worldly goods was a religion that didn't have the power to save.

Well, Mormonism, at least for these folks, had surely required the sacrifice of most worldly possessions. So I prayed, as I strode along the dusty trail, that the Lord would please save them, and all the rest of us who had come so far, in his celestial kingdom. And praying for them, I quickly discovered, made me feel better about Gideon Monson and about where I was going and about what I was hoping to accomplish. In fact, I could feel my heart growing wider and wider—

"Hey, you!"

Looking up in surprise, I realized that I had come to the mouth of the canyon. Further, a man with a rifle was standing there, and he had it pointed directly at me.

"Where do you think you're going?" he asked brusquely.

"Up the trail," I replied, feeling a little irritated by the man's rough manner.

"You have a pass?"

"A what?"

"A pass, Son. Don't you know that Brother Brigham declared martial law? It's been ten days now, so you ought to have heard."

Dumbly, I shook my head.

"Well, he did, and no one goes up-trail without he has orders from General Wells or without he tells me flat out that he has quit the Church and is returning to the sin and wickedness of the Gentiles. Which are you?"

"Neither one. I'm just looking for some folks—"

"Say," the man asked, interrupting me, "how old are you?"

"Eighteen."

The man grinned. "Then if you're a Mormon you're conscripted. You've got to report and get sworn in as a member of the Nauvoo Legion. There's a war going on, you know. Or hadn't you heard of that, either?"

The fellow was being a little sarcastic, but I didn't much mind. I should have known about the conscription. What really troubled me, though, was that I wasn't going to be allowed up-trail.

"I know about the soldiers," I said, my mind racing. "We camped near them, crossing the plains.

"You camped? What do you mean?"

"I came in with Captain Cowley's company, a couple of weeks ago, and now I need to go—"

The sound of rapid hoofbeats beat into our consciousness, and within a moment a horseman loomed into sight, pushing past the stragglers of the emigrant company. As we watched, he pulled his lathered mount to a halt near the sentry.

"Wheat," he said, nodding his head in greeting. "Express for Squire Wells."

"Lo, Port," the sentry replied, momentarily forgetting me. It might have been a chance for me to get by him, too. But I couldn't, not with the man on the horse looking down at me.

He was a thin man, roughly dressed, with gray eyes and jet-dark hair and beard that hung in braids far below his shoulders and chest. In spite of the horse's heavy breathing, the man sat easily and seemed calm as a summer day. Still, I could feel something, almost as though the man was seeing through me, and I could hardly move.

Port—Porter Rockwell. So this was the famous guard of the Prophet Joseph, the dangerous man that folks back east were calling Brigham's avenging angel. I tried to see murder in him—tried, but couldn't, for I don't think it was there. Nevertheless, I continued to stare, and after a moment he turned back to the sentry.

"Van Vliet has left Ham's Fork," Port said softly. "He's going east, and he's sounding like ol' Brig ate him up."

The sentry grinned. "Just like we'll eat up the army, happen they try to come into the Valley. What did he say to Squaw-killer Harney?"

"By gum," the man responded, "*that's* what I've been forgetting! Harney's been replaced by a gent name of Albert Sydney Johnston. I hear he's hard as nails, but he's no butcher, either. He's on his way west now and figures to meet the troops by the end of October. Me, I figure it'll take him a little longer."

Port chuckled, and the sentry laughed with him.

"Wheat," the scout continued, "it was wheat with Van Vliet, all the way. He told Colonel E. B. Alexander, the temporary commander that the government blue-bellies are calling the Old Woman, that the Mormons had been lied about more than any other people he knew. He told him that we're innocent and will fight the army to the last of our extremities. And if my name's Port Rockwell, he's dead right."

"They had *better* believe him!" the sentry exclaimed.

"Some do, some don't. The 10th Regiment are young and full of fire, and when Van Vliet tried to stop them with his warning, they swore they would come in and wipe us out anyhow. They made twenty miles instead of ten the next day. One fellow, Captain Gove, figures the 10th alone can sweep our people from the earth and that the days of Mormonism in Utah are numbered."

The sentry shook his head. "The man's a fool. He's never seen Echo Canyon or the determination of our Mormon boys."

The legendary Porter Rockwell grinned and wrapped his leg around the cantle of his saddle, relaxing further. "Well, at least Van Vliet is convinced our boys are serious, and I do believe he's convinced Colonel Alexander that we are, as well. Van Vliet is reading the words of old Brother Jameson wherever he goes, and they're doing much to spread our cause."

"Brother Jameson?"

"Aye, the same elderly gent as was in the Haun's Mill massacre back in Missouri, where seventeen of our men and boys were murdered. Jameson is still carrying a few ounces of lead around with him from that day. He says he wants to pay it back with usury. Says he prays to God daily to send Old Buck's army along, for he wants to have a chance at them when he's armed.

"Then there was the vote in the southern territories, unanimous, that the Saints would torch their homes and lands and fight from the mountain peaks if the army should come in. Mild and peace-loving Brother John Taylor voiced it well when he thanked God, from the pulpit here in Great Salt Lake City, that the Mormons are determined to be free of mobocracy and to have peace, even if they have to fight for it.

"I reckon that Quartermaster Van Vliet was some startled to see the further unanimous showing of hands when Brother Taylor asked for a confirmation of his words. But now Van Vliet is a believer, and he's on his way to Washington to try and cool Old Buck's heels.

"You know," Port continued, combing his whiskers with his fingers, "I joined up with Mormonism as a youngster, with my best friend Joseph Smith, on the very day it was organized. Yes sir, the Prophet baptized me on the 6th of April in the year '30. But I tell you, even though Brother Joseph told me it would be rough goin' even after our people got to the Rocky Mountains, I didn't figure on all of this."

"Say," he drawled, still seeming to be unaware of my presence, "is Squire Wells yet in the Valley?"

The sentry nodded. "He hasn't passed here, so I reckon he is."

"Then I'm off," Porter Rockwell announced, and with another cry of "Wheat!" he had spurred the horse past the two of us and was pounding past the emigrants down-trail toward the city.

My mind whirling, I watched the man disappear. Then I turned back to the sentry. "Was that *the* Port Rockwell?" I exclaimed.

"One and the same," the sentry replied, still looking at the departing horse and rider. "The purified article. He'd do to ride the river with, too, I'll guarantee. Why, one time—"

"Brother," I interrupted, feeling an increasing urgency to get about my errand, "I must get up that trail."

For a moment I thought the sentry wavered, but then his face set up and he shook his head. "Not unless you have a pass, young feller. I'd suggest that you get down to headquarters, down on Brigham Street, and get signed up. Maybe then you can be assigned to Echo. Otherwise, I reckon you'd better be giving it up."

There are times when a fellow can see that a man can be bluffed, but there are also times when it is just as obvious he can't. This was one of the latter. And so, sorrowing and truly baffled about how I was going to get to Steenie and help her away from her wicked uncle, I turned around and headed back into the dust of the still-descending emigrant company.

I would definitely go down and sign on with the Legion, but I had my reservations about that, too. I had no weapon but my slingshot, no horse, nor no real supplies, and I knew that my chances of getting assigned to the Eastern Expedition were terribly slim. Yet somehow I had to find my way to Steenie.

"Mighty fast trip, wasn't it?"

Startled, I looked up and was surprised to see Gideon Monson, still seated on his rock. Neither had his horse moved, nor the grazing cattle. He was obviously not in any big hurry to reach the valley.

"Sentry won't let me past unless I'm a member of the Legion," I told him. "Brother Brigham has declared martial law, and folks going up-trail have to be apostates or have a pass. Besides, I'm of age and haven't yet signed up for service."

Gideon's hat brim bobbed slightly. "I reckon. But what about that flame-haired gal?"

"I'm going to try and get assigned to Echo. Maybe from there I can find her."

"You don't sound awful hopeful."

"I'm not," I replied, kicking at a rock. "I have no horse, no gun, no supplies. So I have little hope of going. But maybe some other Saint will see her need and help her."

"I thought you loved her."

The challenge was short, terse, and I snapped my head up. "I do, but—"

"Then hang it all, young feller, why you letting that sentry buffalo you? Man loves a woman, he does what it takes to see that she's cared for and protected. He surely doesn't leave it to other folks."

"But the sentry, the conscription . . ."

Gideon slowly unlimbered himself from the rock, setting his floppy, wide-brimmed hat more firmly in place as he did so. "Friend Soderberg," he growled as he creaked to his feet and staggered toward the hanging reins of his horse, "never let it be said that you was overly struck with the brights. You suppose that dusty trail yonder is the onliest way on this green earth over them mountains?"

"No, but—"

"Don't 'but' me, young feller. You want that little gal so bad, go after her!"

"But I have no pass or gun—"

"Hang it all, there's that 'but' again. Young feller, for two cents I'd blaze you a trail back over these mountains myownself. But I don't hardly know if you could foller me."

For a moment I stood still, staring up the oak-clogged slopes that stretched away to the east. My mind was whirling, and I was getting a whole new sense of direction. Finally, I looked back at the old man, who was now seated precariously in his saddle.

"I don't have two cents, Gideon Monson, but I do have this old elm-crotch slingshot and a note from Steenie Bergman."

"You asking me to go with you?" Gideon said slowly, quietly.

"I . . . I . . ."

"Well, are you, or not?"

"I . . . can't ask you to leave your family."

"Kettle-belly here is the onliest family I have, and he goes with me."

"Well, if you don't have anywhere else to go . . ."

Gideon stared off into the valley. "I don't," he said slowly. "I've got no family left alive at all—nothing holding me here but these fool cows. 'Sides, likely the brethren out on the plains could use an experienced hand. So if you wouldn't mind my company . . ."

"I wouldn't. I mean, I'd surely appreciate your help."

Turning his horse, Gideon kneed it forward, and I ran to keep up. Moments later he reigned in near one of the last of the lumbering wagons. Quickly the driver whacked the lumbering oxen to a halt, and then he looked up at the mounted Gideon Monson. "I'm going on a scout," Gideon declared. "Zeph, you and the missus have been good to me, mighty good. I appreciate it, and one day I'll see that you're repaid."

"Gideon, there's no need of that."

The old man reached down into the wagon and pulled out a small pack and long-barreled rifle. "The pendulum always swings," he said as he creaked back upright with his possibles. Then he turned to me.

"Friend Jons, you'll start right now in learning. You see what I just did?"

"Took your pack and rifle out of the wagon?"

"That's correct. But I did it wrong, just so's you'd notice. Did you?"

Mystified, I shook my head.

"Then you'd better open your eyes. Pulling a loaded rifle, barrel first, out of a wagon, is like riding a mule's tail. Both can get you gut-shot. Now, what say that you, me, and Henrietta be on our way?"

"Henrietta?"

Gideon patted the polished, burled stock of the rifle. "Henrietta. She's true as can be, and other than old Kettle-belly here, the dearest thing I have left on this earth – that is, since my Abby-girl and the children was taken . . .

"Tell the missus so long, Zeph," he said, tearing his thoughts away from his past. "I'll look you and the cows up once we all get settled.

"Now leave us be on our way, friend Jons. We have us a splayed-hoofed horse to be catching."

And with that, Gideon Monson urged his horse on its long-gaited way to the north and to the next narrow draw that sliced eastward into the mountains.

And I, with my pack as firmly in place as my determination, set out on shanks pony to do my best to follow him.

Chapter 5

It was cold where Gideon and I hunkered over our small fire, and we were hungry. But the fire helped, and so did the weather, which continued to remain dry. Of course, even as I held my hands over the fire, I knew that the warmth was no substitute for food. But, as Gideon had laconically pointed out, being warm and hungry beat out being cold and hungry six ways from Sunday.

And it was cold up on that mountain. We had been moving for three days, mostly with me hanging onto the tail of Gideon's horse, and we were making tolerable good time, what with having to blaze a whole new trail. But now we were high up, and cold.

That first day, Gideon had led me up what I later learned was Red Butte Canyon, and from the head of Red Butte we had worked our way southeast below Lookout Peak to the top of Killyon Canyon and Little Mountain. Below us a mort of Mormon soldiers had been camped, heading east—so we had stayed shy of them, camping alone. The next day, we had continued east past Fort Big Mountain; had skirted Little Emigration Canyon, Mormon Flat, and Camp Clayton; and had camped above the spring at Kurzy Hollow, just below the mouth of East Canyon. And all the way we had had to take care, for the trail was thick with men and animals heading out to meet the armies of Uncle Sam.

Now we were camped in a little swale high upslope of Spring

Creek, about four miles southwest of the Weber River, and we were hungry. The difference between Gideon and me was that Gideon said little about it, and I could hardly stop complaining.

"Gideon, do you think those fellers down below would spare us a bait of grub?" I asked.

My companion made no reply, so I sat and stared longingly at the fire that winked up at me through the brush and trees below. We were too far upslope to hear what was being said, but there was a large crowd of men down there, and I could occasionally hear voices. Even worse, though, was that at least twice I had distinctly smelled the aroma of frying bacon.

"You think we could go down there and ask to join them for supper?" I asked hopefully.

Almost imperceptibly Gideon shook his head. "Not hardly. Them pilgrims would likely send us back under guard faster than lizards scoot off hot rocks. Besides, one of them might think that thieves had ought to be treated like treasure—buried with care and affection."

"Then could we maybe—just *borrow* . . . some food?"

"You mean thieving."

"Not exactly," I argued. "Gideon, if we're all on the same side, then maybe a little requisitioning between troops would be smiled upon with divine favor."

"Divine favor," Gideon grunted as he pulled himself up from his kneeling position over the fire. Then slowly he hobbled to where his horse cropped sparse bunches of dry grass. At his approach, the horse lifted its head, and with a soft nicker it rubbed its muzzle against the old man's gaunt chest.

Reaching out, Gideon scratched behind the animal's ears. "What d'ya think, Kettle?" he asked the round-bellied animal softly. "Am I hungry enough to become an ordinary thief?"

The horse nickered again and shook its head, and Gideon stared out into the darkness. "Horses is funny animals, friend Jons," he said quietly. "And that goes especially for these scrubby little wild critters that folks call mustangs. Every one I ever saw is smallish, thin and bony, from living off next to nothing at all, and having to travel hundreds of miles to find even that.

"Look at him—grass-bellied, cat-hipped, hammer-headed. Hardly anything at all worth noticing. But there's something there, all right," Gideon grunted, seeming to get more worked up by the minute. "Thing is, it just doesn't show. The spirit is there, and the hardihood, as well as the stubborn clutch on freedom. This little gelding was bred by adversity to survive in a land where only those fitted to it can survive. Kettle here and his kind have been honed by summer drought and winter storm and the fangs of the wolf pack and the claws of the mountain lion to the knife-edge of endurance. Motion is the very meaning of their existence, and in motion they endure. Lookee here, Son. In Kettle's chest are the mightiest lungs on earth, the strongest heart. In his legs are steel springs, his hooves are rock-hard, and buried deep in his lean flanks is the strength to gallop clear to the far edge of eternity and all the way back again."

Once again the little horse muzzled the old man, and again he scratched behind its ears.

"Son," he continued, still not looking at me, "Kettle and I are two of a kind. Neither of us shows much, but as he has been bred to run, I have been bred to become like God. Deep down, I've always known that. Now I've finally found me a religion that teaches I am right. Christ's gospel shows me how to keep the commandments so I can become who I was eternally bred to be—and I am not about to throw it all over for a bellyful of food. No, nor a wagonload of gold, nor anything else of mortal value."

Now Gideon turned back toward the fire and grinned gently. "So if you're hungry enough to steal, Son, you're hungry enough to travel on alone."

He grew still then, and I sat stunned. First, he had said more in that few minutes than he had said in three entire days. But more importantly, he had said things I had never before considered. But he was also right, and I knew it. Like the old man, I had been created to be with God, and to be like God. So was I willing to throw all that away for some foolish, temporary mortal convenience? Not hardly! Not when I thought of it like Gideon put it.

Poking a stick into the fire, I stood up. "Brother Gideon, you are a wonder. What's more, you are right. I am not exercising much faith. My pa gave me a blessing that I would be successful on this little scout, and I suppose that includes filling my belly. I just need to wait until the Lord brings that promise to pass."

Slowly Gideon creaked back to the fire, walking stiff-legged on account of his arthritis. "I call that waiting," he grinned wryly, "living the 'law of the last minute.' For a fact, though, the real name of that law is 'the law of the *true* last minute.' "

"What do you mean?"

"I mean, you and I don't decide when the last minute is supposed to come along. The Lord does. That's why it's called the *true* last minute. Why, I recollect one time . . . "

Gideon suddenly grew still, and he lifted his head slowly until I could see that he was listening, trying to hear something that I couldn't make out.

"What is it?" I whispered.

For a moment he didn't answer, but then slowly he lowered his chin. "Don't know," he replied quietly. "Thought for sure I heard something crying."

It came again then, a faint whimpering that sounded part animal, part human. And that time even I heard it.

"You get a bead on it?" he asked.

"I think," I whispered, "it's off that way, behind you."

Gideon nodded and lifted his rifle. "Me, too. Think I'll have me a looksee."

Well, I don't know why I did what I did then. It made no sense at all, and when I think about it now, it still doesn't. Not unless it was a prompting by the Holy Spirit. Of course, I didn't recognize it as such, but I'm learning that such promptings are most always little more than feelings, small impressions that come into a person's mind like a stray idea. And that is what happened then. A feeling came over me that Gideon and his rifle were not needed out there in the darkness. What was needed was *me*, and I had better be up and getting out there.

"Gideon," I grunted as I rose to my feet and stepped around the fire, "you stay and take care of that arthritis. I'll call out if I need help."

"You ain't armed, Son."

That was true. I wasn't. On the other hand, the same feeling that I was needed out there was making me feel like I didn't need a gun either. Call it crazy, or call it anything else – I don't think I could have possibly stayed by our fire right then. I had to get out in that darkness, and I had to get there in a hurry.

"I'll be all right," I murmured. And without giving my elderly friend a chance for further argument, I slipped into the darkened brush.

As I made my way forward, I was thankful that I hadn't been staring into the flames. A man stares into the flames, he blinds himself for several seconds, and that can be the difference between life and death. On the trail west I had learned to look past a fire, not into it, and fortunately the habit was still with me.

Moving carefully forward, I hadn't gone more than fifty feet when I was abruptly made to halt. The growl that did it was low, animal, and unfriendly. It came from directly before me, and without hesitation I turned to run.

But the brute in the darkness had apparently gotten my scent, and the warning growl became instantly a whine of entreaty. As well, the plea was accompanied by the thumping of a plumed tail upon hard earth.

"A *dog*?" I breathed, instantly forgetting my hunger. "Alone in this wilderness?"

The animal's reply was another whine, another series of hopeful tail thumps.

Searching, I found a sulfur match deep in one of my pockets. Striking and cupping it, I gave close scrutiny to the animal I had found.

Lying there in a dark patch of its own blood was an emaciated creature that looked starved coyote, but that was acting more dog than any dog I had ever seen. I saw that, and I saw also, before the match sputtered out, that this particular coyote-dog had need of human friend far beyond ordinary measure.

"Just so, boy," I said quietly as I reached down and gently scratched him behind the ears. "You need help, feller, and I'm willing to give it if I can. But I've got to get you back to the fire. You willing to be carried?"

The wounded creature responded with further, though noticeably weaker, thumpings of his tail. So, shaking my head, I reached under the animal and eased it into my arms. Rising, then, with my absolutely silent and motionless burden, I made my way back to Gideon and the fire.

"Lawsy," Gideon grinned as I walked in, "you've gone and found some supper."

"Not hardly I ain't," I responded, using some of the old man's own language on him. "This poor brute is hurt, and I'm going to do what I can to help it."

"Son," Gideon said, shaking his head, "that there is a wild prairie wolf. It regains consciousness, you'll likely lose a good chunk of your anatomy, and get the hydrophoby, to boot."

With my foot I scraped a place, near the fire, bare of stones and twigs. "He's conscious right now, but barely. Besides, he may look coyote, but he acts dog."

"That so?" Gideon asked, sounding more interested. "Then likely he's a cross and has been man-trained. What ails him?"

Setting the animal down on the area I had cleared, I bent to examine it and without much trouble found a wickedly broken leg.

It was a cruel wound. Some hours old, it had apparently been caused by a rifle or pistol ball. The radius, or long front bone of the left foreleg, was badly broken near its juncture with the humerus, or upper leg bone. The dog had been licking the wound, so little infection had developed. But to reduce the fracture, and to splint it in such a way as to prevent crippling or gangrene, was going to require the help of far more than my severely limited medical education.

"What you aiming to do, Son?"

"Right now . . . well, to tell the truth, I'm praying."

"Praying?"

" 'Inasmuch as ye have done it unto one of the least of these,' I think the Bible says. Gideon, would you hand me my bedroll there?"

Unrolling the proffered bundle, I sorted quickly through the get-along stuff that Pa had sent with me. For injuries, there was a homemade swab, a wound compress, and a small bottle of carbolic. Knowing that such tools would have to do, and feeling thankful that I had watched Ma do more than a little midwifing, I took out my knife and cut off two short, stout oak limbs from a tree behind me. Then I tore two long strips from the tail of my shirt.

Finally ready, I eased back down beside the shallow-breathing dog. "Are you with me in spirit, good friend?"

The dog whined, licked my hand, lay back upon the earth, and then was still. "Trust in the Lord, you told me," I said with a wry grin to the intently watching Gideon Monson. And then I took up the crude swab and bottle of carbolic and went to work.

An hour later, finally finished, I sank back against a tree and closed my eyes. "Whew! I hope that takes care of him."

"It'll do the trick," Gideon responded, and I was surprised at the tenderness in his voice. "Son, you have a real way with critters. In all my days, I never saw the like."

I opened my eyes and looked at the old man. "Pa has it more than me, and he says he got it from his pa. Maybe it runs in the family. But he can gentle-talk a mad bull into wearing pinafores in five minutes."

Gideon chuckled.

"Likewise," I continued, "back in Keokuk they never brought him a horse he couldn't ride, if he could talk to it a mite before climbing aboard. Come to think of it, I haven't been thrown in some time myself."

"Been on some wild ones?" Gideon asked hopefully, his eyes brightening as he sensed a new friendship forming.

"No," I said, "haven't hardly been on a horse at all, ever in my life. That's why I haven't been thrown."

Gideon grinned and tossed a pebble at me. I ducked, and suddenly I felt good. Gideon had been impressed with something I had done, the dog was probably going to be fine, and I was going to find Steenie and take her back home with me. In short, the world was shaping up as a wonderful place to be.

Sensing my mood, the wounded animal thumped its tail a few times, the small fire crackled warmly, and I stretched back further against the tree. In another two or maybe three days, I would come up with Steenie, and then she and I—

"Hello the camp," a voice called softly from the darkness.

Jerking my eyes open, I was surprised to find myself alone in the small clearing, alone except for the crippled and low-growling dog. Gideon was gone, and—

"Hoist your hands up where I can see them," the quiet voice ordered. "Now!"

Obediently I raised my hands, but still I kept my eyes focused on the rim of darkness where the man's voice seemed to be coming from.

"You alone?"

"Except for this almost dead dog," I replied honestly.

"Other men?"

"Do you see any?"

There was a soft chuckle, and a bearded man materialized on the edge of the firelight. I started then, for I knew him. Or at least I knew that I had seen him before. The trouble was, I couldn't remember where. Nor could I remember his name.

He looked at me, and the single eye of his rifle glared in my direction as well. "Two bedrolls," he said softly, and once again I felt a little shiver of recognition. "You and the dog travel in style, don't you."

"We do."

"But no grub, nor pot for coffee. Friend, I don't understand this a'tall."

"Well," I said, careful not to move my hands, "put down that rifle, take up a rock, and I'll tell you my woeful tale."

"I'll sit, but you've some tall talkin' to do afore I lower this rifle. There's a war on hereabouts, some wild Indians are out taking slaves and lifting hair, and a man can't be too careful. Now, how come you and the dog be rusticating in my own private mountain camp?"

"*Your* camp?" I echoed in surprise. "But there were no signs of previous fires when we—"

"We?"

"We. The dog and me."

"It have a name?"

"Lazarus," I responded, thinking quickly. "If he lives through being shot and my doctoring, he'll have been literally raised from the grave. So, why wasn't there sign of fire?"

"Because I always clean my camps. Now, Son, normally I'm right friendly—but when a man holds a gun on me, especially from ambush, I get sociable as an ulcerated back tooth. You tell that feller behind the rock yonder to come out with his rifle lowered, and maybe we can all make a little medicine."

Turning, I stared as old Gideon slowly rose to his feet, his rifle trained on the man across from me.

"I'll come," Gideon said easily, "but if we're lowering weapons, we had *all* ought to do it. I'd hate like thunder to break your arm."

"Not kill me?"

"Not hardly. I don't hold with killing. Besides, breaking your arm would be a whole lot more beneficial. Give you time to ponder the evil ways of man, and maybe do a little repenting. Now, what's it to be?"

The man, whom I still could not place, chuckled again. "It appears we have here what Dan Jones's friend Kit Carson from down to Taos calls a Mexican standoff. Either hand opens the ball, both hands dance to the tune. I think I'll lower my rifle."

Slowly he did so, and with a sigh of relief I lowered my hands. Carefully then Gideon limped forward until he too was in the light, and then we all glared at each other.

"So, are you Mormon, or otherwise?" the man asked.

"Which are you?" Gideon responded instantly.

The man nodded. "Very well, I'll go first. I'm Mormon."

He watched our reactions for a long-held breath, and then,

apparently satisfied, he plunged ahead. "Name's Ephraim Hanks. I'm on a little scout for the Prophet."

"Ephraim Hanks!" I exclaimed, my memory of my wagon-ride with him and Steenie flooding back, "I met you—"

"Friend Jons," Gideon warned, cutting me off, "it's hard to put a foot in a shut mouth. You forget mighty fast that martial law has been declared back yonder, don't you?"

I gulped, knowing Gideon was right. But still, this man had been very friendly to Steenie, and I felt certain that, given the chance, he would be the same to us.

"We've met?" Ephraim Hanks asked then, exactly as I had hoped he would.

"Yes, sir. The other day. You rode a piece with Steenie Bergman and me. We spoke of the war."

Hanks beamed. "Of course we did. And you're Jons . . . "

"Soderberg."

"That's right, Soderberg. How do you happen to be up here, Son? The way Christena was looking at you and hanging onto your arm, I'm surprised she let you get this far out of the valley."

"Steenie's gone, Brother Hanks. Ben Crost and the whole family pulled stakes and lit out, four days ago. Thing is, I think he forced Steenie to go with him against her will. She asked me by note to come after her, and I'm doing my best to do just that."

"Is this your father?"

Gideon snorted. "Grandpappy, more likely," he growled.

"Is that so?"

"No, sir. I met Gideon Monson on the trail, and he—"

Ephraim Hanks stood up in surprise. "Gideon Monson. *The* Gideon Peabody Monson?"

Gideon's eyes crinkled down at the corners, but he said nothing. Nor did he have to. Ephraim Hanks was saying it all.

"Captain Monson," he said as he stepped forward and held out his hand. "Old-timer, I'm right proud to make your acquaintance. My first wife's father fought under you at the Battle of New Orleans, and I have heard the tale a hundred times of how you took a handful of men and whipped back a regiment of the British, saving his life and the lives of—"

"An old-timer is somebody who's had a lot of interesting experiences," Gideon declared soberly, "some of them true."

"Well, my wife's father swears what he saw you do in that battle was true."

Gideon shook his head. "It weren't no regiment. They was hardly more numerous than we were. Besides, the War of 1812 is a long time past, and everybody was saving everybody's life in that battle. In a war, there ain't never any real heroes."

"Likely," Ephraim grinned. "But I'm still more than a little happy to make your acquaintance. Have you . . . joined the Church?"

"Two years past."

"Why, that's wonderful. Won't my wife be pleased to hear this." Then Brother Hanks turned back to me. "And Ben Crost finally tucked his tail, did he? Well, he didn't act like he had much staying power. And you say that you're after Christena?"

I nodded.

"You sure she wants to be found?"

"The note she left me says she does."

Hanks smiled. "Luck to you, Son. I wish I could help, but I'm under orders and can't do it. I hope you find her, though. With Captain Monson along, I'm sure you will. Now tell me why the two of you are up here on the slope instead of down with the rest of the brethren."

After a nod from Gideon, I told the rest of it, including how Gideon and I had come up Red Butte Canyon, giving the sentry the slip.

Ephraim nodded occasionally, but he was quiet until I was finished. Then he chuckled. "So that's what's been bothering the two of you. No passes, and you've neither of you signed up for the Legion. Well, it'll sure have to be done."

"You mean to stand there, all bold-faced and hairy-fronted, and tell me that a stove-up old fool like me's supposed to sign up for this war?" Gideon exclaimed.

Ephraim looked stunned. "Why, Captain, I . . . I thought you'd *want* to join up."

Gideon snorted. "Not hardly. I'm too old for conscription, too, and you know it! No, sir, I've had me enough of fighting in this life. If Old Buck's army boys want to use me up, why, I'll do like them Lamanite fellers did in the Book of Mormon. I'll lay myself down and make it easy for them. Yes, sir, I am a converted man of peace, ever since I promised the Lord I'd never join nothing else after I joined his onliest true church."

Ephraim grinned. "Then why the rifle?"

"Him," Gideon grunted, nodding at me. "I'm only up here because I want to see the boy find his woman child. Normally I'd say that a feller ought to never marry a woman with the kind of looks he'd like to see on another man's wife. But from the brief looksee I had of Christena Bergman, all bets and uncommonly good advice from an old soldier like me are off. I would say that little sister is a prize worth chasing."

"She is, at that. So, neither of you is interested in stopping the government forces from wintering in the Valley?"

Gideon shot me a warning look, but he needn't have. I wasn't interested in anything but finding Steenie, and Ephraim Hanks could see it in my eyes.

"Because," he continued slyly, "if you'd be interested in helping us out, why, I might be able to work it into our orders so that I could help *you*. Interested now?"

Gideon and I looked at each other, and I imagine he too could see the beam of hope in my eye. With a muttered grumble he swatted his leg with his bedraggled hat, and then he sank down on his saddle to stare into the fire. "Be thankful for fools," he growled to himself. "Without them, none of the rest of us would look like much. You call it, Boy. I'll ride along, whatever it is."

"Then you have a deal," I said to Ephraim Hanks. "So long as it gets me closer to Steenie Bergman."

Grinning, Ephraim nodded. "Brother Al," he called then, "why don't you come on in now."

Gideon started up, and I simply stared as a man rose from

behind the very rock where Gideon had hidden earlier. Then he lowered his rifle, and with a brief nod he stepped into the glow of the fire.

"Gentleman," Ephraim Hanks declared soberly, "may I present Brother Al Bagley. Al, meet Captain Gideon Monson and Jons Soderberg, the two newest *non*-members of the Nauvoo Legion."

And Al Bagley smiled and said hello.

Chapter 6

"Well, boys," Al Bagley declared after we had stuffed ourselves with the best fatback and frybread I had ever eaten, "ol' Eph here has done it again."

"Which is?" Gideon questioned.

"Prophesied. Yes, sir, sometimes Eph out-Brighams Brother Brigham himself. This morning as we were saddling up, Eph told me we'd run onto some reinforcements for our little two-man army, and he thought that we'd about double it in size. Well, here you are, and again he was right."

"This . . . this prophesying happens often?" I asked.

"No, not oftener than every day or so."

I looked with wonder at the bearded man who sat silently across the small fire, picking his teeth with a wood sliver. Ma and Pa were often close to the Spirit, but the process had so far eluded me, and I truly wondered what it would be like. I also wondered how a man could get to be close to the Lord, but I had never seriously considered that it might happen to somebody like me. Mostly, that was because I was too comfortable having faith in the faith of others. I just didn't want to pay the price to develop my own.

"How do you do it?" I finally asked, thinking I might learn some shortcut to out and out becoming righteous.

Eph looked up. "I don't. The Lord does all the work. I just listen and say what I think the Spirit is impressing me to say. Usually it comes out about right."

"Only if your heart is right," Al qualified.

Eph grinned. "Wouldn't know about that."

"Likely," Al grinned back. Then he turned to me. "Son, the kicker to hearing the Spirit is in being worthy. Brother Brigham reminded us yesterday morning, while we were eating breakfast together, of the Lord's warning concerning the Spirit. The Lord told Brother Joseph, in Doctrine and Covenants 63:16, that if a man can be pure hearted, not harboring any lustful or unclean thoughts, then he can *have* the Spirit. On the other hand, if he lets his mind grovel around in the mud of lust and unrighteousness, then he won't have it. The Lord made Joseph that promise."

"There's more," Eph enjoined quietly. "If a feller throws up his hands, so to speak, and gives up to wickedness and lust, he not only loses the Spirit, but the next thing you know, he starts denying the faith. Once that happens, he's apostatized, and the Lord says that from then on he'll be filled with fear."

"Meaning?"

"Meaning," Gideon stated, speaking for the first time, "that a man gets jumpy as a fly-bit bull once he loses the Spirit. He's offended at the least little thing, and he's certain-sure that others are out to get either him or what he thinks is rightfully his. Left alone, the poor soul will be led by the devil all the way down the darkened road until murder is the only option he sees left."

"The Captain's right, Jons, and it's obvious that he's seen this in others."

"Durn tootin' I have. Not only seen it, but heard about it and read about it, too."

"Read about it?"

"In the Book of Mormon. Friend Jons, you need to start reading that book. Every time any righteous man, Nephite or otherwise, lost the Spirit of the Lord and apostatized, he got filled with a spirit of murder and was heaps more wicked than the regular wicked folks he hung around with. Wicked Nephites were always worse than wicked Lamanites, and were always chosen to be their leaders because they were so bloodthirsty.

Way I hear it, wicked Mormons were the ones who led out in the murders of Joseph and Hyrum Smith, so things ain't hardly changed at all, then until now."

Gideon stopped talking, and in my mind I could see Ben Crost, Steenie's uncle. He had acted jumpy as could be the minute I came along, and all of a sudden I began to wonder about that man's thoughts and morals. No, that isn't so. I already *knew* about his thoughts and morals, for he had been trying to force himself upon Steenie for some time. And it wasn't any righteous plural marriage he was advocating. No sir, he didn't believe in that, or the Church, or the prophets. He believed only in himself and was advocating out-and-out lust. And now it became clear as day what had happened to the man. As the Lord had prophesied, he had committed mental adultery, had lost the Spirit, had denied the faith, and was now so filled with fear that he had fled east, thinking that his life was in danger. And so it was—his *spiritual* life. His soul was dying of slow strangulation, and he didn't hardly know it at all.

"Ben Crost's a good example of all this," Ephraim Hanks said, confirming my thoughts. "He's made a lot of boasts about what he accomplished in his past, but a self-made man usually comes to the point where he worships his own creator. Ben has lost the Spirit, and now he worships only himself."

"Anyway," Al Bagley concluded as he nudged a small stick into the fire with his boot, "worshiping the one true God is the trick ol' Eph here has learned. His heart is pure as the driven snow. The Lord knows it, and that's why he blesses Eph with the spirit of prophecy."

For a time then no one spoke, and I looked at the men who surrounded me. I had never before met such men, and each of them was giving my think-box, as Gideon would have said, whole wagonloads of new fodder to chew through.

Finally Eph got up and rolled out his bedroll. "Yes, sir," he breathed as he stretched out, "it was a mortal pleasure taking breakfast from Brother Brigham. He's full of confidence that the Lord will keep the army out of the valley this winter, and so am I. Fact is, I feel better with just the four of us and the

Lord than if I had a whole legion of men behind me. Boys, before our little scout is over, it will be determined whether a legalized government mob can force themselves on us against our will or not. But I say we go in the strength of Israel's God, and the army will not prevail."

"Jesse Earl came in from the plains yesterday," Al Bagley stated, "and he reported that Uncle's boys are marching on very unconcerned and deliberate. He says they are not dreaming of trouble but instead are anticipating fine times in the Valley this winter, walking over our people, hanging our rulers, and ravaging our women."

Eph grunted. "They'll be some surprised where they do winter. In fact, I feel to add my prophecy to Brother Brigham's. If we go out meekly, shedding no blood, that army will never get to the Valley this season. Instead, they will winter in the cold and blizzards of the mountains, where their love for rapine and murder will be somewhat cooled."

"That's a sure prophecy," Al grunted, "because Brother Brigham said it already. That's the kind I could make."

Eph laughed easily. "There, Jons—you see? Prophesying's not much harder than listening to the Lord's anointed servants and then repeating what they say. It's still the Lord who has to do all the work."

Things got very quiet then, and we all sat silently in the mountain swale, thinking. Overhead, the tiny lanterns of the stars glittered in the frosty sky. The black bulwarks of the trees stretched upward as if in sentinel circle, mostly sheltering us from the frigid winds that dropped down from the mountains to the east. Occasionally a log popped in the fire, but other than the sighing of the wind and the occasional distant murmur of voices from down below, there was no sound on the mountain at all.

I looked down at Lazarus, and the animal, sensing my gaze, weakly thumped his tail. I grinned and rubbed between his ears, but I still worried. The dog was not well, and I had no idea how he would live once we departed in the morning. I just hoped that—

"So you doctored the dog?"

I looked up at Eph and nodded.

"Son, you did a fine job, and you've won a true friend. That dog will live, and one day he'll return the favor—with interest."

"Sir?" I questioned, not understanding.

"You've saved his life, Jons. The Spirit whispers that he'll save yours, maybe more than once."

Now I really looked at the man. But he just smiled, laid back on his saddle, and closed his eyes.

"So you're after a girl?" Al Bagley asked then.

"Yes, sir. She left me a note on . . . on something I had given her, asking for help, and I plan on aiding her back to the Valley."

"You give her a ring, or something?"

"No," I said, feeling unaccountably embarrassed. "It was . . . my old slingshot."

I expected laughter, but Al only looked at me. And then Eph spoke from his bedroll. "Funny thing what sorts of foofaraw a woman sets store by. My wives are the same. Little trinkets hooked to memories mean more to them than all the world's wealth. A smile of real happiness from one of my wives is worth more to me than a whole mule-train of pure gold. So, more and more I'm working to give them reason to smile."

"You a polygamist?" Gideon asked.

"That's right. I'm married to Harriet Decker Little and Jane Capener. They're both fine women. Besides that, last winter I met a young woman out on the plains name of Thisbe Read. She was part of the Martin handcart company. If my impressions are correct, one day she will become my third wife."

"Well," Gideon said, shaking his head, "I've heard tell that 'For better or for worse' usually means for good, but Mormons take the cake both for numbers and marital longevity."

"How much?" Al Bagley asked, sounding confused.

"Sticking together for eternity," Gideon explained. "I used to say that you can never trust women, or tenderfeet—but the wife I had was so all-fired wondrous and trustworthy and loving that I'd quit mortality right now if'n I thought she and I wouldn't be together for eternity. Nor would I ever want to try it again with another."

"That's sort of how I feel about Steenie," I said softly. Gideon and Eph looked at each other and smiled, but I didn't mind. I was falling deeper in love by the day, and I didn't see how it could possibly end up any other way than for Steenie and me to get sealed up to each other for eternity.

"Is your little gal truly worth this chase?" Al Bagley asked me.

"Moreso," I said. "Besides being pretty as a picture, which she surely is, Christena is warm, tender, loving, gentle—truthfully, I can't think of an angelic quality that she doesn't have."

"Yep," Al said, "he's sure smitten."

"Learning fast," Gideon agreed. "Given enough time, Jons'll come to find out that a year of traipsing around the mountain don't hardly equal a day of sweetheart'n. But he ain't old enough to know that yet. Way I see it, a man doesn't have sensible thoughts about a woman until he's thirty-five. A'fore that, all he has is feelings, and they run four hundred to the ounce and are mostly blind."

"Is she a smart one?" Al Bagley asked next, when the others had stopped chuckling.

"Questionable," Gideon teased, "seeing who's she's fallen in love with."

"She's smart," Eph declared, finally standing up for me. "I know her, and she's real bright."

"Well," Gideon said, "that's good, Son. Marry a woman with brains enough for two, and you had ought to come out about even."

Everybody but me laughed at that—and I would have, except that I didn't want to encourage too much more of their persecution. But I should have laughed, for it continued anyway.

"If she's all you brethren say she is," Al Bagley declared, "then maybe I'll give young Soderberg a little competition when we come up to her."

"Won't work," Gideon declared. "I've seen it a'fore, and

I'll see it again. She loves Jons, so he'll get hisself hugged for sneakin' a kiss from her, and you'd just get yourself slapped."

"You said she was beautiful?" Al asked.

"Pretty as can be," I told him.

Al grinned widely. "Then I don't reckon she's hardly worth my trouble."

"What? But—"

"Young feller, most women are as pretty as they *can* be. Thing is, that's not usually saying much."

Well, I threw a stick at Al Bagley, he ducked and tossed another back, there was a little more general teasing and poking fun at me, and then Ephraim Hanks grew serious.

"If you catch Ben Crost, Jons, what do you aim to do with him?"

"Beat him to a bloody pulp!" I growled.

"Ahh, the laying on of hands method of teaching the gospel."

I grinned sourly at Eph's humor. "Well, he laid his meat-hooks on me the other night. I would say he has it coming."

"And then?"

The question made me uncomfortable, not because it was asked maliciously, but because I really didn't know. I'd tried to think it out, but as far as I could get was seeing Ben Crost's nose smashed flat. After that, things didn't show up clear at all.

"The man might get real mean," Al put in. "Are you prepared for that possibility?"

Again I squirmed, for truly I wasn't. Pa had always taught us to be peaceable and quick to forgive, leaving vengeance for the Lord. But Steenie was important to me, terribly important, and it seemed reasonable that I needed to put my hand in this pie and pluck out the only plum there. But if it came to violence beyond a good fist fight, I didn't hardly know what I would do.

Gideon, I think, sensed what I was feeling, for it was then that he spoke up. His voice wasn't loud, and it had the squeak of age in it. But nevertheless we all listened intently to his tale.

"I come from the high-ups of the Cumberland Plateau back to Tennessee," he said, talking only to the night. "Me and my folks ran a side-hill farm that was long on rocks and short on crops, just out of Jamestown. Still, we mostly had a good life.

"Then we were set on by a few fellers who were determined to make theirs what we had already made ours. In that fight my older sister died under their hands. But Pa was a peaceable man with a love of God in his heart, so we buried my sister and moved on, leaving what we had to them.

"Trouble is, those same fellers came again, some two or three years later, at our new farm. You see, they had got a place from us once, it had been easy, and they wanted more.

"That time Pa and me stood against them, and one man of theirs went down. But they didn't learn from that, and a week later they came a third time. They shot Pa up real bad, burned the cabin, and thought they had us treed. But I got into the woods with Pa's Henrietta here, and when the last of the smoke had cleared, three more of their men were on the ground dead, including the big old he-bull who had been running their raw-hide outfit. After that they pretty much left us alone."

"You did right," Al Bagley declared. "Even the scriptures tell us to defend our families."

Gideon nodded. "I know. Trouble is, dead men make mighty poor bedfellows. I don't think there has been a day in my life that I ain't seen those fellers lying on the ground. They may have had it coming, but I surely paid the price."

"Unless under very particular conditions," Eph then declared, "bloodshed is never a good idea. The Saints are facing the same thing today. We can have bloodshed, or we can follow the Prophet and avoid it. If we use up that army, then Brigham says we will have blood to our heart's content, and a good measure of it will be ours.

"You see, boys, a man's blood is a sacred thing to the Lord. I don't know how it works, or even why, but blood is terrible important to him. That's why the scriptures say that Christ's blood purifies, sanctifies, and cleanses us from sin. And any murdered man's blood, including Joseph's and Hyrum's, will cry unto the Lord for vengeance until vengeance is taken by the heavens.

"So you see, blood is important to the Lord, or maybe a better word is sacred. If it is spilled unrighteously, then the Lord is bound to see that justice exacts a penalty upon those who spilled it. And we will yet see that penalty exacted upon this nation, for they have spilled the blood of innocent men, women, and children, ever since this Church was founded.

"After the mobbings in Missouri, Joseph prophesied that America would have blood and mobbing to their heart's content, and they will. But to me, it would be a pity if the Saints, in the heat of anger, spilled the blood of those poor soldiers and had to be punished, themselves."

"What about the soldiers who want to spill ours?" I asked.

"Some of 'em might truly want that, Jons. From them the Lord will protect us, if we do as Brigham said. Most of the soldiers, though, are just following orders, and are as innocent as you or me. Trouble is, over the sights of a rifle, innocence is hard to detect. That's why I, for one, will not fire a shot in this campaign."

"But we're making guns and powder . . ."

Eph grinned. "We sure are, and those things will come in handy for hunting, and such, in the years to come. But to use them on people? We won't have to do it if the Saints will do as they've been counseled."

"But the speeches, the factories . . . Why do the Brethren talk about fighting like they do, if they don't really want us to fight?"

"Good question. I'll answer it, and then let's pack it in. Jons, folks have to feel involved to become united, and the speeches and the gun factories are to get the Saints involved. Once we're all united and willing to do what needs to be done to protect our wives and children, to sacrifice whatever needs to be sacrificed, then the Lord will step forward and fight our battles for us.

"We'll slow the soldiers down and make life as miserable for them as we possibly can, and if the Saints will continue to work and prepare in unity to the best of their abilities, then I promise you that there will never be a war. The Lord will fight it and win it for us, and not a shot will ever be fired."

"Is that another prophecy?" Gideon asked.

"Yeah," Al Bagley responded, "that is another one. He said the same thing to Brother Brigham yesterday, and the Prophet blessed him and told him that the Lord had revealed that idea to him. So now we'll watch and see it come to pass."

"You're saying, then, that I won't need a gun on my quest to find Steenie?"

"You don't have a gun?" Al Bagley asked, surprised.

Silently I shook my head.

"Boy, you're crazy. Not to mention the army out there, what if that Crost feller decides to shoot you? He might not take too kindly to your taking the girl back, you know. How you planning on defending yourself?"

"I . . . I don't know . . . "

Al Bagley laughed, but Ephraim Hanks stopped him with a raised hand. "Do what you're supposed to do, Son," Eph then said quietly, "and for the rest of your life you'll never need a gun to point at another man. In fact, the Spirit whispers that if you are worthy, you will one day be a bishop in this Church. And good bishops must be free of the blood and sins of their generation. You keep the commandments and seek the Spirit, Jons, and for the rest of your life, the Lord will fight your battles for you, and you will be free of that blood and those sins.

"Now," Ephraim Hanks continued, "if you boys are ready to turn in, I'll lead us in a word of prayer." He did, and for a long time after that I lay in the dark, thinking. Not about me maybe becoming a bishop. That was too staggering, and I had to let it alone. But I did think a lot about the other. Eph was right about me not shedding blood, and I knew it. I just didn't know if I could hold to that, happen Ben Crost had done something awful to my Steenie. And it was while I was worrying my teeth on that bone that I finally fell asleep.

Chapter 7

"You don't have a horse?"

Feeling even sillier than I had felt about not having a gun, I shook my head in response to Ephraim Hanks's question. "But I'm a good walker," I declared.

"What about your dog? That wound looks mighty serious, Jons. In my experience, breaks like that can take weeks, even months, to heal."

I looked down at Lazarus, who lay on the ground looking up at me. "I guess I'll carry him," I replied. "For as long as it takes."

Eph shook his head. "I don't know, Son. We need to move fast, and I don't think you can do it carrying a worn out coyote-dog. But if you're that all-fired serious, then maybe I can carry it for you, at least until we can find somebody to care for it."

Walking over, he reached down to lift Lazarus but stopped short at the low and threatening growl from the animal's throat.

"Is it just me," Eph asked as he straightened back up, "or is this critter so overly fond of everybody?"

"I don't know," I told him. "Gideon, maybe you can carry him on your horse."

My elderly friend reigned over, and I lifted Lazarus toward him. But again the growl issued forth, and Gideon pulled back his hand just in time to avoid losing a couple of fingers in Lazarus's snapping jaws.

Al Bagley grinned. "Boy, Eph was right. You've got you a

one-man dog, and he'll be your friend for life. I've seen it in others, a time or two. But he's no good to the rest of us, so if you want him along, you'll have to carry him yourself."

"Then I will."

"Jons," Eph asked as he looked down at the dog and me, "did you pray before you worked on that critter?"

"He sure enough did," Gideon responded for me.

Eph grinned. "That explains it, then."

"Explains what?"

"My impression. I feel to tell you that the Lord will work a miracle on that animal. You will yet see it brought to pass. It will heal quickly."

"Truly?"

"Absolutely. Now we'll ride ahead," Eph concluded, "and do what we can to scare you up a horse. You have any preferences?"

I grinned. "Not hardly. Folks say I have a way with animals, so I imagine about anything will do. If it has a saddle on it, I'll be able to ride it."

"You ride a lot?" Eph asked, sounding surprised.

"He ain't rid a'tall," Gideon told him. "But he does have a way with critters."

"Well, like I always say," Al Bagley interjected, "never tamper with the natural ignorance of a greenhorn. Let's go find the boy a horse."

After giving me directions on where to follow, the three rode away, and I was left alone with my new and crippled companion, a mangy but grateful coyote-dog.

"Well, Lazarus," I said as I adjusted his weight in my arms, "it's a fine day for a tramp through the woods. Let us be on our way, as well."

And so we were. It was a beautiful morning for walking, too. The air was fresh and clear as spring water, birds sang in the trees, several times deer bounded away up the slopes before us, and it felt good to Lazarus and me just being alive and in the mountains. I didn't even feel bad that the others had gone on ahead. I knew they were rounding up a spare mount for me, and so in patience I strode along after them.

I thought too about Steenie, wondering where she was and what she was doing. Probably traveling, all right. But a wagon couldn't make as good time as I could, and I knew it would only be a matter of days until I caught up with her.

And wouldn't she be excited then! In my mind I could already picture our reunion, with each of us in the other's arms. What a grand time we would have then. Of course, first I would need to take care of Ben Crost. But I would, by cracky—not maiming him or killing him, I had finally decided—but by teaching him a sound lesson, nonetheless. Yes, sir, what a glorious day that was going to be!

And with that thought in mind, I began to consider the strange turn of events in my life since I had left the Valley. I had met up with the most unusual and most righteous men I had ever known—other than my folks, of course. And they had taught me, too. The thing that was interesting to me was how much better I now felt, knowing that my resolve to live a higher law had been directly related to the company I had been keeping. Sort of made sense, too. Pa always said that the winds of others' words either set a person's ship on course or pushed it out to sea. And right then and there I made up my mind that I was going to be on course. I would get my Steenie, we would marry and settle down, and our children would be taught as these fine brethren had taught me.

With such high and lofty thoughts racing through my mind, I made my way off Hogback Summit, past Jack Beard Springs, through Parker Hollow, and finally into Main Canyon. There I followed the whispering, gurgling creek out into the valley of the Weber River. From that point I turned right, and after what seemed no time at all, I was approaching Echo Camp, at the mouth of Echo Canyon.

"Jons Soderberg! Yo, friend Jons!"

Looking up, I saw Gideon Monson waving at me from the top of a pole corral, maybe a hundred yards away. I grinned, waved back, hitched Lazarus up in my weary arms, and shifted directions. Then I set out to make my way to the corral.

I found the mouth of Echo Canyon to be like one great village. Men were camped everywhere—in tents, willow huts, mud huts, cottonwood bark huts, and even out in the open. Cooking fires were also everywhere, but it was late in the morning, almost eight o'clock, by the time I got there. And by that time most of the fires had burned out. The men were now at work, here and there, building up the defenses of the canyon, getting ready, should it become necessary, to repel Ol' Buck's army of boys in blue.

"Hello, Gideon," I said as I finally hove up at the rough corral and placed Lazarus on the ground. "Been waiting long?"

"Not overly. Put the mutt down, climb up here, and take a look-see."

I did as directed and saw Al Bagley and Eph Hanks standing in the pole enclosure with as scraggly a little gray horse as I had ever before laid eyes on.

"That one for me?" I asked sorrowfully.

Gideon nodded soberly. "It is if you want it."

"Gray?"

"Son, a good horse is never a bad color. Gray, black, dun, I've found the best color for a horse is *fat*, and that one is."

"But . . . but it's so small."

Gideon sighed. "Admire a big horse, Jons, but saddle a small one. You'll ride easier and farther, and that's a purified fact."

"I don't know, Gideon. That horse looks half dead."

Gideon now shook his head. "Boy, for some folks, assets are brains. For you, all they are is baby donkeys. Now you listen to me. When a man gets too old to set a bad example, he hands out good advice, and now I'm handing it to you. That little horse is a good one, and you'd do well to stop your jaw-jacking and accept her."

"All right," I said, doing my best to sound happy, "against my better judgment I'll take your word for it."

"You ain't got no confounded judgment at all," Gideon

muttered. "But you had best be careful anyway. Those boys have a hooraw going—"

"*Her?*" I asked, interrupting my friend. "It's a *mare?*"

"And a fine one, too," Gideon grunted, closing his mouth against me with finality. "Hey, Eph, the kid finally says he's interested."

"Well, Son," Ephraim Hanks said, grinning at me, "that's fine. Come down here and let's see if you can outride her."

I jumped down into the corral, and as innocent as a baby robin I waltzed up to that little gray horse. But I should have been suspicious. Busy as the men in that camp were, I should have realized that there were way too many of them hanging around that corral. For there were, dozens of them, doing this and that and the other—seeming to pay no mind to me or Eph or Al Bagley or the little gray mare.

And I paid them no mind, either. In a moment I was beside my companions, ready to claim my horse. Al had the little gray by an ear, twisting it back and down, and the animal was standing still and motionless before me.

"What do you think?" Eph asked innocently.

"She looks good enough for me."

"Glad to hear it. She may buck a little, but most horses do that. Just hang on, and that will wear her down."

"You don't need to tell him that," Al grunted. "The kid is good with animals. He said so himself."

I looked at the man, surprised a little by his tone of voice. But he grinned at me and winked, and my mind was once again at peace.

"Mount up," Eph Hanks ordered.

And so with great excitement I scrambled onto the back of the little mare. The stirrups didn't fit exactly, but I bent my knees and pulled up the hackamore reins until it felt about right.

"Don't take too short a hold," Gideon hollered, "or she'll jerk it right away from you the minute she bogs her head."

I nodded, starting to feel a little nervous.

"All set?" Al asked.

Again I nodded, and Al turned the mare loose.

One jump, I think, was all she made, but it was all so quick that I couldn't hardly tell. For the next thing I knew, I was on the ground with both hands and one mouth full of dirt. Still, it hadn't hurt me any, and as soon as Al Bagley "eared" the little gray down again, I made another try. It was just as short and sweet as the first ride, but this time it dazed me some, and so I wasn't near so quick getting up off the ground. But Al Bagley eared her down again, and again I climbed back on.

"Never mind the hackamore this time," Gideon shouted. "Just get hold of that old horn and screw down on it!"

I nodded, then looked down at the grinning Al, blinking a couple of times trying to see if it was really him. Then he turned her loose a third time.

And on that ride I did real well, or at least I thought I was doing well. I pulled every scrap of leather off the wooden saddle-horn and managed to ride that little mare through four jumps, and I was starting to think that I might stick. But then the little mare switched ends on me, my foot came loose of the stirrup, and the stirrup flew up and caught me over the right eye, knocking me loose again. Next jump my shirt caught on the saddle-horn, and when I went sailing the shirt stayed behind.

I must have sat on the ground for some time after that, trying to remember where or who I was. For when I finally became aware of the laughter, it had almost died out. Looking up, I saw the top pole of the corral lined with grinning and laughing men, and I knew I had been hoorawed for sure.

Slowly getting back up, I could hardly keep my balance. I took one step, then another—and Gideon was there on one side, while Eph had hold of me on the other.

"He's some wobbly on his pins," Gideon declared.

Al Bagley had the gray by the ear again, and he was grinning, as Gideon later said, like a jackass eating cactus. "You ready for another try?" he hooted, and there were chuckles all around me.

"You bet," I mumbled, and staggered forward.

"Whoa, boy," Eph said softly, "you proved your point, and we all got our chuckle. Now we'll go find you a decent horse . . . "

I broke loose of the two men and limped toward Al Bagley. I think he was some nervous at the expression on my face, but I didn't intend doing anything to him. Not then, at least. Instead, I wanted information.

"Who's is the horse?" I mumbled when I had reached it.

Al released the animal's ear and stepped back. "I . . . I don't hardly know. It's part of a string the Church sent up."

"So if I want it I can use it?"

"Hold on," Eph called. "Jons, we'll be in need of making time, not fighting bad horses. Now let's find you another mount and be moving on."

But I wasn't about to be dissuaded. "Gideon," I asked, "didn't you say this was a fine animal?"

"I did, Son. But – "

"Then this is the horse I want. You fellows need to hurry along, go after it. I'll be up with you by nightfall."

All three of my companions looked at me as if I was crazy. And maybe I was, I don't know. Thing is, I had been shamed but good – and keeping that little mare was the only way I could see of regaining some sort of face – an item of mighty importance to a boy my age.

"You sure?" Gideon asked.

"I am, Gideon, if you are."

"I'm certain," Gideon declared. "She's mustang, and they're good little horses, when they're trained right."

"I'll train her," I stated flatly.

"Then I say let him keep the horse," a man on top of the corral called out.

"I second it," joined in another.

"All in favor?" was the next cry, and that was followed by a wild and cheerful chorus of ayes. The men then applauded and cheered as Al Bagley untied the snubbed-short rope and handed it to me. Five minutes later I was alone with the unsaddled mare, trying to gentle her down.

She had been ridden before, I could see that, for she still

bore saddle scars from some hard use. She had also been ridden earlier that morning, for she had sweat some, and it had mostly dried. That meant, at least, that she had been broke to ride. Good. Then all I had to do was gentle her down a mite, and we would be fine.

Carefully I looked her over, talking softly the while—and the more I looked, the better I felt. I didn't know much about horses, but I was surely getting a good feeling for the gray.

"Her name is Perdition," a man said as he brought me a used saddle and blanket the quartermaster had assigned. "And she's a real son of a . . . Well, that is, she's a real daughter of perdition. Funny thing. I never thought there would be such things as daughters of perdition, but that was before I met this little mare. You be careful, Son. She's mean clear to the bone."

"Perdition," I mused as I looked her over. "Well, first thing to be changed is the name. Instead, little gal, I'll just call you Perdy, because of a truth, I think you are—real perdy."

The horse looked at me and rolled her eyes, so I reached out to pat her neck a little and try to gentle her down. She snapped at me, however, a vicious snap that would have ripped my arm open had she connected.

But she didn't connect, and she was lashing out to give it another try when there was a sort of low snarl from behind me. The next thing I knew, old crippled Lazarus had somehow hobbled into the corral, jumped into the air beside me, and clamped his teeth into the mare's soft nose.

Well, I never heard such a squealing and a ruckus in all my life as I heard then. That poor horse thought she was going to die, and *I* thought the dog was. But it turned out Lazarus knew what he was doing, and in the next few seconds, both me *and* the mare were going to learn that.

I don't think Lazarus had hold of that horse's nose for more than ten seconds, and for five of them she was too surprised to react. Then she squealed and rose up to snuff the life out of the crippled creature hanging from her snout with teeth and pawing hooves.

Only the dog was no longer there. Instead, old Lazarus had

let go of the nose and had launched himself at the mare's exposed belly, taking another nip there.

Well, down she came with another snort to stamp the life out of the pesky dog with those same rock-hard hooves, and again that dog was gone. Crippled as he was, I never did figure out how Lazarus moved so swift and careful. But he did, and the next attack was on the hock of Perdy's near hind leg.

She kicked at that, got only air, and was just spinning to fight when from nowhere, it seemed, old Lazarus was on her nose again.

Well, there was more squealing and more stomping, and that tawny-brown, splint-legged coyote-dog was here and there and everywhere, nipping and snarling and drawing flecks of blood. But in all of that, Lazarus never barked. I learned later that only dogs bark, but that coyotes and wolves snarl and growl and howl. I didn't know that then, but I did know that whatever noises the critter made or didn't make didn't make one bit of difference. Old Lazarus had that little gray mare kowtowed to a faretheewell within a short two or three minutes.

And suddenly it was over. The mare was standing with flared and bloody nostrils, her chest heaving, her head down, and her eyes rolled back, facing the panting dog. And Lazarus, his tongue out and his sides heaving, stood wide-legged, facing the horse.

They stood like that, facing each other, and then the dog did the confoundedest thing I ever saw. Instead of snarling, he whined a little in a low sort of way, and then stiff-legged he moved slowly toward the mare.

She snorted and stepped back, Lazarus stopped and growled, the mare stopped, Lazarus whined and moved forward again, and that little scene was repeated two or three more times. But then the mare didn't move at Lazarus's advance, and the next thing I knew, that dog was up to her and licking the blood from her wounded nose.

Oh, it startled her some, all right, and she jerked back at the first wet lick. But Lazarus growled deep, and in another minute or two he was licking all the blood away, with the mare letting him do it. From there Lazarus moved to her belly and her hocks, and for the rest of the time he was cleaning her up, that little mare quivered all over but never moved hoof again.

It was almost like he was saying, "Friend horse, I beat you, and I'm sorry it had to hurt. So why don't you let me clean up this little bit of a mess I made, and maybe it won't pain you so much any more."

I don't hardly think the dog thought that way. I don't even know for sure if coyote-dogs think. But I did, and I was absolutely astounded. So, apparently, were others, for only then, when I heard a murmuring of voices around me, did I become aware that the crowd had regathered around that pole corral. I looked at them, felt surprised that I hadn't seen anyone, and then one of the men started to clap. Soon all of the brethren joined in, and I clapped with them. We had seen a real show that morning, and I don't think I have ever seen another like it since.

"Friend Jons?"

Turning, I was surprised to see Gideon in the crowd. And next to him were Al Bagley and Ephraim Hanks. So they too had heard the ruckus and had come back to see the fun.

"Son," Gideon called, "that wolf critter's gentled the horse down for you. Now saddle up and get aboard quick, while the mare is still kowtowed. Besides, it's time we were heading up-trail."

Nodding, I took the saddle and walked slowly to the quivering mare. She started to move, Lazarus growled, and from that instant she was still. I put the blanket on, threw the saddle over her, and pulled the cinch-strap under her belly. I then threaded it through the ring, and even when I put my knee against her and snugged it tight, Perdy didn't budge. Of course, Lazarus was right in front of her nose, watching, and I think he was some incentive.

Finally, with wildly beating heart, I stepped into the stirrup and hoisted myself aboard. I felt the mare's muscles bunch, set myself for another awful bite of corral dust, and then slowly let my breath out as I felt her relax.

Then, like I had seen Pa do it, I climbed up and down, in and out of that saddle, several times, just getting her used to me and my weight. I then stepped in front of the mare and led her around the corral a couple of times, with Lazarus hopping painfully along beside us, getting her used to seeing me and following me around.

That accomplished, I climbed aboard again and nudged the mare forward. And to my joy and intense pride, she obediently stepped out. There followed more applause from the pole-top bleachers, with a few offers to buy Lazarus, to which I replied that he wasn't mine but was just traveling with me. Finally someone let down the poles, and we rode out to where I had stacked my gear.

Perdy flinched a little when I dismounted and hoisted my pack, but what surprised me most was when I lifted Lazarus to the saddle and then climbed aboard behind him. That little Perdy mare couldn't hardly stand it, not being able to see the dog. She turned and turned, trying to get her nose close to his, and probably she would have become jittery again had not Lazarus started in to whine and lick her neck. Instantly she gentled down, and from that day forward I almost never saw those two creatures separated.

Lazarus would sleep, and Perdy would stand over him, dozing too. Lazarus would go off on some business of his own, and Perdy could hardly stand it, waiting for him to return. And when she was free, she followed him constantly. Those two critters became the talk of the Legion, and I didn't lose any notoriety from it myself.

So I had the respect and admiration of the men of the Nauvoo Legion, Al Bagley and Ephraim Hanks foremost among them. But the best of all was that I also had a horse and a dog, both of whom mended quickly and gentled down to good service with no trouble whatsoever.

And both animals were destined to play major roles in my life from then on, though of course I had no knowledge of that at the time. I just knew that I was on course to find my Steenie, and that I was more saddled up with good companions than I had ever before known.

Chapter 8

Steadily the wagon moved down the wide draw, pulled by the two straining span of horses. On the wagon bench rode Maria Crost, the lines to the teams in her hands. In the wagon amongst their things, or up on the bench beside her, rode the three children, too small to walk without causing more problems than their walking might solve. Beside the wagon, high on his splayed-hoofed horse, rode Ben Crost, his eyes missing nothing and his determination keeping the wagon rolling steadily forward. And ahead of him, near the heads of the lead team, walked the silent but hopeful Christena Bergman.

She knew that Ben Crost was behind her, and she knew as well that he insisted on following her for two reasons. The first was so that he could be sure that she didn't try to escape. But the second reason, which revolted her mightily, and which poor Maria had no idea of, was so that he could watch Christena walking. And he did watch, of that she was sure. Constantly she felt his hot eyes burning into her back, and it took all the will power she possessed to ignore it and keep moving forward.

But with an inner strength born of righteousness she did move forward, and in spite of her anger and disgust she kept walking, dry-eyed and steadily—and that was one small but significant part of her plan. And to Christena Bergman's credit, she did have a plan.

Wearily she raised her head, staring off across the brush-covered table lands of western Wyoming. Ben had pushed them all, and there had been times in the past four days when she had been certain that she could not take another step. Besides the constant walking, for she had not been allowed to burden the teams by riding, there had been meals to fix, horses to be cared for, and children to feed and clean. Maria had worked as hard as Christena, of course, but Ben had changed and now did no work at all. Instead, he was constantly on guard, watching for the posse he was certain would be following.

And there *was* a follower, Christena was equally certain of that. Not a posse, exactly, but one who followed, nevertheless. Somewhere back there, one day or maybe two, but coming steadily on, was Jons Soderberg, the wonderful young man whose love she carried firmly in her heart. He would have found the slingshot by now, with her note attached, and he would be coming after her, of that she was certain.

In her mind she could see him, standing before her, walking beside her, sitting facing her, and she couldn't help but smile with joy as she thought of him. He was tall with dark, wavy hair. He was quite thin, and he had the bluest eyes she had ever seen. When she looked up into his eyes, which she had done only a pitifully few times, she saw sky and heaven and the wide reaches of eternity—and the depths of his eyes thrilled her to the bottom of her soul.

He also blushed easily, and Christena had taken great delight in teasing him once she had discovered that characteristic. Nor did it seem to matter what she said or did. Almost anything embarrassed him, and like fire the color would sweep up his neck and face, leaving him stammering and silly, and so pathetically vulnerable and wonderful that it took great stamina for her just to keep from hugging him every time he blushed.

But now he was behind her, coming on, and soon he would arrive and take her away—

Her blistered and bleeding feet made her look down, and in dismay she chanced to glance at her hands. Once they had been so soft and white, with perfect nails. But now they were brown, with calluses, and the nails were stubby and cracked.

Would Jons mind that, she wondered? If he didn't, then she didn't care. But if he did—

Lifting her gaze, Christena strode forward. Jons wouldn't notice such things as her hands and feet, and she knew it. Nor would he look with disdain upon her dirty, stringy hair. He loved *her*, not how she looked, and Christena knew that she had to keep that knowledge uppermost in her mind.

"Wilbur," she said quietly to the big horse who plodded along beside her, "Jons is coming, you wait and see."

The horse snorted and shook its head, and a large jackrabbit broke from the brush ahead and sped away, traveling at an amazing speed.

"See that rabbit?" she said to the horse "Jons will be coming just about that fast, and when he gets here, you can bet I'll be leaving that fast with him."

The horse said nothing, and so Christena stopped talking too. But still she dreamed, and still she did her best to plan out a way to stop Ben Crost so that Jons could catch up with them more easily.

Long ago Ephraim Hanks had told her something, and lately it had come forcefully back to her mind. "The secret of victory," he had said, "is to attack—always attack. If an army has ten thousand men, attack. If it is only yourself, attack. If you do that, a way will always open up for you to become victorious."

So, was there a way for her to attack Ben Crost? Was there something that she could do? One thing she knew—she wasn't going to sit by, waiting to be destroyed, either body or spirit, by her step-uncle. But what could *she*, an unarmed woman with no horse, do? What weapons did she have?

Well, she had the love of Jons Soderberg, and she had the truth. Yet she was not so naive as to believe that truth alone would prevail, without any effort on her part. Still, it was a weapon, and if wisely used, it might divert Ben Crost from her. And Jons's love would give her hope until such time as she could determine how to use the truth against her uncle. So she would choose her time, and then she would move. But what time? When? How?

She was not afraid, but she knew what fear was, for she had felt it the night Ben had beaten Jons to the floor and thrown him out of the cabin. That night she had felt fear. And it had grown worse, only an hour later, when Ben had pushed her into her room with the command to pack her things and get them into the wagon. Until the idea to put a note on Jons's slingshot and leave it for him had occurred, she had been terrified. But since then she had been at peace, for she knew that Jons would find it, being led by the Spirit, and would come after her—

"Still dreaming of that stupid, gangly Swede?"

Spinning, Christena looked up into the leering face of Ben Crost, and suddenly she knew that she could hold herself back no longer. She would speak her mind to the man now and worry about the consequences of her words later on.

"You're mighty deep into some silly dream," he continued. "Was it of him?"

"He'll be coming," she answered quietly, firmly.

Ben Crost laughed. "He'd better not, else he'll return again almighty sore and bloody. You saw what happened the last time he came at me."

Christena looked away, but her voice had a ring to it that the man couldn't miss. "You're a coward, Ben Crost, and that's the truth. He didn't come at you, and you know it."

"Why, you impertinent little—"

"Further evidence," Christena said, smiling smugly as she looked back up at him. "Only cowards curse or strike at women."

With an oath Ben regained control of himself, but Christena wasn't through with him, not at all.

"Ben Crost," she declared, speaking softly enough that Maria couldn't hear her, but loud enough for the mounted man beside her to hear clearly, "you have been sorely deceived."

"Have I now?" the man asked sarcastically. "And I suppose you intend to testify to me of the truthfulness of the Church so I can be set straight?"

"Oh, no, dear uncle. Christ said not to cast our pearls before swine, and so I will not even mention those eternal truths that you once considered so important, but which Lucifer has wrested from your understanding. No, Ben Crost, I will speak to you of another truth, and of life, and show you how, by the laws of the one, you have lost the right to have happiness in the other."

"My, my," he sneered, "so you have become the little philosopher, have you?"

Christena lifted her chin. "If I have, you would do well to listen. Ben Crost, coming west to gather with the Saints is a way for all of us to start over. By coming to the Valley, we wipe clean the slate of our past, so to speak. Whatever any of us is to be need have nothing to do with what we were before, but it begins the day we enter the valley.

"That holds for you, too. If you had had courage, done your work and Church callings well, and had been a man of your word, people either would have been thrilled, or would not have cared at all, about what you had done in the past. If it had been bad, you would have been forgiven. If it had been good, you would have received high praise and would have done even better.

"All sorts of people have joined the Church, Ben Crost, great ones as well as those with problems. Some have had trouble with the law, some have been too far into debt, and some just didn't fit into any mold. Others, as successful as you had been, and even more so, have also joined. If you had proven yourself a responsible person, as many of them have done and are doing, then you would have been the equal of anybody in the Church and would have been chosen as leader over many."

"I don't know what you're talking about," Ben Crost growled.

"You don't?" Christena pressed forward fearlessly. "Oh, I think you do. You had a good past, but you made a mistake when you got to the Valley. You assumed that people would see the same importance in you that you had come to see in yourself. But they didn't see it, simply because it is no longer there. You have not put forth any effort to earn it or to continue it, and so the past you brought with you is of no value.

"But now, Ben Crost, and this is what you do not understand, you have a new past; new and terribly evident. You have shown yourself to be lazy, conceited, arrogant, and cowardly, and you're a bully, as well. And there isn't a soul I know who can't see it."

Ben Crost cursed again, but Christena ignored him and concluded her thought.

"People are tolerant, but only up to a point, and the Lord is the same. Because you have chosen to walk in your own light rather than in that of the Savior, you have forced your family to give up Christ's true religion and to leave the Valley. But worse, you have beaten up an innocent young man, and you have forced me to leave my home and loved one against my will. Those things, Ben Crost, push tolerance of good people beyond its limit and force the Spirit of the Lord to withdraw. I fear that the result, for you, will be very abrupt and very, very final."

Ben Crost laughed. "We'll see, my little Christena, we'll see. But was I you, I'd forget the Lord. If he's there, he obviously doesn't care what's going on down here. And I'd not put much store in that scrawny young Swede being a factor in my 'final result,' either. He ever does catch me, he won't last much beyond that."

"You're *pathetic!*"

"Maybe. But I'm also here, and don't you forget that. One of these days you'll change your thinking of me. I'll be coming to you, and you'd better be ready."

Ben Crost pulled his splayed-hoofed horse back by the squeaking wagon, and Christena Bergman strode forward alone. She was furious, but helplessly so, and with all her heart she wanted to cry. Only crying wouldn't help Jons to win her freedom – not yet it wouldn't.

But when they got a little closer to the Green River and the trader Yates's post, then she would get very, very sick. And her pain, tears, and complaining to any who would listen, a complaining not yet seen on this entire journey, would force Ben

Crost to stop at the post so that she could rest and be cared for.

That, she thought grimly and with great determination, was the rest of her plan. And if love and faith counted for anything at all, it would be enough. In the time that diversion gave him, Jons Soderberg would catch up with them and take her away.

Chapter 9

Echo Canyon, at least for the first four or five miles up from the mouth, was a real beehive. Legioneers from all over the territory had been called up and were hard at work at a place called Echo Station, making the canyon as defensible as possible. We met and visited briefly with the leaders of these men – Majors Pugmire and Sharp of Great Salt Lake City, Major D. P. Curtis of Davis County, and Major Munroe of Ogden – commanding among them some 411 men. We also passed a Major Taylor and fifty men from Ogden, and I learned that the horse company who had given me the little gray had been under the command of a Captain Bannion. And there were others, but Eph was in somewhat of a hurry, so we didn't speak with them all.

"Hear the echo?" Eph asked as we rode along. "William Clayton was the first to tell me of it, and of course that's how it got its name. He described it to me as very singular, the rattling of wagons resembling carpenters hammering at boards inside the highest rocks. The report of a rifle resembles a sharp crack of thunder, and it will echo for some time. The lowing of cattle and braying of mules seems to be answered from beyond the mountains, and music, especially brass instruments, have a very pleasing effect, with every note being imitated. Too bad we don't have a bugler with us now, so we could test it out."

As we rode up the canyon, we passed crews damming the stream and flooding the bottom so the government wagons would bog down. Others were digging new channels for the creek so that the water could be used to greatest advantage in future flooding. On the steep slopes, men were hard at work digging rifle trenches and pits, and on top of the honeycombed cliffs that hung several hundred feet above us, others were building stone ramparts, from behind which they could fire down upon the advancing army.

And the army *was* advancing. Expresses passed us twice that day, each with word that the army was within thirty miles of Bridger, and coming on. We also had word that General Daniel H. Wells and his staff were behind us and coming, their destination Fort Bridger, up on the plains of Wyoming. So there was a real hive of activity going on.

Word had also gone ahead about Lazarus and the gray mare, and we drew a lot of attention as we passed by. But lest I get the idea that I had been the recipient of some sort of out-and-out miracle, Gideon went to some pains to tell me that he had seen wolves and coyotes pull the same stunt in the wild, wearing down animals so they could eat them. Of course, that hadn't been Lazarus's objective, as Al Bagley quickly pointed out. And Eph felt certain that the hand of the Lord had been in it, miracle or not. Anyway, it made for a lively discussion and gave me further opportunity to reflect upon the blessings that had so recently come to me.

Another thing—every time we stopped, I found men who had seen Ben Crost's wagon. It was less than a day ahead of us but was moving fast. And more and more Ben was telling folks that he was in a hurry because there were those after him who had orders from Brigham Young to "use him up," meaning, I suppose, to take his life.

Well, that was utter nonsense, for I was the only one after him, and I certainly wasn't under orders from Brigham Young. Nor did I intend to kill him—come within an inch or two of it, maybe, but not kill him. But more and more it put me in mind of what we had talked about the night before, of how a man loses the Spirit, then denies the faith, and ends up being filled with fear. Ben Crost was certainly fitting the mold.

Most everybody also remembered Steenie, and that was starting to trouble me. From what folks said, she did not seem overly anxious to get away from her uncle. Oh, I know I had my note from her, but I couldn't help thinking that if she had wanted to badly enough, she could have escaped. Or said something to the men along the trail so that they would stop Ben from taking her with him. Or anyway talked to one or two of them about *something*. But in all that day, I never met a man who had heard her say a word or give any indication at all that she was not perfectly happy and in agreement with the company she was with and the direction she was going.

And *that* was starting to bother me.

"Friend Jons," Gideon told me after I had worried aloud to him, "women seem passing strange to most men, but that is because they don't understand them."

"Do you?" I asked.

"Mercy, no. But I lived with a good one for nigh onto fifty years, and I did come to understand one thing—womenfolk think different than men do. They run long to feelings and ain't bothered so much by the sense of an issue. To a woman, it's how she feels about something that counts, no matter what color it actually shapes up to be. Why, I've seen a perfectly good woman back up the meanest, lowest-down skunk alive, just because she loved him and believed in him. I've also seen beautiful, lovely sisters turn their backs on the best men the Lord ever made, for the same loco reason. They didn't have any feelings for 'em, no matter the logic of it.

"On the other hand, a good woman will laugh in the face of temptation that would bog a snipe, it is so all-fired bad. And if such a woman sets her sights on the straight and narrow path to celestial glory, then heaven help the poor sorry man who tries to lead her astray. Unlike most men, no matter what is offered, such a sister cannot be bought.

"All's I'm saying, Son, is never expect a woman to do something just because it's what you would do. You'll likely end up disappointed." Then Gideon grinned. "On the other hand, never be surprised if a woman does *exactly* what you would do.

That often happens. But if you press her as to the why of what she did, you'll sure enough end up confused again. Oh, she'll know why, all right, but it won't even be close to the same trail you would have taken to get there. Like I said, womenfolk think different than men do."

"That means," I said, doing my best to understand, "that I shouldn't try to understand why Steenie is still with Ben Crost?"

Gideon grinned. "That's right, Son. You forget the whys of a woman, and just concentrate on the whos. If she's a good woman, then be satisfied with that. You do that all your life, and you'll live and die a happy man."

"I'll try, Gideon, but I'm still worried—"

"Dad-blast it, you young whippersnapper, listen to me! Worrying's like sitting on a rocking horse. No matter how hard you work it, the fool thing ain't never going to get you anywhere. You want to find and help that little gal of yours, stop all the fretting, trust her, and keep your eyes and ears open. Then, when it's time, you'll be worth something to her!"

Well, that ended that particular conversation, and I was still going over it, trying to make heads or tails of what I had been told, when a shot rang out ahead of us, the sound echoing back and forth. With no hesitation, Ephraim Hanks sank spurs to his horse, the rest of us followed suit, and a few minutes later we pulled rein near a clustered group of men.

"I didn't mean it," a large man was pleading. "I just didn't think it would go so far."

Two men held him by the arms, while the others stood around him, glaring. But the big man had no strength to fight them, and he didn't even try. He just wept and told us over and over that it had been an accident.

"Boys," Eph Hanks said as he dismounted, "I'm Major Hanks. Why doesn't someone tell me what happened?"

The big man started crying again, but Eph held his hand up, silencing him. "Well?" he said to the others.

Finally one of the crowd cleared his throat and spoke. "Brother Hanks, Neilsen here just shot William Simmons through the head with his Yeager, killing him on the spot."

"You see it happen?"

"No, sir, but these men did."

Eph turned to the others. "Who of you saw it?"

"I did."

"Me, too."

"So did I."

"And was it like the man said?" Eph asked the three.

"Well, yes and no."

"What do you mean?"

The man took a deep breath. "Sir, Frederic Neilsen here is best friends with William Simmons. He killed him, but he didn't mean to do it."

"That's right," another agreed.

"It can't be," the first man argued. "Man, you saw it. Neilsen pointed the Yeager directly at him and shot. How could he have *not* meant to do it?"

At that a young man about my age spoke up. "It was an experiment, Sir. That was all. We'd been digging those trenches to dam the creek, and Neilsen and Simmons and the rest of us got to arguing about whether or not a person as far away as the tops of those cliffs, where we'll be hiding, could hit a man all the way down here in the bottom.

"Well, Simmons had the idea to climb up there to the top and then have someone fire at him so he could see just how far the ball might fall short. He chose the Dane here, Frederic Neilsen, because he is a former soldier and knows how to handle the Yeager, and because they were such good friends.

"Major Hanks, none of us had the slightest notion that the ball might ever fly so far or so true."

"For some folks," Gideon muttered, shaking his head, "it was too late to get wise the day they was born. I never heard of such tom-foolishness."

Ignoring the old man, Eph looked around at the others. "That the way you saw it?" he asked a lean man in a real funny hat.

"Aye," the man replied, "the kid told it right."

"And you?" Eph asked of the third man who had claimed to be an eyewitness.

"It be like hisself has said," the man replied in an Irish brogue, nodding at the youth. "We've tried to tell these gents that it were an accident, but the blathering fools've not been believing of us."

The man grew still, there were dark looks all around, and a moment later four men came down off the slope with the body of the dead Simmons between them. They laid the man at our feet, and I was very much affected at the sight of him. Except for being so white, he looked as though he would awaken at any second, get up, and get back to work.

Nor was there much blood or sign of damage upon him. The ball, it was quickly determined, had entered in his left temple, leaving a small, bluish hole, and had come out of his right ear, which was also where the only blood showed.

And poor Frederic Neilsen. At the sight of his friend's lifeless body, the Danish convert crumpled to the earth sobbing, and no amount of effort seemed able to console him.

"What do we do, Major?" the man who had spoken first finally asked.

Eph, his hands buried deeply in his pockets, stared upward as if waiting for some sign from heaven. Whether he was or not, I do not know, but after a moment he gave quiet, precise, and simple directions.

"The man's body must be taken to his home for burial. Detail two men to do that, two who were not witnesses to the shooting.

"Because this is wartime and we are under martial law, Neilsen here must be placed under arrest and given a speedy trial. General Wells is right behind us and is on his way to Bridger. He will conduct the trial. All of you who are witnesses must stand ready to testify in behalf of what you saw and know. Do not leave the area, or I swear that you, too, will be hunted down and arrested. Until General Wells arrives, all of you get back to your work. And unless orders are given, there will be no more shooting. Am I clear?"

The men nodded. One then put a blanket over Simmons's lifeless body, and then slowly the men returned to their trench digging.

"Tragic," Eph said as he swung back on his horse. "That is so sad. A man's life gone, and it should never have happened. If we would only learn to use good common sense . . .

"Well, enough of that," he said, shaking his head as if to clear his mind. "Al, I have the feeling that we need to hurry to Cache Cave."

Al Bagley nodded with a wry grin. "Now, that is passing strange. I've been sitting here feeling the same urge myself." Then he turned to us. "Brethren, there are another ten miles to go, and we'll be pushing. Are you up to a hard ride?"

Gideon nodded silently, and I patted a panting Lazarus and told Al that I thought we could stand it too.

So slapping spurs to the horses, we quickened our paces eastward.

Chapter 10

There were three of them, three men who rode up from the south, across the high country, and down into the foothills that made up the north slope of the Uintah Mountains – three stone-faced, weather-stained men who rode slack and easy on their ponies like all men bred to horseback, but whose eyes were narrow-tense and hard and crinkled at the outer corners from a habit of long watchfulness. All were alike in these ways, though in another they differed widely. Two were Ute Indians, renegades who had been expelled from their people and who had then joined with the third man. From him they had picked up many of the ways of the whites – ways of greed and distrust. For the third man, the undisputed leader of the three was white – and not a shining example of that race, either.

He was a mountaineer and fur trapper and trader, one of the remnants of that hardy breed who had tracked out and explored the vastness of western America, risking life and limb to fill their pockets with eastern and European gold.

But by 1857 the great market for beaver and other furs was largely a memory, and so a man with a taste for the wild, free life of the wilderness did what he could to pad his purse and hold body and soul together. Nor was he likely to be particular about how he did it. If the reward was there, so was the willingness to participate. And of late, these same three had found great profit in the running of slaves, Shoshone and Snake Indian women and children, who were much in demand in the Mexican colonies of Santa Fe, Taos, and Abiquiu.

It was a good business, this slave trade, though not as good as it had been when Ute Chief Walker, or Wakara, had been alive. The prominent chief had been one of the greatest traders of human flesh in the mountains, and though Brigham Young and the Mormons had dissuaded him from the practice some years before, others had willingly kept the trade going.

Now Arapeen, Walker's brother, was continuing it, as were other tribal leaders to the south, including Hunkootoop of the Pahvants – and the price was holding steady at $50 to $75 American dollars for children and $100 to $150 for young women. Of course, the Mormons were formidable foes who arrested all who were captured with slaves or who were suspected of selling them. But still the slave-hungry Mexicans came surreptitiously up into the wilderness along the Green, and still men like Vasquez and his two renegade Utes delivered bartered or captured Indian slaves to them.

But this day the three were not traveling for slaves, nor did two of the men think often of them. Instead, they were on a bartering mission to dispose of other illicitly gained goods, and the white leader, José Vasquez, felt certain that they stood an excellent chance of success.

So they had ridden for some time through drought-parched country and thick-timbered slopes, cursing the heat. But it was a day for ducks when they finally hit the north foothills, and all thought longingly of the heat they had left behind. All morning, swift clouds with dark, swollen underbellies had scudded across the drab sky. Shortly after their noon stop the rain had begun, catching the men in the open. Two had wanted to find shelter, but José Vasquez, inexorable, absolute, and always sure, had kept them heading east of north into pale, slashing torrents of water that whipped in windlashed gusts against the leaning forms of horses and men. The storm was no brief blow but steadily drenched the high country of the Uintahs, and so they rode it out, the entire half-day siege of it.

Even in high-buttoned slickers over buckskins, the three

were soaked, miserable, and ugly-tempered when, toward evening, a densely-timbered rise of ground loomed ahead and José Vasquez called a halt. They put their horses directly toward the heart of the timbered stand and broke into a wide clearing with a host of deadfalls at the lee end. Vasquez looked around and then dismounted with a grunt of satisfaction. They would be well hidden here, which was all that concerned him. The mutinous, surly grumblings of the others couldn't make Vasquez bat an eyelash. He knew his men, knew they would be lost without him, and knew that they knew it, too.

They made a cold, wet camp – a miserable camp. The rain had only then begun to slacken into a gray drizzle. The Ute called Knife threw saddle, saddlebags, and canvas-wrapped blanket-roll from his sorrel, then lugged them over to the leeward side of a looming granite outcrop. Where the rock checked the blast of wind and rain it was reasonably dry, and he had seen instantly that it was a good place to spread his blankets. With a weary grunt he dropped his gear and sat down, stretching his bony arms. Yet he did not rest long, for shortly Vasquez was yelling at him to build a fire.

Resignedly, the thin Ute rose to his feet and made a circle of the clearing, limbering his legs and arms. Then he chanced to glance at the rock where he had tossed his gear. Limpy, whose Ute name was Bear Who Walks with Wounded Foot, after a wound a giant grizzly had inflicted upon the huge man's foot many years before, but whose name Vasquez had shortened to Limpy, had taken Knife's place behind the rock and was even then kicking Knife's gear out into the wet.

Knife's hands balled into fists, and he started across the clearing, choking on his anger. Limpy, seeing him coming, swung his huge body to face him, with his bubbling laugh showing chalk-white teeth. Then he whipped off his stolen hat, batting the wet felt against the shining wetness of his buckskins, and tossed it onto his other gear. The rain matted his coarse black hair, roached like a mule's mane, and he ran a hand over it in a slicking-back motion, his wide face still laughing.

"Ungh," he growled with malicious glee as he watched his

traveling companion's stiff-legged approach. "The useless one shows his teeth. Does he think to sink them into the great *Queogand,* the great Bear?"

Limpy's speech was Ute, and he referred to himself proudly by a shortened version of his name. For he was like a bear, big, slow of mind, but cat-quick and deadly when cornered.

Trembling with rage, the much smaller Knife circled his mocking opponent for a moment, a gleaming blade suddenly in his hand. Then he dived headlong for the big, mocking figure.

But Limpy made a fluid, side-stepping motion, and the thin Ute burgeoned past, plowing on his face into the littered gear and mud. Instantly he lunged to his feet, whirled, and went after Limpy again, and Limpy backed away, taunting him.

"The useless one's single metal tooth is more useless than is he. *Weitch,* Knife, is a fool's name for such a one as you. Your mother should have called you *Me-poodg-e-Kan-Nab,* Little Willow, and given you a switch to fight with. Perhaps you might have done better."

Vasquez watched disinterestedly as the fight progressed. He knew the two Utes hated each other, and that bothered him not at all. In fact, there were times when he encouraged their animosity toward each other, for he was able to use it to his own advantage.

Knife bored in again, his blade low and swinging upward, and again Limpy easily deflected it. Then Knife's foot skidded on the wet loam—and his feet, aided by the awkward reactions of his thin, bony body, flailed the ground away and piled him on his face again. He lay there, sobbing in torn breaths, while Limpy kicked him hard on the wrist, sending the blade skidding away from Knife's suddenly numbed fingers. Then the big Ute walked away, laughing.

Knife didn't rise immediately, even after Limpy had returned to the rock shelter. Instead, he lay and nursed his hatred, savoring in his mind the bloody end of the larger man that he knew one day was coming.

Finally he pushed himself up on his hands and knees, then to his feet, avoiding the looks of Vasquez. Wet buckskin moccasins squishing as he moved, Knife walked slowly to the wall of deadfalls and living quaking aspens—there hunkering down among them to be alone with his present shame and his murderous dreams. He rested his arms on his knees, set his teeth into the wet buckskin of his shirt, and listened to the rain pock the few remaining aspen leaves above.

From the clearing Knife heard the mild voice of Vasquez, gently chiding the hulking Limpy. "He had a *weitch*. You had him in the grass. Why didn't you *e-i*, kill him?"

Limpy grunted humorlessly. "A waste of a man's time, to kill such an insect. He is *paquy-nary me-poodg-e kan-nab,* a stinking little willow, and one day he will burn in the *coo-nah* of his own hatred."

"Yeah," Vasquez agreed, speaking in English. "And speaking of burning, I want a fire now! Knife! You get the wood and build up that *coo-nah* now, you hear me?"

The gaunt Ute rose to his feet and plunged ahead, heedless of the wet lash of back-whipping branches, till he found a rotten deadfall. With furious energy he kicked out great chunks of its tinder-dry heart. Bending down, he then picked up an armful of the punk, and in his mind he saw himself and the other two men, a sort of vision of the accumulation of all the days that had passed since he had turned his back upon his people to go with the *tsharr,* the white Vasquez.

He hated himself for that, for thinking he could depart from the wise and sacred traditions of his people. And in a way he hated them for expelling him and for forcing him to join Vasquez. But that was *to-edg-e-tish,* a long time ago, and he wasn't certain he could even remember all those traditions or reasons any more. But he kept his hair right, unlike foolish Limpy, and the little rituals of his mornings were as the people did them.

But now the seeing of the more recent past was in Knife's mind, a thousand or more camps like this one, some colder and more wet, some drier and more hungry. Days and often nights of far-ranging, grueling rides in rain, snow, blazing heat, until he would think he had never known anything but the rocking and jolting back and forth on a sweating *kuvah-u,* horse. Seasons stretched into years of hiding in desert holes or mountain hideaways, where boredom hung like a dead weight and there was nothing to do but throw sticks and *ni-a-witch,* gamble the white man's *wah-pana-kar-ra,* money-rock. Ten thousand days and nights in company with the hated Limpy and the more-than-feared José Vasquez who jumped at every sound and was always more than ready to kill. That was the life Knife had somehow, foolishly, chosen for himself.

"Wagh!" he grunted quietly. Why had he done this? Why had he let himself be led along by the white slave trader? Much better that he be back with his people. Much better that he *pe-oh-a,* that he marry, and be making little ones with a warm and comfortable squaw, a woman who would take care of all this woman's work he was constantly being forced to do.

And Knife truly did want a woman. For the past year or so, he had eyed squaws and girls Vasquez had purchased from Ute bands led by men such as Arapene, trying to think of a way he could purchase or steal one for himself. And though several had been possibilities, none had really taken his fancy. Nor, for that matter, had he been able to work out just how he might persuade Vasquez to part with such a possession. After all, women, especially those who were young and thin, brought good money from the Mexican raiders who came regularly to the southern crossing on the Green. And Vasquez loved money—loved it more than anything else. Knife marveled at that, for to him it held little value. So also did he marvel that women seemed to hold no fascination for the trader. In fact, even big Limpy seemed unaffected by them, and Knife wondered at both of his companions.

For him, the supreme happiness of life would be to be part of a *meah-a-bitch,* an encampment of his people, having a squaw or two to do his cooking, and having sons that he might watch grow into warriors. That was his greatest dream, and it was never far from his mind.

His second-greatest dream, he thought sourly as he rose to his feet to return to the clearing, was to see the huge Limpy dead, the man's *pwap,* blood, staining the grass beneath him.

And Knife knew, even as he did the woman's work of carrying the wood for Limpy and Vasquez's fire, that one day he would see the big Ute *e-i,* dead.

But now they were not even after the women and children who could be sold as slaves, and Knife worried at that. Now they were on their way to see another hated white, another trader whose name was Yates. Within the past year, Vasquez and his companions had, quite by accident, stumbled upon a poorly armed caravan of Mexicans, and after treacherously murdering them while they slept, they had found the caravan to be carrying several hundred pounds of gunpowder.

Caching it beneath the heaped-up bodies of the dead Mexicans for future consideration, Vasquez had gone about his other illicit business enterprises, and when word had reached him, only days before, of the march of an approaching army to destroy the feared and hated Mormons, he had suddenly known what he might do with the gunpowder.

Of course, he could not sell the explosive salt-peter and nitrates to the army himself, for his was a known name and face, and that would be too great a risk. But Yates was an old trapping compadre, an honest man who owed Vasquez a mighty favor for the saving of his life, and now would be the perfect time for Vasquez to collect.

Knife knew all this, and it troubled him—not because of the murdered Mexicans or the pack-mule loads of stolen gunpowder or the approaching army did he worry. No, those things mattered little to him. What troubled the gaunt and bony Ute was that there would be no women this trip, no squaws that he might examine and possibly select from. For Knife had decided, in recent weeks, that when the next passable woman was purchased by Vasquez, he would have her, whether he could afford the price or not. For there were other ways of obtaining things than by *nar-ro-wap,* by purchase, Knife thought, grinning evilly. Vasquez had taught him that, and Vasquez had taught him well.

Trudging back to the clearing with an armful of the crumbling punk, Knife dumped it on a dry place under a spreading pine. Setting his face in frustrated determination, he ground a handful of the heartwood between his palms to make a small heap of loose tinder. Over this he built a wigwam of dry sticks he'd gathered from under a nearby log. Then he reached inside his buckskins for an oilcloth-wrapped packet of matches, one of the few white-man things of which he approved. Striking it, he cupped the orange flare in his palms, and then carefully he eased it down to the punk.

Smoke threaded from the tinder, then a spoon of flame that caught the twigs. A brief moment later, when he had secured a steady blaze, Knife piled on chunks of the rotten wood.

Limpy came across the clearing with swinging stride, whistling cheerfully in the disgusting white man's way, carrying the battered coffeepot full of water. Before Knife had time to wonder why the big man was doing a menial woman's chore with such a cheerful air, Limpy reached the fire and bent as though to set the pot close by.

But then it tilted in his hand, and a stream of water gushed over the meager blaze. The fire sizzled and died in a thin mushrooming of steam and smoke, and Knife came to his feet, no uncertainty in him.

"*Sar-ich katz-te-suah,*" he snarled angrily, "dog of a fool! Do you think I do not *pesuds-away,* do you think I do not understand that you did that of choice?"

Limpy's black brows lifted in the blandest motion of innocence. "But Stinking Little Willow, I merely wished to hurry with the coffee—"

And then the giant Limpy was interrupted as José Vasquez strode heavy-footed across the clearing, an emphatic anger visible in his swinging arms. "Limpy," he growled as he bored in, "this time you've gone too far."

The sodden smack of Vasquez's fist froze Knife in position while Limpy somersaulted backward. The big man turned over once, landed on his back, and stared upward into the rain, trying to comprehend what had just taken place. Then he shook his head, his ugly face distorted, and with a grunt he hauled himself to his feet, ripped open his slicker, and clawed for the dead white man's holstered gun that he wore.

Only, through the ponderous haze of red anger that filled Limpy's mind, his eyes suddenly saw the gun in Vasquez's hand, the gun that had arrived there in the magical way that only Vasquez knew. Slowly his own hand dropped from his weapon, and he stood in the drizzle, staring at the feared Vasquez.

One day, he promised himself while Vasquez stared him down, and while the gaunt Knife grinned evilly from the side, one day—

And little did he know that Knife was thinking exactly the same thing about him.

Chapter 11

Cache Cave, to the south of the head of Echo Canyon, was one of the greatest landmarks of the early West. Small and oven-shaped, set in overhanging rocks, it had been used for many years as a shelter for fur trappers and mountaineers, explorers, and the early Mormon pioneers. It looked to me, when I saw it, to be about thirty feet deep, fifteen feet wide, and from four to six feet in height. It was located above a stream called Cache Cave Creek and was an ideal place to hold stock. In addition, it was situated so that it warmed quickly and provided excellent shelter. Therefore, it was an almost perfect camp.

In the cave and on the rocks nearby were carved the names of a hundred or more people who had stopped there as a testimony of the cave's value, and Eph Hanks pointed out to me that those names included many of Brother Brigham's pioneer group of 1847.

It being evening, we took mess with the Mormon troops stationed nearby. These were under the direction of Hosea Stout, who I was told was also a lawyer and an elected officer of the law down in the Valley.

"So you're a lawyer, huh?" old Gideon asked as we sat to eat.

Hosea Stout nodded matter-of-factly.

"Humph," the caustic old Gideon grunted. "Well, lawyers is good for something, I say."

"Which is?"

"They get you out of the kind of trouble you'd never get in if there was no lawyers in the first place."

The rest of us felt mighty uncomfortable, but Hosea Stout chuckled good naturedly. "Well said, Captain Monson," he declared enthusiastically. "May the Lord preserve me from becoming such. Thank goodness we have the Book of Mormon to remind me of the kind of lawyer I never want to be."

Gideon looked at the man with new appreciation, and I was glad that nothing more was said about that topic.

"Well, Ephraim," Stout finally said as we finished the last of the beef and beans, "how are your wives?"

Eph looked up. "Harriet's just fine, or at least she was when I left. But Jane is feeling poorly right now—she's hoping the little one will be here soon. She was not overly anxious that I be gone."

"No, I suppose not. Did Brigham send you out?"

Eph nodded, and his long beard bobbed gently on his chest, causing me to wonder again that any man could grow a beard of such proportions.

"And I suppose that you will go off on your hook?" Stout continued.

Eph nodded again. "Well, Brother Brigham *did* ask Al and me to do what we could to slow Ol' Buck's boys down."

Hosea Stout grinned. "I wish I could go see the fireworks. I'll never forget how you almost single-handedly saved the entire Martin handcart company from starvation."

"The Lord blessed me with those buffalo. You know as well as I do that buffalo don't wander during storms."

"I know that, Eph. I also know you would never have been led to it if you hadn't gone off on your own hook. You recollect all the blessings we gave to those poor souls that night?"

"I do," Eph replied, nodding soberly.

Hosea Stout looked into the fire. "I'll never forget the sufferings and privations of those people. Funny thing, though. Some were merry and cheerful, some dull and stupid, some sick, some frosted, and some lazy and mean. But one thing they all were—elated at the prospect of more speedily arriving in the Valley. Say, Eph, I left the morning after we gave those blessings. Did that feller you raised from the dead continue to live?"

"You mean Brother Blair? He certainly did. Last I saw him he was still singing hymns."

"And what about the Read family?"

Ephraim Hanks grinned. "They're tolerable well, especially young Thisbe Read."

"Yes," Hosea Stout mused, "I recollect her. Right pert woman. She'll make someone a fine wife. By the way, an express came an hour ago from General Wells. I imagine the express passed you."

"He did, but he didn't stop."

"His news, Ephraim, is that General Wells will reach her later tonight, hold a court concerning that shooting, and then take up the march for Fort Bridger in the morning. Are you sure you wouldn't rather wait and accompany him?"

The question sounded to me to be genuine, and so I was surprised at Eph Hanks's response.

"Thanks for the warning, Hosea. We'll mosey along up-trail directly."

Hosea Stout grinned. "I thought that might be how the stick floated. Well, just be sure you don't shoot at everything that moves. Colonel Robert Burton and his seventy-five or so men are out there flanking the army, we have expresses coming and going twice a day, and there are a lot of Mormon folk still at Bridger and Fort Supply. So, do be careful."

"We will. Have you seen anything of a wagon going east? Man by the name of Ben Crost, his wife, and three youngsters? There is also a girl with them, real pretty thing, sixteen or seventeen years old. You seen them?"

Stout nodded again. "I haven't seen them, myself. But I was told they had passed. They took the northern trail and so avoided the cave here. Problems?"

"Some. The young man here, Jons Soderberg, is betrothed to the girl, and he thinks she was forced to leave the valley against her will."

"So you are Jons Soderberg," Hosea Stout said, looking at me. "The miracle worker. So young and yet so famous. Where's the coyote-dog?"

"Uh . . . Lazarus is down with the horses, sir."

"How're that critter and the horse doing? Orson Spencer brought word that they had quite a fight."

"There's truth to that," Al Bagley declared. "I never saw the like in my life, and I missed some of it."

"Spencer told me it was an amazing thing to see."

"The animals are fine, sir," I told him then. "The dog is healing fast, and Perdy is a smooth horse to ride. She acts a little shy without Lazarus around. But since the dog tamed her, she's been gentle as a kitten with me."

"The mare's a good'un," Gideon said then, speaking for the first time. "Plenty of bottom. I would say she could out-distance any of our other mounts. She's been going all day today, and she never even lathered up."

"Hosea," Eph asked, bringing the subject back around, "is there any news?"

Grinning, Hosea Stout stood and walked to the edge of the bluff. "Same old Ephraim. You sure you don't already know?"

Eph lifted his eyebrows in question.

"Revelation, man. You get as much news from heaven, I think, as Brigham does. I suspect I should be asking you."

"Now, Hosea, you know better than that—"

"Know better? I should smile I do. I'll not forget those starving Sioux Indians back on the plains at Ash Hollow this past February, nor the wounded boy you instantly raised up. The rest of you brethren may not know about this, but after the boy was healed, the Spirit of God rested upon Ephraim, and he prophesied that within three days the entire country around the starving Indians would be overrun with buffalo—which traveling of herds, I might add, never occurs in mid-winter.

"Leaving camp hungry the next morning, Ephraim and Feramorz Little, as well as the men they were guiding, found their way lined with thirty of the most prominent Indians—each with a package of the choicest meat to give the elders. Those Lamanite brethren were real impressed with Ephraim's ability to raise the sick and get news from heaven. Thanking them, Ephraim promised to be back later in the season.

"When he returned two months later, carrying word of the coming of Uncle's army to the Saints in the Valley, Ephraim came upon some mountaineers camping near where the Sioux had been camped.

" 'What'd you do to them Indians?' the mountaineers asked when they found out who Ephraim was. 'They've been looking for you for the past two months, and they've been going up and down the country for miles, every day, trying to search you out. And when an Indian loves a white man like that—'

"Ephraim just laughed. 'Have you boys seen any buffalo since I was here before?' he asked.

" 'Yes,' replied one of the men. 'About three days after you left here going east, one of the biggest herds of buffalo we've ever seen passed by.'

" 'And it saved us from starvation,' put in another. 'Our food supply was about gone.'

"Well, boys, the minute Ephraim put in his appearance among the Sioux, he was given the hero's welcome. And he would get it today, happen he was to visit them again."

"Indians are easy to impress," Ephraim Hanks said modestly.

"Well, I'm not," Hosea Stout responded, "but I've heard that tale from forty directions, and *I'm* impressed."

"If you want, I'll tell you another one," Al Bagley stated then.

"Al—" Eph pleaded.

"No, if we're discussing getting messages from heaven, then this is a humdinger. You want to hear it, Stout?"

Hosea smiled. "I certainly do."

"Last winter, scouting across the plains on his way to help rescue the handcart folks, Eph got in a blizzard and wandered off track. Pretty soon he stumbled on a group of Indians, none of them very friendly looking, and they proceeded to give his horses and outfit the look-over.

"By pointing and tracing lines in the snow, the Indians showed Eph where the road was. Well, Eph was paying attention to that, but he was just as interested in figuring out some way to scare those Indians so they would forget coming after him and planting him deep for his outfit.

"Suddenly he had an idea. Drawing his hunting knife from his boot-leg, Eph also made lines in the snow, showing that he understood their directions. Then purposefully he dropped his knife, but he continued to talk as if nothing had happened. From the corner of his eye he saw one of the braves kick snow over the knife and then stand on it, and Eph knew his little plan was going to work.

"Acting satisfied with their directions, he mounted his horse and started away. After he had ridden about ten yards, with the Indians watching him closely, he stopped his horse and began to feel for his knife. He searched himself well, then searched his packhorse. But of course no knife could be found. So, turning his horse, he rode back to the watching Indians.

"He then raised his hands high above his head and began to speak, half in Sioux, half in English, to the Great Spirit. Then, drawing his eyes to narrow slits, he dropped his hand and pointed with long forefinger straight at the feet of the man who was standing over his knife. He didn't actually look at the man, but still he held that finger pointed, without moving.

"When he asked them which one had his knife, all the Indians shook their heads and said they didn't know, including the guilty party.

"Again Eph pointed skyward and talked to the Great Spirit. Then, like a shadow on a sundial, Eph's long forefinger dropped, slowly moved, and once again pointed straight at the guilty party, who by then was trembling with fright. And that time, Eph followed his finger with his eyes, staring that Indian right into the ground, so to speak.

" 'You have stolen my knife!' he intoned with powerful voice. 'It is in the snow under your feet. The Great Spirit has shown it to me, and he is angry with you!'

"Slowly moving his finger around the group, Eph then eyed

them all. 'Each of you saw him hide the knife under the snow, and the Great Spirit is going to kill you now. When I lift my finger again, the lightning will come and you will burn on the spot!'

"Well, those braves were all shaking like leaves in a high wind, and so slowly, dramatically, Eph began to lift his forefinger skyward. The Sioux looked at each other, they looked back at him, they shook harder and got more frightened, and finally one of them shoved the thief off Eph's knife, grabbed it up, and, pulling Eph's hand down out of the air, forced the knife into it.

"Needless to say, Eph had no further trouble with those particular Indians."

We all chuckled over that story, and Al Bagley was just unlimbering for another when Eph impatiently cut him short. "Hosea, you were going to tell me the news?"

"So I was," Stout replied with a sigh, "though I would rather hear more of these tales. Abraham Hunsaker and the others have been called in from Carson Valley and the Humboldt, and word has it he's bringing with him about 2,700 pounds of gunpowder, ammunition, and arms. The people are abandoning San Bernardino, and at last report all feel good about it. Samuel W. Richards has gone to England to bring back apostles Orson Pratt and Ezra T. Benson, and I've heard that they're closing the mission to the Sandwich Islands and bringing the elders in from there. I imagine you know the rest.

"Oh, yes, one more thing. We've made our first strike at the army. Porter Rockwell raided some of the soldiers at Pacific Springs the other morning, trying to make off with their mules. They got in and out successfully and nobody was hurt, but somehow the attempt to get the stock failed, and now the army is warned. So be careful, Ephraim. They'll be watching for you. And remember, unlike our forces, Uncle's boys are under no such orders to fight a bloodless war."

"True enough," Eph said as he rose to his feet. "Where are the closest government troops now, Hosea?"

"Last express said they were camped on the Big Sandy, some

twenty miles from Fort Bridger. They're calling the place Camp Scott. But we're also told that they're sending scouts out in all directions, so a man just never knows."

"Well, boys," Eph said quietly as we walked down toward our horses, "what say we make a night of it. I have a feeling that by tomorrow, if we ride all night, we can have us a little fun."

I was ready and said so, though I worried a little about missing Steenie's camp in the dark. But she should still have been most of a full day ahead of me, so I put that out of my mind and did my best to concentrate on the assignment at hand.

Of course, Al Bagley was ready for an all-night ride, and he quickly told us so. Gideon wasn't sure he could handle such an errand at his age. He explained that an aging man lost his dreams, his teeth, and his idiotic follies, in that order. But he further allowed that if we were so all-fired ready to show stupid, then he would have no choice but to ride along and keep us from getting ourselves killed, no matter how it pained him.

Eph thanked him for his magnanimity, and right there I picked up another word for my growing vocabulary. More and more I was sounding pure American.

Lifting my crippled dog up before me, I mounted, and with my little mare moving smooth as could be, I rode with my companions forward into the night.

Chapter 12

"Jons, do you think that dog can hold all the horses?"

I looked down at Lazarus. His recovery was coming along amazingly fast, and he could get about without much trouble. He had no speed yet, but when I removed the splint, that, too, would likely change. And in another day or two I would remove that splint.

We were all gathered in a shallow depression at the base of a high ridge, and it was from the top of the ridge that Eph proposed to make a scout of the country. But he didn't want the horses up there getting skylined, as Gideon put it. So they had to remain behind. That meant either I had to stay with the animals, or Lazarus did. And I was of no mind to stay.

"I think Lazarus can watch the horses, Brother Hanks. I don't know if he's been trained to do that, but if he has, then we should be all right."

"Of course he's been trained," Gideon growled as he started creaking up the hill ahead of us. "The dog did what he did down at Echo because he's been trained, and no consarned idjut is going to train a dog to gentle down a horse without also training him to keep that same horse in line once it's gentled. Don't worry about the horses. I guarantee with that Lazarus dog here, they'll be finer than frog's hair."

Eph grinned and nodded, and so together we started up the rocky, brush-covered slope.

It had been a long ride out of Echo, east across the night-darkened prairies. Eph had kept to the ridges and bluffs in case some of the army might have moved out ahead of the rest and were camped in the bottoms. But we had seen no one during all the long night, nor had we seen any sign of fire—just the vast, empty, rolling land.

During the night, we forded the Bear River at Spaulding Grove—and near daybreak, after riding over what Al called Pine Ridge, we crossed the Muddy and stopped for a bait of breakfast. Eph built the fire while I rubbed down the horses, and poor old Gideon stretched out on the ground and never even moved. His ailments were paining him fierce, and I felt bad for him. But he would have none of my sympathy, and so I had to leave him alone.

With daylight we were in the saddle again, climbing the side of a long ridge, and off to the south I could see some high mountains. I had seen them coming west, but for some reason I hadn't learned their names. Now I learned that they were called the Uintahs. On top of the ridge, which for some reason was called Aspen Mountain, the ground stretched away almost level, and it was covered with sage and very little else. Oh, we had passed small pockets of aspen and cedar or juniper, but other than that, the country seemed mighty desolate.

We took another rest at Mussleman Creek, and then Eph steered us across Bigler Bench, then south of Bridger Butte and around Fort Bridger, crossing Black's Fork and Ham's Fork of the Green a little to the south of the fort. Fort Supply, another Mormon outpost, was five miles to the south of us, but we didn't go there, either. Ephraim Hanks had one thing on his mind, and one thing only. He wanted to come up with the army in a hurry, and he didn't want to be interfered with while he was doing it.

The ridge we finally climbed on foot was far to the east of the Green River, Yates's trading post, and even Big Sandy Creek. It was about three miles from what Eph called Seeping Spring, and it was like most other ridges in that Wyoming country. The rock was basaltic, and except for sage and cedars and sparse bunch grass, the rise was barren.

Until a person has seen those wide, western, high-country plains and low flat-topped ridges, they can have no true understanding of the vast and empty land we were in. Of course, along the rivers were stands of cottonwood and willow, but other than that, the scattered cedars, and the endless sagebrush, the country was strangely empty.

For miles it stretched away, appearing flat and monotonous, though actually cut to ribbons with arroyos and draws and lifting volcanic drifts like the one we were on.

And the sky – the wide, eternal sky. Who can imagine such a sky who has never seen it before, stretching like a vast canvas from low and distant horizon to low horizon? And the Lord seemed to use it as a canvas, too. Where we crouched it was sunny, with the hill dropping away in golden hues below us. But off to the north and east a storm had set in, and the clouds were billowing in dark shades of blue, purple, and gray. Here and there streamers of rain slashed down like waving curtains, sweeping the hills and valleys before them, with others staying high and never coming to earth. We could also see occasional flashes of lightning, but it was so far away that the sounds of thunder never did reach us.

The land was inhabited by no one, used by no one but the Indians. And it was useful, as Al Bagley said, for nothing more than to hold the rest of the world together. Of course, the wildlife was there, herds of swift-running antelope and high-bounding muley deer. There were also crows, magpies, badgers, prairie dogs, hawks and eagles, and snakes, though it was so cold that we didn't see any of the latter at all. But I never tired of watching the antelope, their white rumps showing for miles and miles as they fled from us, returned to stare, and then fled again.

Finally reaching the ridgetop, we looked out over the land – and to my surprise, we saw a group of perhaps a hundred horsemen, with packs. They were upwards of ten miles away, but after a time we determined that they were coming somewhat in our direction. So we waited to learn who they were, as Eph felt they would come to us, and I occupied my time with watching a group of a dozen antelope that were grazing down below.

There was one huge buck in the bunch, and I was watching him in particular when Al Bagley interrupted my thoughts.

"A year or two back," he said quietly, "Eph roped a buck like that and dragged it home for dinner."

"Roped him?" I asked, amazed.

"That's right. He lassoed it with his rope and dragged it into camp for the men to eat. George Washington Bean told me about it. On that same trip, Eph killed a mother griz and roped her two cubs, which he carried into the valley and sold for a good profit. I've also been told that he has lassoed buffalo many times, for dragging them to camp alive is much easier than cutting them up and hauling the meat in."

I looked over to where Eph was reclined in the midst of a tall sage, relaxed as if he had been in the most comfortable easy chair in the world. He was watching the distant horsemen but did not seem bothered in the least that they were coming toward us. What manner of man was this, I wondered? Could any human possibly be so strong?

"Does he never feel fear?" I asked.

"If he does, I've seen no sign of it. I've seen him jump on buffalo and ride them until he tired of the sport, then jab them in the ponce and continue riding them until they fell, paralyzed. I've seen him ride alone into villages of wild Indians and come out again unscathed. I've seen him taken advantage of in trades and yet always manage to come out ahead. I even saw him shave off his long beard one night, at Brother Brigham's request. Everyone else scoffed at him for doing it, but Brigham was impressed by Eph's obedience, and in the years since, no one has been more trusted by the Prophet than Ephraim Hanks. Why, Eph has crossed these same plains on missions for Brigham all the way to the states and back, at least fifty times. And single-handedly he took in the first food to the stranded and suffering Willey and Martin handcart companies a year ago, having been impressed by the Spirit that they needed him to hurry."

"By jings," declared old Gideon, who had also been listening, "he's enough to make a good man feel like a sinner."

"What do you mean?"

"I mean," the old man said easily, "that few things are harder to put up with than a good example. Too confounded intimidating. Sort of makes us normal folks feel like throwing in the towel and giving up."

Al shook his head. "That's the funny part, Captain. Eph is so normal in every other way, it's scary. And *he* thinks he's normal in spiritual things, as well. He says there isn't a man or woman alive who can't enjoy the same spiritual freedom, or have the same spiritual courage, that he does."

Again I looked at the distant, silent scout. "How does he do it?"

"Well, he says that he wants to be close to the Spirit more than he wants those favorite little sins that most of the rest of us hang on to. Because he's willing to give them up, he's blessed with unusual protection. This is real personal, and I'm not sure at all that I understand what he's saying. But he has told me on occasion of a man in a gray tweed suit who has promised to watch over him. Eph doesn't know if the man is a spirit of an ancestor, or just who he is. But several times he has seen him, almost always in precarious situations, and never has Eph been injured. That is at least part of what gives him his courage."

Well, again I cast my eyes at the reposing man, and I found myself wondering, as I sat there, if I had such a guardian. I had never seen such a character, but then, I hadn't been overly spiritual in my young life and probably hadn't been worthy.

However, then and there I determined that I was going to become spiritual. I wanted angelic help like that, and I knew it wouldn't come until I was worthy of it.

Towards evening, to everyone's amazement but Ephraim Hanks's, the hundred horsemen reached the base of our hill and established camp at a small spring that bubbled there. We watched as they picketed their horses, set up their tents, and built cooking fires—and I realized that my heart was hammering with excitement as I gazed down at them. They were the army, all right, a company off on some scout. And there we were, four of us, to fight the whole bunch of them. As Gideon grumbled, it was enough to give a man the fluttering fantods, for sure.

After dark, Eph spoke. "Brethren, we've got to go down among them, find out what they're up to, and create a little havoc with their livestock. You all up to it?"

"I am," I said, feeling tremendously excited about the prospect.

"You know me," Al Bagley said quietly.

Gideon pulled himself to his feet. "Well, you know me, too," he said, his voice scraping low like a burro with a bad cold. "When there's heroin' to be done, some coward besides that crippled dog has to hold the horses. I'll be waiting there for you."

Well, all of us knew he was withdrawing on account of his age and slowness, so we chuckled at his humor and watched as he started hobbling down the backslope. Then Ephraim, Al, and I crept down and entered the camp of the enemy.

Al went one way, and I followed Eph the other, until we were crouched beneath the bushy boughs of a huge cedar. We had hardly gotten settled, though, when the crunching of boots warned us that a man was near.

"Sure," an Irish voice boomed from so close I jumped, "an' if the Mormons come tonight, we'll be ready for 'em."

The man stretched his long arms, breathed deeply, and spoke again. "Faith, boys, but it's a lovely land this is. Do ye smell the air of it, the cleanness and the sweetness of it? It's right glad I am to be here."

"You won't be so glad, Patrick, if one of those long-bearded Mormons should get the drop on you."

The man called Patrick laughed. "It's blarney you're blatherin', man. There won't be a Mormon in fifty miles, and if there is, he'd best be watchin' out for the swingin' mits of Patrick Mulhavey."

Several men laughed, and Eph and I listened as the men then talked of their mission, to find a road to the valley somewhere to the south of Echo Canyon. I grinned at that, knowing that there was nothing passable that would admit of wagons. Horses and men, yes, but wagons and team? Not without a lot of work would they find a road through.

Of course, I suddenly thought, maybe there was some open canyon that the Mormon explorers had missed—

With a gasp I realized that the Irish soldier had spat, and what he had unloaded had hit me squarely on the forehead. I wanted to move but couldn't, and so I suffered in silence, waiting for the soldiers to return to their camp.

"Ahhh," he sighed as he returned to the fire, "I did na' think, when Donegal passed behind me, that I'd see another land so fresh and clean. 'Twas my wish to go back to Ireland a rich man, and to have the pick o' the lasses there. But now it's off to fight the Mormons I am, and maybe a wee pretty thing will be found amongst the lot o' them heathen scuts."

"You're dreaming, man," another soldier said as I desperately attempted to wipe myself off with a sage bough. "How can a woman with horns in her forehead be beautiful?"

"Horns? Go on with ye, mon, there's no such thing, even if they *are* Mormons."

Not waiting to hear the rest of that amazing discussion, we crept to the herd grounds, where we met up with a crouching Al Bagley. Both he and Eph Hanks had a good snicker over my recent misfortune, and I didn't blame them, though at the time I didn't see much humor in being spat upon.

As soon as the pickets had gone back to the fires for some supper, we stood and walked among the restless horses, removing the picket ropes, hobbles, and bells. Then, silently mounting some gentle-looking mares, we were off—walking slowly, taking the entire herd of horses and mules with us.

We rode west, far around the ridge and back to where Lazarus and Gideon were tending our horses, and there Eph dismounted and lashed his pack to a government animal. Al did the same, and then they both turned their own horses loose, knowing that their mounts would lead the entire band back toward the Valley, where the Mormon boys could gather them up.

With daybreak we sat on the hill again, watching the soldiers searching everywhere for their missing horses, and we all enjoyed a good chuckle over their discomfiture. Of course, their mission was now concluded, and they would have a long walk back to the place they were calling Camp Scott.

Suddenly the colonel of the group below walked straight toward the hill we were on, and straightway he climbed toward us. I watched him come from the bush I was behind, and I wondered why we didn't get out of there. But Eph Hanks, who was behind a tree, stood still, and the man came on.

Finally, when less than ten feet separated them, Eph stepped out with gun leveled and cried, "Halt!"

"Who're you?" the soldier asked as he raised his hands in surprise.

"We're a platoon of your long-bearded Mormons," Eph replied easily, fingering his own beard as he talked.

"Mormons? We were told they were all to the north and west of here."

"Just goes to show you can't believe all that you're told. Now Colonel, you might just as well call your boys off their search."

The man looked startled. "What? But they're looking for our horses. That's why I came up here—"

"You won't see them, even from here," Eph said. "The entire herd of livestock is well on its way to Great Salt Lake City, where it will be held safely until these foolish hostilities between your people and ours are concluded."

"Great Salt Lake City!" the man stormed. "Man, you can't *do* that! My men must have those mounts, and . . . and . . . by thunder, I'll sing out and the boys will have you surrounded in no time. Now drop that weapon, Mormon, and submit yourself to arrest."

"He'll not do it," Al Bagley said as he rose to his feet some fifty feet away. "You're the ones that are surrounded, Colonel. These woods are fuller of us long-bearded Mormons than a dog is of fleas, and if your boys have any respect for their lives, they'll be hoofing it back to their army post right *pronto*. Being mountaineers, we're real good at shooting down from heights such as this, and few of us are ever known to miss."

For emphasis, old Gideon stood up with his Henrietta pointed loosely at the man – and finally catching on, I stood up, too. Of course I had no weapon, but as it turned out, that didn't matter. The Colonel looked at the four of us and saw four hundred armed and hidden Mormons. He then turned tail and scooted down the slope, and in less than an hour the soldiers had packed up food, blankets, guns, and ammunition and were on their way to their distant post, moving double-quick on their shanks ponies.

And us? We spent the rest of the day gathering up saddles, pack bags, and other equipment, and hauling it all to a safe cache a mile or so south of our ridge. Altogether, it had turned into a dandy sort of encounter with the enemy.

Chapter 13

The next twenty-four hours seemed to me like one continual round of adventure. I didn't have time even to think of Steenie and where she might be, and I was so tired that I could hardly see straight. But except for a couple of quick cat-naps, Ephraim Hanks kept us on the move. We set several fires to burn animal forage so the government troops would have a more difficult time passing by. We hoorawed a couple of small units from the ridgetops, shooting in the air and riding our horses around and around to raise a dust like we were more than we were, thus throwing the fear of the Mormons into the poor souls and sending them scurrying back to their outfits. And, finally, we drove off a couple of herders and picked up fifty head of government cattle which we delivered to some of Colonel Burton's men.

But now it was night again, and we we sprawled out in a spring-fed, grassy swale about twenty miles east of Green River. I was doing my best to stay awake, and Lazarus was helping me by thumping me now and again with his bushy tail. Old Gideon had no dog, however, and he was sound asleep, his soft snores adding a gentle rhythm to the night.

The horses were cropping grass nearby, and every few moments Perdy would raise her head and look in our direction, making certain that the dog and I were still there. Satisfied, she would drop her muzzle and chomp down on more of the delicious feed she had found. Altogether it was a peaceful scene, and it was hard for me to keep in mind that enemies might be near and might even come upon us unawares.

"Al?"

Al Bagley rolled over and grunted at Ephraim's inquiry.

"Al, is it your turn to fix the grub, or is it mine?"

Sighing, Al laid back and closed his eyes. "Yours, Eph. I cooked it the night we picked up Captain Monson and the boy."

"You mean we haven't eaten a decent meal since then?"

Ephraim sounded shocked, and I grinned. I knew he was funning, but my stomach had been growling all afternoon, and now that I was no longer riding, the hunger was truly upon me.

"No, Eph," Al replied, "I didn't mean that. Hosea Stout fed us just forty or fifty hours ago, and that ought to be enough to last a good Mormon elder like you for two or three days, at least."

"Then I'm certain going to need to repent," Eph growled as he sat up. "I'm hungry enough to eat my pack, buckles and all."

"You may have to," Al said quietly.

"What do you mean?"

Now Al sat up. "I mean, I got to looking for our provisions this afternoon, thinking about supper. And unless you have them in your pack, they're gone."

"I don't have them, Al. You were to carry them."

"Then they're lost," Al Bagley sighed.

"Lost," I said, sitting up with the rest of them. "Where did we lose them?"

"If I knew that," Al muttered, "they wouldn't be lost, only cached, and I'd go back and pick them up. When I thought to check my pack this afternoon, I found that it had come open. I reckon our grub is scattered all the way back to Butcher Knife Spring."

Groaning, I lay back down – and Lazarus crawled to me and laid his head across my body. I scratched his ears, feeling bad about our hunger and feeling worse that it couldn't be solved. I was also feeling bad that the search for Steenie had sort of been swallowed up in the bigger issue of the war. I had no idea anymore where the emigrant trail was, or even for certain where *we* were. Nor had I talked to a single person all day who had seen Ben Crost's wagon. He might have been behind us, or he might have been ahead of us, I didn't know. For that matter, he might be camped directly across the next low ridge, and we would get up and move on, and I would never know of it. So, the uncertainty was there, and I was feeling pretty low about it.

But the hunger made it worse, it surely did.

"What you pilgrims intend on doing about it?" Gideon suddenly asked.

"What?"

"About supper, you consarned idjut! You young fellers may be able to go on forever without fodder, but old relics like me have got to eat."

"Same for us young relics," I said softly.

"All right, all right," Al muttered as he struggled to his feet. "I'll go out scouting. Maybe by morning I can scare up something to wrap our bellies around."

"Go west," Eph said quietly.

"What?"

"I said, go west. You won't need to go more than a mile. Then come back and tell us what you've found."

Shaking his head. Al saddled his horse, mounted, and rode away into the darkness. Gideon and I looked at each other. I shrugged, and he nodded knowingly—and then he laid back again and closed his eyes.

"Jons?" Eph suddenly spoke, his voice low and quiet.

"Yes, Sir?"

"You'll be wondering about Christena."

"I . . . I have been, sir. Do . . . you happen to know where she is? By inspiration, I mean?"

Eph shook his head. "I don't, Son. Wish I did—for I think the world of that girl, and of you, too. But maybe that sort of information isn't for me to know. However, the Lord has told me something, and you need to know it. I don't think you are going to find the girl, not galavanting around the country with

Al and me. I think you and Captain Monson had better take off on your own hook, heading back west—if you get my drift."

"You can't help us?" I asked.

"Not while I'm on a mission for the Prophet. But you won't need me, either. You'll see."

Stunned, I lay back and stared up at the darkness that I knew was lowering clouds. I was pretty sure that it was going to rain, but for some reason that was the furthest worry from my mind. I had truly come to depend upon Ephraim Hanks and Al Bagley, and I had felt certain that with their help, Gideon and I would have no trouble finding and getting Steenie back again. Now we would be going separate ways, and suddenly I felt lost and alone.

Somewhere in the distance, thunder rumbled, and the entire night felt heavy and ominous. I had seen no lightning, but again I heard a distant rumbling. Lazarus stirred next to me, then rose to his feet and whined. Seconds later, my Perdy mare came to us, and after she had touched noses with the dog, she lifted her head and stared off into the darkness.

"Horses are better than dogs for smelling trouble," Ephraim said quietly.

"That's so," Gideon agreed, "especially these little wild mustangs like your mare. What do you think she smells out there?"

"Or hears?" Ephraim added.

I didn't know, but by then even Lazarus had his head up and his hackles lifted. I sat tensely, waiting, not even realizing that Gideon had once again disappeared.

"Yo, Ephraim."

The voice was low, and with a sigh of relief I recognized it as belonging to Al Bagley.

"Here, Al."

A moment later the dark shape of Al's horse materialized out of the night, and with a grunt he dismounted. "Boys," he said as he leaned against his saddle, "I must be getting too old for this chasing around the country night and day. I got saddlesores and a sprained finger, and my eyes hurt something awful.

My belly is growling out a Captain William Pitt's Brass Band marching tune it is so empty, and my head is pounding enough to add the whole percussion section to it. The sum of it is, I am tuckered plumb out, and if I wasn't so doggone hungry, I'd unsaddle and go to sleep right now."

"Hypochondriac," Gideon muttered as he stepped back into sight.

"What?"

"You can always tell it," replied the old man. "When a hypochondriac has measles, he spends all day telling you how many."

"Hummph," grunted Al Bagley.

"You must have found some food," Ephraim said, grinning.

"I did. Plenty. The trick will be getting it."

"You speaking of the army?" Eph asked.

"As ever was. I think we could sneak in there and steal it, but I didn't want to try it without I should tell you first. Besides, you said to come back and report, so here I am."

Ephraim thought a moment, then broke into a wide grin. "Better than stealing it," he said, sounding pleased as punch, "why don't we get Uncle's boys to give it to us."

"Eph, you know full well that the U. S. of A. Army isn't about to give their food supplies away to a bunch of rebellious Mormons. So what do you have up your sleeve?"

"You still remember any Sioux or Cheyenne, Brother Al?"

"Some, but more Cheyenne than Sioux."

"Good," Ephraim grinned. "Then let's stage us an honest-to-goodness Cheyenne uprising."

"You mean . . ."

"That's right, Al. You be the chief. You've got the nose for it, the dark eyes and the color, too. Besides, it won't take you but a minute to shave off that puny little growth you call a beard."

"Shave off my beard! I wouldn't shave—"

"Up to you, Al. But if I was as hungry as you say you are . . ."

Well, Al Bagley fumed and fussed, but in not much time he had a tiny fire built and was shaving off his beard. He was already in full buckskins, so Ephraim added a mort of feathers out of his pack and then painted him with charcoal and white paint.

"Lawsy," Gideon said as he watched in wonder, "you do look like the genuine article."

"He can act the part, too," Ephraim said easily as he added some finishing touches. "Al spent a little time with the Cheyenne – two, three years ago. As I recollect it wasn't an intentional visit, but it turned out to be highly educational for both parties. Al got rid of a little extra blood, and old Roman Nose was surely pleased with those two copies of the Book of Mormon he ended up with when Al disappeared.

"All right, Chief. You set?"

"Ungh!"

I grinned, and Gideon clapped me on the back. "Watch close, Bucko," he said. "These pilgrims will either be teaching us a few tricks tonight, or they're about to learn a few new ones themselves. Whichever, I'm mighty anxious to go along and take me a looksee, for I ain't certain this will work."

"You're welcome along," Eph said as he saddled his horse. "Fact is, we might need a few extra 'braves' just outside of the firelight. For effect, of course, and not for any direct action. And don't you fret about whether or not this will work, either. George Clawson and I did this same stunt one night back in '53, and it came off like a charm. Besides which, the impression is powerful that it will work again tonight."

"Well, I haven't heard no Spirit say anything," Gideon said. "All the same, I hope you're right. Of course, I've learned that you can't tell how far a horse will run by the color of his hide. Maybe the same eternal principle applies to made-up Cheyenne chiefs."

"Maybe so," Eph replied.

"On the other hand," the old man continued, "I learned years and years ago that if a feller gets the drop on you, then the best thing to do is to smile and walk away. There's plenty of time to look tough when you're out of sight."

"Meaning?"

"Meaning maybe I'm overly cautious. But some men are so

stingy they'd skin a flea for the hide and tallow. If those soldier-boys don't want to part with their food and start lifting weapons, then I don't recommend pressing the issue."

"Sage counsel," Ephraim said softly. "However, I'm certain that all will be well. Should it turn out otherwise, we'll do as you say."

"And do it *pronto*," Al Bagley agreed.

After Gideon and I saddled up, we all mounted. Ephraim was then given hasty directions to exactly where he had told Al that he might find food, which was less than a mile to the west—and while he went off alone into the darkness one way, Chief Al Bagley, Gideon, and I went another.

We followed a deep ravine that led to the hills some distance above the soldiers' camp, and then we swung toward the camp and halted. Meanwhile, Eph, looking for all the world like an old mountaineer, and armed to the teeth with every weapon he had on this earth—and all of them showing plainly—followed the same ravine down the other way until he came to the trail the soldiers had made heading into camp. Then he turned and, sinking spurs to his horse, rode wildly up the trail and into their firelight.

From where we sat, we could see plainly the commotion he made, with the sentries stopping him and the soldiers spilling out from tents and jumping up from fires to surround him. Finally the commander of the men emerged from his tent to meet the stranger, and at that, Al urged his horse forward.

We pulled up several dozen yards outside the light, and while Al grinned, Gideon and I listened in amazement to Eph's windy tale of the heathen Cheyenne savages that the soldiers had spread camp right in the hotbed of.

"This ol' son's tellin' you pilgrims the gospel," Eph shouted. "Them bloodthirsty Cheyenne dog soljurs would think no more of peelin' scalps from you poor ignorant souls than they would of eatin' a chunk of raw buffalo liver after a hard day's hunt. And boys, raw liver is to them misbegotten heathen Injuns a purr-dee wondrous delicacy."

Right off men started running after rifles and Yeagers, and

the commander started putting more men out on perimeter patrol. But Eph stood in his stirrups and shouted them back in, and he yelled and cussed and kicked up a storm until every man was back listening to him.

Then he started in again to gussying things up, making conditions sound worse by the minute, until that whole entire camp was like a stick-swatted hornet's nest.

"You blinkin' idjuts," he raged. "Don't you know nothing about fighting Cheyenne? Get those rifles out of sight, and do it *pronto!* They get the idea you want to fight, and you'll all be dead. These braves is on the warpath, and they've swore the blood oath not to come back alive if they happen to run into anybody who is hankering for war. Now go on! Get them rifles under cover. You'll all be deader'n the last century if you give them Injuns the idea you want to fight!"

Without a word, every soldier hurried to restack his rifle, even as Eph had cautioned them to.

"That's better. Now listen to me, and listen good. According to the Cheyenne, you're trespassin', plain and simple. This exact spot is sacred ground, and the man who chose it for a camp ought to be whipped good and double-cursed by the meanest Cheyenne medicine man alive, who it so happens is right out there with another two or three hundred other unrighteously wicked warriors."

"Two or three . . . *hundred?*" several gasped.

"Aye, maybe four hundred, the way you boys is spending so much time augerin' with me. And now you pilgrims are starting to get my drift. Why, if you ain't packed up and out of here faster'n chain lightning with a link snapped, then I don't hold out no more hope for your sorry miserable lives than—"

"Oh, no. Oh, my merciful heavens, *no!*"

"What . . . what is it?" the commander asked, looking around.

"Hoofbeats, consarned it. I . . . I . . . Well, boys, that cuts it. It's been nice knowing you."

"Wait a minute!" the commander shouted. "What is it? Who—"

Eph swung his horse back impatiently. "You poor, sorry fools, that's Chief Ugly Face's horse I hear. Now I got to git—"

At that very instant, Al kicked his horse—and with a series of high shrieks and barks, he left my side and galloped down the hill at breakneck speed, letting out yells that would have done justice to a whole nation of Cheyenne warriors.

When he reached the camp, he slid his pony to a halt and began to harangue the bystanders in regular Indian fashion, at the same time swinging his arms and pointing to the mountains, hills, and plains.

By now the whole blue-coated outfit was standing open-mouthed, watching—and the commander, with flushed face, was wanting to know what the Indian wanted.

Reluctantly stating that he would find out, Eph rode forward and began talking with the "chief," using sign-language as well as Cheyenne. Finally he nodded, satisfied.

"Captain," he declared, turning his horse away from the disguised Al Bagley, "he wants you to understand that he owns this whole country as far as the eye can see—the land, the rocks, the rivers, the brush and trees, the birds and animals, and everything else that he can't think of at the moment. Further, he wants you to understand that you will have to pay dearly for the sacred bunch-grass your hungry animals have been devouring—not only tonight, but for the past five sleeps. Otherwise, he will give his five hundred men the word, and you will lose your scalps, just as sure as his name is Ugly Face."

"Andrews," the Captain shouted into the darkness, "are there others out there?"

"There sure are," a man shouted from so near Gideon and me that we both jumped. "There's at least two dozen right over here, and I can hear dozens of others all over the place."

Muttering, the captain shook his head, while Gideon and I both stared at each other, wondered who besides us the man had seen. We both breathed a sigh of relief.

"All right, Mister," the commander asked of Eph, "what does the chief want as tribute? I'm willing to pay anything within reason, for we can't afford to get in a shooting war with the Indians. We're too busy fighting Mormons to let that happen. So find out, and we'll see what we can do."

After the "chief" and the "mountaineer" had had another spirited talk, Eph turned around again.

"Captain, I reckon you're getting off lucky. He says his people are hungry. All he wants is some flour, bacon, beans, coffee, tea, sugar, and tobacco. A good bait of all those items ought to do the trick."

The captain ordered the commissary to bring forth the desired supplies, and the order was immediately filled.

Suddenly, however, the "chief" began to jabber again, at the same time rubbing his stomach and making all sorts of horrid faces.

"What in the name of common sense is the old cuss kicking about this time?" the captain growled.

Eph grinned and explained to him that the wife of Ugly Face was very sick, and he wanted some good brandy to rub on her stomach. And, oh yes, he also wanted a little candy for his children.

Well, there was another order, a government horse was brought forward and loaded with a good U.S. Army issue pack, which was in turn loaded with the mound of foodstuffs, and in a short time we were all sitting less than a mile away in our little camp with everything our hearts could desire for a delicious meal. We cached the liquor, coffee, tea, and tobacco for possible trading later on, and then commenced to eat and laugh, feeling thankful for U.S. Army vittles.

Meanwhile, the captain and his men were also happy and busy congratulating themselves over the clever manner in which they had concluded the deadly threat they had faced.

"Brother Hanks," Gideon said as we cleaned up the last of the bounteous supper, "a lot of folks would do more praying if they could find a soft spot for their knees. But from now on, I ain't waiting for such luxuries. I aim to repent right along, until I get to where I can hear like you do. Why, that little drama was a pure delight to behold, and I thank you for the privilege."

Ephraim smiled. "You're welcome as you can be. What do you boys think you'll be doing tomorrow?"

Gideon looked at me and nodded, saying by his expression that it was my decision. So right there I made it, pure and simple. "We'll be moving on," I said. "I hate to do it, for this has been a wondrous education. But I've got to find Steenie, and I'm not going to do it chasing the army all over creation."

"You follow the Spirit, Son, and you'll find her sure as coyote-dogs growl."

And as Ephraim said it, I suddenly knew with all my heart that he was right. If I could just get in tune, the Lord would lead me to Steenie, and then tell me what to do when I got there.

Chapter 14

When I awakened the next morning, just as light was breaking in the east, Ephraim Hanks and Al Bagley were gone. Rolling over with a groan I sat up, put on my hat, stomped into my boots, and set about building up a fire. Gideon was still asleep, but Lazarus was at his tail-thumping best, whining as though he couldn't stand not being able to tell me good morning. And even my Perdy mare stood close in, tossing her head and blowing joyfully with the light of the new day.

I felt good about the day, too. Even with the two Mormon scouts gone, I felt good. I didn't know where we were going to find her, but somewhere roughly south and west of us had to be Ben Crost's wagon and my sweetheart, Steenie Bergman. No one in the other direction had seen any sign of them. So, given a little luck and a lot of the Lord's blessings, right soon she and I would be together.

Surprisingly, it hadn't rained during the night, but the sky was still threatening, and so I knew it was only a matter of time. Meanwhile, the overcast made things warmer, which helped, and I had no trouble finding dry wood—which also helped. By the time poor old Gideon opened his eyes, I had a cozy fire going, and breakfast was sizzling and smelling wondrously.

"Morning, Gideon," I said cheerfully. "Arise and shine. Daylight's burning out here."

"Looks more like she's ready to drown," Gideon grumbled as he stared skyward. "Friend Jons, I feel somewhat like I've been trod upon by a herd of stampeding buffalo. My pappy always used to tell me that if I woke up feeling halfway between 'Oh, no," and 'My lawsy,' then I had overdid it."

"It was a tolerable long day, with an adventurous night," I agreed.

"Ummph. You maybe had ought to leave me here to go to my eternal reward, for I surely think the crossing of the River Jordan is close upon me."

Looking quickly at him, I tried to tell if he was being serious. "You truly feeling poorly, Gideon?"

"Worse than a calf with the slobbers. Trouble is, I don't reckon the good Lord is going to let me pass away without I should finish up my job getting that little gal back to you. So spread the table, for I'm about to be getting up."

Gideon dragged his blanket and tarp aside, revealing his bony old body in its patched underwear and scraggly socks. Me, I slept in my clothes, but Gideon wasn't of a mind to do that. He told me time and again that my body couldn't get a good sleep unless it got uncovered as a recognition that it was time for rest.

He lay still a moment, gathering determination. Then he propped himself up to a sitting position with arms behind him, and gently he eased his thin old legs off the side of the bedroll. Reaching to a nearby bush, he took his floppy wide-brimmed hat and settled it on his head—and I couldn't help but grin. At night he undressed from the bottom up, and in the morning he dressed from the top down. He told me when I asked him about it that no true man would get dressed or vice versa any other way—so I was trying to make it a habit of my own. And I was making some very minor progress, at least in that area.

Next Gideon took his frayed khaki shirt and fought the stiffness in his arms and shoulders to get it on, and then he fought again with the buttons of it to get them through the right buttonholes—his arthritis being a major obstacle to that endeavor. Next came the greasy leather vest, and with the aid of various snorts and grunts he finally shrugged into that. And only then did he roll over to his knees and slowly push himself to his feet.

I wanted to help him then—with all my heart I wanted to reach in and give the old man a hand. But I had tried it once, and he had snapped at me like a trapped weasel, letting me know in no uncertain terms that he could do this himself. So from then on I let my aging friend alone. But still I ached for him, I truly did. I had come to love Gideon Monson as I loved my own father, and it hurt to see him in pain.

Small things, like still managing to struggle into a shirt or pair of pants, were what gave him pleasure, though, and so I would not offend him by offering my help again. No, I knew that when he needed it, he would ask.

But his struggles also made me proud, too, for the old man was a fighter. And I knew that if he wouldn't give in to the miseries of life, then, by jings, neither would I.

Reaching his arms up and out, with me hearing—but not hearing so much as feeling—the creakings in the joints of his brittle old bones, Gideon stretched. Then carefully he took up his pants and nearly toppled trying to get his right leg in.

With a mumbled oath he hobbled to a convenient rock, sat down, and began to work the pantlegs one at a time all bunched over his feet and around his thin shanks. Then finally he could stand and pull them up into position. Giving a grunt of satisfaction, he tightened his belt. He then fastened the battered silver buckle that looked like it was of home manufacture but that, he had told me, had been given to him by a Cherokee Indian girl back in his younger days. For all I knew of his age, this could have meant before the Revolutionary War.

"I surely ain't so young like I once was," he grumbled while he battled his boots, stomping to push his heels all the way down inside them. "But I can still make it, friend Jons. Now, what's for breakfast?"

The next few moments we spent in silence—silence, that is, except for the lip-smacking time we each had downing those government vittles. I was beginning to think of myself as a westerner in every way—and judging by my new eating and speaking habits, as well as the increasing bow I was getting in my legs, I wasn't far off.

After we had eaten, Gideon looked down at Lazarus. "Jons, you reckon that wolf's ready to go it on his own?"

"It's hard to say," I answered. "But I'll tell you this. I think that *he* thinks he is. Come here, Lazarus. That a boy. Now, let me see that leg . . . Gideon, take a look. He doesn't even flinch when I pinch or twist it. And the wound is no more than a thin red line. Is it possible that he's healed so soon?"

"Well, Son, it's been four, nearly five days—and Eph Hanks did prophesy that the critter would heal fast. I'd say you should take the splint off and see how he does."

I did as instructed. Lazarus trotted off into the sage and back again, and some six hours later he was still going strong, acting as if he'd never even been shot in the first place. So, with my miracle dog ranging before us, we rode south and west across the wide and lonely plains. And as we rode, we saw more and more smoke from grass fires spotting the distant horizon, confirming our suspicion that Mormon patrols were still busily engaged. Then we topped a ridge and learned how truly unlonely the plains of Wyoming really were. For there, angling toward us, were a patrol of twenty or more long-bearded Mormon soldiers.

We all pulled up and eyed each other, and finally the leader, a lean young man with wide hat and twinkling eyes, spurred forward.

"Boys," he said, "if you aren't Mormons, then the Good Lord has led you into a heap of trouble—for you have been delivered into our hands."

"The Lord has preserved us then," I replied, grinning. "I'm Jons Soderberg, lately of the Valley, and this is Captain Gideon Monson, of the Battle of New Orleans fame. Perhaps you've heard of him?"

"Don't allow as I have," the other said.

"Uneducated pilgrims," Gideon muttered from behind me.

"And who might you be?" I asked.

"Major!" somebody in the rear suddenly shouted, interrupting us, "lookee there!"

We all turned to see where the man was pointing, and there was Lazarus, squatting in the sagebrush behind us, eyeing the group of men with skepticism.

"That your wolf?" the leader asked as Lazarus then trotted up and lay down beneath Perdy's nose.

"That's an often-asked question, and the answer is no. He stays with us of his own free will, which we appreciate. Besides which, he's a dog, not a wolf."

"Could've fooled me," the man grinned. "But he's acting like a dog, so I'll let it ride."

"That's awful kind of you," I said easily, with just a trace of sarcasm directed at his condescending attitude.

The man grinned again. "You're a strange kid, but well said. I'm Major Lot Smith, lately of Fort Bridger and headed back from the Big Sandy on a mission that accomplished a little pillaging and burning of the enemy's supplies."

Well, to me it was astounding to learn how many of the brethren were out and about on the plains, doing their own small parts to throw sand into the machinery of the army, thus grinding its progress to an early and winter-catching halt. And the amazing thing was how small most of the bands of Mormons were. This bunch of twenty was the largest I had seen, and yet they were just as confident as if they had been two hundred. That was, of course, because to a man they were convinced that they went in the strength of Israel's God, and that He would fight their battles for them.

"Until this morning," I told Major Smith, "we rode with Ephraim Hanks and Al Bagley, doing the same."

"So ol' Eph is already out. I wondered if he would be. Who's he working under?"

"As far as I know, he's ranging free under President Young's direction."

Lot Smith nodded. "Yes, that would be so. Why aren't you together now?"

I looked at Gideon, but he only blinked a couple of times,

leaving it all up to me. So I told it all, about Ben Crost and Steenie, and about our quest to find them and return her to the Valley.

"That's a tall order, Son. You met anybody who's seen them?"

"Not since Cache Cave. But I figure they have to be on the emigrant road, so Gideon and I are going to ride backward down it. Given time, we'll find them."

"Major Smith?"

Lot Smith turned toward his men. "Yes, Lewis?"

A man rode forward to side with the major, and for a moment or so they spoke in tones too low for me to hear. Finally Lot Smith turned back to me.

"Son, this is Brother Lewis Robison. He's quartermaster-general of the Nauvoo Legion, and he saw something you might be interested in hearing about."

"That I did," the man said quickly. "Lot and I had delivered Governor Brigham Young's message to Colonel Alexander at Camp Scott, forbidding either him or his army from coming any closer to the Valley—and commanding them to surrender their arms and ammunition to me.

"The Colonel declined the Prophet's order," he continued, grinning, "and he said so in a letter we were ordered to return. On our way back to General Wells with Alexander's reply, we rode within a mile of Mister Yates's trading post, down on the Green. Because I'm quartermaster-general, it's my duty not only to requisition supplies for the Legion, but to see that other supplies don't get into the hands of Uncle's army.

"Mister Yates is not a Mormon, but he's been friendly to our people for several years. So I stopped at his post to see if he had any gunpowder and to secure a promise from him that he would sell what he had to us. He was supplied with a few dozen pounds, which I bought all but a little of—as well as two Sharps rifles, which I also purchased. It was while I was leaving that I saw the wagon."

"Wagon?" I asked quickly.

"That's right, Son. It was a civilian wagon, camped down

on the river behind the post. I had the feeling that the folks might be runaway Mormons, so my horse 'accidentally' got real skittish, and before I could get it under control, it had pranced and sidestepped and bucked its way back and forth past their encampment. Sorta gave me a better look.

"But the point is, Son, that I believe they are the people you're looking for—man, woman, young family. There was a young lady with them, too, a right pretty thing. And I noticed that she watched me the entire time I was there, like she wanted to say something but didn't dare."

"Dark hair?" I asked hopefully.

"Dark, but sort of reddish. Real fetching color—and she wore it loose, not up, so it was easy to notice."

Well, my heart was pounding like I had just run ten miles. "It's her!" I breathed. "It's Steenie. Sir, where exactly is their camp?"

"It's on the Green, Son. But you can't go there alone."

Shocked, I looked from Lewis Robison to Lot Smith and back again. "But . . . but . . . I must, Sir! She's been abducted against her will, and she's depending on me to rescue her."

"Besides which," Gideon growled from a little way off to my side, "he ain't exactly alone."

For the first time, Lot Smith and Lewis Robison noticed my companion—or rather, for the first time they noticed my companion's rifle Henrietta, which was easily covering both of them with her single dark eye of death.

"So that's the way the stick floats?" Lot Smith asked, watching Gideon carefully.

"No, it isn't," I declared. "At least it doesn't need to be. After all, we're on the same side, and if you are as you call it, pillaging and burning, then Gideon and I are rescuing. It seems to me that we're both after the same thing—disrupting the army and protecting our own."

"And you say she asked for your help?" Lot Smith asked.

"Yes, Sir." I then pulled the slingshot from my rear pocket, ignoring the men's grins as I did so. That little elm-crotch slingshot was *not* a well-respected weapon.

"She wrapped the note around the fork of this slingshot," I said, holding it up. "Fact is, I have her note right here, if you'd like to read it."

Smith nodded, so I put the old slingshot back, fished the note from my breast pocket, and handed it to him.

"It's a request for assistance, all right," Lot said as he read it. "Thing is, how do we deal with it?"

"You don't," Gideon said quietly. "She's our job, and we'll do 'er just dandy. You brethren have enough to worry over."

Lot Smith looked over at Gideon. "Feisty old cuss, ain't you? You sure you don't want to join my men in our fight with Uncle? You could do the Lord's cause a powerful lot of good and maybe wrap this entire war up by your lonesome."

Gideon merely looked at him.

"Well?"

"After some folks tell you all they know," the old man growled sarcastically, "they keep on talking. You fit the bill, Brother."

"Oh?"

"That's right. In the midst of all that verbal lather you've been whipping up, I said that I figure the boy and me are already in the Lord's cause."

Lot grinned at Gideon's response and turned back to me. "Son, wherever you got this old coot, you hang onto him. He's worth his weight in gold. Now, it seems to me that the best way to solve this dilemma is to work together. You try to ride from here to that camp on the Green alone, with all the government's boys out and about, and you won't have a prayer. But if we combine forces and put our noggins together, why, I think we can get that little girl back for you without much trouble. Either of you interested?"

"If we aren't?" Gideon asked.

"Then likely we'll all have a few problems."

Gideon's head came up. "That a threat?"

"Not hardly. We won't harm you at all. But Uncle's boys aren't very friendly, and what my men and I propose to do between here and Camp Winfield, which is near Yates's post, won't help pacify them at all. On the other hand, if we throw in together, we'll be moving fast enough that the word won't get out ahead of us, and we can lead you directly to their camp. Plus we'll be nearby to help you—that is, should you need it. What do you think?"

Gideon looked at me. "Son, the switching tail is always the one to catch the cockleburs," he said quietly as I looked at him. "The more you keep on joining up with every tomfool scout traipsing about on these miserable plains, the more likely you'll be heading for trouble. Howsomever, it's up to you."

Well, I knew that. And I knew, too, that my decision had better be right. Quickly I pleaded in my mind for the Lord to impress me with what I should do. I waited but nothing happened, nothing except that the more I thought about it the more it seemed like joining up with Major Smith was a smart thing to do. I didn't know if that feeling was an answer, but it was the closest thing to one that I was getting, so I decided to go with it.

"Major, we'll ride along. And Gideon and I will truly appreciate all the help you can give us."

"Good enough," the Major declared. "All right, men, let's move out. We've got work to do."

And so once again, Gideon and I were caught up in the maneuverings of the blossoming Utah War. But at last and at *least* we were finally doing it in the right direction again.

Chapter 15

It was dark, and the smell of rain was on the dusty land. There had been showers, two or three, though not enough to really complain about. But they had left the clean, fresh smell of newly fallen rain behind them, and I breathed deeply of it.

"Ol' Lazarus is doing mighty well," Gideon said quietly from beside me, where we sat on our horses in the darkness. "The Lord surely must have had a hand in the healing of his leg."

"It's hard for me to imagine that the Lord heals animals," I said.

"Why's that? They're his critters too, ain't they?"

Well, Gideon had me there, and I mortared up another stone of gospel truth in my shallow well of knowledge. Actually, I'd never thought of such a thing—but now that I had seen it for myself, it truly made sense.

"Friend Jons," he said then, "this is purely a risky business we're in the middle of. You sure you were following the Spirit when you agreed to throw in with these brethren?"

"No," I replied honestly, "but I was surely trying to. Until I get the hang of it a little better, that's about the best I can admit to."

"Well, I do hope you were right. Trouble is, I have this pain high up between my shoulder blades, and that has me worried. Of course, it might be my bursitis, but I can't tell. I'll say this, though, friend Jons. You and I had better be carefuller'n a couple of chickens on a fox run, or any help you can give that little gal might be nothing more than old wishes."

Nodding nervously, I looked off across the wide, dark land. There was something nagging at me, too, some awful dread that I couldn't place. Maybe it had to do with Steenie, and maybe it had to do with the raid we were about to make. I didn't know, but I was sure tight inside. Of course, like Gideon had said to me maybe twenty times in the past week, "If you don't have a choice, be brave." So I gritted down on my fears and did my best to get ready for whatever was coming next.

"All right, men," Lot Smith said quietly, "these teamsters are drunk as skunks, but the scouts say they have settled down some. So here's the plan. We'll ride forward until we're somewhat in the light, and then I'll do the talking. Questions?"

"Aye," a man called Big James said. Big James was an Irishman, and I had learned that he wasn't Mormon. He just happened to believe in the same ideas of freedom that the Saints did, and so he was fighting with them.

"Sure, an' ye've got a head count, Major, but in case ye've forgotten, it's outnumbered that we are."

"You're right, James. I thought there were twenty-six wagons, but it turns out there are fifty-two. I'd say, with the help of the Lord, that still puts the odds heavily in our favor. Wouldn't you?"

"It's a poor joke ye be telling us, Major."

Lot Smith looked right back at him. "This is not a time for joking, man."

James grinned widely. "Sure and you Mormons are blatherin' idiots, but it's ready to follow you I am. And if it's the Lord ye see fighting beside ye, Major, then tell him hello from Big James of County Cork."

There was a quiet chuckle from the men, and without another word Lot Smith spurred his horse forward toward the blazing fire near the center of the wagons.

"Who goes there?" a man standing with his back to the fire shouted as the column drew close.

"We're here to see the captain of the train," Lot Smith declared quietly. Then he signaled the column to halt.

"I'm the captain," another man said, stepping forward. "Name's Dawson. Who might you be?"

"My name is Lot Smith, Mister Dawson, and my boys and I have a little business with you."

"This is a passing strange hour for business, Mr. Smith. State the nature of it and then be on your way."

Lot grinned. "Very well, here it is. You are ordered to get all your men and their private property out of the wagons as quickly as possible, for my boys and I mean to put a little fire to them."

"For God's sake," the wagon-master exclaimed, "don't burn the wagons!"

"It's for His sake that I *am* burning them," Major Smith replied coolly. "Stack your arms over there, and then come back and stand here – all of you in a group.

"Lee Kimball and Jim Hewlett," Major Smith then ordered, "come guard these men. Bishop Steve Apple, you take a ride down toward Little Mountaineer Fork and set a scout there. Three rounds fired fast will let us know there are people coming. Four rounds will tell us they are soldiers.

"Mister Dawson," Lot then said, turning back to the teamster captain, "are your men making haste?"

"Yes, Sir, they are that."

"Well then, tell them to be double-quick about it. I have little patience with dawdlers and would just as soon burn personal property as otherwise, if it be in the way."

"Men," Dawson shouted anxiously while I grinned with the pure joy of watching this event unfold, "hurry faster. They're going to fire the wagons! Billy Cody, you and Bill Hickock get help with your wagons. You boys can't work fast enough for these Mormon fellers.

"Those two are just youngsters," he said by way of explanation to Major Smith, "but on that wagon bench they're mighty fine teamsters and can move a team with the best of 'em."

There was anxious scurrying then, and we were all watching

that, when from nowhere a mounted blue-coat rode up to the fire from a direction that Major Smith hadn't covered.

"Who's in charge here?" the young soldier asked.

"I am," Major Smith replied as he rode forward. "If you have dispatches, hand them to me."

"I have them, Sir, but they are verbal."

"Well then, sing them out. And remember, Son, if you lie to me, your life isn't worth a straw in a high wind."

The poor soldier, suddenly terrified, for he belatedly realized what was happening at the train and to whom he was speaking, began to shake and his jaws to clatter. And as Major Smith later said, it was from considerably more than the cool weather.

"Big James," Lot Smith then ordered, "take his man's mule and arms, and if he moves, even a little, shoot him on the spot."

"N-no . . . please . . . please don't kill me," the man sobbed.

"Sure and it'll be doin' ye no good to whine," Big James growled as he gave the man a poke with his pistol. "Soldiers' lives are worth very little around here. It'll be only the bull-whackers who get off easily, so stop bawling and stop quivering, or it'll be escaping I'll think you're up to."

The man dropped to his knees. "I'll . . . I'll give my dispatches, please, only d-don't shot me."

"And what are they, man?"

"I . . . I'm from Winfred, and . . . and I'm to tell the teamsters to be on the watch for M-Mormons. The . . . they're . . . *You're* in the field, and the . . . the bull-whackers are to put out g-guards. In the morning there will be . . . four c-companies of cavalry and two pieces of field artillery to . . . to protect them."

There was a round of laughter from the men behind me, and I joined with them. The poor man was so pitiful that he was funny, and knowing that he was actually safe from harm, I couldn't help but enjoy his discomfiture.

"Say there," another man said as he strode into the firelight, "what goes on there?"

Quickly swinging his rifle upon the surprised man, Lot Smith identified himself. "Now mister," he ordered, "where are you from?"

"The . . . the other train," the man responded.

"Then you get back to your train and don't move from there," Lot told him. "Don't do one single thing but wait, and I'll be up directly to take care of you."

The man took off like a shot, and then Lot Smith scattered a few of the men to make certain the first train was ready to burn. While they were doing that, the Major herded the frightened Mister Dawson ahead of him, and another group of us followed the two of them through the sage to where the second train was halted.

"Well," Lot said to the quaking man whom he had sent running a few minutes before, and who was still squatted down next to the closest wagon wheel, "you were wise to be obedient. Now step lively here, up beside Mister Dawson."

Nimbly the man sprang to the side of the captain, and shortly the two teamsters, with several of us lined out behind them, came to the wagon of the sleeping captain of the second train.

"Bill!" shouted Mister Dawson as he furiously shook the wagon. "Confound it man, get up, or you'll be burned to a cinder in five minutes!"

Bill suddenly displayed remarkable activity. He came boiling out of that wagon like it was already in flames. Major Smith then introduced the same program to him that had been introduced to Captain Dawson, and in a short time the arms of the second wagon train were in a pile and the teamsters and others were huddled under guard several yards away.

"It's amazing," Lot said then, shaking his head at Gideon and me. "Our boys appear to have dwindled to a mighty small body, but these sixty or seventy prisoners don't seem to notice it. General Wells prophesied that our numbers would be multiplied in the eyes of the enemy, but I never thought I'd see such a literal fulfillment.

"Captain Dawson," the Major then continued, "what sort of loading do you have? I have need of overcoats and gunpowder and would hate to see such items go up when I fire the wagons."

Hastily Dawson produced his bills of lading, for he truly didn't know what he had.

"Hunt the stuff up, yourself," Major Smith told him. "I'm somewhat busy at the moment."

Diligently, Captain Dawson began searching by the light of the fire, and in not more than a minute he announced that he had found large quantities of saltpeter and sulfur, which he claimed were not less dangerous than powder.

"Well," Lot said, shaking his head, "we'll have to take the risk of injury from it, for we can't separate it, and the train must be fired now. Any overcoats?"

"Not a one."

"Then fire it up!"

"Oh, please, Major, don't make me fire my train," Mister Dawson pleaded. "I've been sick and am not well yet, and don't w-want to be hurt."

Suddenly I became aware of a deep growling, and, looking down, I saw Lazarus staring off into the darkness, the hackles on his neck raised straight into the air.

Gideon, who could somehow see better in the dark than I ever could, was fingering his rifle as he watched in the same direction that Lazarus was pointing. And then, suddenly, he grinned.

"Major," my elderly friend interrupted as he signaled me to quiet my dog, "look smart, now. Here's a fellow coming up that's been afflicted with Saint Vitus' dance or some such malady, he's shaking so badly."

We all looked, and at last the poor soul moved into the firelight, gazing wide-eyed around him as he stumbled forward. "Why . . . why am I bringing in the oxen so early?" he asked with quavering voice. "Are we hitching up the t-train already?"

"No, sir," Major Smith told him, "we're *burning* it already. The oxen won't be needed here any longer, so we'll be taking them with us when we depart. Just bring them up and leave them with my boys, and then take your place here under guard."

"You . . . you're *Mormons?*"

"That's pretty near the truth."

"Well, then I d-don't think much of your methods. I should think you would have c-come sooner, and not waited until I was in bed and asleep and liable to be burned up."

Big James laughed. "Sure and it's a lucky mon ye be, old son. It's busy we are, and the luck of the Irish is with ye that ye even got called up at all."

The man stared, wide-eyed, looking from one of us to the other. "M- Mormons," he gargled in a strange sort of way, "real, honest-to-goodness Mormons. I . . . I never thought . . . "

Suddenly Lot Smith reached up and swept off his hat. "Since I'm bald," he said, grinning at the quivering fellow, "you can see that I have precious small horns. But they're there, nonetheless, and I'm doing my best to make 'em grow. Now, shoo, before I butt you!"

The man, with a squeal, turned and ran, and I stared after him, astonished that he could believe such nonsense. But he did, that was evident, and I realized that he wasn't alone on this earth. There were many who were willing to believe almost anything, no matter how preposterous, so long as it pushed along their own preconceived but false notions of truth. And suddenly it was crystal clear to me why it was so all-fired important that a person learn to go to the source of all truth, to God Himself, to obtain answers. Only from the Lord could a man believe everything he was told and rely on it eternally. And only by relying on the Lord's information to him could a man ever hope to regain God's presence.

Soon everything was prepared in both trains, and we were getting ready to fire them when three shots in rapid succession came from Bishop Apple, down toward the Mountaineer Fork. Tensely we waited, and soon an Indian, a Ute brave, came riding alone into the firelight.

Since we were all awake, he was seeking presents—though I imagine, since Indians don't usually make social visits at such an early hour, that he would have taken what he wanted by grand theft had everybody been asleep. But Major Smith was feeling generous, and the brave went away elated with some flour, some soap, and two wagon covers for his lodge. Nor did he have to fracture the seventh of the great commandments to get them.

And then the major lighted his torches.

"Come, James," he said as he rode toward the wagons. "It seems fitting and proper for the Gentiles to spoil the Gentiles."

Laughing gleefully, Big James took up another torch. Then the two men rode from wagon to wagon in both trains, setting the covers afire. Meanwhile, a couple of the Mormon boys had several of Dawson's men separating two wagons from the rest and filling them with supplies.

"The boys down below will like this," one of the Mormons said, giving the hint to Dawson and the others that we were accompanied by an entire host of others who were camped nearby.

Soon teams were hitched to the wagons of supplies, and the other fifty wagons were sending a bright glow into the Wyoming night.

"By Saint Patrick, ain't it beautiful!" Big James exclaimed as he looked on in awe. "Sure and I never saw anything go better in all my life."

As I watched the billowing flames, I had to agree with him, though it seemed unnatural for the Lord's army to be wantonly destroying government property. However, I knew that our mission was simply to put time and distance between Uncle's troops and the Valley—and that by crippling their progress, so to speak, the hot air they were blowing would naturally cool down.

But now it was on to Steenie, and I couldn't have been more anxious, knowing that every hour of every day could possibly mean the difference in whether I succeeded or not.

Chapter 16

"Vasquez, I won't do it!"

Yates glared from behind the barrels and planks that served as the counter in his low-ceilinged, sod-walled trading post. It was not a large post, and it was overly full of hides, furs, traps, saddle tack, barrels of salt pork and onions, and just about anything else that someone crossing the great American desert might find use for. In short, it was a typical, side-bulging western trading post.

In the corrals down on the flat were a motley herd of horses, oxen, and mules, taken in trade because they were too jaded and worn to make the trip over the mountains to the west or the plains to the east. But Yates was feeding and resting the beasts, and in time most of them would regain their strength. For above all else, Yates was a connoisseur of animals, and he loved and took under his protective wing even the worst possible cases of travel-abused carcasses that came along.

But as if to prove to the world that he could also spot the good ones when they showed up, Yates kept in a separate corral, butted against the post itself where he could keep his eye on them, two horses of an entirely different sort than the beaten-down trades that were down on the flat. These two horse were tall, long-boned and long-bodied, well muscled and well bred. One was a Morgan and Standard cross and the other a Thoroughbred and Hambletonian cross. They were beautiful animals, rare animals, and they were born to run and race. They were also the pride and joy of the trader.

Only now it was not his two prize horses that he worried about. No, now it was the singularly dirty man who stood before him, as well as the two renegade Utes who stood back and behind. These three worried the trader Yates, and they worried him badly.

"You'll do it," Vasquez said quietly, his voice filled with malicious venom. "You owe me, Yates, and I'm collecting."

The man sighed and stared at the floor. "All right, all right," he agreed reluctantly. "But I'll be seen in blazes before I sell the powder to the army. They've got no business here, and they know it. Besides, I already promised the Mormons that I'd sell what I had to them."

"*Promised?* Since when did a promise to a Mormon mean any more than a promise to an Indian?"

Vasquez laughed at his own joke, but the other men remained still. So he grew quiet again, and, picking up a fox pelt, he began caressing it between his dirty fingers.

"So, how will the Mormons pay you? In scrip, or in trade?"

"Trade, I reckon. They're an honest folk, and I don't care how many pounds you have to sell, they'll make it good."

"At how much a pound?"

"I sold them a few pounds day before yesterday at two bits a pound."

"Cash?"

Yates shook his head. "Course not."

"Then it won't wash with the Mormons—neither the price nor the method. You take that train of mules outside and take it to the army today—and don't bother to come back without you have a dollar a pound, gold money."

"But . . . but I can't leave here," Yates protested.

"I'll mind the store," Vasquez grinned. "And Limpy and Knife will feed your animals. Oh, by the way, there's eight hundred pounds of powder out there. That means I want eight hundred dollars. But I'm a generous man, Yates. Anything beyond eight hundred dollars that you can get, we'll split fifty-fifty. So, do your best."

"And if I can't get a dollar a pound?" Yates growled.

Again Vasquez grinned. "Well, then, since you'll have our mules and powder, we'll have your store, and your two pet racers out back to boot. I'm sure, ol' Son, if we lumped everything in here together, with your pet horses tied inside here against the wall, it might be worth eight hundred dollars. Especially if we poured coal oil over the whole shebang and struck a sulfur match to it."

"You wouldn't dare."

Now Vasquez laughed outright, and the two Indians behind him joined in. "*Dare*, Yates? Don't even tempt me. Now, go on. You have until tomorrow night to be back here with the gold. Otherwise, the boys and I will warm ourselves by a nice fire and eat a hearty supper of roast horsemeat. And you can start hauling goods by stolen Mexican mule train again, just like we did fifteen years ago."

Yates shook his head in anger and frustration. But there was nothing he could do, and he knew it. He feared Vasquez, feared him with all his soul. The man was as cold-blooded as any man Yates had ever known. Nor were the two Indians hardly less so. But toward them Yates carried no animosity. They weren't of his culture and could not be expected to think as he did. But Vasquez, who murdered as easily as he took a drink of water –

"Mister Yates . . ."

All three men whirled to the startlingly clear, feminine voice that came from the doorway behind them, and Yates felt his heart sink. He had forgotten about the runaway Mormon family down on the river, and he had forgotten most especially about this lovely girl who was traveling with them. But now Vasquez and his men had seen her, and, as Yates watched the leering expressions on the faces of the three renegades, his heart turned cold as winter ice.

"Well, well, well," Vasquez said as his eyes burned into the girl in the doorway. "Do come in, honey-child."

"Thank you," she said spiritedly, "but I will wait out here until you are finished. Then I will speak with Mister Yates."

Vasquez laughed. "Then you will have a long wait, little sister. Mister Yates is just now leaving on a mighty long journey."

The girl turned back, confused. "But . . . but . . . "

"Christena," Yates said as he came hurriedly from behind the barrels and planks, "you go down and wait with your family. I'll be back from delivering this gunpowder to the army by tomorrow night, and then you and I can conclude our discussion about the young man with the slingshot."

"Slingshot?" Vasquez laughed derisively. "Is some young sprout coming to protect her with a slingshot? Or to fight the army with it? Ha, ha! A slingshot . . . "

"Don't mind him," Yates said as he stepped out through the low door. "You just wait down below with your family, and I'll be back as soon as I can get here. And whatever you do, stay away from those men in there."

Steenie smiled and then beat a hasty retreat from the men inside the post. But as she walked away, her skin crawled, and she knew to the depths of her soul that she had been in the presence of evil men, men more wicked than any she had encountered before in her life. Oh, if only Jons were there . . .

"Well, boys," Vasquez said as Yates rode away with the string of loaded mules behind him, "by tomorrow night we'll be eight hundred dollars richer."

"Unngh," grunted Limpy, "and the little *tsharr* squaw?"

"Ah, yes," Vasquez said with an evil grin as he turned inside the room, "the lady. A likely looking creature. In Taos or thereabouts, she might fetch upwards of two hundred dollars. But I've a feeling that she's worth more than that, much more. If Arapeen, or Hunkootoop even, got a good look at her, well—I'd give my best saddle if one of them redskinned heathens wouldn't give five hundred American dollars to make her their *numero uno* squaw."

"What of the squaw for today?" Limpy asked hopefully. "Until we get her to the *kibah,* to the mountains."

"You don't touch her!" Vasquez ordered. "Not either one of you. Not until we are ready to go tomorrow night. You hear me, Limpy?"

Bear That Walks with Crippled Foot nodded agreeably, for he knew what came of arguing with his white boss. But neither did he worry overly much about his commitment. There was time, and there were ways . . .

Knife, on the other hand, said nothing to either of the others. But his dark eyes were glued to the place out in the sage where the girl had disappeared over a small rise of ground. And he noticed, as he stood there, that his breath was coming much more rapidly than it had in years.

At long last, he knew, he had found the squaw he had dreamed of for so many difficult seasons. She was not exactly as he had pictured her, true. But this white girl with the fire of sunset in her hair took his breath away. Further, she left him with a deep longing in his belly that was like nothing he had ever before known. Yes, he would have her, and with her he would disappear into the mountains far to the south, where he would return forever to the true ways of his people.

"Knife?"

Without turning, Knife grunted that he had heard.

"I mean it," Vasquez growled. "The girl is mine, and I want full value for her when I *nar-o-wap*, when I trade her. Touch her and you're *e-i*, dead. Now get out there and see that our horses are fed and watered."

"Oh, Stinking Little Willow," Limpy added scornfully in Ute, "remove the *timbi-up* and the *carri-nump*, the bridle and saddle, from my pony before you take care of your own. Then make haste to see that my pony is happy with grain and a good rubdown. Afterward you may care for your own. *Pe-nun-ko*, in the future you will do this always, for the ponies of squaws are always taken care of last."

Limpy laughed. "Do otherwise, Stinking Small Willow, and *Tabby* will smile down on an *e-i* fool, a very dead little willow."

Without a word Knife went out the door. But in him was a burning hatred, and anger that startled him with its intensity.

No longer was he one with those two in the white trader's *paquy-nary* wickiup, his stinking lodge. Now it was just he, himself, *towats*, a man of the Southern People, who with his *tsharr* squaw, his white woman, would go off into the mountains to dream his happiness.

From where he stood trembling with anger and determination, Knife could not see the girl's camp. But that did not matter. He knew where it was, and he knew also that before *tabby-moushy*, before sunrise, he and she would be gone. And if that meant that Limpy and Vasquez would have to die, then so be it. He would see to that, and see to it with pleasure. Nor, he decided as he broke into one of his rare smiles, would they die easily. Neither of them deserved that privilege.

Of course, Knife thought as he drew his blade in a motion swift as thought, it would be the one called Limpy who died first. That went without saying. His eyes flashing, the scrawny little man drew his thumb along the razor-sharp blade of the Spanish knife, feeling the narrow slice of it into his flesh.

In his mind he could see the big oaf called Limpy, staked over an anthill and sobbing silently, tonguelessly for mercy as his flesh was sliced and peeled. The mental image felt good, better than good, and from that instant Knife began to plan.

Chapter 17

Trying not to worry about the men she had seen at the post, Christena sank to the wagon tongue. Ben Crost was off looking for a stray cow, and it had been her first real opportunity to get away from her bed and finish her talk with Mister Yates. Of course, he had come to doctor her when they had first arrived, and knowing that a real illness couldn't be faked, she had confided in the trader, explaining to him what she was trying to do.

He had winked in response, told her not to worry, and then had told Ben and Maria Crost that "the poor little thing" shouldn't be moved for at least three days. So for three days Christena had been "recuperating." But now Mister Yates was gone, and Christena felt a deep foreboding about the men up at the post.

"Steenie, what's the matter?"

Christena looked down at the small boy who had spoken. Maria was down on the riverbank, washing clothes. The two younger children were with her, and so Christena and Daniel Crost, Ben and Maria's eldest son, were alone at the wagon.

"Nothing's the matter, Danny."

"Are you all better now?"

Christena smiled. "Yes, I am feeling much better, thank you."

But then, when the boy's face showed his great relief, she sighed. Of all that had happened, this was the worst for her, the guilt over fooling poor Maria and the children. They were so sincerely sympathetic, and they treated her so nicely, that it really hurt her to carry on her charade. Yet there was no other way, for none of them knew of Ben Crost's threats against her, or of his lustful desires. So it was him she was fooling, him she was holding off until such time as Jons would be able to rescue her. Then, when she was free, she would tell the rest of them, and all would finally be right.

For the hundredth time she scanned the horizon to the west, hoping to see Jons riding up to get her. But the land seemed empty, devoid of life, and sighing with discouragement Christena turned away.

"See this?" Danny asked as he held out his hand.

"What is it?"

"Arrowhead."

"Can I see?" she asked.

Danny held it out in his open palm.

"Christena looked, amazed. "That's pretty. Where did you get it, Danny?"

The child waved a hand toward the hill rising north and east of the bluff. "Yonder. There's more of them there, too."

"Could I find one?"

"Maybe, if you look sharp, and if you're lucky."

Feeling unaccountably bored, and certain that Ben wouldn't be back for some time to catch her in such a healthy state, Christena smiled at the boy. "Will you take me there and let me look?"

"I don't know. What would Ma say?"

"She wouldn't mind. It isn't far, is it?"

The boy shook his head. "But you'd be scared, I bet."

"Scared? Danny, what's there to be afraid of?"

"Ghosts of dead Indians that these arrowheads killed," the boy responded seriously.

"Did you see a ghost?"

"No, I never. But that doesn't say they ain't none. You really want to go?"

Christena nodded.

"Okay, and you don't have to be scared. I'll take care of you."

"I'm *not* scared," Christena declared, smiling at her pint-sized escort.

Walking together, the two started up the bluff, toward the sharp-rising hill. Climbing it, they followed the top, descended a narrow draw that headed toward the trading post, and came to a bare level place in the midst of some brush, part way down the slope.

"See," Danny said, indicating a circle of fire-blackened stones almost covered with dirt and sand. "This was where they roasted each other, I bet."

Christena giggled. "Indians didn't do that, silly. You're thinking of headhunters or cannibals. But I'll bet this was a real Indian camp, just the same. Have you come here a lot, looking for arrowheads?"

"Naw, just once. I found some old bones, and I was looking for more."

"Bones?"

"Yeah. Mister Yates told me there were old elephant bones up here, buried in the bank. He even has a big, yellow tusk down at his post, and a picture of an elephant, to show what it looked like."

"An elephant, Danny? There aren't any elephants here."

The boy looked seriously at her. "I know, not anymore. Mister Yates says they lived a long time ago, before even you or he were born. He says they are ex . . . ex . . . well, 'ex' something. It means they are all dead now, like the ones I was looking for. He said a man offered him eighteen whole dollars for that tusk, but he didn't want to part with it."

Danny stopped suddenly, picking up a piece of stone almost as large as a man's fist. It had been chipped along one edge and was quite sharp.

"See this? I'll bet an old Indian made this, too."

Christena looked carefully at the stone. "You're right, Danny. I'm sure that was a scraper, something the squaws used to scrape the fat off a buffalo hide. Ephraim Hanks told me about that. Just think, years and years ago, a busy young squaw knelt right here in this exact spot and scraped a robe, getting it soft and ready for her new husband. It was the first buffalo he had killed since they had been married, and so she was doing her best to make it perfect, just so he would be happy. And I'll bet he was real happy, for she was the prettiest and sweetest maiden in the whole tribe. She was also—oh, look, Danny! I found an arrowhead!"

Christena held it up for young Danny's inspection.

"By golly, you sure 'nuff did. Come on, let's see if we can find some more."

Eagerly the boy began to search, his head down, his attention fixed upon the earth at his feet. Christena, almost as excited, followed suit, and for several minutes they cast about the camp, moving in ever-widening circles, looking for the next arrowhead.

Christena never knew what made her suddenly look up, but when she did, her heart almost stopped. There, not a dozen feet away, his eyes boring into hers and a fiendish grin on his face, was the huge Indian she had seen earlier in Mister Yates's post.

"Unngh," the man grunted, "good for little squaw to come to Great Bear. Save him trouble."

"Danny," Christena whispered, trying to calm her terrible fear.

"Yeah, I . . . Gosh, Steenie," he gasped, "look! A real Indian."

"I . . . I know, and he isn't a nice man, either. When I give the word, Danny, run up the hill and then around and down to the wagon, just as hard as you can. We can run uphill faster than him because we're smaller and lighter. You ready?"

The boy, three or four feet away, his eyes wide with fright, nodded slowly.

Christena took one step backward, and with a gruff roar the big Indian leaped forward. Only he staggered because of the old wound in his foot, and that momentarily slowed him down.

"Run," Christena shrieked, and then she and Danny were off like rabbits, running up the steep hill, dodging past brush and rocks, and straining for the top. Behind her, though Christena feared to look back, she could hear the man's big feet scratching the gravel, she could hear his labored breathing, and she knew that he was coming on.

Off to her left, Danny was also scrambling upward, seeking the top of the steep ridge. He darted past a large boulder, and suddenly Christena had an idea.

"Help me!" she called frantically to the boy. Then, scrambling, she got behind the boulder and started pushing. After a few seconds, Danny joined her, and together they pushed, pushed, pushed—

The rock moved, tilted, and finally began to roll, a slow, ponderous roll—then it fell free and started downhill, leaping and bounding, right at the huge Indian.

He heard it and looked up, eyes bulging, and then he gave a great and twisting leap to one side and hit the scrabble rolling. Down he went, the boulder narrowly missing him as it crashed past.

The Indian started to rise, staggered, and fell again.

"Quick," Christena cried, "another one!"

Scrambling after her, the two got behind another boulder and shoved and pushed. Down it went after the other one, leaping and bounding, followed by a torrent of smaller rocks, some of them flying high as they fell—all of them cascading about the fallen Ute.

"Come on," Christena shouted without looking to see what damage they might have inflicted, "let's run!" And they did, scrambling up the hill, sprinting along the top and sliding and tumbling down the far end. Sprinting, though out of breath, they ran across the flat to their wagon—and there they were greeted by a surprised Ben Crost, who had just ridden up.

"Pa," Danny shouted, "Pa, help! Steenie and me was attacked by an Indian, and he's still a'coming."

"Sounds like a fun game," Ben Crost replied, never taking his eyes off a breathless and absolutely-surprised-to-see-him Christena Bergman.

"Feeling better?" he asked. And then, before she could

answer, he turned his horse away to stake out the recovered cow.

"Good," he then said over his shoulder, responding to her silence. "That means we can pull out with first light. Be ready."

Christena stared, the new horror compounding with interest the one she had just escaped—and with a sigh and a sudden gushing of tears, she slumped back to the tongue of the wagon.

What would she do? Mister Yates was gone. Jons was not there, and it didn't look like he would make it before morning. Could she stall longer? Or would it be better if she just allowed herself to be taken farther eastward, hoping against hope that Jons would travel faster than the wagon and ultimately catch up with her?

Christena didn't know the answers, but she was pondering the issue so deeply that she didn't see Ben Crost, standing by the tethered cow, staring at her with haunted eyes. Nor did she see, back on the slope of the high hill, the smaller Indian called Knife. He was bending quite joyfully over the unconscious form of his huge, former, and hated companion, and he had some rope and his razor-sharp blade in his hand.

To say that he had expected the huge Bear That Walks with Wounded Foot to be so summarily delivered to him would have been an untruth. But to say that he was not prepared to act immediately upon Limpy's unconscious condition would have also been false.

"Unngh," Knife grunted in great satisfaction. "It is a fitting end to my *no-ni-shee*, to my dream." And then, haughtily, he looked off in the direction of Ben Crost's camp, where his other dream slumped on the wagon tongue.

"Get ready, little white squaw," he breathed, "for I will very soon finish what must be done here. Then I come with the darkness and the two big horses from behind the post, to take you to my *put-te-ent*, to my home. Truly you will make a fitting wife for the great Knife. *Poo-suds-a-way-ah?* Do you understand?"

Chapter 18

"Son," Gideon said from where we sat our horses on the rise above the small trading post, "It looks mighty quiet down there."

"Do you think something's wrong?" I asked quickly.

"I reckon. You see the wagon out there on the flat?"

"I see it."

And I did. Not only the wagon, but every detail about it, including the fire-blackened bows and the breeze-flapping remnants of burnt wagon cover. I also saw, in the late afternoon light, that it looked hopelessly abandoned—and I knew in my heart that I had arrived too late.

"Go easy," Gideon called as I spurred my Perdy mare down the hill, but I wasn't interested in going easy. I had the worst feeling in the pit of my stomach, and it was all I could do to hold back the tears. I knew that wagon had belonged to Ben Crost, and the fear was rising in me that I would find him and his wife and children, as well as my Steenie girl, dead.

With Lazarus running beside us, my mare pounded past the sod trading post, past the eerily silent corrals, and over the side of the low bluff that dropped to where the wagon stood, mute and alone. Sliding to a halt, I was off and running around the wagon, looking for something, *anything*!

Only, I found nothing but ruin and desolation. The wagon, with the name Crost carved into the tailgate, had been burned where it stood, and it had been burned long enough before that the fire was out and the charred wood had turned cold. Some of the Crost family's belongings had been scattered about—but most had not, and had burned and smoldered inside the wagon. Still, there were no bodies, no evidence anywhere as to the fate of the family.

In pain and frustration, I kicked the charred wheel spokes, and then the tears finally came and I sank to my knees while Lazarus came forward and rested his head on my lap.

Why had I taken so long? Why had I thought that by coming with Lot Smith's men I would be better off? I *couldn't* have been inspired! Not seeing what had happened here around me. Oh, if I had only come straightway from the Sandy—

"Jons?"

Gideon's cracked voice caused me to look up, and I saw him sitting on his horse back on the low bluff, a little to the right of where I had jumped Perdy over.

"Boy, you'll want to come take a look."

I knew that Gideon had found the bodies, and with heavy heart I pulled myself to my feet and stumbled across the flat and up the bluff. But when I got there, I found I had been wrong, and for the first time I began to feel a little hope.

The single fresh grave was marked with a simple board, and on it was only one name, that of Ben Crost.

"That your man?"

"He was Steenie's uncle," I replied woodenly.

"Then we may be in luck, Son. White folks buried him, which means they didn't all die."

"Yeah, but Ben surely did. I . . . I . . . "

But I couldn't say any more. All I could do was stand there, with silent tears in my eyes, and think of Ben Crost. I had come mighty close to hating him, which Ma had warned me against but which I hadn't been able to stop. I had wanted to beat him, to pulverize him, to make him sob out his apologies to me and to my Steenie. I had even thought of killing him, or at least I had wondered if I could. But now he was dead, gone, and all I wanted to do was cry. It was like a big, empty place had opened inside me, and it hurt, it hurt!

"You all right, son?"

"I . . . I don't know," I sniffed. "I thought I hated him, Gideon. But now I'm sitting here feeling so bad for him that I'm crying. I don't hardly understand . . . "

"It's who you are, Son."

"Who . . . I am?"

"That's right. You're the blood of Israel, boy. You know, a descendant of Abraham, Isaac, and Jacob, which Jacob's name was changed by the Lord to Israel. You're descended straight from them. And Jons, the Lord gave Israel the responsibility to love and bless mankind, and that 'love and bless' sort of blood flows in your veins. Being righteous, like you're trying to be, it'd be wrong to feel anything but sorrow for the man."

"But . . . but he took Steenie, and he had evil designs toward her."

Gideon grunted. "Maybe, but that don't make no difference in how you should feel toward him, especially once you get past the anger. Fact is, the more wicked he might have been, the more you had ought to sorrow for him. Unless the man's repented recently, which doesn't seem likely, then the poor misbegotten fool died in his sins. And that's tragic, Jons, terrible tragic! The whole world ought to sorrow after the death of a man like this."

Well, I could see what Gideon was saying, and of a sudden I began to understand a lot of other things. Like why the Lord was always sending out missionaries. Or why Gideon and Eph Hanks had turned so strongly against the shedding of blood. Or why Pa was always helping folks out, paying special attention to the ones who likely didn't deserve it. Or why Ma was always praying and exercising the bulk of her faith for her enemies. It was their heritage not to hate, but to love and lift and improve the lot of other people. I'd got that from them, being their son and a member of the Lord's earthly kingdom as well, and that was why I'd never been able to imagine, even wildly, the actual killing of Ben Crost.

"He . . . probably had lots of good points," I said quietly.

"Most of us do. It's nice to know that the Good Lord takes all them points into account, ain't it."

"It surely is. Poor fellow. Maybe if I'd got to know him better, I would have liked him. I surely did like his wife."

"Speaking of which," Gideon said, reining around, "where're the rest of the folks that had ought to be here?"

Helplessly I looked up. "Only . . . only the Lord would know that, Gideon."

Gideon looked hard at me. "Yeah, I reckon He would. The trick will be getting Him to tell us. Too bad friend Hanks is not nearby. He seemed to have a pretty good conduit into Heaven."

The old man was interrupted by Lazarus's growling, and we turned to see the dog on the uphill side of the post, facing a heavy clump of brush. With hurried step I ran up the slope and, pushing past the brush, came upon a sight such as I had never imagined, even in my worst nightmares. I was still staring, horrified, when Gideon pushed his little mustang through the brush and stopped beside me.

The man on the ground had been an Indian, of that there was no doubt. But when I say ' had been,' I mean that literally—for his body had been systematically destroyed until it was almost beyond comprehension. He had been a large man, large and very muscular. But someone had somehow overpowered him—and then had tied him, spread-eagled, between four deeply driven stakes, positioning him so that his lower back arched over a red ant hill.

"Whoever did that was good with a knife," Gideon said.

I nodded, but I didn't speak for fear of losing all I had eaten. Yet still I stared, and as I did I found myself wondering at the cruelty that had driven someone to do such as this to another. For there was not a place on the man's entire body that had not seen the slow and patient work of the murderer.

Of course, the Indian was dead, but he had not been dead while the cutting had been going on—and the expression of horror on what was left of his face mirrored that of my own.

"Friend Gideon," I whispered as I rubbed Lazarus's head

to calm him down, "what . . . what do you think happened here?"

The old man shook his head. "I haven't the least possible notion, except that this occurred no later than yesterday. Remember that, Son. Lot Smith and his boys not excepted, we couldn't have got here in time to do a thing about it.

"As for the rest, that wagon looks Indian burned, and this here is sure enough an Indian. But he's been kilt by other Indians, or by folks who want to make it look that way. Either direction doesn't make much sense to me. From the looks of the flat down yonder, Crost wasn't robbed of much. Indians are like that. They're also partial to taking captives of women and children and making them over into their own people. But if that's the case, who in tunket buried Crost, and where is the trader who runs this place? And last but not least, why did this poor soul get used up in such a sorry way?"

Well, old Gideon was only thinking out loud, not asking questions, so I remained silent. But I had no answers either, only that Ben Crost was dead and that Steenie was gone.

Again.

Slowly I turned away from the dead man, my mind whirling and my heart aching with sorrow and fear. Would I ever find Steenie now? Which way could she possibly have gone—or with whom?

Somehow this all seemed my fault, for if I had only been there a little earlier . . . But no, Gideon had said that the man had been dead for at least a day and maybe more. That being the case, I *couldn't* have helped! But if that was so, then why was I feeling so awfully guilty?

With head down, I made my way past the trading post, Lazarus and Perdy following closely behind. But I paid no attention to them, for my head was spinning and hurting so awfully that I couldn't even think. Finally, out of pure pain and anguish, I dropped to my knees and began at last to sob.

Later, when I was pretty well spent, I realized that I was praying. It hadn't been intentional, I don't think. Rather, I was praying because there was no one else I could turn to. Oh,

Gideon was there, but he didn't have any more answers than I did. But God had the answers, I knew that, and from what Ephraim Hanks had told me, if I wearied the Lord long enough, He would grant me what I asked. So now as I prayed, I realized that I was asking only one thing, and I was asking it over and over again. *Which way had my beloved Steenie gone?*

I prayed and prayed but still felt nothing. The shadow of evening started up from the bluff above the Green, and the warmth of the sun was suddenly gone. But still I stayed on my knees, pleading, praying . . .

"Jons, we had best get along."

Looking up, I stared at the old man.

"To where, Gideon? The foxes have holes, and the birds of the air have nests, but I don't hardly know where to go anymore – not now that Steenie has been taken from me again. Oh, lawsy, I just wish that – "

"Son, a wishbone ain't no substitute for a backbone."

"What?"

"You want that little gal, prove it! Stop feeling sorry for yourself. Get up off the ground and get after her."

"But I don't know which way she went."

Suddenly an idea hit me, and, lunging to my feet, I ran to the empty horse corral behind the post. On my knees again I examined the dirt near the gate.

Nothing!

No sign of the splayed hoofprint of Ben Crost's horse.

Jumping up, I sprinted down off the bluff and onto the flat below, and in just a moment or so I saw that the horse hadn't been in that corral, either. Running then to the burnt wagon, I soon found where the horse had been staked. Ranging out, I began walking slowly in a big circle, and in less than five minutes I had found the track heading south along the river, moving at a high lope.

"Gideon," I called, "does hurried trail of splayed hoof mean pursued or pursuer?"

"In this here instance," the old man said as he drew up his

Kettle horse and studied the trail I had found, "it means pursuer. See how the splayed print is over the other?"

"Then friend," I grinned thinly, "the Lord has given us the direction that somebody took my Steenie. I would think—"

But I never got to finish what it was I had been about to say, for Lazarus gave a warning growl, and Gideon and I turned to find ourselves facing the aimed rifles of three bearded men.

Chapter 19

"Which one of you is Yates?"

The men were obviously Mormons, so I did my best to smile.

"Neither of us, Sir."

"Then whatcha doing here?"

I looked closely at the man, wondering what was troubling him. I had been questioned by other Mormons, but never before had I felt such anger or bitterness from the questioner.

"Friend," Gideon said from behind me and off to my left a little, "the boy said neither of us was Yates. We ain't, and that concludes any right you might have had to hound us with questions. Keep pressing, and it'll be the last pressing you'll do."

The three looked at Gideon, saw Henrietta's solitary dark and unblinking eye, considered for a moment or two what they were looking into, and backed off. A little.

"Very well," the man said softly as he lowered his rifle a few inches, "*please* tell us who you are and why you are here at Yates's post."

"Be glad to," I answered. "The past few days we've been back and forth across the plains with Lot Smith and Ephraim Hanks, kinking the government's works—but today we left them and came here, seeking the one I love. Trouble is, the Indians got here first, and now we're trying to work out their trail."

The men consulted briefly, and then the lead fellow began

quizzing us again. "You say you know Lot Smith and Ephraim Hanks? Describe them for us."

Gideon shook his head. "Lawsy, Jons, there's no more pleasure in some folks's company than in a wet dog's. Makes me ashamed to be in the same church as these heathen idjuts."

I nodded, described Eph and Lot, and threw in Al Bagley's description to boot, but even that wasn't enough. I could feel these men's suspicion almost as though it were a blanket that had been thrown over me.

"Well, anybody could've met those fellers," the one man said. "But if you ain't Yates, do you know where he is?"

"We've never seen him in our lives," Gideon replied. "Now for the last time, who are ye?"

"Mormons," the man replied. "My name's Bill Finkman, and these are a couple of the boys assigned to fight this war with me. We have word that Yates has turned traitor on us, taking up with the Indians and selling gunpowder to the army. All along he's told us he would do otherwise, but now Mrs. Crost tells us—"

"Mrs. Crost?" I asked quickly, interrupting him. "You fellers have seen her?"

The man nodded. "We found her and the little ones hiding down river a piece and took her captive. Her husband had been killed by the Indians ol' Yates had taken up with, probably the same ones you mentioned, so we came up here and buried him. Since this morning, the boys and I have been waiting for Yates, for the man has turned traitor and must be dealt with."

"We heard that Yates was a fine man," Gideon declared then.

"Not hardly, not when he tampers with the Indians to turn them against our people, and when he helps arm the troops to come against us. Oh, I know folks such as Dan Jones and Eph Hanks swear by him, calling him liberal in his views and kind-hearted and other such rot. But the boys and I have the goods on him, and he won't be getting away."

I shuddered at Finkman's vehemence. More than anything else I wanted to get away from these men, as far away as I could. Something was wrong with them, something that didn't feel right. But I couldn't leave, not until I had learned from Ben's wife what had happened to Steenie.

"Do you know where Maria Crost is now?" I asked.

"She's at camp with a couple more of my men."

"Will you take us to her?"

The man grinned. "No problem with that, is there, boys? I don't hardly—"

"Say, what goes on here?"

Spinning, we all looked as a burly man started his horse down the bluff behind us, a string of mules following him. Unconcerned, he reached the level and rode forward—and if he noticed that the rifles of Finkman and the others had shifted and were pointed at him, he gave no note of it.

"Howdy, boys," he said as he drew rein, "you here for supplies?"

"You Yates?"

"As ever was."

Finkman grinned. "Then you're under arrest for a dirty, low-down traitor."

"Now wait just a confounded minute—"

"Take his guns, boys."

Without a word the two rode forward and relieved the trader of his rifle. A quick search revealed no hand gun, and so they roped his arms behind him. Then one of the men dismounted and tied Yates's feet under his horse's belly, the other slipped a riata over the horse's neck, and then they backed away.

"Just like that, huh?" the man said bitterly. "No trial or chance for explanation?"

Finkman shook his head. "We're not that hard. You'll have plenty of chance to defend yourself. Now come along—"

"Wait a minute," Yates said, suddenly pleading. "I've got some fine thoroughbred racing stock that needs caring for, out back. And there's a runaway Mormon family that I should tell."

"You have no stock left at all," Finkman avered. "Your Indian brothers took every horse and cow on the place. Likewise, they killed Ben Crost before they left."

"They *what?*"

"You heard me."

"Yeah, I reckon I did. And the girl?" the man asked, sounding anxious.

"Crost's wife's fine, though pretty upset by what those heathen friends of yours did. Traitors turning on traitors. The Lord's using the wicked to use up the wicked, I say. But you'll be seeing Crost's widow soon enough, and you can answer your guilt to her yourself. Now let's ride!"

We started out, and though I wanted with all my heart to talk with Yates, I couldn't do it. Finkman and his boys were still suspicious of Gideon and me, and it felt like we were riding under guard the entire short journey.

"This is awful," I muttered to Gideon as we rode.

"Amen, Son. But when things don't please you, the best medicine is to swallow a little tincture of time. Our chance'll come."

"You actually think this is going to help me find Steenie?" I asked, surprised.

"You were given your pa's blessing, weren't you? And Eph Hanks told you that you would find the gal. Was I you, I'd start believing. That's called having faith, Son."

"Yeah, I suppose it is. But Gideon, these are mean folks we're amongst."

"True enough. Most folks feel just about how they've made up their minds to feel, and these pilgrims have simply concluded to be miserable. That's their problem, not ours. As for being meaner'n hydrophoby skunks, Son, just you remember that hard-boiled eggs tend to be yellow inside."

I snickered through my emotional pain and was told to knock off the chit-chat. In less than two miles more of silent riding, we came upon Finkman's camp. It was located on a small spring in the bluffs along the river, and it was a nice spot, I had to admit.

It was almost dark when we rode up, and the light from their small fire hardly helped. But finally I saw Maria Crost, and seconds later, after I had dismounted, she recognized me.

With a squeal she ran to me and threw her arms about my neck, and that did a lot to help me feel better.

"Jons – oh, Jons . . . "

"Sister Crost," I said, trying not to cry again, "I . . . I'm right sorry about your husband."

"I . . . Oh, Jons, he never had a chance."

"Ma'am," Yates exclaimed from behind me, "what in thunder happened?"

"That's enough out of you," one of the men who had ridden with Finkman ordered, and for the moment Yates grew silent.

"So you know each other," Bill Finkman said to Maria Crost and me as he dismounted and came toward us. "That must mean you're *all* runaway Mormons. Such doings need to be dealt with."

The man's animosity was amazing to me. It was a thing that could be felt, and I hardly knew what to do about it. The thing was, I didn't want to turn my back upon him, no matter what the occasion. I know Gideon felt it, too, for he never stopped glaring at Finkman and the group of men who were with him. And, too, old Henrietta was always on the ready. The whole situation made me wish, for the first time since I had left home, that I carried a gun of my own, no matter what Eph Hanks had told me.

"Sister Crost," I said, "do you know what happened to Steenie?"

"Only that I know who took her, Jons. It was during the night, and something awoke me. I don't know what it was, but I lay in my blankets for some time before I became aware that the wagon under which we slept was on fire and that I was seeing movement out in the dark. I crawled from under the wagon, and there was just enough light from the growing fire for me to see Christena being pushed onto the back of one of Yates's big Thoroughbred horses. She . . . she looked dead . . . "

"No," I cried, "she can't be . . . "

"Son," Gideon said softly, "remember the prophecies and blessings. Besides, it don't make no sense for some fool to haul off a dead body. More'n likely the little gal was only unconscious."

Bleakly, I nodded. "What else?" I asked the Widow Crost.

"I . . . I suppose I gasped with fear and surprise. That was when the Indian, for so he proved to be, stopped tying her and leaped upon the other Thoroughbred, and in a second the two were gone. It was only after I could no longer see them that I started to scream."

"Which Indian, Ma'am?" Yates asked, ignoring the threat of the man who guarded him.

"Yates, so help me—"

"I'll help you!" the bound trader thundered, glowering at the surprised guard. "I'll help your black soul on its way to hades if you don't back down.

"Now Mrs. Crost," he said gently, turning back to her, "you go ahead and answer me. Which Indian was it took the girl?"

"The . . . the little one. I never saw the other one at all, except for just a minute, up by the post. But . . . but I shouldn't have . . . have screamed! Oh, if only I hadn't carried on so when I saw Christena taken."

"Why the dickens not?" I asked, not understanding. "Surely the voice of warning had to be raised."

Maria Crost wiped at her eyes. "P . . . perhaps. But the cry did not bring Christena back. Instead it hastened . . . oh, why did I cry out as I did?"

Maria Crost dissolved into deep, wracking sobs, and it was only gradually that I learned from her how Ben had leaped to his feet at her screams and had pulled the groggy children from under the burning wagon. Then he had grabbed up the rope of his splayed-hoofed horse to give chase after Christena. He had only just gotten it saddled and climbed aboard when out of the darkness came running the dirty, buckskinned white man who had ridden in with the two Indians.

In disbelief that had turned quickly to rage, the man listened to Maria Crost's terrified account of Steenie's abduction. And then, with no more thought than if he had been shutting a door, the man had lifted his gun and had shot Ben Crost from the saddle, killing him instantly.

Stepping to the frightened horse, the man had yanked the reins to settle it down, jerked Ben's boot from the stirrup where it had caught, and then had vaulted into the saddle.

"Limpy!" he had shouted loudly, yelling into the darkness in the direction of the post. "Limpy, you listening to me?"

There was no answer, and so with a string of curses and Ute words that she didn't know the meaning of, the man had spurred Ben Crost's horse viciously and had ridden the squealing animal into the darkness, following after the little Indian and Steenie.

"That was José Vasquez," Yates said quietly. "He's a mean one, all right. I'm sorry it had to be your husband that got in his way. And it was the crazy Ute called Knife that took the girl."

For a moment Yates stared ahead, deep in thought. "So old Knife split the blankets with them, did he? He must have taken a shine to the girl when she walked into the post yesterday. That's good, in a way, because he won't hurt her, at least deadly hurt. He just wants her for his squaw."

"His *what?*" I asked, horrified.

"Squaw. But like I say, that ain't the real problem. The fact that Vasquez went after him tells me something else. It tells me ol' José had his eye on the girl, too, though probably not as his squaw. Vasquez is a slave trader, Son, and that little filly is likely to be worth several hundred American dollars, even from the Spanish. From the Utes she might bring a good deal more. And that, as I see it, is the real problem."

Well, poor Maria Crost was fit to be tied, and I was even worse off than that. Steenie, my Christena Bergman, being sold into slavery? I could hardly comprehend the thought. And worse, I had no idea what to do about it.

"Two things," Yates went on, thinking out loud. "If the girl and Knife are on my two racers, which looks likely, there's little hope that Vasquez will catch them. Lightning is a Thoroughbred and Hambletonian cross, and Dancer is a Morgan and Standard cross. Both of them are bred for distance racing, and they're both good at it. So far as I know, there's nothing alive that will beat my racers."

Gideon, seated beside me, snorted in disgust. I didn't know what had upset him, of course, but I didn't think that then was the time to find out.

"You said that *two* things bothered you?" I asked.

"Aye, that I did. The second is that big Indian Vasquez called Limpy. He could be anywhere, and wherever he is, the man is trouble."

"Not anymore he ain't," Gideon squeaked softly. "Leastwise, I reckon it's him that won't be bothering folks no more. In the brush upslope from your post, staked over an antbed and cut up something fierce, lies the mortal remains of a tolerable big Indian. His moccasins were there, tossed into the brush, and they had a peculiar sort of bell design beaded onto them. I've never seen the like."

Yates looked startled. "That's Limpy, all right. And you say he's dead?"

"For at least all of today. The magpies have been at him, and maybe the crows, too. But all that was after his killer had got through cutting. So yes, friend, he was real dead."

"If he was cut up," Yates said then, thinking further, "that has to have been Knife's work. Torturing with a blade is what he likes to do. There must have been bad blood between them for a long time for this to happen, but with an Indian it's hard to tell."

"Do you know the direction the Indian might have gone?" I asked then.

Yates considered. "Maybe. I know they rode south. Last I heard, Vasquez had a camp way south of here, down on the confluence of the Dolores and Grand Rivers, near the Santa Fe Trail. So, far as it is, maybe he's going there. Fact is, now that I think on it, Knife used to be a southern Ute, from down off thataway. The story is that his people cast him out years ago for killing his mother, but you never know. Taking up a squaw like he's done, he might be figuring on going back."

"He won't make it," I said, "not if I can help it. I'll get Steenie back if it's the last thing I ever do."

"Hold on, Son," Yates said, sudden alarm in his voice. "There's three, four hundred miles betwixt here and that camp, hard miles of mountains and desert, most of it filled with angry Indians and meaner whites. Besides, Knife is on my racer. You'll never catch him, Boy, but you'll likely die trying."

"You'll die trying to leave here, too," Bill Finkman said quietly. "You'll all be going back to the Valley as my prisoners. The Saints don't hold with spies running out here and spilling their guts to the government ninnies about what they saw in the Valley."

"Friend," I said, anger making my voice tremble, "you're sure enough mistaken. We aren't spies, unless it was Ben Crost, who has passed beyond the veil and is of no further threat to anybody. But for us, there is no guilt.

"Now Gideon and I will be going, and you'll be giving me your word that Sister Crost and her children, as well as Mister Yates, will be escorted to the Valley in safety."

"Not hardly, I won't," Finkman snarled, lifting his rifle as he spoke until it was pointed roughly at me. "I said you were my prisoner. You ain't a'going–"

But Bill Finkman's orders were cut short in a terrified scream as a scraggly dog came hurtling out of the darkness to clamp vice-like teeth upon his arm. The rifle exploded harmlessly, and both dog and man slammed back to tussle with each other on the ground. Finkman continued to scream, and Lazarus continued his silent attack, intending, no doubt, to use the man up. But finally I called him off, and with raised hackles and stiff walk the dog backed away.

"You can educate a fool," Gideon said with disgust as he looked at the injured man who was scrunched on the ground. "You can educate him, all right, but you sure can't make him think."

"Brother Finkman," I said as I climbed aboard my Perdy mare and backed her toward where Gideon sat with rifle ready, "swear that the Crost family and Mister Yates will get to the Valley safely."

"I won't swear nothing," the man growled as he nursed his dog-bit arm. "I told you they were traitors and warmongers. Now get them, boys!"

"Anybody raises a rifle will never raise another one."

The voice from the darkness was soft, but it had an electrifying effect upon the men who stood around the fire. As one they lowered weapons and backed up a step or two, and then we all stared in surprise as Lot Smith and several of his men stopped into the light.

"Lawsy," Gideon breathed beside me. "I never thought I'd be glad to see that feller again."

"You boys all right?" Lot asked.

"We are, but . . ."

Lot Smith grinned through his long beard. "We heard it all. I told you we might be of some use to you, and by the time some of the boys get Sister Crost and her children safely back to the Valley, my word should have been pretty well fulfilled. Maybe I'll become as much a prophet as ol' Eph Hanks."

"Smith," Bill Finkman growled, "these people are my prisoners, and I won't have you interfering."

"I am *Major* Smith to you, Finkman," Lot Smith said sternly, cutting the man off, "and I direct you to remember that.

"As regards your charges, you may have a case against Mister Yates, and a fair trail down in the Valley will determine that. Therefore I order you to escort him there immediately. As for the Crost family, I shall take charge of them personally.

"Now, Brother Soderberg and Captain Monson," he said as he turned his attention to us, "you said something, I believe, about taking a ride to the south."

"Yes, Sir, we did."

"You'll be needing fresh horses, I suppose? And weapons?"

"Fresh horses," Gideon grunted, "wouldn't make it. Kettlebelly here will do just fine for me, thank you."

"Do you think I should do the same?" I asked Gideon quietly. "Keep my Perdy mare?"

"Up to you, Son, but my feeling is that one ought to dance with them that brought him."

Well, I looked down at the dingy gray mare who stood motionless beneath me, and I wondered. We had covered several hundred miles in less than a week, she and I—and I knew she had done her best for me. Now I looked again at her stringy mane, her big head and short neck that were joined like the two parts of a hammer, and at her flanks that were hollowed with use and hunger. Perdy was smallish and stunted, and there wasn't much about her that would catch the eye at a first glance. But if a man looked again, which I had had occasion to do quite often in the past five days, he might note the depth of chest and the strength of bone beneath the dirty hide. Or he might notice the trim neatness of legs dropping down to rock-hard hoofs that had no need of being shod. Scrubby, yes, but scrubby proud, as shown by the swelling of that short neck holding that almost-too-big head. Perdy, in spite of the name I had given her, was not pretty, nothing splendid or noble looking. But she was filled with power and endurance in her compact solidity, and the look of eagles showed occasionally in her eyes. I felt certain she would stay.

Besides, beneath the mare's nose squatted Lazarus, his tongue hanging out, his eyes resting upon her. And I knew that he would never forgive me if I gave over the horse he had personally trained for my use.

"Brother Smith," I said, "good ol' Lazarus seems to have spoken, and the mare it is who will carry me, as Eph Hanks might say, into the camp of the Philistines."

"Is that the southern tribe we'll be visiting?" Gideon asked by way of a joke—and to the ring of Lot Smith's laughter, the boys packed a mule with supplies, and we started south into the darkness.

Chapter 20

For Christena Bergman, regaining consciousness was not much of a blessing. She had never been in such pain, and every jolt of the big horse made her wish that she could once again drop into dark oblivion. She was draped over the saddle like a sack of grain, and her hands were secured to her feet under the horse's belly. A coiled bullwhip tied to the pigin strings on the saddle kept knocking her in the head—which was throbbing anyway—and she knew from the taste in her mouth that she had been sick. Worst of all, though, was the fact that she couldn't get enough air. Each jolt of the horse smashed into her abdomen, and gasp and struggle as she would, she could not adequately fill her lungs.

"Help," she cried into the darkness that was just turning gray with morning, "help me please . . . "

Nothing happened—so she drew air, held it, drew in more, and finally let it all loose in a scream of which she felt justifiably proud. There, she thought, that ought to bring that evil and unsympathetic Vasquez back to help her. And Christena knew that the man who had taken her, who had somehow knocked her out and tied her to this horse and abducted her, was the man Mister Yates had called Vasquez.

Again she held her breath and screamed, again and again, until finally she felt the horse dragged to a quivering stop.

Seconds later rough hands reached under and freed the

ropes from her ankles, and then unceremoniously she was pulled forward off the saddle and dumped onto the ground.

"Now you listen here—" Christena started to complain, when a moccasined foot kicked her in the ribs, sending her reeling. Gasping with the new pain, she struggled to her knees and looked at the dim form of the man who had kicked her. She had barely come to the realization that it was not the filthy Vasquez, when his hand slapped her in the mouth, sending her stumbling once again to the earth.

"Squaw no talk," the man stated with guttural emphasis. "Squaw listen to *towats*, to man, and obey. More *at-am-bar*, more talk, and this!"

He slapped her again, hard—and with a sob Christena rolled over on the ground, the salty taste of blood filling her mouth.

Instantly, the Indian grabbed hold of her hair and pulled her to her feet. Then, roughly, he squeezed her arm.

"Good! *Tshar nan-zitch*, white girl, learn fast. You make okay squaw for Knife, maybeso you do what I say. *O-net-shpee*, conceive many sons. But for now you ride. Get back on *kuvah-u*, horse."

Sobbing, wide-eyed, and frightened, Christena struggled to mount the huge horse. She was not fast enough to satisfy the Indian, however, for he slapped her again. He then boosted her into the saddle and quickly tied her feet under the horse's belly—causing terrible cramps in her legs.

Laughing at her cry of pain, the Indian leaped aboard his own horse and kicked it viciously, and the two were once again flying up the gradually lightening trail.

For a time Christena tried to shut out all thought, to force her mind into oblivion. But gradually an awareness of the strength of the beautiful horse she was riding stole upon her. She had truly never been upon such an animal—and after a time she found herself no longer reveling in self-pity but marveling instead at the flow of muscle and sinew beneath her. The horse, a sorrel, was incredibly pretty, and as morning rays crept across the peaks to the east, its beauty became more and more evident.

Christena had seen the horse before, back at the post. She had even admired and petted both it and the one the Indian was riding. So she knew that both animals had been stolen. Yet with strength and courage, the stolen animals galloped along the trail. The girl marveled at that and gradually began to take from the horses a little peace of her own.

The Indian was abusing his mount terribly—kicking it, flaying it with a quirt, and not giving it adequate rest. Christena's own mount, the sorrel, was heavily lathered, and she knew it would be only a matter of time before the horses could run no farther. For her that would be good, and so she pushed thoughts of the horse's pain from her mind and concentrated instead on the animal's courage and her own hoped-for rescue.

The country they rode through was higher, now, and dotted with juniper—more commonly called cedars. They followed a deep canyon, riding high on the rim, and she could see that a dim trail led ahead of them toward the snow-covered peaks. Also ahead were slopes covered with thick stands of timber—pine and fir—and she realized that the Indian was taking her high into the mountains she had heard called the Uintahs.

For a moment she felt panic, wondering how Jons would ever find her there. But then the confidence of the stolen horses struck her again, and instantly she began to feel better. If animals could go forward courageously, then so could she.

"Heavenly Father," she pleaded in a quiet whisper, "I know that thou knowest where I am. Wilt thou please tell Jons and give him the power to find me? And Father, please give me the strength to do what I must do until Jons comes for me . . . "

The sun was an hour high when the Indian pulled off the trail and into a clump of trees. There was a seep there, enough water for the horses and themselves. And so without a word the man dismounted, untied Christena's feet, and ordered her to dismount and build a fire.

Slowly she complied, wondering as she slid down what she would use to accomplish her task. Then, almost in answer to her silent question, the Indian threw a bag onto the ground before her – and within it she found some coffee and some other foodstuffs.

"You fix food," the Indian declared. "Me eat. Then we *ah-be-quy*, then we lie down – together. Later we *ep-weh*, we sleep."

With numbness and horror, Christena worked at building a fire and then fixing a meal from the bare necessities she found within the sack. She wanted to run but could think of nowhere to go. She thought of stealing a horse, but she knew that, after having removed the saddles, the Indian had staked the animals firmly. There would no be time.

Over and over she prayed, pleading that Jons would come quickly and save her. But he did not come, nor did anyone else. She was alone on the mountain with the scrawny Indian who called himself Knife, and she knew that if anything was to be done about her situation, she was going to have to do it herself.

But she could think of nothing.

As the coffee boiled and as the food cooked, Christena sought desperately for escape – and finally she found a little relief, of sorts, in her imagination. In that mental citadel she saw herself in a snug cabin, somewhere back in the Valley with the Saints, happily married to the handsome Jons Soderberg.

Of course he was away somewhere, taking care of a Church calling – so she was lonely for his presence. But the children, four of them, were in bed, and now she was standing outside, the wind in her hair, the glittering stars giving her comfort. Off in the hills a coyote cried, and she smiled at the sound, liking it. Behind her, the windows of the cabin reflected the glow from the fire, and from down in the corral there was a faint stirring among the horses.

Goodness, she would be glad when Jons returned. She needed love, she needed tenderness, and Jons had given her both. Now he was gone, but soon he would be back, and the joyousness of their lives would continue.

Stepping back inside the cabin and closing the door, she looked around the shadowed room, lit only by the lantern and the faint flickering of the fire.

A loft above was for the children, and down below for her

and Jons there was a double bed, a table, some benches, a chair—pots and pans shining upon the wall or near the fireplace, the hard-packed earthen floor—would she ever have a plank floor, she wondered? There was an aroma of cooking food in the air that lingered from their supper, almost as if it was burning—

Slap!

Reeling from the unexpected blow, Christena looked up in shock. The Indian was standing before her, his face dark with anger. At his feet rested the pan of cooking gruel—on its side in the grass where he had kicked it—smoking with a deep scorching. Raising his hand, the man slapped her again, sending her rolling and tasting more blood, and then he strode over to stand above her.

"*Katz-te-suah nan-zitch!* Foolish girl! *Pe-nun-ko*, in the future you will pay attention to what you do, or I shall beat you until you have no face left. Now *wo-tun*, kneel down before your man!"

Stifling her sobs, Christena dragged herself to her knees, and when the kick came she rolled with it and hardly felt the blow. Nevertheless, it stung, and she wanted to cry out with the waves of pain she was experiencing. But she didn't cry out—and when she realized that, she suddenly took perverse pride in her silence. She wouldn't cry out—she wouldn't give the mad Indian the satisfaction! She would be like the two thoroughbred horses—silent, strong, enduring, waiting for Jons to arrive—

She had heard that Indians often beat their wives, but she could not believe that such brutality or cruelty actually existed. Only now the ringing in her head, the salty taste in her mouth, as well as the pain in her side, gave terrifying evidence of what she had heard.

"Father in Heaven," she again pleaded as she lay on the dry grass next to the two saddles, "help me . . ."

"Come," the man growled, still standing by the fire, "spread the blankets. There will be time enough to *tick*, to eat, later."

Staring blankly at him, Christena closed her eyes, willing herself to be somewhere else. Nothing changed, however—and so, steeling her mind against whatever might be coming, she rolled to her knees to stand up.

And saw before her, still tied to the stolen saddle, Mister Yates's well-used bullwhip.

Having mastered the use of the whip while crossing the plains the year before, Christena stared at the whip, realizing that the Lord was answering her prayers—and suddenly she knew what she was going to do.

"Squaw hurry!" the man growled from behind her—and with a low cry, Christena determined to do just that. Quickly, before she could convince herself that the idea was a bad one, she moved. In an instant the whip was in her hand, and in another she was on her feet, facing the man called Knife.

The whip had a foot-long swivel stock and a ten-foot braided lash, and as the Ute watched with surprised fascination, it became instantly obvious that the young woman he had selected to be his squaw knew how to use the weapon in her hand.

She struck swiftly, then, and surely. The whip cracked like the report of a pistol, and the buckskin popper on the end of the lash lifted flesh from Knife's neck. With a cry of pain and startled anger, he stepped back, and the second blow of the lash took him over the shoulders, the third on his leg.

With a growl, the Indian lunged toward her, but Christena stepped quickly aside and struck again. Turning from his misdirected lunge, the man ran away from her in a stumbling run, the popper ripping his buckskin shirt with one last blow.

At that, Knife stumbled and fell. In the same instant, Christena gathered the whip and was fleeing to where her horse was tethered. Anxiously, desperately, she tugged at the rope, finally pulling it loose from the stake. Spinning, she ran for the horse. Then, dropping the whip and grasping the animal's mane, she struggled to drag herself onto its high back.

Anxiously she pulled herself up, throwing her leg as high as she could throw, pulling, straining—

"Woman!"

With a chill of fear, Christena stopped struggling, and slowly her feet dropped and came back to the earth.

"Woman, hear my words."

Numbly the girl turned and faced the gaunt Indian, who was standing with the rope to her horse grasped in his hand. Blood trickled down his neck, and there was a livid streak across his shoulder and down his back. Yet he stood calmly, and she could hear no trace of anger or disdain in his voice.

"Woman," Knife said, his head high and his eyes steady, "I see that I have chosen well. You are *te-a-now-er*, an equal, a warrior fit for mothering many strong sons. I too am fit for fathering many strong sons. This is good.

"You have also brought to my thinking that I must not *tur-reb-by*. I must not throw away the path of honor, the true way of my people. I am not white, and I must forget the ways of the man Vasquez, the white ways of evil."

The Ute stood straight, breathing deeply, and his knowledge of English startled Christena. "The two of us will be one," he continued, "but it will be as it has always been, as such a joining always must be. It will be after the manner of purification and feasting in the wickiups of my people. Until then there will be no fear, and there will be no fleeing. I shall tie you, and if escape is attempted, you shall die. If it is not, then we shall go together, and we shall go in peace.

"Woman, the warrior called Knife salutes you."

Stepping forward, Knife picked up the whip Christena had used against him and solemnly tied the lash end of it around her neck. Then, turning away, he led both her and the horse to where the packs had been tossed to the ground. Taking one of the blankets, he walked to the other horse, pulled the rope from the stake, and led the two animals, with Christena stumbling before them, to a place of shade on the far side of the clearing. Tying the two ropes to his arm and cradling the stock of the whip against his chest, he lay down, rolled up in the blanket, and, so far as Christena could tell, went instantly to sleep.

She didn't move but for a long time stood and sobbed quietly, devastated by the fact that she had come so close to escape and yet had failed. Why, oh why?

Moments later, as her tears gradually dried, Christena took

the blanket the Indian had left for her and spread it as far from her sleeping captor as the whip would stretch.

Then, sitting down and watching him, Christena finally marveled. She knew that it was no longer practical to attempt escape, at least not yet. But she knew, just as well, that the Lord had protected her, and that such divine protection would continue until her beloved Jons would come for her.

"Please hurry, my darling," she whispered as she stretched back on the blanket and finally closed her eyes, "please, please hurry . . ."

Chapter 21

A dust devil whirled across the trail before us, slapping a few tiny pebbles against my face. I winced, but I noticed that neither of the horses were troubled, and that old Gideon simply stared ahead. He was a tough old man, tougher maybe than anyone else I had ever known – old, crippled, in constant pain, but never quitting, never saying die. He was truly amazing, and of a sudden I once again felt glad he was riding with me.

We were still ramming southward, right then following a trail that was probably Indian – and the land stretched empty and endless before us. It was the morning of our fifth day since leaving the camp of Bill Finkman, and the pace old Gideon had insisted on setting had burned itself into my brain until I no longer even thought of it. We moved steadily – not fast, not slow – but at a jogging foxtrot that gnawed away at the miles.

"No long-distance race is ever won by speed at the start," Gideon had said that first morning as we had started into the Uintah Mountains. "Too much reserve energy is burned up in the speed. No, what we'll do, Son, is play to their weakness, their hurry. We'll do an easy trot for an hour, then an easier flat-footed walk for the next hour – and then trot again, and so on. We'll be out of blanket at daybreak every morning, then walk-trot-walk until the sun is overhead. We'll stop for water if we can find it, strip the horses, water them and rub them down, let them eat a little while we do the same, and then we'll rest for two or three hours. In the afternoon, we'll follow the same trot-walk-trot, and we won't stop until dusk. Then an hour's feed, rubdown, and rest for us and the horse, and more walk-trot-walk until midnight or thereabouts. Then we'll camp in the best grass we can find, give the horses a full length of rope, and sleep until dawn. Then we'll start it all over again. If we do that, we'll catch up with 'em sure."

"And what about the trail?" I had asked. "How in the dickens will we follow those fleeing heathen in the dark of night?"

"The dog," Gideon said, nodding at Lazarus. "I've been watching, and he's already got the scent of the trail. Betwixt his nose and the print of that splayed-hoofed horse, we'll not lose 'em."

Well, I knew that old Gideon was certain he was right, both about Lazarus and our mustangs. But still I was worried. Maybe that was because Yates had been so positive that we had been playing the fools when we had declined fresh mounts. And maybe, too, it was because Gideon and I had talked so big about our horses. The look on Yates's face, and on some of the other men's faces as well, had said it all.

"What?" their expression had said as we had ridden out, carrying Yates's crude map and leading a long-legged mule lightly loaded with food and what else they had tossed in, "You're keeping those scrubby, misfit pieces of wolf-bait that must already be worn out from five hundred miles of trailing the army of the United States all the way from Echo to the Little Sandy and back? And you expect to catch the big, strong half-bred and thoroughbred horses that have been hand-picked for their speed and distance? Why, two scrawny little half-dead mustangs like those won't even be in the running against those big horses, bred right and fed right, that have almost, as it were, lived their entire lives in preparation for this race."

Oh, I could hear the men saying that, all right. Trouble was, mostly I believed they were right. Mostly, that is, until I looked down and saw Lazarus ranging ahead of us and pausing frequently to look back and give a soft whine to the mare. Invariably she flicked her ears at the dog, and I could almost hear her say,

"Don't worry, friend Lazarus. I'm getting on just fine – and as long as you set the trail, I'll be behind you."

Lazarus believed in our horses, I knew that – and I also knew that if he had been able to bet, he would have given odds, for that coyote dog knew a thing or two of his own. He had tamed and calmed that Perdy mare to a faretheewell in the corral on the Weber, had seen her take to him and to me almost instantly, and had seen her go all the way to the Little Sandy and back, plus all over the landscape in between, without ever turning a hair. Somehow old Lazarus knew that when Perdy appeared to be done, worn out, finished, the little gray southwestern mustang had only just begun to fight.

There was something else, too – the prophecy Ephraim Hanks had made. I believed that, and I believed just as strongly in the blessing my father had given me before I had left home. From those two sources, I knew that as long as I did my best to do what was right, I would be successful in finding and rescuing Steenie Bergman. And that was the rest of what kept me going.

Every time I thought of Ephraim Hanks, I shook my head. How had the man done it, I wondered? How had he ever learned to be so close to the Spirit of the Lord? He had told me one night that spiritual abilities were like any other muscles – the more they were worked, the stronger they became. When I had asked how to work them, his reply had been simple: "Pray regularly and sincerely without just mumbling memorized words, Son. The Lord truly wants us to talk to Him. Then read some from the scriptures every day, just to get in tune with how the Lord speaks. If we aren't familiar with the sound of his words, how will we ever recognize the message we ask him to send us?

"Finally, you need to keep the commandments, every one of them, and feel bad enough to want to repent every time a slip occurs. Jons, most Mormon folks I know are fairly righteous. They are active in the kingdom and follow the Lord and His leaders. But hardly a one of them but doesn't complain that the heavens seem closed to them, except for an occasional dream or flash of inspiration or instance of divine protection.

"The reason for their lack of ability to get answers from the Lord, I believe, is because in spite of their predominant righteousness, those poor souls still grasp tightly to a few of their favorite, howbeit small, sins.

"But Son, they can't do that, not and grow closer to the Spirit. The Lord is a God of law, and He won't look upon sin with the least degree of allowance. Nor can He respond with great power to a person who is too lazy or selfish to become really pure. That's why He told Brother Joseph that all blessings were predicated upon obedience to law. The more laws we obey, the more blessings we obtain – or in other words, the closer to the Spirit we get.

"I'll tell you, Boy, the trick is to reach a point where you never, on purpose, commit a sin. And when you slip and do something wrong accidental-like, you get rid of it and cry unto the Lord to forgive you just as fast as you possibly can. According to Alma and King Benjamin, Saints who really feel this way have experienced what is called 'the mighty change.' They are adopted as sons and daughters of Christ, and they abhor sin because they have come to understand the pain that their own sins caused the Lord. They can't bear to inflict any more of that selfishness-caused pain upon Him. You see, it has finally become clear to such souls that it is they themselves who drove the nails into the great Being who has loved and redeemed them. Do you understand what I am saying?"

"I . . . I believe so," I told him.

"Good. But remember, all this is just the beginning. Shun sin for long enough, and you will become purified. Become purified, Jons, and the Lord will give you knowledge whenever you call upon Him. That is called receiving personal revelation, and it is what Brother Joseph said we should all strive daily to achieve.

"If you continue to progress, you will receive all the higher blessings that will be promised you when you receive your endowment. After that, as Peter says in the New Testament, you will be given the power and knowledge, by the Spirit of God, to open the heavens and commune with the righteous hosts who dwell therein. That is one of the fruits of paying the price to be close to God's Spirit.

"But for you, young man," Eph had said, grinning, "a more important fruit of diligently seeking righteousness would be that you will be given power to take that sweet little Christena to God's holy altar, to be sealed to her for eternity, and then to go forward in righteousness until you can claim her as yours beyond the grave. Unless you love her enough to do that, all this sashaying around the country makes very little sense at all.

"From my own experience, Son," Ephraim Hanks had concluded, "I have found that paying the price to be righteous is a peaceful thing. I don't have much fear about things anymore, and, as the Lord promised, my confidence is waxing strong in His presence. In other words, I have great faith in the impressions He gives me. If you want such faith and confidence, and if you want the eternal rewards of Christena's companionship, why, I'd recommend that you pursue the course I have shown you."

So for days I had been riding, thinking over and over about what Ephraim Hanks had told me. And the more I thought of it, the more sense it made. For some reason, though, it frightened me, thinking of putting every fault aside. I knew myself pretty well and was mortally afraid of backsliding. Yet I wanted to be in tune with the Sprit of God, and so as I rode I was praying almost constantly. And in spite of my self-doubts, I was doing my best to dredge up those favorite sins, make commitments to the Lord concerning them, and finally cast them off my shoulders by giving them up to Christ.

That was embarrassing, asking Jesus to lift burdens from me that I had committed apurpose. But mile by mile I was feeling better about things, and I had no doubt that the Lord would direct me until I had not only found Steenie but had achieved my spiritual goal as well.

"Time to walk 'em," Gideon said as he reined his Kettle down.

I followed suit, and the horses moved slowly forward into the day, walking that flat-footed walk that Gideon said was a resting for the mustangs. But I hated that slow walk, for with each passing minute I seemed to see Steenie and her abductor drawing farther away.

"At this pace, it seems like they're going to get away," I finally said.

"It does seem slow," agreed Gideon.

"Then why the dickens do you think we are going to catch the evil souls?"

"Because they're starting to go slower than we are."

"What?"

"Apparently you ain't noticed the tracks, friend Jons. The two 'breds are walking quite a bit now, and back there apiece I saw where the splayed-hoofed horse had stumbled. And it wasn't from a rock or a hole, neither. You see any sweat streaks on your Perdy mare?"

Silently I shook my head, for there were none. Reaching out, I rubbed my hand along Perdy's neck, and then I felt back along her flanks. No moisture—only an even warmth. My Perdy mare could do what she was doing all day without working up a real sweat.

"She's dry," Gideon affirmed. "But if we were to ride up to the splayed-hoofed horse, or to the 'breds, we'd see plenty of sweat, as well as flecks of foam at their mouths and plenty of energy-wasting head-shaking. By now, you can bet that all three horses are getting mighty jaded. Besides, the two 'breds, at least, have been fed on rich feed and consequently are overweight with hot flesh. Not so with Kettle and your mare. That gives our horses more pure endurance, you can bet on it.

"Another thing. When a man's being chased, or sometimes even when he just thinks he is, he doesn't cogitate right. That's what guilt does, for guilty men run even when no one's behind them. A guilty man rides his horse too hard and has to stop too often to breathe him. Doing that, he takes too much out of his horse too early.

"The way we ride may be slower, but it is also steadier and

goes on for longer hours. Those fellers started a good twenty hours ahead of us—but Son, these tracks in the trail today are fresh, and I'd say we're less than six hours behind them now.

Gideon paused for a long moment and then concluded. "All the same," he muttered, "those horses'll be something to beat. Both 'breds. Never know just what they've got left when the finish line's in sight."

Sometime later, with me still worrying over Gideon's last unencouraging statement, the time clock in his mind had given its silent signal, and he relayed the message along the reins. Kettle-belly had picked up to a mile-eating fox-trot, and without thought I had urged my Perdy mare to the same gait.

We had followed the Green River south until it had drifted off to the east, and then we left the river and made our way over the Uintah Mountains. That was cold country—cold but beautiful—and I marveled at the hidden lakes and vast stands of timber. There was a little snow up high, but nothing fresh, and it served only to highlight the tracks we were following.

Our only high-up camp was at Iron Springs, and it had been a cold one, all right. I had fussed a little about it, and Gideon had scornfully tossed another log onto our fire.

"Shallow rivers and shallow minds freeze first," he had growled, and I had said no more about the cold.

From Iron Springs the trail had led down Hole-in-the-Rock Canyon and out into the vast and barren country to the south. Actually, it wasn't really barren, for the country was much like that in Wyoming—sage-covered valleys, flat tablelands, and innumerable draws and washes. It was also a dry country, but the season was a good one for traveling—and water, at least during the early part of the day, lay in many of the usually empty arroyos. There were also seeps and freshwater streams, and the trader Yates had marked the best of these on his map. But the men we followed had known of these as well, so Gideon and I had only to keep to the trail they had laid out for us, and we had no trouble.

It was nearly noon when my Perdy mare raised her head

higher and quickened her pace. Gideon was behind me, but as usual Lazarus was out ahead, and so Perdy had no fear.

"She smells water," Gideon informed me.

"Good. I'll bet it's been twenty miles or more."

"At least," Gideon agreed. "When folks say this country gets a six-inch rain, I reckon they mean one drop every six inches."

I chuckled over that, and ten minutes later we topped a low hill and saw what had to be the Green River again, a quarter mile ahead. It was a wide expanse of sandbars and shallow water and deeper-cut channels, but it did look inviting.

I rode to the bank and stopped, and Gideon and the mule soon reached my side.

"It seems high," I said.

"Been raining up-country, I reckon. Yates said to watch for quicksand."

"Do you know the look of it?"

Gideon shook his head. "Never seen any. But I reckon the horses have, or maybe their ancestors. Whichever, the fear of it will be bred into them, so we'll let them pick their way. Put the blankets around your neck, and this bag of food. I'll pack the rest of this."

Undoing the blanket from behind the cantle and draping it over my shoulders – along with our bag of grub – I tickled Perdy with my spurs, and she stepped into the shallow water, splashing some and seeming to enjoy it. For a minute she snorted and bucked at Lazarus's antics, but then she sobered to the serious business of feeling forward for footholds in the gravel, mud, and sand of the bottom.

We came to the first of the deeper channels, and Perdy surged into it, swimming strongly and steadily – and then scrambled out on a sandbar beyond, Lazarus directly ahead of her. That partial crossing had not been bad at all, and with greater confidence Perdy launched into the main current, swimming evenly, following Lazarus. I urged her forward, turned and saw that Gideon and the pack mule were directly behind, and then gave my attention to the crossing.

We drifted downstream some, but at last we reached a sandbar on the far side of the river, and Lazarus scrambled up onto it. Perdy started to follow, then snorted with fear and, before I hardly knew what was happening, had reared and plunged back into the water.

Lazarus leaped as well, or tried to. But the sticky substance of the sandbar mired him, and he could gain no footing.

"Lazarus," I shouted, "come here! That's *quicksand!*"

The dog tried, and Perdy fought the current, the entire time watching the struggling coyote-dog.

"Jons," Gideon shouted as he threw the mule's lead rope to me, "take the mule! Head upstream and hit the bank where those other fellers came out. Now git!"

"But Lazarus—"

"I'll get him. Now go on!"

In anguish I urged Perdy forward, but she fought me and tried to go back. I yanked her head with the reins, yelling and trying not to think of my dog. And the next thing I knew, we were on dry ground and Gideon was splashing out behind me, a poor, bedraggled Lazarus on the end of the rope behind him.

Lazarus shook himself, and to my surprise, Perdy did the same, almost unsettling me. But the water flew, and with that she seemed ready to be on her way.

"Good a place as any for a nooning," Gideon said, not commenting at all on his rescue of Lazarus—and he rode to a small clump of cottonwoods and swung down. Following him, I dismounted, and we spread-eagled our saddles on the ground so they would dry. Hanging our saddle blankets over a low tree limb, we unpacked our mule, unrolled the blankets, and dumped our meager gear out into the sun.

"Don't leave your boots off," Gideon warned as I pulled them off my feet and dumped the water from them. "They'll dry stiff and shrunken, and you'll never get them back on again."

So I struggled, hopping about on one foot and then the other, getting my wet boots back on my feet again. Then I sat down with my back against one of the trees and stared at a hunk of dried beef that I knew I needed to eat. Only somehow I just couldn't.

"Brother Gideon," I said, suddenly having a hard time of it, "you saved . . . my dog. I . . . I thank you."

Gideon chewed for a moment longer, than swallowed. "Glad I was there with the rope, Son. Seeing that over yonder makes whatever I done seem worth it."

Following his gaze, I looked toward the bluff we had yet to climb. And only then did I notice the horses and mule where Gideon had staked them to feed.

Kettle-belly and the mule were cropping grass at the end of their picket lines, but Perdy wasn't eating at all. She was standing still, all atremble, her nose down—and Lazarus was squatted before her, his face lifted against hers.

The poor coyote-dog had nearly lost it back there in the quicksand. But, bless his heart, there he was—giving comfort to a frightened little gray mare who could not abide the thought of losing her best friend.

"And it came to pass that she fell to her knees," Gideon said as tears started from my eyes, "giving Him thanks. Son, we'd better do the same."

And then and there, we did.

Chapter 22

In the hush of dusk dropping toward dark, I sat on a flat-topped rock in a low swale, enjoying the small fire and wolfing down Gideon Monson's recent and only cooked specialty, singed beef and refried beans. Off to the side lay Lazarus, apparently asleep, while next to him the skimpy pack of supplies sat squatly in the dimness. Forty feet beyond, Perdy and Gideon's horse cropped grass in companionable competition with the long-legged mule.

"That mule," Gideon said softly, "he's almighty tired."

I grunted, being too busy eating to say much else.

"We've come three hundred, three hundred and fifty miles by now," Gideon declared. "I don't hardly know if that mule will hold up much longer."

"Perhaps there will be no need," I said then. "The pack's got next to nothing in it."

"Yeah, there is that," Gideon agreed. "Boy, we've got to catch up to them pilgrims pretty soon. Not to mention being plumb tuckered out, we're next to flat out of grub."

The darkness deepened, and I thought about what Gideon was saying. He wasn't the sort to holler out when there was no need, so I knew that he was justifiably worried. It followed, then, that I had better be worried myself.

Lazarus lifted his head and thumped his plumed tail as he looked at me, and I grinned. Somehow I still had all my hope, and I couldn't seem to feel the gloom that had apparently settled upon Gideon. Perdy and Kettle were running strong, the tracks in the sandy trail we followed were deeper and fresher than ever, and I just knew that we were getting close. It was only going to be a matter of hours now, another day at the most, and Gideon and I would confront those heathens and I would have my Steenie back again.

"You positive sure you want to go on?" Gideon suddenly asked.

"Excuse me?" I said, not certain I had heard.

Gideon coughed nervously. "I said, you positive certain you want to keep going?"

"Why do you hesitate now?"

"Son, its . . . uh . . . been five full days since we left Lot Smith, and six since the girl was taken. I . . . uh . . . well, Indians do things to purty young girls . . . "

"Not Steenie," I said flatly.

"But you don't know that!" Gideon argued. "I do. I've seen it afore, way too often. I thought we'd catch up with 'em sooner, and there would be a chance. But it's been too long . . . "

"Would you want me to just walk away?"

The old man poked at the fire. "I know it seems harsh, Boy, but the girl's likely dead now, or worse. If she ain't dead, likely she's been used so she won't *want* to be found. Not especially by the young feller she loves more than she loves life itself. The way I'm thinking, Son, time is the best doctor there is—and distant memories of the good things are a whole lot better than fresh realities of the bad, for both of you."

I noticed that one of my fingernails was cracked and needed attention, so I took out the knife Pa had given me and went to work on it, thinking hard and fast. It was true that Steenie had been gone an overly long time, and the things Gideon had said certainly made sense. I didn't want to see Steenie dead.

And worse, I didn't want to see her used and humiliated. And she would be, I knew that, if her abductor had had his way with her.

There were also the animals to consider. As Gideon had pointed out, the mule was about on its last legs. The same was probably true of his horse Kettle-belly and my Perdy, though neither of them was showing as much strain as the mule.

Besides that, I was tired—bone weary—and so sore it took all the power of my will just to mount up each time we stopped. That being the case, I could hardly imagine the pain that poor old Gideon must have been enduring. For all I knew, the chase was killing him, putting him to death just as certain sure as the Indian called Knife, or his companion Vasquez, would do it. Maybe with his subtle questions he was even trying to tell me that. But whether he was or not, if Gideon died, I would always carry the burden of it on my soul.

Yet he wouldn't stop, not unless I stopped beside him, and I could hardly carry the load of that knowledge, either.

Staring down at my nail, I tried to balance my love for old Gideon against my love for Steenie. She had faith in me that I would come, I knew that, and the old man had faith in me that I would have the sense to know when to give it up.

Truthfully, I did not have the least possible notion of what I should do. The horses were tired, the mule was about to give out, Gideon was caving in of exhaustion and old age, we were about out of supplies, and I was nearly dead myself . . .

"Father in Heaven," I pleaded silently, "what wilt thou have thy servant do?"

Perdy snorted softly, and as I looked up I saw Lazarus trotting over to her. They stood together then, a smallish horse and a scraggly, tawny brown coyote-dog—and in the almost darkness I suddenly realized something. Those two creatures had never asked odds of anything life had ever thrown at them. I had talked big, but ol' Lazarus and my Perdy mare were ready to give it the last ounce of stubborn endurance, just to back up my talk. This was Lazarus's and Perdy's race, too, and it was just as important to them that we get to Steenie, as it was to me.

"Friend Gideon," I said softly, "I can't hardly quit now, not with what you, Kettle, Perdy, and ol' Lazarus have done for me. No sir, with the help of the Lord, I'm convinced that Steenie will be delivered, unharmed, into our hands."

Slowly Gideon shook his head. "Son, as the Bible says, we are troubled on every side, yet not distressed; we are perplexed, but not in despair. Second Corinthians four. And why ain't we? Mostly, Jons, because of you. They say that no man in the wrong can stand up against a feller who's in the right and keeps coming. Those fellers in front of us had best be getting worried, for they've no idea the kind of man behind 'em. I'm only just starting to understand you myownself. If you've got the sort of faith to keep going, then I've about got to go along just to watch those sorry brethren learn their lesson."

"So you think I'm doing the right thing?"

"I didn't say that, but I reckon you are. Further," Gideon declared grinning, "if you always do what's right, you'll please the most important folks, and you'll keep the rest of 'em up nights awondering what you're up to."

I chuckled. "It would be better," I then said carefully, "if you came after me, more slowly . . ."

Gideon snorted. "Not on your life! I ain't that old – not yet, at least. Now, let's hit the hay – or in this case, the sagebrush and gravel. Otherwise, you'll be too tired to travel when I roust you out about an hour from now."

Sounds of hurried doings tapped at my eardrums, penetrating at last to awareness. I came out of my sleep still tired and with a stiffness in my backbone that was getting worse by the hour. The darkness of sky overhead had shifted to a dull gray, and a few stars still fought against the seeping glimmer of the false dawn.

Rising on one elbow, I looked around and saw old Gideon slapping the pack on the long-legged mule. I pushed up, stretched, and took the bucket half full of water that Gideon had placed near me and walked a short distance away for a quick and cold wash-up. And it was while washing my face that I first realized something was wrong.

It wasn't anything definite, just a gloomy feeling, a sense of foreboding. Yet as I thought of it, the feeling seemed to grow, and it wasn't long before it was all I could do to keep from bawling.

Five minutes later, standing by the dead campfire, I watched Gideon hurrying toward me with a tin cup in one hand and some cold beef in the other.

"Gobble these," he growled. "Fast. And kick me when you're through. Hard."

"Something feels mighty wrong," I said.

"Don't I know it! I overslept, and it's near morning."

"I know, friend Gideon," I said, trying to chew dried beef while I talked. "But there's more, lots more. I feel a sense of doom that almost brings chills—"

"Being late's enough, Jons. Those fellers could have fifteen, twenty miles more on us by now, and it's all my fault. I'd of saddled Perdy, but you know how she fights anyone but you."

Gideon grabbed the bucket, emptied it, and shuffle-hurried to the mule, where he stuffed it into the pack. Then he grabbed the lead rope and limped rapidly toward where his horse was standing ground-hitched.

"Well," he snarled back at me, "get the lead out, boy! Like you say, daylight's a'burning."

"But there *is* something wrong, Gideon . . . "

His sour look stopped me from saying more, but that bad feeling was getting worse by the minute. Still, Gideon hadn't felt anything, so what was I worried about?

I swallowed the bite of beef I had been working over, took a long drink of water, and stuffed the rest of the beef into my shirtfront. Then, grabbing up the blanket and my saddle, I ran toward my Perdy mare.

I was tugging at the cinch when I realized that Perdy's head was up and her ears forward, staring off into the darkness. Then I heard, off toward the trail, the sound of Lazarus snarling. But before I had a chance to shout a warning to Gideon, I heard a series of fierce shrieks that sent shivers down my spine and all the way to my toes.

I hesitated briefly, unable to move, and then the shrieks were interrupted by the heavy boom of Gideon's Henrietta rifle.

The shrieks stopped abruptly, there was the faint sound of diminishing hoofbeats, and I could hear nothing more.

Swiftly I finished saddling and swung up on Perdy, and obstinately she rose into the air, head down and back arched, bucking once, twice, three times in her nervousness. Then she leveled into a fast lope toward the trail.

Gideon was standing on a little rise, just finishing reloading his rifle, when I slid Perdy to a stop. Lazarus was walking stiff-legged back and forth in front of my companion, the mule was standing motionless, and there was no sign at all of Kettle-belly, Gideon's faithful little mustang.

"Confound it," he growled as he rammed the rod down the long barrel. "When am I ever going to learn? Brains in the head sure saves blisters on the feet!"

"Gideon, are you hurt?"

"Not hardly. But I got to learn to listen to you fellers who can hearken to the Spirit—especially when you tell me to listen. I don't hear them things much, so I tend to doubt. But every single solitary time I ignore Eph Hanks or you, I end up looking the sorry fool. Now I got *two* kicks coming."

"What? You're making no more sense—"

"Yeah, I am," the old man snarled. "You told me there was something wrong. But oh, no, I wouldn't listen. I'm so confounded used to thinking that when a hen cackles she's either lying or laying, that I forget she might be giving me warning. Now I've gone and lost my horse."

"Kettle-belly is—"

"Away and gone!"

"Somebody stole him?"

"No, he just spooked when that Ute kid jumped out of the brush when I nearly ran over him. The poor kid was scarder'n me and Kettle. I shot old Henrietta into the air I was so startled, my horse pitched me on my noggin, and then the fool animal took off."

"What you going to do?"

"Do?" Gideon growled. "Why, get even with the ornery

critter, of course. I'll make that fool horse walk all the way back to me, all by his lonesome. That'll teach him."

"Gideon . . ."

The old man grinned wryly. "He'll be back, Son. He always ends up tracking me down, given time. But confound it, that's just what we ain't got—time. But don't you worry none about me. I'll ride the mule till Kettle makes it back, then I'll ride like the dickens and catch up with you later today."

I looked forward along the trail that stretched to the far horizon, where the first faint blush of color was creeping up the sky. Lazarus was no longer walking stiff-legged back and forth, so I knew that the Indian boy had to be gone. But out there somewhere were likely to be other of the Utes, perhaps waiting for the boy, though perhaps not. But each would be anxious to obtain a new horse, and maybe even to lift a white scalp.

Trouble was, also out there, knocking off more miles, were the Ute named Knife and the white man Vasquez, and with one or the other of them, or maybe both by now, was my Steenie Bergman. I could not afford to wait.

"Take your time," I said to the disgruntled Gideon. "There'll be no catching up, not the way Perdy, Lazarus, and I will be riding. But fear not, old friend. The three of us, and Steenie, will meet you on our return."

"Now hold on, Son. You can't do this alone! Getting your little gal away from those two heathen will be trickier'n braiding a mule's tail."

With a heavy heart but brave smile I bid my friend farewell, and even while he was protesting I rode away down the trail.

"Consarn it," he shouted after me, "that's the best thing about talking to my horse! He don't talk back, and he don't ignore me . . ."

Gideon was right, and I knew it. I could never do what had to be done, alone. But still—

"Remember, Jons Soderberg," Gideon shouted from behind me, "every fool on this earth is afraid of something. You find what those heathen are afraid of, and you'll beat 'em sure."

With a last wave to my friend and a glance into the brightening sky, I knew suddenly I wasn't alone at all. After all, no less an authority than Gideon himself had declared that I was as in tune with the Spirit as Eph Hanks. I knew that wasn't so, of course, but I *had* felt something back there, a warning that I knew full well had come from above. That being the case, the Good Lord would surely be willing to direct me from where I now was. All I had to do was ask.

And I *was* asking—believe me, I was asking.

Chapter 23

An hour later I found two more bodies, and I didn't know whether to feel relieved or terrified. The first, the splayed-hoofed horse that had belonged to Ben Crost, was lying in the trail where it had fallen, literally having died on its feet. I had noticed the tracks for some time, and though I was no expert at reading sign, I could tell that Vasquez, or whoever had been riding it, had ridden the horse especially hard for the past mile or so. The tracks were spaced wide and deep, and more and more often it had stumbled, so it was no real surprise for me to come upon the horse's dead body.

I was still looking at that and the deep boot tracks leading forward from it when I heard Lazarus's deep growl from maybe fifty feet ahead. Riding forward, I came shortly to the second body. Instantly I knew that I was looking at the man known as Knife—and just as instantly I felt a deep sense of pity for him. He had been shot and dumped aside as if he were no more important than a used blanket, and I had the feeling that maybe he had deserved more. Still, I was glad to know he now had no more power over Steenie.

Gulping and taking a deep breath, I rode around him—and within a few yards I came to the remnants of a camp. It had not been a permanent camp at all but was more like the ones Gideon and I had left behind us each morning. The difference was that in this camp were the tracks of three people—the moccassined Ute, the booted Vasquez, and the smaller tracks of a woman's shoes that had to have been made by Steenie Bergman.

With heart racing, I searched for any sign left by her, any indication that she was still hoping for my arrival. I found nothing but scuff marks indicating that she had fought her abductor, and off in the brush a ten-foot leather bullwhip. I also discovered that the coals from the fire were still warm, and that renewed my excitement. I was close, so close that I could feel it. Now all I had to do was catch up to them and somehow take Steenie away from José Vasquez.

For the first time I wished for a gun, feeling bad that I had taken Eph's word that I hadn't needed one. He had not seen the cold-blooded murders that the man I was following had committed. But I didn't have one, and so I would need to rely on the Lord and my wits, something I had to admit I had watched Ephraim Hanks and Lot Smith do to near perfection.

Perdy moved strong and steady under me as I followed the flowing shoeprints of the two long-legged 'breds. Lope-trot-lope. Lope for half an hour in the smooth undulating stride familiar to anyone who had ever seen a herd of wild mustangs flowing over the land, their backs rising and falling as easy and regularly as water waves. Trot for the next half hour in that swinging double-beat stride that Gideon had told me mustangs themselves favored for making maximum distance with minimum effort.

It was hard, not knowing what was happening ahead, to hold down, to keep from spurring Perdy into full gallop. But the tracks those 'breds left behind looked smooth and steady, and if it turned into a 'long' race, as Gideon had called it, I wanted Perdy to be able to make it. Lazarus, too, appreciated the pace, and though I could never tell if he was tired or not, I knew that he had to be. No animal can cover four or five hundred miles and not be worn by it. And I knew that Lazarus was worn. He no longer ranged far ahead or to the side of us but always ran just uptrail, never more than fifteen feet ahead, no matter whether Perdy was loping or trotting.

When I ran into my first living human of the journey, the

sun was standing at an hour or a little more before noon. He was an old mountaineer, a trapper and prospector, riding a little burrow and leading three others—and he looked like he was heading back into the Uintahs to do his winter trapping. Quick as a flash he had a bead on Lazarus, but at a warning shout from me, he dropped his old weapon.

"Friend," I said as he quizzically regarded me, "have you seen a man and a girl, him of vicious countenance and her filled with fright?"

"You train the wolf?" he asked.

"He isn't trained but follows or leads as he chooses. Have you seen the pair?"

"A trained wolf. Who'd have thought it? You're talking about José Vasquez," the man replied evenly. "I'd make it a shade under two hours ago they passed me. But was I you, I'd turn around while I could still breathe. That's a mean man, Boy. *Mighty* mean."

"It won't matter. I'm still going after him."

The old man shook his head. "Then you'd best start praying, boy. There ain't a man I know who ain't afeared of him, Injuns included."

"Have you a weapon to spare?"

"Against Vasquez?" he chuckled. "Not on your life. He'd kill you and see that your weapon was mine. Then I'd be a dead man myself. And me, I've got some gold to get out of those mountains come spring."

"There's gold up there?"

"Son," he said, sending a squirt of dark tobacco juice shooting over the head of his burro, and then wiping his stained beard with the back of his dirty hand, "out here every prairie dog hole is a gold mine, every hill is a mountain, every creek a river, and every prospector you'll meet is a forked-tongued liar. I tell you there's gold in them there hills, and you'd best know better. Let me be the fool, not you.

"And I'm right sorry about not giving you my extra gun. If you're still crazy enough to go after Vasquez, you'll have to do it with the weapons you brung with you."

At noon I gave half of the meager contents of the feed bag to Perdy, and Lazarus and I chewed down half of what I had left of the dried beef. But there was no water—nowhere along the last miles had we come on a stream or a wash with any leftover moisture in it. Nothing but barren, friendless, sandy country.

"Doesn't seem much like manna," I said to the two animals, "and I don't hardly have no rod with which to strike rock for a drink. But the Lord knows of our plight, and if He's really watching over us . . . "

I could see it far ahead, two adobe and two weathered and burned board buildings that comprised what I thought Yates had said was Fort Rubidoux, an abandoned fur trader's outpost. But Yates had also said there was a flowing well there—water.

And he was right, I discovered as we drew closer—for there was not only a well, but a log that had been hollowed into a small watering trough.

Holding Perdy to a trot and then a walk, I moved cautiously forward. The tracks of the two 'breds led to the trough and then away, but I was still suspicious. Pulling up twenty feet away from the trough, I waited.

Nothing.

Dismounting, I left the mare and walked slowly forward, Lazarus gliding silently at my side. Again I looked around. There was no sign of life anywhere, and that made me nervous. Above me, the tired, seasonal remnants of the cottonwood leaves rustled, and I could hear the slight trickle of water spilling from the well spigot, as it had been somehow diverted past the trough onto the ground.

"You see any trouble?" I asked the dog quietly.

Leaning over the shallow trough, I scooped water into my hands and drank, intending in a moment to go back and lead Perdy forward. One scoop I drank, then another, and I was just starting in on the third when the dog, who had placed muzzle to water just below me, snarled and leaped away.

"Lazarus," I called, "what the dickens is wrong? See, I'm drinking . . . "

With another snarl Lazarus leaped at me—and as I staggered backward I saw, out of the corner of my eye, an Indian woman dart forward from one of the empty buildings and grab Perdy's bridle. She then held something out under the mare's nose, her palm flat, and I jerked around.

"Say!" I shouted. "You get away from that mare—"

The rest of my breath was jolted from me as another squaw leaped onto my back from behind. I struggled to free myself, but the woman, wide and heavy and stronger than I could have imagined, clamped her arms around me. I tried to call Perdy, but only a small sound came forth, not nearly enough—

But Lazarus heard, and his snarl was more than enough to activate Perdy. The mare reared back, jerking her reins. Still the Indian woman hung tenaciously to them. Perdy reared again, and this time the little mustang plunged forward with forehoofs striking. The woman shrieked and went down, and then Perdy was swinging in a fast circle, head high, coming right for me.

"Blow the horns over Jericho," I grunted—and between my stomping on the woman's foot and Lazarus's chewing on her leg, I finally broke free. "Now let the walls of the city come tumbling down!" I shouted as I grabbed the horn and pulled myself into the saddle. And with that, my Perdy mare surged ahead, picking up speed, getting us away from the abandoned fort.

Out in the trail and moving away I looked back, but no one was following. If the Indian women had horses, they were still hidden. The one woman was on her feet—but the other, the one who had been kicked by Perdy, was still flat on her back, which I thought served her good and right.

"You did good," I said as I patted the mare on the side of her neck. "And like friend Gideon, I've sure got a kick coming."

The wind of motion was tugging at me, and gradually I became aware that Perdy was pounding in full gallop, while Lazarus was running effortlessly at our side.

"Easy," I said as I tugged the reins. "Easy, girl. There's no need of such hurry, not yet . . . "

And then I became aware of a nagging ache inside me, under

my ribs – growing, increasing. That was followed by a wave of nausea that swept over me, blurring my vision and constricting my breathing in sudden, dry retching.

I pulled on the reins and Perdy stopped. Then I all but fell from the saddle – and was immediately on my knees by the trail, bent over, while both Lazarus and Perdy stood silently, watching.

"Now I've . . . got *two* kicks coming," I breathed, and that was about all that I could say.

It was the water, I knew. Sensing that I was following him, or maybe even having seen me, Vasquez had poisoned the water and instructed those two women to stay and make sure I was put out of my misery. But the knowledge of his deeds gave me little consolation, for I was more sick than I had ever been in my life.

Pushing two fingers down in my throat, I felt my shoulders shake as my throat muscles reacted in spasmodic constrictions, and then the foul stuff gushed forth. The taste in my mouth was loathsome, and the smell of the mess before me was more so – and all I wanted to do was just fall away from it and stretch out in the trail and die. But not far ahead my Steenie girl was praying for me to come, so I staggered to my feet and to Perdy and then pulled myself into the saddle.

Fingers fumbling, I tied the reins around the horn, and then grabbing Perdy's mane I fell forward. "Get going, good and faithful friends," I mumbled to the animals. "I'll hang on somehow."

Lazarus ran to the front and looked back, Perdy started moving, and the three of us were on our way again.

Time passed, though I had no knowledge of it. Hunched forward, head hanging down, fingers wrapped in Perdy's stringy mane, I rode in a sort of trance, aware of nothing, not even the insistent joggle of Perdy's swinging trot or of the already habitual response of my own muscles that held me in the saddle.

But gradually awareness returned, and I knew both who and where I was. I was on my Perdy mare, Lazarus was out before us, and ahead of us somewhere was a young woman named

Christena Bergman, who was surely waiting for me to save her. And I was letting all of them down. Without a doubt, I was the stupidest fool in the whole world, and I was letting down the best friends I had on God's green earth.

I tried to straighten in the saddle, be less of a spineless blob of dead weight on Perdy's back – and I managed to do so, somewhat.

But Perdy was moving strong and steady beneath me, not even letting down a little – and Lazarus, who had tried to warn me of the poisoned water and had even pushed me away from drinking more of it, was running free ahead.

Suddenly all I wanted to do was cry, to blubber like a little child. For I knew, somehow, that these two friends of mine, the ugly little gray mustang and the scraggly coyote-dog, were saying something to me – saying it in the ceaseless steadiness of stride, in the flex and flow of muscle under dusty gray or tawny brown hide, in the tireless thudding of hoofs or the endless padding of almost silent paws.

"Stop your worrying," they were saying to me. "The Lord has raised us up to do this thing for you, and we are doing it well. Of course you're a fool, but all men are fools, and we hold that not against you. Besides, you're good for some things, such as combing the burrs from our tails, and we rejoice in that. But, Jons Soderberg, you could never do what we do now. So cease your fretting, look to yourself, and let us do this little thing that we have been raised up to do."

So time passed, and slowly I began to feel better. I may have been all sorts of a fool, but I was young and strong, and finally I was straight in the saddle again, doing my best as a balanced rider to help Perdy and my Lazarus dog bring me to my frightened but waiting love.

Chapter 24

In the darkness of the night, back away from the trail and well screened by high bushes, I gave Perdy the last grains of the meager feed bag Gideon had given me. While she ate that, Lazarus and I chewed down what was left of the dried beef.

"And he would fain have filled his belly with the husks that the swine did eat," I said to my two silent companions. "Luke fifteen, the story of the prodigal son. Ma taught it to me. Good friends, are you as confounded hungry as I am?"

Neither of the animals answered, and I swallowed the last tiny bits of the beef. Then I took the end of the rope trailing from Perdy's neck and tied it to my arm.

"Half an hour, no more. Take longer and I'll be gone in sleep, certain."

Leaning back on my saddle, I closed my eyes—but thoughts of Perdy and Lazarus and two long-legged 'breds speeding Steenie away from me chased themselves through my mind, and I could not seem to relax.

"Father," I prayed silently, "thy servant knows he is close to Christena, and tomorrow I'll likely come to her and the heathen Vasquez. I don't know what I'll do then, but thou knowest all things, and I pray that thou wilt open a way . . . "

A few feet away, Lazarus lay with head down on paws, absolutely still. Beyond him Perdy stood, motionless, head low. Both animals were gaunt along the ribs and sunk in some at the flanks. They were dirtied, clumsy-looking caricatures of their former selves that seemed to have died, one on the ground and the other on her feet. They looked finished, done for, ready to collapse into heaps of bone and hide.

But they were not, neither one of them, and I knew it. Each of those wonderful animals was resting. They were relaxed all over, dropped, stretched out, sagged into absolute limpness. That was because, somehow, they knew. The gray mustang mare and the tawny brown coyote-dog that called me his were wasting no extra energy in twitchings or stompings or tail switchings or thumpings or other movings about. They were making the most of a very brief rest. And they were both just about ready to begin to fight.

And by gum, I thought as I looked at them, so was I!

Struggling out of a doze a little later, I dragged myself to my feet. "Let Gabriel blow the trumpet," I mumbled, for some reason thinking more and more of words from the scriptures that Ma had read me. "We are on to find my Steenie . . ."

There was only the dark of night and the trace of trail like a ribbon under faint, cold starlight and the wind of our own motion as we moved at a fast lope into the lonely miles. Off and on I thought of old Gideon and hoped that he had found his horse, and I wondered where he would be right now. At other times I thought of Eph Hanks and Lot Smith and tried to picture in my mind a way that I could trick José Vasquez into releasing Steenie into my hands, the way they might do it if they were with me.

I could not come up with an idea, however, and so I tried during the rest of the time to think of nothing, but just to hurry so that I would be in time. Urgency, therefore, talked along Perdy's reins—and stretching her neck, she responded.

Tiredness was an ache that covered my whole body, and hunger a hollowness that gnawed in my belly. Dizziness took me now and again, and at those times I knew I would never remember the night clearly. But it didn't matter, not anymore. All that mattered was that I find Steenie, and that I find her in time.

Lazarus loped ahead of us, never hesitating, and at times I

watched the dim rise and fall of his paws in amazement, wondering that such poetry could exist. Yet I knew that it did, for the drumming of Perdy's hoofs beneath me pounded to the same primal rhythm. I knew as well that Lazarus's nose was leading him, and not for a minute did I worry that we might pass Steenie in the dark.

And it was dark—though after an endless time, I realized that rocks and bushes along the trail were sharper, more distinct. We kept moving, and sometime later the songs of birds penetrated my thoughts, making me even more aware of the coming of dawn.

Suddenly I felt good and sat straighter in the saddle, as a man should sit. I no longer felt quite so tired, and much later, when the first rays of the sun hit me, I even managed a smile.

"Well done, thou good and faithful servant," I said as I reached down and patted Perdy on the neck. "Now keep those hoofs a'moving . . . "

And Perdy, warmed through to the very marrow of her bones, fully into our race to find Steenie though it should last for all eternity, leaned forward again into a fast, long-reaching lope. Lazarus responded in kind, and we were all eating the wind, gobbling the miles and feeling good as we flew into the morning.

And then I heard hoofbeats behind me. Twisting to look back, I was startled to see an Indian coming up, and coming up fast. For a moment I felt fear, and then I realized that the man was well within range of any weapon he might have wanted to use, and yet he had used none.

Well, I decided, he didn't want to kill me or to stop me, at least not yet. But if not that, then what?

The man pulled his horse alongside, five or six feet away from me. Then he slowed to Perdy's pace, and, yipping shrilly but not looking at me at all, he continued to ride.

And so did I.

Before I knew it, another Indian was on my other side, also riding at Perdy's pace, also shouting his war cry but ignoring me otherwise—and I could feel little shivers of fear going up and down my back. I was surely confused by what the two were doing, but as no harm seemed to be coming from them, I decided that three could play the ignoring game. So I kept my eyes as straight ahead as they did, and I kept Perdy pounding forward. And the funny thing was that Lazarus ignored my Lamanite brethren just as thoroughly as I was ignoring them, and so did my little gray mare. She was intent upon her work, strong and steady, never pausing, and Lazarus was intent only upon leading the way.

There were more Indians now, Utes I assumed, quite a crowd of them, and we all rode together, them shrieking, me riding silently, all of us ignoring each other. It was a strange experience, and I don't expect to ever again see the like. I wondered what old Gideon would do about such an escort and was glad he wasn't along. Then I thought of Ephraim Hanks. He would handle it coolly, I knew that, and I could almost see him in my mind, riding with these folks, paying no attention to them, beating them at their own game.

But I didn't know the rules.

We pounded across a long, brush-covered bench, the dust churning up behind us in clouds, and I was almost starting to relax about the Indians when I felt a sharp jab of pain in my shoulder.

Spinning, I was startled to see the first Ute riding with his lance outstretched, and his cries rang out louder than ever. He obviously thought that by poking me, he had just done something wonderful, but I didn't agree. My shoulder hurt like blue blazes, and I was still trying to puzzle it out when I was jabbed in the other side from another direction.

"Say!" I shouted as I glared back at the second man, "who do you think you are? Now back off."

The whole bunch was clamoring now, trying to get around each other to get at me with their lances and other such implements of war, not to kill, apparently, so much as to touch. And finally it came to me what they were doing. Eph Hanks and Al Bagley had talked one night about Indians "counting coup," being brave enough to touch a living enemy, pull away, and then come back in for the kill. Well, I was their enemy, they could touch me about as they chose, and I knew without a doubt that unless I did something very soon, we wouldn't be traveling much longer under such amiable conditions. The whole tribe would be swooping in for the kill.

Another lance probed my thigh. I yelled out in pain, then somebody else whacked me on the back of the neck, and suddenly another of Al Bagley's stories about Brother Hanks came to my mind.

With a sudden scream of my own, I threw my right arm high above my head. Then, pulling a hideous face, I twirled my arm in a rapid circle beside me. Then I began to bark, at the same time unbuttoning my shirt, pulling it over my head, and wrapping it around my neck.

A quick glance and I felt hope, for as one the Indians were staring at me as we rode, and no one had his lance out and poking at me anymore, either.

"Oh, the lady she died and went away . . . " I suddenly sang out at the top of my lungs, and then with another grimace that exhibited my front teeth in such a way that *anybody* looking on would wonder, I took my feet from the stirrups.

With a quick twist I spun about on the saddle so that I was riding backward, and I felt thankful that Lazarus was leading Perdy, and that she was paying more attention to the dog than she was to me. So far as I could tell, my ridiculous actions didn't even slow her down.

Now the Utes were truly staring, so at the top of my lungs I began orating to them in Swedish, pulling faces, swinging my arms, leaning forward and backward, and doing anything and everything I could think of to look crazy. For that had been the story I had remembered about Eph Hanks. Knowing that Indians feared crazy people, he had acted crazy once in a tight place, and it had frightened some truly hostile Lamanites away from him. My only hope was that the same ruse would now work for me.

And to my dumbfounded wonder, it did.

"*Pe-up,*" one of the Utes shouted as he pulled back until

they were riding twenty or thirty feet from me. They were still with me, of course, but I felt a whole lot better having them with me at that distance than I had felt at the skin-piercing distance we had previously shared.

Still singing and making faces, I righted myself in the saddle, patted Perdy's neck, and breathed a sigh of relief. I was going to make it, and I knew it. The Lord was protecting me, and my friends, even when they were far away, were still managing to save my obviously charmed life.

Crossing the bench, we swooped down through the wash, me way out in front of the Utes—and on the other side Lazarus suddenly swerved and then almost instantly veered back and was on trail again. Looking to the side where he had swerved, I was shocked to see a big black Standard and Morgan cross, gaunt, sweat-streaked, bedraggled, head-hanging, saddle empty, looking ready and more than ready to fall.

One down.

And that meant that the other 'bred was carrying double—that is, unless Vasquez had picked up a second horse from the Utes. But no, there was only one set of tracks stretching before us, one set of big hoofprints upon which the valiant Lazarus had fixed his mind.

Perdy suddenly shifted her lead from right forefoot to left—a sure sign, Gideon had told me, that she was feeling the strain. Her eyes were beginning to show red-rimmed, her chest was heaving, and sweaty lather dampened her flanks and stretched-out neck. But still that reassuring refrain came up from her pounding, rock-hard hooves, and I could hear her saying to me, "Fret not, good friend Jons. You've asked that this be done, and the dog and I are doing it well. Now stop fretting and prepare yourself for what you, alone, must do."

A dark shape appeared in the trail ahead of us, far in the distance, and I wondered. Lazarus and Perdy continued to run smoothly, and as we drew closer I saw that it was a big sorrel, carrying double. Beating down the excitement that surged through my body, I watched the man on the sorrel turn back to look at us.

Instantly he exploded into frantic action, slapping with his rein ends, raking with his spurs. His sorrel mount rallied some, trying, trying – and then broke into a jerky gallop.

I was debating whether to urge my mare forward or to hold my pace, when Perdy suddenly took charge, and I knew that it was no longer my decision to make. She shifted to right forefoot lead again and surged into full gallop, belly low, striving for distance in lengthening stride – the message of urgency suddenly reversed and coming back through the reins from the mare's hammering hammerhead.

"Go," I whispered, forgetting altogether the group of Ute braves who hung back but were yet following. "Go, you gorgeous, wonderful, lovely little mustang . . . "

There was no break in Perdy's long-reaching lope – but I could sense the laboring in it, and I feared. I could feel the extra jolting as the hoofs hit, and the straining muscles no longer cushioned the shocks in instant energy response. Perdy's breath was coming in long, sobbing gasps. Sweat drenched her gray hide, and a dingy froth whipped away from the sidebars of the bit in her mouth. But there was no break, no falter in that steady stride, and I loved her for what she was giving me.

And then I was alone, strangely, and I sensed without looking that the Utes had all dropped back, way back, and were following behind for a different reason altogether now, watching.

Ahead of me, the big sorrel Hambletonian and Thoroughbred cross pounded forward. José Vasquez was lashing with his quirt, jabbing with his spurs. And frenzied, foam-spattering, head high and tossing, wild-eyed, running on nerve and breeding alone, dragging the last burst of power and speed from the great Thoroughbred heart in him, the sorrel began pulling away.

But Lazarus saw, Lazarus with his tongue hanging a mile out of his mouth and his tail dragging deep in the dust behind, saw the burst of speed. With a low whine, that triumphant look of eagles appeared in his eyes, and he stretched out, encouraging the mare, encouraging . . .

And my lovely Perdy heard. With a flash of diving, taloned

raptor in her own red-rimmed eyes, she stretched out to follow her friend. And out of the long past of her kind in the wide and barren land of the far southwest, out of the stubborn endurance bred into her small but powerful body through untold generations, came the greater surge of strength in lean, hard flanks and hammering hoofs, the surge that could not possibly have been there, but was.

Gideon had been right, all along old Captain Gideon Peabody Monson had been right! There was not a finer horse in the whole wide world than the scrubby little gray mare who surged forward beneath me, carrying me after my beloved Steenie.

The sorrel, longer-legged but carrying double, covering more ground with each frantic leap, inched ahead. I watched as bloody froth flew from the horse's mouth. I heard as breath rattled and whistled in his throat. And suddenly I was angry, angry that men would do this awful thing to fellow creatures so wonderful as the horses we rode. But then I noticed that Perdy was creeping up on the sorrel again, inch by inch, and I forgot my anger in the glory of knowing that somehow, someway, because of Perdy and Lazarus and Gideon and so many other little miracles lying in the miles behind me that I could hardly count them, Steenie would soon be mine.

Then the big sorrel stumbled, caught himself, went on, and then stumbled again, badly. And as I swept past in my slowing and reining down of the mare, I saw Vasquez's face, pinched and angry, his teeth bared in a grimace that showed more hatred than ever I thought could exist in another human being. But I also saw my Steenie, her eyes wide with hope and joy of being freed, and of being freed by the man she loved. And if I live to be a hundred, I'll never forget that expression of incredible wonder, frozen into place in my mind as I hurtled past and as she and José Vasquez were in that exact instant being thrown by the falling horse, tumbling to the ground in a hopeless heap.

"Jons!" Steenie screamed from behind me as she scrambled to her feet. "Oh, my darling Jons, you came!"

And then, finally, with Steenie's frantic, hopeful voice ringing in my ears—and with the hope in her eyes glowing like the sun, I pulled Perdy to a turnaround halt and stared back.

Chapter 25

For the number of people who sat astride horses or stood watching, it was amazingly quiet. The slave trader José Vasquez was on his feet, a handgun in one hand and Steenie gripped tightly by the other. Around him, ringing themselves into a half-circle as they rode up, apparently so they could face me, were at least twenty Ute braves. All were heavily armed, and all but two sat on their horses, guns or bows at the ready. The two on the ground, the first to ride up beside me earlier, now stood on either side of Vasquez, and it was obvious that they were prepared to back him in any play he might happen to make.

"Jons," Steenie cried, "he's a killer. I . . . ouch!" Vasquez was twisting her arm though never taking his eyes off me, and his hurting Steenie was making me angry to the core.

"That's good, Vasquez," I snarled. "Using women and children for protection. Now I know why you used those squaws to do your dirty work. You were too afraid to do it yourself. Seeing how you operate, I imagine you shot Knife in the back too. It's easy to see you're sure no ordinary coward."

Vasquez gave me a toothy grin. Lazarus growled low, and with a nudge I urged Perdy forward. We were in a high-walled, desert canyon that ran roughly south, and in the distance, toward the canyon's mouth, I could see the gleam of a wide river. I assumed it was the Grand, the river now called the Colorado—and I realized with amazement that Lazarus, Perdy, and I had come up with the fleeing Vasquez before he could manage to reach his permanent camp at the confluence of it and the Dolores.

Her sides still heaving, Perdy stepped slowly forward, and I found myself in a sort of daze from which I could not escape. Oh, I was aware of everything around me—Lazarus's panting, Perdy's steps and deep intaking of breath, the raucous cry of a crow somewhere in the distance, the nickering and head-tossing of several of the Ute ponies, the stumbling shuffle of the big sorrel as it rose to its feet and wandered from the trail, and most of all Vasquez's consuming anger as he watched me riding slowly toward him.

But the daze I felt was caused by the sight of Steenie Bergman, and more and more she was the only thing I could really see. Oh, she was some dirty, all right, but I expect that I looked the same. Her lovely dark hair with the fiery glow of sunsets in it was disheveled and unkempt. Her dress was torn, and her petticoats showed through in several places. One of her shoes was missing altogether. And as I got closer, I could see burns on her wrists where she had been bound.

Put all those things aside, however, and it will be easily understood what I was seeing about Steenie Bergman, and why I was in a daze over it. Her head was high, her proud chin was thrust out with determination, the mysterious blue-gray of her eyes flashed with unconquerable spirit and the same look of eagles I had seen in Perdy's eyes and the eyes of Lazarus—and her lips, showing red and warm even through the dust and grime of six days' hard riding, formed clearly the words, "I love you."

Dazed with the sight of her, dazed with the knowledge that nothing had changed, dazed with the understanding that a creature so perfect and so lovely could love me—I measured my thoughts!

What did it matter that I faced the most vicious killer I had ever known? What did it matter that half the Ute nation was staring me down, armed to the teeth and ready on the instant for the warpath? What did it matter that I was alone with only a gaunt coyote-dog and a stove-up little southwestern mustang to side me? Or what did it matter, finally, that I was so exhausted I could hardly sit upright in the saddle?

Very little did it matter, and I knew it. What mattered was the girl standing proud and straight before me. What mattered was the dog and horse facing forward with me, not stumbling—but strong and ready to go again if need be.

And what mattered most was that I knew, just as I knew everything else about that moment, that the Lord had brought me there. He had heard my father's blessing. He had heard Eph's promise. And he had heard my cries and pleadings. And, just as surely, the Lord God of Israel had been kind enough to answer. He had given me Gideon Monson, Ephraim Hanks, and Lot Smith. He had given me Lazarus, and he had given me Perdy. And I could see then that he was willing and happy that Steenie and I should give ourselves eternally to each other.

Only there was still the little matter of my somehow getting her away from Vasquez.

"Jons," Steenie cried, "I knew that you would come! I told everybody . . . ouch!"

Vasquez grinned again as he squeezed her arm—but the grin was wiped off his face as Steenie lashed out with her one remaining boot, kicking the filthy slave-trader in the shin.

"There," she shouted as he dropped her arm and grimaced in pain. "You touch me again, you filthy beast, and I'll—"

"Steenie," I shouted frantically when I saw her stepping toward the man instead of away from him, "don't fight—*run!*"

"What?" she asked, looking at me, surprised.

"Run! It's your best chance—"

But by then it was already too late—for the Indian standing behind her suddenly reached out, grabbed her hair, and yanked her close, putting his arm around her neck.

She struggled against him, kicking and swinging her arms, but the touch of a knife under her chin quieted her, and her eyes opened wide at me.

"Jons, please . . ."

And then Vasquez angrily reached out and jerked Steenie

away from the Indian. Then he, too, threw his arm around her neck, choking her into further submission.

"There, you little minx! Now you're gonna watch the kid die."

"Father," I prayed silently, "thou knowest that I come into this camp of the Philistines as unarmed as poor old Samson was. Give me therefore, I pray, the jawbone of an ass—"

"That's far enough!"

Vasquez's gravelly voice stopped me at about fifteen feet, and so I sat on my horse, looking at him. He was big, all right, and evil to the core. I could see clearly the cruelty in his eyes, and suddenly I understood how this man had been capable of murdering Ben Crost and the Indian called Knife. There was a darkness within him, a darkness beyond skin and hair and whiskers that Ephraim Hanks had spoken of at one time, that came from being devoid of God's Spirit. And this man *was* devoid of that Spirit, I could tell that.

"So, it's you who's been followin' us?"

"Partly."

Vasquez grinned. "For her? She isn't worth it, kid, and now you've come a long way just to die."

"He won't . . . die," Steenie gasped, never taking her flashing eyes from mine. "The . . . Lord will fight our . . . battle, and . . . and I'll be going home with him."

Well, I flushed with pride, but Vasquez only laughed derisively.

"Take you *home?* This kid? That'll be some trick, outnumbered the way he is."

"He will," Steenie declared, suddenly struggling again. "I . . . I know he . . . will!"

Vasquez laughed again as he clamped his arm more tightly against Steenie's throat—and again I felt chills at the vileness of the man. He was truly one who deserved to die. Yet Brother Brigham had counseled us to avoid bloodshed at all costs in our war with the army. Was this no less a war? And was I no less a Saint than the brethren on the plains of Wyoming?

In my mind I could hear Al Bagley questioning me about

what I would do if it came to the question of killing or being killed, and again I was brought up short by the answer. I didn't know what I would do. I truly didn't.

But then I realized, abruptly and with sinking heart, that it hadn't come to that choice anyway. I was completely unarmed, and there was no way I could fight and defeat this wicked man who stood so arrogantly before me with Steenie held so cruelly against him. Nor could I possibly fight the Utes who backed him.

"Dear Lord," I pleaded in my mind, "show me the jawbone—"

"Get down off that horse and draw your gun!"

"I . . . I'm unarmed," I admitted quietly and to my mortal shame.

"Jons, noooo . . . !"

Vasquez laughed with glee. "Then get down off that horse and die, you young fool. I've got a wedding to arrange here, between the girl and old Chief Tavagoop, and I don't have time to waste on you!"

"Unngh," the Ute next to Steenie grunted, the one who had held her with the knife to her throat. Then he reached and pinched her again.

"*Tsharr nan-zitch*, white girl, she not *tick-i own-shump*, she not eat enough to be good squaw." The chief laughed, and the other Utes laughed with him. "But *towats* Tavagoop fix that soon enough."

Vasquez and several of the Indians laughed again, but I didn't, and neither did my Steenie.

"Jons," she whispered, her eyes momentarily filled with fear, "*please do something*."

Well, I wanted to do something. With all my heart I wanted to. Trouble was, my mind was an absolute blank. All my prayers had come to nothing, and I had no single clear idea—

"Get down!"

Numbly I pulled my foot from the stirrup, lifted my leg, swung it over Perdy's back, and slowly swung to the ground.

"Dear Father," my mind cried out as I did so, "please show me the way."

"Move away from the horse!"

I did, or rather I took a step to do so. But maybe I had been in the saddle for too long. Or maybe it was still the effects of the poisoned water.

But maybe . . . maybe it was because of something, or Someone else! Whatever the reason, my legs had gone numb—and with my first step, my pins literally collapsed, and I found myself seated ungloriously on my rear in the dust and scrabble of the high-walled canyon floor.

And as I sat there, dazed, I found, too, a stone beneath my hand—rounded and smooth, about the size of a fire-hardened, clay marble.

Vasquez laughed uproariously, and Steenie closed her eyes so that she would not see my humiliation. Even the Ute warriors grinned and chuckled at my foolish ineptness, saying *"Pe-up,"* over and over, and snickering about it.

But me, my mind was racing. In my fall, I had found the stone beneath my hand in the dirt of the canyon floor, and in that instant I felt, too, the awkward pressure of the forgotten object in my rear pocket.

"Lord God above," I muttered, glancing upward, "hast thou shown me the jawbone?"

A shot rang out, and dust plumed upward an inch from my closing left hand. I started, moving my gaze instantly to the grinning José Vasquez.

"Get up," he said with a snicker as he shoved the one single-shot pistol into his belt and pulled out another. "There ain't no time left for praying, but I can't see no sense in making even a fool die on his rump. Now on your feet! *Pronto!*"

Well, I stood, and then with a fixed look and my right hand reaching toward my hind pocket, I started toward him. "Friend Vasquez," I said, suddenly smiling a little and feeling better about things, "let go of the girl and give it up. This day you have been delivered into my hands."

The man was startled, so much so that his jaw flopped

open – and even the Indians took a hurried step or two backward and lifted their weapons a little higher.

"Hold it . . . " Vasquez gurgled as he once again tightened down on Steenie's throat.

"No," I said, still walking, "nor will you continue to abuse my Steenie. Release her, you infernal fiend, and prepare for your Master to impress some new thoughts upon your mind."

As Vasquez's jaws refused to come back together, and as the dusky audience waited spellbound for my own execution, I smiled even wider and drew to a halt some five feet before the vaunted slave trader and my wide-eyed sweetheart.

"Are you ready, you miserable excuse for a human being?" I asked, grinning thinly. "You're a coward through and through, and that's the weakness old Gideon told me you'd have. If folks aren't afraid of you, then you're finished. Well, Steenie's not afraid of you, *Mister* Vasquez, and neither am I! Because you're a *coward*, and I'm calling you."

It was Vasquez's move then, and he made it like the man he thought he was.

It was a pretty good move, too.

But it just wasn't good enough.

He had hardly started to lift his second pistol when Lazarus launched himself from my side, taking dead aim on Vasquez's leg just above the kneecap.

At the same time, my right hand came forward from my rear pocket with the old elm-crotch slingshot that had sealed my betrothal to Christena Bergman. My other hand flicked fast as a snake's head to fit into the sling's worn leather the smooth round stone I had been given moments before, the stone that was the general size and heft of a fire-hardened marble or a cast-iron horse chestnut, the stone that was fittingly native to the high-walled desert canyon.

Thus was I armed.

Vasquez yelled bloody murder as Lazarus clamped down on his leg, and Steenie threw her elbow angrily into his paunchy gut. But as it turned out, I never really needed Steenie's nor the dog's diversionary tactics, not at all. The Lord was with me, and the deed was done almost before it had begun.

Long before Lazarus had clamped teeth on the leg of the startled slave trader, long before Steenie's dainty elbow had driven shoulder-deep into Vasquez's soft solar plexus, my hand had loaded the sling leather, hauled it to full, ear-lobe stretch—and released it with a wicked, whirring "wwhhhrrraaannng!"

The heavenly selected stone took Vasquez squarely between the eyes. His dog-bit yell blended with the thunderous report of his single-shot pistol as his trigger finger jerked to send his shot crashing harmlessly into the earth in front of me. While the blast of the black-powder load was still bounding back and forth between the high cliffs, Steenie jerked free. Vasquez then straightened up, quivered, and slumped at the knees. Then he fell like a rotten tree—trembling and slow, and with a terrible crash that sent the dust puffing even further than my own fall had done only moments before. And when he struck, the slave trader lay cold as the stone with which the good Lord had so deeply impressed his mind.

With some embarrassment, I lifted my gaze from the fallen slave trader to the love-filled but nevertheless dumbfounded stare of Christena Bergman. Nor did I fail to note the almost reverential awe with which the twenty or so Ute warriors were presently regarding me.

"If you'll look," I said carefully, "you'll find that the miserable heathen there on the ground is merely unconscious and likely won't suffer from permanent impairment."

Everyone continued to stare, and so self-consciously I lifted the old slingshot so they could see it better.

There was a universal cry of fear from the Utes, and they would have fled the spot instantly if I had not held up my other hand with the command for them to stop. With abrupt suddenness they did, their eyes wide, and I spoke again.

"Uh . . . actually it has been some time since I fired such a shot from this," I declared, wanting them all to understand. "But it was fairly simple, likely not even of semifinals quality. Certainly it was not such a shot as would have won for me the

'Chief Keokuck' shoot-off, back in Mount Pleasant, Iowa, where Ed and Billie Kitch were judges. Not, at least, two years ago when I actually won it."

Well, the Utes saw that I had said my piece, so still staring, they backed off another step or two, their eyes glued to my slingshot. The chief and the other brave who had flanked the downed Vasquez carefully mounted their ponies, and then as a man the entire group turned horses and spurred frantically back up the canyon.

That left Steenie and I suddenly alone, and neither of us could do much more than stare at the other.

"I . . . I knew you'd come," she whispered, stepping toward me.

"It was a long ride, and . . . well, I took too long."

"Pretty near. When you said you weren't armed, I wanted to break free and thump you one. But my goodness, who'd have ever have thought you were planning on using your . . . er *my* slingshot."

I dropped my eyes. "I . . . I wasn't. It only came to me when I fell on it. I think that was the Spirit, telling me what to do. I . . . Goodness, Miss Steenie, if you ain't a sight for sore eyes."

Now Steenie turned bright red, and her hand went self-consciously to brush a strand of lovely hair from her forehead. "I . . . I surely must be a mess. Jons, I—"

"You look mighty good to me."

"I . . . I do?"

"Better'n anybody I ever saw in my life."

"Just goes to show a person that love is blind. For that matter," she said with a sigh, smiling into my eyes, "you are about the most handsome man I ever laid eyes on."

Steenie came into my arms then, her eyes suddenly alive and dancing . . . and then she batted her long, dark lashes, setting my heart to beating like Perdy's hoofs on a hard-packed trail. Against those eyes I didn't have the chance of a horned toad in heaven—but consarn it, I didn't care, either. I was willing to get lost forever in her love—

Suddenly I felt the gentle nudge of Perdy's velvety muzzle

pushing against my back, forcing me forward against the woman of my dreams. I drew her more closely to me, and in an instant we were holding each other fiercely, our tears flowing freely and our murmured "I love yous" blending over and over together. And while Perdy nuzzled against the two of us, I felt upon my feet the happy thumping of plumed coyote-dog tail—and I knew that Lazarus was pleased, as well.

Truly, I thought, as my arms held the willing and wondrous softness of Steenie Bergman, was I ever a blessed man. The world was a wide and wonderful place, the Lord God of Israel was ruling firmly from His heavenly throne, and the four of us would stand as a witness of that to the end of our days.

And forever after, I knew as I held Steenie close. Forever and ever after, as well.

Epilogue

"Did you have to fight the Indians, Pa? Did you, huh?"

Fondly I ruffled the hair of the small boy and girl who sat spellbound upon my knees—and then I winked at their older sister, who sat on the floor before me.

"Fight them," Steenie answered for me as she turned from the pan where she was cutting apples for a pie to give our needy neighbor. "We very nearly did, Little James, getting away from them. Those poor Indians practically worshiped your father after he wiped out José Vasquez, calling him Heap Chief *Pun-ker-ro*—"

"Tell us what that means, Ma."

"I don't know," she said, giggling, while I frowned at her. "Something like 'The Scrawny Little Man with the Forked Stick and the Go-Fastest Hands in All the World,' or some such nonsense. The way those people pampered your father was an eternal shame, and I was thankful when Gideon finally came and got us out of there."

"Uncle Gideon finally caught up with you?"

"He certainly did," I told them, "just a day later. I thought he'd never get there, I was so tired of being toasted and feasted by the Utes, eating dog and other such delicacies."

"It's a good thing they didn't eat Lazarus," Little James said, looking at the aged tawny brown coyote-dog who was sleeping soundly on the hearth before us. "We wouldn't have anybody to watch over us when we play."

"That's right," I agreed softly, gazing fondly on the elderly canine, who was practically immobilized now from the old gunshot wound that had turned to arthritis after a long and hard-run race. "Besides that, he'd have been way too tough to eat."

"And what about that mean Vasquez?" our daughter Mary Caroline asked. "Did you have to kill him when he awakened?"

"Of course he didn't, Mary Caroline," Steenie answered. "Your father vanquished the powers of evil that day with the one weapon a man such as Vasquez has no defense against—ridicule. The story spread from the Indians outward, the slave trader became a laughingstock wherever he went, and your father's triumph was as complete as Wellington's at Waterloo."

"And do the Indians still love you, Pa?"

I grinned, looking up at Steenie. "I reckon they do, Little Elinor—but they don't love me as much as they love your ma. Never did. Why, old Chief Tavagoop still has a hankering for her, and every time he comes here—"

"If that old fool pinches my arm one more time," Steenie flared, shaking a rolling pin in one hand and putting the other firmly on shapely hip, "then I'm going to take this rolling pin and knock him all the way to kingdom come!"

Wide-eyed, the children stared at their mother. But me? I only grinned as I looked at the beauty of her anger. "Steenie, of a truth it is Tavagoop's only good way of telling you that he approves of what you're eating."

"He's telling me I'm getting fat!"

"Not fat," I grinned. "Just . . . uh, more pleasingly plump."

The rolling pin swooshed closely above my head, the children squealed, and I chuckled. At that instant the door opened, and Old Gideon Monson, the friend of my youth, creaked through.

He was moving steady enough, like always, but slow, very slow, and my heart swelled with worry over him. He did not seem aware of the laboring in his thin old chest that even I could see, or of the aches that surely must be in his stringy old muscles. Or, if he was aware, he never let on. He just allowed his old feet in his worn boots to shuffle forward, and in a miraculous sort of way he followed after them.

"Morning," he groused, teetering toward a chair and plopping himself into it, his walking stick still held before him.

"Morning, good and faithful friend," I smiled. "Have you eaten yet this glorious day?"

Gideon nodded affirmatively but nonetheless kept his eyes fixed firmly on the instantly discovered, rapidly developing apple pie.

"Talk Bible to us, Pa," little James pleaded. "Do it, please?"

Again I ruffled his hair. "Verily I say unto thee, my children," I growled fiercely, "if thou ceaseth not to pester thy father with such frivolity, behold the heavens shall open and an angel shall come down to box thine ears."

"Your own ears, more than likely," Steenie said as she laid the dough over the apples and began pinching the pie edges into shape.

"Amen," Gideon growled. "Amen, brethren and sisters, and amen. Who's the pie for, Miss Steenie?"

Gideon still called her that, in spite of the fact that she was so obviously a Mrs. And Steenie loved him for it, she truly did.

"A needy neighbor . . . " she replied coyly.

"Hummph," Gideon grunted as he pulled himself to his feet. "Fine thing, fixing apple pie and giving the whole blamed thing away. Reckon I'd do better dropping in on the Widow Maria Crost."

"A needy neighbor," Steenie finished, smiling sweetly, "name of Captain Gideon Monson. Unless that same captain's in such a terrible hurry this morning to go visit the lovely Widow Crost that he can't wait for his pie to bake up proper."

Gideon stood still, but a wide grin spread slowly across his wrinkled old face. "I'll be waiting right here, Miss Steenie. You can count on me."

"I always have, dear Gideon," she said, patting his hand. "I always have."

The old man blushed and shuffled his feet, and then abruptly he looked over at me, remembering. "Friend Jons," he croaked, "this Sanpete air must be powerful good for mustangs. Perdy's foal has foaled, herself, this morning. Yes sir, Perdy's a grandma again. The new one's a scrubby little gray colt with stubby neck, hammered head, and the look of eagles in his eye. I thought maybe you might want to get rid of him, he's so dad-blamed ugly."

"Hallelujah," I said as I stood with my excited children in my arms. "I reckon we'd better keep him, if he's that ugly. Shall we go, children, and see this newest wonder that the Lord has sent to bless our family?"

Excitedly they agreed, and Steenie placed the pie in the oven. Then she turned with a secret smile and batted the biggest, darkest-lashed blue eyes in all of Utah Territory at me, setting my heart pounding and reminding me that she too was going to be bringing forth a wondrous addition to our family, a child to replace our little Peter, whom we had laid away to rest the February past.

With a sly wink I set little James down and took my wife's hand. I squeezed it tenderly, and then all of us filed out of our home together.

"Hallelujah," I breathed again as I looked off through the glorious Sanpete morning toward the corral.

"Amen," muttered Steenie Bergman Soderberg as she held tightly to my hand and arm.

And left with the last word, crippled old Lazarus, the scraggly coyote-dog and sometime canine philosopher who was limping silently beside us, shook his head in resignation at the mental condition of the poor fool humans he was bound to live with and protect.

"Aaarrowww," he howled, probably in self-pity—and then he limped off ahead of us to say congratulations to the hard-hoofed grandmother, the beautifully scrubby little old gray mustang mare we still called Perdy.

Historical Note

The Utah War, during which our story takes place, is one of the least understood but most fascinating episodes in Mormon, and American, history. It pitted against each other two forces that, from start to finish, should have been united. One of the fundamental beliefs of members of The Church of Jesus Christ of Latter-day Saints is that the nation known as the United States of America was raised up by the hand of God. Mormons believe that those who founded this nation were inspired and that the Constitution they framed is an inspired document. The Mormons, who had been driven from Illinois in 1846 to settle in the valley of the Great Salt Lake a year later, strongly believed this. In the West they were no longer part of any state in the Union, but they had no desire to break off from the United States. The majority of them were American citizens, and they wanted to remain such.

Therefore, less than two years after they first moved into the Great Basin, the Mormons organized a provisional state government and applied for statehood as the State of Deseret. However, for a host of political reasons, Congress rejected their application, ignored their protests, and organized the Territory of Utah instead.

With a territorial government, the Mormons did not have the right to elect their own officials. Instead, these offices were to be filled by appointments made by the president of the United States.

President Millard Fillmore, acting upon the advice of Colonel Thomas L. Kane, an influential non-Mormon friend of the Latter-day Saints, appointed Brigham Young as governor of the territory. However, the president filled a number of important but lesser offices with politicians from the eastern states. Some of these men had a true desire to serve the people, but many more had their own selfish political ambitions in mind, and they made no attempt to understand the Saints.

Soon after arriving in Utah, three of these men, Chief Justice Lemuel H. Brandenbury, Associate Justice Perry E. Brocchus, and Territorial Secretary Broughton D. Harris, left the territory, angry that the people had not willingly accepted them, and returned to the East, where they spread false reports about the Mormons in Utah. Called by the Mormons and the Eastern press the Runaway Officials, these men claimed, among other things, that they had been compelled to leave Utah because of the lawless and seditious acts of Brigham Young.

Daniel Webster, U.S. secretary of state, investigated, determined that the allegations were false or immaterial, and ordered the three to return West. They refused and resigned, and the issue was dropped.

Meanwhile, the biggest political issue of the 1850s was the question of how much control the federal government should have in determining the domestic affairs of the territories. The issue almost split the Union in the decade before the Civil War. According to the Missouri Compromise of 1820, Congress had the authority to decide whether or not slavery could exist in a territory. After a bitter debate in Congress in 1854, this law was replaced by the Kansas-Nebraska Act. According to this new law, pushed by Stephen A. Douglas and the Democrats, Congress had no right to decide whether slavery could exist in a territory; only the people living in that territory could decide the issue by popular vote. This was called "popular sovereignty," and, though opposed by many, it became law.

Many of the law's opponents linked it with the Mormons and their practice of plural marriage. They hurled this argument at the Democrats: "If the people of Kansas can decide by popular vote if slavery is legal, then surely the Mormons can decide the same question about polygamy by popular vote." Of course, few in the East believed that the Mormons should practice polygamy, so the argument was very powerful.

The Republican Party, organized in 1854, opposed the extension of slavery into the territories and felt that Congress should have power to make slavery illegal. In 1856, when they ran John C. Fremont for the presidency, this was a major plank in their platform. James Buchanan and the Democrats, on the other hand, supported popular sovereignty.

To further their cause and to make slavery appear even worse, crafty Republicans determined to link slavery with polygamy in the minds of the people. Most Americans already considered polygamy a terrible sin, and if it could be linked, in the public eye, with slavery, then both would be made to appear more evil. Consequently, in almost every Republican rally that year, there were banners that read, "The abolishment of slavery and polygamy; the twin relics of barbarism!"

In spite of these contiguous contamination tactics, the Democrats won the election, and James Buchanan was elected president of the United States. However, many times he was accused by others of aiding and encouraging the immoral (as they viewed it) practice of polygamy. This no doubt rankled James Buchanan.

Meanwhile, those appointed to replace the Runaway Officials proved to be better men than their predecessors. As a result, there was little conflict between the Mormons and the federal officials between 1852 and 1855. This situation changed, however, when two new judges were appointed in 1855. One of these was Judge William W. Drummond, and the other was Judge George P. Stiles, an apostate Mormon.

When Drummond, a heavy drinker, an avowed agnostic, and a user of vile and profane language, arrived in Utah, he introduced the woman with him as his wife. Often she even sat with him on the bench. Soon, however, it became known that his *real* wife and family were in Illinois, abandoned, and that the woman with him was a harlot. Since he was adjudicating so strenuously against the "immoral" practice of polygamy, the Mormons were outraged, and they let it be known.

Finally driven to resignation, Drummond returned to the East in a huff in the spring of 1857, soon after James Buchanan took office. Upon his arrival, Drummond made a number of serious allegations against the Mormons. Among other things, he accused them of wholesale murder, immorality, and rebellion against the United States.

At the same time, Judge Stiles forwarded to Washington an affidavit affirming many of Drummond's charges. Thomas S. Twiss, U.S. Indian agent on the Great Plains, felt that the Mormons were gaining too much influence among the Great Plains Indians, so he also wrote and complained. And finally W. M. F. Magraw, a government mail contractor who had been underbid by the Mormons and was angry at them for getting the mail contract from him, wrote Buchanan and made other false charges.

Newspaper editors, knowing that anything abut polygamy or the Mormons was "hot copy," eagerly seized upon these false reports and published them as the true state of affairs in Utah. Some of their stories were outright fabrications, and others were greatly exaggerated. (For example, see the various issues of the New York *Daily Times* of May 1857.) In this manner, fuel was heaped upon the fires of public opinion, which were already burning against the Saints. As a result, the American public was aroused against the "wicked," "immoral," and "rebellious" Mormons, and there was a popular clamor in the North for the government to do something about the "Mormon problem."

In the eyes of many aroused Americans, President Buchanan was neither acting fast enough nor decisively enough in dealing with the Mormons. This view was exemplified by a letter that "Amicus Curia" wrote in 1857 to the editor of the *Daily Times*. Published on the front page on May 27, 1857, the writer says: "Had Fremont been elected, with his anti-polygamy plank in his Presidential platform, you would have seen General Harney out as far as Fort Kearny, a distance of full three hundred miles, with the proper antidote for Mormonism, and a prompt and efficient man en route for Utah to ease GOV. YOUNG of his Gubernatorial honors; but for fear of displeasing the Mormons . . . the whole summer will be spent in talk and . . . feeble, undecided action. . . . Have not the American people the right, and is it not their duty, to demand speedy and decided action on this vital subject?"

Another writer, in the Santa Fe *Weekly Gazette*, stated: "Religious fanaticism, when excited and aroused, is the blindest species of madness, and is regardless of consequences. . . . While we may regret the loss of life that is likely to follow this madness, of these deluded people, yet we cannot but regard their action as a blessing to the cause of truth, for it must result in their extinction as a people in the United States. . . . The day of doom of Mormonism, we trust, is fast approaching."

Of course, the Mormon editors lashed back as best they could. George Q. Cannon, editor of the *Western Standard* in California, wrote: "The editor of the Herald deceives himself and those who believe what he writes, when he says that 'the days of Mormonism at Salt Lake are numbered.' The cannon are not cast, the powder and ball not manufactured, nor the men to use them either born or conceived, that will destroy 'Mormonism.' Mark our words gentlemen, it will live, though all earth and hell array themselves against it."

Goaded by these and other statements and pressures, President Buchanan acted. He did not investigate the charges made by Drummond, Stiles, Magraw, and Twiss at all. He accepted all charges at face value, mobilized 2,500 troops of the United States Army, and appointed a non-Mormon, Alfred Cumming of Georgia, as governor of Utah.

In July, the first troops left Fort Leavenworth on their way to Utah, acting officially as a *posse comitatus* to see that Cumming was properly installed as governor, to preserve the peace, and to see that all federal laws were obeyed by the "rebellious" Mormons.

However, Buchanan did not inform Brigham Young that he had been replaced as governor, nor did he inform the Mormons that he was sending an army west. In fact, he canceled the mail contract to Utah in a deliberate attempt to prevent the Saints from knowing that an army was coming, or why.

With no news but rumors being brought to Utah by returning missionaries and incoming emigrants, the Mormons were left to ferret out the facts of the government expedition for themselves. They quickly learned *about* it, but it was much more difficult for them to ascertain *why* the army was coming.

Because of previous experience with murdering, ravaging, raping, and pillaging mobs in Ohio, Missouri, and Illinois, the Mormons naturally expected the worst. They had been driven from state to state before, even by official armed state militias, and so this threat from the national government was looked upon as the final, ultimate mob. Consequently, the Saints determined to prevent the army from entering the Valley, at whatever the cost.

Historian Leonard J. Arrington writes: "The territorial militia, which was called the Nauvoo Legion, was mustered into full-time service under the leadership of General Daniel H. Wells. This force, consisting of about 3,000 men, was the kind of citizen army that younger officers were inclined to belittle, but which the old professionals never took lightly. As a later observer wrote, it was an 'uncouth, undisciplined, and ragged set of men,' with 'every variety of weapon known to civilized nations,' but it was a group, which in its own habitat, fighting for homes and families, could be ferocious and deadly."

Engaging in guerrilla tactics, the Mormons barricaded Echo Canyon and annoyed and hindered the army in every way possible. Under explicit orders to engage in no pitched battles, groups of Saints destroyed bridges, burned army wagons and supply trains, stampeded and took to the Valley herds of government animals, and burned the grass on the prairies. Without killing or wounding a soldier, they prevented them from entering the colonized part of the territory, forcing the army to spend the winter on Black's Fork, near Fort Bridger.

Men such as Orrin Porter Rockwell, Colonel Robert T. Burton, Major Lot Smith, and Major Ephraim Hanks led these raids, and the accounts in our story are taken from their personal and official records.

It was a frustrating time for the army. Colonel Alexander (known as "the Old Woman"), who was never officially in command, was nevertheless all alone at the front. Concerned by reports of Mormon preparations for war; beleaguered by the guerrilla fighters who were constantly harrassing his troops, destroying his supplies, and stealing his animals; and pushed by anxious [in]subordinates, Alexander finally decided that the safest and surest way into the valley was to avoid Echo Canyon altogether.

Accordingly, under Jim Bridger's direction, he pushed up Ham's Fork, intending to come around and down by the Bear River. But the command, not moving fast enough, finally bogged down as the weather turned foul and then worsened. Numerous accounts of dying animals and struggling soldiers bear evidence to the trial Colonel Alexander and his men endured just getting back to where they had started. And they had lost an entire month going absolutely nowhere. At this point, Albert Sydney Johnston finally arrived to take command, and the only thing left for this angry commander to do was to order his frustrated and exhausted men into winter quarters.

The Mormons, with the help of their God and his weather, had obviously won the first round.

The only soldier allowed to enter the Valley in 1857 was Captain Stewart Van Vliet, who came to arrange for supplies for the advancing army. Courteously received by Brigham Young, he could give no suitable answer as to why the army was coming. Hence the Saints were even more convinced than ever of the "mob" intentions of the army.

But though Van Vliet's mission failed there, it was a huge success in another way. The captain, after spending several days carefully observing conditions in Utah, came away convinced that the Mormons were a good but misunderstood people, not guilty of the crimes charged against them. He was also convinced that the army could not beat the Mormons at war in their own mountain strongholds. Heading east, he expressed these views freely, and word of them began to spread.

President Buchanan had been riding high on the tide of public opinion when he called out the troops to go west, but he soon learned that public opinion is capricious and unpredictable. When by winter the army hadn't accomplished anything but the spending of huge amounts of money and being embarrassed by a ragtag militia, the American taxpayers began to squirm uncomfortably. Shortly, after further "reflection," influential Americans began to publicly criticize the government for sending an army west in the first place.

By January of 1858, congressional leaders and newspaper editors had taken up the cause and were pressuring the leaders of the government to end the "war" and the resultant waste of money and manpower. President Buchanan, acutely aware of the shift in public opinion, began looking for an easy but respectable way out of the mess he and others had created.

At this point Colonel Thomas L. Kane, still the Mormon's friend, was asked by a messenger from Brigham Young to go to Washington to speak to Buchanan in the Saints' behalf. Finding the administration anxious to get the whole affair settled amicably, Colonel Kane left Washington and came to Utah via the isthmus of Panama and California. There he explained to the Mormons that the army was not to be a mob but was sent as an assurance that Alfred Cumming would be accepted as governor.

Meanwhile, Governor Cumming and the other federal appointees had spent the winter with the army at their temporary settlement called Camp Scott, near the remains of Fort Bridger. It was not a comfortable camp, and it was described by Charles A. Scott: "Rather tough times now, not enough to eat and blest with a ravenous appetite: Intensely cold weather, Sentinels have to be relieved every hour to keep from being frost bitten, as it is, when they come off post, they look like venerable patriarchs, their breath being frozen in their beards, eyebrows and even eyelashes. When we are not on guard, six or eight of us have to take a wagon and go out daily to the Cedars about four miles from Camp and haul in a load of wood by hand (because the animals are gone to Henry's Fork for forage)."

After meeting with the Mormons in Utah, Colonel Kane sped east to meet with Governor Cumming; and at the Colonel's request, Cumming came back to Utah with him.

Alfred Cumming was surprised at what he found. Not only were the vast majority of the Saints a sincere, devout, and orderly people who wanted only to be left alone in peace, but they were willing to abandon their homes, burn everything, and move south rather than turn their belongings over to the army.

In fact, even while he watched, all Mormons living from Salt Lake City north were actually leaving. More than thirty-five thousand men, women, and children ultimately packed their things into wagons and headed south, some to Provo and other Utah County areas, and others even farther south. Their abandoned homes, with straw piled high against them, awaited the torch should Albert Sydney Johnston's army force its way into the Valley, and Governor Cumming was astounded to see this.

Finally, he was also astounded to discover that the Mormons were perfectly willing to accept him as their governor and would give him every iota of respect that he actually earned and deserved.

While these things were happening in Utah, opposition to the "war" continued to grow in the East. More and more it was becoming obvious that the war was politically and economically motivated and had very little to do with the Mormons. The main schemer in this was Secretary of War John B. Floyd, an avowed secessionist who used the facade of a Mormon rebellion to scatter U. S. forces and arms preparatory to the impending Confederate Rebellion. Further, in later Congressional investigation, it was shown that he, in cahoots with William H. Russell of the firm Russell, Majors and Waddell, had defrauded the government and others of over $7 million in connection with the freighting of military goods to the West. Truly was it called a "contractor's war." Under an increasing barrage of criticism from all sides, and before he had received Governor Cumming's report, President Buchanan appointed a peace commission to go to Utah carrying a proclamation of pardon. This proclamation stated that though the Mormons were guilty of treason and sedition, all would be pardoned who would submit themselves to the authority of the federal government.

The Mormons, always sustaining the Constitution and the government, laughed this document to scorn. Yet Brigham Young and the other leaders, anxious to end the conflict, saw the value of it. Knowing that it was the administration's attempt to save face, and knowing too who his own people really were, Brigham Young signed it. In doing so, he said: "As to the gentlemen Commissioners, they have no power to investigate the past, but (are) to inquire if we will submit to the constitution and laws of the United States. We always have, and always expect to. I have no (reputation to uphold) – no pride to gratify – no vanity to please. If a man comes from the moon and says he will pardon me for kicking him in the moon yesterday, I don't care about it, I'll accept of his pardon." (*Comprehensive History of the Church* 4:433.)

Meanwhile, the move south continued, ultimately lasting from March until about the middle of May. Governor Cumming, on one trip south with Brigham Young, passed about 800 wagons in one day. "Is there not some way to stop the moving?" he asked the Prophet, to which Brigham Young replied that if the troops were withdrawn from the territory, the people would stop moving.

John R. Young, who was returning to Utah from a mission to Hawaii, described the move south as follows:

> At Parowan, two hundred miles south of Salt Lake City, we encountered a scene that I shall never forget. I remember distinctly the "Exodus," as it was called, from Nauvoo, when sixteen thousand souls left their homes and commenced that marvelous journey of fourteen hundred miles to the unknown valley of the Salt Lake. But that exodus was like a small rivulet by the side of a mighty river when compared with the thirty-five thousand men, women and children that we now met in one continuous line of travel.
>
> Horses, oxen, and cows were harnessed or yoked to wag-

ons and carts; and one family by the name of Syphuis, was moving their effects on a handcart drawn by a pair of yearling steers. Mothers and children walked along as merrily as if going to a corn husking; each family moving its little bunch of cows and flock of sheep, and all starting on the journey to Sonora, in Mexico, or some other place.

At times we were compelled to drive our wagon for miles outside the beaten road, everywhere hearing and seeing evidences that increased my gentile companion's wonderment of the marvelous power held by Brigham Young over this people.

A pioneer teenager penned the following description:

We packed all we had into father's one wagon and waited for the command to leave. At night we lay down to sleep, not knowing when word would come of the army which we thought was coming to destroy us. . . . There were seven of us children in the family.

We put away all our playthings, for the days found us so frightened that all we did was follow father and mother from place to place, looking into their faces for a word of comfort and a look of cheer. One morning father told us that we should leave with a large company in the evening. He said little more. There were packing and the making of bread.

Along in the middle of the day father scattered leaves and straw in all the rooms and I heard him say: "Never mind, little daughter, this house has sheltered us, it shall never shelter them . . ." I did not understand him then, but as we went out of the yard and joined all the other people on the main road I learned for the first time that the city would be burned should the approaching army attack the people.

That night we camped on Willow Creek in the south end of the valley, and at ten o'clock every soul with bowed head knelt in prayer to God. As I dropped to sleep I heard my mother whispering that the Lord had heard our prayers and that our homes should not be burned. I cried and cried, but at last I dropped to sleep.

There is no doubt that it was a trying and uncertain time for the Saints. Many truly struggled, but others were full of faith and gave the army very little attention. John Pulsipher recorded in his diary:

> The U.S. army East of us have wintered very well, & are threatening to come upon us & make a final end of all that will not join them. Truly this is a trying time—Destruction stares us in the face which every way we turn—They that have not the Holy Ghost the Comforter in them, are beginning to tremble. The prophet Brigham is as calm as if there was no danger—says *move South and see the Salvation of God*. And almost the entire people say Amen to it & are as happy as were the children of Israel led by Moses, anciently when they passed thro the red Sea.

So the Saints went south, difficulties were finally ironed out, and, as a final agreement between the peace commissioners and the Mormons, the army was allowed to come into the Valley. According to the agreement, they were to pass through the city unmolested, providing that they not stop and that they camp at least forty miles away. The commission forwarded a letter to that effect to General Johnston, who, upon receiving the news, "took off his hat with the insignia of a general on it, threw it on the ground, stamped on it, and said: 'Damn such a government. Here we starved and froze all winter, and now that we have these (Mormons) right where we want them, they are going to get off without shedding one drop of blood. Damn such a government.' "

Nevertheless, on June 26, 1858, the army finally, and very, very peaceably, entered Salt Lake City. A correspondent for the *Atlantic Monthly*, traveling with the army, described the scene as follows: "It was one of the most extraordinary scenes that have occurred in American history. All day long, from dawn until after sunset, the troops and trains poured through the city, the utter silence of the streets being broken only by the music of the military bands, the monotonous tramp of the regiments, and the rattle of the baggage wagons. . . . The stillness was so profound that during the intervals between the passage of the columns, the monotonous gurgle of the city creek struck every ear."

And gentile editors back East, watching the unfolding drama with amazement, made such comments as:

> Whatever our opinions may be of Mormon morals and Mormon manners, there can be no question that this voluntary abandonment of forty thousand people, of homes created by wonderful industry in the midst of trackless wastes, after years of hardships and persecution, is something from which no one who has a particle of sympathy with pluck, fortitude and constancy can withhold his admiration. Right or wrong, sincerity thus attested is not to be sneered at. True or false, a faith to which so many men and women prove their loyalty by such sacrifice, is a force in the world. . . . When people abandon their homes to plunge with women and children into a wilderness to . . . they know not where, they give a higher proof of courage than if they fought for them.

Thus concluded the Utah War. As historians Richard D. Poll and Ralph W. Hansen put it, at an estimated cost of between 20 million and 40 million dollars, the United States Army received field experience and lessons in geography. The freighting firm of Russell, Majors and Waddell made enough profit to become objects of later Congressional investigation. With "Buchanan's Blunder," the Democratic administration complicated its already difficult political situation, and Buchanan ended up serving only the one term. And while Alfred Cumming became governor of Utah Territory, Brigham Young remained leader of the people.

Though *In Search of Steenie Bergman*, set in the midst of this conflict, is fictional, we used accurate historical information in the book's setting. Ephraim Hanks's exploits, spiritual and otherwise, are documented in his biography, listed below. Lot Smith's adventures were also recorded by himself and published years later.

An interesting verification of Lot Smith's account is given by William F. Cody, who later became famous as Buffalo Bill. In 1857, at twelve years of age, he was a qualified teamster but had had to secure his mother's permission to travel west with Lew Simpson. His account in *The Great Salt Lake Trail* of Smith's capture of the government train is fascinating and adds the detail that Smith had earlier traveled with the train for a few days, posing as a teamster. Cody also recorded that he admired the Mormons for their pluck.

Orrin Porter Rockwell led the first raid on the troops at Pacific Springs, which failed only when the bell mule got caught in the brush. And, with the exception of the Mountain Meadows Massacre, which is not part of this story, the shooting in Echo Canyon took one of the only two lives lost by bloodshed during the war. The other life, that of the trader Yates, was apparently taken by Bill Hickman somewhere near the head of Echo Canyon. Dan Jones verified this murder, and his statement is published in *Forty Years Among the Indians*, also listed below.

In the Valley, weapons and munitions factories flourished as described, and martial law kept people from traveling freely in the mountains. Emigrants, who literally traveled westward side-by-side with the government trains and troops, pushed ahead and arrived in the Valley early, and the songs recorded in our story are two of the many that were sung by the two factions.

Slave trading between the Indians and the Mexicans was a terrible problem for Brigham Young and the Mormons during the early years of Utah, and President Young finally pushed a law through the territorial legislature, making it illegal for Mexican traders to even enter the territory. It is unknown whether or not any Mormon women or children were ever sold into slavery, but not a few vanished at the hands of Indians, and their whereabouts was never again discovered. It is very possible that these became slaves.

Finally, it was quite surprising for the authors to discover that the Saints, in their journals and other writings, called the government by the sobriquets "uncle" and "uncle Sam." We had assumed this to be a more recent appellation and so have no idea where it actually originated.

Our research led us to many sources, and for the convenience of the reader who may wish to pursue further study of the Utah War, they are listed below.

Alber, Sarah Pulsipher. "History." *Pioneer Journals*. Dugway, Utah: Pioneer Press.

Alter, J. Cecil. *James Bridger: Trapper, Frontiersman, Scout and Guide*. Columbus, Ohio: Long's College Cook Co., 1951.

Arrington, Leonard J. "Mormon Finance and the Utah War." *Utah Historical Quarterly*, 20 (1952): 219–37.

_______. "The Utah War." Typescript in authors' possession.

Bailey, L. R. *Indian Slave Trade in the Southwest*. Los Angeles: Westernlore Press, 1973.

Baily, Paul D. *Holy Smoke: A Dissertation on the Utah War*. Los Angeles: Westernlore Books, 1978.

Bancroft, Hubert Howe. *History of Utah*. San Francisco: The History Co., 1899.

Berrett, William E. *The Restored Church*. 15th ed. Salt Lake City: Deseret Book Co., 1955.

Brooks, Juanita. *On The Mormon Frontier: The Diary of Hosea Stout*. 2 vols. Salt Lake City: University of Utah Press, 1964.

Carter, Kate B. *Heart Throbs of the West*. 12 vols. Salt Lake City: Daughters of the Utah Pioneers, 1939–1951.

Carter, Kate B. *Our Pioneer Heritage*. 12 vols. Salt Lake City: Daughters of the Utah Pioneers, 1958–1969.

Carter, Kate B. *Treasures Of Pioneer History*. 12 vols. Salt Lake City: Daughters of the Utah Pioneers, 1952–1963.

Cheney, Thomas E., ed. *Mormon Songs from the Rocky Mountains*. Austin: University of Texas Press, 1968.

Cody, William F. *The Adventures of Buffalo Bill*. New York and London: Harper & Brothers, 1904.

Cooley, Everet L. "The Utah War." Unpublished master's thesis, University of Utah. Salt Lake City, 1947.

Flake, Dennis D. "A Study Of Mormon Resistance During the Utah War, 1857–1858." Unpublished master's thesis, Brigham Young University. Provo, Utah, 1975.

Furniss, Norman F. *The Mormon Conflict, 1850–1859*. New Haven, Conn.: Yale University Press, 1966.

Gottfredson, Peter. *Indian Depredations in Utah*. Salt Lake City: Merlin G. Christensen, 1969.

Gove, Jesse A. *The Utah Expedition, 1857–1858*. Concord: New Hampshire Historical Society, 1928.

Hafen, LeRoy R., and Ann W. Hafen, eds. "Diary of Captain Phelps."

The Far West and The Rockies Historical Series, vol. 8. Glendale, Calif.: Arthur H. Clark Co., 1958.

———. "Documentary Account of the Utah Expedition." *The Far West and the Rockies Historical Series*, vol. 8. Glendale, Calif.: Arthur H. Clark Co., 1958.

Hanks, Sydney A. and Ephraim K. Hanks. *Scouting for the Mormons on the Great Frontier*. Salt Lake City: Deseret News Press, 1948.

Inman, Henry, and Cody, William F. *The Great Salt Lake Trail*. Williamstown, Mass.: Corner House Publishers, 1978.

"Journal History of the Church of Jesus Christ of Latter-day Saints." 1857–1858. Salt Lake City: L.D.S. Church Historian's Office.: Salt Lake City, Utah.

Jenson, Andrew, comp. *Church Chronology: A Record of Important Events*. 2nd ed. Salt Lake City: Deseret News Press, 1899.

Jones, Daniel W. *Forty Years Among the Indians*. Salt Lake City: Juvenile Instructor, 1890.

Langley, Harold D., ed. *To Utah with the Dragoons and Glimpses of Life in Arizona and California 1858–1859*. Salt Lake City: University of Utah Press, 1974.

Lamar, Howard R., ed. *The Reader's Encyclopedia of the American West*. New York: Thomas Y. Crowell Co., 1977.

Larson, Gustive O. *Outline History of Territorial Utah*. 3rd ed. Provo, Utah: Brigham Young University Press, 1972.

McAllister, John D.T. "Diary." Typescript at Brigham Young University, Provo, Utah.

Poll, Richard D. and Ralph W. Hansen. "Buchanan's Blunder: the Utah War, 1857–1858." *Military Affairs*, 25 (1961): 121–31.

Pulsipher, John. "Diary." Typescript at Brigham Young University, Provo, Utah.

Roberts, B. H. *A Comprehensive History of The Church of Jesus Christ of Latter-day Saints*. 6 vols. Provo, Utah: Brigham Young University Press, 1965.

Schindler, Harold. *Orrin Porter Rockwell, Man of God, Son of Thunder*. Salt Lake City: University of Utah Press, 1966.

Smith, Lot. "The Echo Canyon War: Lot Smith's Narrative." *The Contributor*, 4 (1882–1883): 27–29, 47–50, 167–69, 224–26.

Tracy, Albert. "Journal of Captain Albert Tracy." *Utah Historical Quarterly*, vol. 13 (1945).

Tyler, Daniel. *History of the Mormon Battalion*. Salt Lake City: Juvenile Instructor Press, 1885.

Vetterli, Richard *Mormonism, Americanism and Politics*. Salt Lake City: Ensign Publishing Co., 1961.

Whitney, Orson F. *History of Utah*. 4 vols. Salt Lake City: George Q. Cannon and Sons Co., 1904.

Wells, Junius F. (Vaux). "The Echo Canyon War." *The Contributor*, 3 (1882): 50–54, 84–86, 102–5, 146–49, 177–79, 215–17, 270–74, 296–99, 339–43, 380–83.

The Bishop's Horse Race

The Bishop's Horse Race

Blaine M. Yorgason
Brenton G. Yorgason

Bookcraft
Salt Lake City, Utah

Library of Congress Catalog Card Number: 79-54894

ISBN 0-88494-385-2

Printed in the United States of America

10 9 8 7 6 5 4 3 2 1

Contents

Introduction

The setting for *The Bishop's Horse Race* is Utah Territory in the summer of 1888. Historically, besides the entire nation being hotter than a burnt boot, the eastern United States was still recovering financially from a devastating late-spring blizzard. Benjamin Harrison had just been nominated by the Republicans to run against Grover Cleveland, Louisa May Alcott had died, and Belva Ann Lockwood had been nominated for President of the United States by the Equal Rights Party at its convention in Des Moines, Iowa.

In Utah, where the great drought of the nineties was just beginning, the Mormon Church, whose President, John Taylor, had recently died in exile, was reeling under the Edmunds-Tucker Act. This act, passed by Congress the previous March, added to the Edmunds law of 1882 to provide that—

1. polygamy was a felony;
2. polygamy was the same as unlawful cohabitation;
3. no polygamist could vote;
4. no polygamist could hold public office;
5. no polygamist could serve on a jury;
6. The Church of Jesus Christ of Latter-day Saints was disincorporated;
7. the Perpetual Emigration Fund was dissolved;
8. female suffrage was abolished;
9. children of polygamous marriages were disinherited;
10. all Church funds and properties were escheated to the government.

In addition to the above, polygamists themselves reeled when two federal judges held that separate indictments could be brought against a polygamist for each and every time he appeared in the proximity of one of his wives. Some were fined over twenty thousand dollars each on separate three-hundred-dollar charges, all chalked up within the space of a few hours or days. The judges also ruled that wives had to testify against their husbands; they imprisoned those who refused; and they allowed the children to accompany their mothers to the pen, where all were classified as jailbirds. To combat this situation, Church leaders counseled the minority of their members who were living the law of plural marriage to hide out, and elaborate schemes, codes and hiding places were devised to enable members to avoid the long arm of what they considered to be an unjust law. The circumstances depicted in *The Bishop's Horse Race* occurred as a direct result of this atmosphere of fight and flight.

Besides polygamists and federal officials, there were several other elements in Utah in 1888, two of which figure in our story. Among the Mormons were many who were inactive, "Jack-Mormons" they were occasionally called. Many of these, not polygamist at all, found themselves suffering for a principle they weren't even involved in. To ease the pressure and to gain favor with the Feds, it was not infrequent for these people to "spy" on their polygamous neighbors, and occasionally to participate in the "polyg hunts" or "cohab parties" conducted by the territorial marshal and his deputies. These people, of course, caused the polygamists much distress.

The second of the two additional elements dealt with in the story is the outlaw element, those who were using the rugged country of Eastern Utah, known even then as Robbers' Roost, as a hideout and base for their nefarious operations. These men quite naturally carried guns. But outlaws weren't the only ones who went around armed. In a land and a time when most men carried weapons, and when they were essential to survival, violence seemed almost to be a way of life. When weapons and duels were the accepted means of settling disputes, among Congressmen as well as among highwaymen, when the July 23, 1889, seventy-five-round, bare-knuckle fight between John L. Sullivan and Jake Kilrain was billed as the world's greatest sporting event, and when violence, especially in the West, was so casual and off-hand, it is not surprising to learn that Mormons, too, occasionally dealt with each other in physical ways. The remarkable thing, when one considers the buffetings the Mormons received from those around and among them, is that as a people they restrained themselves as frequently and as well as they did.

Now to the story itself, which we hastily admit is fictitious in much of its detail. Still, it should be understood that the story is based upon actual experiences of men and women who recorded in their journals what they saw and felt. A man who was serving as a bishop actually did run his giant horse in such a race, and he ran it for the reasons specified in our story. The raid by the marshals is written as described by those who experienced it, the appearance of the strange old man was also recorded, President Taylor made the statement attributed to him, and the toast made by Hans Weegin is a direct quote of a toast made by Jedediah M. Grant, counselor to President Brigham Young.

In addition, fast days at that time were held on Thursdays, some women got around to washing their hair at least once every three or four years, tithing was paid in kind, bedbugs and lice were nearly as plentiful as beard-bugs, most polygamous husbands (who wore the beards that beard-bugs lived in) did their best to love all of their wives equally, the wives did their best to appreciate all the above arrangements, young people fell into and out of love, and soap and milk were made in the back yard rather than bought from the supermarket.

In short, times have changed. Even so, much of the story you are about to read is, for the most part, occasionally somewhat . . . well, you decide how much of it is true. And while you are deciding, we hope you have as much fun with it as we did.

1

The Mud Hen

The sound of a horse's hooves being sucked out of sticky mud drifted loudly across the late afternoon stillness. The rain had stopped, but still the air was heavy and threatening. The water had puddled in the bottom of the ditch where the bishop lay, and though it was mid-June, he found himself shivering uncontrollably.

Carefully he lifted his eyes to peer through the water-beaded grass which arched above him, trying to determine from one tiny patch of sky the complexion of the whole afternoon. Yet the grayness told him nothing, and he shivered again as a stream of icy water broke loose from the grass and cascaded onto the small of his unprotected back.

Again the sound of the horse came to his ears, this time closer, and desperately he pushed himself deeper into the mud, hoping and praying that he might remain undetected.

In his mind's eye the bishop could see vividly the man on the horse. Hebron Clawson, United States deputy marshal, would be sitting astride his ancient and ugly piebald gelding. He would have his slicker on, though it wouldn't be helping much, being so full of holes as it was. His drooping hat would be more droopy than ever, and his well-worn boots were probably filled with water from brushing through the nearly-ready-to-cut alfalfa. His foul-smelling cigar would of course be in his mouth, but more than likely it would be unlighted, simply because the rain collecting in his yellowed mustaches would have doused it.

Eternal minutes dragged along, and now the only sound coming to the bishop's ears was the constant but irregular dripping of water into the ditch. With effort he restrained an impulse to rise up for a careful look around. He might make it, but then he might not, too. He knew Deputy Clawson too well to take the chance. Far too well. True it was that he had a shoddy appearance, and true it was also that he cared little for the clothes he wore or the animals he rode, for these things were merely necessary tools to aid him in his job. But that job, the job Deputy Clawson did with untiring zeal each day of his life, was done with nothing at all that resembled shoddiness or carelessness.

For Hebron Clawson was a manhunter, or perhaps more appropriately he was a polygamist hunter, and he was very probably the best polyg-hunter in the entire Territory of Utah. For that reason alone the bishop lay quietly in the bottom of the ditch.

Slowly the afternoon dripped along. The rain had started up again, a slow cold drizzle that did nothing but make everything just a bit more miserable than it had been before, and the bishop groaned inwardly at the thoughts of another two or three hours in the bottom of the ditch. His legs were now cramping from being still so long in the cold and wet, and it was agony trying to keep from rolling into a sitting position to knead his screaming muscles.

Off in town a dog barked, a lonesome kind of bark that was more a howling, and the man in the ditch thought of his own loneliness. True it was that he was the bishop, the supposed spiritual leader of the more than seven hundred citizens of his ward and community. And true it was also that he had three wives and fourteen children. Yet still he was lonely, with an aching kind of feeling within him that was impossible to explain or even to understand. He remembered well the day that John Taylor had discussed with him his new calling as bishop, and President Taylor had told him then that it would be the most lonely position he would ever have. How right the prophet had been! Always he was surrounded by people, and yet always he was lonely, for none of them could know of his feelings.

And add to that the polygamy problem. Three wives, piles of loving children, three comfortable homes, and here he was lying in the bottom of a miserable ditch with icy water his only loving companion. Where was the justice? Where was the—?

The nickering of the horse was so close and came with such suddenness that the bishop literally jumped, and as he cursed himself for dreaming he listened as the horse moved slowly in his direction. Silently he held his breath and pushed himself deeper into the mud, pressing even more tightly against the bank where he would be hidden by the overhanging grass. The sound of the horse was now directly above him. With half his mind he wondered how he had been discovered, while with the other half he wondered what he was going to do next. How would his family get along without him if he were in prison? How would the members of the ward—?

With a grunt the horse lunged across the ditch directly above the hidden bishop, and as it strained upward one of its hooves slipped on the mud bank and crashed to the bottom, striking the bishop a glancing blow to his shoulder.

The bishop, tensed anyway, let out an involuntary cry of pain as the hoof hit him. Instantly he realized his mistake and lunged to his feet to run.

The marshal's horse, unaware that anything but a ditch was beneath it, saw the man suddenly materialize at its side. In terror the animal rolled its eyes, laid back its ears, and lashed out with its hind feet in a vicious buck. In the next instant the gelding was fleeing headlong across the field, taking the marshal away from the apparition behind it as rapidly as possible.

Marshal Clawson, his reputation as the most able polyg-hunter in central Utah at stake, sawed the reins desperately against the neck of his fear-crazed horse. Over his shoulder he could see the most famous polygamist in Sanpete County slipping, skidding and sliding toward freedom. Blasted horse! If he hadn't needed it so badly the marshal would have made the animal into instant buzzard bait. Trouble was, it was a long walk home without his horse, and the marshal was not a walker. To his way of thinking, if a job couldn't be done from the back of a horse, then such job ought not to be done. So he held his drawn pistol in one hand, yanked on the reins with the other, and cursed his horse, the rain, and his luck.

The bishop, his lungs feeling as if they were about to burst, pushed himself as rapidly as possible across the alfalfa field toward town. He had no idea where he was going, except as far as possible from the deputy and from the muddy field. Problem was, if he went to one of his homes, that would be exactly where the deputy would look for him. If he went to anyone else's home, there were two things to worry about. The first was that any individual who helped him would be aiding and abetting a known criminal—namely, him. The second thing was that he wasn't certain at all whom he could trust. After all, the reward money on his head was a sizable thing. Fact is, more than once he'd wished there was a way that he could turn himself in just so he could collect it and pay a couple of his bills.

Marshals! Polygamy! Criminals! What a farce this whole thing was! The Constitution of the United States was supposed to grant him freedom of religion. Exercising that freedom, he had done as the leaders of the Church had commanded him and had taken more than one wife—three, to be exact—just like men in the Old Testament had done.

Then the government, bless its political and puritanical heart, had taken upon itself the role of tyrannical monitor of the Mormon religion. All kinds of measures and bills had been introduced and passed in Congress, and good Mormons who had always supported the principle of obedience not only to the law of God but also to the law of the land, suddenly found themselves outside the law and branded as criminals. It was a fine mess—as fine a mess as any he had ever seen—and the good bishop found himself right in the thick of it, playing the role of a fugitive rather than the role of husband, father, financier, and bishop like he ought to be doing. Why, if the marshals would let him alone, then—

The sound of the rapidly approaching horse forced his thoughts back to the precariousness of his present situation, and as he glanced over his shoulder he suddenly knew that he needn't worry about where he was going to flee. The question now, he knew, was no longer if he was going to be captured, but when, and how easy he should make it for the marshal. For that worthy had finally pulled his horse under control, turned it, and was even now fanning its rump with his reins, urging it to greater speed as he flew toward the bishop.

"Soderberg!" he yelled. "Hold up right there! I got this hogleg trained right on the middle of yer yellow back, and if ya don't rein up I'll blow a hole in ya so big your whole blasted ward can drive their buggies through it!"

The bishop, glancing back, could see the pistol all right, but he knew it wasn't aimed directly at anything, not the way that gelding was humping and sliding through the mud and the alfalfa. Still, if Clawson decided to shoot, he could get lucky, and the bishop didn't like the idea of going to the next costume ball dressed as a sieve. Some folks already claimed that he had holes in his head, and there was no point in going out of his way to prove them right.

The explosion of a .45 suddenly thundered in the bishop's ears, and in the same instant he felt a tug at his sleeve and heard the *whap* as the slug whipped past him.

"Oh no," he groaned. "Clawson is shooting for real! I reckon I'd best—"

Another explosion roared in his ears, much closer, though again it was a miss, and he looked over his shoulder just in time to see the marshal's ugly gelding, flecked with mud and foam, come thundering down upon him. The bishop tried to dodge back, to get out of the way, but his feet were as much out of control as were those of the horse, and in an instant he was knocked sprawling into the mud and the alfalfa.

Deputy Clawson, so close to his prey, now suddenly found himself being carried once more in the wrong direction. Hauling on the reins, he looked back in time to see the bishop struggle to his feet, wipe the mud from his face, and stagger off in another direction.

"Confounded beast!" Clawson shouted, whipping his animal once more with his reins. "Git on around there! Most awkward blamed cayuse I ever been astride of. Come nightfall, you mangy critter, and you'll be buzzard meat for sure.

"Soderberg, blast yer Mormon hide! Hold up there or you'll be the deadest dang bishop in all of Sanpete County. Thunderation if I ever saw anybody with as much run in 'em as you've got. Yer yellow streak must be three-quarters of a mile wide just on yer shoulders, and I reckon it get wider as it goes down. All gurgle and no guts! That's what I said before, and that's what I say now.

"Git up, horse! Git them feet under you and git going! Blasted critter's as awkward as a blind bear in a bramble patch. Thunderation, Soderberg, hold up there, I say!"

Bishop Soderberg, cold, wet, tired, and very, very sore, glanced back to see Deputy Clawson on his piebald gelding barreling down on him once again. And suddenly, for the first time since he had been made bishop, the proverbial patience that was supposed to be one of his never-ending virtues climbed on its own pony and galloped off, leaving the bishop alone with his temper and Deputy Clawson.

Now it must be understood that Bishop Jons Soderberg was not a small man, not in the size of his family, not in dreams, not in acquisitions, and certainly not in physical bulk. Fact is, folks in town liked to say that he was big enough to hunt bear with a switch, and likely they weren't far wrong. Of a weekend he'd go to church, conduct the meetings, and then race the young boys home, carrying a cedar post for a handicap. Ofttimes the older sisters would shake their heads in disgust at such goings on, but that didn't slow the bishop down, at least not so's a body would notice. Why, one Sunday he even packed his two counselors home, one sitting astride each of his shoulders, and those two holding that cedar post above his head. So when it is said that if he put his heart to moving something, it usually moved, that ought to be accepted as known fact.

The other thing that ought to be understood is that Bishop Soderberg was by nature a peaceable man, not too easily riled. His calling as the bishop made him even more inclined toward peace, and so despite his size he was known as one who walked away from fighting. In fact, if the truth be known, there were some who were not even that kind. They simply called him a flat-out coward. Marshal Clawson was one of those, and he sincerely believed that the bishop was indeed that—a coward, pure and simple.

That was why, when the bishop skidded to a halt and turned to face the deputy, warning bells did not go off in the deputy's mind. And that was a shame, too, for up to this point the only mud the United States deputy marshal had on him was what his horse had splattered on his legs.

And so now Deputy Clawson grinned, for there was the polygamist bishop, Jons Soderberg, standing there waiting for him, willing to surrender and further the legend the marshal knew was building in the Territory about himself. Only again his blasted horse was moving too fast to stop when it was supposed to, and it was still humping along at a pretty good clip when it reached the fugitive. That was when Marshal Clawson first saw the look of anger and determination showing beneath the mud on the bishop's face. Then it was that the warning bells rang, but by then it was way too late for warnings to do any good—any good at all.

For the bishop, suddenly and unexpectedly, reached out and took hold of the reins of the still-moving piebald on which rode the hapless marshal. With a mighty heave the bishop hauled down on those reins, pulling the gelding's head down almost to the ground. That, of course, stopped the front end of that horse from going anywhere. Trouble was, the hind end of the animal was still set on traveling, and it continued to do so, straight up into the air and on over the top of its buried head.

"Anti-I-over!" shouted Bishop Soderberg as the piebald completed its flip with an awkward and heavy *kersplatt* into the mud of the alfalfa field.

"Eeeeyyyyiiiii!" shouted Deputy Clawson, who suddenly had all options but one removed from his bag of choices. Whereas a moment before he had been about to arrest the most wanted polyg in the county, he now found himself airborne. He flailed his arms and his legs in a vain attempt to lengthen his flight or soften his landing, not caring very much which. Nothing worked, however, and with a *kersploosh* he did a belly-flop in the mud, where he slid to a halt some twenty feet from his still-struggling horse.

For a few seconds he fought to regain his breath. When it returned he started searching for his dignity, which had also been knocked from him. Then, just as he was getting to his feet, a voice behind and above him brought him to a dead stop.

"Deputy Clawson," the bishop said quietly, "reckon if I were you I'd hold it right there. One false move and I'll blow a hole in you so big my whole ward will be able to drive their buggies through it."

Slowly the marshal turned to look, and he felt something within him shrivel up and die when he saw Bishop Soderberg perched on top of his mud-covered horse with the marshal's gun in his hand and a grin on his face.

"Deputy," he continued, "seems to me I ought to do something about terminating this relationship of ours. We just can't go on meeting like this. I mean, what'll folks say and all?"

Slowly then the bishop lifted up the pistol until it was trained on the marshal.

"Soderberg, no! Don't shoot! I wasn't going to kill you! I swear it! I never did aim to hit you! Only scare you into stopping, that was all I wanted, that was all I . . . "

The bishop, as though he heard nothing of the deputy's wailings, continued to sight along the barrel of the pistol.

"Yep, just like I thought. The barrel on this weapon is bent, and the whole thing is covered with mud and dirt. Deputy, you ought to be ashamed, representing the U.S. government with a weapon in such deplorable condition as this one is. Why, I'm of a mind to report you to Marshal Dyer in Salt Lake City for carelessness.

"Of course, I'm a mite careless myself, being caught out here on a day like this without a slicker or a horse. Still, that is no one's fault but my own, as I left my home in much haste, fearing a real bad man was after me. Why, I reckon we can both see what a foolish notion that one was. So I've been careless, and you've been careless, and that seems to pretty much even up the score. Don't you think?

"Now, deputy, we could sit here jawing all day, and I don't mean to be rude, but it seems to me I've enjoyed about all of your hospitality I can stand, at least for today. With your leave, then, I'll be on my way. And deputy, I hope we'll meet again. I surely do. The next time we meet I won't have to borrow your horse. No, sir, I'll have one of my own then, a mover that will sail away from such company as you like a bird from a tree. Until then, adios."

"Soderberg!" the deputy shouted, suddenly angry, "I'll have you for horse stealing, horse stealing and resisting arrest and weapon stealing and insulting a U.S. officer and—and—"

"Temper, my good marshal, temper. Take a moment and clean the mud out of your ears. I'm borrowing, not stealing. Didn't you hear me? Why, what would a man like me want with a bent-up pistol and an ugly, broken-down, sway-backed cayuse like this one? Merciful heavens! Except for this once, I'd not be caught dead on such a critter. No, sir, Brother Marshal, I'm only borrowing. Later on today you'll find this critter tied to the gate by the cemetery north of town. You'll also find this worthless pistol tied to the saddle. And, marshal, don't tarry too long at the cemetery. There's some that say those old polygamists buried in there are restless of a night and prowl around looking for nice juicy marshals.

"Now, once again, adios. It sure is a beautiful afternoon for a walk, don't you think? See you around, Brother Marshal!"

Angrily Deputy Clawson stalked through the mud and the rain and the alfalfa, his eyes riveted on the retreating back of the bishop. Never, never in his whole life had he been so humiliated, so—so—

"Blast!" he swore as he kicked viciously at a clump of alfalfa. "I'll get that man! I'll arrest him if it's the last arrest I ever make!"

2

The Eighteen-Hundred-Dollar Plug

I think that if Pa had known a little more about horses, there wouldn't have been any problems. Trouble was, Pa was only an expert in maybe three things, those being the Church, making money, and getting married, and not necessarily in that order. Not that I'm against any of them, of course, but that day Pa surely could have used a little more savvy about horses. If he had, what I'm about to relate would probably never have happened. But it did, and here is how.

It had been about ten days since Pa had come home from the field all muddied up and mounted on Deputy Clawson's gelding, and about all he'd talked about since then, at least while I was around, was finding a horse that would be faster and stronger than any other horse in the Territory. He was not, he declared over and over, about to lie freezing in another ditch when a fine horse could be carrying him off to safety. So every day Pa was out hunting for horses and dickering on them, which left his wives and us children at home doing our best to hold things together.

This day Ma had pulled me out of bed right early so I could get over to Ammon Hanson's and get a big old wart charmed off my hand. I got there, and he took a hunk of raw bacon and rubbed the wart like crazy, wiped it all off with an old dishrag, and then took the dishrag and buried it somewhere out in his orchard. I don't know how it worked, but it did. I'd had two of them charmed off before, so I didn't doubt for a minute that it would work. It took a week or two, of course, but the warts always went. Besides, it was painless, and since I'm allergic to pain I didn't mind his treatment at all.

When I got home Ma had rounded up my half-brothers Jim and Lyman, two boys belonging to Pa's first wife, Aunt Polly, and Johnny, who was the only son in town belonging to Victoria, Pa's second wife. I could tell that today was going to be as exciting as the rest of them, for Pa had left word for us to get down to the bishops' storehouse to help Elinor, one of my half-sisters, with another day's work on the tithing. Now I don't mind work if it is done with moderation, but it always seemed easier for Pa, as bishop, to get work out of us than to make a work call from the pulpit. Today was even worse than most, though, because we had ninety-six tithing chickens to butcher. Imagine that! I never could understand why some folks couldn't kill and clean their own tithing before they brought it in.

Well, anyway, we had just dumped the first bucket of scalding water, having plucked seventeen of those foul-smelling fowls, when we heard the most gosh-awful thunder of hooves pounding up the lane. It sounded like Pa was on the run again, except that Pa didn't have a horse that sounded like that. Dropping the axe, I found myself, as always, hobbling a step behind the others as they vaulted the woodpile and headed up through the potato patch. That was risky, since Ma had a switch handy for anyone, man or beast, caught running through the ward's "needy garden." Nonetheless we made it, and I was just running around the side of the shed, limping full-tilt, when both horse and rider jerked to a stop practically right on top of me. I stumbled back out of the way, the horse reared in fright, and Pa, yelling at me to watch what I was doing, grabbed leather and clung to that horse with all his might. Again it was obvious that Pa was not a horseman.

After a minute or so Jim got hold of the bridle and calmed the horse, and then Pa lit into me, giving me the worst tongue-lashing I'd had in years. And I reckon maybe I deserved it, too, for I surely did get in the way of Pa and his new horse.

For that is what it turned out to be. After Pa got through with me he turned to Ma, and with the widest grin on his face I'd seen since he'd saved old Hepsi, our cow, from the mud mire, he said, "Hattie, what do you think of my horse?"

Ma didn't answer, not at first. She just stood there staring, along with the rest of us, at Pa sitting on top of the biggest, doggonedest horse any of us had ever seen.

"Gosh," I gasped. "Whose cayuse is that, Pa?"

Without even answering me, Pa swung out of the saddle quicker than chain lightning with a link snapped, picked up Ma, and started twirling her around like they were in the middle of a ball somewhere.

"Well, Hattie," he grinned, "I finally got it. Slickest horse trading I ever did. Why, those gents were sure square shooters, and by golly, they weren't even Saints. Isn't he a beaut! Pure-blooded registered Belgian stallion, not a mark on him, and eighteen hands high if he's an inch!"

"But, Pa," I shouted, forgetting again who I was in relation to who he was, "he's a plug! That ain't no riding horse! Why, look at those feet. They're big enough to plug badger holes and stomp out grizzlies!"

"Hyrum," Pa said quietlike, turning on me again, "curb your tongue. You seem to have forgotten who you are talking to. Just because you are nearly full grown, that does not give you the right to rattle your tongue at your father.

"Now, I'll grant you that he is big, but I guarantee that this horse will outrun any other four-legged, saddle-packing critter in Sanpete County. Why, I've just come from Victoria's home, and before that I came up from Ephraim. And, Hyrum, you and your smart tongue might be interested in knowing that I stopped in at our dairy, and who should be there but Deputy Clawson, looking for yours truly."

"Jons?" Ma asked anxiously.

"It's all right, Hattie. Don't worry. Clawson got the drop on me, all right. But he didn't tie my hands. He just took my reins, held his pistol on me, and ordered me to ride. So I did, and as soon as he was relaxed I reached up, slipped the bridle off of old Ingersol here, and the two of us took off. Well, you never saw such a surprised marshal. I hit that front gate, the one I rigged with the trick weighted latch, and we sailed through it and were off before Clawson even realized that we were gone. By the time he figured the gate out and got through it himself, Ingersol and I were into the trees on the south end of Cedar Hill, two miles away from him and gaining.

"A plug this horse may be, Hyrum. But I'll tell you this: he is the fastest plug I've ever had the pleasure of riding. In five miles I outran Deputy Clawson by nearly three of them. Son, that is riding. In fact, I am convinced that there isn't a horse in the county that this animal couldn't daylight. And that includes those two white mares of Mungus Sorenson's. Yes, sir, this is one fine animal."

By now we were even more amazed, and so we just stood there slack jawed while Pa showed off the points of that high-quality hunk of horseflesh to Ma.

Thing was, we got so wrapped up in Pa's new horse that we didn't hear anyone approaching until the springs creaked in a buckboard behind us. Then we turned to see Mungus Sorenson jumping down.

Now, Mungus was probably the last man I would have expected to see at the storehouse. He was what we called a Jack-Mormon, and he had been since he stormed out of the meetinghouse the day Pa was made bishop. Pa says it was tough on Mungus to watch an outsider be made bishop, for he was sort of aspiring to the position himself. When the authorities in Mt. Pleasant asked Pa to move up from Moroni to lead the Aspen Wells Saints, it was just too much for him. Mungus had spread the word that he would never again set foot on Church property until Pa was released. That was why it was so surprising to see Mungus at the storehouse. And his gloating look had me right puzzled.

"Well, bishop," he grinned, "who in tarnation is so poor that they have to pay tithing with a worn-out, half-dead piece of horseflesh like that?"

We all froze, knowing firsthand of Pa's temper, which was slow to boil but scary when it did. Ma even put her hand on Pa's arm, though as it turned out she didn't need to. Pa simply turned his back on Mungus and began digging out the horse's hooves with his pocket knife.

"Mungus," he inquired, finally looking up, "how have you been?"

"It isn't me that we ought to be worried about, bishop. No, sirree, it surely isn't. Your wife Victoria was just up to the Co-op, and she told us right proudly that you had paid eighteen hundred dollars cash for that nag. Now, bishop, that worries me. In fact, it worries me a lot. I worry because no one in his right mind would ever pay that much for a plug. Only you did, and that troubles me, for I see all these good folks here in Aspen Wells allowing themselves to be led by such a man. And bishop, that brings me to my second concern. Eighteen hundred dollars cash! I wonder where you got that much money? I wonder if we don't need an audit of the tithing office?

"So anyway, I just stopped by to see this horse for myself. I had to find out if what your wife said was true, or if she was fabricating somewhat, like her husband is prone to do."

I don't know about my brothers, but I was so shocked by what Mungus had said and implied that I simply held my breath, knowing that Pa was about to clean his meathouse. Ma looked like she had just been slugged, but when she spoke I was surprised at what had upset her.

"Jons," she gasped, "is that true? You couldn't have paid that much for a horse! Not when . . . "

Without even so much as looking at Ma or at the rest of us, Pa slowly rose to his feet and walked over to where Mungus was standing. It had suddenly grown so quiet that I could hear a bee buzzing somewhere nearby, and the birds in the willows down by the creek sounded closer than they ever had before. I was even aware of a bead of sweat that was trickling down my spine.

Pa stood for a moment, gazing intently into Mungus's face, and then very calmly he spoke.

"Mungus," he said, nearly whispering, "you listen, and you listen hard. Don't you ever call one of my wives a liar again! Do you hear? If you have something to say about me, then drag up your stock and run it around the corral a few times so we can see how the brand lies. But don't you ever malign one of my family again! Now kindly climb back up into that wagon of yours and rattle your hocks on out of here, before I lose my temper and read you from the book."

"Why, yes sir, bishop," Mungus grinned. "Anything you say, bishop."

With that he wheeled around, leaped into his rig, and picked up his reins.

"Say, bishop," he yelled as his team of matching white mares started to turn, "Victoria said you bought that nag because it was fast. You wouldn't care to make a little wager on that, would you? I mean, if it is as fast as your wife said it is, I'd like to see it run."

Without answering, Pa took Ma's arm and walked toward the

storehouse, his face a study in barely controlled anger. With that, my brothers and I hightailed it back to the woodpile and our chickens. We knew Pa would have sent us back anyway, and right then we would have fought mountain lions rather than incur Pa's wrath. Fact is, I was amazed that Mungus had gotten off so easily.

One thing for sure, Pa's new horse had surely muddied the water in the puddle called Aspen Wells. How much, though, I wouldn't learn until later that night.

3

The Eighteen-Hundred-Dollar Kiss

It was hard to believe how quickly word spread about Pa and his new horse. By the time conjoint session for the young people started that evening, the news of his purchase was the main topic of conversation. He, and by implication all of his family, were having their sanity questioned. And that is saying it mildly.

Now, I'm kind of used to talk such as that, having a crippled foot and all, so I have learned to pay it no mind when folks start laughing at me. I mean, if a fellow gets all het up every time some person starts poking fun at him, then he's going to spend his whole life being angry. For a time I went that route, but it didn't take too long for me to see that I wasn't going anywhere. That was when I finally made up my mind that I had too many more important things to do. I wasn't going to waste my life being angry all the time.

So that night when the fellows started making fun of Pa and the rest of us, I just naturally pulled in my horns and started to walk off. Trouble was, Jim and Lyman had never learned how to do that, and Jim especially is one of those fellows who won't be pushed for sour apples.

I've heard some folks say Jim is mean, and it is true that he has occasionally hung kids by their heels in picket fences, leaving them there to rot when they wouldn't let up on him. But mean? No, mostly he just likes to tease. Still, he's rolling thunder when he gets riled. That I will admit.

So that night when Pete Livingston and Curly Sorenson, Mungus's boy, started crowding us, why, old Jim just wouldn't crowd. Pete and Curly started calling us "plugs" when they first saw us coming up the street, and by the time we got up to them there must have been about twenty fellows chanting all kinds of unpleasantries in our direction.

Now to me that seemed like quite a crowd, but Lyman and Jim just saw them as a challenge, as though the odds were about even. Why, one day when three Feds were hassling Aunt Polly and giving her grief, Jim took Pa's pistol and got the drop on them. He then told them to get off the property or he'd whup them all, one at a time or all at once, and it didn't much matter to him which. Well, those marshals knew he was just a boy, but they took one good look at the man-sized pistol he was holding, and they left, every last one of them. Nope, Jim didn't have a single fear-bone in his body, nor Lyman either, for that matter, though he was more quiet about it. In fact, I suspect that if it had been Lyman who got the drop on the Feds, he wouldn't have offered to fight them; he would have just waded in and done it, and then maybe talked about it afterwards. Both my brothers take after Pa where all this is concerned, though Pa did a whole lot of settling down when they called him to Aspen Wells to be the bishop.

Pa did tell us that we ought to avoid fighting as much as possible. But if we were going to fight, he said, we might as well fight to win. He also told us most fights were won with the first punch, and that we ought to land the first one good and hard, the way General Moroni did it in the Book of Mormon. So Jim and Lyman, taking Pa's advice to heart, marched up to Pete and Curly, who were joking and elbowing each other, having a right good time poking fun at Pa, his horse, and all the rest of us. We were outnumbered, they knew it, and they were all set on having a wonderful time giving us a little verbal abuse.

"Hi, ya, Petey-boy," was all Jim said, and he was smiling when he said it, a nice easy kind of smile that was as innocent as a newborn babe. Pete stood there kind of surprised, taken back by the quietness of it all, and I reckon he was still trying to understand why Jim wasn't mad when his nose got spread all over his face. At the same moment, Lyman let Curly have a stiff one in the wind section; Curly doubled over, and then Lyman introduced Curly's face to his kneecap.

Well, things got pretty exciting then, with those two boys, like Samson among the Philistines, smiting their brethren hip and thigh, fist and foot, and head and knee as well.

Right off I could see that while those two heathen brothers of mine were having the time of their lives, the odds were not exactly in their favor, and they maybe could do with a little help. So, making myself as inconspicuous as I could, I limped up behind Hank Forest, who was just getting set to throw himself on Lyman's back. Then I lifted up that heavy-handled cane Pa had given me for Christmas and I began pounding some whole new thoughts into Hank's mind. The next fellow I made an impression on was Spike Mills, and then the three of us, my brothers and I, were back to back and earnestly practicing the laying on of hands.

Well, for the next few minutes we had more ups and downs than a charging caterpillar, and by the time Pa's counselor, Ollie Olsen, came out and pulled what was left of those fellers off from us, we were all chomping dust and picking gravel out of our knuckles.

I don't recall the last time I hurt so bad, and I don't remember the last time I felt so good, either. All three of us—Jim, Lyman, and I—we got to our feet and stood there together, breathing hard, trying to spit out the salty taste of blood and sweat, and, in general, swelling our chests.

Ollie then proceeded to yell at us, I think for fighting, though the way it came out it sounded like he was angry simply because we were the bishop's sons.

When he'd finished, Jim grinned at him, picked up my hat and handed it to me, and then the three of us filed through that crowd of bloody faces and—

And that was when I first noticed Ida Mae. She wasn't doing anything, just standing there staring, her eyes bigger than anything I'd ever seen.

Now I reckon I'd better say a little about Ida Mae. She was Mungus Sorenson's daughter, Curly's little sister, and she was about the cutest little lady I'd ever seen, a pure grade A, blue ribbon girl. Fact is, if the truth were known, I'd had a case on her ever since I first noticed that she was a female, and that had been maybe three full weeks, give or take a day. I didn't know exactly where she lived, never having had the opportunity or courage to find out, but I'd heard she and Mungus and Curly lived on some two-by-twice rawhide outfit somewhere south of town.

So there was Ida Mae, staring at the fellows who had just been feeding her brother a supper of knuckle sandwiches, and suddenly I was sick inside. I'd never spoken to her, never even looked at her when she was looking back, always admiring her from afar, so to speak. And now I realized that all my dreams, all my hopes, all my plans, had been drowned in the blood and sweat of a fistfight. Hang it all, I—

Without warning, something heavy smashed into my skull. I saw Ida Mae, and it looked like she was screaming. Then the ground was coming up at me, and the next thing I knew it was all dark and quiet, my head was hurting like blue blazes, and someone right close by was crying.

With an effort I opened one eye, just enough to see a few stars above the roof of the meetinghouse. Then someone leaned over me, blocking out the stars, and I felt a cool damp cloth wiping my face. Then a hand, all soft and warm, pressed gently against my cheek and my chin, and of a sudden I knew what was happening. Some girl critter had hold of me.

With a yelp of fear I lunged up, and in the instant before dizziness got the best of me I saw the face of Ida Mae, all anxious and worried as she reached out to steady me.

Then I was on the ground again and it was funny how I knew everything that was going on but was unable to do anything about it. Ida Mae was kneeling in the dirt beside me and she was holding my head against her, and the last time any female had done that it had been Ma. Thing was, somehow it surely felt different this time. And I couldn't decide whether I liked it or not.

Suddenly that blasted fear of girls seized me again, and I shoved her hands away and pulled myself once more to my feet.

"Say!" I shouted, sounding much louder than I had intended. "Where are they?"

"Who?" she replied quietly.

"Jim and Lyman is who. And how come I'm here alone with you?"

"That's right," she said thoughtfully. "You wouldn't know, would you? Your brothers are somewhere chasing that dumb brother of mine. When Curly hit you over the head, Jim and Lyman lit out after him like hounds after a rabbit. You'd best get inside now and set yourself down. No fooling, you look worse than third-day porridge."

Well, if she wasn't flattering at least she was honest, and to tell the truth I didn't feel much better than I apparently looked. So I made my way into the meetinghouse and sat there hurting and dreaming for the rest of the meeting. Golly, did my head hurt! I felt worse than a calf with the slobbers. On the other hand, though, wasn't that Ida Mae something! Maybe that big old plug of Pa's was worth eighteen hundred smackers after all.

Lyman and Jim and the other fellows came in toward the end of the meeting, and Jim handed me back my cane. Then the three of us sat there together, and I'll tell a man I was proud as punch, sitting next to those two. We did miss Johnny, who was out at the herd, and Ernest, who was learning to irrigate. Both of them had missed all the fun. Still, it was great being part of a big close family like ours was. Folks can say what they want about polygamy—but me, I like big families.

When the meeting ended, all the young people started filing out through the back door, girls first. It was like a mass movement that I was swept up in, following those girls just like I knew what I was doing. And to tell the truth, I was getting caught up in the excitement as much as the other fellows. Now, like I said, I'd only known girls were alive for about three weeks, and of all the girls in my ward only Ida Mae had taken my fancy. And in that three weeks I'd either been irrigating or working down at the dairy, so this was my first conjoint session, so to speak, where I was aware of the girls. It was fun and it was scary all at the same time.

Once outside, we all stood around shoving each other and generally acting foolish. I was straining my neck trying to locate Ida Mae when some lunkhead pushed me into a whole crowd of girls. They started giggling and I staggered back, and then not knowing what to say I just stood there with my hands in my pockets, feeling the red creep up my neck and across my face. Boy, was I ever glad it was dark!

Well, then all of us, boys and girls, stood around and made

funnies, and Joe Spinner did some fancy walking along the top of Anderson's fence. And then suddenly, as if by some prearranged signal, Joe jumped off the fence and the whole crowd followed him off down the street.

I didn't know what to do, so I ended up doing nothing except just standing there, feeling dumb. Lyman saw me, though, and shouted, "Hey, Hy, come on! Don't just stand there like a bump on a stump. Let's go!"

At that, everyone turned to stare, and I heard a couple of girls giggle, so with burning ears I kicked myself where a fellow ought to be kicked occasionally and caught up. My hands were still in my pockets, and my cane was tucked tightly under my arm where I hoped no one could see it.

I didn't know where we were going at all, but I couldn't think of a good way to ask without looking more foolish than I already did. So I just kept walking, figuring that it would all come out in the wash.

After walking for what seemed like forever (though it was only a block or so), I was shoved into Jim. So I grabbed his arm and asked him where we were going.

"We're walking the girls home, dummy. Wheredidya think?"

Okay, so I wouldn't ask Jim any more questions that night. Still, now I knew, and I supposed it sounded safe enough. I mean, it was dark, and I could remain anonymous in the crowd. No one would notice me, so what did I care if we walked the girls home or not? It couldn't take too long, so there still should be plenty of time to milk Hepsi when I got home.

Then I happened to glance to the side just as two fellows and two girls peeled off from the group and turned down a side street together. I was still wondering at that when Lyman broke off from the crowd and walked away with that Hanson girl, and the way he was acting I could tell he was lady-broke for sure. And now I was getting nervous! Something was happening, and whatever it was, it was getting out of hand!

In the next three blocks the boys and girls peeled off at regular intervals, and it wasn't too long before I realized two things—no, three things. The first was that not only Lyman but Jim too was gone, leaving me alone. Well, not alone, exactly. My second realization was that there were only six of us left. And that brought me to my third realization, the most scary one of all.

I was walking beside Ida Mae Sorenson!

It was too dark to see her very well, but I could tell that up close she was a little shorter than me, and that she had her hair done up in a bun, neither of which I'd noticed earlier. She was walking along with her hands held in front of her, her arms down straight and held tightly against her dress.

And me? I had my own hands as far down in my pockets as they would possibly go. We were awfully close together, so carefully, trying not to draw her attention, I inched away from her two or three feet. That flower water she had on was simply overpowering.

Well, I was just trying to sort out the butterflies when another couple took off for another front door and there were only four of us left. The other two were talking and giggling a little, but you can bet I wasn't. I was as silent as a graveyard at midnight, and a whole lot more nervous. For the life of me I couldn't understand how I had ever gotten into this mess. Here I was, alone, walking along a dirt road in the dark with a girl I had never so much as spoken to until that night. That was scary.

But what was even more scary was the fact that we were coming to the edge of town and I didn't even know where she lived. I could have shot myself for being so dumb. But then we went past some old poplar trees and I could see that there was only one house left.

What a relief! We were almost there. Sensing my ordeal to be about over, I turned into the path, only to stumble over Dave Connaly, who had just turned toward the gate with the Pritchett girl. Now what?

Just then the silence broke, and Ida Mae softly asked, "Where are you going, Hyrum?"

Hyrum? Why, she actually said my name! My heart did a couple of flip-flops as I squeaked, "In here. This is where you live, ain't it?"

"Isn't," she corrected. "And no, it isn't. This is where Kathy Pritchett lives."

Well, I tell you, I was dumbfounded. This was the last house. Anybody could see that. If she didn't live here, then where in blue blazes *did* she live?

She was walking on now, quite slowly, swishing her skirt back and forth as she walked, so desperately I clambered to catch up with her. By now Pa's horse and my fistfight had taken leave from my mind, and I was thinking some whole new thoughts. Something was happening way down deep inside me, something I'd started to feel after the fight, but which I was now feeling a whole lot. It is hard to describe that feeling, but it was like a cross between being sick and being in heaven, or something like that, anyway.

Anyway, I had to know where Ida Mae lived, and the only way I could think of finding out was to ask her. So I swallowed a couple of times, cleared my throat real quietly so it wouldn't squeak, and then I blurted, "All right, if you don't live there, then where do you live?"

And hang it all, despite my throat clearing I still croaked. I couldn't believe how much I sounded like a frog, especially when it was important that I not sound that way. I tell you, I was fast becoming a mental wreck, and I didn't know what to do about it.

Somehow, though, I found the courage to look over at her, and when I did I immediately wished that I hadn't. Why, she was *smiling* at me! Well, I gulped a couple of times, looked around for a rock to kick, and pushed my hands even deeper into my pockets.

Why was she looking at me, and why was she smiling at me? For crying out loud, was I supposed to look back at her and smile myself? There was no way on earth that I could do that.

"Do you see that light up there?" she suddenly whispered, breaking the agonizing silence. "Well, that light is in our window."

I squinted desperately into the darkness, trying to see the light. Normally I had pretty good vision, but still it was a minute or so before I saw, dimly and barely visible, on top of a mountain about a hundred miles away, a tiny flicker of light.

"You mean that light way out there?"

"Uh-huh. That's where I live."

As she spoke, I noticed for the first time that her voice was sounding sticky, like syrup or molasses or something. So cautiously I moved another foot or so away from her.

"Do you walk that far all the time?" I squeaked, not knowing what else to say.

"Only when I want to," she said. And now she smiled at me again, that same sticky smile. "Hyrum, I wanted to tonight."

Well, now, what in tarnation does a feller say to that? "Me, too"?

Not on your life you don't. Not if your name is Hyrum. And mine was. I moved even further toward the ditch, suddenly noticing that she had somehow inched closer to me.

Right then my stomach was tied up in a million knots, I was so full of conflicting emotions. But one thing was for sure: Ida Mae would never know how I was feeling. Just because I liked her was no reason for her to know it. It was a lot more comfortable liking her from a distance. Still, I had to talk to her about something.

At that moment, something that Pa always said popped into my mind.

"Boys," he said, "if you ever lack for confabulation, just ask someone about the Bible."

Well, it was worth a try, so I up and did it. I asked her, I mean.

"Have you ever took to reading the Holy Word?" I inquired, my voice squeaking again.

"Taken, Hyrum, taken. And yes, Father occasionally reads to Curly and me at breakfast. But I've never actually read it myself. Do you read it, Hyrum?"

Well, I'll be . . . ! Here I was, having my first ever real talk with a girl, and suddenly I felt a strange new confidence.

"Why, sure," I blurted. "Pa has us learn a new verse every week. Says it will be good for us if he ever feels to call us into the mission field."

"Oh, can you quote scripture? I think men who can quote scripture are so wonderful! Hyrum, quote me a scripture, please."

I hesitated, and right off she opened her eyes wide and started imploring me again. But I couldn't. Blast! What a time to go blank. And even worse, I got so busy trying to remember some scripture that I didn't even notice that she was working herself toward me again. At least, I didn't notice until she was almost to me. But then, with a bit of fast thinking, I reached down, grabbed a rock, and took a couple of quick steps to throw it. Thus I got away from her again.

And just as I did so, the perfect scripture popped into my mind. It was one Lyman had taught me while we were at the sheep herd the summer before.

"Here's your scripture," I said. "Are you ready for it?"

"Oh, yes," she breathed, and suddenly I got the shivers. This girl was the most unpredictable creature I had ever laid eyes on.

"Okay, but remember, when someone learns a scripture, he's bound to do what it says. No matter what. Do you still want to hear it?"

"Uh-huh."

"All right, here it is. It's found in St. John, chapter 20, verse 17. It reads, 'He saith unto her, touch me not.' That's all I can remember."

Well, she got a funny look on her face, but it only lasted for a minute or so before the moon ducked behind a cloud, and that sudden things were back to normal. We walked in silence for a few yards, and then she spoke again.

"Hyrum, you do know my name, don't you?"

"Oh, er . . . yes . . . it's Ida, isn't it?"

"Ida Mae, Hyrum. But you can call me Ida if you'd like. From you, maybe I'd like that better."

"Oh," I choked. What was happening? Why all the special treatment? Was I imagining things? Did she maybe like me, or what?

Silence again. Silence and darkness.

"Hyrum?"

"Uh . . . yeah?"

"I'm really sorry about Curly hurting you like he did. He had no call to do that. Just because your father's gone and bought an old plug for a riding horse gives Curly no right to—"

"Now hold up right there, Ida Mae. Ingersol might be big, but Pa says he's fast, too. Mighty fast. He ain't no plug!"

"Isn't," she corrected. "Isn't any plug."

"Yeah," I breathed, relieved that she had come around so quickly to my way of thinking. "That's what I said. No marshal will ever catch him now."

"Do the marshals bother him a lot?"

"Well, I should smile they do. Whenever Pa's at home, one of us has to go act as lookout for their dust. He can't hardly rest, and he can't ever get anything done because he always has to move around. I'd say they bother him a whole lot."

She didn't say anything then, so for a month or two we walked along in uncomfortable silence, her swishing her skirts back and forth and me limping along beside her, doing my best to act natural. That was tough, though, for somehow that girl surely addled my thinkbox.

Ma says that I'm right smart, but for all I'm supposed to know I couldn't think of a single thing to say.

Something else that was bothering me was . . . well, me. From all appearances this girl acted as though she liked me, and that was a strange thing to consider. I mean, I've already mentioned my bad foot, but besides that, I'm skinnier than a peeled-off bean pole, and I heard Ma telling Pa one day that my teeth hadn't set straight. In other words, I was ugly. I knew it, everyone else knew it, and I honestly didn't know what I could do about it. Of course, being ugly didn't matter so much when I was around my brothers, for they had about the same problems I did, and each of them, in his own way, was ugly too. In fact, we often talked about that, trying to come up with ways of building our muscles and doing other things to improve our almost impossible looks.

Neither did being ugly matter too much when we were around our sisters, because sisters love brothers anyway, and never give much notice to the way they look. That is, they don't unless a brother happens to get real dirty or wear the wrong color of socks or something to meeting. And mothers? Well, you've heard the expression that some fellow has a face only his mother could love? Somebody said that for a good reason, and that was because it was occasionally true, myself being one prime example, as I have mentioned.

So add this all up and you can understand why I was having trouble understanding why Ida Mae seemed to be enjoying my company so much. There were just too many other fellows, good-looking ones, like Joe Spinner for instance, who could set a girl's heart to thumping.

So I was worrying that over in my mind when, without warning, Ida Mae sneaked up beside me and slipped her hand through my arm. I was so startled by the suddenness of the attack that I jumped at least thirty feet into the air. Yet somehow she held on and managed to look unruffled about it all.

I tell you, there isn't anything in the world that will discombobulate a fellow faster than a pretty girl. And that is especially true if he hasn't gotten at least a little used to the idea that he is near one. I was so nervous that I was like a piece of walking oak, but Ida Mae didn't even seem to notice. She just walked along slowly beside me, swishing her skirts back and forth like she was in the May Day parade.

"Hyrum?"

"Huh?"

"Don't you think the stars are pretty tonight?"

The stars! Good grief! Who had time to think about stars? I was still trying to think of some way to escape, or at least say something funny. It was obvious that she had not gotten the drift of Lyman's scripture.

"Yeah, I guess they are," I replied at last. "They look cold, though."

"Cold? Oh, Hyrum, I don't think so! To me they look warm, full of love, full of life. To me they are so . . . so . . . romantic."

Romantic? I tell you, she'd caught me completely off guard. I didn't know where this conversation was going, but I hoped it took longer for it to get there than it did for us to reach her front gate. Trouble was, that light on her porch looked farther away than ever, and I was beginning to wonder if we were ever going to make it.

"Hyrum?"

Oh, no! What did she want now? That tone she had in her voice was one I'd heard before. Ma used it when she wanted Pa to do something that he found particularly disagreeable, but which he always seemed to end up doing. Hearing her use it on me, though, was about enough to scare the bejeebies out of me!

"Hyrum?"

"Huh?"

"Hyrum, may I ask you a question?" she asked coyly, and I felt the shivers start up my spine. I heard once that if you felt that, it meant someone was stepping on your grave. Well, I could believe it. This whole experience was scaring me to death.

"Well, may I?"

"Er, I don't know," I said lamely, knowing she was coyoting around the rim of something I wouldn't like, but not knowing what I could do about it. She looked at me then, with those big eyes of hers, and suddenly I felt bad. I mean, I felt somehow like I was being mean or something, and that was when I really started to squirm. Why, if my sisters can get me to feeling mean or guilty, then it's all over. I'm too softhearted. I'll do anything to get rid of that feeling. And, unfortunately, that night was no exception.

"Ah . . . I guess you can," I said, hoping that she would fall into a gopher hole before she could ask it.

"Hyrum, have you ever kissed a girl?"

"Whaaaaaaaaaaaaat?"

"I said, Hyrum," and now she looked at me again, setting me to squirming even more, "have you ever kissed a girl?"

"Why, no . . . I, ah—"

And before I had time to stutter out another word, she leaned up and kissed me on the cheek. Not a big kiss, mind you. Just a very solid one.

Well, my mouth came open in shock, but nothing in the way of a scream for help would come out. Good grief! What was going on? This walking a girl home was getting clear out of hand. I pushed my hands deeper into my pockets and quickened my pace, but that didn't do very much good at all. We hadn't made it another fifty feet when she attacked again. Only this time it was a full frontal assault.

She tightened her grip on my sleeve, spun around in front of me, and threw her arms around my neck. Then with all the concentration she could muster she planted a kiss—and I don't mean just a little "Aunt Polly peck" either, but the whole full-grown outfit—right smack dab on my mouth. And I'll tell you, then I *knew* I'd never been kissed before!

For about twenty years or so I couldn't move or breathe or anything else, but then she released me and pulled away slightly and looked up at me with those big eyes of hers shining in the moonlight, and to tell you the truth, I just couldn't handle it any longer.

It's pretty embarrassing to admit this, but like Joseph in Potiphar's house I gave one long wild yelp that expressed everything I had ever felt before, shoved her arms aside, and then I got me out of there. I did feel bad to see her lose her balance and tumble toward the ditch at my sudden departure, but my sorrow was dulled to a remarkable degree by my sense of relief. I hoped that she didn't fall into the ditch, for it was about three feet deep, and full, but then she was a big girl. She could get out by herself. As for me, I didn't even touch the ground until I got to our barn on the other side of town.

As I hunted up the stool and got out the milk pail, I was actually glad that I still had the chores to do. I just couldn't bring myself to walk into that house yet, not with my head still spinning as it was.

Slowly my breathing and heartbeat climbed down out of the loft and I started to milk, all the time rehearsing in my mind everything that had happened. I was just coming to the part where her eyes were shining at me in the moonlight when I heard a noise. Well, my heart dropped clear out through the bottom of my feet, it shook me up so badly. But when I dared to look, I found it was just the cat, who was acting about as scared as I was. So I squirted some warm milk in her face, and then we both settled down.

Except for that kiss, I reflected, the whole evening had been great. I mean, I was still socially retarded, but with a little practice I might have a chance.

"You know, old gal," I said to Hepsi, "it's hard to figure out girls. They simply make no sense, no sense at all! But I'm sure glad Pa bought that horse. I surely am. If it wasn't for that horse, I might never have been kissed, scary as it was!"

4

The Raid

"All right, boys," Deputy McNeely said softly, "move up quiet now. You know how important this is to Marshal Clawson. Hank, you and George get around behind and watch the back. Bill, you take Parsons and watch the sides. We don't want this bird to slip away from his roost unseen."

"McNeely, are you sure he's in there?"

"Yeah, I'm sure. Clawson told me he was; that Sorenson kid saw him go in late last night, and you know we've seen no movement at all this morning. Soderberg's in there, all right. We just have to smoke him out."

"Hey, there's a light!"

"Sure enough. That Mormonite is up early, isn't he? No matter, though. Okay, boys, get in position. I'll fire a shot at 5:00 A.M. sharp, and when you hear it, break in that back door quick. We'll be coming through the front door at the same time, and between us we'll have that blasted Mormonite polyg dead to rights."

In the predawn darkness, McNeely and the other deputies quietly closed in on the home of Bishop Soderberg. In all there were five of them, each heavily armed and expecting trouble—and that may have been why, when there was none, they did what they did.

At five o'clock sharp the sound of a gunshot echoed through the sleeping streets of Aspen Wells. An instant later, Polly Soderberg, who was getting ready to feed her three-month-old daughter Sarah, saw the front door of her home smashed open and her parlor fill quickly with armed men.

Hastily the house was searched, but Soderberg was not there. Nor had be been since midnight, when he had slipped past the eyes of spying neighbors to spend the night with his second wife, Victoria.

Instead they found Polly's daughter Elinor, sixteen, and her son Ernest, who was even younger. Roughly the two were pulled from their beds and pushed downstairs into the parlor, where their mother was being held at gunpoint.

"All right," Deputy McNeely shouted, "where's he at? We know he's in here, and we've got a warrant for his arrest. Now where is he?"

All three remained silent, and it was then that the men, frustrated, went contrary to standing orders and became physically abusive.

When a frantic Ernest, an eye swollen almost closed, found his father almost two hours later, the story he told was almost beyond belief.

Sick at heart, hurting, and more angry than he had ever been in his life, Bishop Soderberg ran desperately through the fields and up to the smashed-in back door of his home. As he burst into the parlor, the sight that met his eyes was overwhelming. Furniture, some of it broken beyond repair, was scattered everywhere. Window panes were broken out, lamps were shattered, the smell of coal oil was everywhere, and in the midst of the rubble he found his wife and his daughter Elinor resolutely cleaning up the room, their faces tearstreaked and grim. Then they explained to the angry bishop, between sobs, what the deputies had done and why.

Jons Soderberg did what he could to help and comfort, and it wasn't long before both Victoria and Hattie, his other wives, were there also, sharing the grief, the anger, and the despair.

Later in the day he saddled his Belgian stud and rode slowly up past his mill and to the Big Springs. The springs were nestled in a little cove at the base of the mountain, and in the entire valley he knew of nowhere that was so quiet, so cool, and so serene. The Big Springs was where he came with all his weighty problems, for he had found that the very atmosphere helped him feel more close to God. The quietness calmed his soul, and the stillness helped him to place things in proper perspective.

For some time he sat on his horse in silence, watching the crystal water gushing out of the rocks. The spring was immense, and had been, according to the older residents, the subject of an interesting prophecy by President Brigham Young. Apparently the first year Brigham had sent settlers to the area the spring had about dried up, and that forced all but two or three to leave for other locations. When Brother Brigham heard of it, passing through that fall, he had stood in his wagon and told the people that as long as they lived their religion there would always be ample water in that spring to meet the needs of the community. Interestingly, Aspen Wells had grown over the years, and so had the spring. Each year, even when there had been drought in the valley, that spring had put forth enough water for the community. Between seven and eight hundred people used the spring now for their entire water supply, and there was plenty for them.

In the west, water was life. One lived where one could get water, or one didn't live. Brigham Young had told the people that no one owned the water, that it was the Lord's, and all who needed it should have access to it. Not everyone believed him, though, or felt as he did. One such man came to Aspen Wells and determined that the Big Springs would be a likely source of wealth. In Pine Canyon, just north of the springs, he dug a tunnel, intending to intercept the water and then sell it.

Stories conflicted about exactly what happened, but the way the bishop heard it the fellow dug in quite a way. The citizens complained to Brother Brigham, and he warned the man away, predicting dire consequences. The man ignored the counsel, and shortly afterward met with an accident in which he lost his arm at the sawmill up Ephraim Canyon. Of course that stopped the digging.

And so the stories went. Whether they were all true or not Jons Soderberg did not know. Nor did he feel that it was important. The important thing was that the people believed them, and shaped their lives accordingly. Brigham Young and the others who had led the Church were prophets; he himself knew that to be true. But a prophet, to be most effective in carrying out the Lord's work, must have a believing people behind him, people who would be willing to do as he felt impressed they should, even when it was difficult or was contrary to their personal wishes. If a man was a prophet indeed, then it could not be that he would be inspired only about religion. One who had actual access to the mind and will of the Lord should be inspired regarding all aspects of the lives of the Lord's children, whether they were political, social, economic, or spiritual. And so the prophets of the latter days had spoken, though there were many who felt inclined to disregard their counsel. The stories helped, though, for they taught lessons secondhand that, learned firsthand by all the people, would have become far too expensive and time-consuming. The bishop wondered whether the story about the Pine Canyon tunnel was all true, and, if so, whether the man's accident was indeed divinely engineered. He grinned a little as he thought how ludicrous it would be for the Lord to cut off the arms of all the men and women who had ever become a little greedy. One sufficed; word spread, and many learned the lesson.

But what about his problem? What about polygamy and persecution? He had done what he had been told to do, both in the taking of plural wives and in the avoiding of the federal marshals. The prophet had promised him that if he lived his religion it would all work out. Well, he had tried, had been doing his best, he felt, but now the law had taken it to him. What was a man to do?

"Father," he said softly, "thou gavest me a family, and thou gavest me the responsibility of caring for them and protecting them. Thou also called me as bishop, and gave me the responsibility of conducting my life in a manner that would be above reproach. But, Father, today my heart is as black as midnight, and for the first time in my life I want to do murder! They've hurt my wife and daughter and son, and as their husband and father I want to strike back! Oh, how I want to strike back!

"Tell me, Heavenly Father. How is it that thou wouldst ever want a man like me for thy bishop? The scripture says thou knowest the end from the beginning, so I know thou knewest this was going to happen, and how I was going to feel. Dear God, please help me. Help me to clear my heart, help me to think clearly, help me to be the kind of man I told thee I would be. Help me . . . "

For the remainder of that afternoon the bishop sought the help of the Lord, and later that night, when he returned home to Polly and Elinor, he spoke reverently of a marvelous spiritual experience. There, in the midst of his anxiety and his frustration, he had felt a spirit of calmness settle upon him like a blanket, filling his whole soul with peace and an understanding that justice would ultimately be done.

In the days that followed, the incident with the marshals was never mentioned outside of the home. Two weeks later, when Baby Sarah died, the neighbors thought it was because of some disease, though no explanation was given. No one outside the family ever knew that the bishop and his wives and children blamed Sarah's death on the shock her mother received at the hands of the marshals. The emotional upheaval brought on by that incident, they felt, caused Polly's milk to dry up, and her little daughter slowly starved to death.

Bitterness toward the law, its founders, and its upholders naturally grew, and Jons Soderberg and his families vowed with a fierce determination that they would never, willingly or otherwise, submit themselves to the power and authority of the mob that called itself the law.

5

Soap Day

A few days after the raid on our Big House, where Aunt Polly lived, Ma shook me awake earlier than usual.

"Hyrum," she whispered, "get dressed quickly, and hurry downstairs as soon as you've said your prayers."

"Why, Ma? What's going on?"

"Soap day, Hyrum. Did you forget?"

"Oh, no!" I groaned. "Not soap day again! Ma, can't the girls do it?"

"Hyrum, I'm ashamed of you! You know those little girls can't stir that thick soap or move that heavy kettle around. Now, hurry so we can do it in the cool of the morning. I don't want to spend all day on it."

Well, I dragged myself out of bed, threw a few words towards heaven, though with my attitude I doubt that they got past the ceiling, pulled on my clothes, and stumbled out to do the chores. I got the pigs, chickens, and ducks fed and watered, and then I went to war with Hepsi.

That morning Hepsi had a sore teat, but in my frame of mind I couldn't have cared less. I just tucked her tail underneath my left knee and commenced squeezing and pulling. At the first good pull on the sore teat, however, Hepsi jerked her tail out and popped me on the side of the head with it. Now, normally that wouldn't be so bad, but it just happened that her tail was filled with cockleburs and dried mud and dung from our recent rain, so you can guess how that felt. Angrily I jerked her tail back under my knee, took more ungentle pulls at her udder, and that blasted cow popped me with her tail again.

"Doggone it, Hepsi!" I shouted, giving her a look that would make an icicle feel feverish. "Cut it out! If you hit me with your tail one more time, I promise you a whole lot of grief!"

For a while I milked while Hepsi and I stared each other in the eye. I knew then that she understood exactly what I was saying, and I know it now. She knew exactly who was boss, and she wouldn't—

Whap!

That third slap was by far the hardest, and I was so mad that I just hauled back and slugged her in the side, as hard as I could hit.

"There! Take that, you ornery no-account good-for-nothing miserable excuse for a flea-infested bovine hay-burner! You dirty sway-backed despicable udder-slung—*Owwww!*"

And that miserable cow retaliated by planting her monstrous splayed hoof right on top of my left foot, smashing it forty feet into the ground.

"Hepsi!" I screeched, jerking and pulling on my foot, trying to get it out from under several tons of ugly beef. "*Hepsi!* You lowdown, mean . . . *Get off my foot!*"

With all my weight I pushed against her leg, and finally she shifted, allowing me to pull my mangled foot loose. Really upset now, I grabbed that sore teat and pulled with all my might, determined to show her that no cow-critter could come it over a human the way she was trying to do.

Well, she kicked at me then, but I anticipated that move and leaned back, laughing at her feeble efforts. Trouble was, I forgot for a moment that I was dealing with Hepsi, and I had an absolute knowledge that she was the smartest doggone cow in the whole county. Quick as a wink, before I could do or say anything, that blasted cow did the worst thing that she could possibly have done.

I had forgotten the milk bucket, which was nearly full and still sitting directly under her. With malice gleaming in her eyes she turned and looked at me and then lifted her foot high into the air. Desperately I lunged, knowing what she was about to do. But I was too late, forever too late, and in an agony of defeated spirit I watched as she plunked her filthy hoof down in the exact center of that pail of milk. For about a hundred years she let the warm milk soak the straw and you-know-what-else off of her hoof, turning our milk a kind of greenish brown. Then gently she withdrew it, being careful not to overturn the pail.

The war ended right there, with our cow the victor, and me, as usual, defeated and in trouble. You see, I knew that Hepsi understood how badly Ma needed that milk, and she knew full well that when I came home without it I would be in real trouble. That was why, when she was angry with me, she would step in the milk. She never did it with Pa, or with Ma, or with any of the others. Just me. And she never did it when the bucket was empty, either. She only did it when it was full. That cow was so mean and so smart that it was scary.

Well, I cleaned out the bucket, stripped Hepsi, gave what there was of the milk to Ma, took my verbal licking, bolted down my mush, and went out to get started with the soap.

Several days earlier I'd had the job of making potash lye from our ashes, so I should have been expecting that soap day would come along. Ma said, in regard to the lye, that she preferred apple wood ash because lye from apple wood made the whitest soap. But Pa told her he wasn't about to cut down our orchard so she could have white soap. So we used scrub oak out of the hills, which wasn't as white but which made the strongest lye a body ever saw.

We extracted it by filling a tub with ashes and then pouring boiling water into it. As the ashes settled we added more ashes and more boiling water, and then we let it steep for a day or two. Finally I'd draw off some of the water, and if it would float a fresh egg we knew it had enough lye. Then we'd boil it down until the water was gone, leaving what Ma called Black Salts. This we also cooked, heating it until the black was burned out and we had a whitish powder, which was potash lye.

Compared to making soap, making lye was easy. I mean, have you ever spent a day, when the sun was hot enough to wither a fencepost, stirring boiling grease over a hot fire with lye fumes burning your nose? If you have, then you know why I groaned when Ma told me it was soap day. There was nothing that I hated worse than making soap on a hot summer day.

I got the fire going out behind our log home, got out the big kettle, and finally had it situated so the fire was around it rather than under it. Ma said that prevented the soap from burning.

"Now what, Ma?" I shouted, always feeling uneasy about the recipe for making soap. In a moment she was there, and we set about making hard lye soap.

"First, Hyrum, bring seven and a half gallons of water to a boil. When it's boiling, dissolve three pounds of potash lye in the water, and then call me. I'll be inside getting up a program for sisters' meeting Thursday night."

"Thursday," I thought as I fed the fire. "Fast day again. It hasn't been too long since I dreaded that day like a plague, but now I don't feel that way. Hyrum, old boy, like your Ma says, maybe you are growing up."

I thought about it then, remembering the feelings of agony and hunger I endured working all day Thursday and then sitting through an eternally long meeting that night. Two months before, though, I was sitting in fast meeting thinking about nothing in particular when I had the strangest feeling that I ought to stand up and say something. Naturally I rebelled, preferring to be thought of as a fool rather than to stand up and remove all doubts. But the feeling wouldn't let me alone, and after a little while I stood up and said some things about how I felt about my folks and about the Church. Right then I got choked up and started watering the pew in front of me, and I surely did feel foolish. But I also felt something else, something that I don't know how to explain. It was the hottest and most special feeling I've ever had, and I felt like I was going to explode, it was so big. And right then I knew, I mean I really *knew,* that Joseph Smith was a prophet and that the church he helped restore was the true Church.

I used to wake up nights and wonder what I'd do if I died and got over there and the apostle Peter or someone told me our church wasn't true. For the last two months I hadn't wondered that. You see, the Holy Ghost gave me a testimony. That's how come I was crying and choking and all that. Pa told me that was how the Holy Ghost affected people, jumping up and down on their heartstrings, so to speak. He said it was surely nothing to be ashamed of; he'd irrigated a few pews and pulpits himself, time to time, and he felt proud that the Lord loved him enough to give him that witness. I did too, and now I looked forward to fasting and attending fast meeting, watching other folks feel the same feelings I'd felt. In fact, I was even starting to feel tolerant of old Sister Adolfson, who rattled on every month about her illnesses and her four hundred or so kids. You see, it dawned on me that with all her rattling on, she was just trying to put into words all those feelings that I'd had and had stumbled over myself. I was just able to get the job done quicker is all. And for that I was thankful.

When the water finally boiled I added the lye, careful to be way back so it wouldn't spit or splash on me. When it had dissolved, Ma came out and slowly added nine pounds of mutton tallow which she had rendered earlier. Meanwhile I stirred and stirred and stirred, the fire burned and burned and burned, the sun got hotter and hotter, and I got more miserable by the minute.

To make myself feel better I tried thinking of happy things, like Ida Mae, for instance. But somehow I just couldn't think of her while I was stirring Ma's boiling lye soap. Now, witches I could think of, and hell and the devil and the Great Salt Lake desert and that sort of thing. But I surely couldn't keep my mind on Ida Mae. Why in tarnation did it take so long for the lye and fat to saponify?

"Hyrum!" Ma called, surprising me out of my gloom.

"What?"

"Drop some soap on the plate, and tell me what it does."

I did; it turned milky around the edges, so Ma had me add a little more lye. When that was finally cooked in, the droplets on the plate remained clear, so I added a pound and a half of salt, which separated the soap from the water and caused the soap to rise to the surface.

I was stirring on that when Ma came out and put her arm around my waist. It hadn't been too long since she'd put her arm around my shoulder, but now when we stood side by side I looked down upon her. Somehow that made her seem little, which was hard for me to get used to. It made me want to . . . well, protect her, I guess. She just seemed so little and so helpless, though I knew that was silly. Why, she could outwork me any day of the week. One day I just watched her, and in that one day she milked the cows, killed and cleaned five chickens, made noodles, churned up some butter, pulled a carriage nearly full of beans, cooked up three meals, helped Pa set posts for a fence, and then got cleaned up and went with Pa to a dance down at the Pavilion. I've also seen her hitch up the team and plow and harrow our field, dig ditches, sew up all kinds of clothes, shear sheep, card and spin the wool, fast days at a time for someone in our ward who was sick, and chew out Brother Anderson for taking the water out of our ditch before our turn was up. (And did he repent quick? Well, I hope to shout he did! No one could face up to Ma when her wrath was up.) Funny thing was, she smiled while she was telling him off, and I really believe that Brother Anderson walked away from Ma feeling happy as well as repentant.

That was why I felt silly thinking that Ma was helpless. I knew better, everyone else knew better, and yet I still felt that way. I couldn't help it. Pa says it's natural for a man to feel protective of a woman, and he says the good Lord made women small and soft so men would want to be protective. Ma told me that the Lord fixed women up so they would want to care for a man and would need a man's protection, emotionally as well as physically. The Lord did it so that men and women would get together and stay that way. Men need to provide for and to protect, women need to care about and to be protected. It's as simple as that, for God made us that way. Pa says that men and women are equal in that way only: They need each other. Beyond that, this equal rights business, like Arizona is stewing about, is pretty much nonsense. Up until the Edmunds-Tucker Bill passed, Mormon women in Utah had the right to vote just like the men. Pa says that Arizona is trying to decide whether to give women the franchise, but Ma says it makes no never-mind with her. She says she doesn't want to be equal with men. It's all right to vote, but beyond that she doesn't want to stoop to the level men usually live on.

So anyway, Ma put her arm around my waist and squeezed, looked up at me with her eyes full of tears of gratitude, and suddenly that old soap job didn't seem so bad after all.

"Hyrum, thank you so much! I know this is a miserable job, but, son, it still must be done. I'm so thankful that Jons and I were blessed with such a fine man for a son. I hope you know how much your father and sisters and I love you.

"Now, Hyrum, old Sister Nielson died this morning, and Polly, Victoria, and I are going down to hold a wake for her. We'll keep her body packed in ice today, and then other sisters will take over until the funeral. Can you set the soap out, cut it, and get it drying alone?"

"Sure, Ma."

"Thank you, son. I surely love you."

"Yeah, Ma. I love you, too."

A little later Aunt Victoria and Aunt Polly drove up in their cart, Ma climbed aboard, and all three of Pa's wives rode off together, smiling and talking and hugging each other just like they were real sisters. I was thinking on that, wondering at the marvel of those three women loving each other like they did when they shared the same husband, when I heard hoofbeats coming down the lane. I stood up to look, and it was Pa and Ernest riding Pa's new horse.

"Hi, Pa," I called. "Ma just left with Aunt Polly and Aunt Victoria. Didn't you see them? Sister Nielson passed away and they were going there."

"I saw them, Hyrum. And I heard about Sister Nielson. It's sad, but she surely has been ill. Hattie says you've been stirring soap since early this morning. Is that right?"

"Yeah, I reckon. Though it feels longer than that."

"I'll bet it does. How much longer before you finish? I'd like you to come up to the mill with me."

"Well, Ma wants the soap all set out and cut up into squares. That will take a little while."

"Ernest, can you cut soap?" Pa asked.

Ernest nodded vigorously, so Pa set him to cutting up my soap, freeing me so I could go up to the mill. I was also minding my little sisters, so Ernest was assigned that task, too, and in a moment I was up behind Pa on that big Belgian stud.

We rode for a time in silence, and to tell the truth I was surprised how smooth that big horse moved. I really enjoyed riding him, and believe me, that was saying something. I *never* enjoyed riding plugs!

As we passed the widow Nielson's place I saw Pa's horse and cart hitched out front, and that put me in mind of Ma, and Pa's other wives. Time to time, the past day or so, I'd been thinking about that, wondering about marriage and polygamy and having a wife or so, wondering what it was like. But that is a hard thing to ask someone about, so I hadn't done it. Now, though, with thoughts of Ida Mae pestering me constantly, I suddenly decided to ask Pa what being married and being a polygamist was like.

After I'd asked, Pa was quiet so long that I decided he hadn't heard me. I was about to ask him again when he finally spoke.

"Say," he asked, "what kind of a question is that from a fellow who three months ago didn't even like the thoughts of a girl?"

Well, I got red right away, and mumbled something about just wondering.

"Wouldn't have anything to do with Ida Mae Sorenson, would it?" Pa asked.

I was getting real fidgety by then, and was wishing with all my heart that I hadn't said anything. But then Pa jabbed me in the ribs with his elbow, squeezed my knee to death with his big hand, and answered me.

"Hy," he said, "being married is like different things on different days. Some days there isn't anything greater. Other days, well, a man wonders. He surely does. Still," and now Pa grinned back at me, "I'd say that most of the time there is nothing better than being married to a good woman. And, of course, being married to three of them is just three times better. Right?

"But, Hy, how does a man tell his son what it's like? I don't know. Most of the time it's a happy, calm, relaxed, comfortable feeling. My wives help me to feel comfortable and relaxed, for with them I don't have to be anyone other than who I am. They know me for that, and they have me convinced that they love me in spite of what they know about me. With them I never have to pretend or impress, and that's a very comfortable feeling.

"It's not an easy thing for a man and a woman to learn to live together, because men and women are so different in so many ways. And the obvious physical difference is just part of that, Hy. There are basic differences in terms of feelings and emotions, too. All these things must be dealt with when a man and a woman are married. Of course, they must be dealt with prior to that also, when boys and girls begin courting. Right?"

"Yeah, I reckon. But Pa, I never knew they were different. I mean—well—"

"That's all right, Hy. I think I know what you're saying."

"Well, how are girls different, then?"

"That is a good question. I hope I can answer it. For one thing, women are closer to their feelings than most men seem to be. They tend to cry more readily, they get their feelings hurt more easily, and so on. And, they like to talk more about their feelings than men do. As a bishop and a husband, I've encountered that situation right frequently."

"Does that mean that women feel more things than men do?"

"Oh no, Hy! I don't think so. It's just that a woman's feelings seem closer to the surface than most men allow theirs to get. As men, we have to recognize that and deal with it when we associate with women."

"How?"

"Boy, you are full of questions, aren't you? All right, here's one way. You and Jim and Lyman shove each other around a lot, in fun, showing that you care for each other. Right?"

"Yeah, I guess so."

"Well, I wouldn't recommend that you do that sort of thing too often with young ladies, Hy. Ida Mae surely wouldn't think you liked her if you started slugging her and pushing her around."

"Gee, Pa. I wouldn't do that with her."

"No, of course you wouldn't, because you understand some of the differences between men and women already."

"Are there any others?"

"Well, yes. But offhand I can't recall—wait a minute! There is one other difference you ought to understand."

"What?"

"It has to do with feelings again, Hy, but in a slightly different way. I've noticed you eyeballing the young gals lately. Why?"

"Huh?"

"Why do you look at the girls, Hy?"

"Oh, scrud, Pa. I don't know."

"Yes you do. Now why?"

"Well, because they're cute, I guess."

"Sure they are. But I've also noticed one or two of the girls looking at you. Why do you think they do that?"

"I don't know, but it sure ain't because I'm cute."

"Yes, that would be stretching the imagination some, wouldn't it?"

Pa grinned at me then, so I knew he was funning. Sort of. Thing was, he was right in a way, and for the first time I got to cogitating about it.

"Hy," Pa continued, "men are generally stimulated by what they see. That's why girls look cute to men, and why men look at them. It's exciting.

"Girls, however, aren't usually stimulated or excited by what they see so much as they are by what they feel. If a woman feels warmth, or love, or security from a man, she is attracted to him. And it doesn't seem to matter much what he looks like. He is still exciting to her."

"Golly, Pa, I never knew that."

"No, I didn't expect you did. But the Brethren in Salt Lake City know it. That's why they've asked girls to be modest in their dress and in their actions. If a girl is immodest or inappropriate, she makes it awfully tough for a fellow to keep his thoughts pure.

"And, of course, that is also why the Brethren have counseled us men to be modest and restrained in our physical relationships with women other than our wives."

"I don't understand, Pa."

"Hy, let me explain it this way. When most boys kiss and hug and so on, especially when they are quite young, they are usually only satisfying selfish desires. It's not likely that they are thinking much about the girl, or about building lasting relationships with her.

"With young ladies, thoughts and feelings are entirely different. Hyrum, from my experience as a bishop I've learned that when most girls become physically involved, it isn't because they are thrilled and excited about the prospects of touching a boy. It's because they desire the security that seems to come with touching. They want a lasting relationship, for that means security. Many girls believe, usually mistakenly, that excessive physical closeness will result in such a commitment that will lead to security.

"As an example, a boy often will hold a girl's hand for the sheer excitement of holding hands. The girl thinks this means that the boy likes her. Actually, all it means is that he likes to hold her hand. If I could somehow teach this to the girls in our ward, I'm certain there would be fewer moral problems.

"Anyway, Hy, when boys insist on being physical, that can cause girls to have as much trouble with the purity of their thoughts as boys have when girls are immodest. And that is why both boys and girls are to a certain extent responsible for helping each other to control their thoughts and emotions. It seems to always come back to the Savior's Golden Rule, which tells us that we ought to really care about each other. Does that make sense?"

"Yeah, though I hadn't thought of it before."

"Well, I seem to have gone off on a tangent. Your question was about what it was like to be married, wasn't it? And I can best answer that by saying that it is like any other job. If a man buckles down to it and works at it with all his heart, developing true love, it will be one of the most satisfying and rewarding things he can ever do. If he doesn't, then it's likely that he'll be miserable."

"But, Pa, how can you love three women? And how can they love you and each other? I mean, I like Ida Mae, but if I saw her with another fellow I'd be upset. How come Ma and Aunt Polly and Aunt Victoria don't get jealous?"

Pa chuckled and didn't answer right off, but when he did, his answer surprised me.

"They do, Hy. They do. Jealousy is a human trait, and all three of my wives are surely human. I recollect the night that Elder Daniel H. Wells asked Polly and me to enter into plural marriage. That was a tough decision for both of us, but Polly is a very righteous woman with a strong desire to be obedient. Ultimately, believe it or not, *she* convinced *me* that we should do it. Together we decided that Victoria would be a likely second wife, we invited her to Sunday dinner, and I began courting her. Hyrum, I'll never forget the look on Polly's face when we left the Endowment House in Salt Lake City the day Victoria and I were sealed. Victoria and I climbed into the buggy to begin our honeymoon, Polly stood on the boardwalk watching us, and, Hyrum, riding away from her was one of the hardest things I've ever had to do. Talk about a woman conquering jealousy, striving for a righteous attitude!

"From time to time since then there have been difficulties, of course, but all four of us do our best to make those difficulties minimal. For instance, I'll never leave Polly's home to stay with your mother if Polly and I are having problems. If I were to do that, jealousies could really develop. Neither will one of my wives pressure me to do something if I have a prior commitment with another of them. We all agreed on this, and it works out very well.

"With three wives, a man surely learns fairness. If I were to ever start showing favoritism for one or another of them, the other two would see to it that I became the most miserable man alive. And believe me, Hyrum, women have the ability to make men miserable if they so desire. So I do my best to be fair. I buy cloth by the bolt and divide it into three equal lengths, and I try to spend equal time in each home. Another thing is that each of my wives is given a quarter once a week so that she can go down to the barbershop and take a bath. Now you'll have to admit that is being very fair and lenient. Most husbands don't do that."

I grinned, thinking of the last bath I had there. It was a hot steamy room in the rear of the barbershop with no windows, so at least it was private. The other thing is that it was the only bathtub in town. Still, I preferred the hole in the creek up by the Swedish Temple. The air was better there.

"So, Hyrum," Pa continued, "I do love each of them. Each of them I love in a different way, yet I sincerely feel that I love all three of them equally.

"Anyway, how can I explain what it's like being married to three women? I don't even know if I understand myself what it's like. They're so different from each other. Polly is quiet, but is an expert organizer. Victoria is much more vocal and is very skilled with her hands. But when I'm with her I always feel like I am in a whirlpool, kind of dizzy with things spinning all around me. Victoria is not an organized person.

"Then there is Hattie. Hyrum, your mother is the softest, most kind and gentle woman I've ever known. She has more love in her little finger than I'll ever have. That's why I called her to be president of the Relief Society. Polly would run a tighter ship, Victoria would do a much better job conducting meetings, but Hattie simply loves and cares her way into the hearts of the sisters here in Aspen Wells. Still, don't let your mother's softness fool you. She's tougher than nails, and she's rolling thunder when she's upset. Do you remember last spring when I took all three of my wives out to Jericho with me to shear sheep?"

"Yes."

"Well, in fun I challenged them to see which one could shear the most sheep, and I promised that whichever one of them did, she would be the one who sat beside me on our way home. The others would have to ride in back with the wool. Well, they laughed about it and things started out pretty normal. Polly went right to work; Victoria couldn't catch a sheep, and then when she finally did she couldn't find her shears; and Hattie wouldn't catch one because she felt sorry for them and thought we were hurting them. But then one of the others said something to Hattie about her thinking she was too good and too dainty to shear, and you never saw a woman get so busy so quickly. She didn't say a word. She just smiled at all of us and fairly flew over those sheep. And when it was all over, your mother rode home beside me.

"Of course, you know how we do things as a family—picnicking, fishing, and so on. And I try and involve all of you as much as possible in my businesses. That's why I'm taking you to our mill with me. I want to teach you how to run the new roller process I just had installed. Doing things together builds family closeness, and, Hyrum, having a strong and closely united family is what life is all about."

"But, Pa, don't you ever feel . . . well, funny? I mean, isn't it embarrassing to have three wives and a whole passel of kids tagging behind you?"

"Feel funny? Well, sometimes I do. I felt a little foolish the day Elder Snow sustained me as bishop. He asked for my wife and me to come up to the stand, and everyone laughed when all three of my wives stood at once and then couldn't decide how to line up in the aisle."

"Golly, Pa, wasn't that embarrassing?"

"Well, I should smile it was, especially when all those folks started laughing. I think I was red clear down to my toenails."

"What did you do?"

"What could I do? Elder Snow had asked us to come up, so we had no choice but to go. So I lined those women up single file, the shortest one first, and I followed them up to the stand. And, Hyrum, it seems like I have been following them ever since."

Pa grinned then, and I did, too, knowing how Ma would bend over backward to do what Pa asked her to do. I also knew that Pa would do almost anything Ma asked him to do. Seemed to me like nobody in our family followed anybody, unless of course you counted the Lord. Pretty much I think we all followed each other.

"Pa, do you think I'll ever be a polygamist?"

"Well, son, I don't know. I don't know how much longer our Church will be able to practice it, with all the pressures we're getting from Washington. Our leaders are underground, our property has been confiscated, all of us have been disfranchised, and none of us dare hardly even live. Of course, this is the Lord's Church, and he is powerful enough to overturn all the governments on the earth if he is of a mind to do it. And that would certainly solve the problem. Thing is, it has been my experience that God most generally leaves problem solving to us mortals. If he does that with polygamy, I couldn't guess what will happen.

"One thing I do know, though. I will follow the Brethren and do whatever they tell me to. If we retain polygamy, I will support it to the death. If we are told to cease the practice of it, then I will take no more wives. Beyond that, after seeing how the law has treated me and my family, I will never submit to them. I will die first! Now, as for you, my boy, I'd recommend a few years and one wife before you start worrying about a whole passel of them. Wouldn't you agree?"

"Yeah," I said, "I agree." And wouldn't it be nice, I thought, if I could someday marry Ida Mae? Golly, she is something!

For the rest of the way up to the mill Pa talked about the crops in the fields we were passing. But I only half listened, for I was day-dreaming about Ida Mae, wondering if she would support me if the Lord ever called me to be a polygamist. I wondered if she could be as strong as Aunt Polly had been.

At last we turned into the lane leading up to the mill, and Pa turned back for a final look at Aspen Wells. As he did so I glimpsed, behind some bushes ahead of us, the piebald gelding of Deputy Clawson.

"Pa!" I yelped, flinging myself off of the horse. "It's the Feds, over by the mill!"

Pa turned, took one quick look, wheeled Ingersol around and was gone in a cloud of dust. In that same instant Deputy Clawson came boiling out of the hawbushes after Pa.

"Get out of the way, kid! Blast it, get out of the way! Soderberg, you low-life coward, hold up there! You're under arrest!"

Well, you know about my bad leg. I tried to get out of his way, I really did. Thing was, I somehow hobbled right into the path of that cross-eyed gelding, and when I got there my leg gave out and I lost my balance. Naturally, I had to wave my arms around a bit to keep from falling, and I reckon I got a mite carried away hollering for help to get away from that stampeding horse.

Of course all that racket and jumping around must have somehow spooked the gelding, for it took off through the hawbushes like it was loco, pitching and bucking and giving the marshal a ride he'll not likely forget. The marshal wasn't silent, either, but I'd best not repeat what it was he was saying. Suffice it to say that I laughed until my sides hurt, and then I walked home, taking a shortcut, sort of, down to the other end of town past Ida Mae's home. The next day when I saw Pa we had a good laugh together. And that was pretty much how it was being the son of a Mormon polygamist.

6

Birds of the Roost

In 1888, Green River, Utah, was known for two things: its frigid winter winds and its proximity to the infamous area known as Robbers' Roost. Several miles southwest of Green River City, the land climbed gradually to the top of the San Rafael Swell, a waterless black horseshoe of a rock nearly eight thousand feet high and about eighty miles long. This was the Roost country.

The south side of the swell dropped steeply into the bitter and alkaline waters of the Muddy and Dirty Devil rivers, while the north side of the swell dropped into the San Rafael River. This in turn wound a snakelike course through the tortured San Rafael country, a land which old-timers claimed was used by the Lord as the blueprint for hell, until at last it spilled itself into the murky waters of the Green River.

Across the Green from its confluence with the San Rafael was a sandy bottom nearly a quarter of a mile wide and maybe three times that in length. It was surrounded on all sides by high sandstone cliffs, was filled with huge old cottonwoods, squawbrush, and greasewood, and the Green at that point had a bottom that was quicksand. In short, it was a lonely and inaccessible area.

Under the cottonwoods, back from the river and beneath an overhanging sandstone ledge, stood an ancient and decrepit cabin. It was windowless, except for the chinks between the rough-hewn logs, and its only door hung crookedly from one hinge, cabin and door resembling nothing so much in character as the three men who sat within.

Their names, which do not matter that much, were Jack Moore, Jim Wall, and John Griffith. Locally, however, they were known as the Boss, Silvertip, and Blue John. Moore, a tall young man with black curly hair, commanding presence, and an overpowering urge for dishonesty, was the Boss simply because he was. Wall, the oldest of the three, was called Silvertip because of the graying around his temples and because of his heavy shoulders and rolling walk, which was much like that of a grizzly bear. Griffith, less a cowboy than the others, was known as Blue John because he had one blue eye while the other was brown. Blue John was an excellent cook and a master with teams and wagons, while Silvertip, not long on intelligence, was still an excellent horse thief. Together, the three of them were anything but a trio of square dealers. And at the moment, Jack Moore, the fiery-tempered boss, was obviously upset with the other two.

"All right, Silvertip," he was saying, unmistakable anger and disgust in his voice, "lead that past me one more time. I sent you to the mines at Cisco to get this horse I heard about. You did get it, but on the way back you sold it. Have I got it right?"

"Yeah, Boss, you got it right as rain. Plucking that nag out of the corral in Cisco was a job I could do surer than a belch after supper. 'Twern't nothing to it. Then Blue John lifts this wagon, we tie our horses to the back, hitch that plug to the wagon, and leave town with nobody the wiser."

"Why didn't you ride the stallion out?"

"Boss, that ain't no riding horse. It's a plug, and nobody rides work plugs. You'd oughta know that."

Moore got a pained look on his face, rolled his eyes heavenward, and said, "When they was pourin' in brains, someone joggled their arm." He went on, "All right, Blue John, you hitched the stallion to the wagon and got out of town first-rate. Now you take it from there."

"Sure, Boss. Like Silvertip said, it all went too easy. And you know I ain't no riding cowboy. That's why we hitched up to the wagon. Why, with a wagon under me I can make a hoss stand up and dance. And that's what the stallion did all day long. He just danced.

"That night we was camped on the Sevier when someone hollered out of the darkness that the posse from Cisco was hot on the trail of the hombres who took their blooded Belgian stallion. That was the first we knowed it was blooded. So we doused our fire and heard the posse go past in the night.

"Next day I pulled the shoes off the horse and we headed north, up through Sanpete, hoping to shake the posse. But somehow they heard about us and was dusting along at a pretty good clip just a few miles back. That was when we ditched the wagon, and that there gave us a little breather, but we knowed it wouldn't be for long. Them fellers surely did want that horse back. So we was hightailing it up past Ephraim awondering what to do when here comes this Mormon bishop all set on buying our horse.

"'Well,' I says to Silvertip, 'this here looks an awful lot like the hand of providence. That there posse is making it hotter'n a burnt boot for us, but I reckon someone up there don't want nobody shortening our stake ropes. I also reckon he wants this here Mormon to enjoy all the blessings a hoss like this one can bring him, posse and all. And Silvertip,' I said, 'if heaven is so set on this man having this here blooded plug, then we ought to set a heavenly price on him.'

"Silvertip, he allowed as how we was using plumb good sense in shaking our tails at that hoss and skedaddling on out of there. So I says, 'Mr. Bishop, sir, this here animal is a highly prized blooded Belgian stallion. He belongs to our boss, but I'd be a mite shy of the truth if I wasn't to say that there is a whole passel of fellers who right this minute wish they were here getting this horse instead of you.'

"Well, the bishop, he comments on the fine points of the hoss, and then he looks in his mouth and asks us for a price. So I look at Silvertip, wink, and say, 'Mr. Bishop, sir, when a man looks over a hoss the way you've just done, then I know that there same gent is as wise as a tree full of owls, and there ain't no use in trying to pull the wool over his eyes. No, sir, Mr. Bishop, sir. You know the value of that blooded stud as well as I do myself, and there wouldn't be no point in quibbling over the price, not for either of us. We understand each other, we do, and that's why I'm willing to sell this beautiful animal to you for the fair price of two thousand dollars gold.'

"'Sixteen hundred,' says the bishop, and afore you know it we had shook on eighteen hundred dollars gold. It took him about an hour to round up the money, and that is what is setting on the table here before you."

For a long moment there was silence in the cabin as Moore sat and eyed the two before him. A fly buzzed in the shade of the room, and Blue John stirred restlessly, uncertain of what his boss was thinking.

Suddenly Moore grinned and spoke. "Eighteen hundred dollars gold, huh? That is a lot of gold, to my way of thinking."

"You bet your pearl-handled pistols it is, Boss. Slickest hoss-trading we ever did."

"Eighteen hundred dollars gold. Say, Silvertip, which is highest, eighteen or twenty-six?"

"Uh, twenty-six is more, I think. Ain't it, Blue John?"

Blue John nodded, getting more nervous by the minute. He didn't know where the Boss was headed, but he had the feeling that he had the bit in his mouth and was being led.

"Silvertip," Moore continued, "I swear you are as chuckle-headed as a prairie pup with the mumps. And you, Blue John, you can't even use stupidity as an excuse. I sent you boys for that horse, that particular horse, for a reason. And that reason was that I know a rancher over near Telluride what will give me twenty-six hundred dollars gold for that blooded Belgian. What I am saying, boys, is that you just cost me eight hundred dollars gold. Do you savvy?"

The grin was gone now, and both men knew they were in big trouble. They'd been around the Boss long enough to know that he didn't carry his pearl-handled pistols for decoration. Moore was tough as boot leather and mean as a barrel full of rattlers, and one time they'd seen him go ten days with a dislocated shoulder without complaint, get it set, and then rob the sawbones who set it.

"Gee, Boss, we didn't know. Honest we didn't. I—"

Moore reached across the table, grabbed Silvertip's shirt, and yanked him forward, at the same time drawing his pistol to cover Blue John, who quietly lifted his hands and backed up against the wall.

"Listen, you two owl-hoots, and listen good. I want that horse back, and I want it back quick. I don't care how you do it, just get it back. Do I make myself clear?"

Silvertip bobbed his head up and down vigorously, while Blue John swallowed and nodded also, knowing he was looking into the blue barrel of death. Moore then released Silvertip, who stood up, straightened his shirt, and reached for the bag of gold.

"What do you think you are going to do with that gold?" Moore questioned ominously.

"Gee, Boss. You said to get the horse back, so I was just getting the money so's we could give it to the bishop when we took away his horse."

"*Give the money back?* By all the powers that be . . . !"

And Jack Moore was so angered that his face turned purple and he couldn't speak. Blue John, recognizing the symptoms of sudden death by lead poisoning, grabbed his bewildered partner, shoved him through the door and toward his horse, forked the saddle of his own bronc, and dusted his tail toward the narrow ford in the river.

Of one thing he was sure right then, and of one thing only. Without that blooded stud, his life and the life of Silvertip weren't worth the price of a plug of tobacco half chewed.

Jack Moore, still trembling with anger, watched the two horse thieves swim their mounts across the river and finally disappear over the far rim in a cloud of dust.

Shaking his head once again in disbelief that Silvertip might actually have returned the money to the Mormon, Moore rose to his feet, picked up the heavy bag, set it atop a roof beam, and then strode through the door and down the trail toward his horse.

Suddenly and without warning an arm was thrown around Moore's neck and he was jerked violently backward, his breath shut off and his arms pinned to his sides. Instinctively he began to struggle, and then he felt the end of a pistol barrel pushing into his ribs. Without hesitation he ceased all movement and lifted his hands well above the pearl grips of his two famous pistols.

"All right, boys," a quiet voice ordered, "move in."

In a moment Moore found himself surrounded by several men, all heavily armed, all covered with a thick coat of trail dust, and all quite anxious, it appeared, to terminate his earthly existence.

Quickly his weapons were taken from him, and then a rope was taken from the nearest saddle. Moore, seeing that, spoke quickly.

"Who . . . who are you gents?"

"Well," the quiet man replied caustically, "we might be angels from heaven, only we ain't. We might be outlaws like you, only we ain't that, either. We might also be the law, but if we claimed that, it wouldn't be true. At least, not exactly. What we are, Mr. Whatever-your-name-is, is a posse from Cisco, the ones who lost their horse. We followed those two friends of yours, and got here just in time to see them disappear over the far rim. So, you'll have to do. Now where is our horse?"

"You followed those two idiots all the way here?"

"Right as rain. Say, but you think fast. Why, I'd be willing to lay a bet that you even know what we are going to do next, what the law says to do to any hombre who steals horses."

"Now, boys, don't be hasty. I didn't take your horse. I swear I didn't. It was Blue John and Silvertip who done it. They—"

"Hank, shake out your rope. I'm fixing to give this owl-hoot a hemp neck massage. I've heard that a stretched-out neck cures a whole lot of common ailments, such as lying and such."

"No!" Jack Moore shouted, pleading desperately now. "What I told you is true, so help me! Those two took your horse, but they sold it to some Mormon over in Sanpete. That's where they've gone now, to get it back."

"Sold it, huh? Well, that would explain why the prints disappeared, wouldn't it?"

"Yeah, that was why, I swear it!"

"Where's the money they got for it?"

"Beats me," Moore lied. "They wanted to get rid of it quick, so they sold it for fifty bucks or so and probably lost that gambling. That's why I was so sore and sent them back. I got nothing out of the deal."

"Jules," the man with the quiet voice asked, "how much do you reckon that stud is worth?"

One of the men in the posse did some quick figuring and then replied: "Well, at least a thousand, maybe fifteen hundred dollars. It depends."

"Could a man tell by looking that the stallion was worth that much?"

"Well, I hope to shout he could! Have you seen the points of that animal? His eyes, his chest, his hips, his—"

"Thanks, Jules. Well, outlaw, fifty dollars, did you say? My, my, my. Hank, shake out that rope, and let's string him up."

Moore watched with fearful intensity as the rope snaked up over a huge limb and dropped back to dangle near him. Casually the man took hold of the loop and drew it loose, then slipped it over Moore's head and tightened it about his neck.

"Hank, dally it up and take in the slack. When you're ready, slap your spurs, and—"

"No! Wait!"

"Yes?"

"I . . . well, ah, I reckon I'd better level with you boys. I mean, maybe Blue John and Silvertip got a little more than fifty dollars when they sold your horse."

"How much more, son?"

"Put the rope away, let me go, and I'll tell you everything."

"What do you think, boys? Is he worth it?"

Jack Moore watched anxiously as each of the men considered and then nodded.

"Okay, outlaw, you tell us. If what you say is worthwhile, then we put up the rope and you ride away a free man. If it isn't . . . "

Hastily Moore began talking, and in a few moments the posse had gone to the cabin and had the gold counted out on the table.

"Well, boys," the posse leader said, "eighteen hundred dollars gold, just like this feller said. I reckon now I'm ready to propose two things. The first is that we let this pilgrim go, provided that he goes east, that he goes in a hurry, and that he never returns. My second proposal is that we take this money, consider the horse sold, and go home. Jules, you put the value on the horse, and it was yours. Is this enough?"

"It sure is!"

"There it is, boys. Besides, it looks to me like that Mormon feller has enough troubles as it is, with those other two owl-hoots after him. He thinks he bought the critter fair and square, so if he can keep it, then I say let him. Are you ready to head back?"

There was a chorus of agreement, and in a few moments two clouds of dust left the secluded bottom of the Green River. Jack Moore, the Boss, was churning up the ground eastward, his holsters empty and his mind filled with all sorts of new resolutions. The posse were themselves headed west, thoughts of home on all of their minds. And to a man they were relieved that the stallion was sold and that they had gotten such a good price for it. Why, eighteen hundred dollars gold was a powerful lot of money! It surely was!

7

A Very Good Runner

In Aspen Wells during the summer of '88 there wasn't much more to do of a night than sit around counting crickets, swatting 'skeeters, and watching the nails rust in the barn door. What recreation there was, folks had to provide for themselves. Drama and theatre were popular, either with local groups or sometimes touring professional actors putting on the shows. Wrestling, Cornish style, was sure to draw a good crowd, as was racing. And dancing—well, folks surely did go for dancing.

Down in the middle of town we had what we called the Pavilion. It was a large log structure with a stage at one end and two big old potbellied stoves on either side. The Pavilion was where we held all the drama productions, and it was also where we held the dances. Summer and winter, folks danced there, no matter what the weather was like outside. On rainy nights mud would get tracked in, and once folks got to dancing the mud dried up and got stomped into dust which rose up so thick it liked to choke a body to death. And on cold nights those stoves would get red hot, and folks would dance in a half circle around those stoves, doing their best to keep at least one side warm. So we had some fine dances, and even us fellers who didn't dance much enjoyed going just so we could watch the other folks acting foolish.

That was why when Pa announced at our monthly family meeting that there was going to be a dance the next night I got so excited.

I simply liked to go. Yet there was another reason, and I reckon I ought to admit it. You see, I was hankering to see Ida Mae again, and I was fairly certain that she would be there.

Now, I'd been over to Aunt Polly's when Lyman and Jim were sprucing up for a dance, though I'd never really done any honest sprucing myself. Yet I'd watched and I was pretty certain that I could handle it. So the next night, as soon as I finished straining the milk, I headed for the loft where I slept. It was Saturday night, but I wasn't about to take time to drag out the wash tub and take a bath. I'll tell you what I did have time for, though, and that was Pa's straightedge razor. Now, Pa was over at Aunt Victoria's eating dinner, so for the first time in my life I began to lather up. To be right truthful I'm not sure that I actually needed a shave, but Jim had been giving me the raspberries about my fuzz for quite a while, so I figured the time was ripe.

Luckily for me, Ma had taken the egg basket down to the coop about the time that I needed to gather up the makings, so in no time I had stripped the washroom and was up in my loft whittling away like I had been born to it. And would you believe it? Nervous though I was, my first shave ended with not so much as the slightest mark on my face—well, except for maybe one tiny slash under my chin.

Now, on my way out to do the chores I had taken Pa's hair grease and stashed it in the ditch. I was sure Pa wouldn't mind my using it, but I didn't want to endure the chiding my younger sisters would throw at me if they saw me putting it on.

So I slipped outside, greased down my hair and my boots a bit, and then lit out. And as luck would have it, who should I meet as I rounded the house but Ma. I thought for sure I had been nabbed, but Ma just looked at me and beamed. Right then I was glad I had a face that at least a mother could love, for there was no mistaking how she looked at me. She cautioned me to be home by ten o'clock, and pointed out that staying out any longer would provide chances for nothing but no good.

I agreed and got away without her noticing that my cane wasn't along, and that was a relief. I headed over to the Big House to pick up Ernest, and Aunt Polly saddled us with our younger sister Martha, too. But that didn't bother us too much, for we could easily ditch her if we needed to.

As we approached the Pavilion I started getting uneasy, thinking about Ida Mae, and by the time we reached the door I was as nervous as a duck in the desert. Once inside, though, I got caught up in the excitement of it all and was able to relax. That is, I relaxed until I saw Ida Mae. There she was, all smiles and sweetness, dancing up a storm with that rotten Pete Livingston!

I hadn't forgotten the welt that had been raised on the back of my head by Pete's bosom buddy, Curly, and knowing that those two were thicker'n bobcats in a gunny sack, I couldn't help but feel distrustful of both of them. But doing my best to appear calm and nonchalant I made a beeline for Ida Mae. I decided to rescue her in style, so I laid my hand on Livingston's shoulder, coughed a little, and said, "Excuse me, but could I have this dance?"

Right off I knew I had made a grave mistake. Pete Livingston merely swirled Ida Mae around so he was facing me, and then he blurted, "Well, if it isn't old Clubfoot Soderberg, hisself! What'cha want, Limpy Leg? Har Har Har!"

Well, I could feel the red creeping up my neck again, but I wasn't going to be put off that easy. So I said, "I would like a dance with Ida Mae, please. I'm cutting in."

"Why, you skinny sawed-off little cripple! You ain't big 'nuff to see over a sway-backed burro, let alone dance with a girl like Ida Mae. Now go sit down like a good little boy, and stop embarrassing the lady here."

Well, I was madder than a rained-on rooster, and I was all set to light into him, bigger than me or not, when he turned his back on me, swept Ida Mae into his arms, and twirled her away. And the look on her face stopped me cold. There she was, after seeing me humiliated, grinning up at that no-account tomcat like there was no other fellow on earth but him.

I stood there momentarily, feeling lower than a snake's belt buckle in a wagon rut, sincerely wishing that I was dead or maybe hadn't come to the dance. Then Ernest and some girl bumped into me, and I decided the best place for me was not in the middle of the floor. So I hobbled over to lean against the wall and nurse my wounds in private.

After a minute or so, though, I noticed Uncle Albert's beaver hat bobbing up and down in front of me in tune with the Virginia Reel.

Now, that would have been fine, except that I happened to know that Uncle Albert was out at the herd, so whoever it was under that hat had to be someone other than Uncle Albert. I leaned a little closer so I could see past all the gray hair, and there on the back of that old geezer's ear was the exact same mole that graced the back of Pa's ear. By golly, Pa had come to the dance! And as if to confirm my thoughts, the old fellow turned around, grinned, and gave me a big wink. Well, it sure was Pa.

I reckon this is the time to explain that Pa was a natural-born actor, and was in as many drama productions as he dared to be in. His favorite role, the one he did best, was playing the part of an old man. Why, when he painted up his face, colored his whiskers, put on his wig, and changed his voice, a body would have sworn that he was older than Moses or one of those other biblical fellers. So there I was, grinning and watching Pa enjoy the dance, when I glanced at the door just in time to see Marshal Clawson saunter in.

Pa saw him, too, and for an instant he froze. All I could think was, "Oh no! Some dirty so-and-so has squealed on Pa!"

But then I saw Pa lean over and whisper to old Hans Weegin, who was sitting next to him. Hans got right up, walked over to the marshal, welcomed him to the dance, and then led him over to the chair he had vacated next to Pa.

Well, I about died. I thought Pa had lost his mind, and I set myself to jump on the marshal so Pa could get away. But Pa never moved a muscle to run. He just sat there, ignoring the marshal and tapping his feet to the music like he was having the time of his life.

That was the first time I'd seen Marshal Clawson up close, and it didn't take me long to realize that he wasn't much to look at. What hair he had was long and yellow, his clothes were dirtier than a squaw-man's blanket, and his boots were so frazzled he couldn't scratch a match without burning his feet. His most distinctive feature, however, was his nose, which was big enough to store a small dog in. In short, Deputy Clawson was uglier'n a fresh-foaled moose, which he mightily resembled. Add to that the fact that he had all the social graces of a used-up horseshoe, and you can see what we were up against.

When the fiddles finally stopped, Pa sat there for a moment watching the folks on the floor getting ready for the next set. Then he turned his head, and if I hadn't known better I would have sworn that was the first instant that Pa saw the marshal. Golly, but my pa was an actor!

For a second or two Pa just stared at him, but then he grinned that warm old grin of his that could make a body feel like he'd just come in out of a blizzard. Extending his hand to shake the marshal's, he introduced himself in a squeaky old voice that made him sound at least a hundred and eighty-three.

"Well, how-de-do, stranger," he squeaked. "Welcome to the dance!"

He then began pumping the deputy's hand up and down, up and down, just as vigorously as he could. He didn't let up, either. He just kept on shaking hands until Marshal Clawson finally got tired of it and jerked his hand free. Then with a muttered oath the marshal began massaging his fingers, which Pa had undoubtedly crushed in his vicelike grip.

"Right pert dance these youngsters are having here," Pa commented. The marshal nodded in agreement, still massaging his fingers and arm where Pa had about shaken it loose from its socket.

"Yer a-talking to Avery Goodrunner," Pa said seriously, and I could tell that old Hans Weegin, who was standing next to me against the wall, was about to bust open, he was trying so hard to keep from laughing. But the marshal never got the joke, it having floated somewhere over the top of his thinly planted yellow hair.

"Hebron Clawson," he said, almost reaching out to shake Pa's hand again. Pa reached out, too, but just in time Marshal Clawson jerked his own back, unconsciously massaging his fingers again. I reckon he recalled the shaking of a moment before, and was not exactly anxious for another go-around.

"You here to dance?" Pa asked suddenly.

"Well, no, not exactly. I'm here, well, I'm here on business."

"Humph! Must be a mighty fine business that would bring a man out to a shindig like this one is shaping up to be. Say, what might your business be?"

"Uh . . . well . . . uh. . . . say, old man, have you lived here all your life?"

"Nope—leastwise not yet. Why?"

"Do you know the bishop? Soderberg, I think his name is?"

"Do I know the bishop? Well, I should smile I do. Him and his Daddy, too. And fine men they are, both of them. Honest, loyal, upstanding, humble, courageous—"

"Courageous!" the marshal shouted. "Soderberg? Why that mealy-mouthed, yellow-backed . . . why, I've never seen a man with so much run in him. If I could be alone with him for two minutes, old man, then you'd see how courageous he is."

"My heavens, sir," Pa squeaked, "you can't be talking about Bishop Soderberg—*our* Bishop Soderberg! Big fellow, strong as an ox, mean as a catamount, handsome as a stage performer? Is that the man?"

"Big, maybe," the marshal replied. "Tall, heavy, pretty much run to blubber and fat, cowardly, and so on. That is about like I'd describe him."

Well, I could see the fire in Pa's eyes, the marshal talking about him that way. But Pa held it in well, he surely did.

"Say," Pa said, "if we're talking about the same man, you'd better not let him hear you talking like that."

"Why not? There ain't nothing he can do to me."

"Oh, I don't know," Pa squeaked. "Why, he might get riled and pull those long yellow mustaches right off. He might do just that."

So they sat there for a few more minutes while Pa commented over and over about the deputy's mustaches and what a fine honest face he had.

"You a Mormon, Clodson?" Pa asked suddenly.

"Clawson," the deputy replied.

"What do you mean, Clodson?" Pa asked, sounding awfully puzzled.

"I said, my name is Clawson!"

"What of it? I don't understand."

"Why, you called me Clodson."

"Why'd I do that?"

"Well," the deputy responded impatiently,"I guess you thought it was my name."

"What was?" Pa asked seriously, sounding downright dumbfounded. I don't know how Pa kept a straight face. I was grinning from ear to ear, and old Hans Weegin was about to bust a gasket.

"What was?" Pa asked again.

"Clodson!" the deputy replied with exasperation.

"But you just now said it was Clawson," Pa said. "And now you say Clodson. You've got me right confused."

"Well, it is. I was trying to—"

Pa then reached over and took the marshal's arm and pulled him close.

"Young man," he said, speaking sternly, "you have an honest face, but it doesn't seem to go very deep. Straighten up now and listen to the wisdom of old age. If your name is Clawson, own up to it. Don't pretend that it's Clodson. A man who is shifty will never get anywhere here in the west, especially not here in Utah. It just doesn't fit a Utahite. Leave all such petty flim-flamming to Easterners like that rabble of oppressors and murderers of the righteous who go around with stars on their chests calling themselves marshals, and who, to a man, have incipient hoof-and-mouth disease. Yes, sir, if your name is Plodson, admit it like a man. Let your nay be nay and your yea be yea, and you'll get along much better here in Aspen Wells."

Well, Marshal Clawson was so flustered that he was turning purple, but Pa was giving him no chance to interrupt, no chance at all.

"Now, Mr. Plumson," Pa continued, his voice squeaking more than ever, "I don't recollect you ever stating your business."

"It's Clawson," the deputy fumed, "and—"

"Now hold on, son. How in the world can your name also be your business?"

"Listen, you old geezer!" the marshal shouted at Pa. "My name is Clawson and my business is United States deputy marshal, and—"

"Son," Pa said as he placed his hand on the deputy's arm again, "you've no need to shout. My age may be great but my hearing is still quite good. So you are a marshal, eh? My, my, my, and you did look like such an honest young man. Still, we all must do *something* for a livelihood. Isn't that true?

"Folks," Pa suddenly squealed, pulling himself to his feet where he stood tottering back and forth, "this here stranger in our midst is Deputy Marshal Clodson, and he has been kind enough to come to our shindig tonight just to be neighborly. Now, he hasn't come right out and said so, but I reckon he'd be plumb tickled if he was to catch himself a polygamist, as I take that to be his main line of work. Neighbors, he seems especially interested in our bishop, so if any of you know of that good man's whereabouts, Plodson here would surely appreciate hearing from you. Now, don't be bashful. Step right up and—"

At that moment a funny thing happened. Pa almost toppled over, saving himself only by reaching out as he fell and latching onto the long drooping mustaches of Marshal Clawson. That worthy let out a yell like he'd been scalped (which he probably felt like he had), pushed Pa off of him, stuttered and stammered for a moment while he made sure that his mustaches were still part of his anatomy, and then he turned with an oath and stalked out the door. A moment later we all heard the pounding of hooves as one deputy marshal, once again minus his dignity, departed the vicinity. That man was getting right irked at my pa.

For a moment there was total silence, and then old Hans Weegin held up a mug of cider from the refreshment table and shouted, "Brothers and sisters, ladies and gentlemen, a toast. To all federal marshals and other minions of the law: may they be winked at by blind men, kicked cross lots by cripples, nibbled to death by ducks, and carried to hell through the keyhole by bumblebees."

There was a roar of laughter, and I could see that Pa had won another round.

8

The Seeds of Opposition

Pa's performance that night beat all I'd ever seen, and most folks there were having a right good chuckle. But then Mungus Sorenson put a sudden damper on things when he and George "Loose-lip" Lundstrom swaggered over and knocked both wig and hat off of Pa's head.

Then Loose-lip, living up to his reputation as a loudmouth, spit a mouthful of black tobacco juice right on Pa's boot. Wiping the drizzle from his whiskers with his shirt sleeve, he grinned and spoke.

"Well, well," he said, "beneath the disguise of an old idiot we find an honest-to-goodness real one."

Instantly the crowd grew silent, and Loose-lip, a little awed at his own bravery, hastily retreated behind Mungus, where he stood looking like he expected at any moment to have the roof fall in on him.

"Well, bishop," Mungus sneered, "you got lucky again. I'm amazed that one of these fine upstanding citizens didn't turn you in. Had I been any closer I would have, but no matter. Sooner or later Clawson will get you." He paused, then added: "Say, how's that old nag of yours doing? Somebody said you'd been out racing him with the tithing chickens."

Two or three people laughed, and Mungus, sensing sympathy from the crowd, boldly continued.

"Now, lookey here, folks. What we've got here is a bishop who is not only stupid but is likely dishonest as well. He sits right here and plays idiot right in front of the marshal, laughing at the danger of it, with never so much as a thought about who'd take care of his family or the ward if he was to get captured. Besides that, he boasts of going out and giving a full eighteen hundred dollars for a plug, and no bishop I ever heard of has that kind of money, especially to spend on a worthless plug. Now I ain't accusing, but I am wondering if our good bishop has been dipping into the tithing funds without us knowing of it."

Now, I'd been around Pa when he was mad plenty of times, but I'd never seen him come so close to boiling over and still manage to keep his lid on. And all I could think of was what Pa kept telling us youngsters over and over again, that we ought to be actors rather than reactors. In short, we ought to be our own men. Pa called it succumbing to social pressure, and right then he was surely showing all of us how to resist it. If I ever saw social pressure I saw it that night at the dance.

"He tells us," Mungus continued, "that he paid that much for the stud so he could keep out of reach of the marshals. He tells us that nag is fast, and he tells us that he bought it from two strangers down near Ephraim. Now, I don't know about any strangers, as no one has seen them before or since, and that seems right incriminating to me. But I do know horses, and there was never a plug born that was good for racing, or for being worth the handsome sum of eighteen hundred dollars gold. That I do know!

"Soderberg, I say that you are either an idiot or a fraud, and my guess would be that you are both. To my way of thinking, there are only two ways that you can prove otherwise. First, submit to an audit of the tithing office and storehouse. Second, race that fool horse and prove to us that it can run. Right frankly, I'm personally willing to bet five twenty-dollar gold pieces that you're too yellow to do either."

"Yeah, Soderberg," echoed Loose-lip. "And I'm willing to go Mungus here one better. I'll not only bet a hundred dollars that you won't take the challenge, but I'll bet another hundred that your old nag couldn't make it from here to Salt Lake City in a whole week."

"Now, hold up," Hans Weegin said, pushing himself forward. "You boys are taking advantage of this here situation. You know as well as I do that Soderberg here is the bishop, and that means he ain't allowed to bet. You know that bishops don't gamble or do none of them other hell-raising things, so how come you're trying to force him into doing something that he hadn't ought to?"

"Shut up, Weegin," Mungus snapped, "before you get thrown out of here on your ear. What's it going to be, Soderberg? Put up or shut up?"

Pa was so angry that I think I could see smoke coming out of his ears, and just when I expected him to snap Mungus in two, bishop or no, Ma stepped forward. Smiling sweetly, she took Pa's arm in a persuasive manner and said, "Jons, have you ever noticed how the scum rises when the pot boils?"

Still smiling then, she led Pa toward the center of the floor.

"What do you say, Jons?" she asked. "Don't you think we're all about ready for another Virginia Reel?"

I guess those boys in the band were fearful of the dance ending, for the music was going quicker than a tie comes off after meeting. As for me, I went back to my corner where I could get the heat off and take a breather. What a terrible night! Ida Mae had disgraced me, her father had disgraced Pa, and what could we do about it? As far as I could tell, nothing!

When I got home Ma was there, and she asked me to go up and say prayers with my little sister. I did, and I thought it was pretty special when she prayed for Pa, asking Heavenly Father to help him resist all his social pressure. The way it sounded, Ma had read the situation about like I had.

Later, long after I should have been asleep, I heard Pa come in the back way. Ma, who was downstairs churning cream, stopped immediately. There was a long silence, and then Pa asked Ma if he could spend the night. Now, you would be interested in knowing that although Ma was Pa's third wife, when Pa had serious problems he usually came to our home. I don't know why, unless it was because Ma could tell Pa he was either right or wrong in the nicest way a body ever heard.

"Hey, Pa," I grinned, leaning out over the loft, thinking to tease him like he was always teasing me. "Old Mungus sure got to you tonight, didn't he? What are you going to do now, go after him with—"

"Hyrum Soderberg," Pa shouted angrily, "be still and get to bed! Your bad manners ill become who you are, young man. To help you learn that lesson, you will consider yourself barred from all outside activities for one month! Do I make myself clear?"

Embarrassed and humiliated, I nodded and withdrew to my bed. Good grief! What had brought that on? I wondered. Pa was suddenly as touchy as a blistered heel. A month! For crying out loud, that was a long time. Especially was it a long time when I was only teasing him. Scrud! When he teased me I was supposed to laugh and take it. If I could, why couldn't he? Sometimes parents are surely difficult to understand.

After a little while he and Ma started talking about what had happened at the dance, and it was easy to tell that Pa was upset, maybe more upset than I had ever seen him. Over the years Mungus had given Pa plenty of cause for grief, but this was the first time Pa had ever let it bother him. Up to then the fact that he was the bishop had always cooled him down, but that night it made no difference, no difference at all. Pa even ignored Ma when she reminded him of who he was.

Apparently several people had echoed Mungus's doubts, some about his money and others about the speed of his horse, and that really hurt Pa. He had always been a stickler for honesty, and more than any man I knew he had made it a policy of going the extra mile. One time some butter spoiled in the storehouse, and Pa replaced it with some of our own, saying that the Lord always blessed those who gave freely, even and maybe especially when they weren't obligated to give. So it wounded him deeply when folks began questioning his honesty. It also hurt him to have folks questioning his judgment regarding the speed of his horse, especially when he was so convinced that he was right.

Ma, sensing Pa's real problem, repeated to Pa his own favorite lecture, the one he gave to me whenever someone made me feel bad about being crippled—the lecture about not letting social pressure pull me down.

"Hyrum," he would say, putting his hands on my shoulders, "does it really matter what other people say or do? Not really, not when you understand that God never makes mistakes. Certainly he made you different, but that was not an accident. He's given you special blessings to compensate for your club foot, and he's left the realization of those blessings up to you. Now, you can either spend your time happily enjoying the discovery of them, or you can waste your days wallowing in the mire of self-pity. Hyrum, people are a lot like chickens. If one is different, no matter why, most of the others will mercilessly peck it to death. When you reach the point where you are unaffected by the silly surface peckings of social pressure, only then will you approach the potential God has given you. And only then will you be truly happy."

Now Ma was using that same logic on Pa, pointing out that God had made him different by trusting him to be bishop. If he stooped as low as Mungus and Loose-lip wanted him to stoop, then he would be betraying God's trust and giving in to social pressure. Mungus and the others were just being normal chickens, she said, so it was up to Pa to rise above the flock and meet the potential God had given him.

Well, it tickled me to hear Ma talk to Pa like that, but it only made him more sore.

"Hattie," he said, "this is different, and you know it! A man does what he must! They've questioned my integrity, my judgment, and my honor. I am bound to protect my honor!"

"Jons," Ma said quietly, "your honor is unscathed. When a fly bites a horse, that doesn't change anything. The horse may flinch a bit, but it is still a horse, and the fly is still a fly. Your honor is as sound as ever. What has really been wounded is your pride."

"Honor!" declared Pa.

"Pride," Ma said gently.

"Honor!" Pa thundered, and right then I pulled my pillow over my head and went to sleep. After all, enough was enough, and I could tell that there would be little else said that night that was worth my remaining awake to hear.

I was still feeling sorry for myself the next morning, licking my wounds about being restricted and not being able to do anything with Ida Mae, when Pa hollered up at me to get about the chores. Then the door slammed, and I knew Pa was on his way to bishop's meeting. Well, it was all I could do to take leave of that feather mattress and drag myself down to the barn. I felt about as limp as a neck-wrung rooster. To me there never was any justice in having to do chores on the Sabbath. To my way of thinking, if the Lord had really wanted the day kept holy he would have had cows stop making milk every seven days, and so on. But he didn't, so I had the milking to do.

Anyway, I finished up and hitched the team just in time for Ma and all the little girls to clamber aboard. "Let's go, Hyrum," she called, trying to get me to hurry with getting the cow-smell off my hands. "We're late! Why, if we should ever walk into that meeting before your father gets up to start it, I expect he would faint on the spot."

Sure enough, we were late again, but there was a pew up front that was empty as could be, and for that we headed. To tell the truth, I quite enjoyed sitting next to my little sisters, as it made me feel important helping Ma while Pa sat up front. The only thing bad about it was hobbling all the way to the front while folks looked at us.

We settled ourselves just as the opening hymn was ending, and out of habit I turned and glanced around to see where Jim, Lyman, and Ernest were sitting. Little did I expect to see, directly behind me, Ida Mae. Not only was I stunned that she would be there so close to me, but I was shocked to see her father, Mungus, sitting next to her. What in blazes is he doing here? I wondered, slowly working my neck back into its socket. Impulsively I glanced up to where Pa was sitting, and, sure enough, there he was, looking right through me. And he was wearing that little smile, too, the one that always meant he was about to do something unexpected. And I didn't have long to wait to find out what, either, for right after the opening prayer Pa rose to his feet and began to speak. I don't recollect all he said, but a good portion of it I'm fairly sure I will never forget.

"Brothers and sisters," he boomed, "welcome to meeting. Welcome especially to those of you who have not made a habit of attending. It's always a pleasure to see the sinner cast off his yoke of bondage and return to the fold."

Pa grinned at Mungus as he said that, and then he continued.

"Since the dance last night, I've done considerable thinking about the subject for this morning's sermon. I'd like to take my text from Proverbs, chapter 16, verse 27, which says, 'An ungodly man diggeth up evil, and in his lips there is as a burning fire.' Now, last night at the dance the whole ward saw a classic example of this scripture. There were those who sought to dig up evil and spread the fiery words of falsehood, and they did their very best to discredit your bishop and undermine his effectiveness.

"Brothers and sisters, I will be the first to admit to mortal weaknesses, and very likely I have many more than a man in my position ought to have. But a liar I am not, a thief I am not, and a coward I am not! All of these accusations were either implied or stated explicitly. As a man of honor I feel duty bound to dispel these falsehoods and lay to waste the weeds of wickedness and deceit which even now are beginning to choke out the simple stems of truth which ought to flourish in Aspen Wells.

"Therefore, after a sleepless night of considering all the alternatives, I have determined to accept the challenge so offensively thrown at me. I will cover the bets made by Brothers Sorenson and Lundstrom. Furthermore, to show my contempt of them and all others who are making wind with such wild accusations, I will extend my bet to any and every other gentleman who might feel inclined to doubt the speed and stamina of my stallion, Ingersol. I will place one hundred dollars in gold against each of you who wishes to bet an equal amount. My bet is that I can ride that Belgian stallion which I have named Ingersol from the gate of our cemetery to the Temple block in Salt Lake City between sunup and sundown of this coming Wednesday.

"Any and all takers are welcome to meet me on the front steps immediately following the meeting, as such business ought not to be conducted within the Lord's house."

Well, you should have heard the sisters gasp. Ma was fit to be tied, and Aunt Polly and Aunt Victoria, Pa's other two wives, were just as upset. I could tell that no matter where Pa spent that night, he would be in a world of hurt.

After the meeting there must have been at least three dozen men take up Pa's bet, and at least as many more wanted to, but weren't allowed to by their wives, I guess. Mungus and Loose-lip were, of course, first in line, and as they walked away I saw Mungus poke Loose-lip in the ribs and grin, saying, "We done it. That's the end of Soderberg. Shake hands with the man who will be your new bishop."

At the moment I didn't understand what he meant, and as I rode home in the wagon with Ma I worried about it. But I didn't worry about that nearly so much as I worried about where Pa was going to get three thousand six hundred dollars gold. Goes to show how short-sighted a fellow can be.

9

Outlaws Within and Without

On Devil's Lookout, a rocky outcropping high in the hills above Aspen Wells, the outlaw known as Blue John sat in the sparse shade of a juniper, better known locally as a cedar tree, waiting impatiently for the return of his twice-slow partner, Silvertip.

Down the steep slope a flock of magpies screamed their displeasure at the world, two or three flies were doing their best to share the limited shade with the outlaw's wildly swinging sombrero, and now and then a welcome breeze whispered through the cedar boughs above. Other than that there was no sound but the heavy scrambling of hooves on rocks as Silvertip's three horses laboriously climbed the hill below.

For thirty minutes Blue John had watched his partner approaching, and now as Silvertip drew near he could see that the man was coated with dust. Wistfully he realized that he looked the same, that both of them smelled of horses, leather, and stale sweat, and that down in Aspen Wells the barbershop had a tub and some warm water which could be his for only two bits an hour.

"Ah, well," he mumbled, "that tub might just as well be in San Francisco for all the good it will do me."

At last Silvertip pulled up, the two horses he was leading snorting and blowing behind him.

He sat for a moment, wiping his face with his bandana. Then he spat in the dust and spoke.

"Sure is hot," he said.

"Yeah," replied Blue John, "and dry enough to make the bushes follow the dogs around. Did ya bring the water?"

"Yup. Here, have a drink."

"I see, Silvertip, that you have two fine broomtails there. That's wonderful, but you went after the stallion. Where's it at?"

"Well, you see, Blue John, I seen that stallion all right, but I have no earthly idea how we're going to get him."

"Why not? We'll get him just like we did the last time. That bishop can't be any harder to steal from than those folks were down at Cisco."

"No, I reckon it'd be easy to steal that nag from the bishop, but stealing it from the whole town is not so easy, and I ain't so sure I want to try it now."

"What are you talking about, Silvertip?"

"I don't know, Blue John. Something funny is going on down there, and I sure don't know what to make of it. They have our plug, all right, but half of the men in town are guarding him with rifles."

"What? Do they suspect us?"

"Naw, nothing like that. As far as they are concerned, we don't even exist."

"Then why, blast it? Why are they guarding our stud?"

"Why, I know it sounds plumb crazy, but word is that tomorrow there is going to be a big race, and that bishop we sold the horse to is going to race that same plug in it."

"Aw, come on, Silvertip. You know that nag ain't no race horse."

"I know it, and you know it, too. But honest, Blue John, that's what they told me was coming off. Funny thing is, most of them fellers down there don't think he can race, either. That's why they're guarding him so closely. They don't want the bishop switching horses or doing something so's the horse can't race."

"Whatsa matter? Don't they trust him?"

"I don't reckon, Blue John. Not when so many of 'em have a hundred dollars gold bet against him."

"Whewee! A hundred dollars each? Does the bishop have that kind of money?"

"Beats me," Silvertip said, shaking his head. "But those folks seem to think he does. They trust him that far, at least. Anyhow, bad as the Boss wants that horse back, I don't reckon we'll get him until after the race."

"Who's he racing against?"

"Nobody. He's racing against time. He's got to get from here to Salt Lake between sunup and sundown tomorrow."

"Why, shucks, that's a hundred and ten miles! I say it can't be done."

"Blue John, you sound like them folks down there. Maybe you want to ride on down and place a bet, along with them folks, against the bishop? Let me tell you, there ain't many horses that could survive a one-day trip that long. I had one once that might have done it. Best horse I ever had. But that Belgian? I doubt it. He's big and he's strong, but I don't think he's that strong. And that bishop ain't no little man, either. He'll wear out that nag in a hurry. Way I see it, those folks are about to make themselves an easy hundred bucks."

"You're right, Silvertip. And the way I see it, it's our job to guarantee that the citizens down there win. Did you learn his route?"

"Yeah, sure. A fellow by the name of Sorenson told me there was only one way he could go, and that was over through Salt Creek Canyon, past Nephi, and then straight as the crow flies past Provo, through the Jordan Narrows, and into Salt Lake Valley. But Blue John, how we going to guarantee that the bishop loses?"

"Silvertip, I reckon the Boss is right. In some ways you're awful shy of smarts. We're after that horse, ain't we? And after they start the race, he won't be guarded, will he? So all we have to do is drift on up the canyon a few miles, drop down on him when he goes past, and the horse is ours."

"Gee, Blue John, don'tcha feel kinda sorry for the bishop, him losing twice, the horse and the money, like he'll be doing?"

"Oh, for—! Silvertip, how in blazes did you ever become an outlaw? Now, come on, let's get riding. We've got to find an ambush site before dark. By the way, these are awful pretty mares. Matched white, ain't they? I reckon we can play our own out, if need be, and then switch to these white critters you picked up, as we chase down the bishop. We'll bushwhack him before he even sees us, and even if he does see two riders bearing down on him, he'll see these white mares and think we're his neighbors. Why, this is going to be easy as whistling."

"Gee, Blue John. How'd you ever think of such a good plan? I wish I could think of plans like that!"

"Oh, it weren't nothing. Now, come on, let's ride!"

Earlier that day, in a back room of the Aspen Wells Co-op, Mungus Sorenson and several of the more-than-eager-to-grow-financially men of the town sat in animated conversation.

"Boys," Mungus was saying, "I tell you, it's in the bag! By sundown tomorrow Soderberg will be in the territorial prison, and we'll have won the bets and collected by default. Everything he owns, including the dairy pasture and that fine brick home, will be ours, and Aspen Wells will be needing a new bishop. The choice is obvious, and yours truly will be ready to accept."

"But, Mungus," questioned Jesse Christensen, "what if Soderberg should win? How do we know he's going to get arrested?"

"Why, that's easy," sneered Mungus. "We've set him up, and since you boys will be helping me, I see no reason why I shouldn't lay it all out for you. Less than an hour from now, Loose-lip will leave for Nephi on the train. Once there, he will telegraph Territorial Marshal Dyer in Salt Lake City, telling him of Soderberg's route through the Jordan Narrows and into the city. By the time the bishop gets past Porter Rockwell's old saloon and into the narrows, there will be twenty to thirty deputies swarming over him like bees over honey. He won't stand a chance of ever seeing the city, let alone reaching the Temple block.

"Now, before he gets to those narrows we'll do everything in our power to slow him down. That's just in case the marshals don't make it or he slips through them. So far that man has been shot with luck, but I suspect this will end it. Tonight my son Curly and the Livingston kid will sneak into Soderberg's tack room, put cockleburs under his saddle blanket, and cut his cinch strap nearly in two. That's just for starters.

"Pain, before daylight tomorrow I want you up on the Divide starting a bunch of fires in that cheat grass. All that fire and smoke will at the very least affect the stallion's breathing, and it might even spook it clear out of the country. Jesse, you take Anson Holman and

Ollie Johnson here, and hightail it up the canyon to the Petticoat Cliffs. You three will be outlaws, so disguise yourselves well. Then when Soderberg crosses Salt Creek, stick him up. Take your time and go through everything he's got, dump his canteen, strip off his saddle, and if the cinch strap hasn't broken yet, break it. Point is, your job is to cost Soderberg thirty minutes, and hopefully more.

"Scar, you take the train to Nephi with Loose-lip, steal a herd of cattle or sheep, drive'em into the mouth of the canyon, and hold 'em there where the sides are so steep that a horse can't climb out of it. A good riled-up herd should cost him fifteen minutes, and, boys, every fifteen minutes counts!"

"Mungus," Jesse said in amazement, "you've sure thought of everything."

"Sure as sow bugs under a buffalo chip, Jesse. And there's one more thing that I haven't even told you. I have a lady friend up Santaquin way, a lady friend who's agreed, for a certain . . . er . . . sum to be on the trail when the bishop rides past."

"Hey, she don't sound like much of a lady to me," Jesse said.

"So what?" questioned Scar. "Mungus, what's she gonna do there?"

"Why, Scar, I'm truly amazed! Everybody knows that a polyg loves women. Especially this polyg! She's a winsome lass, and she'll be lying near the trail with more troubles than old lady Lavine. When Soderberg stops to give the lady assistance, she'll occupy another half hour, and if it works out she'll bring him more grief than he ever thought possible. Can you imagine what a torn blouse and a scream would do to that man? Especially if some properly enraged citizens were hidden close by?"

"Why, hang it all!" breathed Scar. "That poor galoot don't stand a chance."

"He sure doesn't," agreed Ollie Johnson. "Why, it'd take an angel from heaven to get Soderberg past all that and into Salt Lake before sundown."

"Yeah," laughed Mungus. "It would take at least one and more than likely it would take a whole cloudful of 'em to get him through. And, boys, we all know he ain't got that kind of influence. Now when—"

Suddenly the door burst open and in staggered Curly, all out of breath from running.

"Pa," he gasped, "they're gone! Somebody stole the white mares, and they're gone!"

"What? How do you know they've not just strayed off?"

"Because Angie Holman saw some feller on a dark horse leading them up into the cedars. She said he was a big man—looked kinda like the bishop."

"Well, I'll be . . . " Mungus mumbled. "Boys, now those marshals will get the bishop for polygamy and horse-stealing. And, boys, that's not just prison, that's a hanging crime! Loose-lip, when you send that telegram, don't forget to tell Marshal Dyer that Soderberg has stolen our two white mares. Knowing what a coward the bishop is, he'll probably have two of those boys of his riding along on those mares as guards. He's got neither the guts nor the horses to tackle that race alone. I tell you, boys, Soderberg is as yellow as mustard without the bite! Now, let's get going. We've a lot to do before morning."

10

The Race Begins

It couldn't have been much later than three in the morning when I was awakened by the sound of tiny pebbles striking against my window pane. It took a minute for me to get my bearings, and then I staggered to the window to see who was causing all the fuss. It would have been like my brother Johnny to do a thing like that, but as far as I knew he was out at the herd. Still, you can imagine my surprise when I parted the curtains and saw Ida Mae standing in the moonlight, beckoning me to come down.

For about a millionth of a second I wondered if this was one of the activities Pa had restricted me from. But then I was dressed and out that window quicker than holly-be-scat. When I hit the ground right next to Ida Mae my heart was really pounding, and I was trying to think of something to say when she grabbed my arm and began pulling me toward the barn.

"Hurry," she whispered, "and don't talk. I've got a lot to tell you, and no time to tell it in. If Father checked my room, we'd be in a whole lot more trouble than we are now."

By then we were inside the barn, and right off Ida Mae started crying. I'll tell you, there is nothing more discombobulating than to be with a girl when she starts crying. However, I at least had the sense to put my arms around her while she dried her tears, and that was a little slice of heaven for sure.

"Hy," she sobbed, "I don't even know exactly why I'm here. I love my father. He's a good man. I swear he is. It's just that he's so jealous, and . . . well, I just can't stand by and let him destroy himself by ruining another man."

"Ida Mae, what are you talking about?"

"Oh, Hyrum," she groaned, "don't you know? Father thinks your father stole his two white mares, and he's out to get him. Why, not more than an hour ago Curly and that mean old Pete Livingston accidentally woke me, bragging to Father about how they'd hid cockleburs under your father's saddle blanket, and I don't know what all else. Hyrum, what I ever saw in that Pete Livingston I'll never know. So please forgive me for the way I acted at the dance."

Well, she about had to scrape me off the rafters, I was floating so high. I wanted to dance and shout, but instead I mumbled, "Sure," and let it go at that. If I'd said much else I'd have been singing, and I can't carry a tune in a bucket.

"Cockleburs," I said, placing my feet firmly back into the issue. "Well, let's check out Pa's blanket."

Quickly I led the way into the tack room, lit the lantern, and pulled Pa's saddle blanket off the post. And Ida Mae was right. There, carefully buried in the fabric of that blanket, were nearly two dozen spiny cockleburs. I could see that it was going to be a job getting those burrs out, so I walked Ida Mae home, pulling the burrs out as we went. And despite the lateness of the hour, I don't think I ever enjoyed a walk more.

She didn't try kissing me that night, which was a relief in several ways. I'd worried some about kissing, especially since Pa's talk with me, and it wasn't long before we got to talking about it.

Hardly had I mentioned kissing when Ida Mae apologized for pushing herself at me the way she had done. Without waiting for me to reply, she began talking about how her ma had died some six years before, and how she missed having someone who could teach her the social graces, as she called them. That made me think of the things that Ma and Pa were always telling me, so I shared them with her.

Kissing, Ma said, was fun and exciting, but even more it was meant to express feelings of love and closeness. For that reason, it ought to be kept sacred, reserved only for the most special people. According to Ma, I said, kissing was a proper and special way of showing strong affection. But Ma said that if young people kissed too often they would soon tire of it and start looking for other ways to satisfy their emotions.

I then told her about the time when Pa sat all us boys down on a log up in Meetinghouse Canyon, where we were dragging out Lyman's first buck.

"Boys," he said, "a lot of young men acquire habits like that buck right there. They think life is simply for frolicking and for mating, and all young girls are seen as free game. They don't understand that Heavenly Father made mankind to be different, to be above the animals. While we do have some very strong and constant feelings, we are also told that we must learn to control them until we are married."

Pa then told us that before we could really love a young lady we first had to learn to trust and respect not only her but ourselves as well. That self-respect could only come by consistently practicing self-control. He then promised us that if we would always remember our priesthood, and honor it by controlling our actions, then we would never find ourselves mistaking lust for love. Love, he told us, gets crowded right out of a young relationship once a couple begin to focus on kissing and the like.

Pa then did something I'll never forget. Right there in the shadow of a huge pine he placed his hands on each of our heads and gave us a father's blessing, promising us by the power of his priesthood that we would have the strength to be true men as we prepared for our missions and for marriage in the temple.

"You know, Ida Mae," I said, "the other thing I will never forget was when Pa finished the blessings and stepped back onto a large rock there in the ravine. With tears in his eyes he told us how happy he had been each time he rode away from the Endowment House in Salt Lake City with each of our mothers as his new wives. He said that those three days had been the most meaningful days of his life, and that we could enjoy the same eternal blessings and the same special feelings if we made up our minds right then to bridle our passions and to help the girls we were with to bridle theirs."

"Hyrum," Ida Mae said, "you are so fortunate to have parents who are willing to share their wisdom with you. Mother would have, if she were only here. Father . . . well, he doesn't have time to think about it, and I'm afraid to ask him. Do you know why I kissed you that night after conjoint session? My girlfriends told me that boys like kissing, and I thought if you liked kissing, and if I kissed you, then you'd like me. And, Hyrum, I really wanted you to like me."

Well, I just shrugged and kicked at a rock, because I surely didn't have anything to say to that, not anything at all.

"You know, Hyrum, maybe I shouldn't tell you this, but I've kissed a couple of other boys, too. I did it because I wanted in the worst way to be popular. Now, as I think of what your parents have told you, I can see that my girlfriends are not really popular at all. They're just available."

"That's right, Ida Mae. Boys generally don't respect girls like that. They just use them. Too many kids think that to be popular they have to go along with the crowd, and do what everybody else is doing. Shucks, I've listened to Jim and Johnnie for years, and they both have some real stories to tell. But do you know what, Ida Mae? The girls they really like, the ones they take to church or bring home for all of us to meet, are not the ones you would call 'popular.'

"I asked our herder one time, after I'd seen him smooching with that Smith girl, if he was going to marry her. He laughed and told me no, that he just used her when he wanted a good time. He said that when he got married it would be to a girl he could respect. Ida Mae, I've never forgotten that. The thing that struck me as funny was that old Jake felt like he could mess around and do whatever he had a mind to do, and yet he would only marry a girl who had never done such things. Seems to me that the good Lord gave out rules for boys the same as for girls. I know my pa sure doesn't believe there ought to be a double standard."

As we approached her house she suddenly grinned, and looking over at me she spoke. "You know, Hyrum, I've been thinking that perhaps Father has been teaching me some good values after all. Just last week I heard him yelling at Curly, and he told him that kids who were fooling around where they hadn't ought to be would have more troubles than the little worm who accidentally crawled into a convention of hungry robins."

We both laughed, and then I watched from out in the road while she crawled into her window. I'll tell you, that Ida Mae was really something!

I was just getting back through my own window when I heard the folks stirring downstairs, and I hadn't even got the covers pulled over me when Ma called me softly to come down for breakfast.

"Pa," I asked as we were eating, "do you know anything about Mungus's white mares?"

"Nope. Nothing more than that they are certainly fine animals. Why do you ask?"

"Oh, no reason. I was just wondering. Pa, I found some burrs in your saddle blanket last night. Looked to me like somebody had put them there on purpose. Be careful, Pa. I just know somebody's after you."

"Hy," Pa answered, "there's a lot more than one person who'd like to see me lose today. Fact is, I wish there was some way out of this race. That was a foolish thing I did, letting myself be pushed into a corner by Mungus and his crowd. Trouble is, I'm here now, and the only way out is by riding north. Hyrum, your mother was right when she said I was being blinded by social pressure. The minute I gave in, that very minute, I lost control over my actions. Today I am not my own man."

As the sky started to gray in the east, the brethren who had been guarding Ingersol brought him to the barn, gave him a bag full of oats, and saddled him up. And none of them saw the cut in the cinch strap that Curly had made. Anyway, after it was saddled Pa took the reins and together we walked through town and out to the cemetery.

I'd never seen so many folks assembled in Aspen Wells at one time. That is, not unless you count the time those two dancing bears got to fighting down behind the Pavilion. If we had been holding a meeting, that crowd would have set an attendance record.

Old Hans Weegin, one of those who had been guarding Pa's horse, placed his hand on Pa's arm and spoke.

"Bishop," he said, "it's a long way to Salt Lake City. A lot can happen to a man or his horse in a hundred and ten miles. My advice is to ride for your life and don't slow down for nothing or nobody. Use that horse wisely, and if you get all the breaks you might just make it."

As Pa started to climb into the saddle his foot slipped out of the stirrup, he about fell, and the crowd gave him a good hurrah. Stiffly then, and awfully embarrassed, Pa climbed aboard, doing his best to ignore the crowd as he smiled bravely at each of his wives. He knew he was heading for trouble, but he was game to go, just the same. I'll tell you, right then I loved my pa so much that I could have popped my buttons. And it didn't matter whether or not he'd restricted me either. He was still a great man!

Just then I caught sight of Curly and Pete Livingston, and they were both as expectant as two robins watching a wormhole. Well, I grinned and winked at Pa, and he winked back, knowing exactly what I was tickled about. It's funny how disappointed a person is when something he's planned so carefully fails to come off, especially if it's supposed to be funny and is in reality a dirty trick. Shucks! I almost felt sorry for Curly, he looked so sour.

At that moment the first rays of the sun splashed across Pa's hat, and with a loud war whoop he slapped the spurs to Ingersol and off he went. We all stood around and watched until even the dust vanished, and then as if on command the whole town turned and headed home.

11

Tucker Bill and the Crawler

We had just finished asking a blessing on my sisters' morning mush—something it dearly needed, in my opinion—when somebody started banging on the door. Since I'd already eaten I told Ma I'd answer it. As the door swung open I caught my breath in surprise, for there was Ida Mae again, so worked up and worried that I knew something else had gone drastically wrong.

Not waiting for greetings, she grabbed my arm and tugged, at the same time pulling the door shut behind me. "Oh, Hyrum," she gasped, trying to catch her breath, "Father has really done it now! I just heard him talking to another man about your father, and about some lady up at the Santaquin depot. She is going to stage a fake accident up on the hill south of the feed store in Santaquin. Father said she will be lying there in agony and pain as your father approaches. He also said something about her tearing her blouse and screaming, and that would get your father in real trouble! Hyrum, I don't know what got into Father, but I'm scared."

For a moment I stood there, shocked into silence. This was pretty bad, but what could I do? I'd seen Ingersol run, and I knew we had no horse that could hope to catch him now, not after a thirty-minute start. Neither could I send a telegram, for Pa would stay as far away from people and depots as he could. Wildly my mind searched, groping and grasping for an idea, but there was nothing, nothing at all.

"Ida Mae," I said at last, defeated, "I reckon I can't thank you enough for your concern. Sad thing is, there is nothing we can do now. Pa will just have to—"

And that was when I heard the train whistling, up at the depot. For a split second nothing registered, but then my mind reached out and took a-hold of that lonesome whistle, and a glimmer of hope leaped into my heart.

"Come on," I shouted, pulling Ida Mae off the porch after me. "We've got to get to the depot, and fast!"

There was no time to get one of our horses, but as we sprinted up the dusty road, here came Sister Dunn in her shiny new surrey. Not thinking of manners, I grabbed the reins and pulled her to a stop. Almost before I knew what I was doing, I was settling onto the seat next to Sister Dunn, and Ida Mae had climbed in on the other side of the surprised woman.

"Now see here, you—"

"Excuse me," I shouted, grabbing the reins, "but this is official Church business, Sister Dunn. We're working to save the bishop, and we need to get to the depot fast. Giddap, horse! Hyyahh!"

Well, that old horse did the double-shuffle for about five seconds, and then it took off like a shotgunned rooster. I was clinging to those reins for all I was worth, and once when I happened to glance at Ida Mae I was surprised to see that she and Sister Dunn were holding on to each other like each was the rock of salvation. Not only that, but both of them had their mouths open and were scooping up flies like they'd missed their last meal. Simply put, they looked scared. But then I probably did, too, though I couldn't see myself too well. Truth was, I'd never driven a buggy like that before, and it was exciting.

The folks along the street were eyeballing us as we bolted past, and a bunch of little kids barely got out of our way. I could hear some mothers screaming at me, but I didn't stop. I had to get to that depot in a hurry, and there was no time to pause and give explanations.

Things were going pretty good until we rounded a corner and hit one of those excuse-me-ma'ams, and that old bump about did us in. First we tipped onto two wheels, and then we crashed back and were on the other two wheels, and I thought for sure we had lost it. Lucky for us that the horse didn't know our predicament, for he kept fogging it along, and our speed eventually brought us back onto all four wheels again. Before anything else could happen, we were churning to a dusty halt near the already moving caboose of the train.

"Let's go, Ida Mae!" I shouted as we leaped from the surrey. Then I shouted back at Sister Dunn. "Much obliged, ma'am. We're all done now. Thanks for your timely assistance."

"Yes, young man," she answered sweetly, as she whipped her horse around, "and I'm all Dunn, too." She started giggling then at her pun, and Ida Mae and I laughed, too.

The conductor on the Sanpete Crawler was Amos Reed Tucker, and he had been conductor for as long as I could recall. Most folks knew him as Amos, although for me he was "Tucker Bill," a name he had told me to call him years before when I was just a little squirt. I'd always thought of him as my good friend, and right then I couldn't have had a better friend for helping me save Pa.

"Well, if it isn't my good buddy Hy," he said as we entered the door of the caboose. "Why, it's been a month of Sundays since I saw you, young feller. And ain't this the Sorenson girl? What on earth are you two up to?"

"Tucker Bill," I replied breathlessly, "we've got more troubles than a cow in a corn patch. This here's Ida Mae Sorenson, like you said, and together she and I are trying to save Pa before someone hangs up his hide."

"Say, that's right," Tucker Bill said thoughtfully. "Today is your Pa's race, isn't it? I heard tell of it down in Manti, and I hate to say it, but most folks down thataway think your Pa's going to lose. What in the world got into him, Hy?"

"It's not what got into Bishop Soderberg," Ida Mae blurted. "It's what got into my father that has us worried. That's why we have to get to Santaquin, and fast."

"Santaquin! Miss Sorenson, if I owned houses in hell and in Santaquin, I'd live in hell and rent out the one in Santaquin. What could you ever want there?"

"Nothing, exactly," I said, grinning. "It's just that Santaquin is where we have to be if we want to save Pa."

"Now hold up, you two. Let's start at the top and work down on this thing."

So between the two of us we told Tucker Bill about Ida Mae's father, how he wanted to be bishop, and was willing to do anything to destroy Pa so that could happen. We also told him about the problems in Santaquin, and how we had to get there before Pa did, or he was had for sure.

When we had finished, Tucker Bill sat in silence for a moment, and then he spoke. "Well, if that doesn't beat all I've ever heard. And that trick with the woman lying in the dirt and groaning will stop Bishop Soderberg sure as snow in winter. He's got more mercy and compassion for the hurts of others than any man I ever saw."

"Tucker Bill, can we beat Pa to Santaquin?"

"Good question, Hy! Good question! As far as I know, it's never been done. And up to now I'd have said it couldn't be done, either. Thing is, now it about has to be, so we'll just have to change our minds and do it. And by jimbo, we will! Hy, are you afraid of heights? Jiggly, wiggly, shaky, rolling-along-fast kind of heights?"

"Huh?"

"Hyrum, there ain't no way we can do what you need without a full head of steam. We've got to let the engineer, Delbert Yergeson, know of our straits, and then he's got to have help feeding the hopper. Hy, there's no way that I am allowed to leave this caboose, so that leaves just you and Ida Mae. One of you is going to have to climb out and crawl along the top of the five cars between here and the engine."

Well, I gulped and swallowed hard, because I knew for certain who it wasn't going to be. I'd never let Ida Mae up on that swaying walkway.

"Tucker Bill, how do I get up on the roof?"

Ida Mae squeezed my arm and gave me a look that would have melted snowbanks, and right then I would have fought bears in a tunnel at midnight for that girl.

Tucker Bill grinned and opened the door, and before I knew it I was making my way across the roof of the first car, wondering what in blazes I was doing there. We all made fun of that train, calling it the crawler and such, but on top of that car it felt like we were moving at a pretty good clip. And sway? If you've never been on top of a moving railroad car, bumping along on a narrow-gauge track, weaving through the sage and the oak and pines, then you'll never appreciate how I felt. Suffice it to say, I was full of fear and trembling, and would that I might not have been there.

I carefully crawled across that first car, feeling about as wary as a loafer wolf moving upwind into a baited buffalo carcass. There I climbed to my feet and leaped to the second car, and was just falling to my stomach for the next crawl when the train gave a powerful lurch. Instantly I was thrown off the walk, and then I found myself sliding slowly toward the edge of the car. Well, in an instant I was as scared as a bull elk being ringed by a pack of half-starved wolves, and it wasn't just because I was falling off, either, though that was certainly part of it. You see, I knew that if I fell off that train, then it was all over for Pa, and that had me scared. Then, too, Ida Mae was watching, and nobody likes to get killed in front of his girl. So wildly I started grabbing, trying to catch on to something, anything that would slow my fall. But there was nothing, nothing but the smooth wooden top of the car.

Ida Mae was screaming as my feet went over the edge, and I reckon I was praying louder than she was screaming. But I was praying without hope, for I knew I was a goner. There was no way that I was going to stop, and my pounding heart told me I was right. However, it was then that a miracle happened. At the last minute my index finger slipped neatly into a knothole, and instinctively I held on.

Now, I might mention that due to my bad leg I had been forced, over the years, to develop and use my arms and my shoulders, and so I had a lot of strength in them. At that moment I was surely thankful for that strength. By inches I muscled myself back up onto that roof, listening while I did it to Ida Mae, who was crying and cheering me on all at once. I know she thought I was a dead man, and for a time I thought so as well. Finally, though, I was back on the walk, and after a quick wave to reassure Ida Mae, I nervously resumed my ordeal. The rest of the way I had no troubles, and after about a month of terror I dropped down into the tender right behind Delbert Yergeson.

"Mr. Yergeson, sir," I blurted, assuming that he was aware I had dropped in.

I've seen men jump before, but never as high or as far or as fast as Brother Yergeson did that day. You'd have thought I was a ghost the way he looked at me. He recovered quickly, though, and soon I had recounted the whole story to him. Then he grinned and asked me if I wanted to work for my fare, and to tell you the truth that was the first time I had thought of that little item. I agreed, though, and in no time at all I was stoking the furnace and building up the steam in that mobile boiler unit we called the crawler.

"With enough steam," Brother Yergeson shouted, "we might make it, Hyrum. We just might!"

12

The Herder and the Cinch Strap

As Bishop Jons Soderberg pushed his big bay stud across the Divide, he found his mind dwelling upon his own ineptness, both as a horseman and as a bishop. How, he wondered, could a man live in a country where so much depended upon horses and still know so little about them? Yet that wasn't entirely true, and he knew it. In fact, he knew quite a bit about horses. He just couldn't ride them very well. He was a livestock man, an animal breeder, and he was the first to admit it. That was why he had been so impressed with Ingersol that first day down near Ephraim.

A magnificent animal, obviously a worker, Ingersol had impressed him like no horse ever had. He remembered looking into the huge bay's mouth, examining all forty teeth, the grinders and tusks as well as the front ones, and all were strong and evenly worn. The black cavities of the bottom center nippers were clearly visible, which meant that the horse was not yet six years old. In fact, the bishop was certain he was nearer four.

The animal's head was well sculptured and held high, a sure sign of pride. His ears, small and pointed, were wide apart, as were his eyes, which were full, large, and uncommonly alert. His neck was long and tapering, the muscles thick on top and thinning toward the middle. His back was short, but his hips, close-jointed, were long and broad. His withers were located exactly halfway between his ears and the coupling of the hip, and all this gave the bishop confidence that the horse could sustain a man his size. The clincher, though, was the width of the animal's chest and hips. This horse, the bishop knew immediately, had speed and bottom. Yet the really remarkable thing, notwithstanding these fine points, was the animal's deceptive gait. When he moved he looked big and awkward. In the saddle, however, one was instantly aware of the animal's smoothness, speed, and grace. He was literally what was called a "rocking-chair" horse.

Eighteen hundred dollars was an awful lot of money—the bishop knew that. There were many reasons why one didn't pay that much for a horse. The first reason, of course, was simple economics. A horse would have to perform long and hard to recoup such an awesome investment.

Another problem was the image such an investment presented. By nature the bishop worried little about the envious or childish thoughts of others. Because he was a bishop, however, there was a problem. Anything he did, no matter what, that appeared foolish or sinful had the potential of becoming a stumbling block in the path of faith which his ward members were following. He wished it weren't so, yet nevertheless it was a truism that far too many people judged the Church by the actions of their bishop. Obviously that meant their testimonies were weak, but still they were sons and daughters of God, and he was duty bound to live a life that would strengthen rather than hinder their spiritual growth. So that was the second consideration.

The third consideration, however, was the real clincher, and it went opposite to the first two. Besides being bishop, Soderberg was also the most wanted polygamist in Sanpete County, Territory of Utah, and as such he was forever being pursued by federal marshals. As bishop, he felt honor bound to avoid capture no matter what the cost.

After all, it was the prophet, John Taylor, who had recently said: "Avoid [the marshals] as much as you possibly can—just as you would wolves, or hyenas, or crocodiles, or snakes. . . . Get out of their way as much as you can. What! Won't you submit to the dignity of the law? Well, I would if the law would only be a little more dignified."

Undoubtedly President Taylor's feelings had been influenced by his experience forty-four years before, when he lay beneath the bed in the Carthage jail, suffering from wounds caused by four lead balls received when his beloved prophet, Joseph Smith, was murdered.

"Yes," Bishop Soderberg said aloud, "he was justified in preaching rebellion, and so am I! For is not my own baby daughter mouldering in the grave because of the injustice of mobs wearing on their chests the authority of the United States government?"

And so his decision was made. He had paid the eighteen hundred dollars for the Belgian stud, and now he was suffering one of the inevitable consequences. If only he had cautioned Victoria against discussing the price he had paid for his horse! He hadn't, though; the word had quickly spread, and now he was left with only hindsight, a poor substitute for wisdom and discretion.

Always Jons Soderberg had prided himself on being his own man, and rightly so. Now, however, as he raced away from the morning sun, he realized that was no longer true. He had allowed the heavy foot of pride to trample down his well-nurtured free agency. The stinging taunts and shallow laughter of Brother Sorenson and the others should never have affected him.

But they had!

"Jumping blue blazes!" he murmured softly. "As a bishop, as a man of God, why didn't I rise above such pettiness? Like Nephi of old, I am moved to declare: 'O wretched man that I am! Yea, my heart sorroweth because of my flesh; my soul grieveth because of mine iniquities.'

"Dear, dear Father," he groaned, "why don't I ever learn? I promised thee up at the Big Springs, after I was called to be bishop, that I would put away my foolish pride. Why, instead of helping Brother Mungus, I fell into Satan's trap, and have only hedged his celestial progress a little further! Lord, bless Brother Mungus. Help him to—"

Bishop Soderberg winced as his horse lunged over the lip of a deep wash, and suddenly he had to swerve to avoid colliding with none other than Rasmus "Pain" Mumford.

"Whooaahh!" he shouted, sawing back on the reins. "Brother Mumford . . . Pain . . . what are you doing here? And why are you holding that torch?"

Pain Mumford stood flatfooted, his mouth hanging open, feeling the red of guilt and embarrassment flush across his face.

"Why . . . ah . . . bishop . . . ," he stuttered, struggling desperately to stamp out the blazing firebrand. "How'd you get here so quick? Ah . . . I mean . . . er . . . what are you doing out so bright and early?"

Soderberg was thoughtfully silent as realization flooded his mind. Slowly then a smile spread over his face, and quietly he spoke again.

"Pain, you'd best be careful with that fire. Grass this time of year burns easily. In fact, seeing that burning patch over there puts me in mind of the time some owl-hoots fired the prairie out in Wyoming just so they could stampede a few head of stock. Wind changed, though, and they came fair to burning down all of Cheyenne before they got it under control. Of course, they were bad men, Pain. Real bad! And real dead, too, when the vigilantes got through with them. Seems that folks don't like their homes burned down. No, sir, they don't like that at all.

"But I was thinking. Wind right here is coming out of the canyon, blowing across the Divide and straight toward Aspen Wells. Be a real shame if we were to lose our town now, wouldn't it? But of course, that's why you're here, isn't it? To put out that fire. I'll say this, my friend, folks'll be mighty proud when I tell them how Brother Pain Mumford saved our town from the ravages of a range fire. Yes, sir, they'll be mighty proud!"

The bishop then reined around and spurred the Belgian forward, calling back as he did.

"One thing more, Pain. You be sure to tell Brother Mungus how slick you put out that fire. He'll be thrilled to know."

Rapidly then he rode off, leaving Pain Mumford standing in the middle of a slowly spreading circle of fire, leaving him wondering just how much the bishop really did know.

"By golly," Pain muttered in amazement as he moved to contain the fire, "Bishop Soderberg is quite a man. He had me dead to rights, and then he gave me an out. From now on when my hand goes up in meeting to sustain that man, I'm going to mean it. Jons Soderberg is my kind of bishop!"

Jons Soderberg, meanwhile, was thundering toward the canyon, his thoughts racing as rapidly as were the hooves of his horse.

"Pain Mumford," he said aloud. "I wonder what Mungus did to get Pain under his thumb. Why, just last week Pain brought his two finest lambs into the tithing office. Had a good chat with him, too. I wonder if his wife's doing any better. I sent my counselors to see her, but maybe I should have gone myself. Blasted horse race! Got so worked up over this race that I forgot just where my priorities were. Pain Mumford is a fine man. Fact is, I wouldn't hesitate recommending Pain to replace me as bishop.

"Dear Heavenly Father, this race is about the most foolish thing I've ever done. But thou knowest how much I've taken from Mungus, and thou also knowest how much I've taken from Marshal Clawson and the other legal authorities our government has set against us. And . . . well, I know all this is nothing compared to the suffering of thy Son, or even the suffering of the prophets. But Lord, I'm no prophet; I'm just Jons Soderberg, and now I'm in trouble clean up to my eyebrows because I went and got weak when I shouldn't have. I know I've no right to ask for help, Heavenly Father, but I'm asking for it just the same. If there is any way, any way at all for me to get out of this mess, why, I'll . . . "

For a time the bishop rode in silence, deeply concerned about the far-reaching and potentially disastrous consequences of his horse race. Suddenly, though, as he emerged from a clump of cottonwoods, he glanced up, his countenance changed, and he spoke again.

"Glory be, Father," he whispered reverently, "I've never seen this canyon so beautiful. Look at how the sun is splashing so vividly across the peaks of Nebo! And look at those quakies—leaves just dancing in the breeze. And green? I don't remember ever seeing the canyon so fresh, so crisp, so green. Why, even those old cedars set my soul to singing this morning! What is it, Father? What are you trying to tell me?"

His voice trailed off and he rode in silence for a time, totally immersed in the ethereal beauty of Salt Creek Canyon. Soderberg could never remember feeling quite this way, and he was totally without words to describe it. It was almost an emotional thing. In fact, it was affecting his emotions to the point that—

Snap!

Soderberg knew instantly that his cinch strap had broken, and it was only by dint of mighty effort that he was able to hold himself and his saddle onto the horse while he reined in. Awkwardly then he slid to the side, his saddle coming with him, and both he and the saddle fell in a heap beneath the stallion's nervous feet. Extricating himself hurriedly, he began examining his gear to discover the nature of his problem, which he knew was serious. It was obvious that the strap had been cut, and it was also obvious that it had been done in such a way that it could not be repaired. Blast! If only he hadn't given his old double-rigged rim-fire saddle to his sons. That had two straps, and he could have managed. But this new-fangled single-rig—or center-fire, as they were calling it—had one strap only; it was cut, and now he was in trouble. Suddenly he thought of his own belt, reached for it, and remembered that he had left it off that day, wearing his suspenders instead. So what was left to do? Well, two choices were all he could see: The first was to continue bareback, the other was to end the race right here. It was obvious that he couldn't do the latter, but he knew he'd never last the full distance without a saddle. Perhaps, though, it might be possible to pick one up along the way. Oh, if only he knew who'd cut that strap! If only—

"Say, bishop, that young feller did a nice job, didn't he?"

Bishop Soderberg, startled out of his reverie, spun his head to see an old man seated on a rock beside the trail directly behind him. Amazed, the bishop spun to his feet, wondering how he could have ridden past the old man without having seen him. Under inspection the old man wasn't too impressive. His hair and beard were white, and his clothing, though clean, was obviously well worn. His face was wrinkled like an old apple, but out of that face flashed eyes like none the bishop had ever seen before. They were clear and blue, but at times almost seemed filled with a flashing fire. Of course that was silly, but by golly, that was what the old man's eyes looked like. And for some reason he looked familiar, too, though the bishop was certain he'd never seen him before.

Could this be one of Mungus's men? No, of course he wasn't. As quickly as he thought it, the bishop knew that this man could not be a part of that crowd. But if not that, then who was he, and what was he doing in the canyon? And what did he mean about a young feller doing a nice job?

"Howdy," the bishop said, wondering just what he should say. "What young feller did what?"

For a moment the old man sat silently, carefully regarding the bishop. Then suddenly he smiled and spoke, his voice so quiet that Jons Soderberg found himself straining to hear.

"Why, the young feller who cut your strap. He did a nice job. You can't repair it."

"Young feller? Do you know who did it?"

"Well, no, not exactly, though I could tell you what he looked like and even his name if it was necessary. Only it isn't."

"Say, how do you know who it was, old man? Were you there?"

"Bishop, your questions are difficult ones to answer. I was there in some respects, though you may put your thoughts to rest concerning my involvement. I had nothing to do with it, but only observed the deed from a great distance off. At that point I had not received permission to come, and so was still supposedly an impartial observer. Now, however, you have asked for help, so I have been allowed to work with you."

Soderberg looked at him blankly, understanding nothing of what the old man was saying.

"Say," he asked, "do I know you?"

"I don't imagine you do. Though you might, you might at that. Lots of folks have, one time or another. Maybe you read about me. Time to time I kept a journal. Maybe you read that."

"Are you a sheepherder?" the bishop asked, looking around for sign of a herd. "I don't recall passing any sheep."

"Why, I'd guess you'd say I was a sheepherder, all right. At least that business is the only one I've worked at for quite a spell. But you're right. I've not much of a herd around here. It's what you'd call a family flock, but I think you'd have to say it's sort of scattered."

"Why, man," the bishop replied angrily, "that's no way to treat livestock! A herder is the leader of the sheep; he gives a herd guidance and direction. He protects them from danger, takes care of injuries, and so on. How can you do that if you aren't with your herd? It's no wonder they're scattered. How long has it been since you worked with them?"

"Oh, not long. In fact, I work with one or another of them most every day."

"Say, who do you herd for?"

"Oh, nobody local. Why?"

"Well," stormed the bishop, "if you herded for me, I'd want to know that you had left my herd! That's why!"

"Then what would you do?"

"Why, by golly, I'd find out why you left my herd. And if the reason wasn't good enough, I'd fire you! That's what I'd do!"

"Bishop, I like that. I like a man who'll say what he thinks even if the other feller might not like it. And I like a man who cares about his livestock, who cares enough to buy the very best. Like that Belgian stallion there, for instance."

"Well," Soderberg replied, somewhat embarrassed, "I've always said that a man ought to buy the best and only cry once."

"Interesting idea. Very interesting."

"So you like my horse, huh?"

"I certainly do. It is a marvelous animal."

"Well, that makes a grand total of two of us who like him. Not exactly a majority, I'd say."

"No, it isn't. Not normally. Bishop, I understand that you are in a fix. So I am here to help you out."

"So the word has spread out of Sanpete County, has it? Well, old-timer, whoever told you I was in a fix had it pegged about right. For I surely am in trouble. But it isn't the kind of a fix that I can get helped out of."

"Why not?" the old man asked.

"Because it's a fix I fixed for myself, is why. I danced the tune, and now I have to pay the fiddler."

"Now, that is interesting. I was told that your fix had to do with a horse race, not a dance. Maybe I was misinformed."

Jons Soderberg gave the old man a narrow look, wondering if he was funning him. But the old fellow surely did seem serious. Maybe he was, but had just been out at the herd too long. Yes, that had to be it. He'd probably been alone so long that he had slipped a cog. The bishop had seen it happen before, plenty of times, so this poor fellow wouldn't be the first. Suddenly he realized that time was passing, and that he had to be on his way.

"Mister," he said, "I've got to go. I've got me a race to win."

"Hold up, bishop. I'm not through with you. You just said your trouble was a dance, and now you say it is a race. Just what is your problem?"

He was so serious that Soderberg burst out laughing, and in spite of his hurry he turned back and quickly told the old man about his fix.

"So that's it," he said. "Naturally, I'd like to win the race. I think old Ingersol here can do it, and given half a chance, we will. Or we would have, if this cinch-strap hadn't been cut. The real problem, though, isn't the race. It's my ward. I'm just sick about what I'm doing to them."

"What do you mean?"

"Well, a man who becomes bishop has got to be above the little problems that seem to afflict mankind—problems such as pride, arrogance, selfishness, dishonesty, and so on. A bishop sort of makes a covenant with the Lord that he will be the spiritual beacon for all the people in his ward. By letting social pressure push my pride into gear, I've in essence told my whole ward that gambling is A-OK with me. I've also told them, pretty clearly, that Mungus Sorenson is my enemy. Can you imagine that? Why, Mungus is a good man, and I'll tell you, I'm amazed at his leadership ability. Somehow I've got to find a way to reach him. Somehow I have to let him know that we need him, and that we need the rest of the men who hang out with him. Sure, they have a few problems, but so do I, and so does everyone else in the ward. None of us are perfect, and I have come to the conclusion that the Lord doesn't expect any of us to be; all he demands is that we be moving in the right direction. And that is what I'd like to help Mungus understand. If I could work that out, either by winning or losing this race, then I'd do it!"

"Bishop, are you certain that winning isn't as important as helping Brother Sorenson? In your heart of hearts can you declare that to be true?"

"Yes, I can! Last night I couldn't have, nor would I have said so this morning. But now I feel different about it. Trouble is, old man, that I don't know which would help those men the most—winning or losing."

"Winning would, bishop. And because you have conquered your pride and set your heart back in the right place, I'm willing to help you do it. You have learned that a mistake is only a mistake if one persists in it. If one's course is changed, then a mistake becomes a learning experience. You've learned, so I'll help."

"Oh, brother!" Jons Soderberg thought. "That's all I need, a little help from this slightly cracked old egg. Why, if—"

"Listen carefully, young man, for here is what you must do:

"Canter from one,
gallop from two,
ride light in the saddle,
and run from three.

"To Brother Sorenson
be kind *and* firm,
and of a truth
he will come to thee."

Smiling then, the old man lifted his hand.

"Farewell, good bishop. Race well. The animal you have there is worthy of a good run."

Well, to say that the bishop was confused would have been to say it mildly.

"Say," he stammered. "What . . . why . . . how do you . . . who . . . ?"

"Yes, bishop? If you have something to say, say it. I've got things to do that are a whole lot more important than sitting here on a rock listening to you stutter. And, by the way, so do you. So say what you have a mind to say, and then be on your way."

Open-mouthed in amazement, the bishop stared at the old man. For the life of him he didn't know what to make of the old fellow. He'd certainly never met anyone like him.

"Fine," he said finally. "One question. Who are you?"

"Bishop, I've already told you that names aren't very important. I can't tell you mine. I won't even tell you that we're related, for you wouldn't believe that. But I will tell you something that is important, if you'd like."

"I certainly would."

"Very well. You have a broken cinch strap. What do you propose to do about it?"

"Well, I don't know, exactly. I—"

"Merciful heavens!" the old man exclaimed. "Bishop, don't you carry a spare cinch strap in your saddlebags?"

"A spare cinch strap? Old man, I think your own cinch is getting a little frayed. Why would I ever carry a spare cinch strap with me?"

"Bishop, that is a foolish question. You'd carry a spare cinch strap around just in case one of your fellowmen was low-down enough to cut the one you were using. Like that young man obviously was. But you didn't answer me. Do you have a spare?"

"Of course I don't have a spare!"

"Are you certain?"

"Say, I ought to know, hadn't I?"

"Yes, you certainly ought to know. Nevertheless, were I you I'd check in my saddlebags. In fact, let's see . . . yes, I'd check in your right saddlebag if I were you."

"Why? All that bag has in it is my lunch. I know. I packed it myself."

The old man then grinned. "Mighty funny taste you have, bishop. Very few men would eat leather for lunch. Take a look, bishop."

"Oh, for crying out loud! I . . . "

And the bishop, to his total amazement, opened his right saddlebag to find, neatly coiled on top of his lunch, a new cinch strap.

"Well, don't just stand there staring, bishop. Get it changed! You've got a race to run."

Without another word the bishop changed straps. Quickly then he saddled up and remounted, forced a grin at the calm old man, waved weakly, and slapped his spurs to his horse.

"Humph," he said as he galloped off. "I wonder how that old man knew about the new strap? In fact, I wonder which of my wives had the foresight to slip that spare one in? Fact is, I wonder when she did it? But that old man is surely something. I wonder who he works for? Poor old fellow has obviously spent too much time alone at the herd. I do wish he'd told me his name, though. Maybe I could help him. Related, hah! Man must be crazy, thinking I'd believe that. Still, he did look familiar, somehow."

Onward then he galloped, onward through the rocks and grass and trees of the Salt Creek Canyon morning. And as he rode he thought of the old man, and of Mungus and the rest of his ward. What a privilege it was to be called as their bishop! Yes, it took a lot of his time, and yes, he was always giving more than he felt he had to give, but he had been blessed with far more than he had ever given. So far, he had never been able to get the Lord in his debt.

In the midst of his reverie, Soderberg's thoughts were shattered by the crashing explosion of gunfire. Twisting in the saddle, the bishop looked back to see three riders come boiling out of the draw he had just ridden past.

"What in tarnation!" he growled, as he heard the *whap* of a bullet passing somewhere near him. "Why, those gents are firing at me!"

Slapping his spurs to his horse's flanks, Bishop Soderberg urged the animal to even greater speed. For a moment he worried about the horse's ability to respond, but then he glanced back and realized two things. The first, and perhaps least significant, was that he was definitely drawing ahead of his pursuers, and rapidly, too. His second realization was that, even though the three men had bandanas over their faces, he recognized one and perhaps two of the horses they were riding.

That lineback dun with the white splash on its chest just had to be Ollie Johnson's, and the dapple gray looked an awful lot like the cayuse Jesse Christensen rode. Setting his jaw, the bishop grimly acknowledged that Mungus certainly had a great deal of power over these men. The third rider would have to be either Loose-lip Lundstrom or Anson Holman, and he would guess from the way the man sat in his saddle that it would be Anson. How in the world could Anson, being the kind of a man he was, justify this?

For five full minutes the four men rode furiously through the narrows of the canyon. Thundering through Hop Creek they rode across the flats where Heber Ockey was clearing off a ranch. Bishop Soderberg kept to the main trail, splashing across Salt Creek and then skirting the southern tip of the Petticoat Cliffs. He knew he was pulling away from the three men, yet he also knew that Ingersol could not endure the terrific pace too much longer. At least he couldn't if the bishop intended that the horse last the remaining ninety-nine miles.

Suddenly from behind him came another flurry of gunfire, and he twisted again to see the two white mares of Mungus Sorenson come crashing down out of the timber, their riders in reckless pursuit of the erstwhile outlaws. For a moment there was concentrated gunfire, and then the three men from Aspen Wells scattered, heading their mounts into the hills in three different directions.

"Oh, no!" the bishop groaned as he glanced back, "now what's going on? Those mares belong to Mungus, I know that! What is he doing fighting his own men?"

As he watched, the two white mares came together and their riders held a hasty conference. Suddenly they broke apart and wheeled in his direction, intent upon renewing the chase the others had so recently abandoned.

In despair the bishop glanced down at his horse. Ingersol was heavily lathered, and foam was flying from his jaws. Still, he was running well, and Soderberg could detect no weakness in him, no weakness at all. But how much longer could he go like this? How much longer could he keep up his killing pace? If it was Mungus and one of his cronies back on those mares, then they were most certainly after him. Yet if it were Mungus, why had he driven off the other three men? That made no sense, not unless Mungus was trying to protect him. But no, that couldn't be it, either. Mungus would be the last person to protect him from injury or danger. So what was going on?

Suddenly he thought of the old man, the old sheepherder who had stopped him earlier. What was it the old fellow had said? Something about a canter, a gallop, and a run? At the time the old man seemed to be rambling, and the bishop had paid little attention to him. But now he wondered. Could the old man have known? Might that old man in some way have seen these men, learned of their plans, and hurried to meet the bishop? Might it be a trap that Mungus was setting, and the old man had learned of it? It was possible, he supposed, though he couldn't imagine how the old fellow might have done it.

"Canter from one," he'd said. That was it! "Canter from one, gallop from two, ride light in the saddle, and run from three." Well, if that was a warning, then he'd better heed it. Trouble was, what did the old man mean? He had been running from three, now there were just two, and that ought to mean that he could slow to a gallop. But then maybe the old fellow had meant that he could canter from the first problem, gallop from the second, and that he'd better run like blue blazes from the third. If that was what the old man had meant, then he'd better—

The piercing shriek of the whistle of the Sanpete Valley train ripped apart the still air of the canyon; once, then twice, a long and drawn-out whistle that Soderberg thought would have raised the dead. The stallion leaped forward at the sound, and the bishop, who had anticipated no such movement, was almost unseated. Retaining his seat, however, he glanced back to find, to his amazement, that one of the white mares was riderless and was buckjumping back up the canyon. The other was running wildly toward the hills to the north despite her rider's obvious displeasure, and Soderberg immediately realized that he knew exactly what the old man had meant. From these two he could now slow to an easy lope or gallop, rest his mount, and still maintain his lead. It was simple. Only how could that old man have known that the train would come along and whistle when it did? There was no way that he could have known that. Not unless—but no, that was impossible. Still . . .

Ahead now he could see the gypsum quarry, and beyond that was the valley where nestled the city of Nephi. Pulling his watch out, he studied it. He had left Aspen Wells at just a little past six in the morning; it was now nearly seven-thirty, and he had almost beaten the sunrise. If it hadn't been for that cut cinch strap and that crazy old man—

Without warning the Belgian stud leaped sideward, and Jons Soderberg found himself clinging with one hand and one leg to the saddle while the rest of him flopped awkwardly in the air. Briefly he caught a glimpse of a rattlesnake his horse had shied from, and then all he saw was ground and sky and horse and ground and sky again, rapidly and not necessarily in that order. Desperately he pulled himself toward the saddle, using all the strength of his arms to hang on while his horse lunged up the steep hill. After a moment they topped out on the rim, and not until then did the bishop regain his seat. While he caught his breath the horse continued to flee forward, and they covered several hundred yards before the bishop thought to rein the animal in.

"Whew," he sighed as the horse blew and snorted beneath him. "That was a close one. Blasted snake . . . I could have lost the entire race right then."

And that was when he noticed, directly below him in the mouth of the canyon, a herd of milling cattle. It was a big herd of shorthorns, tightly bunched, and Soderberg could tell immediately that anyone trying to get past them on the trail would have problems, at least for a few minutes.

"Say," he thought aloud. "I wonder if . . . ? Uh-huh. Just as I thought. That herd of cattle right there can't be an accident! Now where is the drover? . . . Ah, yes. Now if he'll . . . that's it, now this way a little more, out from behind those trees, and . . . Well, I'll be doggoned. That's Osrow "Scar" Thomas down there! I didn't know he was in with Mungus, too. Glory be! Won't surprises ever cease?"

"Hey, Scar!" he shouted. "Scar, I'm up here! *Hello!* I was just passing by, and I thought I'd best say hello. Wish we had time to chat, but I've got to get to Salt Lake City. Come into my office next Sunday, though. I'd like to have a visit with you!"

Soderberg watched with interest and amusement as the expression on Scar's face changed from one of curiosity to understanding and recognition.

"Soderberg!" he shouted, sounding surprised and sick all at the same time. "I thought you'd been held up back there . . . er . . . I mean, I thought you'd been detained."

"Not hardly."

"But how did you get up there?"

"Scar, I like to travel the high places, not the low ones. I try to keep my eyes up, not down. My father used to tell me, Scar, that it is better to aim at the sun and miss than to aim at a pile of manure and hit it. Scar, from the smell down there, I think you've been aiming a little low."

For a moment the bishop thought Scar was going to charge his horse at the sheer hillside. But then he stopped, looked back up the canyon toward Aspen Wells like he was trying to make up his mind, and then he whirled and rode off, kicking his mount like the devil himself was on his trail.

Back up the canyon the train came in sight once more, whistled, and the bishop waved back at whoever it was in the cab who was waving at him. Wheeling his horse then, he turned north across the hills toward Provo and Salt Lake City, while behind him in the canyon Scar flogged his horse toward Aspen Wells, and the outlaw known as Blue John swore bitterly as he trudged along in the dust of Silvertip's white mare, doing his best to catch up with his companion and his runaway mare.

13

The Trouble with Being Crippled

There are times a man gets so excited about something that he becomes absolutely certain that it will work out. And there are folks who will tell you that if a man wants something badly enough, he'll get it, no matter what. Mostly I suppose that is true, but nothing except death is ever sure-fire. So when I give advice now I always say to think positive but plan negative. That way, if something doesn't work out just right, you won't kill yourself with disappointment and frustration. You'll just keep on trying for the next time. That was one of the lessons I learned that day while chasing Pa with the train.

The other thing I learned, or rather relearned, was that just because a fellow prays about something, even prays with all his heart, doesn't mean that the Lord will necessarily let it happen that way. As an example, all my life I'd been praying about my bad foot, praying either that God would make it better or that he'd make people stop laughing at me and poking fun at me. Well, Pa heard me one night, praying for God to smite Pete Livingston because he'd beat the tar out of me. After I'd climbed into bed, Pa came in and sat down beside me. He tickled me a mite and then told me what he thought about my prayer.

He wasn't mad or anything, though. He just told me he'd heard me and thought, after dealing with Heavenly Father himself for lots of years, that I was praying for something that God might not want to give me. I asked why, and he told me that mostly God didn't like to take away the agency of folks, their freedom to act like they wanted. That had been the devil's idea in the first place, and God had rejected it right off. Then Pa told me that people have the freedom to act like they want to act—they just don't have the freedom to choose the consequences of those acts. Consequences were predetermined in heaven, and that's where blessings and punishments come in. If we do something good, then we get a blessing or so for doing it. If we do something bad, then we lose a blessing and so suffer a punishment. Those are the rules that we all agreed to before we were ever born. God lives by them, and so do we—not because we always want to, but because that's the way it is.

What Pa said made sense, and after I'd thought about it for a minute it came to me just how dumb it was to be going around being wicked, fighting and quarreling, stealing eggs and melons, telling lies, and all that other nonsense. My only reward for that was grief and lots of lost blessings, and to tell you the truth, I can't afford to lose any blessings. I'm the kind of fellow who needs all he can get.

So I asked Pa what he thought I ought to be praying for, and he told me Ma and him had been praying about my bad foot right along, and it had come to them that the Lord had given me that foot as a blessing. Well, that made me grin, for I've been dragging that foot around since who flung the chunk, and since when has it been a blessing? I said as much, so Pa told me about Enoch and Moses, who both had speech problems. Yet God called both of them to be prophets. That didn't make much sense to me, so I asked Pa why God had made those men defective, especially if he knew they were going to have to go around preaching the gospel.

"Hyrum, pretty near anybody can preach. But hardly anybody can be a prophet. That takes somebody who is especially humble and prayerful. If you were a prophet, and all you could do was stutter and stammer, would that make you humble or proud?"

"Humble."

"It's obvious then, isn't it? When God gave Enoch and Moses speech problems, he was in reality giving them special blessings. That was humility, for if those brethren were humble, then the Lord could work with them and make them even greater than they were. If a man has to rely on God, then that same man gets closer to God."

"OK, I guess that makes sense. So what is my great blessing?"

Pa laughed and tousled my hair around a bit, and then he took hold of my shoulders and got real serious.

"Hyrum, how fast can you run?"

"Be funny," I replied bitterly.

"Can you keep up with your brothers?"

"Not hardly."

"There's your blessing. Your Ma and I have noticed that you can hardly wait for anything. When you want something it has to be right now or you get pretty wild. Are we right?"

"Yeah, I reckon."

"Son, that's called not having any patience. Your bad foot forces you to slow down, doesn't it? And being slow automatically teaches a man to have patience."

"But Pa, why is patience such a big deal? What's wrong with being in a hurry?"

"Maybe nothing. Thing is, I have noticed that when a man doesn't have patience he generally doesn't have much tolerance or kindness in him, either. If people aren't as fast with something as he thinks they ought to be, then *bam!* he's had it with them. He has no kindness, no understanding, nothing. Now you know that tolerance and kindness are qualities that Jesus wants us to have. The entire message of the gospel is one of love, of caring. With you, I'd say that the Lord wants you to learn those qualities pretty badly. That's one of the reasons at least why he blessed you with your club foot."

Pa kissed me goodnight then and left, and I thought about what he'd said. And funny thing was, the more I thought about it, the more right Pa sounded. By the time I finally went to sleep I was even thinking about thanking Heavenly Father for my special blessing: my bad foot.

Anyway, there I was on that train, shoveling coal and praying with all my heart that we could catch Pa right quick, when Mr. Yergeson shouted and pointed Pa out to me. And that was when I forgot that God doesn't always answer our prayers right off the way we want him to.

I started pulling on the whistle chain, shouting and waving with all my heart, and then I noticed those two white mares that belonged to Mungus. Right away they started to pitch and buck, and then one man was down and both horses were heading for the trees totally out of control. That was when it dawned on me that Pa was being chased. For a moment or two I watched him, but he was paying no attention to us at all. Suddenly his horse, old Ingersol, jumped sideways and headed up the side of a ridge, and I thought Pa had lost it for sure. We turned a bend then, and I lost sight of Pa for a couple of minutes. When I saw him again he was topped out on the ridge, sitting there watching us. I jerked the whistle again and started waving, but Pa only waved back, sat there for a moment, and then turned and disappeared over the ridge.

When he vanished my heart sank clear down to my boots. I had been so certain that we had caught him, and now I was so disappointed that I was ready to quit.

"Gosh, Mr. Yergeson, I thought we'd caught him there, I surely did. I know he saw me, because I saw him wave. Why do you suppose he didn't stop?"

"Why, boy, that's near a half mile over to that ridge, maybe even a little more. And as I recollect, the last time I saw your Pa he had on his nose a pair of spectacles. From that I'd guess that his eyes are going bad. I think he saw the train, he likely saw someone waving, and he waved back just to be friendly. I'd bet two bits against a hoot-owl's hoot that he had no idea it was you waving at him. Why, he'd never suspect you to be on this train."

"No, I suppose he wouldn't," I agreed. "Only now what am I going to do? Pa's already headed for Santaquin."

"Say, young feller, don't be so discouraged. Did you see how your Pa daylighted those whites when you blew that whistle? Why, already you've done him a heap of good. If I'd been alone I'd have never thought of blowing the whistle. So rattle your hocks, boy, and throw more coal. We've got to get you to Santaquin."

"But you don't go to Santaquin!" I shouted, struggling with another shovelful of coal.

"True enough. But if we hurry we can get to Nephi before the Utah Central pulls out. Then I can talk with old Cale Steiner, the engineer. He's just crusty enough that if he takes it into his head to get you to Santaquin in a hurry, he'll bend the rules to do it."

"Will he really?"

"Sure he will. You ever seen him?"

"No."

"Well, he's a little man. Fact is, he told me hisself that he's so short he has to borrow a stepladder to kick a grasshopper on the shinbone. What I'm saying, Hy, is that after spending his life on the raw end of one joke after another, he just naturally fights for the underdog. Right now, that is you—you and your father. So hustle, boy, and we'll get you there yet."

So hustle I did, shoveling that coal out of the tender and into the firebox faster than Johnnie-be-quick. And we did build up a good head of steam, too. I'll tell you, we were really rattling down that track, black smoke billowing up behind us for a mile. It was a beautiful sight to see.

But then, as we came around a curve just above the gypsum mine, I saw Mr. Yergeson look ahead and gasp.

"Look out, Hy!" he shouted. "We've got us a real problem!"

I looked out the window myself then, and what I saw scared the living bejeebies out of me. There, directly ahead of us, was a herd of cattle blocking off the track.

"It's cows!" I shrieked.

"I'll say it's cows! It's that prize herd of new shorthorns that Swede Jensen just had shipped in. How in thunder did they get loose, and what are they doing here in the canyon?"

Well, I surely didn't know, but then I doubt that Mr. Yergeson was asking me, anyway. Fact is, he was still talking, or maybe he was even praying; I don't know. I do know that I sure was.

"Hy," he shouted suddenly, "hang on! There isn't time to stop, so I'm opening her wide open. Now we'll see if that cowcatcher up front is good for anything or not."

Suddenly the whistle started screaming again, blast after blast after blast, and we were getting close enough to the cattle that I could see their faces when they turned to see what was making all the racket.

I've noticed before, when I've been herding Pa's cattle, that with the exception of Hepsi, cows are so dumb they don't know enough to come in out of the rain, and they're about as fast-acting as wet gunpowder. So I didn't have much hope that our whistle would do the job. Except I guess there were a few smart cattle in that bunch. Maybe it was because they were shorthorns or something. I don't know. But right off a few of them started scrambling up the sides of that cut, doing their level best to get out of our way.

The whistle screamed again, several times, and more of those critters got the message. Why, a body never saw such scrambling and climbing. For being so crowded it was wonderful how many of them managed to get out of the way before we got there. Out of that whole herd we hit only three . . . well, four if you count that one foolish cow who kicked at us and got flipped end-over-teakettle for her troubles. I watched her, though, and after a few seconds she got up and took off, so she wasn't hurt too badly. Still, I'll bet it will be a spell before she tries kicking a train again. I kind of wished that it had been Hepsi.

One thing, though. That cowcatcher didn't work too well. Fact is, it didn't catch a single cow. About all it did was to divide them asunder, parting them to the right and to the left as we passed by. Was it me, I'd have called it a cow-cleaver or something like that. Would have made a lot more sense.

Shortly thereafter, and without further incident, we emerged from the canyon and clattered up to the depot in Nephi. We had barely stopped when Mr. Yergeson grabbed my arm and ran with me to the already moving Utah Central. Quickly Mr. Yergeson introduced me to Mr. Steiner and told him my story, and by the time he'd finished, Mr. Steiner was grinning from ear to ear. Jerking his thumb toward the back he motioned for me to get aboard, and then he pulled open the throttle and we were off.

I jumped aboard and was making my way back through the car when I glanced out the window and about had a heart attack. For there, hauling tail along the tracks outside, were an out-of-breath Tucker Bill and a very frightened Ida Mae Sorenson.

"Oh, my goodness," I groaned, "I plumb forgot about Ida Mae!"

I lunged through the car to the back of the platform, reached out, grabbed her arm and pulled. And while Tucker Bill pushed I was glad once again for the strength of my arms. Ida Mae stumbled and was bouncing along like a barrel rolling downhill, but I held on and after a minute she was there beside me on the platform, shaking like quakies in a high wind. Well, I was shaking, too, but I didn't want her to know that, so I tried to make a funny.

"I don't know about you, Ida Mae, but I'm getting awfully tired of just about missing trains."

She grinned and snuggled up to me, I put my arm around her to steady her (I needed a little steadying myself about then), and together we walked into the caboose and sat down. And for the first time in a long time I found myself feeling self-conscious about my drag-along foot. Why? Well, have you ever thought about what it would be like to be walking beside a girl with your arm around her kind of tight? And instead of moving smoothly all you can do is lurch along, either bumping into her or pulling away from her with every step you take? And that when the thing you want most in all the world is to impress her favorably? Think about it for a minute, and you'll understand why it bothered me so much. Right then I felt as out of place as a .22 cartridge in a twelve-gauge shotgun, and I started wondering just what I was trying to prove, pretending I was normal in the presence of such a special girl as Ida Mae.

Right away my ears and neck started to burn, and I was just coming down with a real bad case of feel-sorry-for-me-itis when Ida Mae looked up at me and spoke.

"Hyrum, when you almost fell off the train back there in the canyon, I thought I was going to die. I've never been so scared in my whole life! And pray? I've never cried and prayed so hard, either. Not ever!"

Well, shock me! What she'd said so surprised me that I didn't know what to say. So I just sat there like a dummy and asked how come.

She looked up at me again, her eyes big and round, and I could see that they were watering up right rapidly. Now what was I going to do? Why had I said that? Why . . . ?

"Don't you know, Hyrum? Can't you tell how I feel about you? In my whole life I've never known anyone who was so kind and gentle, who really cared about other people. Why, you're special, Hyrum, and I like you. I like you very much."

Now my ears were really burning. I couldn't believe what I was hearing. I couldn't believe—

"I was so worried when you started across the top of the train, Hyrum. I mean, with your foot and all I was sure that you were going to—"

Ida Mae suddenly stopped, realizing, I suppose, what she had said. And me, I just dropped my arm from her shoulders and sat there, staring at my twisted foot and wishing I had never been born.

For a long time neither of us spoke, and I didn't look at her to see what she was doing, either. I just sat there trying to think of something to say that would show her how badly she had hurt me. For she had, though for the life of me I couldn't understand why I was so devastated. After all, she had only spoken the truth, and I'd heard it often enough before. I'll tell you, self-pity had come back real quick.

"Yeah," I said finally, making my voice as bitter as I could, working myself into a real mad. "It sure is tough, having to worry about a cripple. And I'll bet it is just as tough being seen with one, isn't it? I must be about as wanted as a polecat at a picnic!"

That started her to crying in earnest, but I didn't look at her. No, sir, I didn't! If I was going to hurt, so was she!

"Hyrum," she sobbed quietly, "I didn't mean—"

"Oh, yes you did, and you know it, too! I know what my foot looks like. And I know what it looks like when I hobble along, too! I'll bet that for a sweet little girl like you it must be a real mortifying experience, being seen out in public with a crippled freak like me. Why do you do it? So people will laugh all the harder when they see how much worse I look when I am with you?"

"Hyrum, I—"

"Oh come off it, Ida Mae!" I stormed, angry now through and through, and wondering that I could have made myself so angry so quickly. "You don't really like me, and you know it! No girl can really like a cripple!"

Suddenly Ida Mae jumped to her feet and slapped me in the face, hard! She was still crying, but now she was mad, more angry than I had ever seen anybody except maybe Pa that time after the marshals abused Aunt Polly and wrecked our house.

"You're right!" she said, almost spitting her words at me. "I don't like you! But being a cripple has nothing to do with it. Or maybe it does. I liked you because I thought you were sweet and kind, because I thought you were a man who had the kind of qualities that I wanted someday in my husband. But no, you're not like that! I'm not even sure that I would call you a man. You're just a mean and vicious boy, just like my brother Curly and his friend Pete. Of course I noticed your club foot. I'm not blind. Everybody notices things like that! Big deal. I've got freckles, and people notice them, too. So what? I don't like freckles, but I hope that people can look past them, just like I looked past your foot, to see what kind of a person is there. And you know, Hyrum, I liked what I saw so much that I decided that you weren't really crippled at all. It was me who was crippled, because I noticed your foot and let it bother me. So I made up my mind that I wouldn't let it bother me any more. I even prayed about it. And you probably won't believe this, but I haven't thought of it since. At least I hadn't until I saw you start out across the roof of that train. And then I only noticed it because I was so worried about you, because I cared so much about you.

"What do you want? Do you want people to close their eyes when you walk past? Do you want people to pretend and to be dishonest around you? Do you want them to lie and say they don't notice your foot when they really do? Hyrum, you can't help it. It isn't your fault that you were born with a club foot. But neither is it theirs, nor mine! No matter what you or anyone else says, you are different, at least to that extent. And because you are, people will notice it. The thing is, instead of hiding behind it the way you are doing, you ought to be proud that you are you, that you have had experiences and feelings that most of the rest of us will never have. But no, not you! Not Hyrum Soderberg! You're too busy feeling sorry for yourself to even notice how much you have to give.

"Let me tell you something! You're crippled, all right. But it isn't your foot. No, sir, Hyrum Soderberg! You're crippled in your mind, and that is the worst kind of cripple that a man can be!"

And with that she turned and marched through the train and into the next car, slamming the door behind her and leaving me alone to choke down my tears of humiliation and ponder what she had said. And I'll tell you, facing up to that was one of the toughest things I've ever had to do. That was because she was right—she was right, and I knew it. And what made me most angry was that I had gone over all that before, myself, and thought I had it licked. I mean, how long had it been since I'd let it bother me when someone stared at my foot? I didn't know, but it had been a spell, that was certain.

Slowly I got up and hobbled back to the platform behind the caboose. What was wrong with me? Why had I acted like that? Why in the world . . . ?

For a long time I just leaned against the rail, watching the country slipping away behind me. The land north of Nephi was pretty arid, growing mostly rocks and dirt. And the brush on the lower slopes of Mt. Nebo was so thick that the rabbits had to climb trees just to look out. Here and there some hardy farmer had practically drowned himself in his own sweat clearing the land of brush and rocks, and was now trying to grow dry-land grain, though most farmers were lucky if they got more than ten to twelve bushels to the acre. Still, they were doing their best to put the land to use, to make it productive—and knowing that made me feel proud.

You see, they were Mormons, I was a Mormon, and that sort of put us all on the same team. Being productive was a part of our religion. So was doing the best we could with what we had and not complaining about what we didn't have. Joseph Smith taught that, Brigham Young taught it, and now Wilford Woodruff, who was Acting President of the Church since the death of John Taylor, was teaching it. You see, we believe that the land is the Lord's (though why he wants some of it I'll never know) and when a man is allowed to use it, even if he buys it first, he is still obligated to the Lord to do the most with it that he possibly can. I think Pa calls that the law of stewardship.

And the law of stewardship doesn't cover just land, either. It deals with everything that we as humans have to deal with. I heard Pa give a discourse on the law of stewardship once, and he explained that the Lord had provided everything for us that we needed in order to be happy, prosperous, and righteous. The Lord made us stewards over everything that affects our lives, and we are under obligation to do the best we can with what the Lord has given us to do it with.

And there was the problem. You see, the Lord had given me my bad foot and had made me steward over it, so to speak. All I had to do was do my best with what I had. And I had been doing my best—or at least it seemed to me that I had. Sure, it wasn't always easy, and sure, I became bitter now and then. But mostly I was handling it. Or at least I was until Ida Mae went and said what she did. Blast! Why does a fellow have to be so gosh-awful dumb? Sometimes I wondered how I ever got past the flyleaf of my first grade primer. Ma would tell me that my pride was getting in the way of my happiness, and it was.

I could even see it. But how is a man supposed to get rid of pride? More and more I was coming to sympathize with Pa.

Shucks! Things would surely be a whole lot more simple if I was dead. For a moment or two I wondered what being dead would be like. I didn't really think about the being dead part, just about what Ida Mae would think if they stopped the train and she came back to apologize and I was gone. They would start a search and would find me lying along the tracks, all battered and broken and bloody, and then wouldn't she be sorry! I could just imagine her crying, saying over and over to herself that it was all her fault, that she really loved me and that she hadn't meant to do it, to say what she'd said. Oh, how sweet is revenge!

I looked down then at the tracks and the ties, speeding away from beneath me. Would it hurt much, I wondered! Probably so, at least for a minute or two. But if I hit right, and didn't try to protect myself . . .

Oh, good grief, I thought! Hyrum Soderberg, how dumb can you get? That's called suicide, killing yourself! And you know what that means. Murder! Beside, if you died, of course Ida Mae would cry. She'd probably even cry a lot. But sometime she would stop, sometime she wouldn't have any more tears for that fellow, poor old Hyrum what's-his-name, who felt so sorry for himself that he jumped off the train. And after she finally stopped crying, then what? Why, you'd still be dead, Hyrum, old boy. That's what. Crying and feeling bad is only for a little while. Dead is for a long, long time.

Yeah, and besides that, it would be just my luck to not get killed at all. I'd probably just get broken up a lot and become a worse cripple than I already was. Then I'd probably have to drag around two bad feet instead of just one. That would likely be how Heavenly Father would punish me for blowing my stewardship over my body. Isn't life tough? As near as I can tell, nothing is ever easy!

Again I looked at the rails and the ties, speeding away from beneath me, slipping away so fast they were just a blur. But then, when they got far enough away, or I did, they could be seen distinctly. Funny, I thought, how much life is like that. Things around a person happen so fast that everything is a blur. It's hard to tell, until something is past or until you've moved away from it, just exactly what is going on. Like my fight with Pete Livingston, which led to my prayer, which led to Pa telling me about my special blessing. You see, it would have been easy for me to say that the fight was a bad thing, because I lost and about got my nose pushed through the back of my skull. But later that fight turned into a blessing because of what it led to. Makes sense, doesn't it? From a distance, things always look more clear.

Or maybe like my fight with Ida Mae. Now that I thought about it, that little girl meant more to me than anyone else in the whole world, except of course my family. Yet there she was, crying somewhere like her heart was broken because I, the fellow who supposedly liked her, had been meaner than a hydrophoby skunk. Now how much sense did that make?

"Hyrum," I said to myself, "you've got to go apologize to that girl! You've got it to do even if she's as cold as the stare of a gila monster!"

But then, just as I turned to go find her, I saw dust off to the east, up along the foothills. My first thought was of Pa, but after a moment I could tell that it wasn't Pa at all. It was those two white mares again. I couldn't believe it. Already they had come this far, and they were still smoking along like Old Nick was after them. Well, in a way that was good, for it meant that Pa was still ahead of them. Now, if only we could—

"Say, young feller. I've been looking for you."

I turned to see who was speaking, and found the conductor walking toward me through the caboose, shaking his head like he thought I was the most impossible person he'd ever seen.

"Cale Steiner told me that we're trying to get you to Santaquin in a hurry. I told him he shouldn't, that it wasn't good for a train to race it like this. But he just laughed and told me it was important. Ha! You don't look so important. Who are you, anyhow?"

"I—uh—"

"Just as I thought. You ain't nobody. Well, no matter. The damage has been done, and now old Steiner will have to pay for it. It's about time, too. Anyway, that's Santaquin just beyond the next ridge. We'll be pulling in in about five minutes, so find that little lady friend of yours and be ready."

With that he turned and walked off, and I heard him muttering about kids, and about how a cute girl like her must have real problems to be willing to be seen with a freak and a cripple.

Because I couldn't do anything else, I grinned, thinking that his high-pitched voice was so bad it would drive a coyote to suicide. Then I set out to find Ida Mae and try to apologize to her for what I'd said.

And to tell you the truth, I was so busy thinking about what I was going to say to her that I didn't even notice, until we were past, the dusty bay horse loping along about fifty yards east of the train.

Suddenly I saw him, shouted with joy, and began running through the train toward the front. That was Pa! We were going to make it! We had caught Pa!

Through the four cars I ran, doing my best to keep one eye on Pa while I watched where I was going with the other. I missed once, though, but I want you to know that I really didn't mean to knock the conductor down. Why, I even apologized as I jumped over his entangled body! In the front car I passed Ida Mae, but I had to get up to the tender and let Mr. Steiner know that I had to get off.

"Hyrum—" she said as I ran past. But I didn't have time to stop, not then.

"Later!" I shouted, and then I was out the door and scrambling up the tender. Only at that moment we entered the cut through the ridge south of Santaquin, and suddenly I could no longer see Pa.

Oh, no! I thought. How am I ever going to get his attention? How am I going to . . . ?

Still scrambling, I made my way across the coal-filled tender and down into the engine, where I stood gaping. There was surely no comparison between this giant machine and the old Sanpete Crawler.

"Mr. Steiner, that was Pa back there, and—"

"Yes, son. I saw him. Looks to me like he is doing all right, too. He's near two miles ahead of those two galoots on the white mares. Now you just relax and keep out of the way. We'll be at the depot in no time."

"But, sir, that's just it. I've got to warn him *before* we get to the depot, not after. Ida Mae said her father wanted that woman to be waiting just over this ridge here, not down at the depot. She'll be laying in the trail, and Pa won't have a chance—"

"Well, why didn't you say so? I reckon I misunderstood when you and old Yergeson were jawing at me back in Nephi. Okay, boy, you're in charge. You say the word, and I'll hit the brakes."

"Uh . . . how long is this cut?"

"It ends just beyond this curve. Another fifty, sixty yards, I'd say."

"All right, stop it just the other side of the cut. That way I can run up the trail and maybe get there before Pa does."

"Sounds good. You need any help? I mean, can you run all right with that foot?"

Well, this time I really grinned, thinking instantly of Ida Mae. Bless her heart, she surely did have a way of making a feller take a good look at himself.

"No, sir. This old foot slows me down a little, but when I have to, I can get along pretty well. Just ask the conductor back there. Thank you anyway, Mr. Steiner, but what has to be done I want to do myself."

He grinned then and shook my hand.

"You'll do, boy," was all he said. "You'll do."

And then he pulled on the brakes. In another moment we'd be through the cut and I'd know if we were in time.

14

Enduring on the End

Pain Mumford leaned against the door frame of the Aspen Wells Co-op, his body racked with a new spasm of coughing. He had been amazed at how his little fire had spread, and there had been a time when he wondered if he would get it out at all. But he had, and now he suffered from smoke inhalation, fatigue, and an overwhelming sense of guilt.

"Mungus," he gasped, tugging once again at his oft-used neckerchief. "I may not know much, but today I received a whole year's schooling in about five minutes."

"What you talking about, Pain?"

"The bishop, Mungus. I'm talking about our bishop. As far as I'm concerned, we had him all wrong. He'll do to ride the river with."

"Oh, no, don't tell me you didn't get the fire built! What'd you do, sleep in?"

"Hang it, Mungus! Stop yelling at me! I've enjoyed all the yelling from you I'm going to. I built your fires, and I was just getting them spread when here comes the bishop, pretty as you please on that big stallion. Right off he guessed what I was doing."

"How do you know?"

"I know he knew! I've seen that twinkle in his eye before. He measures the doings of a man better than any bishop I ever had. And do you know what? Even when he knew what I was doing, he thanked me. Can you beat that? He thanked me for being up there on the job saving the town from fire. Funny thing is, he was right. As soon as he rode off the wind changed, and if I hadn't been there to put out that fire, if I'd run like a rabbit when I first saw him, why, Aspen Wells would have gone up in flames. And Mungus, that hay you cut last week—your whole crop—would have been the first thing to burn."

"But the race? You didn't slow him down, Pain? Not at all? What about our money?"

"What's a hundred dollars, Mungus? Let me tell you something. It was worth a hundred dollars to me to learn what I did about the bishop today. To tell you the truth, I hope he wins."

"Yeah, yeah, yeah. You sound like goody-goody Mumford all right. Today you really are a pain. Soderberg sure sucked you in. I can see that."

"Maybe so, Mungus. Maybe so. And maybe he didn't, either. Maybe I'm just starting to see how bright the light is when you look out instead of in. You know what I think? I think you've spent too much time looking through the dusty fly-specked windows of the Co-op. Step outside, Mungus. Step outside and see how bright life can be when your conscience is clear and your mind is at peace."

"You bet I'll step outside, you spineless traitor! I'll step outside with my boot planted on your backside. I'll mop up the street with you. I'll—"

"Mungus, why do you always think violence will solve your problems? That can only lead to trouble. One of these days someone will clean your meathouse, and I'll be there to hold his hat when he does it. Who knows? Maybe it will be me. Anyway, you make me tired. I'm going home."

"Why, you—"

"Hold it, Mungus. Here comes more good news, I'll bet."

Sorenson brushed past Pain Mumford and into the street, concern clearly visible on his face. What had happened now? Why had his men returned so quickly? What was going on?

In a cloud of dust Anson Holman, Ollie Johnson, and Jesse Christensen plunged their horses to a stop, and Jesse leaped off and ran onto the boardwalk.

"Mungus," he coughed, clearing the dust from his throat. "Something went wrong. Something—"

"Oh, no!" Mungus groaned. "Not you, too? Why in heaven's name did I ever trust you numbskulls? Lay it out, Jesse. What happened?"

"I don't know, Mungus. Things were going just like you said they would. He passed us and we lit in after him firing and scaring him good, just like we were real outlaws. And the bishop was about ready to stop, too. We could tell. But then from out of nowhere came those two white mares you lost, crashing down on us so fast there was nothing we could do. We—"

"White mares? What are you talking about? I thought it was Soderberg who stole those mares."

"Yeah, so did we. But if he did, the men he gave them to turned against him real quick. Mungus, those two hombres were hard men, as cold-blooded as froze-solid rattlers. And they were shooting to kill, too."

"I'll say!" Anson groaned. "Look at this here hole in my arm, if you want proof. Mungus, those were real owl-hoots, men from up the river and over the pass. Those were Robbers' Roost boys if I ever saw any."

"Add it all up," Ollie joined, "and you'd have three dead partners right now, Mungus. We'd all be flybait except for one thing. They weren't really after us."

"Oh, yeah," Mungus growled. "And what makes you so sure of that? It sounds to me like you boys were taken out by Soderberg's own men."

"You're wrong, Mungus. Dead wrong. When we scattered, those fellows hardly even broke stride. We weren't there at all as far as they were concerned. They were after the bishop, and when we last saw them they were whooping and hollering and throwing lead at him like they were born to it."

"Yes, sir, Mungus. Unless Soderberg's stallion is a lot better critter than we think, your worries are over. Fact is, that's why we lit out of there. We didn't want our names linked in any way, any way at all, with the death of our bishop."

"Death!" Pain shouted. "Don't you boys believe it! It'll take more than you or anyone else has to kill that man!"

"Be quiet, Mumford! And get out of here! All the rest of you clear out, too. Some thinking's got to be done, and it seems to me I'm the only one with enough sense to do it."

Earlier, back in the canyon, the two outlaws had experienced similar frustrations.

"Whooaahh! Settle down now, you old mare! Confounded train! What in thunder is that engineer blowing his whistle at here? Crazy nag, ain't you ever heard a train whistle before?

"Blue John, you all right? I don't like saying this, but your face looks like the north end of a south-bound mule!"

Blue John staggered slowly to his feet, his head spinning as he reached up to adjust his hat. "Silvertip," he groaned, "what happened?"

"Your horse spooked, Blue John, and dumped you. That's what comes of never learning to fork a bronc. You and your wagons."

"So where's the horse?"

"Look quick, pardner, and you'll see it hightailing it over the ridge yonder."

"Oh, no! Where am I going to get another nag?"

"Beats the tar out of me," Silvertip replied caustically. "Fresh mounts in this canyon are scarcer than bird feathers in a cuckoo clock."

"Come on, pardner. Give me a hand up behind you. I'm so weak I'd have to lean against a fence post just to spit."

"Yeah, you look like it, too. But sorry, I ain't givin' you no ride, Blue John. I'll chase down your mare for you, but until I get it, you're afoot. You hoof it along after that Mormon bishop feller as best you're able, and I'll be back directly."

"Say, Silvertip. You'd better be quick, and you'd better come back. We're both in this deeper than either of us wants to admit, and we've got to get that there stallion."

"Why, Blue John, you surprise me. All this verbal lather you're working up makes me feel like you don't trust me. You get walking, and I'll be back with your mare before you top the next ridge."

Nearly three hours later, and much further up the trail, a weary and saddle-sore Jons Soderberg forced his mount through a clump of willows and headed it up the gradual slope that led eventually over the ridge and into Santaquin Valley, a part of the larger Utah Valley. For the thousandth time he shifted his position in the saddle, trying to ease his aching muscles.

Forty miles, he thought, and still another seventy to go. How will I ever last?

"Heavenly Father," he sighed," a couple of hours ago I was asking your help to win. Now I'm thinking that just getting there would do fine, no matter when it is. Lord, the scripture says we must endure to the end. But as for your old bishop here, he'd be satisfied if he could just endure *on* his end.

"Come on, Ingersol, you're doing fine. Once we get over this ridge it'll be downhill for you all the way to the Jordan Narrows. Here comes the Utah Central, big fella. Too bad we can't catch a ride. But that's fine, for in the morning we'll be riding it on our way home."

A few minutes after the train had passed, the man and the horse topped out on the ridge. Pulling his mount to a halt to catch his breath, the bishop leaned back, lifted his canteen, and took a long pull at the warm water. Dismounting then, he took more water and splashed out the stallion's nostrils. Pouring more into his hat, he let Ingersol moisten his mouth.

"That's enough, old boy," he murmured softly. "Too much water and a run in this heat would kill you. We'll get you all the water you want in the stables in Salt Lake City. Until then, old horse, just trust me."

Climbing back into the saddle, Soderberg glanced out over the valley. Suddenly he sat up in amazement. The train had stopped below him in the cut, and a few people were milling around outside. But what really surprised him was that not more than seventy yards away a fellow was kneeling in the trail, and that fellow looked an awful lot like his son Hyrum. In fact, that girl beside him certainly resembled Ida Mae Sorenson. There were three other men, too, but those he didn't know.

"What in thunder?" he growled as he slapped his spurs to his horse. "What are Hyrum and that Sorenson girl doing here? I left them back in Aspen Wells!"

15

The Dress or the Stain?

Leaping out the door and through the cloud of hissing steam, I raced up the hill toward where I knew that woman must be waiting for Pa to arrive. A pretty Appaloosa with its reins dragging was feeding on the grass above the trail, and I guessed that would be her horse. Knowing I must be close, I ran as fast as my leg would allow, and in no time I came huffing and puffing through the brush to almost stumble over the prone form of the woman. She was in the trail all right, just like Mungus had planned, and as I looked at her my heart went out to my pa. How could one man survive so much opposition?

The woman's appearance startled me. She was small, smaller even than Ma, and besides that, she was probably the most beautiful woman I had ever seen—Ida Mae excepted, of course.

In the second I stood looking at her, I saw one eye blink open and glance at me, and then quickly close. And if I hadn't seen it I might have doubted that she was conscious at all. She surely looked to be hurting.

Kneeling down, I smoothed back her hair, and as I did so I heard Pa's horse come over the ridge above us and stop, blowing to catch its breath.

"Take it easy, ma'am," I said softly, doing my best not to grin. "You're hurt real bad, but don't worry about a thing. I'll get you to the train."

"Hyrum," Ida Mae whispered, peering over my shoulder, "what are you doing?"

"This lady's hurt bad, Ida Mae. Her horse must have thrown her, and she looks to be busted up something awful."

"But Hyrum, she—"

"Now hush up, Ida Mae. She's hurt, and I'll take care of her. You gather up her things, and I'll carry the poor lady to the train."

At that moment three men rose up from the brush and started toward us, but knowing why they were there, I paid them no mind. I just reached down, gathered that woman up in my arms, and was turning toward the train when up galloped Pa on old Ingersol.

Instantly the woman opened her eyes. "Put me down, you young fool!" she hissed.

"Just relax, ma'am," I said softly, making my voice as innocent as possible. "Don't worry about a thing. I'll carry you to safety."

"But you don't understand! I—"

"Hi there, Pa!" I shouted, drowning out the woman's frantic whisper.

"Hyrum, what in heaven's name are you doing *here?*"

"Got no time to explain, Pa. This woman's hurt bad, but, well . . . Ida Mae and I are taking care of her just fine."

"But—but—" Pa stammered.

"Pa, button your lip and trust your son. Those two hombres on Mungus's mares are already past Mona, and coming fast. These gents here don't appear any too friendly, either. Was I you, I'd slap spurs and light a shuck out of here. It's still a long way to Salt Lake City."

Well, right then Pa was without doubt the most muzzled and puzzled man in the Territory of Utah. But after about ten seconds of staring hard at me, he caught my drift, winked, slapped spurs, and was gone before those three men could say "Aye" or "Nay" or anything else, for that matter.

Quickly I turned and was starting through the brush toward the train when one of the men reached out as if to stop me. I sidestepped and twisted past him, but with an oath the others started for me. Well, talk about being in a pickle! I knew I couldn't outrun them, and with the woman in my arms there was no way that I could outfight them, either. Oh, what I would have given for a few of my brothers right then! It's times like that when a fellow realizes just how much of a blessing a family can be.

"Ida Mae," I said suddenly, "if these hombres take another step, you give a shout for Marshal Clawson. He told me to holler if I had any problems, and these fellers are shaping up to be a problem."

Well, my mentioning the marshal's name surely stopped them, and I reckon that was the first time that marshal ever helped us. It's too bad he wasn't there to see how well he did. It was easy to see that those three didn't want to believe me, but then they didn't dare not believe me, either. It was what I guess you'd call a Mexican standoff. The big one, though—the man who'd first grabbed for me—was licking his lips, and I could tell by his eyes that he was getting ready. Marshal Clawson or not, he wanted another try at me. And if he got one I knew I was a goner. That gent looked mean enough to have a reserved seat in—well, in a very warm location.

Cautiously I backed up a step, then another, signaling with my eyes for Ida Mae to get over behind me. The woman in my arms was quiet, but I felt her body tense, and I knew she was going to move the same moment those other hombres did. But what could I do about it? I couldn't run fast enough to get away from them, and if I wanted to fight I'd have to put the woman down, which I didn't want to do, either. So I stepped back another step, got Ida Mae a little closer to me, and prayed a little harder. I could see no way out of this mess, no way at all.

The big man suddenly grinned and spoke, his voice so cold his jowls were dripping ice water. "Boys," he said, "this young whippersnapper's bluffing us. Ain't no marshal on that train, is there, boy? You and the little gal pull a good bluff, but not good enough! Drop that there woman now, 'cause we're about to tear you apart, and you'll need all the hands you got to defend yourself with."

Nervously I took another step back, looking for some way out. My hands were sweaty, and my mouth felt like cotton. I rolled my tongue around a bit, licked my lips, and wished I had enough moisture there to spit, to show them that I wasn't scared. Only I didn't, and I was. And there wasn't a thing I could do about it, either.

"Come on, boys," the big man said. "Let's get him!"

He took a step toward me, and out of the corner of my eye I saw the other two start forward at the same time. I was about to drop the woman and do my best to defend myself and Ida Mae when from behind me I heard a loud metallic click, the sound of a carbine lever action working a shell into a chamber.

Those old boys heard it, too, and they came to a mighty sudden halt. The big man was staring nervously over my shoulder, and I slowly turned to see the engineer, Cale Steiner, standing in the brush with his Model 1873 Winchester carbine .44–40 aimed right at the belly of one of the men to my side. Quickly I stepped back, and then Brother Steiner swung that rifle to bear on the big man who was obviously the leader.

"Was I you," Cale Steiner said casually, "I'd hoist my hands as high as they'll go. Quick, before I cut loose my dogs and make you as dingy as three head of sheep!"

Those six hands shot upright, and then Ida Mae lifted their hardware from them."

"Fine, miss," Brother Steiner said. "Now, Hyrum, you take that woman down to the train where she can get proper aid. Miss, you take their weapons with you.

"Now you good ol' boys listen, because I'm only going to say this once. Keep your hands in the air, turn around easy-like, and mosey on back into that brush. I'm figuring to turn you loose, but one wrong move and you won't get loose for a long, long time. Savvy?"

They did, for they turned and marched off right regular-like, and Ida Mae and I made our way down to the train. Suddenly the woman spoke.

"Who are you?" she snapped. "And what are you doing this for? Put me down this instant!"

"Oh, no, ma'am, I couldn't do that. You've been hurt far too badly to walk. Just you relax now. Your horse threw you back there on the trail, and you must have hit your head real hard. Otherwise you would remember what happened. My name is Hyrum, and this here is Ida Mae. Together we'll get you to some medical help as quickly as possible.

"Conductor!" I yelled, drowning out the woman's fumings and rantings. "I've got a woman here who's been hurt real bad. Would you get a place ready for her?"

Without waiting for a reply, I lifted her onto the coach, and did she ever put up a struggle! She was madder than a fumigated skunk.

Right off, though, the train started, and by the time I got her fixed out all comfortable on the bench we were going so fast that she had no choice but to remain with us. I mean, only a dummy would ever think of jumping. Right?

"Take it easy," I said, making my voice as sympathetic as I could. "Lie still, and we'll get you to some help in no time. Ida Mae, come sit beside her while I go ask the conductor where the closest doctor is located."

Quickly I stepped back, and with a wink Ida Mae slipped onto the bench beside the woman, taking over swabbing her face with the damp rag someone had offered. In a moment three or four other people had gathered around, expressing sympathy, and then I knew we need worry no longer about what the woman might do. That little lady was trapped but good, and she knew it. Why, after all that sympathy had been shown, who would ever dare stand up and declare themselves a fraud? Nobody, that's who. At least not anybody I knew.

In the caboose I got a cup of water and took it forward to the woman, who seemed grateful for it. As she drank, her eyes bored into mine, but I just smiled back. And my smile was real, too, for I was about as happy as could be. After all, Pa was safe; and, by jimminy, I'd even helped him. Add that to the fact that I was spending the whole day with Ida Mae, we were no longer at odds with each other, and who could have been happier?

Gradually the people went back to their own seats, and after a few moments Ida Mae and I were alone with her once more. As I took the cup from her she asked once again who I was. I wasn't going to tell her, but Ida Mae took matters into her own hands, and before I could stop her, the truth was out.

"Don't you know?" she asked simply. "Why, ma'am, this is Hyrum Soderberg, son of Bishop Jons Soderberg of Aspen Wells."

Well, you'd have thought someone had pole-axed the woman, the way she looked at me. First she turned white, and then she turned red, and for a moment there she was so perplexed I thought she was going to turn inside-out.

"Soderberg!" she gasped. "Then you knew? You knew all along that I wasn't—that I was in that trail to—Say, how much *did* you know?"

"About everything, I reckon. Ma'am, I knew you weren't hurt, and I knew that you were set out there to stop my pa, too."

"Is that all?"

"Well, shucks. I—"

"If you know more, young man, tell me!"

"All right, ma'am. Other than that all I know is what I've heard. And that is that those men who asked you to do what you were doing said some bad things about your . . . well, reputation, ma'am. They said you would tear your blouse and try to destroy Pa, too, and that would end his career as bishop."

For a long time she was silent, and I was feeling pretty uncomfortable. I didn't want to hurt her, but she'd wanted me to be honest, and I had been.

"What you've said is true," she said finally. "But I don't understand how you could have known."

"I told him," Ida Mae said.

"You? And who are you?"

"This is Ida Mae Sorenson," I replied quietly. "She is Mungus Sorenson's daughter."

"Oh . . . merciful heavens, no!" she groaned.

"Ma'am," Ida Mae said. "My father is normally a good man. And I love him with all my heart. But right now he is trying, because he is jealous, to destroy our bishop, and that is not good. I love him too much to let him do that. If Mother was alive she'd have stopped him, but since she isn't, I'm the only one left. That's why I told Hyrum, so we could save his father, and hopefully mine, too. The bishop we had to save from you. Father we have to save from himself, and I'm sure that will be the hardest job of all."

"Well, I'll be switched," the woman said thoughtfully. "You two are really something. Do you know that? Do your fathers know what you are doing?"

"Pa does," I said. "At least he must be guessing right now, for he surely saw me back there in the trail. He's quick, and it won't take him long to put two and two together."

"Miss Sorenson?"

"No, my father and my brother don't even know where I am. There just wasn't time to tell them. Right now I'm probably in real big trouble."

"Yes, you might be, at that. But don't worry, you've done right, and right always works out for the best. Say, did you believe what you heard about my . . . er . . . reputation?"

Well, what could either of us say to that? Of course we believed it. We had nothing to tell us otherwise. So both of us dropped our heads and neither of us answered, and I reckon that was all the answer she needed.

"I see," she said, almost whispering. "But what could I expect? Neither of you know me. And besides, there I was, right in that trail, right where they said I'd be, doing just like they'd asked me to do. Oh, isn't life miserable when you set out to deceive people?"

And then she started to cry, not loudly, but just silently sobbing as if her heart were broken. Ida Mae slipped over and put her arm around the woman's shoulders, and that lady looked more like a little girl right then than anything else. Ida Mae was crying, too, and to tell you the truth I was fighting back a couple of tears myself. I mean, that little lady was really hurting.

Later, when she'd dried up a little and we were talking, she said something that I've never forgotten.

"You kids listen to me," she said, "and pay attention. Have you ever seen someone in a beautiful white dress who had a little spot of food or something spilled on it?"

We both nodded, and she continued.

"When you see someone who has something spilled on their white dress, what is it that you see, the dress or the stain?"

"Why, the stain."

"Right. You see the stain every time. And it doesn't matter how small the stain is, either. In fact, it's hard to keep your eyes off the stain. Now, remember, the same thing is true with a reputation. One spot on it, one blemish, and that's all folks will see. No matter how many good things there are about a person, all people can see is the one spot of dirt in their character. And, saddest of all, that's sometimes all that a person can see about herself, too. In fact, mostly we judge ourselves more harshly than others do. We take what they say about us, magnify it, and then judge ourselves accordingly. I'd been told I was bad so many times that I came to believe it. And since I have believed it, I have acted the part, and so it has become true. Thank you. Thank you so much for helping me to see through your eyes what I was. Run along now, both of you. I'll be fine. And I promise you that I will be no further trouble to either of you. Go on, go be together. Right now I'd say you deserve that."

Neither of us protested that idea, and without a word we stood, Ida Mae took my arm, and we walked away. And funny thing was, I never for one moment doubted that the woman had meant what she said. She had given her word, we believed her, and as it turned out we were right in doing so. But that is another story entirely.

As we walked toward the caboose I thought again of the fight we'd had earlier, and I knew that I needed to apologize to Ida Mae. After all, it was my pride that had caused it, and nothing else. On the platform back of the caboose we stood for a time in silence, staring out at the barren and steep slopes of Mt. Nebo rising to the east of us.

"Funny," I said, finally, "how pretty that old mountain can be when there's so little on it to actually make it pretty."

"Yes," she replied quietly. "It's a lot like some people I know. Their beauty runs much deeper than what can be seen on the surface."

"Ida Mae, I'm sorry. I—"

"I know, Hyrum. So am I."

And so we talked it out, and as we talked we were both grinning and we were holding hands and it was great, standing on that platform while the Utah Central rattled along toward Salt Lake City.

16

What, Him Again?

Hour after never-ending hour Jons Soderberg pushed his mount northward, skirting Spring Lake and Payson, and then riding through Benjamin and into Spanish Fork. As he passed the intersection of First East and Fourth South in Spanish Fork he couldn't help but re-experience the pain of that winter thirty years before when he had stood beside his elder brother, Peter, as they had buried Peter's first-born son. The baby had been born beneath the cottonwood that still stood on the southeast corner of the intersection. Their only shelter during that frigid month had been a draughty wagon box, for they were among the thirty thousand Saints forced to flee their homes when Johnston's Army—in what many were now calling Buchanan's Blunder—had marched against the Mormons back in 1857. Brother Brigham had assigned the members of the South Cottonwood Ward to relocate in Spanish Fork, a community established under his direction only eight years prior to the Utah War. The Soderbergs were among those so assigned. Jons himself, eleven years old at the time, had aided in the birth of his nephew that bitter freezing night in the wagon box beneath the skeletal branches of the cottonwood. Baby Peter contracted pneumonia almost immediately; within a few short days he was dead, and young Jons was experiencing for the first time the bitterness brought on by legal persecution.

How rapidly thirty years had passed, Jons thought, and how little had actually changed! Instead of being eleven, he was now forty-one.

Besides burying a nephew he had now buried a daughter, and he was still being hounded by representatives of the federal government—and that in a country where the Constitution guaranteed its citizens freedom of religion.

Pausing at Hobble Creek just south of Springville, Jons allowed the stallion a few moments' rest as he washed his face and refilled his canteen.

"Just halfway," he groaned aloud. "Ingersol, old boy, you might make it, but I'm not certain that I will."

As he rode down Center Street in Provo he wished there was time to pause for a quick lunch at the Dewdrop Restaurant, and thus give both him and his horse a much-needed rest. But there wasn't, so he nibbled his sandwich and pressed on, saddlesore and more weary than he had ever been in his life.

He crossed the Provo River and rode along the public works road his father and Peter had helped build during their first year in the Territory. Month after month they had traveled from Cottonwood to Provo to build that road, which was eventually pushed all the way into Heber Valley. The job had not paid money, but the men were given tithing scrip which they redeemed at the bishop's storehouse for the food they lived on that first season in the valley.

Both the bishop and his horse, though very tired, seemed to flow effortlessly as they passed through the high grasses on the bench and climbed the hill below Battle Creek. Lehi seemed to loom forever in the distance, but Soderberg knew that it was getting closer. He alternated his horse's pace, using all the skill he possessed, limited though that was, to spare his stallion. He thought about the men on the white mares, wondering where they were. He was certain they must have gained ground while he paused at Hobble Creek, yet that rest had been beneficial for both himself and the horse. He could tell the difference in the way the animal moved, so for that stop he was glad. Yet he worried about the two men, and found himself hoping that they had passed him and would beat him into the city.

Once past Lehi the bishop could see in the distance the Jordan Narrows, and his mind drifted back to the summer of '58, the year Johnston's Army had established themselves at Camp Floyd. That summer Dan Bell, his deacon's quorum president, Terry Baker, the first counselor, and he had organized their first overnight, alone-without-adults excursion. It was a fishing trip to the Jordan Narrows where the large trout from Utah Lake could be caught. He recalled how his father had reluctantly consented to his taking the mare, giving in only when Baker, a head taller than himself, had accepted full responsibility for their safety. He recalled the fun they'd had, and wondered that fun should so often be reserved only for the youth. Why, in all the years since, he had never met anyone with the humor of Baker and Bell! "I wonder how Dan's doing," he thought, "homesteading over in Colorado." And Baker, too, in Los Angeles preaching the gospel at street meetings near an institution of higher learning which had been established there.

In his pocket Soderberg still carried the I*XL (I excel) Barlow-type pocket knife he had found that day in the Narrows. It had been brand new, and he remembered how proud he was when his father told him he would likely never own a better knife. That one, he said, was made in Sheffield, England, by a Mr. George Wostenholm. There was also a double-bladed knife, but the one he found was single-bladed, a perfect knife for the games of mumblety-peg he and the other boys were fond of playing. Again he wondered, as he had so often before, how his father had known the history of that knife, or, for that matter, how he had known any of the countless other things he always seemed to come up with. One of his neighbors, Dale Fielding, used to say that the bishop's father was as full of information as a mail-order catalog, and that was certainly true.

With a start the bishop realized that he had just passed the saloon that had once belonged to Porter Rockwell, and as he glanced back at it he was startled to see a cloud of dust not more than a half mile to his rear. Worse yet, within that dust he could see two white horses! Urging his horse to greater speed, the bishop lunged it across the ridge and into the Narrows, and there he was suddenly confronted with the sight of Marshal Clawson on his piebald gelding.

The marshal was still several hundred yards away, so hastily the bishop reined around and pulled back across the ridge, to be confronted again by the rapidly approaching horsemen. Which way now? Should he try to go up the ridge, which was terribly steep, or should he . . . ?

"Hold up there, bishop!"

Taken back, Soderberg pulled rein, and there sitting on a rock just like before was the same old man he had spoken with in Salt Creek Canyon early that morning.

"Well, bishop, you are doing well, right well—considering. Another twenty-five miles, and you will have won!"

"Wha—why—how . . . ?"

"Bishop, you're stuttering again. Had I known you stuttered, I might have taken care of that, too."

With that, the old man leaped sprightly to his feet. "Bishop, give me a hand. I need a ride."

"Wait a minute, old man. How in thunder did you get here?"

"Why, bishop, same as you. I traveled . . . quick! Now give me a hand up on that stallion of yours. We've got to hurry before those two highwaymen catch up with you."

"Highwaymen? What in . . . ?"

"Ooops!" the old man grumbled. "Slip of the tongue. You call them outlaws now, I believe. Of course, it really shouldn't matter. They're the same breed now as they were back then. Still, if you don't give me a hand, those two whatever-you-want-to-call-thems back there will be on us for sure. Now, let's move!"

"I'm sorry, old-timer, but I've got to climb that ridge there, and I'm not about to carry double while I try to do it. I'm played out, my horse is played out, and I still have a good twenty miles to go before sunset. However you got here I don't know. I've seen so much today that I might believe anything. So, however you got here, you can get yourself away in the same manner. I'm leaving alone, so adios."

"Now, just a minute, youngster," the old man snorted. "Why aren't you going through the Narrows?"

"Because Clawson is in there, and I'm not about to let him get a hold of me."

"Do you want to get past him?"

"Certainly. But—"

"Listen up, bishop. You've been so deep in thought about the Utah War and that Barlow knife in your pocket that you haven't taken time to think about what's been going on around you. I'm not saying more, but if you don't lift me up on that horse you're never going to make it. You've got to hurry, man. You're being timed with a watch, not a calendar."

The bishop stared in amazement. How in blazes had this old man known all that, he wondered?

"Who are you, you old galoot?"

"Like I said before, young feller, names aren't important. I might be anybody. Now, how about that ride?"

Sensing the futility of further argument, and not a little concerned about who this old gentleman might really be, the bishop finally nodded. The old man seemed so doggone familiar. He looked a little like Jons's grandfather had looked, though there were differences, of course.

"All right," he said, holding out his hand. "Get on. But remember, it's midafternoon, and I'm setting no easy pace. I have no time to be troubled with an old man who is grumbling because of aches and pains."

"Don't you worry, bishop. I can't even remember the last ache or pain I had, unless maybe it's been since I began talking to you. But no matter—let's get through those Narrows."

"Old man, I've already told you that—"

"Bishop, get into those Narrows, and trust me, will you? I know that marshal considers you his number one wanted man, and I know he's sworn that he'll take you in. But do as I say, and you will have no trouble with him today. You won't even have trouble with the twenty men he has hidden on the hill behind him. Now ride!"

"Are you crazy?"

"Bishop!"

With that the old man slapped the stallion's rump, and they crossed the ridge again to ride directly toward Marshal Clawson and his hidden men.

"All right, friend," the bishop whispered as they drew nearer. "What am I supposed to do now? Doff my hat and ask Clawson if he wants to ride along with us?"

"Be quiet, you young upstart. You descendants are all alike . . . have to be shown everything. You have no faith, no faith at all. Be silent, now, and just keep riding. You keep your thoughts to yourself and they won't even know we're here."

"Oh, for Pete's sake," the bishop grumbled, not daring to argue further. Instead, he lowered his head, leaned forward in his saddle, and rode cautiously toward Marshal Clawson, expecting at any minute to be fired upon or arrested on the spot. But no, the closer he rode, the less attention Marshal Clawson seemed to be paying to him. When he was no more than fifteen feet away, he half-turned and whispered to the old man.

"What is it? Why can't he see us?"

"Sshhh," the old man whispered back. "Where did you learn to whisper? In a sawmill? He can't see us because he doesn't believe we're here. Don't you remember Paul in Second Corinthians saying if we don't have faith, we don't have sight?"

"No . . . but . . . say, that's not what he said!"

"Well, it's close enough! Now please be quiet!"

As they moved cautiously past Clawson and his deputies and up out of the Narrows, the only thing racing was the bishop's heart. Once on the rise above, however, he breathed a sigh of relief. And then with new-found courage he suddenly turned and shouted, "Say, Clodson, who're you looking for?"

"Oh, bishop!" the old man said reprovingly. "Must you always keep your mug filled with verbal lather? Aren't you ever going to learn that some feelings aren't meant to be spoken? Some thoughts ought best to be placed in a man's pocket and left there."

The bishop, not really listening to the old man, was grinning as he watched the marshal twisting this way and that, trying to determine which of his deputies had called him Clodson.

"Marshal Clodson," the bishop shouted, making his voice high and thin like an old man's, "do you still have mud in your mustaches, or did I clean it out that night at the dance in Aspen Wells? And how about that crooked pistol of yours? Did you clean the mud out of it yet?"

Several men stood up from the rocks to look around, and Marshal Clawson, his face livid with anger, turned his horse from side to side trying to see where the voice was coming from.

"Soderberg, blast your hide! Is that you? Where are you? Show yourself, you Mormonite coward! Show yourself, or I'll—"

"Relax, marshal. The reason you can't see me is—"

"Bishop," the old man interrupted, "say no more. The marshal will soon be busy, and I'm sure you'd rather be forgotten."

"Busy? But how . . . ?"

"Look back, bishop. Look back."

Suddenly there was a commotion of hoofbeats, and into the Narrows thundered Silvertip and Blue John astride the stolen white mares, now lathered and jaded, that were once the pride of Mungus Sorenson. Before they could stop, however, they were surrounded by a host of federal marshals.

"Well, well!" Marshal Clawson shouted heartily. "The telegram said two matching white mares, stolen from Aspen Wells and headed this way. Boys, have you got papers on those pretty broomtails?"

"Ah—well—ah—not with us, Mister," Blue John stuttered.

"Marshal to you, my friend. Your face looks familiar. Have you by chance been decorating the walls of any post offices lately?"

"Me? Why, Marshal, you must be joking. I'm as clean as the day I was born. Matter of fact, however, you have a right good eye. This gent sitting next to me is the notorious rustler and horse thief, Silvertip, straight from Robbers' Roost country. I captured him and these two fine fillies down by Nephi, and I was bringing them in."

"Why, Blue John, you dirty low-down no-account traitor! You'd sell your own mother and grin like a jackass eating cactus while you were doing it! I've a mind to—"

"Hold your tongues, you two," the marshal interrupted impatiently, "and right pronto you reach for some sky."

Just at that moment the Utah Central entered the cut and braked to a stop. Within minutes Ida Mae Sorenson and her unidentified escort had laid claim to her father's horses, and were carefully leading them up into the stock car, directly in front of the caboose.

"Well, bishop," the old man grinned, "what do you think of your son now? I hope you know that almost single-handedly he made possible your success in this race. That is quite the boy."

"Yes," the bishop admitted, "I'm beginning to realize that."

"Well, time surely does have a way of catching up with folks. doesn't it, bishop? It even does me from time to time. I think you'd best let me down now, as my errand is completed and it's time to get back."

With that the old man jumped lightly to the ground, where he stood, grinning still.

"Bishop," he beamed, "it's been a special pleasure making this trip with you. I can't remember when I've enjoyed an association so much. Now remember, keep working on your pride. Pay less attention to what folks say about you, and more to what you say about them. That will also solve your social pressure problems. And bishop, about those boys of yours—they need you, especially at this time in their lives. Most especially right now Hyrum needs you. You were pretty rough on him the other night after the dance. He was only saying what you've been saying to yourself all day long, and I expect a word of apology would go a long way with him. And, by the way, do you really think he should be restricted?

"Now, I'd best be going. We'll see you again, Bishop Soderberg."

"But wait! I still don't know—" the bishop called, and in that instant his mount shied to one side. For a second only his eyes were diverted, and when he looked back to finish his question, the hillside was empty. The old man was gone.

"Well, I'll be . . . !" exclaimed Jons Soderberg. "How'd that old galoot get down into that ravine so fast?" Then, without warning, something slapped his stallion on the rump, sending both horse and bewildered rider flying northward toward the valley of the Great Salt Lake.

17

Rubbing In and Reaching Out

Well, there isn't too much more to say about the race. Pa'd gone so long without eating that by the time he sat down to supper at the Beehive Restaurant in Salt Lake City, his stomach must have thought his throat had been cut. In the Temple-block stables, directly across the street north of the cemetery, stood Ingersol. Ida Mae and I were rubbing down and combing his giant frame, which was so ganted up that he looked like the running-gear of a grasshopper. Still, Ingersol had done his job, and now he was receiving his reward.

As we worked, the telegram, signed by fourteen brethren doing tithing work that day near the Temple block, was no doubt being circulated throughout Aspen Wells. It read simply:

7:15 PM ARRIVED SAFELY STOP SON HY AND IDA MAE SORENSON SAFE IN CITY STOP WILL LEAVE ON TRAIN TOMORROW AM FOR RETURN TO ASPEN WELLS STOP SIG J SODERBERG BISHOP

WITT J BRUCE PARKER
JD HAWKS
RUSS DAVEY
DENNIS CARROL
JERRY JEX
MAX WALTERS
R THOMAS BAILEY
MERIDITH WILLIS
KENDALL JENSON
KARL QUILTER
DICK CHIDESTER
JIM OCKEY
DAVE CONNALLY
DENNIS GIBBONS

That night Pa got hotel rooms for us, and after I said goodnight to Ida Mae I went to our room and found Pa reading the *Deseret Evening News.* I sat down and waited, wanting to talk and yet not wanting to because I was kind of afraid. I reckon Pa was scared, too, or else he had a busted talk-box, because that night he didn't talk about much of anything. I wanted so badly to tell him that I was sorry for being rude, but every time I tried the words just wouldn't come. I was surely feeling miserable. Then Pa asked me if I'd join him in prayer; I did, and when we finished he said goodnight and we went to bed. For a long time, though, I couldn't sleep. My mind kept going over the events of the previous few days, worrying them like a dog worrying a bone. Finally, when I was certain that sleep would never come, it did.

It was midafternoon the following day when the Sanpete Valley Crawler chugged into the depot at Aspen Wells. The trip home was largely uneventful, except for when Loose-lip climbed aboard in Nephi. When he saw us I thought he was going to have a consumptive fit, but he made it into another car and we never saw him again. For some reason Pa still didn't want to talk about the events of the preceding day, so instead he mostly sat while Ida Mae and I visited and got better acquainted. I'd never seen Pa so quiet, and to be right honest I didn't know what to think of him. It seemed a real switch that I would want to make medicine and he wouldn't. Normally Pa was a real speechifier.

As we stepped from the train in Aspen Wells we were surprised by the huge crowd gathering to meet us. It was Pain Mumford who first stepped forward to shake Pa's hand, but he had scarcely done so when Mungus pushed his way forward. Immediately Ida Mae ran to him, pleading, but he shoved her aside as though she were a stranger, reached up, and pulled Pa off the landing.

"Well, if it isn't our good bishop—good 'thieving' bishop, that is! Look hard, folks, for here before you stands the man who stole my white mares and then used them as he relayed himself toward Salt Lake City. Well, bishop, go ahead! Deny it!"

"Father!" Ida Mae screamed, climbing to her feet and running to her pa once more.

"Father, that isn't so! I saw it! I—"

Mungus threw her aside again and turned back, snarling at Pa.

"Soderberg, you low-down—! Turned my own daughter against me, have you? I'll learn you to—"

And with a howl of rage he lashed out like a coiled rattler, his fist landing solidly on Pa's face.

Pa spun to the earth, and the crowd, suddenly silent, parted to give the two men room. Shaken, Pa rose slowly to his feet and held out his hand toward Mungus.

"Brother Sorenson," he coughed, wiping his blood from this cheek with the back of his hand, "as a bishop, I can't fight—"

With an oath Mungus swung again, and once more Pa was knocked to the ground.

Well, I felt sick, and I glanced over at Ma to see her face as white as a sheet. Why wasn't Pa fighting back? Was he a coward? Sure, he was bishop, but Mungus had taken it to him, had hit him first! And it shouldn't matter that Mungus was bigger, either. Pa could take him! Pa was strong enough, I knew that. I could see Jim and Lyman, and they were so anxious to get into it that they could hardly control themselves. Ma could, though, and she had. Those brothers of mine, badly as they wanted to participate, were going to be bystanders, and they knew it. And for that matter, so did I, for Ma had given me the eye, too. Still, I knew just how they felt.

"Pa!" I yelled. "Hit him back! Get up and . . . !"

Pa was starting to get to his feet again when Mungus stepped over and kicked him, a solid boot to the ribs that sent Pa rolling. For a moment he lay still, groaning, and the crowd, stunned, said nothing as Mungus moved forward to kick him again.

Suddenly the voice of Pain Mumford broke the silence.

"Hold it right there, Sorenson! That's it. Now back up a little, real easy. That's the way. Fair fights I don't mind, and mostly I leave a man alone to skin his own cats. But Mungus, that man is a bishop, and he's made him some promises that you and I don't even know about. So this forty-five says you'd best back off until he gets on his feet and decides what he's going to do."

Mungus didn't like it, but he looked hard at Pain and then took a step back, and then another. By that time Pa was on his knees right in front of me, staring off up the canyon. Then he said something so low that I could hardly hear him, and I doubt that many others heard anything.

"Old man," he said, gazing off up the canyon, "whoever and wherever you are, I'm thankful for your help. Yesterday morning you said to treat Mungus fair but firm. Until today I've been more than fair. Starting now I'm going to be more than firm. I hope you're watching!

"Pain, thanks for your help. I'm all right now."

Pa rose to his feet and beckoned for Mungus. "Sorenson," he said, "before I teach you some manners I want you to know that your mares were stolen by two outlaws from Robbers' Roost. They were captured by Marshal Hebron Clawson. Your daughter Ida Mae has them in the stock car with Ingersol, which horse I had the privilege of riding all the way."

With that, Pa hit him. It was so sudden that Mungus wasn't expecting it, and the blow knocked him flat. Rising quickly, however, he circled, feinted suddenly, and threw a hard right at Pa's head. Pa moved under it, though, and smashed a wicked left to the ribs that made the bigger man gasp.

Well, what followed, if it wasn't pretty, was at least quick. Pa wasted no time, and it was soon evident to all of us that he knew what he was doing. Somewhere, sometime, Pa had been up the river and over the pass, and I don't reckon any of us was more surprised to learn of that fact than Mungus, who found himself tied in a knot and hung out to dry on a bob-wire fence.

Mungus fought hard, I'll give him that. But it seemed like whatever he thought of doing, Pa was ahead of him. One time only Pa was hit, but he shook his head, mumbled something about firmness, and that was the last time Mungus touched him.

Two quick jabs to the face, a roundhouse to the midsection, and when Mungus's head jerked forward it met with Pa's knee, which was rising to the occasion.

Mungus went down with a long sigh, and Pa stood there for a moment, head bowed, and the absolute stillness of the crowd was profound. Suddenly, through cracked and bleeding lips, Pa spoke.

"I'm wondering, folks, if there are any others among you who need a dose of this medicine. If there are, step forward. Loose-lip, how about you?"

Loose-lip mumbled something, stepped back into the crowd, and then no one spoke, no one moved. Then Pa turned to me.

"Hyrum, come here. You too, Ida Mae."

Surprised, Ida Mae and I walked out to where Pa was standing. He was a mess of sweat and blood and dirt, and I noticed that he was rubbing his torn knuckles. The people were so silent that the sound of a horse snorting somewhere beyond the crowd startled me. As I drew near I could hear Mungus moaning softly, but Pa was ignoring him, and so did I.

As I got to Pa he put his hand on my shoulder and spun me around so that our backs were to the train and we were facing what was almost our whole ward. Ma, I saw, had moved over to stand by my brothers, and I could tell by their faces that they were as nervous as I was. What did Pa want, I wondered? Why would . . . ?

"Brothers and sisters, for the past week or so I have been acting mighty strange for a man in my position: racing horses, betting, fighting, being prideful, and, worst of all, distrusting those who love me. In all that time only two people have had the courage to flat-out tell me that I was wrong—my wife Hattie and my son Hyrum. Because they had that courage I was rude to both of them, but especially did I mistreat Hyrum.

"During the race Hyrum continued to show courage, but it was then that he showed something even greater than that. He showed—not just to me, but to all of us here—a sincere forgiving compassion for a father who had wronged him. And Ida Mae Sorenson did the same.

"You see, folks, he and Ida Mae accepted the responsibility of righting the wrongs each of their fathers had done, and of protecting them from themselves and from each other, forgiving them both beforehand.

"Brothers and sisters, it is this willingness to forgive and to accept responsibility, not only for one's own actions but for the actions of others as well, that is the measure of a man, and of a woman.

"Hyrum, you are a man I am honored to stand beside. And, Ida Mae, in every way you are a fine woman. Will you both forgive me?"

Well, I looked up at Pa then, he looked down at me, my eyes got all misty, and before I knew it Pa and I had our arms around each other for the first time in a lot of years. We were both crying and I don't remember when I felt so proud of being Pa's son. For a time neither of us could talk, and then Pa told me he loved me. I'd never heard him say it like that before, and suddenly I knew he did, and I knew I never need doubt it again. For a long time then nobody moved, and I just enjoyed being held by my pa.

"Hyrum," he finally said, when we'd both dried up a little, "go fetch me some water, will you, please?"

I did so, and then with all those people watching, Pa knelt down, took out his neckerchief, and began cleaning Mungus's face. He was still fighting emotions, but as he cleaned he spoke again.

"Brothers and sisters, I won that race fair and square. That means thirty-five of you owe me one hundred dollars each, and Loose-lip, you owe me two hundred. The ward clerk will begin collecting that money tonight."

Pa paused, totally serious, and looked around the crowd. Most of them were shocked, and to tell the truth, so was I. Pa was not a betting man, and I had been fairly certain, after what he'd just said, that he would cancel the debts they owed him. But no, he hadn't, and when I looked at Ma she seemed about as sick as I suddenly felt.

"Add my hundred dollars to that," he continued, "and that will give us three thousand eight hundred dollars toward our new meetinghouse fund. With that much, I reckon we can break ground as soon as this problem between the Church and the government is taken care of."

Suddenly, and without warning, Tucker Bill doffed his hat, waved it in the air, and called for three cheers for Pa.

The people roared, and while they did I just stood there wiping my eyes and grinning at Ida Mae.

Within minutes most of the folks had gone, and Pa and my brothers were helping a battered but clean Mungus Sorenson to his feet.

"Hyrum," Pa said, "come here, son, and help me support this man.

"Mungus, put your arms around our shoulders and we'll get you home in time for chores."

"Say, bishop," Mungus groaned as we moved slowly down the street, "what'd you hit me with, anyway?"

"Righteous wrath, Mungus. Pure righteous wrath."

"Was that true, what you said about my mares?"

"Father," Ida Mae interrupted, "the bishop wouldn't lie to you. You know that."

"No," Mungus grimaced, "I suppose he wouldn't. But young lady, that brings me to you. Just whose side have you been on, anyway?"

"Your side, father. I've never been on any side but yours."

Mungus was silent then, thinking about what his daughter had just told him, I reckon. Then, after a long minute, he spoke again.

"By golly, Ida Mae, you're right. I reckon it's about time I admitted that it was me who was on the wrong side.

"Bishop, how in tarnation did you get past all those traps I laid out for you? And why didn't you tell those folks back there what I'd done?"

"Mungus," Pa grinned, tightening his grip on the larger man's shoulder, "those are two good questions. Ida Mae and Hyrum helped me past one or two of the traps, and on the others I had help, too. I'm not saying who, and I'm not saying how, but I had some very special help. Now to answer your other question, I didn't tell them because I didn't think they needed to know. You're a good man, Brother Sorenson, and I feel strongly that the Lord would like to use your leadership abilities in his kingdom. Mungus, will you accept a call from your bishop?"

Mungus stuttered and stumbled and choked and coughed, and I was wondering what in the world Pa was trying to do. But then Mungus looked over at his daughter, she smiled and winked at him, he stood straight and tall (or at least he stood as straight and tall as he could, considering his recent shellacking by Pa), and turned to Pa.

"Bishop Soderberg, I'd consider that a real honor. I surely would."

They both grinned then, and resumed their slow walk down the street.

"Say," Mungus interjected, "that must have been a heck of a horse race, bishop. Some day I'd like you to tell me about it."

"Some day I will, Mungus. Some day I will."

The two men leaned on each other then, walking arm in arm, and I dropped back to walk with Ida Mae. Taking my arm, that young lady looked up, and, with tears in her eyes, she said simply, "Oh,

Hyrum!" Then she leaned up and kissed me, and, by jimminy, this time it was special, this time it was right.

Funny thing, though. Right as it was, that kiss discombobulated me so badly that my tongue got hog-tied and I couldn't make chin music at all, so I just held on tight to Ida Mae and kept walking, doing my best to follow in the footsteps of my pa.

Brother Brigham's Gold

Brother Brigham's Gold

Blaine M. Yorgason
Brenton G. Yorgason

Deseret Book Company
Salt Lake City, Utah

For Mont and Afton Wagstaff and Alta and Huish Yates.
Thank you for your terrific daughters.
We love them dearly.

Contents

Acknowledgments

The authors express appreciation to our rather extended family, who, without much complaint, have allowed us to fictionalize to a remarkable degree the lives of our good ancestors. We also express appreciation to those same ancestors, for we are certain that they would have squirmed with mighty discomfort had they been given any idea of the strange and wild experiences we would one day claim for them.

Introduction

Occasionally it's interesting to consider where our ideas get their birthings and their growth pains. Some, we'll scratch at for months and never even raise a blister, let alone a good story. Others, like this one, spring right out of the woodwork when they're least expected, and they appear full bloom when they do.

Now we don't want you to think that this story is a brand-new idea, for it isn't. We've been pounding folks's eardrums about *Brother Brigham's Gold* for at least four years—ever since we finished *The Bishop's Horse Race*. Furthermore, the story's been in existence for at least two generations before that. We just didn't know of it. But now we do, and we thought it only right to describe the hole in the lattice-work whence it sprang.

Some time ago we went to visit one of our elderly relatives, whose name, for obvious reasons, shall remain anonymous. She lived alone—had done for years—and most folks who knew her considered her somewhat teched. Because of this, we approached her doorstep with great concern.

"You knock," said one of us, being the elder. "Folks say this old bat's crazy."

"No," said the other, having more authority, "she's just eccentric. Besides, she's our relative. You knock!"

"It's your door," responded the first. "I took the last one, two years ago. Remember?"

"That's a joke," the ecclesiastically powerful younger of us replied. "In July this past summer I knocked on a door getting ready for the family reunion. You weren't even there, and I had to carry the burden alone. Now hurry up and knock."

Conversation ended. The elder timidly rapped on the door.

"Well?" someone croaked from within.

"Uh . . . anybody home?" we asked, and gulped, fearing the answer but fairly certain, nevertheless, that someone was.

"Durn fool pesky relatives," the old lady sputtered. "I saw you through the window. 'Course I'm to home. Where else'd I be, stove up as I am? Now come on in and put a cork in the door before the draft shortens my life by another week."

We looked at each other, and one of us, being the elder, graciously opened the door and held it so that the younger could go in first. The younger gave the other a look that would have made an icicle feel feverish, and both of us passed from the view of normal mortality.

Happily, we found our dear old relative relatively pleasant and hardly teched at all, and her disposition was as bright as morning light on a mountain meadow (well, almost that bright, anyway).

"My word and deed," she declared, sizing us up and down through her magnifying glass. "When'd the circus come to town?"

"Circus?" we both responded blankly.

"Must be—I got the two fat men from the sideshow standing in my living room. In fact, I'd lay odds that you two are big enough to be the main attraction. Don't our family ever come small?"

We both attempted a chuckle; she didn't respond, and so without further ado we sat down.

"Have a seat," she said as she watched her sofa sink toward the floor. "Make yourselves to home."

We did, there was a bit more minor chit-chat and good-humored insulting (which seems to be common in our family), and finally the three of us got down to serious visiting. We talked for an hour, sharing tales about the old days when folks still sewed themselves into red long johns come September and when most of them took a bath twice a year whether they needed one or not.

By the end of the hour the old woman was tired and we could see it. As we stood to leave, she raised her hand and stopped us. Then, struggling from her bed and coughing mightily, she hobbled into the only other room in her tiny frame cottage.

"What's going on?" the younger of us whispered.

"Just a minute and I'll pull out my crystal ball and tell you," the elder of us responded. "You've got to learn to be more patient, little brother. These things always come out in the wash."

"That's what I'm afraid of," the younger of us retorted. "Probably all shrunk up and useless, too!"

As we listened, we heard the sound of metal scraping, the screech of old and rusted hinges, and the rustling of some sort of fabric. Moments later our extremely elderly relative was back with a little bundle of yellowed papers clutched in her hands. These she feebly handed to us.

"You boys want a story?" she asked, grabbing onto the arm of the younger of us for support. "Here's a whole handful of one. For years I've kept it secret, doing my best to protect . . . well, who knows what I've been trying to protect! But it's off my shoulders now, onto yours. I've tried once or twice before to shift it, long ago, but it wouldn't go. Too soon, I figured then. Folks just called me crazy. Thing of it is, they still do."

We each looked at the other, and a look of guilt spread across both our faces. Her insanity seemed to be a familiar topic. Fortunately, our antiquated relative seemed to be unaware of our discomfort, for she kept right on speaking.

"Stories, lies or not, die hard. You boys read them papers and then ask folks hereabout what they think of what you've read; most of 'em will tell you everything there is lies. I don't blame them, neither. It's easier to believe it that way. Trouble is, they're right as skunks smell sweet. What you read, boys, is the sum-total truth of the matter. Period.

"I'm thankful that's over with," she concluded as she sank exhausted to her bed. "Fool tale's off my shoulders for good. Now I can do what I been aching to do for some time."

"What's that?"

"Boys, I'm aimin' to pass away!"

"No," the elder of us argued. "You've got too much spunk in you to die."

"I always thought so myownself," she mused. "But I can feel the cold in my bones, just like that old buzzard who was your great-grandpa did before he died. Now take this story and do something with it."

We looked again at each other, not sure whether to be grateful or not for this small yellowed-paper favor.

"Uh . . ." the oldest of us said, hesitating, "we don't normally write other folks's stories. We've got too many of our own to do, and—"

"Just like your great-grandpa, the old goat. You want to be coaxed. I declare, don't families *ever* change?"

"Coaxing's got nothing to do with it," the younger of us retorted. "It's just that because of contracts and projects and syndications, the parameters of our available time frame and the marketability of certain projects have been narrowed somewhat, and would possibly indicate to the more astute observer—"

"No change so's a body would notice," the old woman interrupted, shaking her head. Then, looking at the elder of us, she asked, "Does this flannel-mouth always rattle on like that?"

"Only at certain altitudes," the elder of us responded, giving the younger of us a narrow look, "and when the moon is right. Still, we really shouldn't take these—"

"All right! All right! Two against one ain't fair, but you win! I'll coax. Here, rattle-mouth, take this."

Finally silent, the younger of us reached out and took from the old woman's two quivering hands a heavy, fist-sized rock. "Pyrite," he said after a brief examination, handing the rock to the elder of us. "Lots of iron pyrite."

"Har-de-har-har," the old woman cackled. "I take it all back. Families *do* change. They get dumber. That old crow-bait of a great-grandpa of yours would never have made that mistake. Nor would've your Grandpa Hyrum, who was given that rock by Tabby himself. That there's gold, boys, the genuine article."

Now both of us stared at the bright glint of the metal in the stone.

"But . . . but how . . . where . . . why . . ."

"The answers are in them papers, you chuckle-headed examples of poor posterity. Them and that chunk of gold are the entire shooting match, and they go together. Now, do you want them or not?"

Well, we looked at each other, and it was obvious to us that we were both wavering. The old woman saw that, and being altogether smarter than we'd given her credit for, she grinned and spoke again, and, dagnab it, what she said clinched it for us.

"Boys," she concluded, "I'd like you to write that account out as a book. 'Course I know you ain't the *best* writers around, but right now you're the *onliest* ones this family has. So get after it and do what you can. If the stars are lined right, if you're luckier'n our family normally is, and if the good Lord blesses you more'n He probably ought to, you might get it done. I hope you do, for your Grandpa Hyrum surely wanted it told.

"Now run along before I have to fix you dinner. You look as gaunted up as two stuffed turkeys, and I don't even have enough food around here to keep the mice happy."

Well, we grinned, thanked her for a wonderful time, said goodbye, and, as per her instructions, ran along with her papers. What follows, for what it is worth, is the story those papers contained.

And the fist-sized rock of gold? Well, forget we even mentioned that. We won't guarantee that it even existed, and besides, it wasn't worth much anyway.

1

September 1884

Confluence of Red and Currant Creeks, Utah Territory

Nervously Enock Rhoades stared out into the darkness. He had heard something—he *knew* he had heard some sort of movement. The old tent fluttered in the night wind, the sighing in the pines grew momentarily louder, and painfully he edged himself closer to the door-flaps.

Above him the stars hung like lanterns in the blackness, giving very little light. Down near Currant Creek a night bird called, and from above him on the mountain a coyote sent out an exploratory cry, a lonely wail that served only to emphasize the silence of the mountain night. Enock Rhoades shivered and wished that he had a fire, thought for a moment, and then wished even more that he had never been so foolish as to come alone after the gold.

Gold. Even the thought of it made men do crazy things. And the sight of it, especially in great quantities that were simply there for the taking, well, life itself seemed to mean nothing in the face of such treasure.

Enock thought of himself then, thought of his brother Caleb's reluctance to reveal the location of the gold, thought of his own stubborn insistence, and then wished again that he had never come. It had surely been a crazy thing to do.

The arrow wounds in his side and left leg pained fearfully, he was dizzy and weak from the loss of blood, and deep within him was the fear that he would never make it home alive.

He worried about that, and worse, he worried about the girl who waited for his return, the girl he intended to take to the temple and marry. That was why he had come alone; that was why he had insisted, even when Caleb had pled otherwise, that he be told the location of the gold. With a good poke of that gold, he and she would have the funds to begin a fine life together.

Of course there was also the meetinghouse that needed funding, and with Caleb laid up with a bad leg, he'd been able to use what the Church needed as leverage. But deep down, Enock knew, the real reason why he had wanted to come had been his intense desire to see the gold and to put a poke of it away for himself and his sweetheart.

Well, at least he had found the gold and had mined a small amount, and the leather bag was securely hidden for when he would have the strength to return for it. Only—

Again the wind picked up, two pines rubbed together with a wild screeching, and Enock stared fearfully out into the darkness. Were they there? Had the Utes, who for some reason considered *all* the gold in the Uintahs sacred, tracked him down? Somehow they had trailed him to the mine, and when he had come out with his small poke, well—

As he stared into the constantly moving night, doing his best to keep away the blackness of unconsciousness, Enock thought again of the piece of gold ore he had found in the Narrows the day before and of the excitement he had felt. Pushing forward as Caleb had directed, he had followed Currant Creek to its junction with Red Ledge Creek. He had then pushed his animals up the steep slope, over the ridge, and down Red Ledge Hollow and into Bear Hole Hollow. And there, just as Caleb had described, was the hidden entrance to the old Spanish mine.

As he anxiously prepared to light the candle, he had suddenly been gripped with fear. What if there was nothing there? What if, after all his efforts, this was simply a hole in the rock? No, it couldn't be! Not after what Caleb had told him.

Shaking uncontrollably, he had lifted the stub of candle into the air, stepped forward, and stopped dead, thunderstruck!

He had not been able to breathe! He had not even been able to think. The enormity, the magnitude, of what he had beheld had been beyond his ability to comprehend. Everywhere, above him, beside him, beneath him, gold had glinted in the flickering candlelight.

Slowly he had let out his breath and had stepped forward, reaching out to feel the dancing rock. As Caleb had promised, the basic formation was quartz, rotten and soft, and everywhere it was laced, honeycombed, Caleb had called it, with wire gold. The yellow metal was totally pure, and the long strands were frequently as thick as an eighth of an inch.

With prying fingers he had pulled a chunk of rock loose from the wall. Holding the candle close he had examined it, his heart racing faster. It was even more than Caleb had said!

Setting the candle down, he had feverishly torn the rotten quartz apart, picking out the strips and strands of gold as he did so. Quickly he had pulled another chunk of ore from the tunnel wall, broken it down, and had piled more gold onto his small but growing mound.

For an hour Enock had worked without stopping, burning through three candles, ignoring the dripping sweat that soaked his shirt and blinded his eyes. He had never *seen* so much wealth! Never in all his twenty-four years had he even imagined such a thing. Of course, he had known about the mines, both from Caleb and from his father, John, but still, it was so much more than words could possibly convey.

Enock had paused then and wiped his brow, his eyes never leaving the small pile of gold he had accumulated. He *had* to stop for a few moments. He needed water, and he needed as well the equipment that was on his mules. Then he could begin mining in earnest.

From his pocket he had withdrawn a small leather pouch, upon which he had branded his initials. Opening it, he had stuffed his mound of gold inside. A thousand dollars, he had thought as he had lifted the bag. There had to be at least a thousand dollars worth of gold in his poke!

Stuffing the bag beneath his vest, Enock had turned and made his way toward the entrance of the mine. There had been several hours of daylight left, and in that time he had felt he could fill the packs of both mules quite easily. That would have left him free to travel at night, and the Indians would never even have known he had been there.

At the entrance, he had paused to allow his eyes to adjust to the brightness of the September day. His animals were down the slope in a small copse of aspen, and within minutes he had descended to them.

"Well, gals," he had said quietly as he had carefully packed his poke of gold into his saddlebags, "we've done'er. 'Course you'll have a heavy load going down through Park City and into Salt Lake, but I'll make it worth your trouble, and that's a promise.

"Now stand easy, girl, while I get this cinch loosened. I don't . . ."

Suddenly he had spun around, fear gripping him tightly. He had heard something, some sound that had been foreign to the noisy stillness of the mountain. From the shade of the aspens he had stared outward, examining everything—every rock, every clump of brush. But there had been nothing, nothing but the intense stillness of the afternoon.

Stillness . . .

There had been no birds singing! The squirrel down the slope had stopped chattering, and Enock had chilled with the knowledge that he was being watched! Caleb had warned him of the Indians. Still, until that moment Enock had felt confident he could come and go without detection. At that moment, however, he had wondered if they had somehow discovered him, and—

Whoosh!

Spinning to the sound, he had been knocked forward by the shock of the arrow, which had struck him low in his side. Strangely, there had been no immediate sensation of pain, but the stickiness of blood had been instant, and Enock had known he had been hard hit.

Dragging himself around, he had pulled the old Walker Colt from his pocket, aimed at a likely clump of brush, and fired.

Nothing had happened, but as the echoes had bounced back and forth among the peaks, two more arrows had whispered their fearful way through the aspen grove. Tugging at the shaft buried in his side, Enock had jerked it free. Then, staggering, he had freed the two jennies and had dragged himself into the saddle of his horse.

With a wild shout, he had plunged out of the aspen and up along his back trail. Another arrow had buried itself in his thigh as he urged the horse forward, and a third had barely missed his head as it whistled angrily past. Then he had been free, the horse had been running full out, and Enock, the pain suddenly hitting him, had grabbed hold of his saddle horn, started to tie his wrist to it, blindly given the horse its head, and known no more.

It had been late afternoon of what he thought was the next day when Enock had again opened his eyes, and immediately he had known where he was. Off to the south had loomed Currant Creek Mountain, and so he had not been far from the confluence of Currant and Red Creeks. That had startled him for he had come much farther than he had expected. Still, it would be at least a two-day ride before he could get back to Caleb, and he was in no condition to travel.

He had also been startled by something else, something that might very well mean his escape could be successful.

His mules, and thus his supplies, had followed him!

Grimacing with pain, Enock Rhoades had rolled over and stared upward. Food and shelter had been taken care of, but he also had another problem. What if the Indians had followed his two jennies?

Quietly he had called his horse, thankful that he had trained it to come in that manner. When it did, he had taken up the lead ropes of the jennies, dragged himself up to the saddle, and tried to mount.

He had not been able to do it, but he had managed, finally, to drag himself up and drape his body over the horse like a corpse. Calling quietly to the jennies, he had urged his horse forward, and with the pack animals trailing behind, he had ridden the horse down into the water.

Until long after dark he had let the horse carry him, leading the mules, and by then he had been certain that he was nearly dead. His side felt as though it were about to burst open, and he had known he had to stop. Reaching out he had caught the reins and pulled his horse off onto the north bank of the stream.

In the starlight he had realized that he was on a large horsehoe bend in the creek, and once again he had recognized the location.

Without hesitation he had urged the horse up the steep bank, across a grassy plain that was narrow and flat, and up into more timber. For perhaps thirty yards the horse had climbed, and suddenly he had come out in a small swale, out of which a tiny spring flowed. The swale was surrounded by timber, plenty of dry wood was close, and Enock Rhoades had felt certain that here he would be safe.

With difficulty he had dragged himself from the saddle, fallen, and lain still, trying to stop his head from swirling. At last, with energy he dragged forth from who knew where, he had removed the tent from the mule and had set it up. He had thought of a fire and had not lit one because he had been so tired. He had, however, pulled out his bedroll, and that, finally, along with his saddlebags, he had worried into the tent.

At last, exhausted, he had dragged himself onto the bedroll and closed his eyes, ready to . . .

The gold!

Amazed that he had not thought of it already, Enock had pushed his hand into the saddlebags. It had been there, still in the little leather bag where he had placed it. At least, he had thought, the trip had not been totally useless. At least there was still the gold for his wedding.

Suddenly he had had an idea. He could rest in this place. Here he would be safe from everyone but the Indians. And they would likely come. He knew that.

Only they would be after a man who had taken gold from their lands. If he had no gold, then there would be no reason for them to be after him. He would simply be an innocent passer-by, and he would prove it by letting them search his camp. Of course, there were his wounds, but if he told them he had fallen from his horse and had been stabbed by dead tree limbs during his fall, that would explain everything.

It had all seemed so simple, so foolproof. Only—

In the darkness Enock had pushed the gold back inside his shirt and vest, dragged himself from the tent, looked around, finally seen a fallen tree, and crawled toward it. If it was old and rotted, then perhaps it would provide what he needed.

There was another gust of wind, the two pines screeched together again, and Enock Rhoades gasped with fear and pain. His eyes wide, he stared into the darkness, his Walker Colt at the ready. But there was nothing, nothing but the wind and the grass and the trees and the stars. Slowly he lowered the huge pistol, dropped his head onto his arms to try and stop the dizziness, and suddenly, inches from his head, a tiny twig snapped.

With his breath stopped and his eyes wide with a terrible understanding, Enock Rhoades jerked his head erect, stared into the darkness, saw that the stars before him had vanished, realized that something—no, *someone* very tall—was blocking his view, and with desperate energy he leaped to his feet.

Somehow he had dropped the Big Walker Colt, but his knife was close at hand, and so with one sweeping motion he brought it forward, felt it strike flesh and bone, realized that he was too high, and realized also that he could do nothing else.

For a fraction of an instant time held still while he thought of his death and sorrowed over it and over his loss of the girl who waited. Then, in that slow way that is sometimes given to man as the end appears, he saw a sudden blinding explosion that seemed to fill all the earth with a numbing power. There were flashes of light then, no pain, but lights and a tremendous rushing noise as he was catapulted up and backward through the darkness of a tunnel. Then he saw a light, distant yet bright, and he was moving toward it and suddenly his soul felt peace. Slowly his eyes glazed over, and that light was the last thing the mortal Enock Rhoades ever saw.

The Utes had come again.

2

June 1889

Strawberry Flats, Utah Territory

When I squatted across the fire from Zenos Hill that morning, gold was the furthest thing from my mind. It was frosty cold despite the month, our breath hung misty in the air, and I wanted to get warm. Besides that, the mules had strayed.

"They're plumb gone," I said disgustedly as I shifted to get out of the smoke from the sagebrush fire.

"Umph," grunted Zene, exhibiting his usual way with words. Zene was about the darkest-skinned Lamanitish Indian Mormon I'd ever seen. He'd been baptized at age eight and promised that he'd become fair and delightsome, but it must've taken only on the inside. Outside he was still regular dark Indian brown.

Zene was twice my age or thereabouts, and the way I heard it, Zene's Mormon pa and his wife had come upon Zene down by Ephraim when he was real young. Zene's Indian ma had died, his Indian pa was away on a hunt, Zene had been crying, and the tribe of Utes, not liking all that noise, had tied him to a tree, piled brush about him, and set it on fire. That's when the Hills rattled up in their wagon.

Well, the fire was scattered pronto, and when the deal was done, Old Man Hill had bought that little Indian kid for something like an old cow, a broken pistol, and two bags of flour. The Hills adopted Zene as one of their own, and he was raised pure white and pure Mormon. And he was, too, on the inside. But like I said, he could mask it pretty easily with his outside, and ofttimes he seemed to take real delight in doing so, that morning being a prime example.

"You reckon them mules went back to Aspen Wells?" I asked, still pushing to get a discussion going.

"Umph," he grunted again, and I could see I wasn't getting much enlightenment. Talking things over with Zene was pretty much like having a conversation with myself. Still, I liked Zene, I liked him a lot. I reckon that was because I knew he liked me. He never bothered me about my gimped-up foot, he never teased me about Ida Mae Sorenson, and he never took pity on me, like some folks did. He treated me like a regular fellow, made me work hard as he did, and I appreciated that a whole lot.

Zene had married a white girl named Amelia Hicks, who folks said was a mighty fine woman, and it seemed like he and she were set on raising a whole tribe of their own. They had six little boys, whose names made a rhyme when they were said fast: Nick, Nuck, and Chuck; Daver, Deve, and Dal. They also had two fine-looking little girls, but I never could tie no rhymes to them, so I don't remember only the name of one, which was Emma.

"I reckon one of us'll have to go back for those mules," I ventured, hoping he'd send me. We were both herding sheep for old Andrew Aagard, but Zene was the herder and I was just the camp tender. Still, with Pa in prison for polygamy, our family had fallen on some hard times. All of us kids had dropped out of school to go to work, and all of us were thankful for anything we could get. That meant Lyman and Jim were out on the west desert, Johnny had found work herding horses for Scott Cook down in the San Rafael area along the Green River, and Ernest, who was still too young to get a real job, was being paid a few pennies a day to read to Deaf Man Hibbard, down in Aspen Wells, which folks were now calling Fountain Green. I reckon I should call it that myownself, the town, I mean, so from here on I will. Anyway, my sisters Mary, Elinor, and Laura had even found work, either working at the Co-op, clerking for A. E. Christensen at his general store, or working as hired girls for some of the richer folks up north in Provo. All the little kids, of course, were still at home.

And, naturally, working kids also included me being chief cook and bottle washer to a Mormon Indian sheepherder, which was awful unlikely employment, and not too gainful either, for that matter.

I'll admit, though, that I really liked the job. In some ways, of course, it was boring. I mean, watching those woollies wrap themselves around acres of high-country grass was about as exciting as watching the first 4,300 heats of the national desert tortoise races, out to Ely, Nevada. On the other hand, that very propensity of the sheep gave me a great deal of free time, and I used every minute of it that I could.

My Pa was an educated man, though unschooled as far as formal education went. Still, he had a mind that was respected by folks far and near. He was intelligent and observant and was quick to lend either a strong back or his amazing wisdom to whomever might be in need, and I longed to be as wise and to be thought of with the same respect.

"The best of all things is to learn," Pa had said to me one day as we rode toward his dairy in the Big Meadow down south of Fountain Green. "Money can be lost or stolen, health or strength may fail, but what you have committed to your mind is yours forever."

I believed that, for I had seen how he had grown, and I could see within myself the beginnings of such a change as well. So I was doing all I could to learn more. I was on my third reading of the *Book of Mormon,* my second reading of Frederick Farrar's *The Life of Christ,* and my first reading of the writings of Tacitus and Blackstone's *Laws*, and I couldn't wait for a chance to get back to Fountain Green and pick up some new books. Then, too, there were my family and Ida Mae Sorenson, and I was tolerable anxious to see them as well.

Trouble was, Zene knew that, and he enjoyed watching me squirm.

"Well," I ventured, stretching up to my feet and looking down across the sagebrush-covered flat toward the Strawberry River, "reckon I'd best get moving, providing I aim to catch those ornery mules this side of Fountain Green. Hope that's the way they went. I'm not hankering to tangle with your people over on the reservation. Sure as bear sign smells bad, that's the truth."

Zene looked up at me with an expression I'd never seen before, and right off I knew I'd said something wrong.

"My people are Mormon," Zene stated softly, in one of the longest speeches I'd ever heard him make. "But those are Ute mules, and that's where they'll be."

"Zene, you're an Indian and you know it," I stated, not even thinking about what he'd said concerning the mules. "You'd ought to own up to it and be proud of it."

Zene looked at me again, his black eyes like burning coals.

"How'd the marshals catch your pa?"

"What?"

"The marshals," he repeated. "Tell me how they caught your pa."

Slowly I shifted until I was out of the smoke. "What for?"

Zene looked up from his steaming cup of scorched water and glared at me. "Mules'n polygamists are about alike," he muttered. "Least I'd bet they are. You want to find those mules, then talk."

I'd never seen Zene look as he did then, nor had I ever heard his voice go so low and gravelly. "Shucks," I said nervously as I hunkered back down, "I hate to do that. Too embarrassing."

"Umph," Zene grunted unsympathetically.

"He . . . he's not only my pa, Zene, but he's the bishop, and that office ought to be respected. I hate to drag his name around any more'n I have to."

Zene took a sip from his tin cup in response. Finally, seeing he wasn't going to let up, I plunged ahead.

"Those dirty marshals took advantage of him!" I growled angrily. "Dressed up as women, they did. Clawson and that other one from up to Salt Lake—Dyer, I think. How Pa ever thought Old Clawson looked feminine beats me, but he did.

"The marshals wave to him down in town, he waves back, grins with all his masculine charm before those genuine beauties, and sashays right on over to make their acquaintance.

"Well, simple as that, they had him. Had a regular arsenal hidden up under their skirts. They threw down on Pa, he jerked his hands up into the air mighty pronto, and those two legal Lily Langtrees had the last horselaugh, I'll tell you that.

"First we knowed of it was when Old Hans Tinker brought Ma the word. The marshals were already on their way to Provo by then. Pa's still in jail, too. Him and his third wife and their new baby, who they're going to use as witnesses against him. And they'll all three rot there unless one of us can spring Pa's bail, which doesn't look any too likely.

"Now, what's all that got to do with mules?"

"Mules and cohabs," Zene repeated. "Predictable as thunder follows lightning."

"What's that mean?"

"Cohabs are drawn to women," Zene explained, waxing truly eloquent, "and mules are drawn to home."

Well, I shifted to get out of the smoke again and took another long look at the Indian herder.

"That's what I said," I declared. "So if you've chomped this around long enough, then I'll be on my way back toward Fountain Green after them—"

"Ute mules aren't home in Fountain Green."

"Those are. They're Old Man Aagard's and his home is—"

"Brother Aagard bought them from the Utes out in the Basin," Zene declared. "Home's there."

The Basin, I thought. *That's the reservation. I wouldn't go out there for—*

"You'd better hurry," Zene said quietly. "Currant Creek, Red Creek, somewhere along there you'll find the mules."

"Now see here," I declared. "I don't care if you are the herder. I ain't going onto that reservation. Right now them Utes are thicker'n bottle flies at a buffalo shoot, and the way the government's been running 'em around with new reservation boundaries every month and such truck as that, they're a mite stirred up, too. The way I've heard it, they've got every trail into that reservation sealed off tighter'n a sun-shrunk cowhide. I heard that just last month they found two arrow-shot fellers up there, so full of feathers they'd have flown, happen they'd been launched.

"No sir, Mr. Hill, you're the Lamanite amongst us, not me. I'll leave traveling among your heathen kinfolk to you."

Zene looked up at me, his dark eyes burning, took a last gulp from his tin cup, and rose fluidlike to his feet.

"Maybeso whiteskinned pup wantum smashed head," he said quietly, slipping suddenly into the Indian lingo used by all the Utes from out on the reservation.

I stared at him, surprised. From him I'd never heard that kind of talk, and abruptly it dawned on me that I'd offended him, twice.

"Zene," I said, "I'm sorry. I—"

"Heap long day," he grunted. "White pup go, findum mules all same don't. Come back withoutum maybeso getum bashed head anyway. Me decide later. White pup all the same dumb bishop. Predictable. Like mules."

Scornfully he turned away, and I stared after him wondering if murdering an Indian came under the same statute as doing-in a regular human being. Probably get me six months, I decided, if I did it the cold-blooded way I had in mind. Accordingly I dropped the plan and went to saddle the swaybacked, crow-bait cayuse Old Man Aagard had given me for a horse.

That done, I swung up and pulled the animal around so I could see Zene. He was intently studying the far horizon, so I angrily pounded my spurs into the horse, and me and that animal took off for the eastern borders of the land of the Lamanites.

And I'll say this much more, and then be done with it. I decided that morning that there's nothing so useless as a splendid education squandered on a dumb-tongue Indian sheepherder who is stupid enough to go back to being something he never even was! Unless it was, as the old saying went, teats on a boar pig. Wings on a garden mole. Buttons on a pocket gopher. Or maybe, I thought grinning, hobbles on a dead horse.

No sir, as far as I was concerned, Mr. Zenos Hill could take a long flying leap, and I'd not care at all. I was done with being his tender, for good! I'd get those mules, and then I'd be gone.

For an hour I rode as hard as I could, and that animal was about the roughest running cayuse I ever sat astride. It was gaited like a hybrid buffalo and was thinner than the running gears of a desert grasshopper. Every time its hooves plunked down it felt like my eyeballs had impaled themselves on the roots of my upper molars and my vertebrae had all compressed down toward the saddle. I'll bet I lost a good four inches in height during that hour. It was, in short, one rough ride.

Blast! Why couldn't Old Man Aagard at least give me a decent horse? It wasn't because he was broke, I knew that. I'd once heard Pa tell Ma that before Mr. Aagard came over from the Old Country, he'd talked some elderly sister into sewing his underwear full of five- and ten-dollar gold pieces. Once here he'd played broke and picked up houses and stock and things for a nickle and a song. It wasn't long before he had played himself into being one of the wealthiest men in the county.

In spite of all that wealth, I had the worst horse in maybe *three* counties to ride, and it made me mad. I'd spoken to him about it once, asking for a better mount, but he'd yelped like a young stud whickering over a bellyful of sour oats, so I dropped it and only cussed him every time I climbed aboard the quarterdeck of that mangy creature.

Of course, I was in a pretty ornery mood that morning, I'll admit it, and that made things seem worse. Normally I don't begrudge folks their good fortune, for I've had considerable of my own—not money-wise, but good fortune, nevertheless. In fact, Pa's arrest was the first setback any of us Soderbergs had had since the great horse race of the year before. I'd been getting on fine with Ida Mae, I hadn't worried any more than a little about being crippled, and things just seemed to be going good. I'd even got the job tending camp for Zene when I needed it.

Still, now I was headed smack into the middle of the Ute reservation, and deep down I had a bad feeling about it. In fact, the farther I rode the worse it got, and it come to me that I was heading for a setback like nothing since old Brother Brigham's seagulls had sailed into those anti-Mormon crickets back in '48.

All morning I rode, following the Strawberry eastward until I came to Stinking Springs. From there I cut northeast up Pine Hollow, crossed the top, and worked my way down Wildcat and into Deep Creek Canyon, still going east. That country across the top was rough and rumpled as a messed bed. It was cut by a thousand nameless draws, crossed by another unmapped thousand gulches and arroyos. And up there it was dry. It was scant of water as whiskey was scarce at a Shouting Baptist prayer meeting. It was badlands, getting worse. And still I rode on, following those mules and cussing them every inch of the way.

Course, it was my fault they were gone, for I'd staked them out the night before and had been too lazy to put the hobbles on. I'd learn, but often that day I found myself wondering when. Besides, who'd ever have thought those two stubborn critters'd make such long-legged tracks for their reservation home?

I was feeling bad, too, about what I'd said to Zene. He was a good man, and one of the best friends I had in all the world. Being away from Ma and my little sisters and having my pa in jail and my brothers scattered over half of creation was bad enough, but now I'd gone and alienated myself from Zene as well, and I truly did feel lonely.

What it came down to, I suppose, is that I was out and out homesick. I truly did miss my family. Pa says that a child is given a family as a point of reference. What I think he means is that this is an awful big world, filled with all sorts of folks with problems. It's pretty difficult trusting *any* of them completely. With a family, however, it ought to be different. In a family everybody loves everybody, so everybody can be completely trusted. When a kid grows up in a good family, no matter how bad his troubles are, he can always turn back to his family for love and trust. That's what things are like in my family, and that's what Pa means by a point of reference.

For instance, my family is tolerably large and, what with Pa's three wives and three houses, it is sort of spread out. Still, us youngsters, no matter which of Pa's wives is our mother, all call each other brother or sister, and the other mothers are simply Aunt so-and-so. We think of each other as a family, too. If one has a problem and the others hear about it, why, we all just naturally come a-running.

Pa says the bunch of us are especially handy to him. If one of us sees or hears that the federal marshals are making a raid to catch themselves a certain plurally married bishop (which same plural marriage became truly illegal two years ago when Congress stuck their pious and interfering noses into the practice of religion and passed the infamous Edmunds-Tucker Act), why then Pa just naturally gets a prompt and fair warning that the minions of the law are coming. With that in mind, it's easy to see why Pa makes the unlikely brag that the more wives and children he has, the safer from the marshals he is.

So as a family we're close, mighty close. It gives a body a good feeling just knowing there are a few folks out there who love him and can be depended upon. As far as I've been able to tell, there isn't any trouble too big that a few of us Soderbergs can't handle it.

That's why I was crossing that mountain in pursuit of Andrew Aagard's mules, that's why my brothers and sisters had all gone to work, and it was also why I was feeling so lonesome and homesick. I surely did miss that bunch of Soderbergs who were my family, and I could see no end to my separation from them.

It was coming onto dark when I finally spotted our pack animals. They were both grazing peacefully on some lush grass down on what I figured to be Currant Creek. I rode up slow-like, expecting trouble and wishing my younger brother Ernest was with me, for he's better at sneaking up on ornery critters than any other two-legged human being I've ever met. He is also pretty good at imitating animal sounds; sometimes he even does better than the animals themselves. Fact is, under certain conditions I can sound like a few critters myownself. However, when it comes down to scary or tight situations, Ernest either has more innards than a cornered bobcat or he isn't quite bright. Whichever, he's a handy kid to have around, and I suppose that of all my brothers, it was Ernest and his sunny-bright disposition that I missed the most.

Anyway, I rode carefully up to those mules expecting all sorts of trouble, and I was almost mad when they acted joyful about seeing me.

"Dad-gum it," I growled as I threw my rope over the head of the one I called Lizzard on account of her being so sneaky-like and mean-quick about things, "why didn't you miss me at six-thirty this morning instead of now? And you, Aristotle, why'd you have to follow this slimy critter Lizzard. I've told you plenty how she'd just get you in trouble. Now see, I was right. It's coming on dark, and here we are smack-dab in the middle of the reservation. I'm nervous, and you two ought to be. I hear tell Indians love mule meat more than about anything else."

Well, I snubbed them up and reined around to start back, and suddenly I had this powerful feeling I was being watched. The skin on the back of my neck started crawling, my hair stood straight up, and, I'll tell you, I was worried as a snow-bound buffalo bull in wolf country.

Up on the ridge a coyote yipped at the first stars, and a bat dove through the twilight above me after some fleeing insect. Somewhere down the creek a nighthawk called out soft and lonely-like, and of a sudden I knew I wasn't going back across that mountain, not that night, at least. With that haunt feeling upon me, the odds against me making it safe were about equal to the odds against that Lizzard-mule of mine being agreeable. Or an old maid showing good sense in the company of a sweet-talking man. Blast! The way I was feeling, the whole thing could get skimpier than tracking bees in a blizzard.

"Come on, hoss," I whispered, and even my whisper cracked, I was so nervous. "Let's g-get up into them trees and hole up till daylight."

Without a murmur those animals agreed, and quick as that we were skedaddling up that slope and into the black of the pines. I gave the swaybacked cayuse its head then, hoping it could see better than me, and we rode real quiet for the next five minutes.

Then Lizzard-mule got contrary and started pulling off to the right. I hauled on her lead rope to pull her back, she set her haunches, I yanked the rope hard, she opened her mouth to bray, I kicked her muzzle hard with my boot, she jumped away and pulled harder and set herself to bray again, and finally I gave in. She wanted so bad to go that way, fine! We'd all go.

And we did. For maybe thirty feet. The ground dropped away and sudden-like we were in a deep swale with trees rising black all around us and new grass growing belly-deep to the horses. And after we'd stopped and it got quiet, there was even the laughter of a small stream that I later discovered was a spring.

"Lizzard-mule," I said softly as I looked around, "I've been misjudging you right along, and here-and-now I apologize. This is about as fine a camping site as I ever saw. You've sure enough led us home for the night."

Moments later I had the saddle and the other gear stripped from my old horse, and it and the two mules were all staked out proper. I had hobbles on all of them, too, trail hobbles that I rigged on the spot. I may learn slow, but I do learn.

Dragging the saddle with me, I walked over to one side of the tiny swale, and there, where I somehow sensed it would be, was a pile of rocks set perfect for hiding a fire from anyone farther away than a few feet. Well, that set my spine to chilling again, for there was no way I could have known about those rocks, and I stood for a long time staring out into the darkness, wondering what it was I was feeling. My craw was so shrunk up it wouldn't chamber a piece of pea gravel, and I felt about as yellow as mustard without the bite.

Trouble was, all three of my critters were grazing real peaceful, and I knew that their senses of approaching trouble were to be trusted far more than my own. Despite I was feeling chousy as a screw-worm steer about whatever it was I felt was watching me, I knew I should trust my animals. So, setting my saddle down and dropping myself onto it, I did.

It was the fire, though, that finally tied it all together. Anyone who has ever been out alone in the far-up hills at night will say there isn't anything friendlier'n the bright flames of a fire. There they are, licking hungrily at anything a body can toss into them and lighting up a few feet of the world at the same time, making at least that little area of light civilized again, making it into a place where a man can relax and feel secure. A fire's a wondrous thing, I'll say that.

Anyway, I'd put together a tiny hatful of one there in those rocks, had water heating up, had checked the animals, and was out searching for a little more wood when I found what I now figure was my first clue. I reached for a wide piece of dead, white wood, picked it up, and realized I was holding the skull of an animal, a mule, I figured. I hauled it back to the fire, and sudden my skin started in to prickling again. For there, smack in the forehead of that poor critter, was a bullet hole that was at least fifty caliber wide.

Carefully I looked around again, staring out into the darkness. But my animals were still quiet, and suddenly I knew what it was. A haunt. Animals don't usually pay haunts much mind, but people-folks do, and I was one of that nervous species!

Searching carefully I moved out from the fire again, circling, for I had a feeling about what it was I was going to find. And sure enough, back in the trees I came on what had to be the remains of a tent and a bedroll. Second clue. I had been right. Someone else'd camped here, and the evidence was truly pointing toward the distinct possibility of foul play.

Way I figured it, someone had died there where I was camped, and I was feeling the haunt of it. Only a matter of time, I was certain, and I would come on the remains of that poor pilgrim himself, whoever he was.

Only that time I was wrong.

I searched high and low for the next couple of hours, found another shot-up mule skull, third clue, finally slept until daybreak, and commenced to searching again. Two more hours passed, and I was beginning to feel like if I didn't soon light a shuck out of there I'd be up to my hip pockets in Indians and no room to swim.

Disgusted and more than a little nervous, I sat down on an old log to try to reason things out one more time. I stared at the pack mules and my old horse, which was saddled and ready to go. I stared around the swale. I stared at the bullet-holed skulls. I stared at the remains of the tent and bedroll. No matter which way I twisted things, I couldn't puzzle it out.

Someone had died there sure, and I couldn't find him. Or them.

The skulls looked to be seven, eight years old. The fabric of the tent was rotted but still there, and that left me with a number of possibilities. Either the man had escaped and never returned for his gear, or he hadn't escaped. That also left a couple of alternatives. Either the killers had disposed of his body, or the wild animals had done so. Either way, robbery hadn't been the motive. Otherwise, why would the killers have left his gear and killed two good mules besides.

Indians, I wondered? Maybe, but—

Suddenly the mules lifted their heads and I came alert myownself, shifting on the log to see where it was they were looking. I leaned way out, and that old log, long rotted, of a sudden gave way beneath me. I yelped in surprise as I sank into the soft red pulp and then scrambled quick to get away from a whole army of big black carpenter ants that were swarming about. That was when I saw the small leather bag.

Clue four, and bingo!

For an instant I just stared. Then, real slow, I reached down and hefted it. Heavy. Gold, I wondered quickly? No I decided as I shook it slightly and heard no sound of clinking coins. Nor did it feel like coins. Turning the old pouch I saw the letters ER had been burned into the leather. ER. Initials, most likely. Other than that, there was nothing on the pouch that could tell me a thing.

Carefully I drew the top open and gazed inside. I was still staring, my breath stilled, when I heard a twig snap behind me. That was when I finally remembered that all three of my animals had been staring into the trees behind me.

"Maybeso white pup findum sacred money-rock."

Spinning with the sack still in my hand, I stared into the dark, cold eyes of my friend Zenos Hill.

"Zene," I whispered, "what are you—"

"What do, sacred money-rock?" Zene growled his question and stepped forward, and that was when I noticed the Winchester he held. Interestingly, it was pointed straight at me.

Looked like I'd been wrong about that Ute Indian, I thought. The Mormon white on the inside of him hadn't taken. It wasn't anywhere near so thick as I'd supposed.

"Speakum up, white pup!"

"I . . . uh . . . I don't know *what* I'm going to do with it, Zene. I only just now found it, and to tell you the truth, it was the last thing I was looking for."

"Umph."

"It was! Way I figure it, some poor soul was murdered right here in this very spot. I was looking for his remains when I sat down on the gold. See, I even gathered up the skulls of his mules and what little was left of his tent and bedroll. Don't you see?"

Zene didn't answer. He just stared at me out of those eyes that had suddenly gone so hard and flat and black.

"By the way," I asked, trying my best to get him to talking, "what'd you mean, sacred?"

"Carre shin-ob," he whispered. "Heap bad place! Money-rock from there sacred to Ute."

"No kidding? I never heard of it."

"Umph!"

Well, whether Zene believed me or not didn't change anything. I hadn't heard of it, or the name, at least. I had, however, heard about that gold. Or at least I thought I had. From time to time there were rumors in town of lost gold mines and rich strikes and fabulous

Spanish treasures here and there, and I suspicioned the gold I held in my hand was a bit of that.

My brother Ernest and I had talked time and again of finding some such lost mine, dreaming of easy wealth as most young fellers are likely to do. Lots of folks believe that the West is filled with buried treasure, and I like to think so myownself. In any country where there is danger, as from the Indians or from bandits, or where folks have to travel light and fast and might have a little trouble, they are apt to bury gold or whatever they value highly.

Sometimes they'll pick likely places to hide their goods, sometimes mighty unlikely ones, such as the Mormon Saints who dumped their fine china and other valuables down into their privys when they were being driven from Nauvoo. Now who on earth would ever look in such a place as that for treasure? Only polecats and maybe a few mobocrats, who were both of the same breed anyway, I reckon.

Anyway, sometimes the owners got killed, and sometimes they lost their nerve and never came back. Gold can look almighty nice, but a few hundred miles of sun-blistered desert or ragged-edged mountains full of angry Apaches or Utes can look mean enough to take the shine off almost any amount of gold. So there a treasure sits, waiting for the first feller with guts and smarts enough to go get it.

Ernest reckoned he was such a feller, and who was I to argue? He thought I was too, and I didn't argue with that either. Of course, Pa argued plenty, for he didn't like us wasting our time dreaming of lost gold and other such truck. Whenever he heard us, he'd shut our chatter down quick.

"Gold," he'd say, "is a hard-found thing, and even harder to keep. Lots of folks, good folks otherwise, will turn to murder for the sake of gold. Brother Brigham advised the Saints to be farmers and to leave gold and its troubles to the gentiles. Boys, should the unlikely need ever arise, my advice to you would be to do the same."

I thought on that now, thought of the heavy sack of gold bullion in my hand, saw the hard look in Zene's eyes and steady rifle he held watching me, and then and there I decided that Pa had been right.

"Sacred," I said quietly. "Well Zene, if that's the case, this stuff surely doesn't belong to me."

Carefully then I laid the pouch down on the rotted log. "Maybe you'd do me a favor, Zene, and see that it gets back to your people before someone else gets hurt."

Zene said nothing, so I turned my back to him and walked to my horse, my skin crawling the entire time. I mean, anyone who has walked thirty or forty feet with a hard-eyed Indian standing behind him pointing a rifle at his back will understand why I was jumpy as a bit-up bull in fly time.

Quickly I mounted, and though I didn't want to do it, I couldn't help myself—I was upset, and so I looked back. I had to take one more look at Zene, one more look to convince me that my old friend had turned against me.

It wasn't the gold I was upset about—it wasn't the gold at all. If it was sacred to the Utes, that was fine with me. I respected that. Some things were sacred to me, too, and I didn't like folks making a mockery of them. Besides, the gold *was* on their land, or at least I thought it was. So by right it should have been theirs.

No, it was Zene himself that upset me, turning redskin so sudden-like as he had. That's why I turned back, so's I could argue with him one more time.

Only, where Zene had been, nothing at all remained. Even the sack of gold with ER branded on it was gone. That mountain was silent and empty as the day after the good Lord had divided the light from the darkness.

Gathering up the lead ropes to the mules, I turned the old horse I rode, and all of us, horse and mules and myownself, departed from that swale posthaste.

"Lizzard-mule," I growled as we topped the rim and dropped down toward Currant Creek, "I take back my apologies! You are a stubborn and evil animal. You lead me into the valley of the shadow one more time, and the next thing you know'll be the *last* thing you'll know. That there's a promise!"

3

Strawberry Flats Sheep Camp

It was early afternoon when I came down off the hills and started across the flat toward the sheep camp on the Strawberry. I'd been moving right along, both because I hated to leave Mr. Aagard's sheep alone and because I wanted to get shut of that reservation. The way Pa always said it suited me just fine. "The sooner the quicker," he'd yell when he wanted us to hurry, and, like I said, I couldn't agree with him more.

Of course, I knew the dogs could handle the sheep. But still, I'd been hired, I'd taken Old Man Aagard's money, and I was beholden to him for paying it. So, now that Zene was gone, I figured to pack camp and trail those woollies up into the Grandaddy area at the head of Rock Creek myownself.

Of a truth I was worried about Zene, but I was a whole lot more worried about his wife and kids. I'd have to tell them, of course, but blast! How would I do that? How could a kid like me tell a good woman that her husband had turned Indian on her? That was the bone I was worrying over as I topped that last little rise above the camp.

Drawing rein in a hurry, however, I just sat and stared. The camp was there, all right. But so was Zene's horse, grazing peacefully at the end of its picket rope. Zene was there too, sitting on his campstool and staring into the fire.

"No," I whispered as I stared, "this *can't* be! I ain't never rode so hard in my life, and that horse of his doesn't even look lathered!"

Nudging the horse forward, I rode down the slope and up to the fire, where I stopped again, staring down at the herder. Zene, however, didn't move, didn't even look up.

"How'd you get here so quick?" I finally asked.

"Rode," Zene answered, still not looking up.

"You got rid of that gold mighty fast," I declared. "You'd of had to, to beat me back."

"Umph."

"You weren't alone, were you." It was a statement. "Other Indians were there with you."

"Umph."

Well, I could see that Zene was back to his usual elocutionary ways, so with a frown I dismounted and set about taking down the tent and packing our gear. I'd finished, had the mules loaded, and was all set to mount up myownself, when Zene, who had not yet moved, finally spoke.

"Hy," he said quietly.

My back was to him, and at the sound of his voice I hunched like I'd taken a Ute bullet between the shoulder blades. He'd never called me Hy before, only kid and, lately, white pup.

"Yeah," I answered, doing my best to growl it.

"I'm afraid I owe you an apology."

Now I turned to look at the Ute herder. Suddenly he didn't sound like a reservation Indian anymore but was back to his old self. To say I was confused would have been putting it mildly.

"What for?"

Zene dropped his gaze and stirred at the fire with a stick. "You offended me yesterday, and you apologized."

"Yeah, I know. I meant it, too. The apology, I mean."

"I know that, and I appreciate it. Thing is, Hy, I also offended you, and I've been too stubborn to apologize."

"Zene, you don't need—"

"Hy, a boy has a right to be proud of his father, and yesterday I took that away from you. Your father is a fine man, and I truly admire him for living the Principle when it is so hard. I don't know if I'd be strong enough to be jailed for my beliefs or not. I hope I would, but I just don't know."

Zene poked at the fire again, and I stood there hipshot like my old horse. I felt like saying something, if only to ease off on Zene. To the best of my knowledge that was the longest speech he'd ever made, for he was of the firm opinion that if the ears were bent more often than the mouth was opened, the health of the scalp would be highly improved. But now he'd gone in real deep, and I didn't see how I could help.

Nor could I fault what he'd said. Sure us Soderbergs were having it a little rough, but despite the fact that we missed Pa and truly needed him, there wasn't one of us that wasn't busting our buttons with pride over Pa's strength and courage. No sir, Pa and Aunt Victoria and the baby were in jail because Pa and she held their beliefs and their family sacred, and Zenos Hill's ridicule or not, I was proud of Pa, proud of our family for sticking together, and I wouldn't abandon him or them nohow.

"Zene," I finally said, "your words were maybe harsh, but no more'n my own to you. Besides, such a little thing as what you said couldn't tear me away from Pa. He was disgusted with himself for being caught by those femininely attired marshalls, I was disgusted with him, and I reckon the whole family was disgusted. That doesn't change anything at all. We're still a family, and no matter what those marshals do, no matter even what Congress does, it won't change anything. Pa says our family is an eternal entity, and I believe it with all my heart.

"Besides," and now I grinned, "you were right about Pa and me being predictable. Ernest is telling both of us that, all the time."

Looking up, Zene smiled. "You'll do, Hy," he said quietly. "You'll do."

Slowly then he stood up and began fiddling with the double diamond I'd used to hitch the pack to Lizzard-mule. "It's hard, Hy, being an Indian and living in the middle of a lot of white folks. Mostly they treat me good, but now and then one of them makes certain I remember who I am, or was, or am supposed to be. I suppose you feel the same, being a cripple."

"Yeah, sometimes."

"I thought as much. I guess that's why I took to you. Thought you'd understand." He paused and looked over his shoulder. "Actually, I've never been an Indian, Hy. Not since I was about one year old. I was just born with their features, something I can't do much about. Like your leg, I reckon. I always thought that you accepted me as a man like yourself, nothing more, nothing less. That's why what you said hurt so much. I'd never expected it from you."

Well, I hung my head, and I don't recall ever feeling so low-down rotten.

"What's the bail against your father?"

"A thousand dollars."

"A *thousand?*"

"Yeah. Kinda high, ain't it."

"It is. But your father's a big man hereabouts. The marshals want him bad—figure to make an example of him."

We both looked at the trailing smoke from the fire. A thousand dollars was a vast amount of money, more than I could come up with in *five years* of camp tending, let alone one summer. Just thinking of it discouraged me. Pa's bail was steeper than a barn roof, and all the ideas I'd had of springing him from the calaboos when I found that gold came up gritty as dry-washed sand. Nothing smooth about any of them. Not with the gold gone back to the rightful owners. I—

"Hy, you should know I trailed you because I got worried about you. I didn't even mean to sneak up on you like I did. That just, well, it just happened is all. And I surely didn't intend to rob you of that gold. It wasn't mine, and I never thought it was."

"That's fine," I said, for truly I did not care that much about losing it. "At least it got back to the rightful owners."

Again Zene looked at me. "You really think I know those Lamanitish folks, don't you."

"Some," I admitted. "But so do Pa and my brother Jim. Zene, I ain't accusing you of being Indian or anything else. As far as I'm concerned, the only thing you are is one of my best friends. And as far as that gold goes, I'm with you. If it is sacred, then it ought to be treated as such. I'm just glad you were there to inform me."

Zene's eyes were glittering again, and I couldn't tell exactly what he was thinking. Fact is, I couldn't even tell if he was happy with what I'd said, or angry.

"Well," he finally growled, "you'd best be moving."

Now I raised my eyes and looked at Zene again, happen I hadn't noticed that with everything else he was also going blind. Either that or he was angry and setting in to have more words with me. Anybody, even a blind Mormon Indian, could see that I'd already struck and packed the tent and other gear, and he could also see that the only thing left to pack was his own campstool. My rough-gaited horse was even still saddled.

"Hand me the stool," I said, doing my best not to show my own sudden flash of anger. "Do that, and the onliest thing left to move will be you. This underprivileged camp tender will be long gone."

"Not with me you won't," Zene said quietly. "Here's where we go separate ways for a spell. While you're gone, I'd like you to pick up this list of supplies. And, happen you get to Fountain Green while you're away, stop in and say hello to my family."

"What? But—"

"Take this with you," he went on, reaching into his vest and grasping something. "I imagine the gold you found will cover your father's bail and then some."

Then Zene handed me the small leather pouch branded ER and filled brim-full of the purest gold bullion I'd ever seen. I stared, took the gold, and awkwardly made my thanks. Zene grunted stoically and packed his camp stool, and I was ready, as a matter of Strawberry Flats fact, to go and free my pa.

4

Provo—Territory of Utah

I followed the river past Bridal Veil Falls and down into Provo late the next day, and all the way into town I rode slow and stared. I'd been there before, but that still didn't change things. Provo was a *big* town, with nearly ten thousand folks living there, and I could hardly imagine a town as big as that.

The streets were wide and lined with trees. Homes were set well back, and all of them were fine homes, brick or adobe, and their trim-work was painted. There were also businesses everywhere, and to a feller like me who was used to the Co-op and maybe one or two other small stores and the blacksmith shop, it was a place to see.

Anyway, my first stop was the assay office, for I wanted to get that gold weighed and out of my hands. I mean, a feller never knew what sorts of antisocial criminals he might run into, and I wanted the gold safe.

The assay office wasn't much of an office, just a cluttered, dirty cubbyhole with a flyspecked window, a counter, and two tables. The man who ran it was small, hardly bigger'n a minute and a half. His name was Doolin. He had thin wispy hair and small beady eyes, and right off he made me nervous. Still, he took my gold quick enough.

He hefted it like he was weighing it, looked at the sack and then gave me a funny look, emptied the gold onto his scales, and worked himself around so his body was somewhat between me and what he was doing.

Now, I may be from a small town, and I may also be young, but right off I could see what this little feller was trying to do. The needle on the scales was in sight, my gold was even in sight, but the weight side was hidden behind him, and I knew immediately he was using his hand to make those weights go where he wanted them to go.

"Well, young feller," he whined all happy-like, "you've got yourself quite a fortune here. Comes to, let me see . . . yes, three hundred and two dollars and—"

"Mr. Doolin?"

"Yes?"

"Turn around, real slow, and while you're at it, take your left hand away from your scales."

Well, what followed was the biggest quiet since Giggles La Monte decided to show up for church on Easter Sunday. And seeing that Giggles hadn't heard a preacher, wore a hat, or been seen abroad in daylight for six years, that was some quiet.

"Say," he squeaked, and now his voice was truly high-pitched, "you haven't any right to come in here like this, giving me orders! I told you what the gold was worth, and I run a fair scales."

"Well," I replied, lifting my arm and hand, the one that had my old coat draped over it, and thrusting my hidden finger toward him, "maybe you do, and maybe you don't. Stand away from that scale and let's see that gold weighed square!"

"I won't do it!" he squeaked. "You have no right—"

"Mister, you got more guts than Custer's bugler blowing the second charge at the Little Big Horn. 'Course, you got about that many brains, too. This Navy Colt that you see in my hand says I got all the right in the world. Now *move!*"

That Doolin feller looked at my hidden finger, saw in his mind the pistol I hoped he'd see, and like some rare form of scrawny whiskered bird, he flittered right away from that scales.

The balance needle moved far over on the register, floated back and forth, and finally settled to a stop. "Read it," I ordered.

"S-sixty-four ou-ounces," he stuttered. "T-troy weight."

"Very good. And at twenty dollars an ounce, that comes to . . . let's see . . . yes, twelve hundred and eighty dollars. Pay me, please."

"No sir," he declared, growing suddenly defiant. "I won't."

Well, I was in a fix, and I knew it. I couldn't very well shoot the man, for my finger wasn't loaded. Nor did I know how much more of a bluff he'd go for. Still, it was all I had left, and so . . . "Mr. Doolin, lie down on the floor with your face away from me."

"Wh-what for?"

"I'm going to have to shoot you," I answered easily. "I don't mind that, but I do hate to see a man's face when he's dying. The eyes bulge out, the tongue rattles in the throat and turns the face a sickly blue, and all sorts of other ugly things happen. I just hate to watch that, so lie down with your face against that desk."

"Wait a minute! Wait a minute! I've thought it over, and maybe if we just came to a compromise—"

"Mister, you got my gold. Just under five and a half pounds of it. Happen I don't have my money, *all of it,* within, say, sixty seconds according to that big old Regulator clock of yours, you'll be lying on that floor and feeling just as dead as that brave and foolish bugler of Custer's ever was. Pay up!"

I never did see a man who was so tight as that Doolin feller. He started to get my money and then happened to see the leather pouch, which I'd made the mistake of leaving in his possession. His eyes saucered up wide, and suddenly he stopped counting.

"Where'd you get the gold?" he demanded in a high squeaky voice.

"Found it," I answered.

"Them your initials?"

"Not hardly. Found the sack, too. Now let's have the cash and a receipt."

"No sir, young feller, I won't pay you. I've got to report this."

"Mister," I finally said, "I've plumb run out of patience. Lie down against that desk!"

"You'll never get away with this."

"Maybe, maybe not. But anything's better than coyoting around the rim of this thing with you all night long. Lie down!"

Doolin looked at me, and slowly he lay down. I stepped closer; his eyes were saucered up. I twisted his head so he was looking at the desk. I saw his body start to shake, and I was in a pickle for sure. My aimed finger was shaking worse than he was, and I knew this bluff was nearly up. For crying out loud, if only—

That was when I remembered one more of my birth defects, one that'd come along for the ride with my club foot. My tongue was extra nimble, and I'd learned as a tiny boy that I could make the strangest clicking sounds with it that a body ever heard, sounds that no one else I knew could make. I could do a single click, or a roll of them like a rattlesnake. I could click out tunes, and I had one sound that Pa said sounded just like the click of a pistol. I tried that then.

Click!

Doolin jerked, and suddenly I laughed out loud. "Mr. Doolin, I have a better idea. Shootin's too good for thieving assayers, but coming down the trail today I ran onto a little critter that seems like mighty appropriate company for a fellow like you. Lie still while I put him on your back."

"No!" he screamed. *"No!* I—"

"I mean it!" I thundered. "Lie still!"

He did, and I reached onto his counter and took from it a short length of half-inch rope, which I dropped onto his back, at the same time making my rattlesnake roll of clicks.

"Wh-what's that?" he shrieked.

"Oh-oh," I whispered as I wriggled the rope. "Don't move, Mr. Doolin. Was I you, I wouldn't even breathe. Rattlesnakes are mighty touchy, and—"

"R-rattlesnake?"

"Yes, but—" Now I clicked again. "Don't move," I whispered urgently as I twisted the rope. "The thing's coiling up, and is eye-balling the back of your ear. Oh-oh, it's getting ready, and—" I rattled again, and suddenly I could hear the small man sobbing.

"No . . . no . . . no . . ." he sobbed, "I can't stand snakes. I'll pay, just as you asked, only get that—that snake—"

"Mr. Doolin," I answered, "I'll let you up just one more time. Happen you don't pay immediately and give me my receipt to boot, I will force-feed this rattlesnake to you head-first. Then you and it will have a biting contest to see who can poison which the quickest. Am I understood?"

"Y-yes sir," he whispered through his sobs.

"Fine. Now let me get hold of this snake . . ."

I lifted the rope slowly from Doolin's back, clicking my tongue a couple of times while I did so, and then I stepped back. "All right, you can get up, but remember, this Navy Colt is watching you carefully, and my rattlesnake is lonely for companionship. Get moving."

With terror in his eyes and sobs of fear still in his throat, Doolin rolled over and stared up at me, and when I signaled with my hidden finger, he scrambled to his feet like a fire had been built under him. Instantly he started in to counting again, and it wasn't more than thirty seconds before I had the full $1,280 in my hand.

I thanked him kindly, picked up my receipt, assured him that I'd never recommend his business establishment to another soul, and backed out of his office. Finally me and the old horse were on our way. I had a bad feeling about that Doolin fellow, though. I couldn't help it, I just did. He and I would meet again, I was sure, and when we did, grief would come of it.

5
Territorial Prison—Provo

I put all but a little of my money into an account in the First National Bank, stuffed some more into a used moneybelt I purchased from the bank manager for two bits, and got a draft for a thousand dollars. Then that spavined horse and I made our way out Center Street to the jail where they were keeping Pa and Aunt Victoria and the baby.

The man in the office was big and some run to fat, but he looked competent. He had his boots up on the desk, and his main occupation seemed to be swatting flies. When I walked in, he didn't even look up.

"Umph," I said, imitating Zene.

"He'p you, sonny?"

Well, I hadn't been "sonny" to anybody for near two years, and that got my dander up. I don't know why I was so sensitive about my age, but I was, and it usually got me in trouble. "I reckon," I answered softly. "Fetch me your Boss. I don't do business with office boys."

The man got real quiet. Slowly his boots came down, and at last he swung around to look full at me, his eyes squinting. "Do I know you?"

"Not yet. Where's the Boss?"

"You're looking at him," he said, rising until he'd reached his full eighteen feet or so of height. I stared up at him, and, well, it wasn't too hard to tell that man could make mincemeat out of me eight days out of seven. Besides, if he was the Boss, he was the man I needed.

Yessir, I'd pushed hard enough for one day. Then and there, I smiled. "I should have known it," I said easily. "You do look like a man with authority. I'm right sorry."

"Umph," he grunted, and I thought how amazing it was that such a simple word could be so widely used by so many different people.

"I'd like to bail out my Pa."

"Your Pa a polyg," he asked, "or a horse-thief?"

"Those the only two kinds you keep in here?" I asked.

"Usually, though we got one murderer, one feller who's been selling the bed of Utah Lake for land development and doing a booming business, and Shin-bone Sally, who was picked up last night for soliciting inside territorial boundries, which puts her a minimum of two hundred miles off course, at least according to the laws of man. Which of the first two is your Pa?"

"There's some that claim both," I answered, grinning again.

That made the man smile too, and I discovered then that he was missing one of his two front teeth. I'd surely never forget him.

"What do *you* say?" he asked. "About your pa?"

"I don't say anything, but you boys have him locked up for unlawful cohabitation, and nothing else that I know of. I've got his bail."

"Cagey, ain't you." the man said, grinning wider. "Who's your pa?"

"Jons Soderberg."

"The bishop? Well I'll be. I mighta knowed it. You two talk alike. Bail, huh? I heard tell he was going broke."

"Not so's you'd notice. Who do I pay?"

"Cash money?"

"Same as. Bank draft."

"Lemme see it."

"You the man I pay?"

"I said I was the Boss, didn't I? I'm deputized and bonded both. Now let's see the color of your draft."

I handed the draft to him. He walked to the window and examined it carefully. "Where'd you get this?"

"First National Bank. It says right on it."

"Not the draft," he said, looking down from his lofty height and giving me the dark and evil eye. "The money for it."

"Found it."

"Smart, ain't you."

"I get by. I'm also passing honest, and that helps. When do I get my Pa?"

"Honest, huh. You know, young feller, I believe you are. There's too much brass in you to be otherwise and live very long. You sign this draft, I process it, and you pick your pa up in the morning."

"The morning! Why so long?"

"Rules. What you aiming to do about the woman and the kid?"

"Is there bail on them?" I asked.

"Nope. They're witnesses."

"Then for now I reckon they stay, though I surely hate to see that happen. This thousand-dollar draft is just for my pa."

Again the deputy looked at my draft. "You Hyrum Soderberg?"

"I am. Now give me a receipt for that draft, please, and I'll be back in the morning—eight o'clock on the nostrils."

"Eight-thirty."

"Fine. Let's have the receipt."

Well, that big, tall buzzard eyed me over, grinned again, pulled a tattered book of receipts from his beat-up desk, and wrote one out.

"This your name?" I asked when he tore it out and handed it to me. "Tinsdale?"

"Says so on my birth record," he answered.

"Fine, Mr. Tinsdale. I'll expect my pa to be a free man come eight-thirty tomorrow morning."

"Not free, young feller. Only loose. He's still got to stand trial. Otherwise you lose all this money." He grinned even more widely, showing that big gap in his teeth again, and so without another word I turned and walked out.

I took a room in a house on Academy Street, called that on account of it ran past what was shaping up to be the new home for Brigham Young Academy, which had been operating now for maybe fifteen years. With two meals, the room I took came to six bits, and I figured it was well spent. Then I went to the S. W. Sharp livery, stabled my horse, dickered over a couple of theirs, and finally gave ten dollars for a nag that looked even worse than the one I rode.

Come morning we'd have to make our way south to Fountain Green, and there were three ways to do it, if you counted walking. Pa hated walking very far, so I counted that out. That left horses or the train. If Zene was right, then Pa was predictable, and I reckoned he'd be so tired of being cooped up that eight out of eight chances he'd choose to ride a horse. That's why I bought that second animal.

For a time I walked around Provo, and truthfully I'd never seen so many busy people. The town was booming. There were land speculators in from the East, townfolks figured they had money to burn, and the *Enquirer*, Provo's newspaper, said it all with its headlines of "Boom! Boom! Boom!"

They had new resorts out at the lake; rail cars were running out there every thirty minutes and jammed every run. There were housing tracts springing up everywhere, and I had no doubt that there were at least a dozen other fellows besides the man in jail who were also selling the bottom of the lake to gullible and unsuspecting buyers. Of course, they were throwing in for free the twelve feet or so of water above the land, so maybe it wasn't such a bad deal after all.

The Provo Woolen Mills on First North and Second West covered nearly the whole block, making it the biggest building I'd ever seen. Taylor Brothers Furniture was packed with cash-paying customers. There were both an east and a west Co-op that were both big businesses. And the Palace Saloon and other such establishments looked like they couldn't have handled another customer if they'd found one. Like I said, Provo was booming, and there weren't even any mines to help it along.

For a time I just looked around, but I had an idea, and though it made me feel mighty reluctant and uncomfortable, I finally made my way into the west Co-op building.

"May I help you?" a woman asked.

"Uh . . . I reckon," I answered, feeling conspicuous as a buffalo chip in a punch bowl.

"Well?"

"Well what?"

"How can I help you?"

"I . . . uh . . . well . . ."

"Let me guess. You want something for a girl."

Embarrassed, I dropped my eyes. "Yes ma'am, I do."

"You want jewelry maybe? Or a book?"

"No, that ain't exactly what I had in mind. I just . . ."

"I know!" she exclaimed. "You want something frilly-frally!"

Then I really turned red. I don't know if it was because I was thinking of buying Ida Mae someting as personal as frilly-frally clothing, or if it was because that woman-clerk had figured me out. But whichever, I was embarrasseder'n a fox caught feather-mouthed in a henhouse.

Well, that woman showed me things such as I'd never before seen nor even imagined, and it took me a good ten minutes to convince her I was after something a great deal less . . . well, frivolous. Finally, however, she went to a rack of dresses.

"How big is she?" she asked.

"About like you, only maybe quite a bit thinner," I answered honestly.

Right off I could tell I'd made a mistake. That woman went white as a January blizzard, her lips thinned down to nothing but red lines, and her eyes narrowed off until all I could see were black slits. "One moment, sir," she hissed, and her voice was so cold I could have sworn her jowls were dripping ice water.

"I mean . . . I . . . uh . . . ," I stammered as she glared frostily at me, "I mean, maybe a little taller. Not much, but a little."

Well, she looked at me as though I had no more social position than an onion, turned, and, with a glacier-like flourish, whipped out the prettiest blue taffeta dress I'd ever seen.

"This," she declared haughtily, "is far too expensive for such a *boy* as you. Still, I feel obligated to show even an uncouth person like yourself our *finer* products. Now if you'll please step to the back with me—"

"I . . . I'll take that one," I blurted.

"This one? My dear boy, don't add further insult to my day! This is a fine dress, but *very* expensive. Now in the back—"

"Ma'am," I said, "I'll take that one. Wrap it, please."

Well, the woman looked at me and I pulled out a twenty-dollar gold piece and laid it on the counter. She stared at it and of an instant was all smiles once more.

"Yes sir!" she beamed. "Right away, sir!"

My next stop that evening was at a small bookstore just down the street from the Co-op. I walked in and nearly lost my breath, the sight was so grand. Along both walls were shelves, and those shelves were all lined with books, more books than I could hardly imagine. Like I've already explained, I had a hankering for learning, and I'd promised Pa and Ma that I'd do some reading while I was up with the herd. And though I'd already finished or nearly finished Farrar's *The Life of Christ*, Tacitus's *The Annals and the Histories*, most of the Book of Mormon for the third time, and was well into Blackstone's *Laws,* I intended to make my promise more than good. If I couldn't go to a proper school, that surely didn't mean that I had to go forth upon the face of the land in total ignorance.

Ambition was strong within me. I wanted to see, to become, but most of all, to know and to understand. Most of what scholars took for granted was new to me, and so I read at every opportunity, and herding sheep, at least, provided plenty of free time.

So I had read a little, and the wider my knowledge became, the more I realized my ignorance. It is only the ignorant, I decided, who can be positive of everything, only the ignorant who can become fanatics, for the more I learned, the more I became aware that there are shadings and differing points of view in all things.

Thank goodness, I remember deciding one night after reading the life of Simon Gerty, whom the Americans considered a renegade but whom the British almost deified, *thank goodness that God has the capabilities to judge that man, him and all others*. For myself, my goal was to avoid judgement unless it was thrust upon me, to accept the good in all men, and to learn good things from all who had good things to teach.

Therefore I sought knowledge from every conceivable source, for in knowledge lay not only power but freedom from fear. Pa had told me once that generally speaking, folks feared only what they did not understand. I believed him, and because I didn't want to live a life filled with fear, I tried always to seek knowledge, develop wisdom, and grow in understanding. One of the best ways to do that was by reading, and so I read.

For maybe an hour I browsed through that bookshop, and when I left I carried with me Plutarch's *The Lives of the Noble Grecians and Romans,* all three volumes of William Russell's *The History of Modern Europe,* a fine volume by John Gilmary Shea entitled *The Story of a Great Nation,* and a bound volume containing all the past year's issues of the *Juvenile Instructor* magazine, which was published by the Church.

Taking my books and Ida Mae's dress, I went up Academy Street to the new Academy building, where I stood for a time looking up at the huge spires that were even then under construction. The original Brigham Young Academy had burned down in '84, and the huge building I was looking at was scheduled for completion in another two, maybe three, years.

It was a beautiful edifice, stretching high into the air and covering what seemed like acres of ground. Looking at it sort of made me wonder what wondrous things I might learn in there that would go along with all that I was gleaning from my books.

At last, being truly tuckered out, I returned to the rooming house and turned in, climbing into the softest feather tick I'd ever felt. It surely beat all hollow the rocks and sticks of Strawberry Flat.

Then, just before I went to sleep, I thought of that beady-eyed little man called Doolin who ran the assay office. He was trouble, and I knew it. Thing was, I just didn't know how much. Had I known, I'd not have slept at all. But I did, like a log, and at a quarter of nine the next morning I watched as Pa was led out of the jail and into the office where I waited.

He looked bewildered, but then I reckon I looked some misty-eyed, so neither of us mentioned the other's discomfortable appearance.

"Howdy, Pa."

"Hyrum, what're you doing here? Is . . . is your Ma . . . everyone . . . all right?"

"Everyone's fine, Pa. Or at least so far as I know. I came to take you home. Didn't the deputy tell you?"

"Tell me what? Hy, you know they aren't going to turn me loose. Bail's too high. I could just as easy fly as raise a thousand dollars."

"I know, Pa. I took care of it for you." Then I turned to the big gap-toothed deputy. "Could you give him his things, please? We've got to get along."

"But Hy—"

"Not now, Pa. I'll tell you later. Mister?"

Well, the deputy grinned down at both Pa and myself, and slowly he handed Pa his personals. Pa took them, looking like he was in a trance.

"You . . . you mean I'm free?" Pa asked.

"Yes sir," Deputy Tinsdale declared. "Until your trial comes up, you surely are."

"Then . . . then might I see my . . . I mean, might I see Victoria Copley and her baby?"

Deputy Tinsdale grinned his Cheshire-cat grin. "Well, Soderberg, you almost had a witness against you. Almost. But now, so far as I know, Miss Copley is a single lady, and I see no problem with you visiting her for a few moments."

"Thank you," Pa said humbly. "Might my son here come with me?"

"No, I think he'd best wait here," the deputy said.

"As you wish. Will you escort me?"

"Certainly. Young Soderberg, can you handle my fly-swatter for a few minutes?"

I nodded and took up the swatter and the big Deputy Tinsdale led my Pa off down another hall. As they went through a big door I heard Pa telling the Deputy somewhat concerning my leg and the good things it had done for me. Well, I'm only human, and my head swelled a little. Had Ma been there, she would have taken me back down a notch or two. But truthfully, I don't think praise is always a bad thing. For instance, anytime that someone tells me I'm great, I'll bust a gasket proving he's right. That helps them and it helps me as well, for I become a better person. So, as you might have guessed, I do like praise.

A few minutes later Pa came back. He looked a little emotional, but I understood that, and so I paid it no mind. I handed the swatter back to Deputy Tinsdale, thanked him again for his help, and Pa and I walked out of that jail. For a moment Pa stood still and breathed deeply, and then I led him to the horse I'd bought for him the night before.

"This cayuse still alive?" Pa asked as he saw the animal. He sounded pretty disgusted, but I reckon he was still used to his eighteen-hundred-dollar plug, and so I didn't get my tail up.

"It ain't bad for ten dollars," I said easily. "Would you rather take the train?"

"Train?" he snorted. "When I can ride and breathe in all this fresh air? Not hardly."

"Fine. I figured as much. Now let's rattle our hocks on out of here."

Pa looked at me again, shook his head, and swung aboard. I did the same on my own pile of bones, and we were just starting to ride when a voice we both knew stopped us cold.

"Hold it, Soderberg, or I'll blast ya!"

Pa and I reined around, and there riding slowly toward us on his ugly piebald gelding, was Deputy Marshal Hebron Clawson, yellowed mustaches, filthy dirty clothing, huge bulging nose, and all.

"Soderberg," he growled when he had pulled to a stop facing us, "you're under arrest for breaking jail, not to mention numerous counts of unlawful cohabitation, etcetera."

"Hello, Deputy Clodson," Pa said quietly.

"That's Clawson."

"That's what I said, Plodson. Looks like you're missing your new duds."

"Duds?"

"You know. Skirts and petticoats and such other unmentionables as only women and people like you would wear."

Well, right off the marshal's face turned beet red, trying to match his nose, I guess, and I could see he was going to be about as sociable as an ulcerated back tooth.

"Marshal Clawson," I said, "I—"

"Soderberg," he growled, ignoring me, "get off'n that horse! *Now*!"

"Clawson," Pa replied easy-like and quiet. "I'll not do it. I've been bailed legally, and I'm going home."

"Bailed! Soderberg, you're so dad-blamed broke you couldn't raise a blister, let alone the thousand I demanded they set for your bail."

"So that high bail was *your* doing?"

"You're blamed right it was. You're sneakier'n a weasel after weiner pigs, and I ain't *about* to let you slip away from me again. That's why your bail's so high. Now dismount!"

Marshal Clawson glared at Pa, Pa glared back, neither said anything, and finally, when Pa wouldn't look away, Old Clawson dropped his eyes.

"I might've known," Pa said. "Come on, Hy, let's—"

The air was filled with the sudden click of a pistol hammer being pulled to cock. Pa and I both looked back, and Clawson's big .44 was aimed right at Pa.

"Down," the marshal ordered.

"Marshal," Pa repeated quietly, "I told you, the bail's been paid."

"And I told you there was no way you could raise that money."

"You're right. I didn't. It was raised by Hyrum here. Now if you'll excuse us . . ."

"In a pig's eye. Now git down!"

We got down, and Marshal Clawson bellered out to the deputy in the jail, asking would he please and pronto make an appearance outside.

"What do you want?" the gap-toothed man asked after he had ducked his way through the doorway and raised himself up again outside.

"This man says he's bailed."

"He is. Why you holding a gun on him?"

"Well, I . . . uh . . . . He paid a *thousand dollars?*"

"The boy did. Bank draft. Now Clawson, put that pistol away before I arrest *you* for throwing down on a peaceable citizen."

Well, Marshal Clawson looked about as cheerful as an old bull elk surrounded by sixteen wolves and a blizzard closing in. He growled and glared and did his best to look evil and instead looked only miserable. At last, however, he took that .44 off cock and put it back into his pocket. As for me, I was having whole new thoughts about the gap-toothed giant who had clipped Clawson's wings.

"Satisfied?" Pa asked.

"Where'd you get the thousand?"

"I told Mr. Tinsdale," I answered. "If he wants to tell you, I reckon that's his business."

"I don't," Tinsdale said quietly, winking at me. "Like I said, young feller, Marshal Dyer has resigned, so for the time being at least, *I'm* the Boss around here."

"Yes sir," I agreed, "you surely are. Adios, friend."

Pa nodded too, and then we remounted. "Have a nice day," Pa said politely to Marshal Clawson. That worthy scowled, and we spurred those two flea-bags eastward on Center Street. Within minutes we were raising a dust southeast around the lake toward Fountain Green and home.

It felt good, it did, riding once more with Pa, and even Marshal Clawson's parting yell that he would trace my money and get us both back in jail couldn't dampen our spirits.

I looked at Pa, and he was grinning, and for the first time in months I started feeling real good myownself. Pa had that effect on folks. He is the sort, Pa is, who makes a laugh out of being alive. Not a joke of it, mind you. Just a grin, a sly chuckle, or an outright belly-shaker that makes him, as well as the folks about him, feel good—especially when things are curdling to clabber in a hurry and it appears that there isn't anything funny to be found between Salt Lake and Manti. That's usually when Pa will open up with a shout or a shoulder clap or just a friendly bear hug to get things "elevated" as he calls it. Yessir, it was surely great being back with my Pa.

For some time he just rode and grinned, every now and then swinging his hat in the air and breathing deeply. Me, though, I was troubled, and Pa soon saw it.

"What's wrong, Hy?"

"Oh, nothing, I guess. It's just that I'm so upset at Marshal Clawson I can hardly think straight. I don't understand how you can be civil to him."

"He's only doing his job, Hy."

"Maybe, but if you ask me, he's doing it almighty poorly. Almost anybody I could think of would make a better marshal than Clawson."

"Well, you may or may not be right, but whether you are or not, I surely understand how you feel. However, there might be another side to it, and I'd like you to consider it."

"Pa, he's had you locked up, and—"

"I know, Son, I know. But think what it would be like without any law at all. Right now in Fountain Green, Hebron Clawson may be one of the most important men in our lives."

"Oh, come on! I—"

"I mean it, Hy. That man is all that stands between us and savagery. He's the thin line of protection, and when he mounts that piebald gelding and rides out, his life is always on the line.

"Now I know that this polygamy thing is hard on our family, and I'm certain it is just as hard on hundreds of other families who are living the Principle. But Hy, think what it would be like if we *weren't* living it. Would Hebron Clawson be our enemy then? Would he?"

Slowly I shook my head.

"Of course he wouldn't. Under those conditions, we'd be free to come and go, do business, buy goods, love our families, go sparking with a cute young gal, and we could do all of that because he is there. He is our first line of defense—in many respects, the only line."

"Defense against what?"

"Against savagery, Hy. The savage is never far from the surface in any of us, but because we know the law is here, we fight it down. I don't lose my temper and strike somebody at least partly because Hebron Clawson is there. The drifter with the chip on his shoulder avoids trouble, also because Marshal Clawson is there.

"The Athenian Thucydides, in his *History of the Peloponnesian War,* describes what happens when the savage within us is allowed to run free. He writes that men, because of greed and ambition, lust for power over others. That lust is carried out in continually greater excesses and atrocities, continuing until every vestige of normal civilization is done away with and all people are filled with the desire to take each other's lives."

"That sounds like the folks who were the last of the Jaredites and the Nephites."

"Exactly, son. People don't change. Once they allow Satan to rage within their hearts, freedom is destroyed and the evil of savagery and oppression reigns continually.

"With the exception of polygamy, we have freedom, you and I and your ma and the others, because Hebron Clawson and other law enforcement officers are out there with a badge. To tell you the truth, I think he is a fine man to be wearing it."

"Pa—"

"Hy, let me finish. I know Marshal Clawson has made mistakes, but who of us hasn't. Still, he's dedicated, he hangs on like a bull-terrier pup, and he won't buffalo for sour apples. His judgment's a little lacking sometimes, but so's mine, for that matter.

"Some people believe the law to be a restriction, Hy, and it is, but only against evil. Laws, if they are proper ones, are made to free people, not to bind them. As you know, improper laws cause pain, but never proper ones. They are only to tell us what we may or may not do without transgressing upon the equal liberty of any other man."

"It says that in Blackstone."

"I know, Hy. I read it years ago."

"You did?"

"Of course. Where do you suppose I got that idea? And I'll tell you something else. The longer I live, the more sense it makes. If this polygamy issue wasn't up and about, why, things would be just fine between Hebron and I. He's a good man, Hy. He's just on the other side of the fence when it comes to plural marriage, and he's bound by his oath of office to do his job, just as I'm bound by my oath to support and sustain my wives and my children."

"Who was that Athenian feller you mentioned a moment ago?"

"Thucydides."

"He's a man I've never read."

"You should, son. I have his book at home, and you're welcome to borrow it any time you like. Thucydides was a fine thinker as well as an able war correspondent, and a man can learn much from him."

For a time we rode again in silence, and I spent the time thinking about Pa and myself. Here I'd been bragging about wanting an education so I wouldn't be arrogant or bigoted or fanatical, and first thing I knew, in spite of all my reading, I was. Pa, though, who had gone through only the sixth grade, was intellectually and emotionally where I hoped one day to be, and again I was thankful that the good Lord had given me such a father.

We were clear down near Spanish Fork when Pa finally spoke again. "I don't want to ask, Hy, but I've got to. Where'd you get the money for my bail?"

I looked at Pa and could tell right off that he was serious about knowing. I'd thought all along of making up some whopper, just to spare his credulity, but now that it was on me, I couldn't do it. Sodербergs just didn't hold with lying, not in any from at all.

"From gold," I answered quietly.

"Gold?"

"Yessir. And I know you've told us never to go chasing gold, but I didn't. Chase it, I mean. Honest I didn't. I just sat down on that rotted log and there it was. I was surprised as—"

"Whoa, Hy. Now start at the beginning. Right now you're blubbering like a calf with the slobbers, and I can't make heads or tails of what you're saying."

Well, I grinned and took a deep breath, and for the next few miles I told Pa about my remarkable discovery. When I'd finished, Pa said nothing, and for another few miles we rode in silence once more. Finally, however, Pa spoke.

"First off, Son, you're a truth-teller. You always have been, so I believe you completely, and I have no doubt that Zene will verify your story. Still, I'm afraid you've got a serious problem."

"But why?"

"Greed, Hyrum. And possibly revenge. A few years ago a man disappeared up in those mountains, a man whose last name was Rhoades. The rumor had it that he had found a great deal of gold, much more than a fortune. Word'll somehow get out that you've found some of his gold, and you'll have more troubles than you ever dreamed possible."

I thought then of the beady-eyed Doolin at the assay office, and suddenly my skin started to crawl.

"What'll I do, Pa?"

"I don't know as there's anything you *can* do. But was I you, I'd get back to the herd, and quick."

"I'll go tomorrow. First thing."

"Maybe you ought to go today."

"Pa, I've got to see Ma and the little girls. I miss 'em awful. I also want to see Ida Mae. I bought her a pretty little frilly-frally, and besides, I miss her terrible."

Pa grinned. "I understand, Hy. Only, this time I think you—"

"Pa, I've just got to see her!"

Pa looked at me and shrugged. "Well," he said, "I taught you to skin your own cats. Reckon I ought to let you be about it."

He didn't say any more, and so we rode in silence.

"Pa," I suddenly asked, "what about Aunt Victoria and the baby?"

Pa looked off into the distance, and for a minute or so I thought he hadn't heard me. Finally, however, he answered. "How have the families been doing?"

"Uh . . . okay, I guess."

"Hy, I want the truth."

"We've managed, Pa, but I suppose it's been rough on Ma and Aunt Polly. We're all working, though, and—"

"Hy, I can't let that happen to my families. I need to be there to support them. If my case comes to trial, they'll convict me. I'll go to prison, and I won't be there where I'm needed."

I looked at Pa, wondering what he was getting at. I'd asked about Aunt Victoria, one of Pa's three wives, and—

"Do you see what I'm saying, Hy? I've got to jump bail, go into hiding, and run my homes from there."

"But Pa, that thousand dollars is a whole lot of money. You jump bail and you'll be throwing it all away."

"I know, Hy, and some day I'll pay it back to you. Right now, though, I can't risk a conviction and a three-year sentence. Besides, if I disappear, then the territory'll be forced to let Victoria and the baby go. After all, there won't be anybody for her to witness against."

That made sense, and though I was some bothered about losing that thousand dollars, I reckoned it would be worth it if Pa could go free. Besides, what was a thousand dollars? Riches is all. I'd been rich two or three days, but that wasn't enough to make it a habit. No sir, I still thought and felt and looked broke, so I might as well *be* broke to go along with it.

Again we rode in silence, with Pa now and then pointing out something that he wanted me to see and consider. When I was younger I loved that, but then I went through a spell where I hated it. I felt like every time Pa said something, what he was really saying was that I was dumb and didn't know enough not to eat rocks. Of course, that wasn't true, and now that I have a little more wisdom, I've come again to where I truly appreciate Pa. In spite of being human, he is a great man, and I can hardly get enough of listening to the things he has to tell me. In fact, I think that's what God meant when He said to honor our parents. Finally, by jings, I think I do.

Much later the two of us pulled rein on the hills above Salt Creek Canyon. The Sanpete Crawler was chugging up the grade below us, and I wondered if this was Amos Reed "Tucker Bill's" run. His eyes were going bad on him, and lately he'd only been working days.

We watched until all we could see was the black smoke belching up from beyond the hills, and then we hit the trail and went down into the canyon ourownselves.

Seeing the railroad tracks and the creek and that trail put me in mind of Pa's race, and I was thinking on that when Pa finally spoke.

"Makes a man think of the race," he said.

I nodded, pleased that our minds thought together like they did.

"Mungus is making a fine counselor in my bishopric," he said. "You and Ida Mae surely turned him around."

"With the help of your fists," I said.

"Usually," he responded, "I don't hold with fighting. Brother Brigham taught against it, and it generally doesn't accomplish anything. You remember that."

"I will, Pa. Still, Mungus would've never paid you no mind at all if he hadn't learned to respect your good right hook. Seems to me a knuckle sandwich would be a wonderful diet for old Marshal Clodson, too. Maybe *that's* what would teach him his judgment."

Pa looked at me serious-like, and suddenly we were both laughing. We laughed like that all the way to the top of the divide.

"How are you and Ida Mae getting along?" he suddenly asked.

"Last time I saw her, things were great."

"You like her a lot?"

"Yeah, I do. She's cute as a button, and she treats me right."

"How do you treat her?"

I looked at Pa. "Okay, I reckon. Probably even a lot better than that. To be truthful, I'm scared to death of her, and so I treat her pretty much like I would treat the king or queen of England. Is that good enough?"

Pa smiled. "I imagine it is. Just be certain that, for so long as you remain together, you treat her like a queen, and I guarantee she will always act like one for you."

For a few moments we rode silently. "Pa?" I finally asked.

"Yes?"

"Can I ask you a hard question?"

"Of course. I don't know if I can answer it, but I will try."

"How come the Lord doesn't let women hold the priesthood?"

Pa looked at me and saw immediately that I was serious and

wasn't interested in one of those dumb jokes about holding priesthood holders. "Why do you ask?"

"Well, lately I've been reading a book about Jesus, and it seems to me that of all the people who surrounded Jesus, the women were strongest and most steadfast. I know the apostles were great, but many of them wavered a little, at least right after Christ died. There is no evidence that the women ever did."

"What book are you reading?"

"Farrar's *Life of Christ*."

"That's a fine book. I'm glad you're reading it."

"Well, it is enlightening in lots of ways. Anyway, reading it got me to thinking a lot about Ida Mae and Ma and Aunt Polly and Aunt Victoria and my sisters, and I don't know that there are any finer people in all the world. I mean that, too. I'm not as good as them, not in hardly any way at all. So why did God single me out and give me His power, and leave them out in the cold? Why, for that matter, has He *always* done that with men and women?"

"Are you sure He did?"

"Well yeah! I mean, I know you say that Ma holds your authority hand-in-hand with you, and those are dandy words, but in lots of ways they don't cut ice, and you know it. You and I were ordained, Ma wasn't. You conduct all the affairs of the ward, Ma could never be a bishop, and on and on. That's what I mean. Why did God leave them out? Especially when womenfolks seem so much more righteous."

Pa rode quietly for a minute. Then he drew rein and I pulled up beside him. "I don't know that women are always more righteous than men," he said quietly. "But I *have* noticed that most women seem more inclined to want to be righteous. And you are right about the ladies in our family. In my personal opinion, they are much more deserving of God's authority than I am. That's why I think He gave it to them."

"What? But Pa, you know—"

"Hear me out, Son. God gave those sisters His authority just as He did us, but He gave us completely different assignments. Man's is limited and given only according to personal and immediate worthiness, and seems to be to conduct and preside and hopefully represent. Women's authority, on the other hand, is universal and is the power to conceive and nurture and give love to God's newly born children."

"Pa, every woman on earth can have babies."

"I know. And that seems to say something for their level of spirituality and worthiness in the premortal existence, doesn't it."

"I . . . I don't understand what you are saying."

"Hy, you already pointed out that you have noticed your mother's and Ida Mae's great personal worthiness. Isn't it possible that women, in the premortal existence, and I mean *all* of them, had developed to such a high degree spiritually that God gave them, in a blanket sort of way, the power and authority to bear His children into mortality?

"And if that is so, and it is my opinion that it is, then it seems to me there is *no way* that any woman should ever need to feel second rate to a righteous man, one who not only had to prove himself premortally but must do it again here in this life as well."

"And of course," I added, "if a man is *unrighteous,* then it would be impossible to feel second rate to him anyway."

"Absolutely. Now there is another problem that I should mention. We are beset by groups composed primarily of selfish people who claim that the bearing of children is demeaning and is an odious burden. These people would deny the God-given power to create life and are now even denying the sanctity of that life itself. Hyrum, these people are inspired by that same enemy of righteousness who once sought to overthrow God Himself. There are not many of these selfish people now, but I fear that they will multiply and grow more loud, and one day they will deceive even some of the elect of God. Make certain, my son, that you are not one of those who is so deceived."

"I'll be certain, Pa. Someday I really want to have a homeful of children."

"Good. Though they are a trial, children are also a great crowning blessing. Now, let me conclude this, and we'll be on our way. I believe, Hyrum, that *both* men and women have been blessed with great power and authority from God, gifts indicative of His love and trust. They are just here on different missions."

"I reckon what you are saying could be true," I said thoughtfully. "Still, those powers are surely not the same."

"Of course they aren't. But then, neither are men and women the same."

"Yeah, I remember when we talked about that last year."

"Good. Now remember, Hy, what I've told you isn't scriptural. As I've thought about it, however, it certainly seems to make a great deal of sense. What do you think?"

"Well, like you say, it seems reasonable, because I surely don't think God would favor me above a person like Ida Mae."

"No, He wouldn't, and that *is* scriptural. God is no respecter of persons. I believe that doctrine with all my heart and soul. I also believe the scripture that says that neither the man nor the woman can be without each other in the Lord. According to that statement, *no* gender is most important. It's comforting to me to know that, to understand that my God loves and honors and respects *all* His children."

We sat for a moment in silence while I thought about it all. Pa did have a way with words, and truthfully, though I wasn't certain I understood all he had said, I surely couldn't fault what he had.

The horses shifted restlessly in the afternoon heat, a long-eared jack-rabbit shied from a clump of brush a few feet away and bounded off to safety, and suddenly Pa spoke again.

"Hy," he said, pulling his horse around. "Suddenly I have a funny feeling. Seems to me it'd be a good idea if we split up and head into town from different directions."

"What's wrong, Pa? I bailed you out legal."

"I know. I suppose it's the gold that's worrying me. That and Hebron Clawson's threats. I've been nervous ever since he moved his wife to town and set up his base of operations there. Let's split up. You swing around and come into town by way of the depot, and I'll mosey around by Polly's Peak and come down that way."

"You going to Aunt Polly's?"

Pa nodded.

"I'll go home, then. Will I see you tomorrow, before I go back to the herd?"

"Unless things get hot I'll stop by your ma's. Hy, you be careful."

"I will, Pa. You do the same."

"Don't you doubt for a minute that I *will* be. Thoughts of those prison doors clanging shut would turn a ghost pale. Me, they plumb petrify. You can bet I'll be careful. And Hy, thanks for the bail. Words like this come hard to me, but . . . well, I love you, Son."

I blinked back my sudden tears. "I love you too," I said quietly. "And Pa, I'm proud of you. I truly am."

We separated, and had I known what was to befall, I'd have not been grinning so widely. Problem is a man can't read the future, so he marches into terrible trouble with a smile on his face and nary a care in his heart. And maybe that's the way things are meant to be. It's surely most often the case, I'll say that.

6

Ida Mae's Home—Fountain Green

A few minutes later, as I approached the depot, I was startled to see Marshal Clawson's piebald gelding tied to the hitching post. At first I doubted it was his, for I knew he could not have ridden to Fountain Green faster than Pa and I had done. Then I remembered the train, and I knew how he had arrived so quickly.

Now I was glad Pa and I had made the decision to go by horse. No matter what Pa had said, riding on the same train as Marshal Clawson would have been somewhat less than wonderful, and that was a fact. Pa would've been skittish as the last flea on a drowning dog, and there was no telling how old Clawson would have reacted. Yes sir, I was glad we'd come the hard way.

Skirting the depot, I wondered whether I should go right home or go see Ida Mae. I debated with myself for maybe three seconds, and the decision made, I was instantly riding up the long lonely road to Sorenson's place outside of town.

I reckon Ida Mae saw me coming, for when I swung through the gate, she was on the porch, looking pretty as a field of new spring daisies. It's hard to explain what being around that girl did to me, but it was somewhat considerable. Just the sight of her got me all prickly under my skin, and she'd not even said yea or nay.

Her hair was down that day, something I'd not often seen before, and there was a lot of it, for a fact. It was all long and deep dark brown with red in it, and there were lots of curls cascading around her face and over her shoulders. They looked kind of like a fiery halo when the sun was behind her. Then she smiled at me and I forgot all about her hair.

Ida Mae had a smile that would've melted a revenue collector's heart. Her lips were bright red and full, her teeth gleamed white when she smiled and laughed, her nose was thin and turned up pert on the end, her cheekbones had somehow become a little more prominent in the past year, and all of that made her face seem more angular and lovely than ever.

And her eyes, oh my goodness if she didn't have the most wondrously mysterious eyes. They were a bright blue that somehow could turn to gray or green and could sometimes even be flecked with yellow. They were framed by the longest and the darkest lashes a body ever saw, and they danced, all the time they danced with their own sparkling light. When she looked at me, sometimes it gave me the fluttering fantods, for it felt like she was looking right through me. That was bad, but what was even worse was that when I got close to her that day, I saw a brightness, like a hot fire or something, that I'd never seen before. Spooky, that's what it was.

"Hyrum, what a surprise!"

I swung off the old horse, and Ida swept off the porch and without so much as a by-your-leave she was up to me and had both of my hands in hers before I could even be proper and remove my battered hat.

"H-howdy," I stammered, mesmerized by her incredible eyes.

"You look fit," she said, pulling back a little but not letting go her grip on my hands. "I don't reckon you came home sick or injured."

"You look mighty fit yourself," I said, grinning sheepishly. "Fitter even than I remembered."

Ida Mae suddenly blushed, and I was glad there weren't any mirrors hanging from her porch. Sudden I was sweating like a hog-butcher at frost time, and I know I was red from the crown of my hat clean to the soles of my boots. I couldn't believe I'd said what I had. I was glad I had, mind you, but still I could hardly believe I'd managed it.

"So what brings you back from the herd?" she asked, breathing deeply to cover her embarrassment.

"Business," I answered, not wanting to get too elaborate.

"Business? Hyrum . . ." and now there was so much honey in her voice I was afraid her tongue would stick to the roof of her mouth. Howsomever it didn't, and she kept on, ". . . that word has a *very* mature sound. Uh . . . what *sort* of business are you doing?"

Sweeter than ever. Oh my! How could a feller *ever* keep secrets from a woman like her? "Well . . . uh . . . I reckon I had to go into Provo and go Pa's bail."

"Bail?" Now her eyes opened wide, and looking down into them

I supposed I could see all the way to China, they seemed so deep. "Your father's out of jail?"

I nodded.

"How wonderful! My father will be so pleased. My, how he dislikes conducting all those meetings."

Well, I grinned and was stewing on what we could discuss next, this had all been so pleasant, when that Ida Mae girl rared back and hit me with her next question, the one I'd hoped she'd never ask.

"But Hyrum, his bail was a thousand dollars. Where on earth did you ever get that kind of money?"

Quickly I dropped my gaze and shuffled my boots in the dust, wondering how best I could answer her. Nearby a chicken clucked softly as she pecked in the dirt for her own sorts of treasure, and from out back came the noise of hogs worrying each other for the coolest spot of mud in the pen.

I heard all that, was aware of Ida Mae's hands holding my own, thought about how pleasant her touch felt, and suddenly I knew I couldn't tell her all of it. Like Pa had told me, gold came ready-packed with greed and grief and misery, and I didn't want to dump any of that on Ida Mae.

Still, I couldn't lie, and not be true to all my ma and pa had taught me. "I found a little money someone had stashed," I answered quietly, looking directly into her eyes.

"Stashed? But Hyrum, wouldn't that be theirs? Whoever hid it, I mean?"

"It would've, but this was stashed a long time ago, years and years, and that poor pilgrim won't never be back."

"Won't ever."

"That's what I said. By now he's long dead. That's why Zene and I decided the best thing to do with it was to go Pa's bail."

Suddenly I remembered what I had in my saddlebags, so reluctantly I let go of Ida Mae's hands and turned away. "That reminds me. There was a mite left over, so I picked you up a little something with it."

I handed Ida Mae the package. She took it, her eyes wide and serious, and slowly she opened it.

"Oh, Hyrum," she whispered as she lifted that frilly-frally dress up to her. "It's . . . it's . . . oh my, it's lovely!"

She held it like it was a dancing partner or something, spinning around with it again and again, and I stood there grinning like a jackass eating cactus. Suddenly, however, she stopped spinning and threw her arms around my neck, and once again I was the startled beneficiary of the munificent contraction of her oral orbicular muscles. Kissing, I was beginning to think, was such a wondrous occupation that a man ought to give careful consideration to entering into it on a full-time basis. Especially could he go into partnership with such a pair of lips as graced the beautiful face of Ida Mae Sorenson. Yes sir, I—

"Hyrum, did you know this is the first store-bought dress I ever had?"

I didn't, but I don't think she really wanted an answer. Leastwise she never waited around for one.

"This'll be *perfect* to wear to the dance tonight. Hyrum, you'll escort me to the dance, won't you?"

"I . . . uh . . . well, Pa suggested that I get back to—"

"Hyrum," and now her voice was sticky-sweet again, "you simply *must* take me to the dance! Why, I'll be wearing *your* dress."

She reached out then and put her hand on my arm, soft-like, and squeezed. I felt the gentle pressure from those slender fingers, and suddenly I knew they had closed on my arm and my will like a number 6 lynx trap.

I don't know, now that I think on it, why her words and her squeeze were so important. Nor do I understand why they affected me so. After all, the dress wasn't mine anymore at all, it was hers. And I *did* need to return to the herd. Still, Ida Mae made it seem like her wearing *my* dress to the dance, and me coming along with it, were about the most important things to happen to either of us since who flung the chunk.

"I'll go," I said, grinning widely again. "It'd give me great pleasure to accompany you. I'll pick you up at eight."

Ida Mae smiled sweetly and hugged that dress close to her in a way that made me think she was wishing it was me. I turned red again and hurriedly climbed back aboard Andrew Aagard's broken-down horse, and that was the way we parted.

All the way down the road I could hear her sweet voice singing "Darling Clementine," and all the way down that same road, I was grinning and feeling rosy as a chapped papoose. It was truly wondrous how good that little lady made me feel.

7

The Pavilion—Fountain Green

The dance that night was held in the Pavilion, a big log building that sat back a little way from what folks were calling State Street. We in Fountain Green did about everything in the Pavilion except fix supper and go to church, and I reckon they could've done those there too, had they wanted. The floor was thick planks that had been hand hewn; there were two possum-belly stoves, one on either side; there was a stage at one end where traveling theatrical groups put on their thespian performances and where the band sat when dances were in progress; and there were two coatrooms near the front door, one for men and one for women. The men's coatroom wasn't much shakes, but I'd heard tell the women's room had setees and chairs and was a wondrously comfortable place. 'Course I'd never been in it, as you can understand, but that's what I'd heard.

I picked up Ida Mae in Pa's surrey, a fancy rig he'd bought when we could afford such luxurious trappings. And it *was* luxurious, with long fringes around the top and isinglass curtains and spokes painted bright red and trimmed with black. It was up for sale, but so far Ma'd found no buyers. That was why she let me take it.

I'd had a good visit with Ma and had told her all about the gold and what I'd done with it. She was pleased for Pa, of course, but she was worried plenty about me. She felt about gold like Pa, I reckon, and she was certain there was trouble ahead for me. Between them they had me some nervous, but when I saw Ida Mae in that frilly-frally dress, all my worries vanished. She was truly a vision to behold.

"Evening, ma'am," I said sheepishly.

"Good evening, Mr. Soderberg," she answered, and with a flourish she twirled and handed me her cape. Her brother Curley was watching all of this, and when I went to drape it over her shoulders, he rolled his eyes, grinned, snickered a little, and walked away.

Well, I got beet red, and it was a miracle I got the cape on her at all, I was so ventriculated. Finally, however, we were in the surrey and on our way to the dance.

"Do you like the dress, Hyrum?"

"Uh . . . yeah. I mean, that's why I picked it out. I always liked it."

"Silly. I mean, do you like it on me?"

Well I should smile I did. 'Course, I'd have liked burlap bags had Ida Mae been wearing them. In the past year she'd filled out in all the right places, and what she did for that dress was truly remarkable.

"Well?"

"I . . . I don't reckon I've ever seen a prettier gal," I responded finally. It sounded lame as a horse that'd thrown its left hind shoe, but by gum it was honest, and I reckon Ida Mae knew that.

"Hyrum," she said, taking hold of my arm and snuggling up close, "you do say the sweetest things."

"Yeah," I sighed, breathing deeply, "reckon I do."

And so, snuggled up next to *that* little slice of heaven, we arrived altogether too soon at the dance.

That dance was a lulu, too, as a matter of Fountain Green dust-stomping fact. The town band numbered four men and two women: two guitar pickers, two fiddle sawyers, one banjo-picking man that did licks like I'd never heard before, and one man who called and thumped the tambourine. We could hear the music from about a mile away, and by the time we got to the Pavilion, even our horse had found the rhythm.

Ida Mae hung her cape in the women's coatroom, we stepped out on that floor, and the way folks's heads turned to gape at Ida Mae, you'd have thought she was governor of the whole territory. Talk about belle of the ball! She was it that night, and for sure.

We managed to do-si-do our way through one Virginia reel and one square dance, and then by dingleberry if Pete Livingston didn't cut in. I didn't begrudge him none, though, for he'd only made it through one round of the next dance himself when *he* was cut by Miller Hansen, so called because there were so many Hansens in town and he was our miller.

From him Ida Mae whirled to old Hans Wegian, called that because he was a Norwegian. That brought up Hans Tinker, our local repairman. He was followed by Andrew Aagard, my Boss, and then by the banker, Harrison Short, who was always trying to get ahead of Brother Aagard in the lofty world of high finance, something everybody but him knew was impossible. When that dance was over, Ida Mae needed a rest.

Brother Short brought her to me, and she was flushed and laughing and basking in all the light of adoration. The way folks were carrying on, it made me proud just being seen with her. I could tell that I wasn't the only one who'd noticed her stunning good looks.

"Folks," the tambourine man called out after we'd all had a couple of minutes breathing time, "the next dance is a special number, named after the little lady in the blue taffeta dress. Pick your partners, square them off, and let's begin the Ida Mae!"

Well, I stared at the caller, Ida Mae grabbed my hand, and the next thing I knew, we were the head couple in the center square on the floor.

"One, two, three, four," the man called out in cadence, thumping his tambourine against his fist, and with the first screech of the fiddles we were into it.

Gents form a circle, Indian-style,
Ida in the middle and the gents go wild!
Ida Mae, Ida Mae,
We're in love with Ida Mae!

Well, all around us folks were laughing and whooping, and even sour old Dutch Hanner, so-called because she was from Holland, was smiling and tapping her feet. I'll tell you, that was a round, and I was skipping through it just like the rest of them.

Heading down to Shanty Creek,
Hide your eyes and we won't peek,
Do-si-do in the big barn dance,
Ain't no gal that's got a chance.
Drinking corn and salty dogs,
Chasing through them soggy boggs,
Fox in the henhouse I don't care,
'Cause chasing Ida's free and fair.

Fare-thee-well, Betty Lou
Fair-thee-well, I say—
Ain't nobody chasing you,

We're in love with Ida Mae.
Ida Mae, Ida Mae,
We're in love with Ida Mae.

The caller stopped calling then, but the banjo and the guitar players started in on their licks, folks were really stomping, and the dust was rising so thick a body could hardly see across the floor. Nobody minded, though, and the dance just got hotter than ever.

She's gonna lead and we're gonna follow,
Bay like a hound-dog through the hollow,
Run, run, fast as you can,
She can out-call a hog-eyed man.
She can swim and she can climb,
Ida's making double time—

Again the music swelled, and even with my gimped-up leg I was fairly flying. Ida Mae's face was lit up like a Christmas tree, and I'd never seen anyone look so happy nor so beautiful as she did.

All the boys from miles around,
Foller her from town to town,
Round the tree and back again,
She can't lose and we can't win.
Do-si-do, Cotton-eyed Joe,
Swing to the middle and I don't know,
Foller that girl in a hollow log,
Wind up kissing an old groundhog.

Fare-thee-well, Jansey Ann,
Fare-thee-well I say—
We're going to catch her if we can,
We're in love with Ida Mae.
Ida Mae, Ida Mae,
We're in love with Ida Mae.

Just then, as I took Ida Mae and swung her around, I looked over to the door, and honestly, I about fell over. There, big as life, was my Pa and Ma. "By jumping jehosephat," I murmured happily, "he's with Ma, and he ain't even in disguise."

"What's that?" Ida Mae gasped happily.

"Nothing. Pa's here, is all."

"Oh good," she laughed, not really understanding, I'm sure,

about Pa's courage in showing up at a dance, and then we were off again.

Swing her high and swing her low,
Swing to the middle with a backhand roll,
Swing her up and swing her down,
Chasing Ida round the town

Fare-thee-well, mother dear,
Fare-thee-well I say—
We'll get back some time next year,
We'll be chasing Ida Mae.
Ida Mae, Ida Mae—
We're in love—with—Ida Mae.

Well, the dance finally ended, with Ida Mae safely in my arms, and as we both staggered toward the side, laughing and gasping for breath and being back-thumped by about everyone there, I don't think I'd ever been so happy. Despite that gimped-up old leg, I could really dance. But even more important, I could dance with Ida Mae, and that was what made it all so terrific.

"Oh Hyrum," Ida Mae gasped as we stood close together, "I had no *idea* you were such a dancer. That was *wonderful*!"

I grinned sheepishly, the fiddle-players launched into a waltz, and for the next three or four minutes Ida Mae and I drifted happily around that old plank floor, close to each other as I'd care to get, completely oblivious to the world around us and the cares it maintained. I was happier'n a centipede without bunions, and the way I felt then, I didn't care if the night never ended.

When the music stopped, we drifted toward the door where I'd seen Pa and Ma. Happen they'd taken in my fancy footwork, I was figuring on doing a little boasting. Howsomever, when Ida Mae and I got to the door, things serioused themselves down right quick, and I didn't do any bragging at all. Fact is, I didn't say anything. I just gripped Ida Mae's hand, she gripped mine, and we stared.

There were Pa and Ma, all right. But some ways behind them, looking miserable as ever despite he had his lovely wife with him and was dressed up in his Sunday best, was our own Deputy Marshal Hebron Clawson, in the flesh.

8

The Pavilion—
Fountain Green—
Again

"H-hello," I said to the Marshal as I gripped Ida Mae's hand and did my best to stall the man until Pa might see him. Only Pa didn't look. I was shaking like an aspen leaf in a high wind, and I didn't know what else to say.

Marshal Clawson looked at me, scowled like he'd just bit into the greenest apple on the tree, grunted, and turned away.

Ida Mae looked up at me, and I shrugged desperately, for I was truly at a loss for words. I didn't expect her to help, but I was praying hard enough that I half hoped a legion of angels would come down and go to work on the marshal. They didn't, of course, but I was standing next to one that I'd not even thought of, and she took over for me.

"My, what a lovely dress," Ida Mae said sweetly to Marshal Clawson's wife, Amelia.

"Why, thank you, my dear," the woman responded, smiling. "Yours is beautiful too."

"Thank you. Hyrum gave it to me just today."

"How sweet. He has very good taste, in girls as well as in dresses."

Well, I colored up at that. I think Ida Mae did too, and so I made another stab at conversating with the marshal. "Nice dance, isn't it," I declared hopefully.

"Umph!"

"Good band, too."

"Umph!"

"Folks're really raising the dust."

"Umph! And *umph*!"

Well, I was getting disgusted with the man, but apparently I was no more disgusted with him than was his wife, Amelia. After the last "umph" she jabbed him with her elbow, and with a whisper that could be heard for a country mile, she called him to repentance.

"Don't be so rude, Hebron. Talk to the boy."

"But—but—"

"No *buts*! *Talk* to him!"

Hebron Clawson looked at her, looked back at me, and then with a sort of sickly grin finally spoke. "Pretty warm, isn't it?"

Well, I was about to make some inane remark of my own when Ida Mae suddenly answered him, and right away I could see the drift of her conversation. Not only that, but I hoisted my own sail and did my best to help it along, knowing that the more we talked the better Pa's chances were. Happen, that is, that he saw us, which so far he hadn't.

"What's pretty warm?" Ida Mae asked innocently.

"Why, the weather," the marshal responded, sounding surprised.

"What weather?" I asked, slipping quickly in.

"Why, this weather."

"Well, how's this different from any other weather?"

"Well, it's warmer."

"How do you know it is?"

Marshal Clawson looked at me with a strange look in his eyes, while his wife beamed happily as she watched the dancing from beside him.

"I—I suppose it is," he answered.

"Isn't the weather the same everywhere?"

"Why, no—no; it's warmer in some places and colder in others."

"What makes it warmer in some places than it's colder in others?"

"Well you little crippled pipsqueak! I ain't a'gonna—"

Marshal Clawson got another elbow in the solar plexus, and right away he was back in our conversation with all his heart and soul. "I reckon," he sputtered, "it's the sun—the effect of the sun's heat."

"Makes it colder in some places and warmer in others? Marshal, I never heard of such a thing."

"No, no, no. I didn't mean that! The sun makes it warmer."

"Then what makes it colder?"

"I—I believe it's the ice."

"What ice?"

"Why, the ice, the ice that—that was frozen by—by the frost!"

I could tell that the Marshal figured he had just won a major victory, and I probably should have let him claim it and just walked away. But I was enjoying myself so much, and I had just read a book about weather patterns besides, and so I was pretty anxious to show off. Then too, so far as I could tell, Pa *still* hadn't noticed us, nor had anyone else, and so I needed to give him more time.

"Have you ever seen ice that wasn't frozen?" I asked quietly.

"No—that is, I believe I haven't."

"Then what are you talking about?"

"I was just trying to talk about the weather. Amelia said—"

"And what do you know about it? What do you know about the weather?"

"Well, I been in it enough, so I ought to know something, you young whipp—"

"No sir, you don't, and that is a blue-tailed fact. Yet you come into this dance and begin to talk about the weather as though you owned it, and I find that you yourself don't know a solitary thing about the matter you yourself selected for a topic of conversation. Marshal Clawson, you don't know one thing about meteorological conditions, principles, or phenomena; you can't tell me why it is warm in August or cold in December; you don't know why icicles form faster in the sunlight than they do in the shade; you don't know why the earth grows colder as it comes nearer the sun; you can't tell why a man can be sun-struck in the shade; you can't tell me how a cyclone is formed nor how the trade-winds blow; you couldn't find the calm-center of a storm if your life depended upon it; you don't know what a sirocco is nor where the southwest monsoon blows; you don't know the average rainfall in the states or even in our territory for the past year; you don't know why the wind dries up the ground more quickly than a hot sun; you don't know why the dew falls at night and dries up during the day; you can't explain the formation of fog; you don't know one solitary thing about the weather, Marshal Clawson, and you are just like a thousand and one other people who always begin talking about the weather because they don't know anything else, when, by the Aurora Borealis, they know less about the weather than they do about anything else in all the world, sir!"

Well, the poor marshal was staring at me with his mouth hanging open, his wife was still smiling, though *mighty* stiffly, it looked like, and even Ida Mae had grown pretty quiet. Then with a loud and disgusted "*umph,*" the marshal turned away, and Ida Mae and I were alone once more.

"Where'd you learn all that?" she asked breathlessly.

"In a book. Would you look at my Pa. He *still* hasn't seen the danger, and—"

"Hyrum, how did you *remember* all that?"

"It's a trick Pa taught me. All it is is a matter of concentration. Focus on what you read, and once it is read, it will always be yours. I've been learning scriptures that way, too. Did you see ol' Clawson's face?"

"I'll say I did. He was humiliated."

"I know. Served him right, the sneaking coyote."

Now Ida Mae looked up at me, and her voice was quiet and earnest. "It may have, Hyrum, but I don't know. I hope you won't regret humiliating him like that."

"Why should I? He can't touch me. I'm no polygamist."

"You say you've been learning scriptures?"

"Yeah, and—"

"Hyrum, have you learned yet the scripture called the Golden Rule?"

Quickly I looked at the little gal who stood beside me, and suddenly I was feeling terribly guilty. I even— "Oh no!" I gasped. "Ida Mae, I think we've got trouble!"

Pa *still* hadn't seen the marshal, and was now right in front of him, laughing and visiting with Ma and a couple of other folks, while the marshal, right behind, was chewing on his dirty yellowed mustaches and just aching to reach out and clap some irons on Pa. He looked plumb miserable; his tight-fitting old suit didn't help him none, and his poor wife, standing next to him and reading his mind every bit as easily as I was, looked miserable too.

Then the band started up again, and Pa, with a laugh, took Ma's hand and together they headed for the center of the floor.

Well, I reckon Pa's flagrant violation of the Edmunds-Tucker Act had gotten to the marshal. Muttering, he gripped his fists together and started after my folks. Just then I caught old Hans Wegian's eye and he gave me a warning look, and I knew that once again it was up to me. Clawson had decided to arrest Pa, and somehow I had to stop him long enough so that Hans Wegian could warn Pa and get him out of there.

I nodded, took Ida Mae's unsuspecting arm, and dragged her into the path of the determined but misbeguided marshal.

"Marshal Clawson," I said bravely, doing my best to hide the quiver that was in my voice, "I apologize for not properly introducing you a few moments ago. May I present Miss Ida Mae Sorenson. She has requested from you, sir, the honor of the next dance."

Well, Marshal Clawson did a double-take and Ida Mae about clobbered me, but the whole entire plan, got together in considerably less than a minute, worked better than I'd ever dared to dream or hope.

Realizing what had happened, and seeing that he was fairly stuck with Ida Mae's truly ravishing beauty, Marshal Clawson decided to take advantage of the promising situation. Drawing himself up to his pompous best, sucking in his ample belly (which was evidence of his prosperity in the cohab hunting business), and smiling through his dirty old mustaches, the portly Marshal Clawson bent forward in a low and courtly bow of acceptance.

"Ma'am," he declared as he descended, "it would be my honor—"

And at the extreme depth of his bow, and in the middle of his little speech, we all heard something rip.

Instantly the marshal's mouth was closed and he was up again, his face even more red than usual. He backed up a step, then another, and while Ida Mae and I stood there staring, he called frantically to his wife.

"Amelia," he whispered loudly, "let's get out of here."

"What?" she answered indignantly. "Nonsense! We've only just arrived. I won't go to a dance and leave again without dancing."

"But—but—" he whispered frantically, "I tore my pants!"

"Nooooo. Let me see."

Mrs. Clawson stepped back and looked down, and the poor marshal almost swung down on her.

"Amelia, don't—"

"My goodness," the woman said, sounding surprised, "you certainly did. You should have listened to me about that suit. You've grown some in the last ten years."

"You're right," the marshal hastily agreed. "Now let's get out—"

"Don't worry, Hebron. I can fix it. I have a needle and thread, so come into the ladies' coatroom with me, and—"

"But Amelia—"

"Come on! Don't just stand there with your underwear airing out. Hurry!"

Well, Mrs. Clawson checked inside the ladies' coatroom, found it empty, and informed her husband of that fact. Then while Ida Mae and I did our best to keep from bursting our gaskets, and while everyone else tried to keep from noticing, she dragged the reluctant deptuy marshal through the door and out of sight.

Quickly Ida Mae and I stepped to the door, and without even planning it, both of us pressed our ears to the wood.

"Hurry up, Hebron," Mrs. Clawson was saying, "take them off!"

"But Amelia—"

"Do it!"

Ida Mae grinned at me, and I grinned back, for through the closed door we could hear the scuffling sounds as Marshal Clawson pulled off his boots, dropped them to the floor, and finally dragged off his britches.

"I'd never have guessed it," I whispered to Ida Mae, grinning, "but that man's so henpecked he moults twice a year."

"Hyrum," Ida Mae responded with mock indignation. "that isn't being henpecked. That's simply bowing to superior strength and wisdom."

"Yeah," I nodded, thinking again of what my Pa had told me up on the divide. "I reckon most women *are* superior in one way or another."

"*All* women," Ida Mae responded teasingly, and with a smile at me she signaled that we should listen once more.

"For pete's sake," Marshal Clawson growled a few seconds later, "hurry it up."

"I am hurrying," Mrs. Clawson answered. "I just need to thread this needle . . . There! Now it won't take but a minute or two."

For a few seconds there was silence, and then the marshal spoke again. "Amelia, hurry it up. What if someone comes in?"

"They won't," she replied quietly, and suddenly I had the most wonderfully evil idea I'd ever had. I looked at Ida Mae—she knew right off what I was thinking, and her eyes opened wide in protest. I winked, and suddenly I knew she would go along with me.

"I don't want to hurt him none," I whispered quickly. "Let's just scare twenty years off his growth."

"He *does* need to go on a diet," Ida Mae agreed, getting into the fun of it.

We grinned at each other. I straightened up, lifted my voice to a falsetto, and then I spoke. "Well dearie," I squeaked loudly, "I'm for a rest in the coatroom."

"Me too," Ida Mae sang out sweetly, making herself sound totally exhausted. "I'm so hot I'm about to *die!* Here, let me get the door for you, sweetie. That coatroom's just the place at a time like this."

We shuffled our feet a little, put our ears to the door again, and instantly we knew our dirty little ruse had worked.

"Amelia!" Marshal Clawson yelped desperately, "there's *women* coming!"

I grabbed the doorknob and gave it a little rattle, and Mrs. Clawson came to the immediate rescue of her terrified husband.

"Quick, Hebron," she ordered, "get into that closet!"

We heard her open the closet, shove the marshal inside, and slam the door closed behind him. I pushed the coatroom door open a tiny bit for further effect, Ida Mae and I started to congratulate ourselves for doing this one up proud, and suddenly things on the dance floor got real quiet.

Surprised, Ida Mae and I looked at each other. The band squeaked to a stop, for an instant the air was deathly still, and then from inside the coatroom we heard a furious pounding.

"*Amelia!*" the marshal's voice suddenly thundered, seeming to come from everywhere around us, "lemme in!"

"Hush, Hebron," his good wife called back.

"Open this door!" Clawson screamed, his voice pleading desperately.

"I can't Hebron. Those women are coming in."

"But Amelia," he wailed, "you gotta. This—this ain't no closet!"

"What? But Hebron—"

"Amelia, I'm in the *ballroom!* That—that *door* came into here!"

There was a roar then from the crowd, a mighty cheer, and Marshal Clawson suddenly pounded around the corner and thundered past us, all dressed up in his holey socks, red longjohns, and the upper half of his tight-fitting suit. The applause rose to just slightly short of deafening, and suddenly I was applauding too. Looked to me like Marshal Clawson wouldn't be pestering my pa any more, that night at least.

"Would you care for the next dance?" I asked Ida Mae politely.

"I'd be honored," she replied sweetly, and so together, with no more cares at all, the two of us waltzed back into our own little portion of heaven.

9

Hattie Soderberg's Home—Fountain Green

"Hyrum? Hyrum, wake up!"

Ma's voice sank into my tired brain, interrupting one of the finest and sweetest dreams I'd ever had. Ida Mae and I were down south of town, riding close up to each other in the surrey. I was home from my mission, and we were fixing on getting married . . .

"Hyrum!"

"Yeah, Ma, what is it?"

"Get dressed. Quick."

Well, the tone in her voice wasn't one I liked to hear, for she sounded afraid. Throwing back my covers I leaped up, pulled on my shirt and my pants, grabbed my shoes and socks, and headed for the ladder.

"What is it, Ma?" I asked as I climbed down from my loft with my back to her. "Is something wrong?"

"I'll say it's wrong," a man's voice answered.

Surprised, I spun my head and was startled to see Marshal Clawson standing there with his big old shotgun out and pointed at me. Even more surprising, and frightening as well, was who stood behind him. It was beady-eyed Mr. Doolin, the man from the assay office up to Provo, and he was jumping up and down like someone'd put a burr under his saddle.

"That's him," he shouted over and over. "Arrest him, Marshal. It's him. He held a gun on me, he tried to kill me with a rattlesnake, and he murdered for that gold. I know he did! Now I've earned that reward money you promised me. I have, I surely have!"

"Shut up," Clawson growled at Doolin out of the side of his mouth. "I know who the little crippled pipsqueak is, more's the pity.

"Off that ladder," he ordered then, holding his scattergun on me.

I stepped down slowly, and by then Ma was beside me, her face filled with grief. "Hy," she cried, "I told them it wasn't you! It couldn't be! You found that gold fair and square, and . . . and . . ."

"Back off, lady!" the marshal snarled. "That kid's caused me more grief and trouble than I can say. Besides aiding and abetting and the charges this man here has filed, I aim to prosecute him for defamation of character. He humiliated me in front of my wife, and I'm certain he had something to do with what happened in the . . . the . . . well, later on at the dance. No ma'am, I'm taking him in, and he's earned every bit of the misery he's gonna get."

Well, I thought about Ida Mae and that Golden Rule scripture, and right about then I started wishing with all my heart that I had been a little less smart and a little more wise. Usually, however, when we begin wishing for that, it's way too late. I know it surely was for me.

"But—but you can't just walk into a person's home and take him away," Mother sputtered incredulously.

"Shut up, lady. I'm the law, and I can do about what I want!"

"But—but—"

"It won't do any good, Ma," I answered quietly. "They'll believe what they want to believe. In spite of how Pa feels about him, Marshal Clawson doesn't like Pa, or me either, for that matter. I forced this Doolin fellow to be honest, and so he doesn't like me any more than Mr. Clawson does. Altogether, this must look like a good way to even up a few scores. That I really did find the gold doesn't even matter—"

"Find!" Doolin screamed. "Find, nothing! You killed for that gold, you smooth-talking young murderer! You killed Enock Rhoades, just like you tried to kill me, and then you stole it, just like you *did* steal from me!"

"Mister," I said, turning on him, "you say that once more in front of my ma, and scattergun or not, I'll clean your meat-house up thoroughly!"

Doolin backed up, whimpering, and then I turned to Hebron Clawson. "Marshal, I do have a receipt from him, if that—"

"I'll say he does, forced from me at gunpoint! Marshal, I demand that you arrest this young man right this instant!"

Well, Clawson looked at me. I shrugged and started to turn away in disgust, and suddenly the marshal moved. "Don't do nothing stupid, Soderberg," he growled. "This here double is bored full choke both tubes. She's loaded to the brim with number-one buck.

One false move and you'll look like somebody drove a snubbing post through your brisket, sideways. And frankly, I'd like that. Now where's your pa?"

"I don't know," I snarled angrily. "I haven't seen him since last night, just after you made your hurried departure from the dance."

Marshal Clawson growled hard and lifted his shotgun threateningly, and I thought he was going to brain me right there. Finally, however, with a supreme effort, he got himself under control. "No matter," he muttered. "We'll get him. Stolen bail money's no good. Now you're both in trouble. You were young when Rhoades was killed. How'd you do it?"

"Marshal Clawson, I don't know what you're talking about. I never knew that Rhoades feller, and—"

"Liar," Doolin screamed. "Marshal, he's lying. Look at the bag he had his gold in! You'll see."

The bag! I'd not thought of that, but now . . . ER—Enock Rhoades. *That's* who that bag belonged to! I recalled the story now, or at least a little of it—Caleb Rhoades's brother disappearing when he was after secret gold. But that had been so long before, how could they suspect me? I couldn't have been more than eleven or twelve. Why hadn't they—

"Give me the bag, Soderberg!"

I looked at Clawson, then at my ma, and then over at the weasel-eyed Doolin. Then with a sigh I pulled that leather bag out of my pocket and handed it to the marshal.

"See," Doolin cried excitedly, "there it is, just like I said. See, there are those initials. ER."

"I see them," Marshal Clawson growled. "Now pipe down and lemme think. Soderberg, how old are you?"

"Seventeen, going on eighteen."

"That would have made you eleven going on twelve. Young, but you could have done it, especially with help. Ma'am," he said, looking at Ma, "where was your son the summer of '84?"

I looked at her, tried to warn her, but it did no good. Ma was a perfectly honest woman, and even if she *had* seen me she'd have said what she said. After all, it was the truth.

"Let's see," she answered thoughtfully, doing her best to remember what I was desperately hoping that she'd forget. "He . . . he was herding for Mr. Soderberg, up in the Uintah Mountains. That's right. I remember it clearly. That was his first summer as camp tender."

Clawson and Doolin looked at each other darkly, and then Clawson asked my mother one more question.

"Was he alone?"

"Alone? Of course not! He was herding with Dale Allred, God rest his soul."

"Is that man dead?"

"Yes, this past winter. We heard he died of consumption."

"Well," Marshal Clawson said as he prodded me with the shotgun, "that cinches it up tighter'n thirty-nine bugs in a bed. You and that other feller did the job, and as soon as he died, you made a beeline for the stash. Pretty cool, young feller, but it won't wash with me. You are herewith under arrest for the murder of Enock Rhoades, and for the alleged robbery of Mr. Doolin here. Now let's get down to the jail."

He pushed me ahead of him, and behind me I heard Ma cry out like she'd been hurt, which I guessed she had.

"Hy," she wailed, "say it isn't so. Say it, and I . . . I . . ."

"Ma!" I yelled out, "You know me. I didn't do it! Help me, Ma. Get Pa. This ain't right—"

Clawson smashed me in the back with the muzzle of his shotgun, and I didn't say any more. I couldn't. But I'll tell you this: I made a vow then and there that I was going to get out of that jail, and when I did, sure as a belch after a big meal, I was going to clear myself, and then Doolin was going to pay dearly.

10

The Palace Saloon— Provo, Utah Territory

Felix Ethelbert Friendlessman sat alone at a table near the back of the Palace Saloon, drinking slowly. He was frustrated, he was angry because he was frustrated, and his mood was growing darker by the moment. Somehow that old fool Caleb Rhoades had eluded him again, had vanished without a trace, and eight days of steady tracking and searching had not turned up so much as a new set of hoofprints. The old man had simply vanished.

Again.

Friendlessman stared at his drink and forced his mind to shut out the sounds of the tinny piano and a woman's shrill laughter. In age he was just past thirty, but he was so fiercely intent as to appear more than that. His dark eyes gleamed like live coals. Buried deeply in his head, they seemed to move constantly, making those who knew him think of the eyes of a stoat or ferret. He was full bearded, both hair and whiskers black as stove polish except where silver had touched his temples. His nose was thin and finely formed, his ears were small and lay tight against his head, his body was wire-tight and nervously strung, and his manners were impeccable.

A brilliant, erratic man, Friendlessman was handsome, witty, and elegant, an athlete and an intellect, fawned upon by those who knew little of his true nature. He had been called the Thomas Jefferson of his home county in Pennsylvania, and he was adored by women, yet he was a perjurer, a hypocrite and a manipulator.

When he had been younger he had gathered about him, as a means of furthering his own professed identity—for he was truly hungry to be recognized—what was considered by many to be the intellectual and artistic elite—actually a group of bored men and glib-tongued libertines who talked much of art, literature, and music but who were without any deep-seated convictions upon any subject aside from their own prejudices. Mainly concerned with their own posturing, they were creatures of fad and whim, seizing upon this writer or that painter and exalting him to the skies until he bored them, and then shifting to some other, with the same results. Occasionally the artists upon whom they lavished attention were of genuine ability, but more often they possessed some obscurity that gave the dilettantes an illusion of depth and quality. In most cases, what was fancied to be profound was simply bad writing, bad painting, or deliberately affected obscurity.

Yes, Felix Friendlessman was hungry. Not food-hungry; he cared little for that. Instead, his hunger was for wealth and power. In eastern Pennsylvania he had achieved moderate success in both farming and in intellectual circles. Still, he had felt restricted, not able to acquire the wealth or fame he sought. Others were always there before him, others who fought strongly to protect their own positions of strength. And no matter how he fought back, Felix Friendlessman always found himself left out of the biggest deals or the rarest circles of influence, just short in every race for positions of prestige and power.

Then had come the letter from Wyoming Territory, and his life had been forever changed. Friendlessman recalled the letter, written by the kid he had hired for a brief month in the cold spring of 1882. The kid, whose name was Harry Longabaugh, had moved on, to New York, then back to his home in Phoenixville, and finally west to the territories of Utah and Wyoming. In the letter he had told of his travels and of his new friend, a young man called Robert LeRoy Parker. That had meant nothing to Friendlessman, but according to Longabaugh, Parker had evidence that there existed a fabulously wealthy gold mine near the cities of Ashley and Price, in Utah Territory. Furthermore, if Friendlessman would come west, Longabaugh and Parker would point him in the direction of this mine. This was to be in payment for Friendlessman's kindness, given when Longabaugh had been down and out and only a penniless kid.

For a moment Friendlessman had held the letter and debated, but even in that brief hesitation, he had known that he was going west.

Gold! That was what he needed. Mountains of it. With wealth like that, none of the so-called elite would ever stand in his way again. And so, five years before, Felix Friendlessman had sold his property and had come west, seeking for himself the wealth of Caleb Rhoades's fabulous secret gold mines.

Leaning back, Friendlessman sipped his drink and recalled with bitterness the past five years. He had found Longabaugh, and from what he and Parker—who now called himself Butch Cassidy—had said, he had determined that the mines were supposedly on the south side of the Uintahs, both low down and high up. Yet nowhere in that area, Whiterocks, Ashley, Fort Duchesne, Price, or anywhere in between, could he find a single soul who could, or would, tell him more.

Discouraged, he had hunted down Parker again and had found him working at the FS Ranch, up in Wyoming. That had been in '85. Friendlessman had questioned him closely, and Parker had been very reluctant to give out any further information.

"Can't tell you no more," Parker had said.

"Why not?"

"That gold is sacred to the Utes."

"Sacred?"

"That's right. There's some old tale about Spaniards forcing the Indians to labor in the mines. There was a rebellion, the Spaniards were all killed, and now the mines and the gold are taboo."

"But you aren't an Indian."

"Nope," Parker had replied, "but I respect 'em."

"And you really are foolish enough to believe there is gold?"

Parker had looked hard at him, glanced around, and lowered his voice. "Listen carefully. I'll tell you this once, and if you ever say I said it, I'll flat-out deny it. One day I was heading up here to Brown's Hole, and I was crossing the mountains above Ashley to avoid meeting folks. It started to rain. I rode up a side canyon, dismounted, and crawled into some bushes. I'd been there maybe ten minutes when I became aware of an old tunnel behind me. I crawled in, lighted a match, and knew right off I'd stumbled onto something big. There were bones scattered around, human bones, and mounds and mounds of mined gold ore.

"I was just looking at it, holding a fist-sized piece of ore in my hand, when behind me I heard breathing. I turned, and in the light from my nearly dead match, I saw this big Ute. He wasn't armed, but still I didn't try nothing foolish.

"'Do not touch the gold,' he said in perfect English, 'for it is sacred. There is only one white man who can take it from here, and you are not he.' I believed him, set it back down, and asked him who the man was, and why. He told me, and told me too that I would be all right as long as I left their gold alone. I have done so, Mr. Friendlessman, and recommend that you do the same."

"But why?"

"The curse of God is on them that take that gold," Parker had answered solemnly. "I respect that curse."

Parker, or now Cassidy, had meant it, too. He'd apparently seen the gold since, and yet he had never touched a nugget. Still, in that same conversation he had hinted at a man called Rhoades, so as a last resort Friendlessman had gone to Price, bought some property, and concentrated on watching Caleb Rhoades. And that, finally, had given him his big break.

Vividly he recalled the dying Indian he had found on The Strip near Fort Duchesne when he had been trying to follow Rhoades out toward Whiterocks. He had almost passed the Indian by, for he felt no compassion for the man at all. Yet a sudden thought that this Indian might know something had prompted him to stop and to give aid. As things had turned out, it was one of the luckiest decisions of his life.

He had given the man a drink, and the Ute, with almost his last gesture, had ripped a small medicine pouch from his neck and handed it to the surprised Friendlessman.

"Sh . . . shin-ob," he had mumbled with his last dying breath. "Carre shin-ob . . ."

He had then died, Friendlessman had pocketed the pouch and had gone to notify the authorities concerning the dead Ute, and with one thing and another, it had been several days before he had gotten around to seeing what the Indian's medicine power had been.

The sight of the huge gold nugget had rendered him speechless, and it had also propelled him into what had become the one passion, the single true obsession, of his life. Longabaugh and Cassidy had been right! In spite of the fact that no one would talk of it at all, there was gold, a great deal of it, and nearby!

In the course of the next year, following one pitiful clue after another, Friendlessman had determined that Caleb Rhoades did indeed know where the gold was, but he was not talking. Still, Felix Friendlessman was certain that one day, in one way or another, he would find Rhoades's gold, and the wealth he craved, nay, *deserved*, would at last be his.

Thus were Friendlessman's thoughts as he sipped his drink and cursed the luck that seemed to constantly follow Caleb Rhoades.

Rhoades lived near Price, a town he'd helped to found, and for years it had been assumed that his frequent trips to the mountains were for hunting. But he always had money, a great deal of it, always gold, and his hunting trips always seemed to begin at night. Gradually Friendlessman convinced a few other men that Caleb Rhoades was not hunting but was going to secret gold mines, anciently discovered by the Spaniards, and gathering his wealth from them.

These men, who had come in with the railroad or to work in the coal mines, had been as anxious as Felix Friendlessman to find an easy way to wealth. Thus they had carefully laid their plans to follow Rhoades. They would wait near his small farm out on the Price River; he would set out and they would follow. And they had done this, time and time again. Yet each time he would disappear into the darkness and the mountain, and they would be left behind, both looking and feeling very foolish.

Lately the others had grown tired of the search, and that was fine. Felix Friendlessman had not. He would follow Rhoades alone until the gold was found, and then there would be no one he need share it with, no one but himself. He would not even share it with young Longabaugh, who had only recently taken upon himself the sobriquet "Sundance Kid," chosen because he had spent the past eighteen months in jail in Sundance, Wyoming. Why, even young Parker, or Cassidy, had turned to outlawry, and that very week the papers had reported that he had robbed the bank at Telluride of over ten thousand dollars. No, their pathways had diverged, his and Cassidy's and Longabaugh's, and Felix Friendlessman would never stoop to outlawry. There were easier, if no more legitimate, ways to wealth.

So he'd kept after Rhoades, actually set out alone to find his gold and take it from him, twice. But the first time he had become lost in a thick stand of willows, had left his horse for a moment to find the trail, and had come back to discover that his expensive pistol had been stolen from his saddlebags during his absence.

He had stared around, into the silence of the willows, and had shivered with wonder and even a little fear. Rhoades had been there all the time, playing cat and mouse with him! The old man was a wonder, he truly was!

Actually humbled and yet filled with bitterness, Friendlessman had been unable to do anything but mutter his thanks when, two weeks later, Caleb Rhoades had shown up on his doorstep with the missing pistol in his hand.

"Found this up a side canyon," the old man had said quietly, smiling as he spoke. "Knew it was yours, figured you must have lost it."

And now there was this last incident, the last straw, so to speak, the event that had brought him, finally, to Provo and to defeat.

He'd set out again, carefully, making certain that Rhoades did not know he was being followed. There was no moon, so he had followed closely, guided by the sounds of Caleb Rhoades's horses and mules' hooves striking stone on the hillsides and in the rocky creekbeds. When the clamor of the horses' hooves would stop, so would Friendlessman. When the sound would start again, so would he, carefully, quietly.

All night he had followed the tortuous path, knowing that at last he had managed to stick to the trail of the wily Rhoades. He'd known it would one day happen, and the sense of satisfaction he had felt was almost overwhelming.

At last the sky began to gray in the east, and Friendlessman drew rein in a clump of trees so that he could see without being seen. He could still hear the animals ahead of him, knew that he was close, and knew as well that he didn't want to get *too* close.

Rhoades and his animals were just beyond a small ridge that rose before him, and so patiently Felix Friendlessman waited, knowing that shortly they would come into sight, climbing the face of the next hill.

At last they did, and Friendlessman stared in wonder that turned to horror and anger and frustration and disgust. For there, making her way up the far slope, was not a horse and two mules as he had supposed, but instead an old Ute squaw, climbing slowly, banging two rocks together with her hands as she noisily moved forward.

For Felix Friendlessman, that had ended it. He could not bear to see Rhoades again, could not bear the humility he would feel when the old man would look at him and smile and nod in greeting.

No, it was time to go! Time to get on to San Francisco, where two of his former associates were doing so well. He'd thought of returning to Pennsylvania, but he could not, *would* not, go back, not until he could do so in the manner he felt he deserved.

Therefore—

"I'm telling you," a whiney voice declared, "he found the gold!"

At the word gold, Felix Friendlessman's head came up, and instantly he was listening. The man who was speaking was small, with wispy thin hair and bright beady eyes. He seemed to be drunk, yet he was still upright and was desperately trying to convince a man next to him of the truthfulness of his story.

"It was Rhoades's gold, all right," he went on, banging his fist weakly on the table. "The pouch had ER on it, for Enock Rhoades. I myself weighed it out at over twelve hundred dollars. It was pretty, mostly wire and five-niner pure."

"Ha!" the other man shouted. "Doolin, you do tell the tales."

"It's true. I swear!"

"Show it to me."

Doolin dropped his head. "I can't. The marshal took it for evidence. But that crippled kid done Rhoades in and probably knows right now where them mines—"

Friendlessman waited no longer. Quickly he stepped to the staggering Doolin, put his arm around him, and started him away.

"I'm sorry," he said politely to the man who had been arguing, "but he does carry on when he's in his cups. Why, I'll bet he's been muttering some foolishness about gold mines. It's a persistent nightmare of his."

The man stared drunkenly, finally nodded, and turned back to the bar, and Felix Friendlessman steered the little Doolin from the Palace Saloon and toward the hotel.

"Come, my inebriated friend," he muttered as he dragged him across the street. "You and I have a great deal to discuss, a great deal indeed."

11

July 1889

Ashley-Vernal—Utah Territory

Leaning against an awning post in front of the general store, the outlaw Jack Moore watched as three men worked to change the sign on the bank across the street. The old sign, which read "Bank of Ashley," already lay in the dust. Now the men struggled to straighten the new one, which read "Bank of Vernal." Moore watched, but he cared little for which was used. His cares concerned only what was inside the bank, and he cared about that very much indeed.

Slowly he scratched the stubble on his jaw, glancing up at the cloudless sky as he did so. It was hot, probably the hottest day of the year so far. And it was only the first of July. Lowering his eyes, he pushed up his hat, wiped the sweat from his forehead, and looked again at the men who were trying to hang the sign. He wished they would hurry with their task and be gone. They were a complication he didn't care to deal with.

Down the street, the man known as Blue John, on account of his one blue eye, lounged in the shade of the hotel veranda. His feet were propped up on the railing, and he seemed to be asleep, but Moore knew that was not the case. Blue John was ready to move in on the bank and waited only for his signal.

Again Moore lifted his hat and wiped at his forehead, wondering for the thousandth time how much money the bank contained. He'd heard that the young fellow who was calling himself Butch Cassidy had taken over ten thousand from Telluride. That was a real haul. He doubted that there was even half that much across the street, but anything was better than the twenty cents he had in his pocket.

Pulling out the makings, Moore fashioned a cigarette, thinking as he did so how thankful he was that the man called Silvertip was not there. Silvertip, whose real name was a thing that was never mentioned, just didn't have what it took to be an outlaw. He was strong as a bull, but when it came to brains he was three bricks shy of a full load. The way Moore saw it, Silvertip's head was stuffed fifty-fifty with sawdust and cement. And given thirty days to do it, he still couldn't figure out how to pour creek water out of a wet boot. No, not even with the directions printed on the heel. And from what Moore had heard, Silvertip was the smart one in his family.

That combination of bedrock head, powerful body, and a strange inbred stubbornness made him about as safe to handle as a black Spanish bull. To get between him and wherever he might be going was deemed as sporty as standing barefoot in front of a trailherd stampede. Or lying naked across the tracks in front of the Sanpete Valley Crawler. Or crimping dynamite caps with your side teeth. Crossing Silvertip was as bound to lead to the rigors of mortis as shooting yourself through the roof of the mouth with an eight-gauge goose gun.

So now Jack Moore thought of Silvertip, smoked his cigarette, wiped at the sweat on his face, and felt only relief that the man had finally and of his own free choice gone his separate way.

Across the street, the three men were finally finished hanging the sign. One at a time they climbed down from the roof and entered the bank, probably to get paid. Moore thought of that, felt a momentary sense of loss that the three were getting some of the money he already considered as his own, and then forced the thought from his mind.

Be generous, he told himself. Let them have a little something. After all, it couldn't be very much, and he'd likely lose more than that on women and poker.

Glancing down the street, he saw that Blue John had lowered his boots from the railing. He still looked relaxed, but that was deceptive, and Moore knew it. Blue John was a grim man, lean and hard as jerked reservation beef, with hair and beard the color of snow melting in a chinook. He was never completely relaxed even when he looked to be—no man rode the owlhoot trail very long after he stopped expecting trouble, and Blue John had ridden that self-same trail for nigh onto eight years.

Moore shifted his gaze again and looked at his new horses. They were strong, had lots of bottom, and if held to their gait would run all day and then some. They were the most superiorly fine horses he'd ever managed to steal, almost as good as that blooded Belgian the Mormon bishop had managed to wrangle from him the year before.

Still, these broomtails were about as good, and with them he felt certain he and Blue John would shortly be safe and long gone from the newly named city of Vernal, bank money, stolen horses, and all.

His gaze shifted once more, attracted by movement in front of the bank. The three workers had stepped out onto the boardwalk, stuffing their money in their pockets as they moved. One of them said something funny, the others laughed, and Moore found himself itching to draw his pearl-handled revolver and relieve all of them of their new burden.

They stood for a minute in conversation; then they stepped off into the powdery dust of the street, mounted their dusty broncs, and were soon departing. Moore watched, saw them all out of sight, saw that save for an old woman and a few scratching chickens, the street appeared empty. Slowly he stretched and straightened from the awning post, flipping away his cigarette as he did so. From the corner of his eye he saw Blue John lift himself to his feet and light a cigarette of his own, and he knew the time was at hand.

Carefully he stepped down into the dust of the street, moving slowly so as not to attract attention. The sun struck him like a hot iron, and suddenly his mouth was cotton-dry. This was always the way it was, and in a strange way he liked it, the feeling of fear that turned to exhilaration when the job was done. Blue John had told him once that he never felt fear, and Silvertip, when he'd been asked about it once, looked blankly at Moore and asked what fear was.

"Silvertip," Moore then asked, "don't nothing ever faze you?"

"Why sure it does," Silvertip had replied, smiling openly. "Now don't press me, Boss, and I'll think of it directly."

Moore had given up. Silvertip, who would wrestle a boar grizzly barehanded just for fun, would go down grinning wherever he was when his bullet came along, and he probably wouldn't even be worried about it. Neither would Blue John, who by his own admission had the grit of a bear-dog and who would bet the devil that hell wasn't hot. No, the question wasn't them. The question, for a blue-tailed fact, was Jack Moore, him as the others called the Boss.

Moore was almost across the street and could hear Blue John angling in behind him when he first became aware of the clatter up the road. Turning, he stopped in amazement, staring at the spring wagon that was churning up the dust toward him.

"What the . . ." he heard Blue John muttering behind him, and then Jack Moore's own jaw fell wide open. Many things in this world were purely amazing, but nothing could beat the stupefying fact that, of all the days to show up, and of all the moments to appear in this one all-important day, good ol' Silvertip had chosen to appear just as he, Jackson T. Moore, and Blue John McGuire were about to pull off the biggest, most grand hold-up of their entire lives. Why, the chances of that happening, in Jack Moore's amazed and hastily considered estimate, were about two times double ought divided by zero.

"Boss," Silvertip shouted as he slowed the team to a stop in the middle of the road, "I got news! For you too, Blue John."

The two would-be bank robbers stared hard at the man they had thought was gone from their lives and wondered what worse could go wrong. Shortly they were to find out, for there was an altogether second rock in their road to robbing the Ashley-Vernal bank.

"Silvertip," Moore growled as he glared at the hulking man in the wagon, "if brains was leather, you couldn't saddle a bug!"

"Now Boss—"

"I mean it! I don't mind you being ignorant, but you sure don't have to work so hard making a perfect job out of it. You're so doggone dumb you couldn't teach a setting hen to cluck! Now what in thunder do you mean barreling up here and yelping our names so the whole blamed territory knows what handles we go by?"

Silvertip looked slowly from Moore to Blue John and then back again, and suddenly his face broke into a happy smile. "Say, you fellers were fixing on robbing that there bank, weren't you."

It was a statement, not a question, and it caught them flat. Moore and Blue John stared at each other. Moore felt the itch in his hand again, the itch to draw his revolver and blast away. Desperately he fought to control it, and slowly his fingers lost their curl and his hand fell away from the butt of his gun.

"Silvertip," he whispered hoarsely, "I asked you what is it you wanted. Happen it's nothing but a social chat, Blue John and I are some busy. Now let's *hear* it!"

Again Silvertip looked from one to the other, his smile still on his face. His answer, when it came, was as easy and uncovered as though he were admitting he had forgotten to close the backhouse door. Moore and Blue John looked at him three long drags, and Blue John, finally, flipped his foul-smelling cigarette away.

"You came all the way here to tell us *that*?"

"Sure did, Blue John. Been pumping this rig since before daylight. I got that wire from Mr. Friendlessman, down to Provo. He figures he's got the man who can take us to all that Injun gold."

Blue John looked at the dust that nearly covered his boots and shook his head disgustedly. Moore, just as purely amazed, hawked and spit to clear the gather from his throat.

"Silvertip," he finally growled, "do you have any idea how long Friendlessman's been looking for that gold? Or how many final surefire leads he's come up with in that time? Or how many horses and mules he's wore out tromping around in them mountains? Or how many Injuns he's had laughing at him all that time? Or how loud, for pete's sake, ol' Caleb Rhoades has been hee-hawing and hoorahing him these past five years?"

"Five," Silvertip answered.

"Five what?"

"Five years. You asked how long Friendlessman's been looking, and you just said the answer yourself. Must be so if you say it. You're always right. As for how many leads he's had, I don't reckon—"

"Silvertip!" Moore thundered, "get out of here before I . . . I . . ."

"But Boss, ain't you and Blue John coming with me? Friendlessman said this time it was a sure thing, and—"

"No I ain't coming! Blue John and I got work to do here! Now git, you chuckleheaded moron, before I—"

"But Boss . . ."

Moore, his face livid, turned his back on the still-protesting Silvertip and stormed into the bank, with Blue John directly on his heels. Instantly their pistols were out, and they were ready.

"All right," he shouted as Blue John closed the door and stood against it, "everybody get their hands up! This is a hold-up!"

There was no movement, and Jack Moore stared at the teller's cage and the office beyond, suddenly aware that there was no teller. Nor, for that matter, did there seem to be anybody else.

"Boss," Blue John asked quietly as he moved into the room, "where is everybody?"

"I don't know. I ain't seen anybody leave."

"Maybe they're at lunch."

Both Moore and Blue John spun about in surprise, their guns leveled at the innocent Silvertip, who had come in behind them.

"What're *you* doing here?"

"Golly, Boss. I just reckoned you might need some help."

"We don't, you dolt. Now—"

"Boss," Blue John's voice sounded urgent, "you hear that?"

"Hear what?"

"I don't know. Sounded like knocking, sort of."

Jack Moore looked around. "Since when do folks need to knock before they can go into a bank? Besides, see for yourself. There ain't nobody at the door at all."

Blue John shrugged, and then, while Moore and Silvertip watched, he stepped behind the teller's cage and peeked into the office.

"Boss," he whispered loudly, "there truly ain't nobody here."

Moore, deep in thought, suddenly brightened. "Boys," he said, grinning, "it's the perfect set-up. For a minute there I was confuseder than a blind dog in a butcher shop, but by jingo, I just found the bone. I got it all figured out."

"Tell us, Boss," Silvertip pleaded earnestly.

Moore gave Silvertip an evil look and then turned to Blue John. "The way I see it, these folks have been called out on some sort of emergency. So, let's us take advantage of the situation. There can't be no superiorly wondrous time to rob a bank than right this minute, when nobody's home to object. Blue John, you keep a watch on the door; Silvertip, you get the cash out of the teller's cage; and I'll strip the vault. Now go!"

With a happy smile, Silvertip stepped behind the cage and reached for the drawers, and Moore ran into the office, ready to open the vault.

"Boss," Silvertip suddenly called.

Moore, already examining the vault door, ignored the man's call.

"Boss, I got me a little problem."

"Little," Moore muttered as he looked at the door, "you don't know the half of it, you imbecile. You don't have the brains—"

"Boss, there ain't no money here!"

Jack Moore, just tugging at the edge of the vault door, which he had discovered was loose, stopped. So, too, did his breath. "What?" he whispered painfully.

Blue John answered him. "Blazes, Boss. Silvertip is right. These teller's drawers are empty!"

Urgently Jack Moore ran out of the office and, one at a time, yanked out all the drawers and tossed them onto the floor. "Cleaned out," he muttered. "Why in the . . ."

Hastily he moved back into the office while his two subordinates followed. "It can't be," he mumbled as he gripped the edge of the vault door again and started to swing it open. "They were workers, is all. They were hanging the sign . . ."

With the door open, Moore and the others stared incredulously into the vault. Then, almost mechanically, they moved inside. The vault contained nothing but bare shelves and trussed-up bodies, and carefully they untied the teller and bank president, both of whom lay bound and struggling on the floor.

"Oh, thank you," the president gasped as he rubbed his hands, "I thought nobody'd *ever* come. Those three cleaned us out! I've got to get a posse right away or they'll get off scott free."

Then, while Jackson T. Moore and Blue John McGuire and Silvertip stared in amazement, he ran out into the street, screaming for help at the top of his lungs.

The teller, still seated, sat and slowly rubbed circulation back into his wrists. "Boys," he said, "you've no idea how glad I was to see you come into that vault door."

"You . . . you mean those three pilgrims who hung your sign *robbed* you?"

"Sure as horsehair grows in winter they did. But we'll get 'em, don't you worry about that. Meanwhile, although the bank's closed, I'll do my best to help you with *your* business. What was it you wanted?"

Jack Moore stared at Blue John and then at Silvertip and finally looked back at the teller. I don't reckon you can help us anyway," he sighed. "We was just fixing to make a small withdrawal."

The teller laughed bitterly. "Well, you're right as rain about that," he declared. "We've already been withdrawn to about our limit. Sorry, boys, but thank you again for setting us free."

Dejectedly, Moore and the others stepped out into the street, where they stood watching the posse form down near the sheriff's office.

"Who'd have thought it?" Moore growled. "Them sign-hangers! Them dirty, no-account, thieving sign-hangers. I knowed we should've blasted them! I had me a feeling, but oh no, I've got to go be the nice guy. Talk about a Pecos swap if I ever seen one, hanging the sign and then robbing the bank. Ohhh, them dirty miserable low-down—"

"Golly, Boss," Silvertip said happily, "ain't it wonderful?"

"What, you numbskull?"

"Why, seeing that there posse taking off down there and knowing it ain't after us. Gives a man a right peaceful feeling. I'd most forgot what it was like. Why, now we can meet Mr. Friendlessman and go looking for all that gold. Come on, we can use the wagon."

Moore, finally driven beyond the tautly stretched limits of his frustration, was just getting ready to whip out his pistol and terminate Silvertip's benign stupidity when there was a clatter of hooves from behind him. Spinning, he was shocked to see a man ride his horse out from the narrow alley beyond the bank, the alley he had been certain that, only moments before, had been empty.

The man rode forward, drew rein, and sat looking down at the three outlaws.

"Well boys," he drawled quietly, "you was lucky, luckier'n you'll ever guess. Now was I you, I'd climb into that wagon and ride. I'd say the man with the silver hair has a truly fine idea."

Moore slowly turned so that he was facing the stranger, ready to draw. But there was something that stopped him, something—

Backing up a step, Moore eased his hand and looked the man over carefully, trying to discover why he sensed such great danger from one who appeared so singularly alone.

The stranger sat his horse like most men of the time, like a lean sack of loose oats. His long legs reached straight for the ground in the let-down stirrup leathers. Cradled under his offside was the ever-present Winchester. Slung across the cantle were his suggin and slicker, probably encompassing in their slender girth most all that the man held personal in the world.

Coming to his clothes, the pattern held. The trousers were faded blue, low-hipped, shotgun-barreled as to leg, and a man could bet his last twenty cents that their waistband was stamped "Levi Strauss." The full, choked tops of the Levis would be stuffed inside the pull leathers of sixteen-inch Texas boots, and if those boots failed to support cartwheel Mexican rowels, a man would lose the pockets that held his last twenty cents. His coat was black broadcloth, as was his vest. His shirt was white, or at least had been so at one time, and his bow-tie was black and neatly tied. The hat, too, was out of the clothier's bible, a genuine Six-X beaver Stetson, flat-crowned, four-inch-brimmed, and held on by a string under the chin.

As to his face, it was lean and leathery, surrounded by a long beard and even longer black hair that was stringy and streaked heavily with gray. He seemed a bit oldish, maybe, but it was impossible to tell exactly *how* oldish. Fact is, he might have been forty, and then again he might have been twice that. It was just impossible to tell.

He fitted, all right, and yet he didn't. There was something in his eyes, some glint or gleam—

"Who're you?" Moore demanded angrily.

"I'm your judge and jury," the man drawled, his voice more quiet than ever.

"Sure you are," Moore snapped. "And I'm Albert Sidney Johnston, back from the dead at Shiloh. Mister, you talk or I'll drill you."

"No talk needed," the man replied quietly. "And you won't be drilling anybody. Case has been tried and the verdict's in. You've done been found guilty."

"Guilty?" Moore cried, "guilty of what? We just went into the bank to do a little business and found it had been robbed. We was the ones set those fellers loose!"

"Mister," the man said, and Moore noted the hardness that had suddenly appeared around the edges of his voice, "I've been watching you eyeing that bank, so cut the act. You might be heros to these folks, but I know the kind of withdrawal you had in mind. Besides, when you put your foot out to steal them two horses yonder, you did not step into just *anybody's* cowchip. You lit hard with both brogans square in the middle of the grandaddy pasture flapjack of them all. Mister, them horses yonder are *mine*!"

"Wh-what horses?" Moore asked weakly.

Faintly the man smiled. "That's why you ain't pushing up daisies already. I hate to shoot genuine heroes. Nor do I take to wiping out folks who are smart enough to see the error of their evil ways. And mister, I reckoned right off that you was a mighty smart man, quick to repent and anxious to do so. Now the three of you climb aboard that rig and rattle your hocks on out of here. Happen you choose to do otherwise, why, come this time a minute from now, you'll be staring at the sky and seeing nothing but nothing."

"Now lookee here," Moore blustered, "you can't go around telling folks what to do! Blue John, get our horses, and—"

"*Whoa!*"

Moore stepped back, startled by the loud order and even more startled by the terribly sudden and horrifyingly unexplained appearance of the man's big Colt revolver.

"I reckon," the man went on, his voice once again quiet, "that I'll have to read to you from the book. For the last time, them're *my* horses. One of you touches either of them again, it'll be about as safe as kicking a loaded polecat. Comes to them horses, I'm touchier'n a teased snake. Them're my favorites. Now git into that wagon!"

"But—but our gear," Moore demanded, sensing defeat but still fighting against it.

"Chalk it up to interest on the use of my horses," the man said. "Just credit the account of a feller you might call Orrin Porter Rockwell."

Jack Moore stared, and then felt his mouth go suddenly dry—very, *very* dry. He heard Blue John suck in his breath and turn and climb quickly into the wagon, and instantly he was scrambling aboard himself. Defeat, after all, was nowhere near so hard to accept as he had thought.

"I—I thought you was dead," he whispered as he settled onto the seat.

"Not hardly," the stranger declared.

"But you are! Or I mean, he is . . . I mean . . . Listen, I got friends who was at your funeral, and that was ten, eleven years ago!"

"Do tell," the man responded calmly. "Makes an interesting dilemma, don't it."

"What do you mean?"

"Just what I said, a dilemma. If you're right and I'm dead, you got nothing to fear. On the other hand . . ."

"Mister, who *are* you?"

Slowly the stranger leaned over and spat. "I've said all I intend to say. It's up to you to either call or throw in your hand."

"You're right," Moore growled, "and I ain't about to throw—"

"Moore," Blue John muttered, "it doesn't matter *who* he is. That .44 is real enough, and it's already out and pointed your way."

"Maybe so, but if this gent ain't Port Rockwell—"

"Mister," the man said quietly, "it ain't in you, and you know it. You'll never know who I am, and you'll likely die wondering."

"By thunder," Jackson T. Moore growled, "we'll see about that! I'm gonna—"

"Mister Moore," the man interrupted flatly, "you're already sucking on the front sight of this gun, and if you want the rest of it, here goes. That sound you hear is a single–action Colt revolver being cocked. The next sound that you *don't* hear will be your bodies flopping out of that wagon and into the dust. You got that rig ready to roll, amigo?"

It developed that Mr. Jackson T. Moore's mother had not wasted her cooking on any feeble-minded children. He had got the point of the hard-looking stranger's discourse, and instantly he had the reins and was nodding yes.

"Good. Now *git!*"

Silvertip looked from Moore to Blue John and back to Moore. Both men nodded quickly and vigorously, and so Silvertip, his face wearing a happy smile, climbed aboard, took the reins from the trembling Moore, and reached out and ticked the wheeler with the popper of the whip. He added a kind word for the off-wheeler, and the wagonload of outlaws turned and headed leisurely, in spite of Jack Moore and Blue John's urging instant greater speed, west from the empty Bank of Vernal and Taylor's General Merchandise, Vernal, Territory of Utah.

Happen they'd have thought about it right then, Moore and the others would have known they were going after Friendlessman's Indian gold. They didn't think about it, of course, for two of them could think of nothing but the empty bank and the dark-faced man who was behind them, he of the lightning draw who had claimed to be the notorious marshal Porter Rockwell. The third man, Silvertip, thought little about anything but taking care of his horses, and he certainly wasn't worried. He was merely happy, for he was once again with his friends.

Still, the three were definitely going gold hunting. For them, it was about the only option left.

12

Jailhouse—Fountain Green

"Hyrum?"

Surprised at the sound of Ida Mae's voice, I started up from my bunk. The jail I was in was small, about ten by twelve feet. It was a single room with one heavy door and two small barred windows up near the ceiling. As near as I could tell it had been made of logs and then framed over with sawed lumber, and altogether it was a pretty dismal place. There was no office to it—the marshal's office was across the street, and once the door was shut, I was alone and more lonely than a man can imagine.

In the room was a bunk and a stool and a bucket, and scattered on the bunk were several issues of the *Deseret Weekly,* which I had been reading off and on ever since I had been locked up the day before. I'd also been reading the graffiti that had been scratched on the walls, and in some ways, that graffiti was a whole lot more educational than the *Deseret Weekly*.

I got two meals a day, which the marshal's wife, Amelia, brought to me, and other than that I got nothing and saw no one. Ma had been down and had talked to me twice, and my younger half-brother Ernest had come and talked to me for a few minutes the day before. But I couldn't see them even when we talked. The window was too high and I couldn't get to it.

"Ida Mae?" I asked, wanting to be sure it was her.

"Oh, Hyrum, are you all right?"

"Yeah, I'm fine."

"Is . . . is it bad in there?"

"Not too bad," I grinned. "I feel about as homeless as a lost poker chip and as lonely as a Wyoming winter sky, but other than that, I don't mind it."

"Oh, Hyrum, I can hardly stand the idea of you being in . . . in *jail!* You would never do *anything* so evil as what they're accusing you of, and I think that awful Marshal Clawson is a disgrace. Oh, how can you bear it in that tiny room?"

"Well," I answered, feeling mighty good that Ida Mae was so concerned about me, "it is somewhat confining. I reckon I can handle it, though."

"You are so brave, Hyrum. I'm . . . well, I'm very proud of you. I know what it means to you to be out and working, and now that you're cooped up in that little . . . little hen-house of a jail, well, now I see even more what kind of a person you are."

I shouldn't have to say that I was getting puffed up in my pride as a bloated heifer, but I was, and I couldn't help it. Now, we take care of heifers when they're bloated by sticking them, and I had no way of knowing that the Good Lord takes care of people the same way. In other words, I was getting ready to be stuck, and I didn't see it coming at all. No sir, in spite of my being in jail, I was still just a happy kid who was basking in the light of his girl's adoration and looking to maybe impress her a little bit more.

"It really isn't so bad, Ida Mae," I said modestly, "even though I do take kindly to open lands and sunshine and the far, lonely winds. I like to look far off. Then it seems like I'm free, even if I'm not."

"What do you mean?"

"Well, in a lot of ways I suppose I am more free than many others, but when you think about it, Ida Mae, are any of us who know something, who have an understanding of one thing or another, ever totally free again?"

"I don't think I understand what you're saying."

"Ida Mae, even when a man isn't bound by walls, he's still bound by knowledge and understanding. Those things tell a man that he is surrounded by duty; duty to the things he knows, duty to family and friends, duty to folks about him, duty to his church and country, duty to the law—such-like. If he ignores that duty, then there is no way that he can call himself a man."

Ida Mae was still, and I wondered for a moment or so if she had gone. "Hyrum," she suddenly said, "you really believe in this duty, don't you."

It wasn't so much a question as it was a confirmation of fact, and I squinted up at the window, wishing that I could see her and explain to her with my eyes as well as my words how I really felt.

"Yes I do. Without duty, Ida Mae, life doesn't make any kind of sense."

"I suppose. But you said law. Do you still feel duty to the law, even after you have been treated so shabbily by Marshal Clawson?"

"Of course. If folks are going to live together, they have to have rules and abide by them. The law is those rules. Now, there are always mavericks who can't or won't ride a straight trail, and so we as people need someone who can ride herd on them. I suppose that is who Marshal Clawson is.

"Under the right conditions, the law doesn't work against a man, it works for him. Without it, every house would need to be a fortress, and no man or woman would be safe. Like Pa says, almost everyone would revert to savagery, and we would all be either victimizers or victims. In fact, I'll bet that when Adam and Eve first got their eyes opened, they likely started making laws so they could live together.

"The law will work for me, too. When I go to court I'll get Zene Hill to testify for me, and this stupid charge won't hold water at all."

"Do you think folks will believe an Indian?"

Ida Mae's question surprised me, and I didn't know how to answer it. "I reckon," I finally said. "Why shouldn't they?"

"Oh, they *should,* but folks being what they are, I wonder if they will."

"Well, I don't wonder about it! Zene's a fine man, and probably a better Christian than 80 per cent of the people here. You'll see. When the conditions are right, the law will work for me and I'll be released pronto."

"And what if the conditions aren't right, like with polygamy?"

Well, Ida Mae had hit squarely the question that was ripping apart the Territory. Conditions were indeed bad, and evil, uninformed men had manipulated the law until we as a people were truly under siege. Pa had told me that hardly a day went by without one or more men, and sometimes even their wives, being sent to prison for adultery or fornication or unlawful cohabitation, whichever ridiculous, trumped-up charge the judges decided to press.

For instance, according to a torn-out news item on the wall of my jail, on Monday, last November 19, 1888, in the First District Court at Provo, Judge Judd had sentenced the following brethren: Hans Nielsen of Chester, Randolph H. Stewart of Moab, Jens Hansen of Gunnison, Eli A. Day of Fairview, John F. F. Doius of Ephraim, Oluf C. Larsen of Ephraim, Wm. Christiansen of Pleasant Grove,

John Spencer of Indianola, Samuel S. Cluff of Provo, Alfred Turner of Lehi, Richard Jenkins of Nephi, Oluf J. Anderson of Castle Dale, Albert Jones of Provo, Orlando F. Herron of Pleasant Grove, Soren C. Jensen of Mt. Pleasant, Lorin Harmer of Springville, and Wm. Gallup of Springville. All were convicted of unlawful cohabitation or adultery, fined up to three hundred dollars each, and sentenced to prison for terms ranging up to fourteen months. From what Pa had told me, that sort of thing goes on five days out of every week.

Then there is the issue of all the Church's property, which the government had seized and placed into receivership under the very greedy hands of now ex-Marshal Dyer. The government had done that because of claims that we are not, under the current laws of the land, a legal entity, which of course is nonsense and religious persecution in the land of the free besides.

Last November Dyer had received over $750,000 worth of Church property, including the temple in Salt Lake City and everything else he could lay hand to, and the crook was demanding a fee of $25,000 for handling it, to be paid, of course, by the Saints.

"I asked Pa about all this," I finally answered, "and he told me that our duty is to always follow the prophet, no matter what kinds of pressures Satan and his minions bring to bear. Pa says that Joseph Smith once prophesied that God would never let the prophet lead the Saints astray. Of course, you know that the prophet says to fight the plural marriage issue peacefully and to work through the courts to finally get the law changed."

What happens if the government won't change it?"

"Who knows? One way or another it will work out."

"But Hyrum, what if they keep throwing people in jail? Do the Saints just keep fighting them and suffering?"

"I don't know," I answered, leaning against the wall. "I've thought about it a lot, and I just can't imagine that the Lord will let that happen. Either the government will change the law or the Lord will open a way so that we can obey it without breaking God's law in the process.

"In Farrar's book about Jesus, he discusses the time when Jesus was forced, by Peter's innocent ignorance, into the position of paying a redemption and temple tax on his own temple and when he was already preparing to give his very life as the ultimate redemption. Farrar says 'He paid what he did not owe, to save us from that which we owed, but could never pay.'

"Jesus taught Peter that He, the Son of Man, should be exempt from the tax, but that if it was paid, it must be done freely and not compulsorily, as should be the case with the living of all religion. Then he told Peter that the tax would indeed be paid but not in the normal way. Peter was told to go and pull a fish out of the water, take a coin from its mouth, and pay the tax.

"Peter did so, Ida Mae, so that Jesus might obey the eternal laws of charity and self-surrender and yet still maintain his God-like majesty in the face of mortal law.

"Ida Mae, I truly believe that same type of thing will happen to us. The Lord loves the Saints for this great sacrifice they have been willing to make, and one of these days, in the very midst of our most difficult struggles, God will instruct President Woodruff to throw in his hook and pull out a fish. Some amazing new development will then occur, and we will once again be known as a law-abiding people, both of God's laws and of man's. Then I can truly speak to you of my duty to the law and mean it."

Ida Mae was quiet, and it was not difficult to hear the chuckling of the small creek that ran behind the jail. Oh, how I longed to be out there, either fishing or just sitting with my feet in the cold water, day-dreaming. I had spent many an hour in such pleasant circumstances, and—

"Hyrum?"

"Yeah?"

"I . . . I'm very proud of you. Yet I can't bear to see you remain in that jail. It isn't fair. I'm going to get you out. Somehow . . . yes, somehow, I will surely see that you are free!"

"Ida Mae, I—"

"I mean it! Sit tight, and I'll be back as quickly as I can find help."

Then she was gone, and I was left alone in the tiny jail, feeling proud as punch that Ida Mae Sorenson was my girl. Yet I was about to get stuck like a bloated heifer, and I had no idea of it at all. Nor was I ready. But then, who of us ever is?

13

Jailhouse—Fountain Green—Again

"Hyrum, why . . . why did you do it?"

Surprised, I stared up at the window. "Do what, Ida Mae? Go to jail, you mean?"

"No, I mean . . . I mean, why did you *kill* that man?"

Well, I can hardly express my surprise and . . . and *hurt*. It hadn't been four hours since Ida Mae had been telling me how awful it was that I was cooped up and how proud of me she was for not fighting it. And now suddenly I was guilty until proven innocent, and my heart was running over with a bigger ache than I had ever before felt.

"Ida Mae!" I said, my voice filled with exasperation, "I told you what happened! I didn't kill nobody—"

"Anybody, Hyrum."

"Yeah, that's what I said. Nor did I help anyone to get killed. I found that gold just like I said, and—"

"Now I understand why you aren't really fighting it. You are guilty, you know it, and you know it would do no good to try and prove otherwise."

"Oh for pete's sake—"

"Hyrum, you can talk straight with me. I still care about you, very much. I won't get angry or anything, and I really think it would be good if you told the truth. That's the first step in repentance, recognition, I mean, and—"

"For crying out loud, Ida Mae, I *am* telling the truth. What makes you think otherwise?"

"Why, *everbody* says it had to be you, and—"

"*Everybody*? Who is everybody, other than old Clawson and that beady-eyed Doolin from up to Provo?"

"There are others, Hyrum, very influential people. But I don't want to talk about it if you're going to shout."

"I'm not shouting!" I yelled, hardly even able to control myself. "I just want to know who's the dirty underhanded sneak who thinks I'm a murderer."

"He isn't dirty *or* underhanded, and you are too shouting. In fact, he's the opposite. He is a perfect gentleman, something I haven't seen around here in some time. His grammar is absolutely wonderful, and his manners are . . . are . . . well, they're superb!"

Though I hated like blue blazes to admit it, Ida Mae had me there. I'd picked up a tolerable amount of poor grammatical and social habits during my brief mortal probation, and everything I was reading made me more aware of them. Time and again I'd determined to improve, but habits, once adopted, are hard to shed, and I'd found that to be especially true of my verbalogical difficulties. Given time, though, I'd do better. I'd made myself that vow, and knew I would. But convincing Ida Mae of it was something else altogether.

"What in tarnation are you talking about? Who is this . . . this . . ."

"I'm talking about help, Hyrum. Help! And you might be interested in knowing, *Mr*. Soderberg, that he has offered to help get you out of jail."

Well, that was all I needed, help from some feller who was going around telling folks . . . no, telling *Ida Mae*, that I was guilty. Happen he *did* use language that was so polished a feller could skate on it, I could care less. That was *my* girl he was tearing me down to, and I didn't like it one little bit!

"He? He? Who in thunder is he? What's this hombre's name?"

"Felix Ethelbert Friendlessman."

"*Felix Ethelbert Friendlessman*! Ida Mae, that ought to give you a clue right off that the man can't be trusted. I'd say you'd best watch out for him. There ain't a self-respecting man on earth who'd tell *anybody* he was called by a handle like that."

"Well, how rude! And he even wants to *help* you."

"I can tell," I snarled. "He's most surely helping me with you."

There was quiet for a moment, and when Ida Mae spoke again, her voice had a whole new tone to it.

"I declare. I do believe you are jealous."

Now that got to me quick. She was correct as a schoolmarm's manners, or maybe this Friendlessman feller's manners too, and though I hated to admit it, I hated even more for her to know it.

"Well," I growled, changing the subject as fast as I could, "I *would* appreciate all the help I can get, getting out of here. This jail's fast becoming pure misery."

"I'm sure it is," she answered, apparently as eager as I was to change the subject. "What on earth do you *do* in there?"

"Sometimes I sleep. Sometimes I think. And now and then I even think out loud. Most of the time, however, I read."

"Read? What on earth is there to read? Did the marshal give you your books?"

"No, but there's a whole pile of *Deseret Weekly*s, and those poor misbegotten pilgrims who have spent time here before me have scratched a good deal of literature of their own on these walls. Reading what they wrote has been an education all by itsownself."

"Hyrum," Ida Mae said, sounding shocked, "you aren't reading *that?*"

It wasn't difficult at all to catch the vivid edge of disgust that was lining her voice, and I caught it. Made me feel badly, too, it truly did.

"Of course I'm reading it," I replied, forcing a lightness into my voice that I did not feel. "A man needs to be educated, doesn't he?"

"You surely can't call all that . . . that *filth*, an education?"

"Filth? Now Ida Mae, that's being a bit harsh. I admit there's a touch of roughness here and there, but a feller's just got to skip over that. Pa says that's what a man has to do in life, too.

"Actually, I was thinking more on some of this other stuff. One feller must have had bad feet, for instance, for he wrote that the only difference between an oak tree and a tight shoe was that one held acorns and the other held corns that ached. Ida Mae, that there is truly an educational thought."

"I don't get it."

I grinned. "Yeah, it is some deep. Another feller must have been a poet, for there's a whole pile of these limericks. What do you think of this one?

There once was a man named Deeth,
Who sat on his set of false teeth.
Said he, with a start,
'Oh, bless my heart!
I've bitten myself underneath.'

"Now Ida Mae, that's terrible fine literature, as you've surely got to admit."

"I'll admit no such thing!"

"Well, you should. It's better than a lot of stuff folks are passing off as literature these days. They write to make money or to aggrandize their own names before the world, and then they can't understand it when folks don't buy more than one or two of their books. The way Pa says it, if a man takes pen in hand to write something for other folks to read, he'd surely better have something significant to say. Otherwise he's not only wasting his time and money, but he's wasting the time and money of other folks as well. Besides that, he's fiddling with their minds, maybe even preventing them from learning something important that they might otherwise have learned, and that is a heavy responsibility indeed.

"Say, here's one written about us folks."

"Us folks?"

"Yeah, us Mormon folks. See if this doesn't make a little more sense.

There once was a young Mormon priest
Who lived almost wholly on yeast.
'For,' he said, 'it is plain,
We shall all rise again,
And I'd like to get started, at least!'

"Hyrum, that's the dumbest thing I ever heard."

"Educational."

"It is not," Ida Mae declared disgustedly. "If you call that an education, then I'd recommend that a person ought not to have any education at all."

Well, I could tell that Ida Mae was getting riled again, but for some perverse reason I didn't much care. I mean, what did she *expect* me to do in that jail? Metamorphosize? Besides that, being in jail hadn't improved *my* temper too much either. I was there when I hadn't ought to have been, and there was some Felix feller outside who was impressing my girl all over the place, and because of that I was touchier'n a busted tooth and didn't care who knew it.

"I don't know, Ida Mae," I said, feeling evil but enjoying it. "Way I see it, education's like a mother's love or a married lady's morals. A feller don't dare question either one, especially in public. Now you just come out against education, and if folks had heard you, why you'd never get elected to nothing in this whole country. Not *ever*. Same with religion. You could likely stand in favor of them owl-hoots who stole your pa's and my pa's horses, or maybe giving free liquor to the Indians, and be better off. Me, I'd rather run on a ticket of kicking stray dogs and pistol-whipping little old ladies than to utter a derogatory word against education or religion. Seems to me, Ida Mae, that you ought to be a little more open-minded."

"Well, I declare!" she stormed. Something banged against the side of the jail, like maybe her toe or something, and she cried out like she might have been in pain.

"Hyrum," she stormed, "I can't even *begin* to imagine what I ever saw in you! You are . . . you are absolutely *despicable!* It's a wonder I recognized the gentleman in Felix at all. I've surely never met one before. So good day, Hyrum Soderberg! And *good riddance!*"

And then she was gone and I was still grinning, only suddenly I was feeling miserable as a calf with the slobbers. Dropping back onto the bunk I sighed, picked up another *Deseret Weekly,* and read where maybe they had caught that feller in England they were calling Jack the Ripper. Then I laid down the paper, stared up at the ceiling, and sighed again.

Blast! What was wrong with me? That little gal was the best thing in my whole life, and here I'd driven her away. Driven her! Made a feller wonder if maybe someone hadn't jiggled the good Lord's arm when he poured in my brains. Blast again! Teasing her had been a sure-enough foolish thing to do. Now I truly *did* feel lonely, and there was no one to blame but myownself.

Yes sir, I surely did give me one miserable day. I'd been stuck but good for my puffed-upedness, and believe me, the gasses of my pride were dissipating fast. Somehow I had to get out of that jail, and I had to do it soon. Even if it was with the help of that Friendless fellow, or whatever his crazy name was. It was the only way I could see of finding out who *had* killed Enock Rhoades. Once I found that out, then maybe Ida Mae would believe me again.

14

Jailhouse—Fountain Green—Still

"Hyrum?"

Quicker than a New York minute I was up on my bunk and as close to that window as I could get.

"Ida Mae? Hey, I'm sorry! I didn't mean—"

"Hy, you numbskull, this ain't Ida Mae. It's me. Ernest!"

"Oh," I growled sullenly. "Well, why didn't you tell me sooner, you little pipsqueak? You trying to make me look stupid or something?"

"Doesn't look to me like you need much help," Ernest replied. "Besides, I ain't little."

"Then you must have growed some since they locked me up. Yesterday you didn't come no more than hipbone high to a mired duck."

"Oh yeah? Well your head's so hollow you had to hold your hands over your ears to keep from going deaf from the noise of the one single lonely thought you had all last month."

I started to make another reply, even more nasty, but finally thought better of it and sank back onto the bunk. I could have said something, I surely could have, but Ma says us Soderbergs have been given quick tongues, and we have the responsibility of blessing folks with our words or of cursing ourselves by tearing those same folks down. I was tearing Ernest down and was so angry I didn't even know it. Thank goodness for an occasional cool breath of sanity and understanding.

"I'm sorry, Ern," I said. "I reckon this jail's just getting to me a little."

"I reckon," he replied, apparently also feeling bad about the tone of our conversation.

"Sure good of you to come see me."

"That's okay. It's better'n weeding Ma's garden."

I grinned at Ernest's honesty. He had to be one of the finest kids a body ever saw. And smart? Why, he was full of information as a mail-order catalogue. Like I might have said earlier, out in the hills he'd spook a normal person. He could count the sweat beads on a mule deer's lip at four hundred yards, and he could hear and just plain *feel* things like he was part varmint. Gave a body the fluttering fantods, just watching him moving through the brush.

I'd heard Pa telling Ma one day that I was some that way myownself, and I *do* feel things now and then that other folks seem to miss. But Ernest, well, I didn't hold even half a candle to that kid. He was something.

"Well, I still appreciate you coming."

"Hy, what do you do in there all day?"

Seemed like everybody had the same question. Might be a good idea if everyone in town got locked up a day or so, so's they'd know. Then I wouldn't have to spell it out so often.

"Read," I answered. "That and sleep."

"What do you read?"

"Papers and stuff that's on the walls."

"Walls?"

"Yeah. There's lots of poems and other literary explorations. Like this one:

> *Thursday's sure a long, long day,*
> *All filled with draggin minutes.*
> *I'd never thought so before being jailed,*
> *But there must be a* million *in it.*

"That feller knew what it was like. I hate it in here. I truly do."

"That's why I came to see you. Some fellers might be fixing to bust you out."

"What?"

"Deaf Man Hibbard told me to tell you."

"Deaf Man Hibbard? How would he know?"

Ernest giggled. "Hy, can you keep a secret?"

"I reckon."

"Swear it by every drop of blood in your body, Hy. You tell, and you have to cut off *every* finger, one at a time, and let your blood *all drip out!* Swear!"

Good grief. Where had he ever heard that gory stuff? Made a feller wonder what the world was coming to. "All right, I swear. Now what is this deep, dark secret?"

"Hy, Deaf Man Hibbard ain't deaf."

"What?"

"It's true. And I just today found out myownself. You know Ma's had me going over there for the past year to read to him, don't you?"

"I know. Pa says you was asked because you made your words good and he could make them out a little. Me, though, I always figured Old Man Hibbard was desperate for human companionship and finally settled on you, which was somewhat shy of the mark."

"Hy, you want this news or not? Happen you don't, I've got some *real* important things to do, like slop the hogs and take a nap."

"You've got a way, Ern, of getting straight to the point. I take it all back and humbly ask you to continue."

"Okay, I will. This morning I was over there to Deaf Man Hibbard's place, reading to him as usual. Old Lady Hibbard was fussing about like she always does, grumbling and growling and scurrying hither and yon with her broom and dustmop, fairly making that place sparkle.

"Sudden she stops in front of Deaf Man and motions that she wants him to go down to the Co-op to pick up some dry goods. Deaf Man, he just stares like he's trying hard to understand but somehow can't get the job done. Finally the old lady gets angry and gives up, motions that he's a useless so-and-so and that she'll go herself, wraps herself in her shawl, and out the door she goes.

"Well, Deaf Man he watches that screen door for maybe two or three minutes, and sudden he turns to me. 'Ernest,' he says, "I've got to let you in on a little secret. I'm not deaf. Fact is, I can hear as well as you."

"Hy, that stumped me. All my life that old man's been deaf, and here I thought all this time I was doing some great Christian act, reading to him like I did. 'But,' I says to him, 'you've been deaf ever since I knowed you. Did you have a miracle or a priesthood blessing or something?'

"'Nope,' he says. 'I never was deaf. Never would take a blessing for it, either. Ernest, about twelve years ago that woman I'm married to finally wore me out. She'd been fussing and yelling and nagging at me for near forty years, and I just couldn't take it any more. I considered the options—murder, suicide, divorce, leaving home, and so on—and every one left something or other to be desired. No matter what I did, I'd break one or another of the Lord's commandments and end up on the short end of the eternal stick.

"'Then one night I thought of going deaf, thought my way through it and couldn't see any major drawbacks, and decided that was the thing to do. When morning came, I was stone deaf.'

"'For real?' I ask him. 'Of course not,' he replies. 'But the same as, nevertheless. And Ernest, these past twelve years have been the happiest years of my life. It's wondrous how comfortable a man's home is when he can relax there.'

"'So why are you telling me?' I ask. 'Because,' says he, 'I heard some fellers talking. Folks do that around me. They figure I'm deaf, and that's about the same as not being there at all. So they just go ahead and talk. Sometimes its plumb embarrassing, but last night it was more informative.

"'You heard of this Friendlessman fellow?' 'No,' I says, 'I haven't.' 'Me neither,' he continues, 'not until last night. But I was up at the depot, and this Friendlessman was there, along with another man who seemed to be from up around Provo way. They were talking to George Loose-lip Lundstrum, and they were being mighty secretive. They stopped talking when they saw me sitting there, but Loose-lip said I was deaf. That satisfied them, and they continued.'"

"Ernest," I said, staring up at my window, "*I've* heard of Friendlessman. Ida Mae thinks he's mighty wonderful, but she might not, happen she knew he'd teamed up with Loose-lip. She doesn't like that man at all."

"Yeah, I recollect Loose-lip and her pa were closer'n two bobcats in a blanket, hunting lost gold all the time and chasing all over these hills on all sorts of fool's errands."

"That they did, and Loose-lip didn't like it at all when Pa and Mungus got to be friends. Mungus's wild days ended in a hurry. Anyway, what'd they have to say?"

"Hy, that's the strange part. All of 'em are convinced you know where that lost gold mine is, and they're going to bust you out of here and make you take 'em to it. Deaf Man Hibbard says they've wired some fellers out on The Strip. Hy, *do* you know? Where the gold is, I mean?"

"Of course I don't know. If I did, do you think I'd have quit gathering gold at just enough to go Pa's bail?"

"No," Ernest replied thoughtfully, "I don't reckon you would have. Hy, where's The Strip?"

"Out by the reservation. It's a strip of land that both Indians and whites claim, so it's a sort of no-man's land. Outlaws hang out there when they're not down to the Roost and out in The Hole. Figure the law won't touch 'em there."

"Outlaws! That's what Deaf Man Hibbard figured, all right. Anyway Hy, Friendlessman wired these fellers, and they should be here in the next few days."

So Ida Mae was right. That miserable Friendlessman *did* plan on breaking me out, only illegally, which she surely wouldn't believe. And here I sat, helpless as a frozen snake. Oh my, oh my, oh my. Life surely was getting complicated.

"Ern, I've got to get out of here, and quick. I don't have a clue to where that mine is, and if they get me and I can't lead 'em to it, then I'm a dead man for sure. Have you told Pa about this?"

"Can't. Pa's gone into hiding again. I told Aunt Hattie, though."

Well, that made me breathe a sigh of relief. At least Ma knew. And if anybody could get me out of that jail, it was Ma. She was little and dainty, but I'd seen great big men back down and crawl away when Ma got her dander up. There's just no stopping a good woman who knows she's in the right, and Ma usually was.

"What's she going to do?"

"I don't know, Hy. Last I saw her she was heading for the bank."

The bank? Now, that was a thought. Maybe Ma had some idea to borrow my bail. Trouble was, she'd be dealing with Banker Short, and everybody knew he was tighter'n a woodtick in a lobo wolf's tail. Money went into that bank, but so far as I'd heard, none had ever come out again. Just foreclosures and such as that. Still, there wasn't another place on earth where Ma could go. So all I could do was wait and pray and hope that Banker Short would come through.

15

Jailhouse—Fountain Green—and Still Again

"Hyrum?"

"Yeah," I said, scrambling up from my bunk. I'd just been reading in the *Deseret Weekly* about lost Spanish gold mines down in California and of how the padres were in the country long before the Americans, had located lots of rich veins of ore, and had enslaved the Indians to work the mines for them. Reading about it out in California made a feller wonder if maybe they were true, all those stories about gold up in the Uintahs.

"Hyrum, this is your mother."

"I know," I grinned. "How are you?"

"Worried, Son. Are you getting along all right?"

"Sure, Ma."

"What are you doing to occupy your time?"

Now I smiled again. I'd been right as rain. *Everybody* wanted to know about that. "Reading, mostly," I answered.

"Good things, I hope."

"Ma, would I read anything else? Marshal Clawson wouldn't get any of my books, but I've got piles of *Deseret Weekly*s in here, and there's poetry and lots of philosophy and such."

"Poetry?"

"You bet. There's even a poem in here called 'Ode from a Polygamist's Wife.' Want to hear it?"

Ma giggled just like a little girl. "Of course I want to hear it. Who's the author?"

"Some feller named I. M. Anonymous. Here it is:

I make a dress of cheesecloth,
You buy a dress of silk.
I wear mine most every day,

Yours in the closet wilts.
I patch mine when holes appear,
I must ignore the silt—
Everything should be thoroughly used,
Or else I'm filled with guilt.
And when the dress won't hide my bones,
Is tattered as an ancient quilt,
While your dress is scornfully thrown away,
Mine's used to strain the milk.

For a long moment there was silence, and at last Ma spoke. "My goodness, Hyrum. Maybe there *is* someone else in this world who understands. I've truly never felt so broke, nor have I felt so keenly the need to have money."

"Ma, we can get by."

"Hy, I went to see Brother Short about your bail. He turned me down flat, the pompous so-and-so."

"That's all right, Ma. They can't hold me here forever. I've been thinking that we could get Zene to come and testify for me. He saw me find the gold, and he knows how surprised I was by it. If he told that, then they'd *have* to let me go."

"Zene's a long way away, Hyrum."

"I know he is," I replied dejectedly. "He's also Indian, and I suppose there's a good chance folks wouldn't believe him anyway."

"I don't think Marshal Clawson would believe him," Ma said thoughtfully. "I think there's something more behind your arrest than the obvious. I'm worried, and I think we need to get you out of there as quickly as we can."

"Well, maybe that Friendlessman feller will get me out."

"Yes, and that's just what I'm afraid of. Hyrum, after listening to what Ernest told me, I'm afraid of that man. Somehow I feel that he is behind all this. He is evil, and I know it."

Well, I couldn't have agreed more, but I didn't say it. Probably would have looked like I was being jealous again. Which, as a matter of Fountain Green jailhouse fact, I was.

"So what are we going to do?"

"I don't know. I'll go see Brother Short again tomorrow. They've set your bail at two thousand dollars—"

"*Two thousand dollars!*" I shouted. "Ma, it ain't fair! I didn't kill that man. Everybody ought to know it, and now everybody's falling all over themselves calling me guilty. Mormons, non-Mormons, everybody! Even Ida Mae told me I needed to fess up so I could begin to repent. Criminentely, Ma, it's disgusting how pious folks suddenly are. Makes me feel like never setting foot in our ward meetinghouse again!"

Outside it was real quiet, and I could hear the cheeping of the baby barn swallows that were in the nest high up on the back of the jail. "Hy," a deep voice suddenly said, and instantly my heart was in my throat.

"Pa, is . . . is that you?"

"It is."

"I didn't know you were there. I . . . I'm sorry. I—"

" I just got here. But Hyrum, you don't have to apologize for honest feelings."

"But Pa, you're the bishop, and I know what the Church means to you. I wouldn't have said—"

"Hy," Pa interrupted, "listen to me. Of course you're right. I love the Church, and I've covenanted to do all in my power to see that it prospers. But Son, I am me, and you are you. That's obvious, but the meaning of it is that because I have a testimony of the gospel it doesn't necessarily follow that you also have one. Testimonies must come individually. No one can take his from another person, no matter how much that person loves or is loved and respected. Do you understand?"

"Yeah, I guess. What I don't understand is how a person who has covenanted through baptism to be Christ-like can do the things that some of these folks are doing to me! How can a church with people like that in it be true?"

Pa chuckled lightly. "Son, that's a powerful question, and better men than you and I have struggled with it."

"*You have?*" I asked incredulously.

"Of course. How do you think I feel when a member of my ward, whom I've just spent hours laboring with, either working in his fields or providing financial assistance or counseling with his children, runs straight to Marshal Clawson or one of the other deputies with the information that I'm spending a little much-needed time with one of my three wives and *our* children? Don't you suppose I struggle with that?"

"I don't know, Pa," I growled, "but I surely would! If I was you I'd cut 'em off! Creeps like that don't deserve to be in the Lord's church."

"And that, Hyrum, is the point."

The voice was now my mother's, and I looked up at the small window, waiting for her to continue. "Hyrum, your father and I have discussed this much, for, as you know, there is a great deal of persecution being waged against those of us who live the Principle, both from within the Church and without. We can deal with it, of course, but only because we have come to understand a principle that we now want you to understand."

"Hy," Pa continued, "we're going to make two statements that will sound like one, but are not. Listen carefully and we will explain. First: the gospel is true. Second: the Church is divine."

Well, mentally I scratched my head. They did sound the same, and I would—

"The gospel," Pa continued, "is the revealed word of God the Father and his Son, the Lord Jesus Christ. That word is eternal, and because it never changes except as God or his Son direct, it is total truth.

"The Church, on the other hand, is a divinely inspired organization made up of all sorts of men and women, not one of whom is perfect. It changes continuously, the people within it make all sorts of mistakes and do all sorts of foolish things, and it is anything but true. The organization is truly Christ's organization, but the Church itself is only a vehicle, with imperfect members. The Church is designed only to preach and promote and administer the eternal truths and ordinances of the gospel; it was never meant to *be* the gospel."

"Do you understand?" Ma questioned. "When you are confronted with the faults and evil deeds of Church members, then you must see that you are viewing the weaknesses of people, and not the gospel or the church of Jesus Christ. The Church is the vehicle through which mankind learns the truths of Christ's gospel and obtains authority to administer God's ordinances."

"Hyrum, does what we've said make sense?"

"Yeah, it does, though I reckon I'll have to think on it some."

"George Lundstrum is an example," Pa went on, "of what I am speaking of."

I thought of Loose-lip and grinned, for as bad as he was, somehow I could not bring myself to be afraid of him. He just didn't—

"As you know, Hy, George has been baptized and ordained to the priesthood. Now he has chosen to ignore it. In light of that, I would like you to consider this thought: Joseph Smith told us that no man, once he accepts the gospel of Christ, can ever return to neutral ground. From the moment of his acceptance, through all eternity, that man is either for Christ or else he is against him. No man can *ever* return to neutral ground. Now, where would you say that George is?"

"Pa, I don't want to judge—"

"Hy, the Lord said that we must not judge 'with unrighteous judgment.' That does not mean that we must not judge at all, for only by judging can we make decisions regarding our own lives. Now what about George, at least as of today?"

"Well," I said quietly, "the way it looks to me, he's against Christ."

"Yes, he is. Now of course he can change, and I for one hope that he does. I'm certain that the Lord still loves George and one of these days will see to it that the man is humbled sufficiently to make him at least consider such a change. But here is the great question: because George Lundstrum is a Church member and yet is choosing to ignore the gospel and to live wickedly, does it therefore follow that the gospel of Jesus Christ is false?"

"No, I don't reckon it does."

"You're right, Hy. Now suppose there were a *thousand* George Lundstrums, all laughing at the Saints and doing their best to make them appear foolish in their beliefs and in their faith. As far as the eternal gospel of Jesus Christ is concerned, what would that change?"

"Nothing, I reckon."

"Exactly, Hyrum. Nothing. Now remember this. When an elephant walks through town, all the dogs bark. But that neither changes the identity of the elephant nor of the dogs. There is a little noise and a little discomfort, but when it is all over, the elephant is still an elephant and the dogs are still no more than loudly yapping dogs. Do you get my point?"

"Yeah," I said, grinning. "I do."

"Good. Can you be an elephant?"

"You bet your sweet buttons," I declared firmly.

"Fine. Now remember that the way of elephants is to step carefully so that they do not injure the little dogs. Even when the dogs bite, elephants do not bite back. Such must always be the way of a disciple of Christ.

"And remember this as well. I am using dogs and elephants only as an analogy. I do not intend to call people who disagree with us, dogs. Actually, some of the finest men and women I have ever known choose to remain outside our church or choose to become inactive within it. Of course, I disagree with them and they with me, but they are still fine people and have the right to live as they choose. Someday God will see to it that active Mormons also have that right, and then we can live peacefully and happily as well.

"Now, I've got to leave, Son. Will you be all right in there?"

"Yes sir."

"I expected as much," Pa declared. "Hyrum, both your mother and I are proud of the way you're standing up to this. No matter what happens, you have a family that believes in you. When worst comes to worst, as it very well might, we will be there pitching in beside you, and you can count on that!"

"Thanks, Pa," I whispered, suddenly so choked up I could hardly talk. "And thanks for coming. I know it was a risk—"

"Oh, pshaw," Pa growled, and I could tell that he was grinning and doing his own best to cover up a few tears. It's funny how us men-folks try to hide our emotions, but we do, and I don't reckon it's going to stop, not at least in this generation.

"Meanwhile," Ma said, "your father needs to be going."

"Bye, Pa," I muttered.

"Bye, Son. I love you and pray that God will bless you."

"Yeah, I pray so myownself. Take care, Pa."

In the stillness I heard him move quietly away toward the willows that lined the creek, and when he was gone, Ma spoke again, "He's a good man, Hyrum. I am a lucky woman to be his wife, and you are a lucky boy to be his son. It seems that, in spite of our trials, we are very lucky people.

"Now, what are you and I going to do to solve that ridiculous bail? Banker Short is the only man in town who has access to that much money, and I don't know how to shake him loose."

"No he ain't, Ma."

"Isn't, Hyrum. Will you please learn to speak properly?"

"I'll try. Anyway, Ma, Old Man Aagard probably has lots more than two thousand."

"Why, you're right, he does. Many times that. If there was one man in town who could afford it, that one man would be Andrew Aagard. But you know how he feels about lending money. He just won't do it. Even your pa tried to borrow from him, figuring it was a fair return on the money he'd once lent Brother Aagard. Brother

Aagard didn't see it that way, however. Jons got lots of advice but no money."

"Yeah, Old Man Aagard's so tight he wouldn't pay a nickel to see a hundred-dollar earthquake. You should see the horse he's been having me use. Doggone thing's gaited like a hybrid buffalo. That's probably why he's trying so hard to get Jim to marry his daughter Ellen. Maybe he figures it will be cheaper to have her gone."

"Hyrum!"

"Well, maybe she eats a lot."

"She could eat all day and not eat as much as you do. Now stop carrying on so shamefully about Brother Aagard."

"Yeah, I reckon I ought to hold my tongue about him. He *did* hire me, and besides, maybe he will also be family one of these days, happen Jim gets his way."

"Ellen is a lovely girl. I hope it works out."

"So do I, Ma. It'd be nice to have money in the family for a change."

"Hyrum!"

I grinned. "Ma, you know I'm joshing. I wouldn't want another man's money. It'd sure be nice, though, if we could get a little of it for long enough to get me out of here."

"It would, but we can't—not from him *or* Brother Short."

"I'll say amen to that! Banker Short is worse than Old Man Aagard ever thought of being. He wouldn't loan a feller a nickel unless that same feller got all the angels in heaven to go on his note."

Ma giggled again. "Hyrum, you're just awful."

"I reckon," I said, feeling pleased to have been so judged. "It's too bad, Ma, that we just couldn't make a bet with those two and then see that they lost. Brother Short is a betting fool, and Old Man Aagard likes a little game of chance now and then himself. You recollect they were the first ones to line up after Pa announced he wanted to race his horse Ingersol."

"That's right, Hy," Ma replied, sounding like her thoughts were a thousand miles away. "That's right. Of course, the Lord doesn't hold with gambling, and you know how much trouble your pa got into with *his* bet."

"Yeah, but Pa still did it."

"Yes, he did. Much to his own sorrow. No, I don't believe gambling is the way. There must be something else . . .

"But don't you worry. I'll have you out of there before

Friendlessman can break you out, and that's a promise. Just relax, and maybe you can write a poem or two of your own on that wall while you're waiting."

I grinned again, Ma left, and I sat down with a pencil, ready to begin my career in creating fine literature.

The polygamist's wife was a honey,
Though she hardly had any money.
But she glowed like the sun,
Getting by on just none,
And the results were really quite funny.

Not bad literature, and prophetic too, though at the time I didn't know that at all.

16

Hattie Soderberg's Home—Fountain Green

Hattie Soderberg stood in the middle of her small log home, gazing about. What did she have that could possibly be worth two thousand dollars? Why, even the house was worth less than five hundred—at least Jons had paid much less than that for it just a couple of years before.

Two thousand dollars! Why had Marshal Clawson ever put that much bail on Hyrum? Meanness? No, that wouldn't be likely. Probably he thought Hyrum really did know where the gold was, and wanted to stop anyone from getting his bail. But that wouldn't stop her, Hattie knew. One way or another, she was going to raise that money—

"Ma?"

Startled, Hattie looked down at LaRue, who at seven was her youngest child.

"Ma, will Hyrum have to live in jail for the whole rest of his life?"

"No, silly," Lucille answered quickly, while Hattie's thoughts drifted back to her son. Lucille was ten and considered herself very mature. "He'll only have to stay until his trial. If he's found not guilty, they'll have to turn him loose. If they decide he's guilty, they'll shoot him."

"Will not," LaRue fumed.

"Will so! Won't they, Ma?"

Shocked, Hattie realized what the girls were arguing about, and instantly she lashed out at them. "Hush, you two! I won't hear such talk as that! Lucille, how can you bear to say such things?"

"Well, it's so, Ma. Pa said that's what happens to people who murder."

"Hyrum didn't murder!"

"I didn't say he did. I only said that's what would happen if they decided he was guilty."

"Well he *isn't!* I'll get him out on bail, and then he can go find out who killed that poor man. Maybe then the marshal will believe him."

"But Ma," Lucille questioned, "where are you going to get all that money?"

"I . . . I don't exactly know. Hyrum said something to me today, and I might have the beginnings of an idea. I'm going to go see Brother Short again in the morning, and—"

"Banker Short? " LaRue exclaimed. "But Ma, he's closer with a dollar than the satin on a can-can dancer's seat!"

"LaRue! Where do you hear such terrible things?"

"Hyrum taught me," LaRue answered proudly as she looked up and smiled. "He's my favoritest brother."

"He's your only brother," Lucille declared scornfully."

"He is not! There's Ernest and Johnny and Jim and Lyman and—"

"I meant *whole* brother, dummie. Half brothers don't count."

"They do too!"

"Betcha they don't."

"Betcha they do, don't they, Ma?"

"Of course they do," Hattie slowly answered.

Bets. The girls were fighting each other with bets. It *was* a powerful way to fight. That's what Hyrum had said. Bet and bet. And even though the Lord frowned on gambling, maybe . . . "Now, you two stop arguing and get on those dishes," Hattie ordered. "If I'm not back when you finish, then peel some potatoes for dinner. Please."

"Oh golly, Ma. Do we have to?"

Hattie Soderberg gave Lucille a withering gaze, and instantly the girl dropped her eyes. "Okay, okay. We'll do it. Will Pa be here?"

"No, he's gone into hiding again."

"Is he out in the desert?"

"No, I don't think so. He went to Sa— Listen, it doesn't matter where he is. Just remember him in your prayers."

"We will. Where are you going?"

"To see Brother Short," Hattie replied as she tied on her bonnet. "I may have one other stop as well. Now be good, and I'll see you in a little while."

And with that, Hattie Soderberg gathered up her skirts and her courage and determinedly set out for the bank.

17

The Bank—
Fountain Green

"Hattie . . . uh, Sister Soderberg, I think we've been through all this. Naturally I'm pleased to have our bank considered by the bishop's wife, but frankly, two thousand dollars is far more than we are prepared to go."

Hattie Soderberg gazed levelly into Harrison Short's eyes and didn't say anything.

"I . . . uh . . . I realize you want to get young Hyrum out of jail, and I believe I understand why. After all, I *am* a father, and . . . and . . . But my dear sister, where there's smoke there's fire, I always say, and well, perhaps he ought to stay right where he is until a judge hears all the facts—"

"Are you judging my son guilty, Brother Short?"

Suddenly the man coughed. "Of course not. I . . . uh . . . well, to be perfectly frank . . ."

"I wish you would be, sir."

"Uh . . . yes, of course. To be completely candid about it, you are too great a risk for us to make such a loan."

"You don't believe I would pay you back?"

"Well, actually I didn't say that. I have no doubt that you would. Or would intend to, at least. No. It's just that . . . that . . . well, you're in no position to do so. Your husband is in hiding, it's no secret that his affairs are in a shambles, and now that Hyrum is in jail you have no income at all. You have no collateral that is worth anything near two thousand dollars, and frankly, unless Hyrum does know where that gold is, I'm certain we would never see our money again. No, Sister Soderberg, the bank simply cannot extend itself in such an irresponsible manner."

"Very well." Hattie paused and gazed directly and openly into

Banker Short's eyes. "Then, Brother Short, I would like to propose a *different* sort of business arrangement."

Harrison Short, unused to women taking such a forward and direct approach, was suddenly cautious. It had been his experience, infrequent as it had been, that such women usually had something on their minds that would not be good for him. Furthermore, in spite of his caution, such women usually prevailed. Nevertheless, he *was* curious.

"Uh . . . what exactly did you have in mind?"

"A bet, Brother Short, I would like to make a small bet with you."

Harrison Short smiled. "Surely, Sister Soderberg, you cannot be serious. I'm a banker, not a gambler."

"Even on a sure thing?"

"Have you forgotten so quickly how near to disaster your husband came just a year ago?"

"No. Neither have I forgotten that you were first in line to place your bet against him."

Harrison Short started to turn red. "Well . . . uh . . . well, that bet did seem like a sure thing. However, it wasn't, and truthfully, madam, I have learned my lesson."

"I'm speaking of a *very* sure thing, Brother Short."

For a full sixty seconds Harrison Short, his gaze level and his expression blanker than that of a hard-boiled egg, stared at Hattie Soderberg, trying to make her drop her gaze and her confoundedly tempting conversation. But she wouldn't, and so at last he capitulated.

"What, exactly, is this 'sure thing'?"

"Brother Short, I would like to bet you that tomorrow morning, when you come to work, you will be wearing polka-dotted underwear."

"What?"

"Would you like me to repeat myself?"

"No," Harrison Short declared, settling back in his chair with a slight smile on his face. "You mean here, at the bank?"

"I do. Tomorrow."

"Uh . . . Sister Soderberg, I don't wear polka-dotted underwear. Ever!"

"You will tomorrow."

Harrison Short drummed his fingers together as he gazed past

Hattie Soderberg and out of the window. The day was nearly over, and he had to get down to the field to irrigate one of his farms, a farm upon which a payment was nearly due. There were also those headgates he had to buy and that new buggy his wife was pestering him about, the one that was going to cost even more money than had Andrew Aagard's . . .

"How much is the bet for?" he finally asked.

"Two thousand dollars."

"*Two thousand dollars!* But . . . but you have no collateral. How can you cover such a bet?"

"I'd say that was my problem, wouldn't you?"

"Not altogether. If I bet, and win, how can I expect to be paid? And when?"

"Tomorrow, when the bet is concluded. But Brother Short, you won't win."

"You seem very confident, Hattie. Is there some trick to this little wager? Some play on words or something?"

"None." Hattie smiled brightly. "I'm simply willing to wager two thousand dollars that tomorrow morning you will wear brightly colored polka-dotted underwear when you come to work."

Harrison Short now smiled himself. "Sister Soderberg, I hate to do this, but you have made the wager, and I think you must be taught the lesson. I will take your bet. Be prepared to pay."

Hattie Soderberg smiled sweetly as she rose to her feet. "I'll be prepared, Brother Short. But you'll be the one who pays. Good day."

"Good day, Sister Soderberg."

18

The Bank—Fountain Green—Again

Harrison Short couldn't concentrate on a thing. Work was piled a foot deep on his desk, and all he could do was look from the clock on the wall to the door and back again to the clock. His secretary kept looking back at him, expecting him to get at the dozens of tasks she had laid out for him to do. And he'd tried, he really had. But all he could do was pick at them, first one thing and then another, not really accomplishing anything toward the completion of any of them. All he could think of was his wager with Hattie Soderberg.

Nor had he slept much during the night. For hours he had gone over that bet in his mind, and nowhere could he find a flaw, a weakness, a way that Hattie could trick him. He couldn't imagine that it was an honest bet, for it was was too sure, too simple. Yet that was all he could discern about it. The whole thing *was* sure, and very, *very* simple.

Again he looked at the clock. Nearly ten-thirty. Of course, she hadn't set a time, but he did wish she'd hurry. Not that he really wanted to win, though indeed he did. But even more than that he was curious; he wanted to know how she would come up with that much money. Especially when she needed that exact sum so badly to get her son Hyrum out of jail.

And that brought up another thing. Was it possible, he wondered for maybe the thousandth time, that the boy *did* know the location of that lost mine? Under given conditions, he knew that all things were possible, even that. Could *that* be where Hattie planned on getting her money? After all, he'd checked on her the day before, and she *had* visited the jail. Maybe Hyrum had told her—

"Good morning, Harrison."

Startled, Harrison Short quickly lifted his eyes. "Hattie, I didn't see you come in."

"Yes." She smiled. "I noticed that you seemed rather distracted. And I understand perfectly. It *is* difficult to lose such a large sum of money. You *are* prepared to pay, I assume."

"Uh . . . Sister Soderberg," Harrison Short replied, making his voice as gentle as possible, "it's you who must be prepared to pay."

Hattie Soderberg laughed. "I fear you are mistaken, sir. You see, I wagered that you would wear colored polka-dotted underwear to the bank today; you did, and now you must pay."

Harrison Short was surprised but admitted to himself that he truly admired the woman's gall. "No, Sister Soderberg," he declared, "I did *not* wear polka-dotted underwear, and it is you who must pay."

"Sir," Hattie Soderberg asked, her face suddenly more serious, "are you certain?"

"Of course I'm certain! I'm wearing those . . . uh, my underwear, aren't I? My underwear is white!"

"Brother Short, I don't believe you."

"What? But . . . but . . . this is ridiculous! I say my underwear is all white, with no colorful polka-dots, and so it is. Now be a man and . . . I mean . . . uh, well, just pay the money!"

"I'm sorry, but with such a large sum at stake, I simply cannot accept your word. I'll have to ask for proof before I even consider concession."

"Proof? Woman, my word is as good as—"

"Proof, Brother Short. Proof, or immediate payment in full!"

"But . . . but . . . how . . ."

"Show me."

Harrison Short stared at the woman who stood calmly before him.

"Sh-show you?"

"That's right. I'm not asking you to remove your trousers entirely. Simply lower them for a few seconds. That will give me ample time to discern the truth."

"Well, I never! Sister Soderberg, such a request is . . . is downright *immoral!* I will do no such thing!"

"Then, sir, I must ask you to pay me immediately, for it is obvious that you *did* wear polka-dotted underwear, and that you fear—"

"I did not, I tell you! But neither will I—"

"Brother Short, folks do their banking here because, first, it is the only bank in town, and second, because for the most part, they trust and respect you. Now by nature I am a quiet woman, but if I get riled up, I will start screaming like a she-bear in a dog-fight. On the other hand, if you show me your underwear and it is white, I will pay you and be gone before you can brush off your shirt. What do you say, Brother Short? And remember, men come quickly when a lady starts screaming, and I have a voice you will think came out of a split cannon muzzle. I'll count to three; take your time.

"One."

Desperately Harrison Short looked about, but there was no help in sight, no help at all. Nor, thankfully, were there many people in the bank. The teller was busy with a man at the window, there were a couple of folks by the door, and his secretary, thank goodness, had her back to him. Oh, if only—

"Two."

A quick look into Hattie Soderberg's cold, level eyes told Harrison Short that he was only seconds away from terrible embarrassment and even possible social destruction. Nor would it matter that he was in the right. Folks would claim that he had taken advantage of a woman, that he had known all along of her plight, that she had been duped because of her desperation—

"Three."

With a grimace of pain, Harrison Short closed his eyes tightly, rose to his feet, and pulled his suspenders over his shoulders; then he unbuttoned his trousers, jerked them down to his knees, and just as quickly yanked them back up, trying his best as he did so to shut from his mind the sound of some commotion over by the door and the sight of Hattie Soderberg, smilingly watching his humiliation.

"There," he growled as he worked feverishly to redo his buttons, "are you satisfied?"

"I certainly am," Hattie Soderberg replied brightly. "And Brother Short, I apologize for doubting your word. You are truly an honest man. Here is your money."

Hattie Soderberg reached into her purse, pulled out a thick wad of bills, and placed them carefully on Harrison Short's desk. "If you would like I will count it out for you. However, I can assure you that the two thousand is all there."

Harrison Short slowly sank to his chair behind the massive desk, too stunned to speak. "N-n-no, that . . . uh . . . that won't be . . . be necessary. I . . . uh . . . I will take your word."

"Good. Thank you, Brother Short," Hattie Soderberg declared, and quickly she turned and started toward the door.

"Hattie . . . uh . . . Sister Soderberg?"

She paused and turned. "Yes?"

"I . . . well, I don't understand."

"What do you mean?"

"I mean you lost. But doggone it, how could you afford to do it? I don't understand."

"It's simple, Brother Short, I didn't lose."

Harrison Short slowly picked up the bills. "Sister Soderberg, this two thousand dollars says you did. Yesterday you came in here broke and desperately needing this exact amount of money. Today you happily give it away on a very foolish bet. That, sister, is called losing. It's also called insanity. To me, the entire episode is very confusing. Would you please be so kind as to explain it?"

Hattie Soderberg stepped back to the desk. "Well," she replied in a confidential tone, "since you asked so nicely, I will. And Harrison, I promise I will also keep it quiet. I can't guarantee the silence of the others, but you have my word concerning myself."

"O-others?"

"Well, other, I mean. You see, I bet you two thousand dollars that you would wear brightly colored polka-dotted underwear this morning; you showed me your white drawers, and I won."

"Lost."

"Won. Did you happen to notice Brother Andrew Aagard?"

"Well, yes I did see him. But—"

"Did you see him fall to the floor in a faint?"

"Faint? No, by thunder, I—"

"Brother Short, last evening I bet Andrew Aagard *four* thousand dollars that you would pull down your trousers in front of me, right here in the bank, sometime before noon. He laughed, told me you were too pompous ever to do it, and made the bet. Yet you did, he fainted—with laughter, I think—and I won."

And with that, Hattie Soderberg smiled sweetly, gathered her skirts up, turned, and left the bank, its dazed owner, and the still gasping but slowly reviving Andrew Aagard altogether behind. She was on her way to the marshal's office, and that poor soul was about to be as shocked as the rest of them. And that little detail didn't bother Hattie Soderberg one tiny bit.

19

The Lane—
Fountain Green

"It's a lovely evening."

"Yes it is, my dear. And it is doubly so because you are here to share it with me."

Ida Mae smiled into the gathering darkness and shivered a little with the excitement she was feeling. Felix Friendlessman stood beside her, very near, and she had never felt quite so conscious of a man's presence.

"Thank you," she replied, almost whispering. "You do say the sweetest things."

"My dear," the man stated firmly, "I would never say them if they were not altogether true." Then, without warning, he placed his arm around Ida Mae's waist and drew her close.

Ida Mae gasped a little with surprise, and suddenly she was aware of the desire she felt to have this man hold her even more tightly and say more of those sweet things to her. She had never had such an experience, not even with Hyrum, and now this man—who was much older and much more polished and refined than Hyrum—was giving her the attention she had always craved. It was exciting, it made her feel like a woman, and with a start she decided that all those things equaled love. She was falling in love with this tall, dark-haired man from back east.

"There," he suddenly whispered, pointing with his free hand, "there was a meteorite, a shooting star. Did you see it?"

Ida Mae gazed up into the dark, star-filled sky. "I didn't. I'm sorry, I was—"

"No, don't apologize. Just watch for another. It is said that if one makes a wish during the fraction of a moment when such phenomena are visible, then that wish will surely come to pass."

"But how can a person wish so fast?"

"Simple, my dear. Have the wish in mind, think of it constantly, and wait for another meteorite to show. Shall we do it?"

"Oh, yes. And I have just the wish in mind."

"Tell me."

"Oh, no," Ida Mae declared. "That would be bad luck. Even *I* know that."

"Well, do as you please. But since I don't believe in such things as good and bad luck, I'll tell you *my* wish."

"Would you? Really?"

"Of course. My wish is that you and I might go on, like this, forever."

"Oh, Felix . . ."

"Don't say anything, Ida Mae. Just think about what I've said, and let us both hope for another shooting star."

Eagerly Ida Mae stared up into the darkness, her mind floating gleefully and her whole being almost dizzy with excitement. In the grass around them a thousand crickets sang their own love songs, while above them a bat flitted by, dancing in a manner that was suddenly terribly beautiful. Somewhere in the darkness a screen door slammed, there was a distant murmuring of laughter, and Ida Mae would have sworn she had never been so happy.

Almost reflexively she snuggled a little closer, and suddenly she was in the man's arms and their lips were together and she had never before experienced *anything* so wonderful, so breathtaking!

"Felix," she whispered when at last they separated, "I . . . I can hardly speak. What you have said is . . . is . . . well, I don't have the words . . ."

"Then hush," the man declared quietly. "Don't speak. Just think of my everlasting love and know that my coming absence will give me greater pain than I can endure."

"Absence?"

"Why yes, didn't I tell you? Very early in the morning I must leave on business, and I will be gone for several weeks. There is a chance that I will be gone even longer."

"Oh Felix . . ."

"I understand, my dear. I feel the same, and my poor heart is nearly broken with grief. I would almost rather die than be separated from your sweet presence. It is just that this trip has been arranged for so long, and it is so vitally important to *our* future . . ."

Ida Mae's mind whirled. Why, this was like a dream, but it was happening so fast, so very fast. Still, what harm could there be in that? He was such a good and sweet man, and he made her feel so, well, so *special*. Yes, she *did* love him, and would gladly wait for him always.

"There is also the matter of my dear grandmother," Friendlessman continued. "She is gravely ill, and there is no one left but myself. I must see to her."

"Oh dear, I do hope that it isn't serious!"

"Well, I'm afraid that it is. Very serious, in fact. Nevertheless, I have considered staying because of you—"

"No, you must go to the dear old soul!"

"But Ida Mae—"

"Yes, Felix," Ida Mae declared firmly, "you must! I would expect nothing less of such a dear man. And don't worry about me. I am well able to care for myself, and I will wait eagerly, no matter how long you are gone from me."

Felix Friendlessman held her tightly once more. "My dear, sweet Ida Mae, how like an angel you are!"

They kissed again, and then Felix Friendlessman drew away. "My dear," he said sadly, "I really must be going, but know this: I will return."

"I . . . I will be waiting." Ida Mae whispered.

Friendlessman took two steps away and then suddenly turned, almost as though he had forgotten and suddenly remembered something. "Ida Mae, there is one other thing. I have almost concluded the arrangements for securing the release of young Soderberg."

Ida Mae started, thinking suddenly of Hyrum. It was strange that she had hardly thought of him since she had been with Felix. Yet now that she did, there was such a feeling of guilt—

"There has been a great deal of expense for me in doing this, my dear, for I have hired several men to break him out during the darkness tonight. Yet still—"

"Break him out? But . . . but I thought he would be going to court."

"Ida Mae, if he goes to court, he will spend the rest of his life in prison, for he is guilty as sin. Therefore, I have encouraged him to flee."

"To flee? But—"

"My dear, I have done this because of his obvious guilt. Still, he was only eleven when he made this terrible mistake, and I do not think he should be forced to pay for it all the rest of his life. Therefore, I have convinced him to leave immediately upon his release, with the hope that the marshals will let the matter drop. I hope," Friendlessman continued gently, "that it will not be important to you that you don't see him. Possibly for quite some time?"

"N-no," Ida Mae stammered, "no, of course it won't."

"Good. I have told Hyrum to return to his sheep camp in . . . in . . . oh my goodness, I seem to have forgotten . . ."

"The Uintahs," Ida Mae declared helpfully.

"Yes, yes, I knew that, but I have forgotten exactly where . . ."

"Last time Hyrum and I talked," Ida Mae volunteered, "the camp was on the Strawberry Flats."

"That's right. That is near where he allegedly found the gold, isn't it? Oh, if only he had enough decency to admit his guilt. It would make things so much more easy. For him, I mean."

"Yes, I feel the same, poor boy. I can't imagine why I ever thought that he and I . . ."

"Now Ida Mae, don't say those things. You were innocent. How could you know what he was really like? Besides, I am certain that there are many qualities about him that are good and decent, qualities that a pure young lady such as yourself might find irresistible."

"Oh Felix, you are so sweet to defend him as you do."

"Well," Friendlessman smiled, "my motives are not entirely selfless. Quite honestly, I am thinking primarily of you, for I know how close the two of you have been. Ida Mae, that is why I wish to be of help."

"Thank you, my dear."

"You are most welcome."

"Will . . . will you get in trouble for breaking him out of jail?" Ida Mae asked fearfully.

"Possibly, but I hope that no one will find out I have been involved. I have considered meeting with the marshal and the justice of the peace, but frankly, I do not think they would understand. Anyway, before morning . . . Well, needless to say, plans have been made."

"But you do not mind taking this . . . this risk?"

"Ida Mae, how could I mind? Such a risk is as nothing so long as it makes you happy and so long as ultimate justice is served."

Friendlessman smiled sincerely, and Ida Mae beamed with pride that she should be privileged to know and to be loved by such a fine man.

"Uh . . . do you suppose Hyrum might move his sheep camp in the near future?" Friendlessman suddenly asked.

"Why yes. In fact, I am certain that it has already been moved. Hyrum told me that Zene would be—"

"Zene?"

"Yes. Zene Hill, the herder. Hyrum is only the camp tender. Anyway, Zene was heading the herd up toward Wolf Creek Pass, and, according to Hyrum, they will summer in the Grandaddy Basin."

"That's right," Friendlessman said thoughtfully, forgetting for the moment that Ida Mae was even there. "That's what he told Doolin, as well. But there is no doubt that the gold would be lower down, near where he was camped. That's where we must concentrate our efforts—"

"Gold? Efforts? But Felix, I don't understand. Your grandmother . . . she is . . ."

Quickly and sincerely Felix Friendlessman laughed. "My dear, you are delightful! How quick your humor is. I see now that I must look forward to a lifetime of teasing. But, more importantly, you will never know how it thrills me to see that you are so interested in my aged grandmother. Thank you, my darling!

"Now truly I must be off. But first, I would give you this small trinket as a memento of my love."

Ida Mae stared as Felix Ethelbert Friendlessman took her hand, held it out, and slipped a small ring onto her finger. "There," he said. "Do you like it?"

"Oh, yes . . . yes!"

"Good. May you think of me each time you see it on your finger. Now *au revoir,* my sweet, until we are together in each other's arms again."

Ecstatic and filled with sweet dreams concerning the nebulous future, Ida Mae kissed Felix to seal the promise of the ring and then stood dreamily as he vanished into the darkness.

"Oh my dearest," she murmured softly, "I love you so, and I promise that I will wait until—"

"Ida! Ida Mae! You'll never believe what happened this afternoon!"

Spinning around, Ida Mae was startled to see her brother Curly come bounding across the fence toward her. "My goodness, Curly, you startled me."

"You think I startled you, wait until you hear about Hyrum and his Ma and Brother Short. That'd startle anybody!"

"Hyrum? Brother Short the banker?"

"Yeah. I can't wait to tell Pa, this is so good. Hyrum's Ma bet Brother Short that he would take down his britches or something, and Brother Aagard was there, and I don't know how it all worked out, but anyway ol' Short done it and she got tons of money from Old Man Aagard and she bailed Hyrum out of jail and he's gone and—"

"Hyrum's gone?" Ida Mae asked quickly, her breath catching.

"I'll say. Gone as the wild geese in winter. Would I like to have been there in that bank."

But Ida Mae was no longer listening. She was hurrying down the lane, searching vainly for Felix Friendlessman, hoping to prevent the true love of her life from wasting his time, his efforts, and his money to secure the release of an evil and unrepentant boy who was no longer even around.

20

Granary and Jailhouse—Fountain Green

"Silvertip, you idiot, stop whistling!"

The outlaw Silvertip looked up from where he was working on the rigging of the harnesses. "Ah, Boss," he moaned, "my ma always told me to whistle while I worked. She was real smart, and—"

"Well don't do it now, you imbecile. Why do you think we're doing this in the dark? We're trying to keep people from knowing about us. Do you suppose your whistling helps?"

Silvertip sat in the moonlight, surrounded by harnesses and the running gear of a wagon, and shrugged. "Beats me," he replied honestly. "But say, Boss, if I can't whistle, what *can* I do?"

Jack Moore looked up at the star-filled sky as if praying for divine relief. Then, without waiting for such aid to manifest itself, he growled, "I don't know, but I'm fairly sure you'll think of something." Then he spun about and stalked toward the granary where the others were planning.

"Did you get him to shut up?" he was asked as he stepped through the door.

Moore looked at the questioner, the man named Felix Friendlessman. "You can't hear him whistling, can you?"

All listened, and suddenly Blue John threw his hat onto the floor. "You're right. He ain't whistling. Now he's out there singing 'Streets of Laredo.' I'm telling you, Boss, that man ain't altogether here, if you know what I mean."

"I do," Moore answered. "Trouble is, I just couldn't help myself from bringing him along."

"But Moore," Loose-lip Lundstrum added, "we've got troubles enough without a man like that to ruin it for us."

"Don't I know it," Moore replied sourly. "If you'll recollect, this wasn't exactly my deal. Nor did I ask Silvertip to come into it. That there was Friendlessman's doing."

"Yes, it was," Friendlessman stated quietly. "He was the only way I had of getting to you and Blue John."

"I understand that," Moore agreed. "I also understand how terrible hard it is to get shut of somebody like Silvertip. Yes sir, especially when that somebody looks at you with eyes that would make a kicked hound feel happy and asks only to warm his hands in the flickering warmth of your companionship. Yes sir, Mr. Friendlessman, I understand fully why Silvertip is here. I just don't like it.

"Nor do I like taking on Bishop Jons Soderberg again. I've had enough dealings with that man and his kith and kin to last me a lifetime. That feller's got him a purely direct connection to the powers of heaven, I swear it, and a man can't fight that for sour apples. When I heard we was after ol' Soderberg's son, I voted to drop the whole idea and go to barbering out in California or to butchering up in Oregon or Canada."

"But Moore," little Doolin whined, "think of all that *gold!*"

"I have thought of it, a whole lot, and the odds in favor of us seeing one ounce of it are poor as a desert grasshopper."

"You think that," Doolin argued, "because you didn't see any of the gold. I *did!* That kid had it, and he knows where the lost mine is located."

"Maybe, maybe not. But you fellers are getting set to spring that jail and unleash a storm that'll make a Wyoming Blue Norther look like a Saturday afternoon picnic. You'll have the law after you; you'll have the Mormons after you; the good Lord will probably join in with a few of His angels, happen He still favors the bishop as much as He did a year ago; you'll be hip-pocket high in angry Indians; and ol' Caleb Rhoades will probably figure in there as well.

"What I'm saying, boys, is that come this time tomorrow, all them forces will be snapping at your tails like a trapped weasel. No sir, gold or not, Mr. Doolin, I'm not altogether sure this gambit is worth the risk."

"Are you through, Jack?"

All eyes in the room turned toward the still form of Felix Friendlessman.

"Yeah, I reckon, other than to say that I got a bad feeling about things. This is going to end in a whole lot of pain and trouble, and you all will remember that I said so. That's all."

"Good. You might be interested in knowing that I heard about your encounter with the man in Vernal who claimed to be Porter Rockwell. I also know about last year's posse and the promise they made you out at the Roost. Something about sending you dancing up the golden stairs on the end of a rope, as I recall. Seems to me, Jack, that your choices are most severely limited. Need I go on?"

Slowly Moore shook his head.

"Good. Then I recommend we get on with our plans. As soon as Silvertip has the harnesses rigged to the running gear and the team harnessed, then we go. Blue John, you work the horses. You're the best man with teams I ever saw. The rest of you, pay attention. The old jail was dragged to that spot by the creek. It's made out of logs, and the folks who dragged it left their iron hoops buried in the wood. We will use those hoops the same as they did, for our ropes and chains. With all of us as well as the team pulling suddenly and together, the jail should come apart quite easily.

"Moore, when it does, you get inside and throw down on young Soderberg. Pop him on the head if you must, but no matter what else, he cannot be allowed to escape or to shout for help, nor do I want him hurt badly. If we can get away with no more noise than the breaking down of the jail, then the lead we build will be significant and should be sufficient.

"Now, are there any questions?"

"Yeah," Blue John said quietly, "I've got one or two. The Boss mentioned the law and the Mormons, and I'm altogether as worried as he is. Clawson's not too hot, but I truly fear that bishop. He ain't all human."

Friendlessman smiled coldly. "So the Great Blue John is afraid."

At those words Blue John stiffened, his fingers curled above the butt of his pistol, and there was a sudden stillness in the room as all eyes went to him and his gun. "Friendlessman," he whispered, "I don't take that from *any* man, let alone a city-slicker dude!"

There was instant silence. Blue John was ready to draw, and he would have, too, except that when Friendlessman's left elbow jerked and he started, he suddenly found himself staring into the yawning mouth of a left-handed .44 that had come from nowhere into Friendlessman's hand. His own pistol, meanwhile, was still only half-way out of its holster, and so Blue John let it slide slowly back down.

"Nor should you," Friendlessman replied, still smiling icily as though nothing had happened. "My point, Blue John, is that you of all people should have no need to fear."

"What . . . what's that supposed to mean?"

"Just this. Hebron Clawson is inept, and from him we have little to fear. Besides, Loose-lip here will stay behind and plant plenty of seeds of cautious wisdom in the marshal's ear. That should take care of him. Nor, for several reasons, do we need to fear the Mormons."

"Why not?"

"First, the bishop is in hiding. He's out of it. Second, I have made great strides in developing a, shall we say, romantic association with young Soderberg's girl. Ida Mae is naive and innocent, very lovely, and firmly convinced that I am breaking the young man out in order to save him from certain conviction. I am more than confident that, come morning, she will explain all that to the proper church authorities as well as to Soderberg's family. They will merely sit by, then, and wait for all this to blow over and for young Soderberg to return.

"Any more questions?"

"I have one," Doolin whined. "How are we going to split the gold?"

Friendlessman gazed levelly at Doolin. "Why," he replied softly, "I'd say that would depend on who does what during the recovery of it and who is left among us after it is recovered. Wouldn't you agree, Mr. Doolin?"

Hastily Doolin nodded, and shortly thereafter the small group was moving through the darkness toward the rear of the tiny jail. Quietly they moved through the creek and up to the building, and there Blue John turned his team, stretched out the harnesses, and silently went to work.

The tugs from the horse collars and hames were connected to the singletrees, which, of course, were attached to the doubletree, and that was firmly in place atop the tongue of the running gears. These, consisting of the front wheels and axle stolen from a heavy wagon that had been found nearby, were used to secure the chains.

Quickly Blue John looped the chains over the axle and back to the iron hoops imbedded in the rear wall of the jail. Silvertip, Friendlessman, Loose-lip, and Doolin worked rapidly to secure their ropes, which were then checked for tightness. Moore pulled his pistol and made ready, and suddenly Silvertip broke the silence.

"Boss," he said innocently.

"Quiet," Jack Moore whispered angrily.

"I'm sorry," the big man whispered back. "But Boss, I don't like this at all. That boy in there's a good boy, and besides, his pa's the bishop in these parts. You know it don't do no good to go against the likes of them, what with all that happened last year, and—"

"Will you shut up!" Friendlessman hissed. "Boys, get ready!"

They all did, including the reluctant Silvertip, and then the signal was given.

As one the team snapped the harnesses tight and the men on their mounts raked them with spurs, sending the animals lunging ahead. The old jail skidded slightly, creaked, and groaned, and with a loud tearing sound the rear wall burst out and disintegrated. The horses plunged forward, carried along by their own momentum, and Jack Moore, ignoring his struggling partners, stepped through the dust and into the sagging remnants of the jail.

"All right, Soderberg," he growled, "Get outa that sack, and . . ."

And for the second time in not too many more days than that, Jackson T. Moore found himself holding a loaded gun on an empty room. Hyrum V. Soderberg was long and permanently gone.

21
The Sorenson Home—Fountain Green

"Ida Mae!" I whispered loudly.

Hearing no answer, I stood silently outside Ida Mae's window, wondering what in Job's turkey I was doing there. I'd set out for the herd after saying good-bye to Ma and the girls, thinking to get back on my job with Zene and work from there on who killed Enock Rhoades. But I'd felt so bad about my rudeness to Ida Mae that I had doubled back so I could see her and apologize and maybe warn her concerning just what kind of a miserable rascal that Friendlessman feller was. But now it was the middle of the night, and I had already tossed two pebbles against her window besides calling her name, and nothing had happened. And with my luck, nothing would. Not unless I woke her pa or maybe her brother Curly and got shot for my efforts. I'll tell a man, I was feeling lower'n a snake's jaw in a wagon track.

"Ida Mae," I whispered once more, just for luck. Still nothing happened, and I was just turning away when I saw the curtain move at her window. Then the sash lifted, and Ida Mae pushed her head out from between the curtains.

"Who is it?" she whispered, straining to see down into the darkness.

"It's me," I said, stepping out from the haw-bushes where I'd been hiding. "Hy."

"Oh."

Well, there wasn't much excitement in her voice, but I'm the eternal optimist. Pa always told me to look on the bright side of things, and I did then. She might not have been very enthused to see me, but at least she hadn't called me names or pulled her head back in or yelled for her pa.

I was just gathering my thoughts to apologize when she suddenly disappeared from the window. Not knowing what she was up to, my mind instantly began telling my heart what a fool I'd been, and I was having a fairly major battle with myself about whether or not to flee from the premises when I heard the front door creak open.

After what seemed an eternity but which was probably not more than five or ten seconds, I saw Ida Mae's form beside the lilac bush near her door. With one hand she motioned for me to be quiet and with the other she signaled for me to follow, and like a lonely little lost puppy, I hastened to obey.

"Ida Mae," I stammered when we had reached the corner of the tack shed, "I . . . uh . . . I came to say I was sorry."

"I heard you were out of jail."

"Yeah, Ma got me out."

"I heard about that, too. The whole town's laughing about what your Mother did to Brother Short, but I think it was just awful! What a horrible way to get money! I don't understand how a woman could *do* such a thing."

"Now hold on, Ida Mae. You're talking about my ma now, and I won't stand for it!"

"Well, I'm sorry it is your mother, but I *still* don't understand how she could do that. Besides being lewd, it was an immoral way to get money—"

"Listen," I interrupted, feeling all sorts of emotions that I was not liking at all. "That was a deal where nobody got hurt. Brother Short is two thousand dollars richer for dropping his trousers and is altogether more popular than he's been in years. And Brother Aagard was at our home all evening, laughing his head off. He told Ma that he'd gladly give another four thousand to see two or three others in this community with *their* pompous purity let down.

"Finally, Ma has already told Brother Aagard that she will give at least the two thousand back the minute I appear in court for my trial. Brother Short has finally decided to become friends with Brother Aagard and will likely give him back his money as well. So you see, everything *is* working out for the good.

"Besides," I continued, searching frantically for some way to get at least equal footing in our conversation, "happen it was up to you to get me out, how would *you* have raised the money?"

"Truthfully," Ida Mae replied scornfully, "*I'd* have let you stay. From what Felix has told me about poor Enock Rhoades and his murder, you deserve everything you're getting."

Well, by this time I was more frustrated than a starving sparrow watching an empty wormhole. As Ida Mae gathered her shawl even more closely about her shoulders, I desperately tried again.

"Dad-gum it, Ida Mae, I told you I was *innocent*. I never even knew a murder had been committed until this week!"

"Yes." Ida Mae responded, looking off down the lawn as though I was not even there, "Felix was right, as usual. He told me that a sure sign of guilt was when a person kept bringing up his own innocence. Hyrum, you surely do keep digging yourself into a deeper hole."

"Ida Mae, you're daft. *You* brought it up, not me. And besides, that Friendlessman feller ain't altogether clean hisownself."

"Hyrum, don't you talk against that man!"

"Somebody's got to. I'm telling you, Ida Mae, there's something about Friendlessman that smells fishier than Friday in St. Patrick's parish."

"That shows all you know! Why, he told me that he's been working for days on how to get you out of jail—he was planning on doing it tonight, a little later on. I've tried to find him and tell him ever since I heard you were out, but I couldn't. He's off somewhere putting himself at great personal risk and wasting his money to secure your release. And a thankless task *that* will be, the poor soul."

Well, I was getting plumb sick to my stomach, and I was starting to feel mean again. I knew why Friendlessman wanted me out of jail, but how on earth was I ever going to convince Ida Mae of what I knew? I mean, it's bad enough when a feller's girl tells him that his mother is lewd, but then to have her fall head over heels for a purely dispicable excuse for a man, well, that's *really* tough.

"Ida Mae, I have a thing or two to say that you need to hear, and I don't want you to take it wrong. I ain't saying it because I'm jealous, though I'll own up square to the fact that I am. But mostly I'm telling you this because I like you. A lot."

"It hadn't better be about Felix."

"Well, as a matter of fact, it is. Ida Mae—"

"Hyrum, I won't listen to this!"

"Ida Mae, have I ever lied to you? Have I? You know doggone well I ain't never told you nothing false before. Not ever!"

"Oh, but you have terrible grammar!"

"Maybe. But my heart's clean and innocent, which is more than I can say for Friendlessman, no matter how fine he can speak."

"Hyrum, I'm warning you!"

"Hear me out, will you? Please?"

"Well . . ."

"Please? Just for a minute?"

"Oh all right, but hurry!"

"Thank you. Ida Mae, I have proof, confidential but reliable, that Friendlessman is pure crooked. For honesty he's ganter than a bottleflied colt, and he's tied in with some thoroughly mean hombres, including a Mr. Doolin, who happens to be the man who tried to steal my gold and who got me arrested."

"Which you thoroughly deserved," Ida Mae declared. "You'd best put up that proof you mentioned."

"Well, uh, I can't," I mumbled, mentally cursing Ernest's dumb oath. "I made a blood vow never to tell how I came about that knowledge, and—"

"And you expect me to believe *that?*"

"I'm hoping you will. Ida Mae, there's more sand in one of Ma's biscuits than there is in Friendlessman's craw. I'm telling you, he is purely a cowardly crook, as is Doolin and who knows how many others. Why, they've even got old Loose-lip Lundstrum tied in with them."

"Hyrum, I won't listen to another word of this. I've never heard such a rambling pack of lies. Felix warned me the other day that you'd try to do this, and now I can see how truly wise he is. And mentioning Loose-lip isn't going to make me believe you either. You *know* I don't care for that man, so naturally you'd throw his name in for effect."

"Ida Mae," I pleaded, "it's all true! They figured on busting me out of jail so they could drag me into the mountains and have me show 'em where Enock Rhoades's gold is hidden. Happen I couldn't take 'em to it, which I can't, they'd likely kill me."

"Oh, Hyrum, stop being so . . . so melodramatic! Murder you? What a lot of nonsense."

Well, I could see that I wasn't making much headway, and even worse, I could see that Ida Mae had been stricken harder than I'd thought. I don't know what Friendlessman had, besides that he could color up the facts redder'n a Navajo blanket, but it surely did seem to be what it took. I'd never seen anyone so confounded moonstruck in my life as Ida Mae Sorenson. Maybe it was time I tried coming into this from another angle.

"Ida Mae, I . . . uh . . . I thought, well, I had it in mind that you was my girl."

"Whatever gave you *that* idea?"

Brother, talk about a cold, cold voice. Ten minutes with her and a feller'd end up with frostbite or his death of pneumonia. Still, I'd gone too far to back off now. Frostbite or not, for her sake I had to go through with it.

"Well, we've had a lot of talks about it, and a couple of times we've even kissed."

"That, Mr. Soderberg, was long before I knew what you were really like."

"Ida Mae," I growled, "I told you before, and I'm telling you for the last time, *I'm innocent!* How in blue blazes could I have—"

"Don't you swear in front of me!"

"Oh, for crying out loud, that ain't swearing!"

"Isn't!"

"Yeah, *isn't!*"

"And stop shouting!"

"Well you . . ." I stormed, finally and most completely losing my temper, "I ain't *shouting!* But I am most assuredly ready to start! You . . . you're ornerier'n a rat-tailed horse in fly-time. I sincerely wanted to warn you, I truly did. I know what Friendlessman is like while you don't, and let me tell you, he's so crooked you could twist him into the ground like a corkscrew. But no, you won't listen! Instead, you fight me, and all I get is . . . *this!* As far as I'm concerned, you deserve that miserable misbegotten whelp of a hydrophoby skunk. More and more it's beginning to look like you and he are two of a kind! Good night!"

Well, Ida Mae gave me a look that was as cold as the stare of a gila monster, gathered up her gown or whatever it was she was wearing, and headed back to the house. Me, I strode back myownself, grabbed the ground-hitched reins of Old Man Aagard's sway-backed cayuse, scrambled into the saddle, and spurred the horse hard down the dark road.

Blast! Why on earth had I *ever* thought that little gal liked me? Sometimes it seemed like I didn't have the brains the good Lord gave a stinkbug. Trouble was, I truly did love Ida Mae. She was a fine girl, and I loved her in spite of everything she'd said and done. I'll say this, it surely was discouraging.

22

Hyrum's Bedroom Loft—Fountain Green

That ribbon of road stretched off into the warm June moonlight, and I followed it blindly, not even thinking about which way I was going. I was churned up inside worse than a fresh batch of Ma's butter, and that was some churned up. Fact is, I felt awful. It truly looked like everything was over between Ida Mae and me.

Like I've said before, that little lady meant a great deal to me, falling only behind my family in that regard. Nor do I think that's much different from folks everywhere.

Pa says that when kids start to become adults, they fall in and out of love pretty regular. It's painful, but Pa says it's necessary, for that is how a person discovers what trusting means and who truly and completely loves whom.

Once that discovery is made, trust is established, two folks pair off and get married, and the family as the point of reference—something that I think I mentioned earlier—is established once again. Then those two who are now joined together can sort of let their hair down in front of each other. They each see the other's true person, and they love and trust in spite of all the superficial daily annoyances.

Then when babies come along, they too feel the trust, and as they grow they always know there is a least *one* place where they can find security and support.

As far as Ida Mae and I were concerned, I suppose I was still learning who really loved me and who I could trust. But now I was in misery, for all along I'd had such good feelings about her. I'd been certain as death and tithing that I loved her, and here I'd learned that I couldn't trust her at all! She'd turned against me like I was kith and kin of Governor Lilburn W. Boggs (the good Christian gentleman who had issued his extermination order against all Mormons in Missouri, back in 1838), and that was about the same as saying I was linked up personal with the devil. It made a feller want to lie down and lick his wounds, it pained that bad.

"Well, ol' hoss," I growled, "I reckon you and I ain't needed too badly here in Fountain Green. Not after tonight. Suppose we take these supplies Zene asked for and get on up to the herd—"

And that was when I realized I had accidentally ridden home. I hadn't meant to. I'd meant to leave town and strike out for Zene Hill's sheep camp up in the Uintahs. But now that I was home, the thought of my feather tick was too much, and I couldn't turn away from it.

Of course, the house was dark, for it was near two in the morning. I put my old horse in the corral, took off his saddle, and rubbed him down, and then I headed for a few hours of real comfortable sleep.

Once on the porch I carefully removed my boots and then quiet-like I opened the door and stepped into the inky blackness of the kitchen. Quietly I closed the door and latched it, and carefully I threaded my way past the table and chairs and over to my ladder. With my boots under my arm I went up and into my loft, careful to make no sound that would disturb Ma or the girls, who would be sleeping below.

For a moment I thought of lighting a candle or lantern, decided there wasn't any point in it, stripped off my duds, and hit my knees for a quick good-night to the Lord.

I reckon it could be said that I was a praying man, for Ma and Pa have taught me well, and off and on through my young life I've had to lean pretty heavily on the powers of the Almighty. I believe in prayer, I've had many prayers answered, and yet lately I'd noticed that my prayers were getting scarcer'n ducks in a desert, and they were mighty thin on content when I did say them. Seemed like I was just too all-fired discouraged and there were too many things going on against me for me to take the time to pray.

I did pray at night, I mean usually, but every time I did, it made me think of something Pa had once told me. "Prayers," he'd said, "are like telegrams. Most folks send 'em at night so's they can get the low rate. The Good Lord probably answers them the same."

Gave a body something to think about, it did, especially happen he was interested in a real powerful answer. But that night I wasn't, though I surely should have been. I was just miserable and tired and feeling worse than a poorly sheared sheep about my fight with Ida Mae. So I whipped through my prayer, pulled back the covers on that big wide feather tick, crawled in on the side where I always slept, twisted my pillow until it was comfortable, snuggled down under Ma's soft sheets with my back to most of the bed, closed my eyes, and—

Suddenly a soft arm came out of nowhere and snaked itself around my shoulders, and instantly an altogether too feminine body snuggled up against my backside!

Well, for an eternity or so I froze up solid as Nephi Robertson's stock pond in January. Then a soft and sleepy voice that I'd never heard before started whispering into my ear, and I realized that I was in real trouble.

"Hi, sweetheart," this altogether feminine voice purred, and I could feel an awful lot of warm breath in my ear and on the back of my neck. "I thought you weren't coming over."

Well, I was speechless as an Egyptian mummy. It was obvious as little red apples on a big green tree that I wasn't alone in my bed, and I should have been, I truly should have been!

"I'm glad you came," she went on. "This loft is so awful—tight and cramped and untidy. It just *isn't* what I'd expected. I'm so glad you're here to make it comfortable."

Well, saying such things about my room was plain rude, and that made me mad! That there was a fine loft, with the best fixings Ma and Pa could provide. Besides that, it was *mine,* and I wasn't about to let no female hussy go running it down.

I was just ready to tell her, too, but then she kissed me on my neck, and of a sudden rooms and rudeness were altogether forgotten. I was out of that feather bed faster'n chain lightning with a link snapped.

"Wh-wh-who are you?" I whispered haltingly.

"Why dear, I'm your new wife."

I caught my breath. "L-lady, I ain't got no wife, new or otherwise!"

There was a instant of total silence, and then that loft of mine was pierced with the doggonedest scream a body ever heard. It was so loud it would've driven a whole pack of wild wolves straight to suicide. The way she was carrying on, I even gave suicide some thought myownself.

Instead, however, I controlled my shaking fingers, struck a

match, and tried to light my lantern, and all the while that lady was screaming like a scrub calf caught in a briar patch.

I finally got the lantern lit and dropped the chimney down, and my chin near broke a hole in the floor, it hit it so hard.

There was this woman, a total stranger, kneeling in the middle of *my* bed, with *my* covers wrapped up around her, screaming that *I'd* attacked her.

Well, I saw and heard that, saw that her eyes had saucered up big as barn owls, saw the cavernous pit where her mouth had probably once resided, saw that she was still yelping like a run-over sheepdog, and suddenly I realized that I was standing there all exposed in my red long-johns, the ones that had one of the rear drop-seat buttons missing. Worse, I was gracing the vision of some strange and likely evil woman whose morals weren't no straighter'n a willow in a high wind.

Quick as I could, I grabbed up my covers and threw them around my unclothed form. Then I realized that the screaming had grown abruptly worse.

I looked, and discovered to my horror that the quilt I had whipped around me was the self-same quilt that had originally been covering the frantically screaming woman. Now, of course, she was screaming more but was covered with a great deal less, and that was a purely naked fact.

For an instant I considered sharing my quilt, for from the sudden way she had huddled down she did appear to be mighty cold. However, right off I knew that would never work, not her and me together under the same quilt again. No sir, Ma hadn't raised no foolish children that lived in *my* loft. Happen I tried that, I reckoned there'd be a lot worse than screaming going on. Why, I'd be about as welcome under that quilt as a polecat at a Sunday school picnic.

So, being the wise and true gentleman that I am, I settled on the next-best course of action. I picked up my trousers and started climbing into them. That done, I figured on giving my quilt back to the screaming stranger, and then we'd both be happy.

I'd have done it, too, but just as I was fixing to do so, I saw Ma come churning up the ladder with her broom in her hand. The sight so unnerved me that I dropped the quilt, and quicker'n scat that woman was off the bed and onto the floor, with them covers up and around her once more.

By cracky, I thought, that woman could certainly galvinate.

She'd got under that quilt faster'n a lizard off a hot rock. I'd not seen anything move so swift and shameless since Euphemistic Lynn Barnes had gone to treat his saddle gall in the dark and got the undiluted sheep dip out of the medicine chest instead of the soothing, comforting bear grease.

Then that woman, now that she was once more covered, commenced to screaming again, and I decided that her resemblance to Euphemistic was even greater than I'd first supposed. My recollection was that he'd hollered some too.

"What is it?" Ma gasped as she tried to adjust her eyes to the light from my lantern. "Who is it, Cordelia?"

Then she glimpsed me, her eyes hardened, and instantly I knew I was buzzard bait. Without hesitation Ma was onto me, whacking me with that broom, joining her screaming with that of the woman Cordelia, and instantly my room was noisier'n an empty wagon running fast on a hard-froze road.

"Ma!" I screamed myownself, and about then Lucille and LaRue were up that ladder and they were screaming too, and both of them little female wildcats who had always and heretofore been my sweet little sisters had also lit into me and were biting and tearing me further asunder with every passing mouthful.

"Ma!" I yelped again. "Its me. Hyrum! Ma, its your *son!*"

At that Ma slowed down enough to look, saw that I was telling the truth, and gasped, and then her lips thinned down with anger and she started swinging that frightful broom again.

"Hyrum, you . . . you . . ." she sputtered angrily. "Why, this is *awful*! What on earth are you doing in bed with Cordelia?"

Well, I thought of several answers, but I didn't give them because I was too busy ducking that swinging broom and pulling my legs out from between fiercely chomping teeth. Why, the whole up-scuddle made a feller wonder about what I'd said earlier concerning families and love and trust and about kinfolk coming to the rescue whenever there was trouble. If this was what it was like to be rescued, then I never wanted to be involved in such a horriferous extricative event again.

"Ma," I yelled, "it's *my* bed and *my* room. I don't even know this woman! And I *surely* didn't mean to go climbing into bed with her! It was *dark!* Now doggone it, *leave me alone!*"

That must have done it, for Ma suddenly stopped and stepped back and looked at me. Then, as I winced from the loss of a major portion of my left thigh to LaRue's dripping jowls, Ma reached out and pulled both LaRue and Lucille away.

"For heaven's sake, Hyrum, I . . . "

It was impossible for either of us to converse, however, for Cordelia whatever-her-name-was was still carrying on noiser'n a strong wind blowing over an empty barrel bung.

"Cordelia!" Ma finally shouted, "Will you please be *still!*"

That did it, too, and for the first time in what seemed like a hundred years, my room got quiet.

"Well?" Ma asked, stern as I'd ever seen her.

"Well what?" I countered.

"Well, what are you doing here?"

"It *is* my room."

"Maybe so, but you are supposed to be on your way to the herd."

"I decided not to go tonight. Besides, who is this woman, and how'd she come to be in my bed?"

Ma looked strangely at me, looked down at Cordelia and then back at me again, and it seemed, thank goodness, like maybe her eyes had finally been opened to the light of truth and understanding. "Well for heaven's sake," she declared. "You *wouldn't* know, would you."

"No ma'am," I agreed quickly, "I surely wouldn't. Now *what* wouldn't I know?"

"Hyrum, your Pa has taken himself another wife. Please meet your new Aunt Cordelia. Cordelia, meet my son Hyrum."

Well, I was shocked, to say the least. You'd think Pa had him enough troubles with three wives and every marshal in the territory after him for having them. Of course, with Pa a body could never tell. He seemed to like trouble, maybe even to thrive on it. Like I've said before, my Pa has maybe three interests in this world: the Church, money, and lovely women. And no doubt about it, this new wife was lovely. I guess he figured four wives would be altogether better, for escaping from the law, than three.

"When was this decided on?" I asked.

"While you were in jail. Both Jons and I forgot to tell you. Polly, Victoria, and I got telegrams from Jons while he was hiding in Salt Lake City, giving us the details and asking our approval. We talked it over and decided in favor of it. Cordelia came into town late today on the train.

"I told her that since you were away, she was welcome to stay here in your room until Jons could find her a better place. She seemed quite happy to accept, and she dearly loves your room."

Well, I looked down at Pa's crouching new wife, Cordelia, and recollected what she'd said about my room whilst she was snuggled up against my back. She knew right off what I was remembering, and sudden she was redder'n a fiery sunset after a dust storm. That did my heart good, seeing her embarrassed. Sort of put us on equal footing, if you know what I mean.

"Aunt Cordelia," I declared magnanimously, "I'm pleased to make your acquaintance. You are most welcome to my cramped and untidy room. Whilst I spend the night outdoors where the air is not so stuffy, I would be honored to have you stay here."

Aunt Cordelia got redder, but then politely and very subdued, she replied, "Hyrum, I . . . I'm sorry about . . . about . . . Well, I accept your hospitality with pleasure. And now, well, I can tell that your room is much more spacious than I had at first supposed. Thank you."

Ma gazed from Cordelia to me and back again, somewhat confused I imagine. The little girls sat down on the bed and started to giggle at Cordelia huddled on the floor in Ma's quilt, and we were all finally starting to smile when of a sudden there was a terrible pounding on the door.

"Open up in there! Hurry it up! Open up or we'll break down the door."

"Who is it?" Ma called.

"Never you mind, lady. Just open up and let us in!"

"Ma," I whispered, "I gotta get out of here."

"Hyrum, what have you done?"

"Ma, I ain't done nothing but find a little gold. I think it's Friendlessman and those outlaws, and they're after me!"

Ma gasped. "Oh my word!" Then suddenly she was angry again. "Well, I won't have it! I simply won't stand for this! Hyrum, I'll get the door and will do my best to keep them busy. Cordelia, take Hyrum's shotgun there—you do know how to use it, don't you?"

"I do," Cordelia declared, rising to her feet with the quilt still firmly in place.

"Good. Let's hope you won't have to. Hyrum, load it for her. You little girls get into your beds downstairs. Quickly.

"Now Hyrum, as soon as the gun's loaded, you get out that window. I've seen you do it for Ida Mae, so I don't imagine you'll have too much trouble now."

Well, I grinned. Its purely amazing how much a mother's apt to know about her children. And mine was a wonder, I'll tell you that. "Okay, I'll go. And Ma, thanks for trusting me."

Ma looked up at me, reached up and softly touched my face, and then she hugged me. "I love you, Hyrum," she whispered, and then she was on the ladder and going down.

Quick as I could I grabbed a handful of shells, loaded two into the scattergun, handed both gun and extra shells to Cordelia, saw that Ma was downstairs watching me, saw too that she was holding Pa's pistol out in front of her, and saw finally that her hands were very steady. Feeling proud as punch of that little lady who was my ma, I grabbed my boots and shirt, waved and smiled at Ma and at Pa's new wife, blew out the lantern, and was out that window and gone.

I heard the door open around front, I heard Ma's cold voice order those men to stand tight, I heard Cordelia's firm voice echoing Ma's, and I knew Pa had got him another good woman. I was glad there were still some around. Gave a feller like me a little hope, happen things continued to stay sour between Ida Mae and me.

Instantly those men were quieter'n a used-up feather duster, and I waited to hear no more.

Thanking the Good Lord that I had a family I could trust and depend upon happen there was trouble, I was off and away across our night-dark pasture, my bare feet making no sound at all as I ran.

23

Brush Canyon—Sanpitch Mountain, Sanpete County

There was a new moon above me, and the small amount of light suited me fine. I knew where I was going, but those hombres back at the house didn't and so the darker it was, the better.

In my bare feet I ran to the back fence of the pasture, and there I stopped long enough to pull on my boots. That done, I was through the barbed wire and climbing the gentle, sage-covered slope to the west of town, going just opposite to the way I hoped they'd expect me to go.

For maybe thirty minutes I ran and walked, and that old crippled clubfoot of mine hardly slowed me at all. In fact, I suppose it helped, for all my life it had forced me to develop muscles on my muscles just so I could drag it along.

It's passing strange how things like clubfeet and other problems usually also turn into blessings. It sort of verifies the Lord's promise in the book of Ether, where He says that He gives men weaknesses so that they will be humble, and then if men *will* be humble, He will make their weaknesses become strong unto them. Now I'm not saying I am humble, but I am saying that my gimped-up leg hasn't lost much because of atrophied muscles. No sir, it carries me right along.

Finally I came to a small hill at the mouth of Pole Canyon, one that seemed to stand sentinel over all that passed below. I didn't climb it but angled up the slope toward the north, worked my way through some fairly thick scrub oak, and so crossed the ridge and dropped down into Spring Canyon. There I stopped for a drink at what folks called the Big Springs, those that had given Fountain Green its name.

There were a whole passel of stories about those springs, which came gushing out of the side of the mountain like a big green fountain, and I'd heard them since I was knee-high to a short stump. First, the springs seemed to bear no relation to the snow-pack on the Sanpitch Mountains, which lifted above them. Folks had speculated for years as to their origin, and no one seemed able to decide where the water truly came from. Some fellers had even poured dye into the waters up above, and none ever came out in the springs.

That led to the other story, which was probably my favorite. According to that account, when President Brigham Young, whom folks usually just called Brother Brigham, first called settlers to the northern end of Sanpete Valley, it had been drier'n the dust in a mummy's pocket, and the settlers had been pretty nearly droughted out. In fact, only two or three families had managed to stay.

When Brigham Young heard about it, it was told that he came south from Salt Lake City, stopped his buckboard down below the Big Springs, stood up, and, looking up at the mountain, declared that so long as the settlers in our town lived their religion, the springs would always be of sufficient size to supply the needs of the community.

We must have been doing all right living our religion, too. The town had grown from a couple of families to sixty or seventy, and each year the springs had grown larger. Truthfully, we always seemed to have plenty of water, and in our country that was saying something. Made a body feel good just thinking about that. Maybe there was a little hope for us recalcitrant sinners after all.

There were a lot of stories around concerning Brother Brigham and his prophecies, and who was to say which of the stories, if any, were correct? He'd been dead since 1877, and to the best of my knowledge he'd made no public appearances since then, either to confirm or deny what folks were saying he'd once said.

Lots of the stories of his prophecies concerned gold and gold mines, and I've always found it interesting that for a man who tried so hard to keep the Saints away from gold prospecting and busy on their farms, so many prophecies abounded about the nearby locations of the fabulous wealth he was always telling the Saints to ignore.

For instance, the story is told that in Salt Creek Canyon, which is just north of Fountain Green, Brother Brigham pulled his team to a halt one day so that his animals might drink. They were then at the confluence of Salt Creek and Hop Creek, and as his horses guzzled the water, the Prophet is supposed to have stood up in the wagon, looked around, and pointed north up the canyon. "Brethren," it is claimed that he said, "someday the Saints will find gold up there, more gold than is found in any other mine in the territory. The location of that deposit is within one mile of where I now stand."

Well, there was always a little placer gold turning up in Salt Creek, and Loose-lip Lundstrum and a few others had churned up the mountains for miles around in their search for the mother lode, but to the best of my knowledge no one had ever found Brigham Young's deposit. Of course, Loose-lip and those others weren't exactly what might be called Saints, and the active Mormons were too busy making a living to go burrowing around in the hills after improbable wealth, so maybe that was the problem. After all, Brother Brigham *had* said Saints.

From Spring Canyon I kept moving north, climbing partway up a steep ridge and then moving across the brush-choked sidehill until I finally came to the edge of the small defile that most folks called Brush Canyon. By then I'd been pretty torn by all the scrub oak, and my clothes were ragged as one of LaRue's dolls. I was also tired as blue blazes, for I'd come near five miles over mighty rough foothill country. I'd done it in the dark of night, and such a climb would wear a body down even if he didn't have a clubfoot. So just where the ridge dropped off, I squatted down into a soft, inviting sagebrush, and there I took my first real breather.

Behind me, up on the slopes of Sanpitch Mountain, a coyote took his last couple of yips at the sinking moon. Then it was silent and I sat still; my own breathing was the only sound on the quiet hillside.

For sometime I closed my eyes and rested, thinking of that woman Cordelia who was Pa's new wife. That had been something, her thinking I was Pa and snuggling up against me like she'd done. It had truly startled me, but now that I thought on it, I grinned. No sir, it hadn't felt altogether bad. In fact, it made a feller understand a little why folks seemed to look forward to marriage like they did. In a way I even looked forward to it a little myownself, happen I could get through my mission and find a gal who would love me as much as Cordelia seemed to love my Pa.

And that got me to thinking of Ida Mae. Though I'd had no right, I'd thought all along that when my mission was over, why, she and I would happily enter into the state of wedded bliss together. I'd even seen a wedding dress in that Co-op in Provo, and I'll tell a man, it was a thing of surpassing beauteous wonder: veil, trail, and the whole regale. I could even imagine Ida Mae in it, providing of course that she'd be willing to wear it with me beside her. Which event now didn't look too likely, I had to admit.

Way over east the sky had taken on a rosy cast behind the East Mountains, or the Wasatch Plateau, which was what the mountains on the east side of Sanpete Valley were properly called. I watched as the mountains grew into focus, knowing that I had to cross over into them, and knowing too that the odds against my succeeding were only just barely short of stupendous. Especially would it be difficult with Friendlessman and his boys on my trail like they were.

Down in Fountain Green a rooster crowed, a dog barked, and somebody's door slammed, and in the intense stillness of the morning I heard the screech of a pump as someone drew water for their breakfast.

Here and there a light showed, for the town was still in darkness, and suddenly I got a real lump in my throat. That little town wasn't much on size. In fact, it was downright small. I'd even heard folks joke about that, one saying that when his pa had died, the town had had to hold an election for mayor, sheriff, justice of the peace, and town drunk, all at once. Another had said that when Fountain Green was surveyed, the man hadn't even bothered to use a scope. Pa always said that in Fountain Green a man could have his face shaved and his shoes shined at the same time, and the barber shop was across the street from the shoe shop. I didn't know about that, but I did have it on good authority that when our town's first and only sightseer stopped by last summer and asked for a local map, they gave him one and furnished a magnifying glass to go with it.

So, like I said, as far as towns went, Fountain Green was small. Still, it was home, and that means something to a man. It was where the folks that I loved lived, and it was where I felt at home and secure.

Down below me the smoke lifted from Cornelius Collard's blacksmith and wheelwright shop, and I thought of the last time he'd fixed Ma's wagon and wouldn't accept any pay. Down the street was John Green's brickyard, where he had molded, fired, and then donated all the brick in the ward tithing office. Then around the corner was Rees Lewellyn's home, which also served as our post office. Brother Lewellyn was a fine man and a real leader, and folks were already talking of running him for the Territorial Legislature. Besides that, he was Pa's friend, and he did all he could to keep Pa informed about the activities of the marshals. Then right below me was Pa's mill, which he called the Phoenix Mills and which was just beginning to come to life. Ole Sorensen ran the mill, and he did a good job of it, too. The winter before, he had gone out of his way to teach me all about milling, and I thought the world of him for that. A boy can always tell which adult folks like him; the ones I've mentioned liked me, and I can't even say how such an understanding helped me on the way to growing up.

So looking down on that little village made me think of a whole lot more than a few small cabins and adobe homes, several barns and corrals, and a couple of withering businesses. That's why I had that lump in my throat.

It was coming on real daylight by then, and I decided it was time to get down into the old tunnel in Brush Canyon where I planned to hide out for the day. I stood to go and started to turn, and just then a sudden movement above and behind me caught my eye. I looked, and there, not more than three hundred yards off, a man sat on his horse staring at me.

Suddenly he lifted his rifle, but I was already in the air and diving down the hill when the *whap* of the passing bullet assailed my ears.

How had they found me? How on earth had they tracked me in the dark and going opposite to where they should have expected me to be going? I didn't know, but that bullet had been evidence enough to convince even an eternal optimist like myself that they had. I hadn't fooled them one little bit.

Down the slope I hurriedly scattered leaves, hoping to confuse them a little and maybe gain some time. I rolled a big rock off toward the bottom, and then, careful to keep my feet on rocks and dead wood, I quickly descended in another direction. I went fast, but I was careful as conditions permitted, and I did all the things Pa and Zene had shown me in the way of hiding a trail.

At last I came to the mouth of the old tunnel I sought, and there for a moment I paused. The tunnel had been dug years before by a fellow who had come into town, learned that we all got our water from the same spring, and decided to tap into it, divert it, and sell it to us out of *his* canyon.

The story went that he'd dug, the bishop had warned him, he'd kept on digging, and then even Brother Brigham had warned him. Still the poor fool had kept on digging. By then he had quite a hole into the side of Brush Canyon, and folks said they could hear the water through the rock, he was that close.

Finally he'd been warned one last time, some said by Brigham Young again, and he had laughed and declared that it was his canyon and he could dig as he chose. Just days later there was an accident, either at a saw mill up Ephraim Canyon or in the tunnel, depending upon who was telling the story, and when things had settled, the poor misbegotten soul was minus one arm.

Well, it's pretty tough swinging a single jack with one hand, so that was the end of that fellow's attempted piracy of the Big Springs. The way it looked to me, it didn't seem to be a very wise proposition, going against Brother Brigham Young. Nor any of the rest of the brethren either, for that matter.

Samuel Brannan, who I read recently had died a pauper down in Sonora, Mexico, last year, had tried that and had also lost. When Brother Brigham settled the Saints in the valley, Sam Brannan had come along and declared that the place to go was California. Brigham Young had said no, Samuel had argued yes, the Saints had stayed, and off Samuel Brannan had gone to prove the Prophet wrong. Well, he did have lots of experiences that the world would probably call successful, but none seemed to last, and worst of all, he never seemed able to throw a rope around being happy. Finally, as I said, he died alone and a pauper down in Sonora, a witness to the fact that it doesn't pay to fight against the prophets of God.

Carefully I worked my way down the side of the gaping mouth of the tunnel, moving through the thick brush, doing my best to break no tree limbs and skin no bark. They had a tracker with them that must have come from the high, deep woods, and it was going to be difficult enough to shake him if I was perfect. Mistakes would kill me sure.

At last, near the floor of the tunnel, I found good footing. I leaped out and came down on a large rock just behind the thick stand of oak that hid the tunnel from view. So far, so good. Happen they didn't know of the tunnel, I just might get away with hiding there. Happen they did know of it, well . . .

Stepping backward, I pulled a few oak limbs down to better cover the small opening I had jumped through, and then I stooped and shuffled maybe a dozen feet back into the tunnel and sat down to wait it out. I could have gone deeper, but there had been a cave-in, and I didn't want to chance another one. Besides, the deeper I crawled the more I knew the hole would feel like a trap, and I didn't like that feeling at all.

I dozed for a time, and it was maybe two hours later when I heard the first of the men. Right off I knew I had been correct about that tracker. My attempts at hiding the trail had been futile at best.

"Boss," a voice called from somewhere above me, "I think he came this way. There's a scratch on this rock that looks fresh, and I reckon it's him."

"Good work, Blue John," another voice called from farther off. "Silvertip, get Friendlessman and Doolin. He's gone this way."

There was silence then for maybe thirty minutes, and I was surely starting to sweat. A fly buzzed in the tunnel, around and around and around, and watching it, I felt more trapped than ever. They'd find me sure, and there was nothing I could do about it. I debated making another break for it, gave that up as suicide, thought of giving myself up, decided that was suicide as well—just the delayed kind—and so I simply sat, hoping for a miracle and knowing there wasn't going to be one.

"Boss," the voice suddenly called again, this time from on past the tunnel mouth, "this kid's a slick one. I've lost him again."

"Stick to it," the Boss's voice called out, sounding so near to me that I actually jumped. "He can't vanish into thin air."

"Boss, you know that and I know it. I just wish the kid who's vanished knew it. I tell you, cripple or no, this Soderberg kid's some spooky. I'd have sworn that Friendlessman nailed him first off this morning, but there ain't been no sign of blood, not anywhere. Then there was that false trail he made with the rock, made like a wounded man might make, and at the bottom it wasn't no trail at all. I tell you, he's slick. Now he's come to here, and whoosh, he's just lifted up and gone."

"It can't happen!"

"Maybe it can, happen a feller believes in haunts."

The one called the Boss laughed, and it was not a pleasant laugh to hear. "You can't be serious," he said scornfully.

"I'm getting serious."

"So am I," the Boss snarled. "And I'll haunt you, happen you don't raise that kid's trail mighty quick."

There was another brief period of silence. I sweated some more and thought on what those two had said to each other, and then from across the canyon on the north slope, another voice called, a high, thin, reedy voice that I'd never forget as long as I lived.

"Say, Moore," the man whined, "there are tracks over here, and they look to be fresh. I'll bet the kid came this way."

Doolin! Why that miserable little skunk! More and more I was growing to dislike that man.

"Blue John," the Boss shouted from nearby, "get over there and follow that trail."

"Oh, for . . . " Blue John's voice called out from so close to the tunnel mouth that I was surprised I couldn't see him. "That ain't his trail, Boss. It can't be! I've followed it to here, and I'll lay odds the kid's within fifty feet of me right now!"

Fifteen feet would be more correct, I thought as I wiped my forehead, hunkered down, and looked around for some rock to duck behind. Fifteen, or maybe even ten. That Blue John fellow was *close*.

"You go on over there, Blue John," another voice suddenly declared, a deep booming voice that sounded kind and friendly and not at all like an outlaw. "See what Doolin has found. Moore and I will stay here and keep looking."

"Yeah," Blue John growled, addressing himself but doing it loudly enough so that I could easily hear. "And a fat lot of good that will do, you knucklehead. Silvertip, you wouldn't know dung from wild honey happen you stood neck deep in it.

"No, boys," he called out, "I'm staying—"

"Blue John," a new voice suddenly ordered, the same ice-cold voice I'd heard order Ma to open her door, "you go join Doolin! Now! Moore, you go with him. Silvertip and I will stay right here and watch the slope. That way we'll have everything covered so tight that even a rabbit couldn't move without being seen. One way or the other, we'll get the boy this time."

There was a scurrying in the brush as the man descended past the tunnel, and instantly I breathed easier. That Blue John fellow had about located me, but now with a little luck, maybe—

"Friendlessman," the deep booming voice of the man known as Silvertip suddenly called, "you reckon he's holed up right around here somewhere? You reckon maybe he can even hear us?"

"Of course I don't," that snow-chilled voice stated flatly. "Why would he have stopped here, when he might just as easily have kept on to his destination?"

"Uh . . I don't know. I just thought maybe . . . well, maybe he's got him a hole or a cave or something."

"In this canyon? You ninny, of course he's in a cave, or more properly, a tunnel. We all know that, and we know as well that it is in Gammett Canyon, not here. Why, in this gully we could *see* a cave, providing there was one. Which there isn't. This ravine isn't large enough to conceal a rabbit burrow, let alone a tunnel."

Now how had they known about my tunnel in Gammett Canyon? I'd not said a word to anyone, and even Ma and my new Aunt Cordelia hadn't known where I was going. It made no kind of sense, but it did give me a great deal of concern.

"But Mr. Friendlessman," the outlaw Silvertip argued, "there's patches of thick brush that could hide anything. Like maybe that there patch of oak right below you."

Well, my heart nearly stopped, I was that scared. I knew what was below that Felix Friendlessman, and it was no more and no less than me, hidden up in that old and concealed tunnel. If anyone got any closer than Blue John had done, they'd literally fall into my hiding place. Trouble was, there was nothing I could do about that, nothing at all.

I stared at the entrance where the morning sun filtered down through the oak leaves, and I wondered how far I could get if I made a break for it. Not far, I feared. There were rifles behind me and rifles across the canyon, and I was fairly boxed.

No, the only thing to do, if they even gave me the chance to do it, would be to surrender peacefully and then to wait for another time. There were a lot of miles to cover before the Uintahs, and maybe—

"Well," the cold voice of Friendlessman asked, "are you going to check out that brush or aren't you?"

"Mr. Friendlessman, I was only suggesting—"

"Silvertip, look into that brush!"

"Yes sir," Silvertip replied immediately, and I heard clearly the scuffle as he rose and started down the slope toward my thicket.

It's purely amazing how sound carries in a mountain canyon. I could even hear the man's breathing as he approached. I could hear the tune he was suddenly humming, and for the second time I thought of this particular enemy as a man, a person who might, at another time and in another place, be my friend.

In the gloom of the tunnel I looked again for a better place to hide, considered crawling back into the debris from the cave-in, and gave it up. That way I would be trapped for sure, and happen the roof gave way again, I'd also be dead. No, at least with the outlaws I'd have a chance.

Outside, the man was within just a few feet of the tunnel mouth, and I knew the game was up. He was still humming "Sweet Betsy from Pike," he was already at the edge of the brush, and he had just parted the first of the limbs when from the earth beneath him, almost under my own nose as well, broke forth the most awful yipping and wailing a body ever heard.

It was a she-coyote yelp of anger and pain and fierce determination to protect her young, and it burst so near to Silvertip, as a matter of Brush-Canyon Sanpitch-Mountain fact, that the outlaw believed he had stepped on the very coyote that was giving the wild-crying alarm.

With a shout of surprise and fright he lunged backward; the trees closed up again, there was a flying up of earth toward his retreating form, and suddenly a small body hurtled into the tunnel and crouched down, staring outward.

There was more yipping and snarling; Silvertip kept moving away, and suddenly he laughed and spoke.

"Mr. Friendlessman," he called, "I reckon I was right. There *is* a hole down there, a coyote hole. Mrs. Coyote's to home, too, with a whole passel of pups. Reckon that means the kid's gone. No wild animal will stay holed up and quiet like that if it's close to a human."

"I suppose you're right," Friendlessman agreed, and abruptly he issued new orders. "Let's cross over. I'm certain that the kid has moved into Gammett Canyon, and that's where we'd better go as well."

I listened as they left, but I didn't move my eyes from that still-crouching form, I didn't move them at all. Nor did the small body move until the two men had crossed the bottom of the canyon and were thrashing their way up the north slope. Then it slowly turned toward me . . . and grinned.

"Howdy, Hy," was all it—he—said.

24

Fountain Green Vicinity—Sanpete County

"Criminentely, Ern, how'd you get here?"

My younger brother kept grinning, but at last he spoke. "I declare, Hy. You're predictable as rain water running downhill. I knew right where you'd be, and it looks like Ida Mae did too."

"Ida Mae?"

"Yeah. I reckon it was her told Friendlessman and the others that you'd likely hide out over here. Nobody else knew, and them boys came a-fanning it right on your trail. *Somebody* surely told them. Hardly gave me time to lead them astray."

Well, I studied on what Ernest had said, and bad as it made me feel, it did seem right. I'd thought they had a good tracker, and they did. But even good trackers have a hard time of it at night, and like Ernest had said, those boys had come a-fogging. Besides that, it surely answered my question about how Friendlessman had known I would be hiding in a tunnel. Yes sir, I'd been pointed out, and it had to have been by Ida Mae.

She and I had talked of this tunnel often enough, for it was where Pa hid out if things got real bad between him and the marshals. It wouldn't be any trick at all for her to put two and two together. Of course, she'd never been to the tunnel, and so far as I knew she didn't even know it was in Brush Canyon; I'd only told her that it was north of the Big Springs. That's why those hombres had been looking in Gammett Canyon. Somehow they'd assumed a tunnel would be in a larger canyon, and that assumption had saved my bacon.

That, and Ernest.

"Little brother," I said, "I surely do admire the way you coyote around these hills." I shuffled forward to shake his hand, and as we gripped, the breeze brought a whiff of something that smelled powerful awful.

"Ern," I gasped, "You're whiffy as the national skunk convention. Where in tarnation you been?"

"In a coyote hole. Where'd you think I yapped from out there? Horseback or something?"

"I . . . I don't know."

"That hole was the only place left between them outlaws and the tunnel, and given about three seconds to make a decision, I took it. Gave me the idea of yapping, too."

"Well, Ern, you did it up good. You the one who laid that trail out across the canyon?"

"You bet." Ernest was proud, and I didn't blame him. For a runt-sized kid, he'd done more than fine.

"Now those boys won't be in Gammett long, Hy. I had to dead-end the trail and get back here in a hurry. Seems to me we'd best depart."

"Shanks-mare, Ern? You know I don't have much foot speed, and this gimped-up leg is about as wore out as the path to the privvy in chokecherry time. I just don't—"

"Just to the bottom, Hy. No farther. I got ol' Ingersol tethered there, and he'll carry us both."

"Ingersol! Ernest, what'll Pa do when he hears—"

"I told Ma to ease it to him gentle, happen she sees him again before we get back. Besides, when Aunt Hattie came and woke us up and told us about you and them fellers who were after you, I knew there wasn't an awful lot of time to spare on getting approval. And Pa always says that it's easier to repent than it is to get permission. I was just sort of applying his teachings. Now I reckon we'd best be on our way."

I reckoned the same, and shortly two young Soderbergs were hoofing it down the gully to where Ernest had hidden Ingersol, Pa's Belgian stallion that had run over a hundred miles on that one day the year before.

"How'd you ever catch this plug?" I asked after we were mounted and moving easy-like down the deep gully toward town. "He's kid-shy as any horse I ever saw."

"Luck," Ernest replied. "I've been around horses all my life, and what you say, big brother, is the gospel truth. Horses altogether are peculiar, and this one in particular, well . . . it's come to me that no matter how spavined or broken down horses might look, no matter how gentle is the look in their eyes, all horses are a little *loco en la cabeza*. Ever since I was throwed by that fool mare belonging to Deaf Man Hibbard, which is the slowest looking nag I ever saw, I've watched horses careful as rattlers in a sack. They'll go out from under you or come down on top of you or just plain up and run off from you for no good reason at all. And that's if it is your own personal horse, one you happen to know like a brother. Coming to a monster like ol' Ingersol here, which I've never rode nor even throwed a blanket on, well, it's Katie bar the door, for sure."

"So how'd you catch him?" I asked, grinning.

"It was tough," Ernest grumbled. "I walked up, took his reins in my hand, climbed up on the fence, and swung aboard."

"He was saddled?"

"And rearing to go. I reckon Pa had him ready for a quick getaway happen ol' Clawson or some other marshal showed up while he was asleep."

"I hope they don't," I breathed.

"Yeah, me too. If they do and if Pa can't find his getaway horse, and if he ever gets out of jail after they throw him in again, I reckon we'll both be dead men."

"You're a comfort, little brother, you surely are."

Ernest was silent, so I kicked Ingersol into a run, and moments later we were down on the lane running from the Big Springs down into Fountain Green. I was some worried about Friendlessman and the others seeing us, but as we rounded the first turn in the road we came onto old Deaf Man Hibbard driving his wagon full of water barrels back home from the springs.

Quickly I pulled Ingersol to a walk beside his wagon, and for the next few minutes we had perfect cover. To anyone up on the mountain, it would look exactly like we had all been after water. Or at least that's how I hoped it would look.

"Hello, Brother Hibbard," I called.

"Eh?" he grunted, cupping his hand to his ear and staring at me.

"I said hello," I shouted, and suddenly I remembered that the old man was no more deaf than I was. Why was he—

"Speak up, sonny, I can't hear a word the way this rig is rattling about."

"Brother Hibbard, Ernest said quietly, "I told Hyrum about you."

Deaf Man Hibbard looked hard at Ernest, my younger brother squirmed behind me, and at last the old man grinned. "Well, a man never knows," he laughed. "Besides, I'm so used to being deaf that sometimes I forget I ain't. Whew! Which one of you fellers is polluting the morning breeze?"

"It's me, I reckon," Ernest answered. "I got a little scented up back there on the hill."

"Well, get that horse to the lee-side of this wagon. Deaf or not, I never claimed to have lost my sense of smell."

I smiled, reined Ingersol around, and soon we were riding smoothly again.

"Ern," Deaf Man Hibbard then asked, "did you tell Hyrum about Loose-lip and those others?"

"Yes sir, I did."

"Is that you they've been chasing around up there this morning?"

"Yes sir, I reckon so."

"Looks like you two was a match for 'em."

"Anybody'd be a match if they had Ern with 'em," I said. "Out in those hills he disappears quicker'n a full-blooded Indian."

"So I can tell by the odor," Deaf Man Hibbard declared. "Coyote holes, skunk holes, nothing's too good for young Ernest, I take it." Then, "What you aiming to do now?"

"I've got to get back to the herd," I answered honestly. "Maybe from there I can figure out who killed that Enock Rhoades feller."

"Well, good luck, young man. And look sharp. You're about as wanted by now as your pa is, and that's some wanted."

I grinned and pulled rein, Deaf Man Hibbard clucked his horses down the road, and Ernest and I sat and watched him go. "Now what?" Ernest asked.

"Now," I answered, unbuckling my money belt as I spoke, "I've got one quick stop. Then I'll be on my way."

"One stop?" Ernest asked as I counted out a double handful of silver dollars from my belt and stuffed them into my pocket. "Hy, I hope it ain't to see that no good Ida Mae Sorenson. That girl's useless as—"

"Ern, don't you say no more. Happen anybody runs Ida Mae into the ground, it'll be me. Besides, her home's close, just through the field. It'll only take but a minute, and then I can pick up Old Man Aagard's horse and be gone."

Ernest didn't say anything to that, so I kneed Ingersol around and a couple of minutes later we were coming to a stop in Ida Mae's yard. I dismounted, and when Ida Mae came to the door I was standing in almost the exact same spot as I'd occupied just a few hours before.

"Good merciful heavens," she snapped, "haven't you given yourself up yet?"

"Not hardly. Can I talk to you back by the tack shed?"

"What about?"

"I'll tell you there. Come on."

I started walking, and reluctantly Ida Mae followed. I rounded the corner so that Ernest and whoever else might be watching from the house couldn't see, and then I leaned against the wall of the shed and looked at her.

"Well?" she snapped again as she stopped in front of me, and I could see that she was surely put out. I reckon she'd hoped I would hasten up to ol' Friendlessman and plead to be captured. Now that I hadn't, and now that he hadn't come up with me anyway, Ida Mae was probably figuring out some other way to get me into Friendlessman's graspy little paws.

"Well what?"

"Well, what do you want?"

"I just wanted to take a good look at you," I answered honestly. "You are awful pretty when you get riled."

Ida Mae colored up quickly, and to cover it she stamped her foot and glowered at me. "Hyrum Soderberg, that isn't funny!"

"Wasn't meant to be. Neither was what I said last night, both about liking you and about my innocence. So far I ain't . . . haven't done anything wrong. No killing, no robbing, no nothing. Not even anything exciting. I was just kind of hoping that you'd changed your mind and had decided to believe me."

"I haven't, and I'd suggest that you place yourself into the hands of Felix or his men right away. Believe me, Hyrum, they have your best interests at heart, and it will be for your own good."

"And if I don't, then you'll do your level best to point out to them where I might be hiding, just as you did last night."

Well, she colored up again, spun angrily away, and started walking back toward the house, and I knew Ernest had been right.

"Hold up a minute," I said quietly. "I'm not quite finished."

"Well, hurry it up," she declared frostily as she stopped. "As far as I'm concerned, we have nothing left to discuss."

Quietly I took out the silver dollars that I had removed from my money belt, and slowly I counted out thirty of the big coins. These I stacked carefully on the windowsill of the tack shed. Though she still had her back to me, the sound of the coins proved too much for Ida

Mae's curiosity to withstand, and she half turned so that she could see what I was doing.

"Pick 'em up," I said when I had finished. "They're for you."

"For me?" Ida Mae frowned as she turned the rest of the way back and started toward my three stacks of coins. "What for?"

"Remember Judas in the Bible?" I asked her. "The same wages for the same work."

I watched her face go pale, and then I nodded, touched the brim of my old hat in farewell, and hobbled past her and around the corner of the tack shed. I did not look back, nor did I think I needed to. She had surely got the message.

25

The Divide and the Wasatch Plateau—Sanpete County

"Hyrum," Ernest shouted as I appeared in sight, "hurry it up! There's riders coming from town, and that piebald gelding out in front looks awful familiar."

I looked, and sure enough, there was Marshal Clawson's horse and the good marshal himself leading a group of about five other horses and riders, and they were all pounding the dust toward Ida Mae's place.

"Look out," I yelped as I swung up onto Ingersol, "we've got to skedaddle, and quick!"

Ingersol took the bit, and instantly we were out of there and headed toward the Divide. I didn't stop to realize that I had nothing to fear, and I think most other folks would have made the same mistake. When a feller gets used to running, then he always will, even when there's no need to do so. I'd been bailed out legal, my trial wasn't for another two weeks, and there was nothing on earth that Marshal Clawson could have wanted me for. Yet still I was running.

"Hy," Ernest asked after we'd gone maybe two miles, "I was just wondering, why do you suppose ol' Clawson is after you?"

"Beats me," I replied. "I reckon it's because his heart's just naturally colder than an Eskimo woman's feet."

"Has he got anything on you?"

"Not that I know of."

"I wonder if—"

Ernest was interrupted by the distant shouts of Hebron Clawson, and when we finally understood them, we grinned and slowed ol' Ingersol's pace a mite.

"Soderberg," he was screaming, "you lousy dirty polygamist, hold up there, so help me, or . . . or . . ."

"Ern," I said, grinning, "Clawson thinks he's chasing Pa."

"But that ain't so, Hy."

"I know, but this is Pa's horse, and from the back . . . Say, I'll bet one of the marshal's spies—some active member of Pa's ward, no doubt—saw Ingersol at Ida Mae's, knew that Mungus was Pa's counselor, put two and two together, and came up with about nine."

"I'll bet so too," Ernest called into the rushing wind. "Now what?"

"Well, let's let him run until his horse is good and winded and then let him catch us."

"Hy, you're gritty as eggs rolled in sand. What'll you do if he's after you too?"

"Take that chance, I reckon. If he isn't, we've helped Pa out a little. If he is, I'll rely on you to help me out. You've done good so far, and I'll bet you've got another rescue or two tucked away, happen I need them."

Ernest grinned, and so for another mile we stayed just out of rifle range of Clawson and his deputies.

"Soderberg," the marshal finally screamed at the top of his lungs, "you'd best stop, and I mean pronto."

I reckoned it was time myownself, so I pulled back on the reins, dragged the just-warming Ingersol to a stop, and pulled him around to face the lathered mounts of Marshal Clawson and his deputies.

"Soderberg," he panted, straining to see through the cloud of dust his sliding horses had created, "I arrest you for unlawful cohabita—"

"Howdy, Marshal," I said easily, doing my best to force the quiver of fear from my voice. "I appreciate your yelling. Otherwise I'd not have known you were trying ride with us. Is there something I can help you with?"

Clawson's face was a study, and I'd have laughed if I hadn't been so afraid that he'd haul me back to town and lock me up where Friendlessman and his cronies could try again to get their greedy little hands on me. He looked from me to Ernest, then at Ingersol, who was hardly breathing heavy, and then back at me and Ernest again.

"I . . . uh . . . I . . . Well dad-gum it," he sputtered, "where's your pa?"

"I don't know," I answered truthfully. "I ain't seen him in some time. Ern and I were just giving his horse a little workout, and I happened to hear you yelling."

"And your pa wasn't never with you?"

"No sir. He doesn't even know we're working his horse. I'll swear to that, and so will Ern here. Ain't that so, Ern."

"Right as rain," Ernest declared. "Pa, he's probably long gone, over to Emery County or down to Robber's Roost. Ma says that's where he likes to hide because no marshals dare go down there."

Clawson's face turned beet red, and with his big nose and his straggly yellow hair and mustache, he suddenly reminded me of one of them circus clowns. I grinned a little, and Clawson suddenly turned on me.

"You figuring on leaving town?"

"No sir, I'm not."

"You look like you are to me, and that there is against the conditions of your parole. Maybe we'd best ride back together, all of us. Let's go!"

Well, I was surrounded, and I couldn't see any way out of it. Clawson and his deputies were sober as the ladies at a Thursday night testimonial, and I reckoned they meant business. Fortunately they had all put their weapons away when they had discovered we were not who they had expected, but they were all around us, and—

"Say!" shouted one of the posse, "who turned loose the skunk?"

"I don't know," another complained, "but things sure are foul!"

"I don't smell nothing," a man next to Clawson declared.

"Well, come over here, and—"

"Boys," I said, "it's my brother Ernest that's odoriforizing the air. He got in a tangle with a whole passel of polecats this morning, and we were hoping the fast ride would sort of air him out."

The men stared, and then as one they pulled their mounts around until they were all near the marshal. "Clawson," one of the men stated, "that kid's considerable whiffy on the lee side. If we ride back with him, I aim to lead out with him following far behind."

"I'm with you," another declared. "I wouldn't—"

"Hy," Ernest suddenly hissed while the men were complaining, "look down the valley!"

I did, and my insides suddenly went cold with fear. About two miles back—maybe a little less—and coming fast was a boiling cloud of dust. It was still too distant for Clawson and his men to have seen, but my little brother could count the flies on a window-sitting pie-crust at two miles, and I didn't doubt his ability now. With dreadful certainty I knew that Friendlessman and his men were churning up that dust cloud, and with just as dreadful certainty I knew that unless we got out of there, and pronto, I'd be magpie fodder for sure.

"Hang on," I whispered back to my younger brother. "We're about to depart."

"Now?" Ernest whispered questioningly. "But Hy—"

"Have to!" I whispered acidly. "Seems to me there ain't no superiorly good time that a cripple and his runt-sized brother could pick to bid adios to the marshals and the outlaws of Sanpete Valley. Not unless you'd prefer to see me pushing up daisies and alfalfa and maybe join me there yourownself."

"I wouldn't," Ernest answered quickly, and I could tell he was grinning again. "Let'er rip, big brother! I'm hanging tight."

"Here, you two!" Clawson growled. "What are you whispering about?"

"Not much," I answered brazenly. "We were just deciding it would be a wise thing to accompany you back to town, happen there might be Indians or other malcontents about."

"Malcontents? What's that mean?"

"Bad men, marshal. Like maybe those fellers yonder who are fogging it toward us."

Clawson and all his men turned their heads to look, and instantly I sank my heels into Ingersol's sides as far as they would go. With a wild snort he crouched down, and then like a shot we were gone—through the huge gap that Ernest's scent had opened up for us, up a small rise, and down the other side and away.

"Hey!" we heard the marshal or someone else yell, and by then it was too late. Ingersol was running flat out, and like Pa had told the members of our ward the year before, that big old plug could *move!* Clawson and his men plunged after us, but by the time they reached the top of that small rise and started firing, we were nearly out of range. A few shots whapped by, but they weren't as close as they sounded, or at least that's what I told Ernest, and by then we were out of range and hauling out.

I never did see a horse that could run like that Belgian plug. His big old feet pounding against the earth sounded like thunder, the dust he churned up was something awful, and his legs were so long that from a little way off it didn't look like he was running fast at all. But he was, he truly was, and the wind in our faces that was taking Ernest's scent away told us so immediately.

Across the Divide we raced, and by the time we entered the mouth of Water Hollow, we had outdistanced the marshal and his deputies by nearly a mile. Friendlessman's men were hardly even in sight. Ernest was shouting and whooping it along, and I was enjoying it a little myownself. However, I had me a worry, and I didn't know what to do about it.

For a time I kept Ingersol running full out, but then as the bottom of the hollow grew steeper I slowed him down and sort of gave him his head. The animal still ran, but now he picked his own way, and I didn't have to concentrate so much.

"Ern," I said then, "we've got us a problem."

"Lots of them, looks to me like."

"I mean an immediate one. I'm heading for the Uintahs, and I don't know what to do about you and Pa's horse. I mean, I need Ingersol desperate bad, and I don't feel good about setting you afoot clear up here in Water Hollow. Neither do I want to take you with me. Things could get bad, and—"

"Things are already bad, big brother. Besides, I ain't going home, not without Pa's nag."

"Why not?"

"He'll murder me is why. Against outlaws and Indians and marshals I've got me a fighting chance. Against Pa I ain't got none at all. Him I don't dare fight back."

"He'd get over it," I declared without conviction.

"Not so's you'd notice he wouldn't. Hy, let me go with you. Pleeease?"

"Ern, what'll Aunt Polly say?"

"You're right, by jings! That's another reason I can't go back. Ma'll kill me too. I didn't get down to the tithing office today to kill all them turkeys Terry Johnson donated, and she said just last night that I'd better or face the consequences. Hy, you wouldn't want me to die twice, would you?"

Well, Ernest sounded so funny with his whine and his serious pleading that wasn't serious at all that I couldn't put him afoot. I knew if I did the marshals would probably find him and drag him back on the end of a rope so he wouldn't offend their olfactory senses, and that might even slow them down a mite. But doggone it, I was lonely, and Ernest was better at weaseling through the brush than most anyone I ever knew. Time might come when I needed his help and for sure. Like that very morning, when I'd never have gotten out of the old tunnel if it hadn't been for Ernest and his quick thinking.

"All right," I growled, "I'll take you along. But remember, it was your idea, and one of these days you'll have to face both Pa and Aunt Polly. Coming with me is only delaying the inevitable."

"I know, I know. Maybe if I'm up there all summer, things'll blow over."

"All summer! Good grief, Ern, you can't do that! I'm thinking a few days, no more, and even that's pushing things. Agreed?"

"Hy—"

"I mean it, Ern. Agreed?"

Ernest spit off into the brush, and I knew he was disgusted. "I reckon," he finally grumbled.

"Good. Now we still need to figure some way to get word to Pa and your ma that you're with me."

"What for? They'll figure it out, and you know it. The way Ida Mae's been so full of verbal lather lately, she'll bust a gut getting it spread around town that she saw us escaping together. Sooner or later that'll get back to 'em."

"Ern, I warned you—"

"Doggone it, Hy, I got to call it like it is! You know I'm right."

I did, and that bothered me. Ida Mae would likely do exactly as Ernest said, and somehow I couldn't get upset at her for it. In spite of everything, my thirty silver cartwheels included, I still loved that lady and truly hoped that some day soon she'd come to her senses and be my girl again.

All morning we pushed ahead, up Water Hollow and over the top into Big Hollow, which we followed down and through The Gap toward the tiny community of Milburn. After skirting town we headed up Dry Creek to the top of the East Mountains, which as I said were really called the Wasatch Plateau, and then we turned north along the rolling top and rode through the heavy stands of pine and quakies.

The air was sharp and clean. Now and then a mule deer bounded off and down into some secluded draw. Twice we passed summering herds of sheep, camp-robber jays followed us off and on, several times we passed trees that had been scratched and marked by territory-establishing bears, and altogether it was a beautiful ride.

There is no more beautiful country in all the world than the top of that plateau, and if I were to die today, I'd go to my reward convinced that I'd already seen God's greatest kingdom at its finest. I mean, a man can stand on the rim of one of the canyons that drops steeply away from the top, with thick stands of pine marching down all around him, and the blue of shadow is so thick in the bottom that he can't even see where the timber ends.

And quiet? It's like the day after the earth was created. Even breathing sounds loud and out of place, and many's the time I've found myself holding my breath without even realizing it, just listening to the beauty and feeling the power of the silence.

Every little way we'd come to a giant snowbank melting in the warm summer sun. Those banks are forty to fifty feet high, with tiny rivulets dancing away from the bottom on all sides. Downhill those little freshets join up, and by the time they've dropped a few hundred yards they've become some of the prettiest little streams a man will ever see. The water is crystal clear and sparkling in the sunlight, and it's cold enough to cause headaches happen a feller drinks too much too fast.

There're fish up there as well, fine native trout that flash from rock to rock when a shadow of danger appears. They fight like crazy when hooked, and spread out and fried up right those fish make some of the best eating this side of anywhere.

And beaver? Goodness but they build up that mountain with beauty. Some folks claim beaver are nuisances because they chew down a few trees, but let me say this: Those quakies grow faster than any beaver can ever chew them down, the trees'd die anyway after a few seasons of growth, and the dams the beaver make with the trees, well, those dams stop flooding, provide catch basins for the topsoil that the streams would otherwise carry away, provide habitat for fish and other water critters, and finally turn deep eroding canyons into grass-filled meadows that feed herds of wildlife and are places of surpassing beauty besides. No sir, God didn't make any mistakes when he created mountains like that Wasatch Plateau.

Of course I may be a mite prejudiced, but happen someone ever sees those mountains, he'll know what I'm talking about, and he'll know my prejudice is well placed.

At the first beaver dam we came to, I reined Ingersol over, rode him into about two feet of water so he could take a drink, and then I spoke.

"Ern, ain't this a pretty place?"

"Yeah, I reckon," he answered, sounding uninterested.

"Doesn't it make you think of clean things?" I asked.

"Clean things?" he responded, sounding puzzled. "I don't know that it does, Hy. Like what, maybe?"

"Like you, maybe," I answered, and with no further ado I pushed my younger brother off Ingersol's back and into the water of the pond.

He went quickly under and came up even faster, sputtering and fussing and wiping water from his face, madder than a rained-on rooster.

"Doggone it!" he snarled. "What'd you have to go and do that for? I oughta—"

"Because you smelled so bad, Ern. I had to do it, don't you see? Ingersol and I couldn't take no more. Now and then this horse likes to go slow, but with you up here it just wasn't possible. Every time he'd slow down, your pleasant scent would catch up, and the horse and I would both get dizzy. Still, I'm mighty sorry I had to do it."

"Well, you should be. You might at least have warned me so I could be holding my breath. I like to have drowned."

"Oh, I wasn't sorry for you, Ern. I didn't mean that at all. I was just feeling sorry for the fish and the beaver in this pond. With all that awful scent in the water, them poor critters'll probably be laid up for a week."

"Why, you dirty no good, low down . . ." Ernest growled, and then he started in to really throwing the water. I couldn't let that go on, so I ground-hitched, or I mean water-hitched, Ingersol, and then I was in the water fighting back, and when we climbed dripping and laughing onto Pa's horse a few minutes later, we were both tolerably cleaner.

We slept under the stars that night, huddled together under Ingersol's saddle blanket. We'd even had a couple of fish for supper; so as far as roughing it went, we weren't too bad off. Still, I knew that with Ernest along I needed more supplies. I just hoped we could get to Soldier's Fort and the general store before the next night.

All the next day Ernest and I rode north along the top of the mountain, drinking in the beauty and thinking hardly at all of the men who must surely be following. We didn't do anything special to hide our trail; we just counted on Ingersol to keep us out in front. And that he did.

Late that afternoon we descended the slope of Spanish Fork Canyon and rode into Galula, a railroad town that wasn't more than a few shacks and a saloon. Turning east we pushed on up the canyon, and it was coming onto sundown when we came over the top and rode into the town of Soldier's Fort.

As towns went it wasn't much, but it was a whole lot more than Galula had been. There were several shacks scattered back on the hills, and there was a railroad station and building, several saloons that lined the main drag, and one general store.

Soldier's Fort, which was called that because soldiers from Johnston's Army had established a post there years before, was in reality a railroad town, or at least that was the case when we were there. Whatever, it surely wasn't the typical Mormon frontier settlement, which had straight, wide streets; clean, well-built homes set back uniformly from the ditches; very few saloons; and an atmosphere that was so quiet a person could usually hear daylight coming.

Soldier's Fort, on the other hand, was what some folks called a Gentile town, and in most ways it was just the opposite of the Mormon communities. Men had been killed there, or at least that's what folks said. And though times were changing and violence was no longer so easily tolerated, it was still pretty firmly entrenched.

For death to occur was natural, and in a violent land a violent death was more to be expected than otherwise. Such was even the case in Mormon communities. Of course, what I'm saying does not necessarily mean that men would die by the gun or the arrow, for there were multitudes of other ways to die, each just as violent.

To fall ahead of stampeding cattle, to be gored by an angry steer or cow (which had happened to my Grandmother Caroline one morning when she went out to milk), to be thrown and trampled by a wild horse, to be frozen to death or to die of thirst, to fall off a steep mountain trail in the iciness of winter—these were the order of the day. And there were dozens of other ways that I haven't even mentioned, all just as deadly and each just as easily accepted.

Outside of Mormondom it was customary to settle disputes between men with weapons, and it had been so for hundreds of years. In my time the pistol was the most accepted weapon, and so it was the one most often used. There were even cases where disputes were settled in such a manner among Church members, but fortunately such instances were rare and were quickly dealt with.

Murder was quite another thing from two men holding a powder-burning contest between each other, and that was one of the reasons why folks were so het up about what I had been charged with. Murder was more than a crime against an individual; it was also a crime against society, against its accepted customs, its way of thinking. To permit a murderer to go unpunished would be to tear a hole in the fabric of the society we were trying to build, and so it was vital that murderers be caught and disposed of according to law.

"Ern," I suddenly said, "we've got to get you a few things. Let's stop at the general store."

"You got any money?"

"A little."

"I'll tell you, Hy, it's mighty handy having a brother that's rich."

"I'll bet," I grinned, and with that I pulled rein in front of the store, a ramshackle building of weathered wood that had never yet seen a coat of paint. I stiffly dismounted, stretched, and moved out of Ernest's way so he could jump down, and then the two of us went inside.

There's nothing on earth like an old general store, and these days they're disappearing so fast that folks a few years from now will hardly know what they were. The smell hits a feller first, that and the darkness. It is the smell of food and leather and salt and dry goods and who knows what all, but it is one of the finest smells I've ever encountered. The darkness isn't so fine, for it is caused by too few windows, and those few are likely coated black with fly specks. In those days the land was alive with flies, and there wasn't much a body could do about them except ignore them as best he could and try not to eat or breathe more than a dozen or so a day. Like I said, in those days, flies were *bad*.

After our eyes had grown accustomed to the dark, Ernest and I stepped forward to the counter, which ran all the way around the narrow inside of the store.

"Help you?"

A smallish, friendly looking man rose up from behind the counter.

"You bet," I replied quickly. "I need a couple of blankets for my new hand here, who is otherwise known as my younger brother. He could do with a new shirt and a pair of those made-for-boots Levi Strauss trousers. Can you fix him up?"

The clerk looked Ernest up and down, grimaced, and then winked. "I reckon so. He's a mite small, but so are some of them Chinamen we get up here working on the railroad. If nothing else, I've got a fine Chinese cone hat he'll surely enjoy."

Ernest made a face. The man grinned, and then, while he scuttled toward the back to put our order together, Ernest and I looked around. On the counter were baskets of eggs—three dozen for a quarter. There was a big jar of butter, quite soft from the heat, that sold for twelve and a half cents a pound. There was cheese both from nearby and from New York and a bucket of hulled corn hominy with mosquito netting over it to protect it from the hordes of flies.

On the floor were barrels of flour of two grades, white and with shorts, and meal, very coarse—the kind that made a man sometimes want to scratch his back. There was a barrel of withered apples, sacks of soft potatoes, turnips, cabbage, and one withered pumpkin. And back of those were barrels of molasses and vinegar and a barrel of salt pork with a big stone on top to keep the pork under the brine.

There were also kits of mackerel of two grades—big and fat, and otherwise. Additionally there were dried codfish hanging by the tail, hams, shoulders and slabs of breakfast bacon, strings of red peppers, and, finally, fresh meats, mostly venison, which were also protected from the flies with more netting.

Back of the counter on the shelf were large boxes of big square soda crackers, crocks of honey, coffee—green Rio and Mocha (folks had to parch it and grind it themselves), tea, starch in bulk, bottles of catsup, cayenne pepper, and soda and cream of tartar instead of baking powder. There were also spices, rice, and two big jars of striped candy.

Further back were things for women, like bolts of cloth, white dishes, steel knives and forks and pewter spoons, jars, milk crocks, pans, wooden tubs, pails, brooms, and those conspicuous pots that always end up under beds. There were also things for the men, such as Levi trousers and shirts, boots, hoes, rakes, spades, ropes, kegs of nails, a whole shelf of tobacco, and one entire wall of leather goods and saddle tack. All in all, a man could find about anything he might ever need in one of those old general stores.

"There you go, young feller," the clerk finally said as he rolled the clothes and two cans of peaches up inside the blankets. "That'll be three dollars and eleven cents."

I gulped at the high prices, paid him, and grinned as he handed Ernest a stick of candy. Ernest almost didn't take it, because he didn't want to play the role of a kid. But it was peppermint, his favorite kind, so sheepishly he reached out his hand and snagged onto it.

Moments later Ernest and I were back on Ingersol and headed out of town and on up the mountain, eating out of the same can of peaches and happy as two kids who didn't know any better had a right to be.

It was nearly dark by then, but we pushed Ingersol on anyway, turning north and following the White River into the mountains beyond.

I wanted desperately to reach Strawberry Flats, but it was long after midnight when we came at last to a small seep where I had camped once before, and I knew we could go no farther. Ernest was asleep against my back, I could hardly hold my eyes open, and ol' Ingersol was about done in. I drew rein and helped Ernest down. Then I took the saddle from Ingersol and let him roll, and then while he drank and cropped at the thick grass, I rubbed him down. That finished, I spread out the blankets, Ernest and I curled up together between them, and the last thing I heard was a coyote somewhere out in the darkness who was complaining of insomnia. Poor critter, I thought as I yawned widely, it's pretty tough being tired . . . And then I was gone, and the silence of the night was the only sound left.

26

Strawberry Flats—Utah Territory

"Hy, wake up!"

Somewhere far off I heard Ernest's urgent whisper, and groggily I opened my eyes. The sun was an hour high, and that told me right off how tired I'd been.

"Hy, we've got trouble."

I rolled over, looked at my brother, and saw his eyes staring straight ahead. I followed his glance, and abruptly I sat up. Around us on all sides, seated on their horses but still and silent as a treeful of owls at noontime, were nine Ute braves. They were watching us as intently as we were watching them, and the only difference between them and us that I could see was that they had weapons of one sort or another, all leveled in our general direction, and we were unarmed.

Instantly my mouth was cotton dry, and as I climbed slowly to my feet I noticed that my palms were wet with sweat. Ernest was already standing, and before I could do anything about it he stepped forward and solemnly raised his hand in the universal sign of peace.

"How!" he declared.

There was continued silence, and all nine men sat without expression. "How!" Ernest tried again, louder, and this time also there were no visible results.

Well, I should maybe have mentioned previous to this that none of us Soderbergs were known for our patience and long-suffering. And to be perfectly honest, Ernest was the worst of the lot. Of course *I* could see that in a situation like this prudence was the better part of valor. I mean, I was old enough to understand that they had us so far outnumbered there wasn't even a chance of a Mexican standoff, a fair and even draw. Even before anything started, I could see that we had gone down to a burning defeat.

Ernest, though, was too young to understand that, and I reckon the fact that the Indians had ignored him was just too much for him to bear. Before I realized what he was about, he reached down, grabbed a fist-sized rock, and let fly at the Indian who sat on his horse directly in front of us, an old man with almost snow-white hair.

"Ern!" I cried in alarm, but I was too late, way too late. The rock was already on its way. Ernest's aim was a little low, however, for the stone struck the pony on the withers and bounced up, smashing into the jaw of the ancient brave.

There was a terrible squeal from the horse, who was already into the air and sunfishing around, and that and the blow from the rock became the perfect combination to unhorse that elderly Indian.

I saw him fall, heard his grunt, and saw the dust puff up from where he had hit; I saw that he didn't move, and I knew that my younger brother and I were dead men. Rifles were suddenly lifted and brought to bear on us, bows were bent with arrows at the ready, and I was already saying my prayers and seeking forgiveness for all I had done that might have been wrong, when that Indian who was on the ground rolled over and sat up.

He shook his head to clear it, felt his jaw—and his posterior, which is what he had used as his point of contact when he had so rudely greeted the earth, and then he rose slowly and somewhat staggeringly to his feet. Without looking to the right or the left he fixed Ernest with his dark and fierce scowl, drew his huge knife from its scabbard, and started forward.

"Run, Ern," I whispered urgently.

"I'll be darned if I will," he snarled. "I ain't scared of no Indian!"

"Do it! I'll do my best to fight them, hold them up. Get on Ingersol and they'll never catch you."

"I ain't running from no old Indian!" Ern declared. "Especially one so rude as that one is." Then, defiantly, he reached down, snagged another rock, cocked his arm, and let fly.

The Indian ducked and came on. Ernest grabbed a third rock and stood ready, his face filled with defiance and anger and absolutely no fear, and suddenly the ancient brave stopped, lowered his knife, and started to laugh.

I was shocked, Ernest was just as surprised, and before we could do anything other than just stare, the group of braves were laughing and pointing at the tottering Ute who had been knocked from his horse. And, strangely, he seemed to be laughing the loudest, enjoying the joke on himself, whatever it had been, most of all.

Suddenly, as if someone had given a signal, though I certainly saw none, all of them stopped laughing and were still. Then the old man who had been thrown from his horse smacked himself on the chest.

"Me Tabby," he declared proudly. "Me the sun!"

Well, Ernest probably didn't know enough to be impressed, but I did, and my mouth probably fell open, I was so surprised. Of all the people my little brother could have picked to knock from his horse, he'd had to go and pick one of the greatest chiefs of the entire Ute nation, an old man who was the long-dead Chief Wakera's brother. Oh, no! How come we had to go and have all the blessings . . .

Suddenly Chief Tabby stepped forward and grabbed Ernest's arm, twisting it a little. Ernest flinched but then held his ground and stared up at the wide-faced Ute. "You brave warrior," the man declared."You be my son!"

"I will not!" Ernest retorted, pulling his arm away. "I already got a pa!"

"Him?" Tabby asked, motioning toward me.

"No sir, that's Hyrum. He's my brother."

"Brother. Ungh. He no brother. He coward. He no fight."

"He would've," Ernest declared, "happen you'd tried to hurt me. Why, Hy's worse than a den of riled rattlers and harder to stop than a wounded grizzly! He's a warrior for sure."

The old man looked doubtful, so Ernest motioned for me to step forward. I did, and after about the second step I heard gasps from the Indians around me, and I saw Chief Tabby's eyes go big in his weathered face. Then quickly he took a step back, then another. I stopped, and there was a rapid exchange between the Utes. I took another step forward and extended my hand so the chief and I could shake, and again Tabby recoiled in fear.

Ernest was as surprised as I was, but he was more blunt. "What's the matter?" he asked. "I told you, he's my brother. He won't hurt you none."

Tabby still stared, but at last he stuck his shaking finger out and pointed at my crippled foot. He chattered again so that neither Ernest nor I could understand him, and then finally he reverted to his limited English. "Him great medicine," he declared. "Him favored by great Spirit Mormonee call God with foot that is not like foot of other mans. Him filled with power!" And again he backed away.

"Hy," Ernest whispered, "you reckon they're scared of you?"

"Seems like it," I whispered back. "Ern, I'm getting awful jumpy."

"You're a poor liar," Ernest answered without looking over at me. "You could sleep in a sack of snakes without twitching. What do you reckon's going on?"

"I don't know. Just tell this ancient chief we ain't meaning to look his Ute gift horse in the mouth, and that you're right thankful that he wishes to be your pa. And tell him that we're glad to leave him our undershirts and our blankets and our single can of peaches with no hard feelings. I don't know about you, little brother, but I feel sort of surplus to this entire hastily called meeting. It ain't uplifting to anything but my hair. Now be nice to him, but hurry up, and let us be long gone!"

"Well then," Ernest answered, "I'll second that. Motion's now been moved and carried, and we're off."

We both took a step backward, the Utes stopped talking and stared at us, we took another step toward our horse, and old Tabby raised his knife again.

"You go," I said low-voiced. "Just jump on Ingersol and take off. I'll keep 'em busy for awhile."

"You make leaving you sound slick as a Kansas City snake-oil salesman," Ernest replied. "Hy, I can't do it. We had 'em there for a minute. Don't you think we can bluff 'em along again?"

"I don't know, Ern. Indians are notional, but I'd say you might be right. A bluff seems to be our onliest chance. Happen it works, we may live. Happen it doesn't . . ."

"So how'll we do it?"

"Just like what you was doing before. I reckon we'd ought to play my bad foot and my strength for all they're worth. Tell the old Chief I won't hurt him if the others will put down their weapons."

Ernest grinned, and suddenly he stepped forward. "O Tabby," he said dramatically, "you are right. Hyrum is filled with great power. Just yesterday we came to a great cliff that we could not get down. Hyrum saw this, and so he took me in one arm and our horse in the other, and he carried us both to the bottom."

There was a great intake of breath, and I was shocked that these powerful men could believe such a pack of lies. I was also embarrassed that my own little brother could come out with them so easily.

"I will show you," he went on. "He wishes for two braves to come and stand on either side of him."

There was a gasp. Tabby looked around; then he signaled, and two warriors reluctantly slid from their mounts and moved carefully toward me. Well, I grinned, for this was an old game of Pa's, and because I'd had a weakness in my legs, I'd practiced it some myownself. I'd been blessed by the law of compensation, for while my legs were born weak, they were weak no longer, and I truly did have some real power in my arms and shoulders.

Stooping down, I wrapped my arms about those two stout Utes, felt them shaking with fear, and then I rose up with the two of them leaning rigidly against my shoulders and actually making little whimpers of fear.

"You see, chief?" Ernest declared. "He has great power. Now he has them, and if you'd like, he will throw them so high that they'll smash into Tabby, which you call the sun. Of course, they'll die, but that's up to you. What do you say?"

"Ern!" I hissed, "that's the dumbest thing I ever . . ."

"My brother says he would rather not kill these men," Ernest declared quickly. "He says that good warriors should live."

"He is wise," Tabby declared softly. "Wise and good. It is enough."

Relieved, I lowered the men to the ground, and they madly scrambled back up on their horses. There was another long silence, and I could see that if I didn't do something quick, we'd likely be there staring at each other all day long. Stooping, I gathered our two new blankets and the remaining can of peaches, and stepping forward, I placed them upon the ground.

"Gifts," I declared, "for the great Chief Tabby."

I stepped back, Tabby stared, and then slowly he stepped forward and took up the gifts. "Me thankum great warrior Hy-mum," he said awkwardly. "Me thankum Little Warrior too. How you called, Little Warrior?"

"Ernest."

"Enn-nest. Good. Good Indian name, Enn-nest. Come. We go."

He turned, and one of the braves leaped down and helped him aboard his pony. Ernest and I looked at each other and shrugged. Quickly I bridled and saddled Ingersol, and moments later we were on our way, surrounded by Chief Tabby and his eight Ute warriors.

For hours we rode, across Strawberry Flats, over the low hills to the east, and down the Strawberry River, almost the same way I had gone when I'd chased down Old Man Aagard's mules and found the gold. Thinking of that, I was amazed that only a little over a week had passed. So much had happened that it seemed like months, and it was hard to wrap my mind around the fact that circumstances in my life had changed so quickly.

Before I'd stumbled onto that gold I'd been a pretty normal young man, head over heels in love with a gal who loved me and doing my best to earn a little extra cash so our family wouldn't be in such dire straits. Now I was still the same age, but most of the marshals in the southern half of the territory knew of me and were after me, a gang of outlaws had sworn in their wrath to take me and force me to lead them to some gold I didn't know anything about, and the girl I still loved had turned against me and would no longer even talk to me.

Talk about change! Pa had always said that gold was a hard-found thing, was even harder to hold, and always came hand in glove with trouble. Now, for a fact, I could say "Hallelujah, amen" and mean it wholeheartedly.

We turned south along what I think was Willow Creek, followed it up for some time, and then rounded a bend and came face to face with the camp those Ute braves were calling home. There were a few tipis and a couple of brush wickiups, some dogs and dirty little kids that had to announce our arrival all at once, and a couple of old men and several squaws who just stared at us.

We dismounted, and Tabby in great solemnity took us to his tipi and bade us welcome. There were two women there, I think both of whom were his wives, and with short instructions he sent them scurrying. He hauled out his pipe then, and though I am thoroughly against the use of tobacco, I did puff on that foul-tasting weed and send smoke off into the four directions so that he would know that my heart was good toward him.

Ernest did the same, but I noticed the smell of the knickinick in the pipe pretty much turned him green. And if it hadn't, the meal the women served up a little later surely did.

Now I need to say that as a whole the Utes seem to be a sincere and wonderful people. Still, they surely don't live life as we do. Nor do they seem to want to, and as far as I'm concerned, that's fine. Folks should have the right to live according to their traditions. But that doesn't change the fact that it's hard for a couple of fellers like Ernest and myself to sit down and be perfectly comfortable with them.

As far as my own tastes went, their filth was awful. Chief

Tabby's oldest squaw passed the antelope hair around in the lid of an old chamber pot that looked like it had been used all day for its natural purposes, and it was all Ernest and I could do just to take it in hand and pass it by. Later we had some stew that we ate with our fingers, and I knew full well we were eating one of the little dogs I'd seen running around earlier. And of course they expected us to stay the night, sleeping on those vermin-infested robes.

Both of us were reluctant but couldn't see any way out, so after dark we retired. In the lodge where we tossed and turned and tried to sleep were also six or eight more dogs, but before morning a couple of litters of pups had come into the world on our beds and had increased the number so materially that Chief Tabby, the aging proprietor of the wickiup, thought it necessary to have his wives remove the mess while he knelt and lead out in offering morning prayer.

"See," he said as he thumped himself on the chest, "Tabby prayum good. Brigham say prayum, Tabby prayum. Tabby good Mormonee."

I was impressed with Tabby's innocent faith, and to this day I believe him to be a good and kind man who was probably closer to the Spirit than I am. I thought then of Brother Brigham's prophecy that the Lamanites would one day be redeemed and become a delightsome people. Frankly, I believe that to be true, and I think that, in their own way, they already are. I just hope that white folks, even good-intentioned ones, don't ruin them first.

Still, as far as the saying goes that cleanliness is next to godliness, it looks to me like the Lord is going to have to accept those folks on their own terms and not His. Happen, that is, that His terms are somewhat akin to my own. And that there opens up a whole new can of worms, which can I'm not climbing into at all.

"Hy," Ern said quietly after more stew had been served up to us for breakfast, "we've got to get out of here before I starve to death."

"But they've given us plenty of food," I protested.

"Yeah, and all these dogs are getting fat from mine. How can you stand to eat that stuff?"

"Easy," I lied. "Dog meat's good for the system."

"Dog meat? Oh *no,* I th-thought that was v-venison. That's the only part I've been eating."

Ernest started gagging, and I decided my brother was right. I'd enjoyed about all of Tabby's hospitality I could stand. Rising to my feet, I smiled at the toothless old woman who seemed to be the boss wife. She smiled back and cackled something that must have been meant to amuse me, and I snorted in response, smiled and nodded at the still-breakfasting Tabby, stooped, and went out through the door-flap and into the clear air of the morning.

Ernest quickly followed. Together we walked to where Ingersol was tethered, and I began saddling him up. I had only just started, however, when a rider came churning up the creek, threw himself from his heavily lathered pony, and rushed into Tabby's wickiup.

Ernest and I looked at each other, shrugged, finished saddling and bridling Pa's horse, and suddenly Tabby appeared, striding toward us.

"Ho, Mormonee brothers," he called in his old man's cracking voice. "Bad thing happen. Heap bad thing. No good for Indian. No good for brothers. Enn-nest come, Hy-mum come, showum maybe so quick."

"What is it?" Ernest asked quickly. "What's wrong?"

"Goum with braves," Tabby said. "They showum!" And with that he turned and pointed off toward the mountains to the north. We mounted, the messenger and three other braves joined us (the messenger on a fresh horse), and soon the whole bunch of us were headed back down the creek.

"What you reckon it is?" Ernest asked as we rode forward.

"Beats the dickens out of me. That brave looked worried, though, and for that matter, so did the chief."

"Yeah, he looked anxious as a young buck lifting his first scalp. What do you reckon it has to do with us?"

I didn't particularly like Ernest's choice of metaphors, for scalping was not an altogether dead art, no pun intended. He had hit the spike square on the head, however, and I couldn't help him.

"I don't know, Ern, I surely don't. Howsomever, I do have me a bad feeling, and the last time I felt this way, I found my poke of gold. I truly don't need any more trouble like that."

"Me neither. I'm getting fidgetier'n a chicken drinking out of a rusted pie tin with a herd of hungry coyotes waiting in line behind, and I ain't exactly anxious to know why."

"Yeah. Happen I know Indians, little brother, this is going to lead to where she squeezes down like a tight-choked side-by-each."

"Like a what?"

"A double-barreled scatter-gun bored full-and-full."

"Ah."

"Yes sir, Ern. I'm feeling miserable as a steer in a herd of heat-struck heifers. A man can't sleep a full night in a Ute wickiup full of vermin, smoke himself over a green-pine fire, and feed himself on half-cooked dog to boot without building up for himself some trace of what every *real* Indian is born natural with—a sixth-sense nose, touchy as a blistered heel, for impending disaster. I hate to say it, but I do believe we're heading for trouble."

Ernest didn't answer, so we rode in silence for a time and lived with our unhappy thoughts. We went down Willow Creek, crossed the Strawberry, and rode on into the wild and tumbled country that formed the western end of Currant Creek Mountain. We were climbing then, through cedar and sage, up into thick hillsides of pinion and oak, and finally into the quakies and pines and firs of the high-up country along the flat top of the mountain.

Skirting a mess of huge boulders that had gathered from who-knew-where, our guide turned abruptly and started down the sharp edge of a dry wash that dropped steeply away to the north. We followed, and Ingersol took that hairline trail like he'd been born to it. We came to the bottom, rode out, and crossed what had to be either Wildcat or Deep Creek, and right off we were climbing again.

"I'm beginning to see why that messenger's hoss was so lathered up," I finally said. "We've come a far piece."

"Amen," Ernest replied. "You don't suppose there's any way we can rig two saddles onto Ingersol, do you?"

"What's the matter? You getting sore?"

"Hy, I got saddle sores on my saddle sores. Besides that, I'm like to split right in half, Pa's hoss is so wide."

"Well, don't fret. We're likely nearly there, wherever *there* is. Then, once we get back to Zene and the herd, some of that sheep dip we'll have to use to kill Tabby's dogs' lice will do wonders where you're galled."

"Yeah, and kill me, to boot. You ever been really galled?"

"Once."

"What was it like?"

"Ern, being galled's a mighty personal thing, and a feller doesn't discuss it. I will say this, though. Bear grease is the thing. Don't never let my ma talk you into putting some of that white Dr. Shields Cure-All Wonder Powder on it."

"Why not? Does it hurt?"

"No, not so's you'd notice, but it sure spreads the word that you've been galled. Everywhere you walk you leave little white clouds, and Ern, that there is a purely embarrassing experience."

Ernest giggled, and suddenly, from up on the mountain, we heard a distant gunshot.

"Oh-oh," I breathed. "I've got that bad feeling again."

The Utes had heard it too, and all of them pulled rein and bunched up together, talking to the messenger. Finally after what seemed like hours of discussion, all grew silent, and the messenger, a tall man with a scar on his face, turned to us.

"Bad," he grunted, "heap bad, Utes good Indians. All-the-same Mormonees. No fightum Mericats. Very bad."

"Mister," I said soberly, "I am confuseder'n a blind bear in a bramble patch. What exactly is the trouble?"

The tall Ute looked at me, then up the mountain, and then back behind him and down the slope. "Me good Indian," he declared with finality. "Utes good Indians. We goum back. No fight. You go, heap strong, you fight."

"Fight? But what—"

"Heap Chief Hy-mum, little warrior Enn-nest, fight bad Mericats. No should be here. We driveum out, more bad Mericats come. You driveum out, bad Mericats no getum angry with Indians. You strong. You Ute's friends. Saveum Cale, all-the-same helpum Utes. There."

He pointed up the mountain, and I had a sinking feeling like I'd never had before. He was sending Ernest and me up there alone, into what I had no idea. "Now see here," I protested, "I don't think—"

"We go," the scar-faced man declared, and before Ernest and I even had a good idea that they were leaving, the warriors had gone. We were alone on the mountain with not an idea in the world as to why we were there or what we were expected to do.

Mericats was the Ute word for Americans, as opposed to *Mormonees,* which is what Tabby and all the rest of them called Mormons. I'd heard Pa talk of that and of the Ute way of speaking, which he had picked up somewhat during what folks called the Blackhawk War, back in the early '70s. Even with the crazy lingo, however, there was no mistaking that tall Ute's orders. There was someone up there needed fighting, and if the Utes did it, they'd be in real trouble from Washington. Happen we did it, however, we'd likely be in trouble only with the law. And since that was already the case . . .

"Ern," I said softly, "Pa used to allow that if you wanted to collect stuffing for a featherbed, you'd put two young cock birds in the same pen of pullets and stand back with your cotton sack spread wide. He guaranteed you a toteful of ticking fodder inside five minutes flat."

Ernest nodded his head. "Yeah, I recollect. He also says that it takes only two growls and a back-leg scratch to turn a nice sociable sniffing into a first-class dogfight."

"You're right, Ern. He does say that. Now I reckon we've had our two growls and are only waiting for the leg-scrape."

"Yes," agreed Ernest as he suddenly strained his eyes up the slope, "and big brother, yonder she comes."

27

Windy Ridge—Utah Territory

"Ern," I whispered, "who is that feller?"

"Don't you know?"

"Would I be asking if I did?"

"Reckon not. That's Friendlessman, him that's been sparking Ida Mae."

"Friendlessman," I breathed as I stared up the slope. "So that's Felix Ethelbert Friendlessman. Don't look like much from here, does he."

"Nope, not much. Is that his name for true?"

"It is," I grinned.

"Man's folks ought to have been whipped," Ernest declared soberly.

"Don't see why," I argued. "The Felix and the Ethelbert parts are okay, but the Friendlessman fits him like a glove. Altogether, I'd say they go together mighty well. I'd also say that the name's about right for a fellow like him."

"Maybe you are right," Ernest replied slowly. "In fact, I do believe you are."

We were down on our bellies on the slope, looking upward through a patch of sparse brush. Ernest had kept watch while I had sneaked Ingersol back into some oak and tied him, and now we lay together, watching.

"What's he doing?"

"Watching, like us."

"Yeah," I responded, "but who? He ain't seen us, has he?"

"Naw, he ain't even looked down toward us. He's watching something on the other side of that ridge."

"What, you reckon?"

"I don't know, Hy. Can't see through hills yet."

I grinned, Ernest smiled back, and suddenly I was glad he was there with me. He was young and he was small, but come to what we seemed to be doing, there was nobody, only Pa and maybe Zene Hill excepted, that I'd rather be with.

Time and again I'd been hunting with Ernest when he'd spot game and instantly get a strange look in his eye. Johnny, one of our other brothers, always said that Ernest was daft and stranger'n a lost wolf whelp. He claimed Aunt Polly doted on Ern, claimed in fact that she *had* to because he was teched.

Me, I didn't believe that. Not after I saw Ern track down a deer Pa had shot, *after dark!* He said he smelled it out, and I for one believed him. Like I said before, that kid was part varmint, and he could spook a man sure.

"What you reckon we ought to do?"

"Well," I answered, "since you can't see what's over that ridge, and since neither can I, it seems fitting that we Indian on over there and see what Scarface sent us up here for. With Friendlessman involved, we know it's going to be bad, and that's certain as mud clings to Sunday shoes."

"You want me to go alone?"

"No thank you, little brother."

"Afraid for me?"

"Nope. For them fellers up there. I saw what you did to them poor pilgrims the other morning, Ern, and being naturally soft-hearted, I don't want to see them come to any more grief than they already have. No, you mosey along, and I'll do my best to follow."

Ernest grinned, and seconds later I was being hard-pressed to keep up with him as he wormed his way silently up the slope. Thirty yards along he paused and waited for me to catch up. I did and then rested until my breath was nearly back to normal.

"You part Ute?" I gasped.

"'Course not, but here and there I learned me a thing or three."

"You learned 'em good," I declared. "You don't make no more noise than a winnow of wind in fresh wolf fur."

Ernest looked back at me, and his face was serious. "Don't mean to," he said quietly. "Let's go."

We did, and shortly we were on the ridge, about fifty yards below where Friendlessman was crouched gazing down into the ravine below. There was another shot, from somewhere below us and off to our left, and then someone shrieked with joy.

"I think I got him!"

Well, it was no trouble at all for me to recognize that whine, and suddenly I was storming mad. That there was that miserable little Doolin again.

"Hey Doolin, tell you what. You walk down there and make sure!"

That was the one called Blue John. He was also below us, off to the right a little, and I figured he was holed up behind a twisted pinion I could see down the slope.

"Now see here," Doolin whimpered, and then Friendlessman spoke.

"Be still, you two. We're in no hurry; we've got plenty of water and he doesn't, so let's let the sun do our work for us. Meanwhile, shoot only to wound, not to kill. Remember, we need him."

"I'll say," someone growled from right above us on the slope. "Especially since we lost that crippled Soderberg kid!"

Well, Ernest and I hunched down like we'd been shot at. Neither of us had seen Loose-lip Lundstrum up there, and the closeness of his voice gave us a shock.

"You see him?" I whispered almost silently.

"No, but I think I can see that feller down in the bottom, the one these owlhoots are shooting at."

"Where?"

"Down there between those rocks, the pink and yellow ones. A moment ago the shadow got darker for a second, and I'm sure it was the feller they're hunting, shifting position."

"I've got Loose-lip spotted," I whispered. "He's in that manzanita right up there. I saw his head move."

"Yeah, I did too. Wish we had Pa's rifle."

"I wish we had any kind of gun," I hissed. "I wouldn't kill no one with it, just maim a little. I feel mighty naked up here unarmed."

"I've felt that way my whole entire life, Hy. I wish Pa'd give me a gun. I can use one sure."

"Yeah, and maybe too fast, Ern. You know the Lord don't hold with shooting folks up."

"I know, I know. But there're times . . ."

For an hour or more we lay without moving on that bare-boned ridge, and it was hot enough to raise a blister on a rawhide bootsole. Things in general were touchier'n a teased snake, but somehow Ernest and I had to keep our thinking straight and hang onto the only cards we held. We simply couldn't afford to make any wrong moves.

We had three of those outlaws within fifty feet of us in three different directions, and maybe more than that who hadn't spoke up yet. In short, we were surrounded and had crawled ourselves right into the middle of it.

Still, faint heart never filled an inside straight, as Pa sometimes said, and I'd be doggoned if I was going to stampede as though I had bought a ticket to Hades and was running to catch the first train out of the depot. No sir. Somehow we were going to find us a way to get to that feller down in the bottom and get him out of there. Trouble was, I just didn't know how.

"Hy, you hear that?"

"Hear what?" I asked, straining my ears against the silence of the late afternoon.

"Horses. I reckon I know where these outlaw fellers hid their horses."

"So?"

"So the way I see it, we need horses. You have Ingersol, but I need a horse, and happen we get that feller out down there, he'll need a horse hisownself. Besides all that, those outlaw fellers don't need no horses at all. Fact is, we'd all be considerably better off if every last one of them was set afoot."

"I see what you mean. Think you can get to their horses?"

"Can birds fly? Or snakes crawl? Or you forever and always beat me at checkers? I hope to shout I can. Can you?"

"Maybe, but I doubt it."

"You want to try?" Ernest asked sincerely. "You're older, and you're maybe the best sneak in the family."

"Except for you," I declared. "Next to you, owl feathers and milkweed fuzz ain't in it. You could outstalk a housecat wearing goosedown shoes. No, you go, and you'd best do it fast. Night's fixing to come on, and I've got me a feeling these fellers are starting to get anxious."

There was a sudden shot from down below, the first that had been fired in over an hour. A white puff danced away from the rock down in the bottom of the draw, and I knew I had been right. Those fellers *were* getting anxious.

"I'm gone," Ernest whispered. "I'll get Ingersol too. When these fellers take off, happen things work out and they do take off, you be ready to shag hide down into that bottom."

"Aye, aye," I grinned, "and 'Yes sir' to boot."

Ernest smiled wide and twisted around, and seconds later he was slithering back down the way we had come. He was loud about it as a buzzard's shadow scraping mesa rock, and I surely did feel proud as I watched him go. Why, in a spot where a noise as loud as a cricket's cough could cost a man his life, that little brother of mine fairly sailed along.

I turned back to look, and suddenly I saw a figure rise on the hillside directly below me. The man stood crouched over, and then, carefully, he eased down the slope, screened by a wide old juniper.

Right off I could see that he was trouble to the feller who was hiding down below, but it took me a minute to figure what I could do about it. Then I noticed a small boulder a little above me on the slope, and I knew.

Worming my way up to it, I hunkered low against the hill and took a small stick; then I carefully eased the stick down and commenced to push the boulder. At first nothing happened, but then the rock gave a little, teetered, and finally fell loose and began to roll. Instantly I rolled too, under a small bush, and there I waited.

For a second or two the rock clattered; then it bounced into the air, made no sound, and crashed down, and suddenly that feller below me started shouting.

"Hey!" he whined, and right off I was grinning. *"Hey!* What you trying to do up there? Kill me?"

"Oh shut up, Doolin," Loose-lip snarled. "It wasn't nobody at all. The rock just came loose is all."

"Yeah? Well, it nearly got me, and now the old man knows right where I am!"

"Maybe he wouldn't if you didn't make so blasted much noise," the man called Blue John declared quietly from down below. "I declare, you're worse than Silvertip. Now be still and wait for Friendlessman to give the orders. Then we'll all move in together."

There was more grumbling from below, and I only felt bad because my rock had missed. Now I know I'd promised Pa that I'd be an elephant during my stroll through life, and I know too that elephants aren't supposed to step on the dogs; meaning, I suppose, that we true Christians are to be properly considerate of those who are trying their best to do us in. Still, I felt mighty badly about rolling that rock down at Doolin. At least I felt badly about having missed with it and not putting the poor misbegotten soul out of his misery.

So, next time, I vowed. Next time—

Suddenly there was a deep booming shout from off below, the sharp crack-cracking of a pistol, the thunder of hooves, and then that same deep bass voice cried out loud enough that all the mountain could hear.

"Blue John, Boss, *help!* Some two-bit kid got our horses!"

Instantly Doolin and Blue John and Loose-lip and even Friendlessman, high on the hill above me, were on their feet and running. Friendlessman even passed so close that I could have reached up and caught him. I didn't, and right away I was glad, for on Friendlessman's heels came another man who was probably the one they called the Boss. Anyway, they were all hotfooting it down the back of the ridge, and so without further ado I was on my way myownself, sliding down the face of the ridge toward the nest of boulders where the unknown man had spent the day hiding.

28

Windy Ridge— Utah Territory—Again

"Mister," I called quietly as I neared the bottom of the steep slope, "don't shoot. I'm friendly."

There was no response, so I moved forward through the shadows and cautiously approached the tumbled boulders where Ernest said he had seen movement.

"Mister, you in there?"

The only answer was the cry of a crow from somewhere far off, and I grinned, knowing that was Ernest's way of telling me that things had worked out. Slowly I moved up to the boulders, crouched down, and squinted into the darkness.

"Mister," I said low-voiced, "I'm friendly, so if you're there, sing out. Happen you want to leave, we're going to need to do it in a hurry."

"I'm here, son," a quiet voice answered from way up under the rocks. "Who're you? And what became of those bushwhackers?"

"Name's Hy Soderberg," I answered. "And my brother Ernest lured them off. Now let's be gone, for I've a bad feeling that they'll be back."

"Oh, they'll be back, all right. Felix Friendlessman's like a bulldog when it comes to hanging on to a bad deal."

"You know him?"

"'Course I know him, worse the luck. Son, we got us a problem, a real bad one. My horse fell on me and then spooked, and so far I can't walk on my leg at all. Can't tell if it's broken, but it might as well be. You got a horse?"

"Yeah, but not here. Happen we make it, Ernest and the horses will be waiting up at the top of this draw. Can you get to me?"

"I can, but what good will that do?"

"If you can get out of there, I'll try and carry you to the top."

"Noooo," he said slowly, his voice filled with disbelief. "Son, it can't be done! I'm a big man, near one sixty. You'll never make it."

"Maybe not, but I'm open for suggestions. You got a better one?"

The old man chuckled. "You got a way of aiming direct, haven't you. Well, let's get at 'er and see what you can do."

There was a quick shuffle, and soon the man was there beside me, struggling to his feet. He was big, all right, not as big as Pa, but big. He was hard, too, and a body could tell he'd spent the last fifty years or so doing plenty of hard work. He had a long beard and lots of hair, and it was mostly gray with just a little black left in it. I reckon that's why Friendlessman and the others had called him old, for his eyes, his face, his hands, none of that looked old at all.

"How you aiming to do this?"

"You'll have to sit on my shoulders," I answered as I moved around in front of him. "Then—"

"Hold on there! You . . . you're a cripple!"

"Yes sir," I answered, looking right at him. "Have been since birth. Now shall we get on with it?"

Well, his face reflected his doubt, but, like I'd pointed out previously, neither of us had too many options—happen, that is, that we both wanted out of that draw together. "Here," I said, squatting down. "Get on my shoulders."

That old man pulled himself up to his feet, took hold of my shoulders, squeezed like he was testing to see whether I was prime or not, and then he hiked himself aboard. "All right, son," he breathed, and I could hear the pain in his voice. "I'm there. Now let's see if you're up to your brag."

I grinned and rose to my feet. "No brag," I said. "Just facts. Ern told Chief Tabby—"

"You saw Tabby?"

"Yeah, him and maybe eight other braves. That ain't counting all the folks at the village where we slept."

"You *slept* with the Utes?"

"We did, with old Tabby himself, and I ain't ever going to brag about that, either. It was awful."

"Was one of the Utes tall, with a long scar down the side of his face?"

"He came in today. In fact, he's the one that led us here."

"Ungh," the man grunted, exactly like the Utes had done. I listened for him to say more, but when he didn't, I went on with my little tale.

"Anyway, Ern told Tabby that I could throw two of his men clean to the sun. That was stretching it a bit, but ol' Tabby took it in, and I reckon I did too. You hang on for yourself now, leaving my hands free, and I'll do my darndest to get us out of here."

I started out, climbing slowly but easily, doing all I could to keep from getting winded. The way was rough, but that was almost in my favor. I had plenty of good footholds, and where the slope was steep and loose, the bottom of the draw was firm and staggered like a set of stairs. Except that the steps weren't even—it was almost like climbing into the tower of our meetinghouse.

"I'll be dad-gummed," the old man breathed after we'd climbed maybe thirty yards. "Young feller, I do think you might do it. Where'd you learn this stunt?"

"My pa. He'll carry two men and a cedar post on a dead run and still beat most of the kids in our ward. I used to look at him and figure there wasn't a stronger man in the world. Then one day I decided I wanted to be strong too, and so lately I've been working on it. Pa's given me some pointers about balance and lifting, and that's helped a good deal. Still, he beats me all hollow with what he can carry."

"Who's your pa?"

"Jons Soderberg. *Bishop* Jons Soderberg."

"The polyg from over in Sanpete?"

"One and the same."

"Well, don't that beat all. The *Tribune* says they arrested one of Soderberg's sons for the murder of Enock Rhoades. Your brother?"

"Nope. Me."

"You? But I thought they had you in jail."

"Th-they did. Ma got me out . . . on bail. Mister, normally I like ch-chewing the cud like most fellers, but not now. I just got to quit talking. This hill's . . . getting steeper'n the price of imported ginseng at the Co-op, and I just gotta . . . save my breath."

What I'd said was true, too. I was panting like Lyman's dog after it had been chasing rabbits, and for the first time I was beginning to have my doubts. That hill loomed above me maybe fifty more miles, and I truly didn't know if I was going to make it.

"You're right, young feller. I'm sorry for making all this chin music. Just one more question and then I'll be through. Did you kill that young Rhoades feller?"

I snorted and almost threw the old man down. "'C-course not," I grunted. "Would I have . . . admitted to being who I was if I'd been guilty?"

"Then how's come you got arrested? The *Tribune,* which I don't hold much truck with anyway, never did say."

"I th-thought you only had . . . one more question."

"I did! But dad-gum it, this here's important."

"So's getting out of here," I panted. "I . . . I'll tell you all about it . . . when we do."

"All right, all right," the old man muttered. "Reckon I can wait."

He did, and in an agony such as I had never before felt, I pushed myself and that old man up the slope. I could see the top by then, and that gave me a little hope. I could also see blood when I spit, and that scared me. My chest had never hurt so bad, and my legs were like sticks of wood that felt like they were going to break into pieces with every step I took.

I staggered, almost fell, stumbled forward, staggered again, and was thoroughly ready to admit defeat and lie down and die when the rock to the side of my head suddenly exploded. I jerked back, heard the powerful boom of the rifle explosion, and saw more rock chips go flying from the impact of another slug. Right off I was no longer quite so tired.

For the rest of the way up that draw I fairly ran, and that's something for a crippled kid who's packing a big old man on his shoulders. The man I carried was whooping and hollering like he was astride a racehorse, and I'd have joined in and whooped some myownself if I'd only had the wind.

Finally, maybe thirty feet above me, I glimpsed the frightened face of my little brother peering over the edge. "Ern," I gasped, and then something smashed into my leg and I was down and the old man was gone from my shoulders and I was rolling. I slammed into a rock, shook my head to clear it, and lunged to my feet, but instantly my leg buckled and I was down again.

"Hy, what's wrong?"

"I don't know, Ern. I must've wore my leg plumb out. It don't hurt, but I can't use it for sour apples."

"If it don't hurt yet," the old man called out from where I'd dropped him, "it will. You've been shot, young feller."

"Shot? But . . ." I looked down then, saw blood all over the rocks, and realized that the old man was right, and then I found out even more how right he had been. Instantly the pain set in, and it wasn't too long before I was wishing harder than ever that I'd never seen that blasted gold. Trouble, trouble, nothing but trouble. And I hadn't even stolen it.

"Hy, can you crawl?"

"Yeah," I gasped, "I can crawl. Trouble is, I can't crawl and carry the old man too. Ern, we're in a real fix, and—"

Another bullet smacked into the rocks beside me and whined away, and involuntarily I cringed.

"Son," the old man called, "don't you worry none about me. Get yourself on out of here!"

"But—"

"I mean it. You done all you could, and I'm beholden. Now scat!"

"Hy," Ernest called, "do as he says. Rattle your hocks on up here as best you're able. I'll take care of the old man."

Well, the old man snorted in disbelief, but he didn't know Ernest like I did, and so he was entitled. Before we were through, though, my brother and I were going to make that old buzzard a believer in Soderbergs, and that was for sure.

I inched my way up the bottom of the gully, which fortunately was dark with shadow, and I shook every time a rifle exploded and a bullet whined away from somewhere nearby. I came abreast of the old man, did my best to smile at him, crawled on, and suddenly I heard a whirr in the air behind me. I turned in time to see the old man open his mouth in surprise as the rope Ernest had tossed settled squarely around him.

"What the—" he called out.

"Sorry, mister," Ernest answered, "but it's the only way. Make sure it's under your arms and get ready. I'm going to pull you up."

Grumbling, the old man worked the loop down under his arms and pulled it tight. "Where'd a kid learn to throw a rope like that?" he asked of no one in particular. "First toss and downhill to boot, and it was right on the money. Maybe he ain't a kid. Maybe he's one of them midget fellers that does trick roping in the sideshows.

"Say, young feller, is that brother of yours a midget?"

Well, I was hurting something awful, and I was so weak that my head was swimming. Still I had to grin, the old man was that serious. "He is s-some shy of full-growed size," I answered honestly but weakly.

"Then how's he going to haul me out of here?"

"Mister, don't let Ern's size . . . fool you none. That kid's got more gall than a grizzly bear's bladder. He . . . he'll get the job done, providing it's do-able at all."

I started crawling again and heard a grunt behind me, and next thing I knew, that old man was past me and skidding up that hill slicker'n a Bible-thumpin' preacher with the devil on his tail. I followed fast as I was able and ignored as best I could the two or three rifle shots that whined by; moments later I was lying on the far side of that ridge holding my leg and doing my best not to bawl with the terrible pain of it.

"Ern," I moaned, "I . . . I got to bandage this."

"Can't do it, Hy. Not now. Them outlaw fellers will be coming, and we've got to make tracks. Plug it up with something and let me help you up onto Ingersol."

I scowled, but Ernest paid me no mind. He just took my arms, staggered, and then lifted me and started pushing me upward. Next thing I knew, I was astride Pa's big horse. Ernest did the same thing for the old man, and while that was going on I tore a strip from my shirt and stuffed it down into my pants and over that ugly-looking bullet hole. It wasn't much of a patch, I reflected, but for then it would have to do.

Ernest had chosen two fine mounts, and once he had the old man into the saddle of one of them, he scrambled aboard the other. "Come on," he urged, "let's get—"

"Hold up there," the old man ordered. "Where you figure on going from here?"

"Who cares, as long as it's away?"

"I do. It just so happens I know these mountains better'n I know the back of my own hand. We go thataway." And with his finger he pointed upward.

"But . . . but that's up into the high country," Ernest protested.

"That it is. We climb and Friendlessman will have to climb too. That's hard work when a man's afoot, and hopefully he'll get tired and give it up. Besides that, I've got somewhat of a hole up there a piece, and I aim to crawl into it and pull the edges in after me. Are you boys ready?"

We looked at each other, Ernest allowed as we were, and scant seconds later we were fogging it out of that country like three turpentined cats. Or dipped sheep, maybe. Or Euphemistic Lynn Barnes, now that I thought of it, who had run full-bore for an hour after he'd lathered up his saddle gall with undiluted sheep dip. Whichever, those horses were moving flat out, and soon, despite the fact that two of us were crippled, we were long gone from the unhealthy vicinity of Windy Ridge, Territory of Utah.

We rode until after dark and were high up and still climbing. I was pretty tuckered out by then, and it was all I could do to keep my thoughts in one place, let alone stay in the saddle. I'd long since stopped feeling all the pain, but I was weak from the loss of blood and knew that I couldn't go very much further.

What really worried me, though, was that I knew the old man was even worse than I was. To this day I don't know how he stayed in the saddle, but he never complained, never murmured. He just kept on riding, reeling and swaying and somehow every time pulling himself back aboard. Every so often he would give Ernest directions; most of the time, however, his teeth were clenched tight, and I did my best to ride that way myownself.

Finally, just after we had topped out on some ridge that was covered with boulders and a thick stand of timber, I saw the old man sway and sag down, and suddenly he was gone from the saddle. His horse shied and danced away, and I knew we'd come to the end of our trail.

"Ern? H-hold up. The old man's . . . down."

Ernest heard me and turned back, and together we rode to where the old feller lay sprawled in the dirt and rocks of the ridge. Ernest jumped down, and I started to do the same. The next thing I knew I was on the ground myownself, and Ernest was holding my head and patting my face.

"Wh-what happened?"

"Hy, Hy," he said softly, and in the dim light I could see the tears that were streaking his face, "I . . . I thought you'd bought it sure."

"Naw," I whispered, "there's l-lots of fight in me yet. H-how's the old man?"

"Still out. Hy, what we gonna do?"

"I don't know, Ern. Reckon we got no choice but to keep on going. Those outlaw fellers will be coming sure, and Marshal Clawson won't be far behind them."

"We can't do it, Hy. Not like this. You're in no shape to travel, and it's for sure this old feller beside you ain't. No sir, we've got to stay here."

"Here? But Ern, this ain't no p-place to camp. Besides, we've got to get on to . . . to . . . Oh doggone it, little brother, I don't know what to do."

There was a moment's stillness, and finally Ernest spoke. "I've been thinking, Hy. I hate to admit it, but we've got to have help. You and I might could have done it, but not now, not with you all shot to doll rags. Not especially with that old man in such a bad way."

"You're right, Ern. There's also another little rock in the road that I ain't mentioned, and I reckon I ought to. We're onto the reservation for real now, and the Utes won't like that. Zene Hill told me how riled up they were this summer, and I don't imagine anything's changed. I don't reckon we'll be lucky enough to run into a tribe of good Indians twice running, no matter *how* fine our luck's been so far."

Ernest sat still and let the silence mushroom. "Criminently!" he finally said. "I never even thought of that."

"I have, and I'm scared."

"Hy," Ernest suddenly declared, "I'm going for help!"

"What?"

"I mean it. It's our onliest chance."

"But how'll you do it? It's dark, and neither of us has a ghost of an idea where we are. No, I think we'd best—"

"Hy, I'm going. I'll take Ingersol and give him his head, and I know he'll take me home."

"But that's more than a hundred miles! It's got to be!"

"Better'n two, ain't it?" Ernest asked, and I could tell he was grinning. "Hy, I'll get you and the old man set up in a camp, stake out your horses, wrap your wounds as best I can, and then I'll be gone. Come on. Let's get over into those rocks."

Well, we did. Ernest got a small fire going, and by its light he washed and wrapped my wound and splinted the old man's leg. Then he went through the saddlebags of the two horses he had borrowed from the outlaws. Besides the bedrolls and two canteens, he found more than a pound of jerked meat, three cans of peaches, and a pistol and one round of ammunition. It wasn't a great haul, but it beat finding nothing all hollow, and I was thankful.

"You set, Hy?"

"I reckon. You sure about this?"

"I'm sure," Ernest answered, sounding confident as a skunk going for a stroll in the moonlight.

"All right. You be careful, little brother."

"I will. I'll even tie myself into the saddle, happen I get tired. I ain't stopping, Hy, until I fetch help. That's a promise!"

"It's appreciated," I whispered, suddenly choked up with emotion. "Ern, uh . . . t-take care."

"I . . . I will," he sniffed.

"Ern, I . . . well, I sure do love you."

"Yeah," he responded brokenly, "I love you too."

There was quiet then, brittle as glass. A log popped on the fire, and the old man stirred and groaned and was still again. "So long!" Ernest whispered. Then he scrambled onto Ingersol and lifted his hand in farewell, and with that he and that big old horse were gone into the darkness with all the noise of a couple of cutthroat trout sliding out of a sundapple and into deep water. Yes sir, that little brother of mine was something, he truly was.

29

Hilda's Basin Creek— Utah Territory

Ernest rode Ingersol like he had never ridden another horse in his life, and for the first time in that same life he was beginning to feel like maybe horses, or at least this one particular horse, was something other than an enemy.

"Hey ol' boy," he called softly into the darkness, "you and me, we're gonna do it, ain't we. Yes sir, I can tell that you feel it too. We got to do it. Happen we don't, Hy and that old man will be dead as a couple of cans of corned beef."

Ingersol seemed to respond, and Ernest grinned. In the black of the night he was certain he saw the big horse's ears flap back, and he took that as a sure and certain sign of brotherhood.

There was also the route the big Belgian was taking. Right away Ernest had given the horse its head, and right away he could tell that the horse was weaving down the mountain and heading in the general opposite direction from what the old man had led them earlier.

"Good for you." Ernest whispered as he patted the Belgian's thick neck. "You and me, we're two of a kind. No matter what, we'll make it."

Ernest rode then in silence, steadily and with his eyes wide open and alert, and deep within him he felt better and better right along. He could do it! Yes sir, he and Pa's horse were a team, and provided the two of them could last, in one way or another, help was assured for his older brother.

"Ingersol," he grinned a little later, "for a time there, I figured we had about as much a chance as a one-legged man in a kicking contest. Now, though, I reckon we can do it. Yes sir, we surely can. This'll take a while, all right, but on the other hand, it'll be a piece of cake. Let's get on after it!"

All night Ernest rode down the mountain. He crossed Shale and Iron Mine Creeks, thundered across the meadows at the top of Wolf Creek Pass, splashed through Wolf Creek itself, and then turned and made his way down Trail Creek. Ingersol then turned, climbed Vat Creek Ridge, and continued south along the ridge that separated Bill's and Jimmie's Basins. Finally he dropped off again and followed Hilda's Basin Creek, and by then day was coming on and Ernest was finding it hard-pressed to stay even halfway alert.

If he had been, what happened next would never have occurred, for Sanpete County farm boys are smarter than ordinary run-of-the-mill outlaws, especially run-of-the-mill outlaws like Loose-lip Lundstrum, who was not a good outlaw and was a terrible Mormon besides.

But Ernest was swaying with fatigue in the saddle, the willows right there were tolerably thick, and for the life of him he didn't see George Loose-lip Lundstrum stooping down on the bank of Hilda's Basin Creek and scooping himself up an early-morning face-wash and drink.

Loose-lip saw Ernest, however, or rather he heard him coming. Hastily he mounted one of the two horses the outlaws had managed to recapture, and which it was currently his turn to ride, and from that vantage point he discovered the identities of the approaching rider and gigantic horse.

He thought of signaling his compadres in crime, who at that moment were slightly behind him, and suddenly he thought better of it. Nosiree Bob! That kid and his family had caused him grief enough for two men, and here was his chance to get even, but good.

Kneeing his horse closer to where Ernest would pass, Loose-lip loosed the piggin strings on the saddle and took up the rope that was tied there. Quickly and expertly he shook out a loop and held it ready, and then he waited, holding his mount quiet with tightened knees.

The big stallion and its small burden came on, Ernest too tired to see and the wind wrong for the stallion to catch the scent of the waiting enemy.

Loose-lip grinned his wolf-like grin and thought of what Friendlessman and the boys were going to say when he showed them his catch. They wanted the boy, that was certain. But there were two or three of them who would be more than excited to see that horse. Loose-lip remembered vividly the race of the year before, and he knew more than anyone else in Fountain Green the full story of that horse. Now, he thought quickly, he could get that nag back for the boys who had originally stolen him, and things would be truly fine.

Finally Ernest and the stallion trotted past, and expertly Loose-lip flipped an overhand loop, cinching the dozing youth low over his arms. Instantly Loose-lip threw two hard dallies around his saddle horn, sat his horse back on its hocks, and waited.

Ernest cried out, flew high into the air, and came down on the flat of his back, breath-bursting hard.

Suddenly Loose-lip paled. The boy wasn't moving, and he knew full-well that Friendlessman didn't want any of the Soderbergs, or that old man either, killed. Not yet, at least. They still had things to tell, and it was almighty hard to tell them when a feller was dead.

"Hey," he accused the flattened youngster, "you ain't kilt!" The declaration was rewarded by a stirring from Ernest, together with a little creative language that would have surprised his mother and maybe brought a tight smile from his Mormon bishop father, happen either one would have been there to hear it.

The affront relieved Loose-lip's fear of having killed the boy, and so with an oath of his own that was truly profane, he spun his horse about and dragged the boy, still on the flat of his back, across the sandbar and through the willows to where Felix Friendlessman and the others were squatted down over a small fire, planning.

Loose-lip had fully expected the big stallion to follow, for he knew that horses liked company and they also liked to remain close to their riders, especially far away from their home corrals. But Ingersol wasn't any run-of-the-mill horse, not by a long shot. For an instant only the animal hesitated after Ernest had been unhorsed, and then with a buck and a snort it was off and gone into the willows downstream.

Loose-lip finally realized that the horse was gone, and so he cursed again, but still he wasn't really worried. The animal wouldn't go far, and he and the others could rope it down any time they chose. Of course Loose-lip Lundstrum didn't know Ingersol very well. He only knew *about* him, and that was nowhere near enough.

Meanwhile Ernest was spitting sand and rock and other bits of mountain debris, and slowly he came wobbling to his feet. Loose-lip, greeting his fellows with his hoarse laugh and his brag of roping "the smallest and meanest of all the Soderbergs," made the reflex cowboy motion of slacking his loop. He had brought the kid back to the others and had busted him good doing it. By all rights the little brat had ought to stand still and shake where he was. But, as has been mentioned, Ernest Soderberg wasn't any run-of-the-mill kid. He was Soderberg through-and-through, Sanpete Mormon breeding, courageous missionary stock, full of faith as a Book of Mormon prophet, and slick in his think-box as a greased snake. He came up shaking, all right, but not from being busted and dragged. Ernest Soderberg came up mad clear through!

"Who's that?" Jack Moore asked of the glaring boy.

"The youngest Soderberg brat. Found him sneaking past and thought maybe you fellers would like to ask him a few questions. When you're done, I got you another little surprise."

"Where's your brother?" Friendlessman growled, looking up from the sketch he had drawn in the dirt.

"Up there," Ernest answered, nodding his head in the direction of the mountain.

"Dead?"

"Not so's you'd notice."

"You'll take us to him."

"Ha!"

"You will." Friendlessman turned away and began scratching again at his plan, totally ignoring the roped and beaten kid. But that was fine, and Ernest was glad. Why, the man was puffed up as a frog in a cream can. More and more this was beginning to look like fun.

Ernest had felt the slack that Loose-lip had unwittingly given him, and with his coyote's instincts for the sliding maneuver, and silent as a sleeping baby, the boy slipped the noose and stepped from it. He was free then, but the thought of fleeing had not even occurred to him. Ernest Soderberg had other solutions in mind.

Leaving the empty loop behind, he glided down the length of the lariat as it lay on the ground trailing behind Loose-lip's horse. Picking up the rope no more than ten feet from the owner's saddle, the boy swiftly coiled its length until he had the loop up to his hand again. Beyond Loose-lip, the others were commencing to crowd in on Friendlessman, who was showing them where he was certain that Hyrum and the old man were holed up.

Ernest heard two or three things said about his brother that brought the furies to his blood, and that was enough and more. Yes sir, he was fairly itching to get on with what he was about to do. Nothing would distract him now, for the weapon of deliverance was at hand.

Directly at his feet was a large and meandering clump of mountain prickly pear, thorny cactus of the sort that had given more than one man a lot of grief. It was an old patch, but many of the leaves were big and thick, and Ernest was glad for that.

Stretching his foot, he managed to break loose a big, thorny, pear-shaped leaf. It wobbled, appeared about to fall the wrong way, then wobbled back and fell right at Ernest's feet. Reaching down, he grabbed it and juggled it until he had it by the broken joint. Hefting it, he eyed the target. Distance seemed about right. And trajectory. Time to be moving, for sure.

Quickly he shook out a smallish loop of the rope, whirled it once, and threw it to fly over the head and settle mid-body of Loose-lip Lundstrum. In the identical moment and with all the accuracy his amazingly natural abilities gave him, Ernest shoved the thorny pear of the prickly cactus up under the tail of Loose-lip's unsuspecting and quietly standing horse.

The poor animal squealed as if shot, and then it jumped like it was dying from the same nonexistent bullet. And for that matter, it probably felt like it was.

The horse went up not only straight into the air but horizontally sideways and out from under its dirty rider as well. When the poor creature lit once more upon the earth, it did so in full gallop and still squealing. And as Loose-lip had not bothered to unwrap the dallies from about his saddle horn, he was nearly cut in two when his horse reached the full length of lariat going away from him.

The wrench jerked the man out of midair with a hair-raising scream that was cut off somewhere just shy of dead center, and then it slammed him down onto the hardpan of the stream bank with fearsome force. All that saved his miserable life was the application of the ancient law of irresistible momentum against movable body, and move he did. Loose-lip followed his runaway horse at the far and worst end of his own dallied rope, bouncing and slamming about like a barrel rolling loose downhill.

He struck dirt, rock, sand, gravel, more cactus, adobe mud, natural gas, and everything but oil, and he surely would have been worn down to a human nubbin had not the horse turned in its own fright and run back toward the startled group of outlaws.

Doolin and Friendlessman dived frantically for cover, but the Boss, Blue John, and Silvertip, well versed in the fine art of subduing panicked horseflesh, ran out to wedge Loose-lip's horse between their own bodies. In that manner they slowed the animal and finally brought it to a stop only scant seconds before the hapless outlaw would have been ground completely lifeless.

Even so, all hades was immediately owing.

When the rock chips and streambed detritus had ceased flying and the gritty dust had settled again to earth, it was not alone the worn-raw parts of George Loose-lip Lundstrum's hide that were missing.

Not only the big Belgian stallion Ingersol but now even little Ernest Soderberg who had ridden him were both gone entire from the bank of Hilda's Basin Creek, Territory of Utah.

"Now that," Silvertip reflected softly as he stared about at the empty wall of willows, "is *my* kind of kid."

"Bah!" Blue John growled disgustedly, and together he and Silvertip and Jackson T. Moore began administering some much-needed aid to the hapless George Loose-lip Lundstrum.

30

Various Locations—
Utah Territory

The friendly proprietor of the general store at Soldier's Fort was not at the moment feeling very friendly. Others in his narrow store obviously were, though.

"Say Frenchy," one of the dozen men called as he waved a bottle drunkenly in the air, "grubstake me to another bottle of that there snake-oil whisky you got out in the back! It's like to do me in."

"That there Turley's prime gin," another man howled, a big man with a thick, black beard and a shirt that hadn't seen a location other than the wearer's back inside the last six months. "The demons get you, there's still a smile or two left in the bottle."

"Yes," the proprietor muttered, altogether afraid of the big man and his crowd of companions, "and it's a foolish rat that goes back to the same poison. No sir, boys, I grubstaked Tranch here and a couple of the rest of you enough and more, and all I ever seen from it was more empty promises. You want more of my goods, let's see *l'argent,* the cash money."

"Aw, Frenchy," the man with the bottle whined, "trust us. You know that gold's up there. That Lundstrum feller swore it when he came through! Why, they've got that kid and the old man trapped—"

"Trapped?" Frenchy Dupont declared with scorn in his voice. "Did you see how Lundstrum looked when he staggered in here? I'd of swore he'd trapped a she-grizzly in the back of a cave where she had two cubs to protect. And he was whining like a puppy full-up with porky-hog quills the entire time he was here. Boys, I'd as soon be caught in a room with no doors and no windows and eighty-three angry catamounts as to be up there with Friendlessman and them others."

There was a snort from the big man in the filthy shirt, he who was called Tranch. "Yeah, and that's why you're clerking in this hole of a store instead of out there where the *real* money is. Now Frenchy, I've run plumb out of patience—"

The door suddenly screeched open and a man entered, a big, clean-looking man who had a black beard streaked with gray. He wore a black broadcloth suit, the kind a minister might wear; he had a white shirt and bowtie, and his hat was low-crowned and flat-brimmed, the kind worn by most preachers. He was rangy, sort of, and somewhat gaunt. As mentioned, he stood fairly tall above his bunions and had wrists like the knucklebones on a four-year-old steer and hands the size of stove lids. He was gangly, maybe, and lanky, but both Frenchy Dupont and even dirty-shirt Tranch got the distinct suspicion that the Good Lord had not cut the gawky figure standing before them precisely to fit the cloth of the ministry.

The man nodded pleasantly at the others and then turned his back and began examining the leather goods that were hanging on the wall.

"Hey, preacher," Tranch sneered, "you're lost. The church is down the road."

"Yeah," the man with the empty bottle agreed sarcastically. "About forty miles."

"Better get to it," a third man giggled. "You're liable to miss your meeting with all the other sisters."

There was crude general laughter, and several of the men clapped each other on the back.

"Hey, boys, maybe this feller's a Mormon preacher."

"No, an upstanding preacher-man like this?"

"Well," Tranch declared, "if he is, then for sure we've found ourselves a female pansy."

"Boys," Frenchy Dupont whispered, "don't start any trouble."

"Frenchy," Tranch laughed, "you worry too much. That pansy ain't gonna cause no trouble for us. Why, he's on his way to church. Ain't that so, preacher?"

The black-suited man in the beard slowly turned and gazed at the crowd of men. "In a manner of speaking," he replied gently.

"Ha!" Tranch declared, turning from the man and forgetting that he was even there. "What'd I say? Man's a coward, pure and simple. Now Frenchy, about them supplies."

"Tranch," the store-keeper replied, "I told you already. I've grubstaked you for the last time. Besides, you fellers don't have a ghost of a chance of finding that gold. I told you what Lundstrum looked like, and it was considerable worse than I said. Additionally, that kid stopped down the street two . . . no, *three* days ago. He was riding that big Belgian stallion he and that other kid had ridden out on, and he stopped at the telegraph office."

"So what?"

"So this: I don't know where he sent his telegram, or to whom, but I'd take odds he was calling for help."

Tranch laughed derisively.

"You wouldn't laugh," Frenchy declared, "happen you'd seen that Lundstrum feller. He wouldn't say much about what happened, but it looked like he'd been throwed so high that St. Peter had whittled his initials in his boot-soles. I'm telling you straight, he was so beat up he had to lean against the counter just to spit."

"Anybody can get lucky, and those two kids did. They won't hurt us. Why, once we get that gold, we'll just plant 'em shallow without a reading. Won't nobody be the wiser."

"Maybe. But the one got lucky with Lundstrum was the little kid on the stallion, all by himself. And he was little, too. No more'n knee-high to a long stirrup. Think what those growed-up fellers who are trapped up there could have done had they tangled with him. Boys, you'd best watch your P's and Q's."

"Bah!" Tranch sneered, suddenly pulling a pistol. "Frenchy, I'm tired of asking and I'm tired of waiting. Fill up a burlap bag with bacon and canned goods and other supplies, and don't forget a couple of bottles of that Turley—"

"Is there a problem here?" the tall man in the black suit asked, stepping forward. He had a mule-skinner's whip in his hand, one he had been examining, and none of the others had noticed that he had been listening to the conversation.

"N-no, sir," Frenchy Dupont stuttered, as afraid for the tenderfoot as he was for himself. "I don't need no help at all, especially from you. Me and these boys were just working out—"

"See here, preacher," Tranch growled, thrusting himself forward and thumping the black-suited man on the chest, knocking him back a step, "keep your long skinny nose out of things that ain't none of your affair."

"But I thought—"

"You ain't paid to think, pansy. All you Mormons and preachers is alike. All gurgle and no guts. Now shove off!"

"Did I hear you say," the man turned to Frenchy, suddenly ignoring the glowering Tranch, "that the boy who stopped at the telegraph office rode a big Belgian stallion?"

"You did."

"Did he or the young feller who was with him earlier happen to mention a name? Like Soderberg, for instance?"

"They didn't, but they did say they was brothers. They looked kin, too, and they—"

"Say," Tranch shouted, "what is this? I told you to beat it, preacher, and when Tranch says beat it, he means—"

He never got the rest of the order out, for one of those stove-lid fists smashed full bore into his own sensitive proboscis. It showered bright red blood, but that was only the beginning. Tranch had only just noticed the new coloring of his shirt when the other stove-lid tunneled into his midsection, which was softened and bulging from years of holding quart upon poison quart of snake-oil Turley and other nefarious brands of booze.

Tranch doubled over; on his way down he met a long, wide-boned kneecap coming up, and the next thing dirty-shirted Tranch knew, he was flat out on the floor, covered with blood, and with not a desire in all the world to get back up.

"Well," the preacher said almost apologetically as he leaned over him and tossed away his pistol, "you *did* say to beat it. Frankly, I couldn't think of a better thing to beat.

"Now," he declared sternly, rising to his feet and looking at the other men, who were suddenly very sober, "I did tell you I was going to do a little preaching. Happen the bunch of you and your misfortunate partner aren't out of here in sixty seconds, the sermon will proceed. I will commence reading all of you from the Book."

The men looked at the tall gangly man in the black suit, and they were puzzled indeed. With one look the man was milk-toast as they come. With the other he looked gritty as fish eggs rolled in sand. If they cocked their heads one way, the feller appeared so helpless he couldn't drive nails into a snowbank. Cocked the other, he appeared like he might haul hell flat out of its shuck. All of them decided instantly that in a tight election, they wouldn't bet on him either way.

One thing was certain, however, and Tranch's cronies decided they would take bets on it all summer. That black-and-gray bearded man hadn't been raised in the territory. No sir. He wouldn't know a whiffle-tree from a wagon-tongue or a whey-belly bull from a spring-bred heifer. He was as out of place there as a cow on a front porch. As far as the decking of Tranch was concerned, the preacher had been lucky indeed.

"Let's take him!" one of the men shouted, and they started toward him. Suddenly the door screeched open again and another man entered, a small man in range clothes who had the swarthy skin of an Indian.

"Excuse me," he said softly as he removed his hat, "but this looks like a lopsided dance. Would you mind if I bought a ticket and joined in?"

The tall, dark-suited man grinned. "The more the merrier," he declared, and then he turned again to face the men.

"What is this?" one shouted. "A preacher and an educated Indian? Come on, boys, let's learn 'em a thing or two!"

And so they tried. They surely did. He of the bottle broke it off at the neck and took one swing with the jagged edge; the next thing he knew, he was lying in a whole lot more broken glass on the boardwalk out front, all of it fly-specked windowglass, and that general store was getting more light than it had seen in years. He started to get up and then saw the man of the stove-lid fists gazing levelly at him, so he quietly laid himself back down in the glass. It was, he suddenly decided, an altogether more comfortable bed than he could find inside.

From that moment the battle truly raged. Fists splattered into noses, ears, and bellies; blood flew, and so did bodies; and of a truth the black-suited man and the Indian were having a mighty fine time of it. The Indian was not large, but he was faster almost than sight, and he jumped those men one after another like a roadrunner jumps a rattler, pummeling them into the floor. He whom they called the preacher, meanwhile, was smiling with pleasure as he picked a man up and easily threw him into a knot of the others, sending them rolling like ninepins. Then, before any of the men were even certain what had happened, stove-lid fists were tapping them on their jaws or behind their ears, and one after another they rolled over and lay still.

Then it was quiet in the store, and the one they had called the preacher straightened and started to turn to see how the Indian had gotten along.

"Jons," the Indian hissed. "Behind you! A gun!"

The black-suited man quickly reached out to the counter and then turned, ready. Tranch, staggering to his feet, was drawing his spare pistol from his rear pocket, and in his eyes was the desire to kill. Suddenly something ice-like and painful curled around his wrist, and he screamed. His hand flew upward; the pistol discharged and blew a hole in the ceiling, and then it went clattering from his deadened grip.

With terror-filled eyes he watched as the tall black-suited man wielded the mule whip like he'd been trained to it all his life. First an open gash appeared on one of Tranch's cheeks, and then, more quickly than he could imagine, his other cheek was laid open. He raised his hands to protect himself, then watched in horror as the trigger finger on his shooting hand vanished with a sharp snap of the whip, and then he screamed again.

Long and loud his cry wailed, continuing until a sharp slap brought him momentarily to his senses.

"D-don't hit me with that again," Tranch wailed in fear as he gripped his bleeding hand.

The man did not answer. Instead he laid down the whip, took out his white handkerchief, and began to bind the man's mutilated appendage.

"Wh-who *are* you fellers?" Tranch then whispered, his face pale with shock. "Who'n—"

"That's Zenos Hill," the man in black answered quietly as he finished with the hand. "My name is Soderberg, Jons Soderberg, from Fountain Green. Those two young fellers you plan on killing, the ones up on the mountain? They happen to be my sons and Zene's friends. Just thought you'd like to know. When you kill 'em, you'll be coming over me and Zene to do it."

Carefully then he stepped back, picked up the whip, and placed it upon the counter. "I'll pay for the damage," he said to the stunned storekeeper.

"The dickens you will," Frenchy Dupont chortled. "No matter what this costs, it won't be near what I'd of paid for a ticket to see the fight I just saw! That Tranch is a mean man, and he's had that coming for a long time."

"Well," Zenos Hill declared, "he surely won't be shooting anyone for a spell."

"If we can't pay for the damages," Jons Soderberg said, "then I'd surely like to buy a horse. That, a saddle and blanket, a bridle, and a good rifle with plenty of ammunition. And yes, I'll take the whip here, too. Happen we get visitors up there on the mountain, I do want to receive them properly."

The men on the floor stared, and then hastily they scrambled to their feet and, with Tranch leading out, departed.

Moments later Jons Soderberg and Zene Hill stood in the street, waiting for a horse to be delivered.

"I'm glad you happened in," Jons Soderberg said quietly. "They had me a little outnumbered."

"I doubt it," Zene Hill replied.

"You here for the same reason as I am?"

"I reckon. A feller stopped by the herd this morning on his way up to, as he said, 'gather in the gold.' I brought him back in somewhat less than glowing health and thought I would send a telegram and let you know of the situation while I was here. I was some surprised to see you."

"Ernest sent me a telegram already," Jons Soderberg replied, "and I came a-running. I have two fine boys on that mountain, and until this is over, I aim to stand beside them."

"You want help?"

Jons looked at the smaller man. "The older boys are scattered all over the country, Zene, or they'd be here as well. I reckon you know that. If you can spare the time, and if Andrew's herd can get by for a day or so without you, why, I can't think of anybody's help I'd rather have. I know that Hyrum would feel the same."

The two men looked at each other and grasped hands, and then together they turned and strode up the rutted street of Soldier's Fort.

The saloonkeeper in Nephi laughed outright, and so did the five men who stood at the bar. "You fellers want to know what?" he asked, waving a glass in the direction of the two young men who had just walked in through the doorway.

"Do they still have that Soderberg kid pinned down up in the Uintahs?" the tall one asked quietly once again.

"Either pinned down or dead, and I hope he ain't dead. Maybe he deserves it, but if he's dead, it'll be mighty tough getting him to lead us to the gold."

"Us?"

"Yeah. Me and the boys here are figuring on joining that little war. The odds are good—just a kid and an old man. They're both hurt, and the stakes are high enough to make it interesting."

"Who's the old man?" the other of the two near the door asked quietly.

"Beats us. Likely some stray the crippled kid snagged onto for help. What's all this to you young fellers?"

"Well," the tall one answered as he lifted his hat and scratched his scalp, "we figured on going on up there and maybe getting involved just a mite ourownselves."

There was a chorus of laughter from the five who were standing at the bar. "Young fellers," one of the men scoffed, "you're a mite too late. What that boy's bought hisself on that mountain is one life less than a Mexican standoff—maybe two, happen the old man gets in the way. No sir, there's maybe half a hundred fellers up there right now. We figure to be on our way as soon as the train comes through, and the train's sold out. There just ain't no room for two more."

The two young men looked at each other, and then carefully they stepped apart. "You fellers notice the cracks in the ceiling?" the taller of the two suddenly asked.

The men, as one, looked up, saw no cracks, dropped their eyes, and found themselves staring down the yawning muzzles of two Colt .44s.

"Grab yourselves some of those cracks you don't see," the shorter of the two said quietly. "Good. Now with your right hands, reach down, each of you, and unbuckle your gunbelts. Careful now . . . gently, gently . . . that's the way. Now drop them to the floor.

"Bartender," he continued, "take your shotgun in your left hand and bring it around front of the bar, real easy like."

The two young men watched as the orders were flawlessly carried out. "You brethren are doing right fine," the short one continued. "Lyman, gather up their weapons."

"Now see here—"

"Mister, we do see. We see five growed-up men ready to head out into the hills to kill some poor innocent crippled kid and a beat-up old man. Well, we ought to let you at 'em just so they could learn you a *real* lesson. But time's short, so we'll have to do it ourownselves. Take off your boots and your britches, all five of you."

"Our boots and britches! Now, that's right unneighborly, boys."

"Yep, it is. But so is killing folks. Now get on with it!"

"Jim," the taller of the two young men questioned, turning to the other, "what for you want their boots and trousers?"

"You ever heard of tenderfeet, Lyman? Naked tenderfeet? If these fellers ain't the bashfullest tenderfeet yet, they will be by the time they get home, crossing all them rocky roads barefoot and in their long johns. They'll also have missed the train. Gather up their boots and britches, Lyman, and we'll give'em to John Ord. If these fellers want 'em back badly enough, they can fish them out of John's watering trough, up east of town."

Lyman grinned and began gathering up boots and britches. Jim, meanwhile, held his .44 steady, and the men did not move.

"You fellers won't get away with this," one of the men fumed.

"Oh, I think we will." Jim smiled laconically. "We ain't stealing, we're just evening up the odds."

"The odds? What're you talking about?"

"That boy on the mountain, mister. His name, in case you don't know, is Hyrum Vincent Soderberg. Just happens that last name's ours too. We're a couple of his brothers."

There was a deathly quiet in that high-ceilinged saloon, and the muzzles of the two .44s looked wider and darker than ever.

"Now," the tallest of the two brothers said quietly, "if you'd like to serve papers on us, we'll be right up on that mountain, just a-waiting to open an extra session of court. If you're feeling lucky, why, look us up and do it."

Johnny Soderberg cussed as thirty-eight head of horses skirted the brush-built neck of his makeshift corral and thundered away.

"Blast," he said as he smashed his hat against his dusty Levi Strauss britches. "Second time this week! If I don't get them horses rounded up, Brother Cook's going to fire me."

Hopefully the young man rode to the corral and looked inside. Seven. For two days he had chased that herd, and all he'd managed to catch was seven head.

The sun along the Green River was hot, and Johnny reached up and wiped his forehead. Off in the cottonwoods a chorus of cicadas split the morning air with their shrill buzzing, and a wandering breeze bent the grass on the bar of the river before him. But Johnny didn't notice that—he didn't see the beauty of the place at all. He'd failed to round up thirty-eight of Brother Cook's horses, and if he didn't have them by the end of the week, he'd not get paid. That meant that with his mother in prison the little ones would go hungry, and Johnny just couldn't stand—

"Johnny!"

Quickly he spun around and stared at the bluff above the river.

"Johnny, come quick! I got news!"

"Mattie Butts," he muttered in surprise. "What are you doing way out here?

"Just a minute," he called, turning his horse and spurring it into action. "I'm coming!"

Moments later, Johnny reined his mount in on the top of the bluff overlooking the muddy Green River. Swinging to the ground, he lifted the young lady down and took her into his arms.

"Mmmm . . ." she mumbled, trying to work her way free.

"That's what I say, sugar. I been seeing your pretty-eyed face in my dreams for nigh onto a month now. Our wedding is still an eternal sixty-nine days and three hours and twenty-six minutes off, and I'm powerful glad you came to see me! Let's have another kiss—"

"Johnny, for heaven's sake, this is important!"

"I'll say it is! Now let's—"

"Johnny, listen to me! Hyrum's in trouble, and everybody thinks Ernest is up there with him."

Johnny Soderberg was suddenly all business. "Up where?" he asked as he released the girl and stepped back.

"The Uintahs."

"Well, he's supposed to be working there."

"Johnny, he's been in prison for murder since you left, which was a trumped-up charge if ever I saw one, and there're folks after him trying to kill him. Ernest sent a telegram for help, and I thought . . . well, I hoped you'd want to know."

"You came all this way alone?"

"It was the only way to reach you, Johnny, and I knew it was what anyone else in your family would do. I took the train to Thompson, and then I borrowed a horse and rode south . . ."

Quickly Mattie explained, and within five minutes Johnny was on his way to the railroad, escorting beside him the courageous girl. When a Soderberg needed help, a lonely and frightening ride for a young woman who was marrying into the family was expected, for frontier women were anxious to stand beside their men and never cower behind them. Johnny knew that, and for the first time he also knew that Mattie Butts was a woman he could be truly proud of.

Additionally, in Johnny's mind, thirty-eight uncaptured horses belonging to Scott Cook suddenly seemed awfully unimportant. Those animals had gotten along fine for nearly a year, and another couple of days wouldn't make any difference at all.

U.S. Deputy Marshal Tinsdale sat in the coolness of his office at the Provo Jail, swatting flies. Outside, the sun beat down mercilessly, and he was glad that the walls of the jail were thick. Even so, the heat was bad, and he was forever—

The sudden beating of hooves against the hardened street caught his attention, and he was already watching as the door to the jailhouse swung inward and Marshal Hebron Clawson stormed into the room.

"Mr. Tinsdale," he said. Sweat dripped from the ends of his dirty yellow mustache and stained his already filthy shirt. "I just got word, and I got to get me a posse right away."

"Whoa," Tinsdale urged as he swung at another fly. "Come at this from the beginning, Clawson. You got word about what, and you need you a posse for who?"

"Mr. Tinsdale, I ain't got time for this! I got to catch that train!"

"The only thing you'll be catching is my boot in the seat of your pants," Tinsdale said easily. "Now let's hear it all, from the beginning."

Marshal Clawson ground his yellowed teeth in frustration. "Oh for—" he growled, but when he looked at Deputy Tinsdale he did not continue with his complaint. "Yes sir," he said quickly. "The whole story. I just heard down at the saloon that some fellers have that murdering Soderberg kid pinned down up above Wolf Creek Pass. He's wounded bad, I hear, and I figure if I can get me a posse and get up there pronto, then maybe I can get him before—"

Suddenly he stopped and stared upward at the giant who had risen before him. "B-be . . ." he stammered, "b-before . . ."

"Is that the boy who came in here and freed his pa?" Tinsdale asked sternly.

"Y-yes sir, it is one and the same. He killed that poor Enock Rhoades—"

"Has that been proven?"

"Well no, but—"

"Clawson, that kid wasn't more than ten or eleven when Rhoades disappeared!"

"I know, Mr. Tinsdale, but he had his gold, besides which—"

Deputy Tinsdale slammed his huge hand down on the desk. "Besides which, that Soderberg kid ain't no killer! I talked to him here, twice, and he don't have the eye for it! I know! Now who has him pinned down?"

"M-Mister Doolin," Marshal Clawson stuttered. "H-him and a fellow name of Friendlessman."

"Doolin? Friendlessman? I can't be hearing this! Clawson, you are dumber than I thought, and that is some dumb. Doolin, as you ought to have heard, is a known crook. Friendlessman, on the other hand, has remained on the right side of the law, but only just barely. Only a month ago Caleb Rhoades reported that Friendlessman was hounding him worse than ever, breaking into his barn and trespassing upon his property. On this very desk I have a warrant against him.

"Clawson, I order you onto that mountain to arrest those two men and any others who may be with them."

"Mr. Tinsdale, I won't do it!"

"You won't?"

"No, by thunder, I won't. That Soderberg kid and his pa and the rest of that miserable family have given me more unrighteous grief over the past three years than any man had ought to take in a whole entire lifetime. Whatever that kid's getting up there, he purely deserves! I just won't go!"

"Very well," Deputy Tinsdale responded mildly, "I suppose you are right."

Marshal Clawson looked up at the huge man, his face a study in surprise. "You . . . you mean I can gather my posse and—"

"I didn't say that," Deputy Tinsdale said as he held the flyswatter out to the filthily clothed marshal. "I merely said that you were right. You won't be going onto that mountain. You'll stay here, swatting flies, while *I* go."

"But . . . but . . ."

"No buts, Marshal, but a word of warning, nevertheless. Jons Soderberg was arrested for unlawful cohabitation and for nothing else. In my own opinion that does not make him a criminal. Now there are folks who say the Edmunds-Tucker Law is constitutional and a fine law, but there are others, just as smart, who say the law itself is illegal and shameful. Happen that second bunch is right, and I personally am amongst them, why then you and me and every other polyg hunter in the territory could be imprisoned for harassment of innocent, law-abiding citizens. My advice, marshal, is to go easy on that good bishop. And marshal, he *is* a good bishop.

"As far as Soderberg's son Hyrum goes, both you and I know that murder charge was trumped up. Caleb Rhoades himself told me he knew the identity of the Indian that had killed his brother. Did you catch that, marshal? Indian. Spelled I-N-D-I-A-N. Not S-O-D-E-R-B-E-R-G.

"Now, take this flyswatter, hold it in your hand like this, and use it liberally. Flies you may chase down freely, but not Soderbergs. Happen there is any trouble at all while I am away, you will be back there swatting flies *behind* bars instead of up here where I am sure you would prefer to be. Do I make myself clear?"

Apparently he had, for as the gap-toothed Deputy Tinsdale was making long-legged strides toward the railroad station on the south end of town, with his hastily albeit carefully selected posse following, he could hear behind him the very rapid slapping of the flyswatter against the walls and desk of the Provo jail.

Marshal Clawson was certainly a good hand against those flies, Deputy Tinsdale thought, grinning. Of course, with those filthy clothes he could probably be arrested for entrapment, but still . . .

Hattie Soderberg was busy straining the milk she had just taken from Hepzibah, the family cow. "LaRue," she said sternly, "hold that cheesecloth tight, for heaven's sake."

"I am, Ma, I am!"

"Well, it isn't tight enough. I'm in a hurry, and—"

"Sister Soderberg, excuse me."

The timid voice behind her surprised Hattie, and she almost dropped the container of milk she was holding.

"Oh!" she said, spinning around. "You startled me, Ida Mae."

"I . . . I didn't mean to. I just . . . well, I need to talk to you for a minute—alone, if I could."

"Very well, dear." Hattie turned to hide her smile, and with a wave of her hand she gave quick instructions to her daughter. "LaRue, hand Ida Mae the strainer, and you run along.

"Now, hold it tightly, Ida Mae. That cloth has a way of pulling free every chance it gets, and you know what the milk is like then."

"Uh, Sister Soderberg, I—"

"You may call me Hattie, my dear. All of the girls in the ward do."

"Thank you, ma'am. I . . . don't really know where to begin, but I've said some pretty cruel things, and I must apologize."

"Cruel things? I'm afraid you'll need to clear those up with Hyrum."

"No, I don't mean . . . I mean . . . well, I said some terrible things about you as well."

Now Hattie Soderberg slowly stood upright and gazed into the eyes of the young girl. "About me? Whatever for, my dear?"

"It was when you raised the money to pay Hyrum's bail. At the time, I thought it was a horrid thing to do to Brother Short, and I said as much to Hyrum. I said things to a few others, as well."

"Words on the wind, I take it?"

"Yes'm. I feel just awful and want to apologize. I hope I haven't done you damage."

"Of course you haven't. I did what I did with my eyes wide open, and I knew there would be criticism. That there has been so little has surprised me. Still, I do feel badly about what I had to do."

"You do?"

"Of course. What good Latter-day Saint woman would feel good about gambling or about deceitfully using two fine men? Thank goodness Harrison Short and Andrew Aagard are understanding people. Both of them know it was the only means I had of raising that money, and neither of them has been anything but kind and sweet.

"You see, my dear, when a mother is put in a position of protecting her child against overwhelming condemnation, especially when she knows of his innocence, she will go to nearly any lengths to save that child. Even now I would do it all again if it meant I could free my Hyrum from the clutches of those evil people."

Ida Mae stared at the container of milk. "Are . . . are you sure he's innocent, ma'am?"

"Ida Mae, I have known that boy for quite a while now, and he surely isn't perfect. Still, to my knowledge he has never lied to me. As far as I know, Hyrum Soderberg doesn't have an evil or dishonest bone in his body."

"But Felix said—"

"Ida Mae, I'm going to tell you something that you must swear never to reveal. Do you so swear?"

"Why . . . uh . . . yes, I guess I do."

"Very well then. I would like to tell you about Polly's son Ernest and Deaf Man Hibbard."

For the next fifteen minutes, a very sober Ida Mae Sorenson listened intently as Hattie Soderberg taught the young lady about her son and about a man who was supposedly deaf but who had overheard one Felix Ethelbert Friendlessman and one Loose-lip Lundstrum and one Mister Doolin of Provo plotting to kidnap and possibly kill her son.

Ida Mae gasped when the other had finished. "Are you certain?" she asked.

"As Hyrum would say, I'm as certain as flies head for new butter. If you'd like, ask Deaf Man Hibbard yourself. But make sure he's alone or you'll never get a word from him."

"No," Ida Mae breathed. "I . . . I don't think I need to do that. Deep down I've known it all along. It's just that . . . well, Felix is so convincing, so refined . . . "

"Ida Mae, Hyrum could be just as refined if he didn't have to support our family. Did you know his goal is to read at least six books this summer? He reads books that I can't even pronounce the titles to, let alone the authors. He has a fine mind, Ida Mae, and given the right friends and the right chances, one day the world will hear of him.

"Now, however, he may never get the chance to learn all the things that seem to set his mind afire. I have heard that he is seriously wounded, and Friendlessman and the others—"

"Wounded?" Ida Mae gasped. "Hyrum is *wounded?*"

"Yes, so I have heard."

"But they wouldn't—"

"Ida Mae, did you think they would chase him down for fun? Did you think that this was some sort of children's game? Those men are selfish—evil. They are murderers, and they will stop at nothing to destroy my son. In fact, he has been in a battle for his very life since the moment he rode into Provo to bail his father out of prison. He is alone in that battle, and I'm certain he feels that loneliness even more strongly since you have abandoned and condemned him.

"I am on my way now to catch the train to Spanish Fork and Soldier's Fort. If I can get no closer, at least he will know that I stood by him as well as I was able."

"Oh, Sister Soderberg," Ida Mae sobbed as she threw her arms about the older woman, "I'm so sorry. I never should have . . ."

For a moment the two women held each other tightly; then Ida Mae pulled away, wiped her eyes on her apron, turned, and ran to the gate. "I'm going to him," she declared as she climbed onto her father's white mare. "Hyrum needs me now more than ever before, and I'm going to find him."

"But Ida Mae . . ."

Without waiting to reply, the determined young lady spurred her mare and was gone.

31

Hades Pass, Uintah Mountains— Utah Territory

"Do you think they're still coming?"

"It's hard to tell."

Exasperated, I looked at the old man. "I know it's hard to tell," I growled. "I was just wondering what you *think*."

"At a time like this, it doesn't much matter what I think or even *if* I think. Like I told you, a fellow can't never tell."

"Criminently," I grumbled as I poked the fire, "you wouldn't admit water was wet."

"Not if I was drowning," the old man answered grimly.

I stared at the old man and realized that he wanted to say no more, so I threw another branch onto the fire.

Four days had passed since Ernest had gone, four days in which the old man and I had seen no one. Both of us had started to regain our strength, though things were mighty slow going. I was still hobbling and reeling around like a pup trying to find a spot to lie down on, and the old man moved like he was drunk as a fiddler's clerk. Still, as far as being our old selves was concerned, both of us were coming close.

"Do you think he made it?" I asked as I flipped over the mess of fish we were roasting for supper.

"Your brother?"

"Uh-huh."

The old man looked at me, then reached out and poked a small stick of his own into the fire. "Might've," he replied quietly. "I know one who didn't, but yours might've."

"One who didn't?" I asked.

The old man ignored my question, so I asked it again. "What'd you mean, one who didn't?"

"Brothers," the old man answered obliquely. "Yours was small, but he was knowing as a bunkhouse rat. Maybe he did."

"Ern's slick, all right. 'Course, so's that Friendlessman feller."

"That he is," the old man mumbled. "Besides that, he's shuffled himself in with a powerfully stacked deck. I'll tell you this, young feller: you *do* pick the enemies."

"I didn't pick 'em. They came after me—them and who knows how many others. It all started the minute I found that blasted gold."

"Gold can do strange things to a man, all right. It can destroy friendships, tear apart families and loved ones—all sorts of things."

"Yeah," I agreed. "I truly understand what you're saying. You know, that poke of gold cost me my girl, and it nearly cost me my friendship with Zene Hill."

"Zene Hill's your friend, huh? I know him. Indian, ain't he?"

"He surely is. He's also white and delightsome as any man I ever met. The Indian side of him, though, that's what shows up first. Why, he don't leave enough tracks to trip up an ant. I've learned things from Zene that ain't written down anywhere in a book, like how to float pack horses across a swollen stream and how to track game and how to doctor a mule or horse what's been snakebit and a lot of other things.

"Another thing I learned is that there isn't anybody who wants to hear about the hard times you've had, so if anything goes wrong, just keep it to yourself."

"Good advice. Speaking of Indians, did you know they're out there now?"

"I didn't know, but I reckoned they might be, since this is their land. Are they friendly?"

"Who can tell? They're notional folk, sometimes willing to give you their very lives, other times just as willing to laugh and take yours. These ain't friendly, but we've done nothing suspicious, so they ain't killing mad yet either."

"Why're they out there?"

"Watching us. They don't know about us, but they do know that most of them other fellers are after gold. That gold's sacred to them. Right now, they're waiting for us to make a move, but once the waiting ends, it's Katie bar the door.

"In my time, young feller, I've had my share of doings with Comanches, Kiowas, Arapahos, Cheyennes, Utes, and almost every kind of Indian there is. With most I got along fine; but when he's fighting, no Indian needs take a back seat to any man. I've heard that a European general called the Indians the finest light cavalry under the sun, and I believe him.

"When a man travels in Indian country, he'd better just sort of sift through gentle-like and take up no more room than need be. When you're on their land, as we are now, it's best to keep out of sight and sleep without a fire, unless it can be well hidden. On top of that, a man had better do a little praying, happen he's a praying man. And the deeper a man gets into Indian country, the more of a praying man he becomes. Young feller, where Lamanites are concerned, you just can't afford to miss any bets."

I sat silently, thinking of all he had said. Tabby had befriended Ernest and me, but why? And what of Zene Hill? How did he fit in with all this? As if reading my mind, the old man suddenly spoke again.

"What'd Zene Hill tell you about that gold you found?"

"Well, first he took it from me—said it was sacred to the Indians. Then when he found out what I was going to do with it, he gave it back, the whole poke."

"Gave it back, did he? What *were* you going to do with it?"

"Get Pa out of jail, and if there was any extra, give it to Ma to help her out. I done 'er too, except for a bit I gave to Ida Mae Sorenson."

"Seems like a good use. Young feller, tell me straight—did you kill for that gold, or have anything to do with the killing?"

Reaching down, I turned the fish over on the rock we were using for a frying pan. "Mister," I answered, looking him squarely in the eye, "I was eleven years old when that happened, so what would you think? No, I didn't kill, and I didn't even know there'd been a killing until just before I found that gold."

"Then how'd you find it?"

"It was crazy," I answered, frowning, "the worst streak of luck I ever had. And the gold didn't change my luck, either. It was almost three weeks back when I was hunting Andrew Aagard's mules. It came on dark, I needed a place to camp, and those mules took me to a swale down near where Currant Creek flows into Red. It was a dark night, but there was something besides dark in that swale. I could feel it. Ma says both Ern and I have the gift—I think she means for feeling things beyond the veil. I don't know if we do or not, but right away I knew *something* had happened in that place. I started looking around, and before long I found the remains of a tent and a bedroll, two mule skulls with bullet holes in them, part of a pack frame, and, the next morning, inside a rotten log on which I'd sat to rest, I found that poke of gold."

"What'd it look like?"

"The gold or the pouch?"

"Both."

"The gold looked mostly pure. It was in long, thin strands, almost like string. There were some other shapes too, like chunks, and a little rock was caked on them, but not much."

"So he did get there," the man murmured. "That does say something. What about the pouch?"

"It was long and narrow, made of leather that had mostly gone black and hard, and it had ER tooled into it. That's what Doolin from down to Provo got so het up about."

"I know Doolin. He's a bad one. He's also a coward, but that just makes him more dangerous. You do pick 'em, young feller."

"Him and Friendlessman and how many others? Old man, looks to me like the two of us are up to our navels in crooks who want that gold." I paused and looked the old man square in the eye. "And I *still* don't know who you are. You got a name?"

"I do, but it's not very important. Old Man's good enough, I reckon."

"Maybe, maybe not. I have a feeling about you too."

"A feeling?"

"Uh-huh. Kind of tight, here in my stomach. Makes me wonder *who* I can count on."

"Well, son," the old man said, leaning back, "Brother Brigham told my pa never to count on nobody but the Lord and his own good sense. Seems like sound advice."

I stared even harder at the old man. Was he trying to tell me something? Was he trying to set me up? Who was he, really, and why had Friendlessman been shooting at him? They were all good questions, but I had no answers, and that worried me a great deal.

"Well," I said as I forked over a fish to the old man, "I don't know if you're after that gold or not, and to be honest, I don't care very much. Personally, I don't want any more of that gold at all. Every bit of this trouble started down in that swale on Currant Creek when I found the first poke."

"You don't want the gold?" he questioned, eyeing me closely.

"No sir, I don't."

"You just don't know, young man. Either that or you are a liar. *Everybody* wants free gold."

"There isn't any such thing," I said quietly. "Everything has a price, *everything!* And the price of that gold is just too high."

The old man squirmed around and adjusted his hurt leg. "Hyrum, you seem to be uncommon smart, so let me warn you. Stick to what you've just said. Don't go chasing after the gold up here. It's cursed, and it only brings misery to the folks who aren't supposed to have it. I know. I've seen it happen time and again . . ."

The man stared off into the darkness of the trees, and for a minute I thought I saw tears in his eyes. But the smoke from the fire was blowing his way, and I decided that that was what had caused his waterworks.

"I felt it too," he said quietly as he finally peeled some baked fish from its bones and began to eat, "and now I know where, and why."

"What did you say?"

"Nothing, young feller. I was just thinking out loud. Somehow that sacred gold causes trouble for folks, and there isn't *anybody* who escapes it."

The quiet wrapped itself up and around us. I studied on what the old man had said, and finally I spoke. "Well, this has been a wondrous review, up to a point, but it seems to me we have skirted clear around the real issue."

"Real issue?" asked the old man.

"Yeah, you know, the answer; the Rosetta stone of the whole thing."

"The what?"

"Rosetta stone, old man: a piece of black basalt found in 1799 near the Rosetta mouth of the Nile, bearing a trilingual inscription in hieroglyphics, demotic characters, and Greek, famous for having given the Frenchman Jean-Francois Champollion the first clue toward deciphering Egyptian. It was a truly important piece of rock."

"Kid," the old man growled, "I went to the fourth grade. Not through it, just to it. We didn't get to that rock. We didn't even get to the Nile. All I remember about Egypt is a picture of Cleopatra advertising cigars. Now, if you'd care to come again with your complaint that my poor memory missed the real issue, I'll give it a whirl on that basis."

Well, I grinned, for occasionally I did get a mite carried away with the things I had read. Still, it was fun, and fun just might be the only thing I got out of that wonderful education I was giving myself.

"Okay," I responded, "think of it this way. Since neither of us has a Urim and Thummim to provide a pure translation of what I have just expostulated upon, here she goes in more simple terms. The moving finger writes, and having writ, moves on. I see its surreptitious cipher engraven on the rock of time. I see the basaltic key appear and unlock the secret meanings of the message. Its words stand forth in letters of fire and brimstone. They are simple words, simple even to folks such as you and me. They say, 'Having each of us got the other to this point, and beaten off the savage foe, what then proposes the unknown man with the game leg?' "

"How's that?" demanded the old man, his eyes wary and yet curious.

"I said," I replied quietly, "that I still don't know who you are or why you are here, and you've never yet suggested what you think we should do happen those fellers come at us again."

The old man bit down on my question hard. He chewed doggedly but it would not chew. Finally he spit it out dejectedly.

"Those are good questions," he admitted.

"And the answers?"

"I ain't told you who I am because—"

Whap!

Both the old man and I rolled into the darkness as the rifle slug tore our fire apart. "What in the . . . " I muttered.

"Hyrum?"

"Yeah, I'm over here."

"Work your way down to our horses. I'll try and meet you there."

I grunted to acknowledge the old man's whisper, and immediately I set off into the darkness. My eyes were blind from staring into the flames, and I cussed myself for breaking such an important rule. Twice I slammed into boulders and once into a fallen log, and then gradually my eyes adjusted to the dark and I was able to make better time.

Our horses were down off the hill in a small stand of pine, sheltered and with good grass, and from a few yards away that clump of pine didn't look thick enough to hide a jackrabbit. I hoped it had been good enough to hide our horses.

In the darkness I worked my way down the slope, slipped through the notch in the boulders that had become my own trail, entered the trees, and found nothing there. The horses and saddles were gone!

"Ssst," I whispered, staring about me. "Old man? Where in blue blazes are you?"

I listened, and nowhere could I hear a response. For a moment I felt fear, and then, suddenly, I got mad. The old man had played me for a fool, and now I could see it clear as day. He'd crippled himself up and let me do for him, and gradually, without ever telling me who he was or what he was about, he'd wormed out of me the location of where I'd found that gold.

Yes sir, that made me mad as a razorback hog stropping himself on a fencepost. Hone me down enough, by gumbo, and I would fix it so that old man would hear from me again!

Uphill, he'd said. That was the way to flee. All right, I'd go uphill. Happen I ran into the rest of the outlaws, well, that was just more the pity for them. I couldn't look out for *everybody* on this mountain!

Back I went up the slope, struggling, quiet as I could with my gimped-up foot and bullet-holed leg, and I was almost back to the fire when I heard voices. I hunkered down, inched forward, and found three men seated at our fire and eating *my* fish.

I was hungry, and seeing those fellers eating set my stomach to growling. Then wasn't the time to do anything about it, however, so I tightened my belt, opened my ears, and backed off, waiting. I didn't know any of those men, with the notable exception of one Mr. Doolin, whom I had previously become acquainted with. It was him that was eating the biggest fish of all.

"I wish Friendlessman would get here," he whined as he chomped on my dinner.

"I guarantee you he will," a man said quietly.

"I'll second that," a deep-voiced giant of a man declared. "If Felix Friendlessman wasn't hotter to get to that young gal down in Fountain Green than a hungry dog to grab a knucklebone, then my name ain't Alpha."

"Alpha, you say?" asked Doolin as he worked on his fish. "I thought your name was Silvertip."

"Nope. That there's just a handle, because of my hair. She's *Alpha*—the first letter in the Greek alphabet. My mother was an educated woman."

"Too bad she didn't pass it along," the quiet-voiced man said.

Silvertip smiled at him and said nothing.

"What's the rest of it?" Doolin asked idly.

"You knuckleheaded pea-brain," the quiet voiced man declared. "Don't you know that out here in the west a man's name is his own personal business?"

"Blue John," the big man said easily, "it's all right. I don't mind. If this feller Doolin's on the wrong side of the law, and if I'm on the wrong side of the law, then why shouldn't he know?"

Blue John rolled his eyes and said nothing, so Silvertip went on. "My name's Garrett, Mr. Doolin. Alpha R. Garrett."

"I don't suppose I should ask what the *R* stands for?"

"I sure wish you wouldn't. It's embarrassinger'n *Alpha*."

"Don't see how it could be," Doolin wheezed. "Tell me, please?"

"Silvertip," the quiet-voiced Blue John warned, "I wouldn't do it."

"Ah, Blue John, he asked nice."

"Maybe. But you tell him, it'll be the same as telling every runny-mouthed granny in the Territory."

"Gee whiz, Blue John—"

"Oh, go ahead, you numbskull. You ain't got the sense to spit downwind. I don't know what else I should expect. Just remember I told you what would happen if you revealed such a shameful thing as that to this flannel-mouthed weasel."

Silvertip grinned. "I'll remember, Blue John, I surely will." Then he turned to Doolin. "He don't mean nothing bad. It's just his nature to be suspicious and cantankerous. It's Rachel."

"What is? What's Rachel got to do with anything?"

"That's what the *R* is for. My full name's Alpha Rachel Garrett."

Doolin, his mouth full of fish, stared. "Why, that there's sinful," he finally muttered.

"Not according to my mother."

The men sat quietly, thinking over what Silvertip had told them. So was I, but I wasn't about to make any comments, not from where I was hiding.

"Do you mean to sit there and say," one of the men suddenly spoke up, "that your actual true name is Rachel Garrett?"

"Alpha Rachel Garrett. My mother wanted it all there. It's wrote square in the Bible and all. You see, Pap, he wanted a gal, and so did Mother. 'Course, I didn't come out with the right plumbing, but they decided they'd do their best with what they had. They covered me up with a double set of wet-pants and let my hair grow, and it was years before folks figured it out, myself included."

"Your folks wasn't educated," Blue John declared. "They was crazy!" Then he stood up and looked around. "Doggone it," he growled, "I wish Friendlessman would get here! I thought he was just stringing that Sorenson girl along."

"He was," Silvertip answered, "except I think the string's got mighty thick. From all I've heard, that there is a fine girl."

"Not too bright, though," Blue John responded. "She couldn't be, letting herself be hoodwinked by a man like Friendlessman. Blast! Where is that man? Now that we got the Boss down there with their horses, those two pilgrims are fairly well grounded."

Well, that gave me a start! That old man hadn't taken our horses after all. Which meant the horses were still around, and probably the old man too. That brought the score back to zero-zero, and we were in a whole new game that seemed an awful lot like the last one. The way it looked, if I was finally going to get me and maybe even that old man to safety, I was going to have to resteal those already-stolen horses.

Easing back into the dark, I stood up and listened. Nothing. Not a sound that might tell me where horses would be hidden. Oh, if only Ernest was here, I thought. He could hear bees snoring at five miles, and horses breathing at ten.

All right, he wasn't, so I had to think. Pa had always told us to reason things out. Most folks don't take time to do that, and they usually end up on the short end of the stick, acting on their emotions. I could have done that very thing when I heard what those outlaws said about Ida Mae, for it made me angry enough. But I could also have been dead. This way I wasn't, and there was still a small chance, hidden down . . .

The cove!

If I were going to keep several horses for a few days, I'd put them into the small cove I'd found down near the lake below us. There was plenty of good grass there, and no end of water, and whoever watched them had weeks' worth of deadfalls for firewood. Yes sir, that would be the place. It was also close to where the old man and I had hidden our own mounts, so they wouldn't even have needed to saddle them up to move them. That was why they'd done it all so quiet. I'd wondered about that, and now I knew, or at least I thought I did.

Hastily I started down the steep hill, going as quietly as possible. Then I thought, what the heck? If I was sneaking they'd likely hear me anyway. It'd only been dumb luck that the three at the fire hadn't heard me. On the other hand, if I just walked up like I wasn't hiding anything at all, then I could likely get close enough to cause some real headaches for the one called the Boss who had been left as guard.

That's exactly what I did, too. I wasn't armed, but I wasn't unarmed either. As the fire came in sight, I reached down and picked up a solid-feeling pine limb with a round knot on one end, and that was what I carried into the camp.

"Blue John," Jackson T. Moore said as he lifted his cup of coffee and turned to face me, "I was just thinking that maybe one of those two fellers might sneak up here and—say, you ain't Blue Jo—"

He didn't finish his sentence, at least not right then. The heavy knot on the end of my limb caught him square on the chin as I swung it upward. He did too, swing upward I mean, coffee, gurgled mouthful of sentence, everything, and the last I saw of him he was diving for pearls or other such treasure in some two or three inches of Heart Lake shallows.

"You're right," I said quietly. "I ain't."

Smiling grimly, I rolled the man onto his back so he wouldn't drown. Then I took his pistol and threw it out into the lake, instantly feeling bad that I'd done that because I was still unarmed. Then I turned and moved through the lush meadow grass to where the horses were tethered. I had no trouble at all picking out the mount I had been riding, for with the blaze on its face and its two white stockings, it did show up.

I saddled the horse, swung aboard, and started looking around for the old man's. That way I could lead it to him and help him mount, and we could be off again. I circled that meadow twice before I finally admitted what I hadn't wanted to admit all along.

I'd been right all along, and that dirty old man was just that—a dirty, sneaking old man. While I'd been eavesdropping up above and taking out the hombre who was at present totally committed to shallow-water swimming lessons, that old man had snuck down, stolen his own blasted horse, and taken off. He'd not thought of me, he'd not tried to help me, he'd not even told me he intended to leave me behind.

Suddenly I was mad enough to chomp a chunk out of an ax! That old man had done it to me, and I wouldn't stand for it. No sir, I'd trail him if it took until I was eighty and he was in Hades, and not the pass I was dropping off of either. I deserved an explanation, and he, by gumbo, deserved to give me one.

With that decision made, I turned the other two horses loose, whapped them with my hat to set them running, and found where the grass had been crushed in a pretty straight line. Then downhill into the darkness I followed.

32

Grandaddy Basin, Uintah Mountains— Utah Territory

With the first gray light of dawn, I squatted beside my small fire and thought. A fish roasted in the coals, and I was grateful for it, though with four more I'd have been four times as grateful. Above me rose a steep slope, and I adjusted the yarrow dressing on my throbbing leg and pondered the slope thoroughly.

There was no trail up it at all. Here and there were rocky outcroppings and there were clumps of brush, a maze of fallen logs, slides of broken rock, and scattered aspen. It all ended at a wall of rock thirty feet high or more, an old fault line that extended along the face of the mountain for over half a mile. And what buffaloed me most of all was that the old man's tracks led exactly to where I was camped. Then they started up the slope, and—nothing.

He'd had to climb it, though, for there was no other way he could have gone that made any sense. Trouble was, climbing it didn't make any sense either.

I planned my route carefully, for I was going to climb that hill myownself, aiming for what seemed to be a fracture in the face of the rock, a shadow only, a possible way to the top without going around to the far end. If that old man could get up through those rocks, then so would I.

In the saddle I started out, holding the reins up tight and weaving a precarious way up through the obstacles on the mountainside. Twice I paused to give the horse a breather, and both times I tumbled rocks down behind me, hoping to slow down those outlaw fellers who would be following.

Finally I rode near the high rimrock, and there my heart sank. The shadow had been just that, a shadow. There was no crack that I could see, and no way up but around.

Weary and discouraged, I turned the horse, felt it resisting, fought the reins even harder, and suddenly had a thought. That horse was likely mountain-bred, and if it had it a notion, why, who was I to argue? It kept pulling toward the cliff, and that was also where I wanted to go.

So—

The shadow was still a shadow, but directly behind it, invisible from more than a few feet away, was a steep fissure up through the cliff. Looking up at it I had my doubts, but dismounting I examined the ground and found the hoof prints from the old man's horse, and so on foot I started to climb.

I had a rough go of it, too, but no more so than my horse. I kept hold of the reins, and that mountain horse I'd borrowed lunged up right behind me, going where I'd never have guessed a horse could go. But it did, and shortly we topped out on one of the flattest and prettiest tabletop mountains I'd ever seen.

A trail led off through the trees, so I followed, not right on it but a few feet off to the side. Zene had told me once that Indians and other antisocial sorts baited those trails, and one was safe only if he wasn't on it.

Suddenly I noticed a small stump showing the marks of an ax. Carefully I walked the horse over and stepped down. The stump was about four inches in diameter and had been cut off about a foot above the ground. Nor was the wood of the cut white any longer, but gray. It was not new then, at least not this season.

Either that was cut for firewood, I thought, or it had been cut for a pole. My guess was firewood, for even the chips had been picked up.

I walked my horse in a widening circle, and it took only a few minutes to find a small lean-to and the remains of a fire. The bits of charcoal lying around had been worn smooth by wind and rain, and so I knew that the fire was old.

He's been here, I thought. *That old man has been here, and this was his fire.* Again I rode in widening circles, but now I found no tracks. I studied the distant ridge where the sun shone bright upon the sullen and silent rocks; then, filled with an idea, I started toward it. On the plateau there was no sound except the footfalls of my horse—that and the sound of the wandering wind, a wind uncertain of itself, prowling among the trees as if looking for something lost.

Again and again I drew up to look about, to listen, and to watch the trail behind. For all its beauty, there was an eerie something about this plateau that made me wary—something I had not felt on the Wasatch Plateau. I had the feeling that eyes were watching me, eyes that might be looking along a rifle barrel.

I changed course several times, veering suddenly to put a rock, a tree, or a bush behind me. I was trying to offer no target for a marksman, and my sudden changes would be useful, I knew, in making my trail difficult to follow. Instinctively, I chose the way that would leave the fewest marks behind, for I felt that even if I was not followed now, I soon would be.

Here and there I passed pits in the earth, diggings made by the old man or someone else in an endless search for wealth. Some of the holes were small and shallow, others much larger, and many had the appearance of great antiquity. I thought again of the Spanish padres who had come into this land so long ago, the black-robes who had enslaved the Indians and bled the land of both gold and life. Perhaps it was their ghosts I felt, theirs or the trusting Indians who had been slain by them.

Quite suddenly I dropped over a small ledge, and in front of me lay a tiny lake, its blue waters ruffled by the wind. I skirted the shore and, seeing that the water was shallow, rode in and walked the horse close to the shore for several hundred feet. I left the lake by a small stream that came down the ridge toward which I had been traveling, and I followed it upward.

In the woods along the course of the stream and in the clump of pine I was in there was no sign of man, but on the flanks of the ridge beyond the creek I noticed a hatch of sage sparrows hopping and flitting over something on the ground. Riding swiftly upward to the place, I found horse droppings that were still soft and, when broken open, faintly warm in the center. The old man had been there, then, and not an awful long time before.

Until dark I searched for further sign but found none at all. That old man could hide a trail, and more and more I was admiring his skill. That didn't mean I liked him any better, but I did appreciate his way in the woods.

In the gathering dusk I made camp in the corner of the ridge, picking up dry wood from old deadfalls that would make an almost smokeless fire. It was a good camp, too. The cove was higher than the land in front of it, offering a good view for perhaps a quarter of a mile. The camp itself lay in a slight hollow under fir trees that would help to spread any smoke the fire might make. Nearby, a stream tumbled toward another lake, and by feeling carefully under the rocks of the stream, I managed to catch a half-dozen small trout. After I had roasted them in the coals and eaten them, I felt considerably better about everything—everything that is, except the old man, the festering bullet hole in my leg, and, way back in my mind, Ida Mae Sorenson.

Four miles away, another fire burned fitfully behind some rocks on an open hillside. A slip of a girl sat huddled over it, doing her best to keep warm. Nearby, her father's white mare chewed contentedly on the thick grass, and for the first time in her life, Ida Mae Sorenson found herself envying a horse.

"Peppy," she whispered to the animal, "You'll never know how lucky you are. I'm so cold and hungry I feel like I'm going to die."

Out on the mountain a coyote began serenading the moon. The stanza was picked up by another of the small carnivores, and soon an entire chorus was yelping a cappella. Ida Mae shivered from more than the cold, put two great chunks of wood onto the fire, and stared fearfully around her.

"Peppy," she whispered, "how can you be so contented? I've never seen anything so dark as this mountain. I'm scared to death! How can Hyrum stand to be up here all the time? I . . . I've never thought about . . . what it would be like to work with the sheep. Oh dear, I—"

Suddenly from nearby came a shrill scream of death as a small animal became the evening meal of a larger predator. Ida Mae was instantly upon her feet with a limb in her hand, her breath stilled, staring outward. The silence was intense, and suddenly she could hear the clear and unmistakable sound of bones being crushed by powerful jaws. She shivered again, and, her eyes wide with fear, she ran to the mare and clung to its neck.

"Oh, Peppy," she breathed haltingly, "what am I doing here? How did I ever think—"

Suddenly she thought again of Hyrum, and in her mind she saw his quick and ready smile, his shuffling walk that he tried so hard to hide, the pain in his face as she told him of Felix, and the deep courage of total despair in his eyes as he told her to pick up the thirty silver dollars, hoping in that way, because there was no other way left, to finally get her attention. Never before had she felt as she did at that moment, nor did she ever wish to feel that way again! She would do *anything* to make things up to Hyrum. Even if he never spoke to her again, she would spend her life trying to be a better person because of him. She owed him that; perhaps she owed him even more. Hadn't he been the one who had brought her father back into her life?

"Peppy, I'm more scared than I've ever been, but I'm staying! I mean it! If I can help Hyrum in any way at all . . . besides that, my heart's about to break with sorrow and loneliness for that young man. Oh, Peppy, how could I have been so blind? I just . . ."

And once again she trembled in fear as the chorus of coyotes began their shrill yipping at the thin new moon.

Not quite three miles away, and at the base of the steep hill Hyrum had climbed earlier, yet a third fire burned. Felix Friendlessman squatted there, staring up into the darkness. "You idiots," he snarled, "how could you let them do it again?

"Let them," Blue John repeated quietly. "Friendlessman, take a look at Jack Moore there, and tell me once more that we let them."

Felix Friendlessman sensed the pulsing of danger within Blue John's voice, saw his fingers curled over the butt of his pistol, and intentionally he cooled the atmosphere. "Oh, I know you did what you could. It's just hard to believe that a crippled boy with a bullet hole in his leg and a crippled old man could manage to steal and stampede your horses. Twice!"

"Well, like I said before, that Soderberg kid's a slick one—always has been. He and the little one that almost killed Lundstrum are two of a kind, and a rare kind at that."

"I like 'em," Silvertip suddenly declared. "Like I've always said, I like kids like that."

"Shut up," Blue John ordered. "Look at the Boss lying there, and then say you like 'em."

Silvertip looked to where Jack Moore lay on a pallet of blankets, moaning softly. His face was swollen and black and blue, and he looked the picture of perfect misery. "Ah, the kid only broke the Boss's jaw," the big man responded easily.

"Yes, and like to drown him, to boot."

"No he didn't. I could see where Soderberg turned him over so he wouldn't drown."

"Well, maybe so," Blue John admitted. "Still, poor Jack Moore won't never eat a regular meal again. I'd like to know what that crippled Soderberg kid clubbed him with."

"I don't know," Silvertip admitted, "but still, I like him for it.

The kid's brave, and he won't quit nohow. I truly do like him, and, like I've been saying since we tried to bust him out of jail, I hope he wins out."

"Blast it, you . . ." Blue John swore. "I never did see a man so doggone dumb and loyal in my entire life!"

The big outlaw looked at his partner and slowly shook his head. "I never could see what was so dumb about being loyal," he frowned. "But then if a man isn't bright he wouldn't see it, would he?"

Blue John stared up at Silvertip and turned as Jack Moore groaned pitifully; then he shook his head disgustedly and was silent.

"Well," Silvertip declared brightly, "I don't reckon the Boss ought to complain none, even if his jawbone *is* broken. He'd have done the same thing to the Soderberg kid as was done to him, and he probably wouldn't have kept him from drowning, either. The way I see it, when we signed on to become outlaws, we knew it was liable to get a mite dangerous. Now it has."

"You meaning to suggest," Blue John questioned, his heavy voice scraping like a burro with a bad cold, "that we're all doing this by choice?"

"Yep," Silvertip replied smugly. "We was all maybe forced into it in the beginning, or maybe we fell into being owlhoots all accidental, but none of us was ever forced to *stay* in it."

"Why, you're balmier'n you look, man. It's no wonder you was named Alpha Rachel. You think we need you to tell us about outlawing?"

"I reckon *you* do, at least."

"Why, you're nervier'n a busted tooth," Blue John snarled, and his fingers curled toward his gun. Suddenly a loud metallic click sounded in his ears, and his hand froze in mid-air, suspended, waiting.

Felix Friendlessman got slowly to his feet, and his .44 Colt revolver was out and not moving. "That's enough," he said quietly.

"No it ain't. I'm going to put this moron out of our misery."

"Not now you aren't. Look around you, Blue John. We've already lost two good men, and that leaves just the four of us. Believe me, we'll need every man before this is over."

"We won't need this—"

"Blue John, already the vultures are gathering to the scent of the carcass. Lundstrum talked continuously about us and the kid and the mine, and when I was down in Provo today, men were gathering to the railroad from far and near."

"So what? I don't—"

"Ida Mae Sorenson's gone too. No one knows where, but she's gone. There's also talk that the Soderbergs are gathering and heading here."

"Not the bishop?" Silvertip interrupted. "Why, that feller's thorny as cactus! I hope we don't have to tangle with him again. Once in this life's more than enough for any man!"

"For once," Blue John growled, "I agree with this idiot. If that bishop is on his way here, then I'm on my way to Canada."

"Nobody is going anywhere," Friendlessman said quietly. "He may be coming, and he may not be coming. If he is, we'll just have to take care of him."

"Judging by his two young sons," Doolin stated, "that bishop will be dangerous. We'll have to kill him too."

"Lots of luck," Silvertip drawled easily. "It can't be done. Me, I'm with Blue John. Let's either leave altogether or else leave the Soderbergs alone and go look for that gold ourselves."

"You are not the first who has had that foolish idea," Friendlessman stated, "nor would you be the first to fail. No, to find that gold we must first find the kid. Now, if you are thinking of flight, listen to this. I also heard talk about the law today. Maybe they are coming as well, and they are looking for five men who have pinned that kid down.

"You see, Blue John, our only chance is to remain together, for only then will we be strong. Additionally, we've got to work fast, very fast, and it will take every one of us to do it. Now leave that pistol in its holster and let's do some planning."

Blue John glared at Friendlessman, Friendlessman looked calmly back, and slowly the thin outlaw relaxed. "All right," he said quietly, "what do we do?"

"We follow them."

"Up that? No way, not in the dark, at least."

"Are you certain their tracks go up?" Friendlessman asked.

"Not theirs," Blue John replied. "His. The kid's tracks go up that hill, and the tracks of that old man start up, then vanish."

"Can't we follow them?"

"I told you, not in the dark."

Friendlessman walked to the base of the hill. For a long moment he stared upward; then he took a step to the side, then another, and suddenly he spun about, his face filled with excitement. "How much light do you need before we can start up that hill after them?"

Blue John gave the man a sharp look. "Why are you so anxious?" he questioned.

"I've been here before," Friendlessman replied, "right *here*. I just didn't realize it until I saw that cliff above me. Boys, right now we are within five miles of the richest deposit of gold ore in the world."

"How do you figure that?" Doolin questioned. "You ever seen the mine?"

"No, not exactly. But I saw Caleb Rhoades vanish one afternoon from right here, and less than four hours later he appeared again with two mules loaded with gold."

"Well, I'll be forever . . ." Doolin breathed excitedly, poking his stick into the fire and jumping to his feet. "Let's get up there after them."

"Don't be stupid," Friendlessman growled. "We could all be killed. There are old mines and glory holes all over this country, some that don't even have bottoms to them. Besides, there are that old man and the Soderberg kid, both of whom are likely expecting us. No, boys, we stay here until first daylight. Now, let's get some sleep."

Doolin watched as the men gradually crawled into their bedrolls and fell asleep. *Stupid,* he thought. *It isn't me that's stupid, it's them. I saw the gold, and that Soderberg kid had seen it too, and I ain't waiting around another night when I can get at it now. Besides, why should I share it with them, anyway? What have they ever done for me?*

Carefully Doolin eased himself from the log upon which he sat. No one moved, and so without a sound, he slipped into the trees and away. He thought of taking Friendlessman's horse but decided against it because of the noise. If the gold was really within five miles, he'd walk to where it was and use the kid's and the old man's horses to pack it out. Yes sir, he was finally on his way to becoming a mighty wealthy man.

33

Grandaddy Basin, Uintah Mountains— Utah Territory—Again

At first I thought it was the wind. Somewhere out in the forest was a distant wailing, a sound unlike anything I had ever heard. It woke me from my sleep. I listened and almost pushed it out of my mind. Then it came more loudly, and suddenly I knew the cry was human, the cry of a man in trouble.

Carefully I arose and made my way up the hill behind my camp, coming finally to the level plateau I had crossed the day before. The trees around me were thick, rocks were plentiful, and deadfalls made progress increasingly difficult. Besides all that, the moon had set, and under the trees it was darker'n Lucifer's disposition. Yet I was making progress, for the man's screams and cries for help were getting louder, though he himself sounded weaker all the time.

I hurried, wondering what might have befallen the poor soul. The voice sounded familiar, and suddenly I thought of the old man. Was it he who screamed? Might he be in mortal danger?

Plunging ahead I stumbled over a deadfall, rolled down a small incline, lunged to my feet, and pushed on, my heart filled with fear for the old man. Suddenly a group of boulders loomed ahead; I skirted them, and on the other side I found the man.

"H-help!" he whined over and over as I cautiously approached.

I paused, staring into the intense darkness, unable to see a thing. "Where are you?" I called.

"Oh, thank the Lord," the man gasped. "I'm here, in this hole. Get me out!"

Well, right away I started grinning, for now there was no disguising the thin, reedy voice of beady-eyed Mr. Doolin, my erstwhile enemy. Nor was there any disguising the genuine fear he felt.

"Aren't you Mr. Doolin?" I asked.

"Yes, *yes!* Get me out of here, quickly! I can't hang on much longer, and—"

"It's awful dark," I said, "I can't see you. Tell me where you are and what happened."

"Oh for . . . There's no time, man! I'm falling! Help me, please help me!"

"What happened, Mr. Doolin? How did you get into that hole?"

"I . . . I fell in! I heard something—someone *laughing*. It . . . it frightened me. I ran . . . I . . . I fell in. Oh, *help me!* I think this is one of those bottomless pits, and I can't hold on . . ."

"Hold on? Mr. Doolin, I don't understand. What are you holding on to? If that is a bottomless pit, why aren't you still on your way down?"

"There's a tree lying across the hole, and I'm hanging on to it. Now give me a hand, man, or I'll fall. My hands are slipping, and you've got to hurry. Please . . ."

"So that's a real bottomless pit, is it? I've heard of them, heard they're all over the mountain up here. Some are old mines, but the others, the blackest ones with the cold air up near the tops of them, are old volcanic tubes that drop all the way down to the fires of hell. I once heard of a man who fell into one of them. He screamed all the way down, and folks say that two weeks later the echoes of his screams were still coming up. Mr. Doolin, is there cold air in that hole?"

Doolin gurgled and sputtered, and I crawled a little closer to the hole, picking up a couple of pebbles as I did so.

"H-help! I . . . I can't hold . . ."

While Doolin was crying and pleading, I tossed the two pebbles past him into the blackness of the pit. Satisfied, I grinned and sat back. "Is the air cool, Mr. Doolin?"

"Yes. *Yes!* Now help me, for—"

"Oh dear, I was afraid of that. There's no doubt that you're hanging above one of the bottomless holes this mountain is famous for."

"Are . . . are you sure?"

"Sure as can be."

"Well then, help me! Give me a hand so I can get *out!*"

"I can't get to you, Mr. Doolin. I just tried, and the side started to crumble. So far as I can tell, there's no other way for me to reach you. And we surely don't want *both* of us incinerating in the fires of hell, do we?"

Doolin groaned. "Do we?" I repeated quietly.

"Oh please! Help me—"

"Do we?"

"N-no," he answered weakly.

"Good. I hoped that you'd understand."

"But . . . but . . . oh, please help me!"

"I can't do it. Too dangerous. Why don't you just swing your legs up and around that old log and then hoist yourself up and crawl out on top of it?"

Doolin gnashed his teeth like a man who could stand a thing no longer, and I was reminded of how the scriptures say that in the last days there would be weeping and wailing and gnashing of teeth among the wicked. More and more I was seeing evidence of the scriptures being fulfilled.

"I tried!" Doolin wailed. "For heaven's sake, man, don't you think I tried. The log rolls every time I do that, and . . . Man, help me. My hands are slipping again."

"Mr. Doolin, I'd like to, I truly would. Trouble is, I'd be afraid of another bullet in my leg if I got you out."

There was instant stillness, and then, after maybe ten seconds, Doolin spoke again. "W-who is this? Who are you?"

"It's only me, Mr. Doolin. Hyrum Soderberg. You know, the evil, vicious killer you tried to cheat and whom lately you've been trying to eliminate."

There was a long gasp and then a choking sob from the weasel-like man in the hole. "H-Hyrum . . . Mr. Soderberg, I . . . I'm sorry, I truly am. Get . . . get me out of here, and I'll swear you are innocent before every court in the land. I will, I mean it! I'll even leave the mountain. Immediately! You can have all the gold. I don't want any at all. I just . . . Oh, my fingers are going! Help me! *Help me!*"

"It's an interesting thing to think about, isn't it, Mr. Doolin?" I asked casually as I leaned back and prepared to philosophize. "The endless fall, the volcanic fires? And think too of the reward you'll be facing for all the dishonest deeds you're so famous for at that assay shop. Ah, Mr. Doolin, you've been calling upon the Lord pretty regular the last little while, and that's good. You'll likely meet Him soon, and I think it is a fine idea to let Him know that you are on your way.

"How do you think He'll respond when He hears how you've

hounded a poor crippled kid like myself, one with a pure heart who's never on purpose done any real harm in his whole life? I'll bet He'll—"

"He'll judge you for murder too," the little man whined. "You let me die and it'll be murder, and you know it! Now help me, please . . ."

"How can I murder you, Mr. Doolin? I've never touched you, and I can't even see you!"

"Yes, but you'll let me fall—"

"Straight to the devil, I expect."

Doolin cried again, sobbed some more.

"You are a thief, Mr. Doolin. Is that not so?"

"No! I never—"

"Mr. Doolin, the truth! Remember the hole gaping open below you, and let me hear the truth."

The man groaned again. "Yes," he whispered, "yes, yes!"

"And you tried to steal the largest portion of my gold from me?"

"Y-yes . . ."

"And I am but the lastest in a long line of victims?"

"W-why are you doing this?"

"Satisfaction, Mr. Doolin. Am I not right?"

"Yes, yes, *yes!* Now *help* me! I can't—"

"Mr. Doolin, I am sorry to hear that," I said, interrupting his plea, "but you see, I knew it was true. Thieves are always known. To a man with little money and no honor, the obvious way to riches seems to be theft. Thievery, however, is a crime only for the very ignorant and in which only the most stupid ever indulge. There is a crass vulgarity in theft, Mr. Doolin, a definite indication that a man lacks intelligence and wit. Without even considering the moral implications, Mr. Doolin, the penalties of theft far outweigh any possible gain."

Doolin was silent, and so for a moment or two I let him stew. "Did you mean what you promised?" I finally asked.

"Oh yes, yes!"

"And if I let you live, you'll leave this mountain immediately, close up your shop in Provo, and go somewhere back east or out to California with all the other crooks?"

"Close . . . close my shop?"

"Of course. That must be part of the deal."

"All right, all right! I'll do anything you say."

"Swear it!"

"I . . . I swear!"

"And Mr. Doolin, there's something else. Us Soderbergs are naturally contrary, and it just isn't in us to lie down and roll over. Real honestly, we don't care whether school keeps or not. One of us gets mishandled, the rest of us will still keep a-coming. Now you do as I've said and leave, everything will be fine as oriental silk. Happen you decide otherwise, you'd better start going to Sunday School and acting like it. Otherwise, the law will be around, and so will *we*. You hear?"

"I . . . I hear."

"Very well," I said then, rising to my feet. "I now decree that you will not die tonight. See you around, Mr. Doolin."

There was a strangled cry. "You . . . you can't—"

"No, Mr. Doolin, you're wrong. I can. Adios."

Again he screamed. There was a slight scuffling sound on the log, and Doolin's scream was cut short in a desperate gasp. I heard his fingers slip further, and suddenly with a soul-piercing screech, Mr. Doolin, hopefully lately of Provo, was gone.

34

Between Lodgepole Lake and Fern Lake—Grandaddy Basin

The thud came about when I'd expected it to come, not more than two seconds after Doolin's hands had lost their grip on the log. I heard him hit, heard his scream cut short in surprise, and then I heard him moan and fall to the earth in what sounded like a swoon. I looked at the hole and grinned wickedly, for the tossed pebbles had told me the hole was not more than seven or eight feet deep, and *all* holes have cold air in them, for cold air always settles.

Doolin had expected to drop a long way, and I'd done my best to help that expectation along. I reckon when he'd fallen only a foot or two and hadn't been hurt at all, the shock was just too much for his weasely system to endure.

"Like I said," I murmured into the darkness, "see you around, Mr. Doolin. And next time, you'd better think twice before you take on a Soderberg."

Slowly I made my way back to my camp, careful to avoid the same problem encountered by Mr. Doolin. In spite of my brave words, I'd been shot full of luck as far as Doolin was concerned, and I knew it. I hadn't dug that hole, and I certainly hadn't led him into it. And there *were* some deep holes around, very deep ones. If he'd fallen into one of them, I don't really know what I'd have done. Probably helped him, I reckon. I couldn't have lived with myself and done otherwise. Of course, maybe I couldn't have lived with myself then, either. He was surely a miserable little man.

When I was nearly to my camp, however, I got my own set of fears and chills and fluttering fantods, and for a minute or two I felt sorry for Mr. Doolin. Off in the woods, sounding high up but somehow real close, I heard laughter, or what sounded like it. I stopped, waited, heard only the wind, decided I must be imagining things, started on, and then heard it again.

Haunts, I thought, the same haunts that had driven my friend Doolin into his "bottomless" pit. Why was it that everywhere I went I ran into haunts? I stared about me; the wind whistled through the pines; down at camp my horse snorted and stomped its hoof; and I knew it would do no good to go seeking the haunt out. Haunts can't be sought but have to come out on their own. If this one wanted me to, I'd see it soon enough. Until then . . .

At camp I checked things out, and everything seemed to be as I had left it. I settled down for a little more rest, heard that crazy laughter again, worried about it, stared up through the trees at the few stars, and grinned again when I thought of Mr. Doolin. Like I'd promised my pa, I'd been gentle as an elephant tromping through a herd of nasty-biting dogs. I hadn't hurt him at all. Nor did I feel truly evil for allowing him to think what he wanted concerning that same subject. Somehow it just didn't seem possible to go around correcting everybody's misconceptions. Still, I truly hoped that he'd had enough, for I knew that next time he might really get hurt. However, I fully believed that I would see him again, and then his lesson would come much more severely. His kind simply do not learn *anything* easily.

How still the night! How strange the sheen on the dark waters of the tiny lake! How bright the distant stars!

Down at the lake the water lapped quietly against the rocky shore, and beyond that, little moved, little stirred—only the water and the wind blowing down from the high peaks, and me as I wrapped my blanket more tightly about myself and waited.

Tired as I was, I was in no mood to sleep, and my ears began making a check on all the tiny sounds around me, sounds that had seemed nonexistent until I focused on them. They were sounds of birds, of insects, or of night-prowling animals, and all were familiar to me. But in every place some of the sounds were different. Dead branches make a rattle of their own; grass or leaves rustle in a certain way; yet in no two places are the sounds exactly the same. Always before I slept I checked the sounds in my mind. It was a trick I'd learned from Zene Hill and was something I'd do till the day I died.

I thought of that then and wondered again if I was going to die. Those fellers were still after me, the old man probably had me marked as well, my leg was not yet healed, and I was alone on the mountain with nowhere to go.

How much could a person endure? How long could a man continue? These things I asked myself, for speaking to myself is a habit I developed when I was younger and lonely and so self-conscious about my crippled leg. Yet even as I asked my questions, the answers were there before me. If a man be a man indeed, he must always go on, he must always endure.

I thought then of an account written by the Greek historian Herodotus wherein he detailed the courage of a certain man taken captive by the Spartans. This man had one foot locked in the stocks, which were made of wood bound by iron. To escape, he measured his foot against the size of the hole, cut off the offending front portion of his foot with his own hand, withdrew his mutilated appendage, and for three days eluded capture and made his way back to his own lines. To me, that and not giving up to death is the way of a man.

Death seems to be an end to torture, to struggle, to suffering, but of course I knew when I thought about it that such was not the case.

Still, death is very much an end to some things: to earthly warmth, to the light of a morning sunrise, to the beauty of a running horse, to the smell of damp earth after a rain, to a mother's smile, to the walk of a woman when she knows someone watches, to the savoring of a fine book—with death, these things would be in my past, and I would have moved into the realm of spirits.

No, I would not die. I was not ready. There was too much I had yet to do, to see, to feel, to learn. I yearned to serve a mission, to give myself to a cause that was greater than anything I could ever of myself be. I yearned also to have a wife, to hold closely in my heart a woman of my own, and to feel of her love while I gave her all of my own. I yearned as well to sire a family of fine sons and lovely daughters, to watch them grow, to ache with them in their sorrows and rejoice with them in their triumphs. I yearned too to have them feel toward me as I felt toward my own father, for such love and deep respect was truly a powerful force.

I yearned to laugh, to see the humor that existed all around me. Only the past winter I had read a copy of Mark Twain's new novel, *The Adventures of Huckleberry Finn,* and I had enjoyed myself almost more than I could imagine. Laughter to me was a tonic easing the common burdens of my life, and for some reason I did not feel that I had laughed in my life anywhere near enough.

I yearned finally to strengthen my mind and my spirit, to increase my testimony of the divinity and of the atoning sacrifice of Jesus Christ, and to understand His Gospel of salvation. I would do this by prayer and by reading the profoundest thoughts penned by the greatest men and women of all ages. I yearned to read the Talmud and the Koran and the writings of Confucius, and especially to study our own scriptures ever more deeply, for in those works are the most inspiring thoughts ever written upon the face of this earth.

Having read them, I intended to make those thoughts mine, for by thinking them, by praying over them continuously, and by treasuring up in my heart such immense amounts of wisdom, I would be lifted so that I would become a better man than I otherwise might have been.

For all these things I yearned deeply, and so I would not give up. Not yet.

In the dimness of first dawn I broke camp and rode slowly toward the towering mountains before me. Once or twice I saw the tracks of the old man's horse, or traces of them. But I was not worried. The trail was difficult to follow, but the problem was not one to worry about. There was simply no other way for the old man to go but straight ahead, and so there I rode.

My leg throbbed with an endless pounding, and twice I stopped to bathe the festering wound in a cold stream, grimacing in pain as I attempted to squeeze out the vile fluids of infection that the yarrow compress seemed to be bringing out. Such efforts helped a little, I thought, but I knew that I needed medical help, and I needed it badly.

The trees around me were spruce and alpine fir. Occasionally when I rode out on some knoll, over the tops of the trees I could see the peaks and ridges above timberline, where I was certain I was going.

White streaks of snow showed on the bare rocks; above, on the peaks themselves, were the remnants of ancient glaciers, the ice and snow of many winters. Here and there a stunted fir or a lightning-struck tree would indicate an effort by the forest to advance beyond the limit set for it, an attempt to encroach upon the lonely domain of the lichen and the moss.

I circled another lake, one I was certain was called Fern, and then I climbed again, gradually moving southward toward a projecting arm of East Grandaddy Mountain. Grassy meadows opened and closed around me, tiny lakes were everywhere, and as I climbed, the forest grew thick and still. I was in the drainage of the East Fork of Rock Creek, and I knew that Zene Hill would be somewhere nearby, probably to the north, herding Old Man Aagard's sheep. He would also be alone, and I felt bad about that, for I was not where I had taken money to be.

I came suddenly upon the remains of another old campfire, and here again I saw what looked to be the suggestion of another track, scarcely to be made out. Yet it was fresh, and I was certain it had been made by the old man.

Carefully I studied the site, going from place to place with my eyes only, holding my horse still. On a limb hung a pothook made from a forked branch, such as Zene had taught me to use. It showed wear, and evidently it had been relied upon more than once. Here, I felt certain, was another of the old man's camps, one he had used while prospecting in the area.

A small lake was close by, and a spring ran a trickle of water into it. The shore was rocky, but trees came almost to the edge of the water.

I pulled up the horse inside the trees to consider. I was in a small basin, surrounded on three sides by steep mountains, except at the point where I had come through, and undoubtedly also at the point where the stream exited. Once outside, the stream cut more rapidly to join a larger stream, and that, I was certain, ran finally into Rock Creek.

I returned to the campfire and looked all about. So far as I could tell, the trail ended there, except for the walk to the edge of the lake. Might the old man have entered the lake and walked along it to hide the way of his passing?

Suddenly thunder rumbled, and I looked up, surprised. A thunder shower, one of the afternoon storms that frequent the Uintahs, was boiling my way, and I knew I was going to get wet. More thunder rumbled, lightning flashed rapidly, and yet there in that cove in the towering mountains I felt somehow secure.

I thought again of the laughter I had heard the night before. Had it been the old man laughing at me? Of course I didn't know, but deep-down I was certain it had been the old man, who had somehow known where Doolin and I were and what we had been doing.

I took another circle around the dead campfire, searching. But there was nothing, nothing at all. I tried again, still farther out, but the results were the same.

The storm was building, a slow, sullen storm that could burst with unbelievable fury at any moment. Moreover, somewhere about were Friendlessman and what was left of his gang. I knew of two who would be gone—Doolin and the one they called the Boss. I'd also noticed that Loose-lip Lundstrum was missing when I'd watched them eating my fish two nights before. But then, so had Friendlessman been missing, and I *knew* he was still around. So the gang had been cut by two, I hoped, and maybe by three. That still gave them three armed men, tough men as well. And who was I to fight alone and unarmed against such—

I felt the shock of the bullet before I heard the explosion, and the next thing I knew I was lying upon the hard earth of the mountain. There was a great pain in my stomach, and I was certain I had been gut-shot. Still, they would be coming, and I must not wait for them there.

Reaching out I gasped with pain and began to crawl, and strangely, I got stronger the farther I went. Looking down finally to my wound, I found that the slug had hit my belt buckle and had only grazed across my stomach. I later learned that it had hit the pommel of the saddle even before that. Once again I had been lucky. Or blessed, maybe, as Ma would say. Like I mentioned earlier, I'd had recent troubles with my prayers, somehow avoiding saying them. But now I'd become a real believer, and the past few days had brought me closer to the Lord than I'd ever been.

It's passing sad how it takes such heavy trials and nefarious tribulations to humble a man. Still, such difficulties do bring humility, and I reckon it is good that the Lord has *something* that can get the job done. Anyway, it seemed like maybe my tiny amount of faith was paying off.

I pushed myself to my feet, caught my breath with the pain, and looked about for the horse. Then I realized it had run off, and suddenly I knew I was alone now, truly alone. If I was to get out of this, I had only the Lord and my wits to rely upon. That meant that, happen the Lord chose not to get involved any further, I was in real trouble.

Still, us Soderbergs are doing folk, so I put my good leg forward, pulled my bad leg after it, held my hands to my throbbing stomach, and started out for the high-up cliffs that rose before me.

35

East Grandaddy Mountain Bench—Utah Territory

The thunder pounded upon its great drums, rolling cataracts of sound down off the wide reaching cliffs and exploding them against the quivering forests below. Lightning shot in vivid streaks across the sky, huge flashes of light that seemed not like the lightning seen in the lowlands but like a heaven of flame gaping open above me, giving me a view of the blazing heart of some other world.

Yet the rain did not come. The atmosphere was charged with electricity, and the streaks of flame seemed to bound and rebound from the peaks above me.

I looked down at the tiny lake below. A sullen sheet, it lay open to the sky, shining like a great bowl of mercury. I lay in a nest of boulders backed against the towering cliff, and I knew it would end there—from that point I had nowhere to go.

The clouds drifted about, now settling over me, now tearing themselves apart so that I could peer through and glimpse the dark trees, the great craggy rocks, the bleak grayness of the lake.

"Dear Lord," I whispered as I stared downward into the gloom, "this is surely one time when I could use a little help. If you could just temper a little with the elements . . ."

A bullet suddenly smashed into a nearby rock, and as I rolled away the clouds split open and the rain came, a hard driving rain that swept with sheets of fury down the cliffs and into the staggering trees. I stared up, amazed, and then, realizing that I was about to drown, I rolled over again, scrambled under a huge boulder that had fallen from the cliff above, saw a small hole or crack in the cliff, and instinctively dove into it.

For a second or two I slid downward; then I was brought up short against a fairly level rock or floor. For a moment I lay still, listening to the storm outside, and then gradually I became aware that I was in a cave, or at least a cavity, in the rock.

"So you found it," a voice suddenly declared from the darkness, and with my heart in my throat I spun about to stare into the blackness before me.

"Who—"

"Hyrum Soderberg, in spite of my warning, you've come to this place like a bee goes to honey. I even tried to frighten you and the others away last night in the dark, but no, you wouldn't frighten."

"The insane laughter was from you?"

"Of course. And it might very well have been insane, for I couldn't bear to think of you being destroyed like my . . . my . . . . Oh, how I wish that I had never heard of this gold!"

There was the scratching of a match, a flicker of light as a lantern was lit, and suddenly I found myself gazing upon the old man who had abandoned me two days before.

And that wasn't all I was gazing upon, not by a long shot. Everywhere about me was the glitter of gold. The walls, the ceiling, even the floor, were laced with it. Moreover, there were mounds of bars, anciently smelted, stacked against one wall in three huge piles. Each of those bars was about a foot long, maybe four inches wide, and maybe two or two-and-a-half inches high. Roughly, I guessed there must be over a hundred of those bars in the three piles.

Near the piles of smelted gold were several pieces of old Spanish armor—breastplates, helmets, swords, and a single pike, and several smaller pieces of armor that must have covered arms and legs. What I really stared at, however, were the bones, the complete skeletons of at least four men, who lay just beyond the armor.

"Yes," the old man said, "you're looking at one of the sacred lost mines of the Utes. There are actually several of them, and this one is perhaps the least of them all."

"Who *are* you?" I suddenly asked.

The old man smiled. "I think you know, for you've suspected it all along. I am Caleb Rhoades, who sent my younger brother to his death. That's why I tried to escape you, my young friend. As I said, there's a curse upon this gold, or maybe it's a blessing. It depends on how you look at it. Nevertheless, this gold can be used only by the Indians, who do not use it selfishly, or by the Lord, for the building of his kingdom, and that's not selfish either. If it's sought for by others, no matter who they are, it always brings disaster.

"Until he died, this gold was Brother Brigham's, and he stewarded it for the Lord. But now they don't send for it any more, and I alone am trustee. I take a little now and then, bless lives here and there, and use a very little for my own needs. I suppose when I die it'll go back to the Indians until they and the Lord decide to bring it forth once more."

"Tell me about it," I asked, still awed by what was so brightly spread before me. "Tell me about this gold."

The old man smiled and shifted, and it was only then that I discovered he had hurt his leg again. "Yes," he said, noticing my gaze. "A rock fell on it, and I fear I'll be joining my Spanish brethren here, who were interlopers just as much as me. I don't sorrow over that, but over my wife, who hates so much to be alone."

Old Caleb Rhoades sighed and looked up at the roof of the mine, where myriads of strands of ore flickered and danced in the lantern light.

"Gold," he breathed. "Doesn't the very word itself create visions and dreams? And truly those visions are nothing when compared with the reality of this.

"Young man, this gold is part of a vast belt of quartz that runs in a gray vein across and through the entire width of these mountains. It is in such an unusual formation that for years prospectors have stumbled across it and haven't seen it at all. Yet the Indians did, and for untold generations they made use of it as ornamentation in their worship and their ceremonies.

"Then came the black-robes, the conquering padres. They enslaved the Indians and forced them to mine deeply and without thought to safety. They thought only of gold, of the wealth they were sending back to their homeland, and to them who had come so far in search of this wealth, no price was too great to pay in the taking of it.

"For years that went on, until the Indians could stand it no longer. Then came a rebellion, short and bloody, and the black-robes were slain where they stood. These four fell here; I've found the remains of two more outside. One group of them made a desperate stand further down on Rock Creek. I've found other remains over above Whiterocks, and who knows where else they fell?

"Some, of course, must have escaped, for there are stories that they returned and were again driven away. Following that, except for a few wandering parties, the Spanish came no more."

"So how did the gold become sacred?" I asked.

"By the blood of the Indians that was shed both in mining it and in driving the black-robes away. So it was told me by my friend Happy Jack, a Ute who knows as much about this gold as any man alive. According to him, the Utes call the mines Carre shin-ob, which means 'There, the Great Spirit,' or 'There dwells the Great Spirit.'

"According to Happy Jack, Old Chief Walker or, more correctly, Wakera, had a vision some time before the Mormons appeared here in the West. In the vision he was shown the yellow metal and was told that he was to guard it until the big hats came, and then was to give it to them.

"Wakera thought Bridger and the mountain men were the big hats, but they laughed at his tale of a vision and so got nothing. Then when Brother Brigham came, leading the Saints, he was also told of the vision. Brigham Young did not laugh, and Wakera gave the gold in the mines to him."

"So how did you learn of it?"

The old man smiled. "Brigham Young couldn't come to the mines personally, so he called my father, John Rhoades, who took an oath upon the Book of Mormon that he would never reveal the locations of the sacred mines to any other man. For several years he came alone into these mountains, taking out mule trains of gold for the Church. The Utes protected him in this, and things prospered. Then he became ill, and Brigham Young, needing gold again, agreed with him that I might come in his place. Old Wakera agreed as well, and I took the same oath as my father had taken.

"I continued taking gold from these mines until Brigham Young's death in 1877, and since then I've come here always by stealth and always alone. Yet I take little of the precious money rock and use it only for my own small needs and to help a few others. Truly I dare do nothing else, for I fear my oath and the curse."

"Yet you revealed this mine to your brother?"

"No, not this one. I told Enock only of a small mine I myself had prospected out and excavated. I did not think the Lord would think that mine was sacred, but obviously I was wrong, and my brother paid for my mistake with his life."

"You know the man who killed him." It was a statement, not a question, and old Caleb Rhoades looked quickly up at me.

"Yes," he said quietly, "I know. I just did not know where, and I did not understand exactly why."

"Who was it?"

"The Ute who rode into Tabby's camp after you, the tall man with the scar on his face. I think that scar was given him by my brother. He is a hard man, but I know his heart, and he is not a bad man. He simply did what he had been charged to do so that the honor and integrity of his people would be protected.

"You see, the Ute only watched until Enock went into that mine and removed the gold. Once he had done that his doom was sealed, for the Indians have sworn that no man will live who takes this gold selfishly."

"Well," I said finally, "I'm confuseder'n a blind buffalo bull in a bumbleberry bush. Why didn't you tell me who you were? And why didn't you tell me about who had killed your poor brother, instead of making me try to defend myself?"

Caleb Rhoades sighed. "I feared for you, Hyrum Soderberg. I truly did. I thought if you knew who I was, you would also try to force the secret of the gold from me. Many others have, you know, including Felix Friendlessman."

"I told you I didn't want the gold."

"Yes, you did. But at that time you had never seen such a sight as this—millions of dollars literally lying about for the taking. Now that you do see it, young man, do you not wish to take at least a little of it with you?"

I looked about me again at the glittering walls and ceiling, at the smelted and stacked bars, at the incredible, incalculable wealth. From the floor I lifted a fist-sized rock and hefted it, gazing at the gold that was laced through it. "Tell me about this gold," I said quietly. "What sort of gold is it, and how did it come to be here?"

"You've asked the right person," the old man said. "I've studied the subject for years. As you can see there is more gold here in this mine than there is rock. Most of it is wire shaped, extruded through small openings in the surrounding rock during some past era of great volcanic heat and pressure. And that, by the way, is when and how *all* gold is formed, in the pressured and fissured rock above huge and unbelievably hot volcanic batholiths.

"There is also leaf gold here, crystaline structures formed within pockets in the quartz vein. It's formed in the same way, only under slightly different circumstances.

"Near here I found a mound of tiny gold nuggets that were almost like kernels of corn. With those nuggets I also found the bones of a slain Spaniard, and so I left that entire fortune where it lay. I have no idea how those nuggets were formed, and I have never found them in their natural setting.

"Finally, the few actual geologists and mineralogists who have seen this gold call it five-niner gold, meaning that in its natural state it is .99999 pure. Truly there is more wealth here than any man on earth has ever imagined."

The old man took a deep breath, lifted a handful of golden detritus from the floor, held it up, and let it cascade down, sparkling in the lantern light as it fell.

"Are you not now tempted, my young Hyrum Soderberg? Can you not imagine the power and glory such wealth would bring you?"

Again I hefted the rock I held, tossed it into the air, caught it, and saw the gleam of the gold within it; then I tossed it toward the four whitened skeletons.

There was power indeed within that gold, and honor and glory as well. But power, riches, honor, and glory, those were transitory things, here and quickly gone. Riches were a claim to distinction for those who had no other right to it, just as the claiming of ancestry is most important to those who have done nothing themselves. Yet often the ancestor from whom such people claim descent would never be allowed in their homes.

Great families were often founded by pirates, freebooters, or energetic peasants and farmers who happened to be in the right place at the right time and took advantage of it. The founder would, in many instances, look with as great a disdain upon his descendants.

No, to me the goal of life could not be what Caleb Rhoades had described. To me it was to see, to know, to learn, to understand. Never could I see a far mountain peak or an unread book of good quality or the pure innocence of a tiny child's face but my heart would stumble and my throat grow tight.

Up to a point a man's life is shaped by environment, heredity, and movements and changes in the world about him. Then there comes a time when it lies within each individual's grasp to shape the clay of his life into the sort of thing he wishes it to be. Only the weak blame their parents, their race, their times, their lack of good fortune, quirks of fate, or, as in my case, accidents of birth for what they become in life. Everyone has it within his power to say, this I am today, that I shall be tomorrow. And then to succeed, the wish must be implemented with deeds.

"Any man would be a fool to claim that the sight of such wealth doesn't tempt him," I answered honestly. "Of course I'm tempted. Still, I'll take none of it with me, for I don't want the troubles that would accompany it."

"Is that your only reason?"

"No, not altogether. My father has cautioned me all my life never to seek gold, for so the prophets have counseled. Because I love my father and honor our prophets, I'll respect that. My father has also shown me, within our own small ward, the misery of those who have allowed themselves to love wealth. Laying aside the troubles that come with it, I don't want the misery and smallness of spirit that the love of gold seems to bring. And Mr. Rhoades, I fear that if I took even a little of this, I could learn to love it very quickly."

"And so, with hardly any thought, you choose a life of poverty?"

"There have been many thoughts, Caleb Rhoades, and of a truth I made this decision long ago when I decided who I truly was and who I wanted with all my heart to be. Nor will I be poor. You see, my gold is out there, in the morning sunrise on a mountain stream, in a V of geese winging north in the spring, in the trembling of an aspen leaf in the late fall, in the bugle of a bull elk on a frosty morning. It's in a noble passage of literature penned by a man who was grasping for the same almost unattainable heights of soul as I am; it's in an inspiring verse of scripture from the lips of God himself.

"It's also in the face of my mother and father, in the dignity and courage of their lives; it's in the love and pride I feel for my brothers and sisters, and in the trembling I once experienced when I felt the power of the Spirit of God. Finally, it's in the awesome glory of the temple of the Most High, where someday I will go.

"No, Brother Rhoades, I don't lust for this gold. Certainly I could use it, for my family is struggling terribly. Yet I'll get along without it, and one day I'll be the stronger for doing so."

I sat silently, and Caleb Rhoades stared at me, his eyes alive in the dancing of the light from the lantern. "Perhaps," he said finally as he lifted the gold-laced rock and tossed it back to me, and his voice was quivering as he spoke, "p-perhaps we *will* get out of here."

"We will," I declared strongly. "If there is a way, we will."

There was a sudden noise at the entrance to the old mine. I turned and heard a scuffling and sliding, and then with a cry of fear a form slid to the floor beside me. It looked up, and open-mouthed, I found myself staring into the bruised and muddy face of a bedraggled Ida Mae Sorenson!

"Oh, Hyrum," she cried out as she scrambled to her feet, and seconds later she was trembling within my arms.

"It's all right," I told her gently as I stroked her face, not even wondering how she had found us, and at that moment I was finally certain that it was all right.

36

East Grandaddy Mountain Bench—Utah Territory—Again

The afternoon broke in a crimson flood upon the storm-shattered mountains, massive shoulders of granite thrown out from the fires of the earth's beginning.

Through the mists that were left from the rain I watched the men move slowly up the slope, small figures spread in a line, all moving toward me, all armed and ready. There were at least ten of them that I could see, and the magnitude of their numbers staggered me. Where had they recruited so many, and how had they come so quickly?

It wasn't happening the way it was supposed to happen. There were the cliffs behind me, and I needed more time, time to get away from the trap that the cliffs had become. But the men were driving me now, and I knew it; they were running me, making certain that I wasn't going to move around them.

It was late afternoon, three hours and a little more until sunset. The sun poured through the mists of the rain, creating a brilliant rainbow that arched up and away to the east. The light splashed golden on the rocks below, and I realized that there too was the gold I truly sought, and in fact already had.

"Ida Mae?" I said softly.

"Yes?"

Just hearing her voice did my heart good and made me believe that what I was planning might work. I hoped it would, for more than ever I wanted to live now, wanted to grow older with her, to share my life with her.

"Don't you forget. When I lead these fellers away, you help that old man down through the rocks. He'll find the horses; you help him onto one of them and then you climb on another and the both of you get away from here as fast as you can get."

"But Hyrum—"

"Ida Mae, I'd dearly love for you to stay, but don't you do it. It's hard enough worrying about my own hide. If I had to worry about protecting yours as well, especially since the only weapon I have is this old Spanish pike—well, you understand, don't you?"

"I do."

"Good. I'll meet you soon as I'm able."

There was silence on the mountain, and somewhere off to my left a marmot whistled shrilly. From farther along another answered, and then Ida Mae spoke again.

"Hyrum, I . . . I . . ." She paused, and I could tell that her voice was shaking with emotion. In my mind I tried to picture her, to see how she was looking at me. But I couldn't do it. All I could see were those outlaw fellers, coming forward—

"Hyrum, I love you!"

"I love you too," I said quietly, savoring the thrill that surged through me at her words. "Now go," I said, and then I moved. Hobbling forward, I staggered through the rocks, trying desperately to move away from Ida Mae and old Caleb Rhoades. A rifle shot rang out, a rock nearby shattered as the slug whined away, and then I was on my stomach and crawling. I could not go fast, yet I went steadily, and it is amazing how much ground a man can cover when he feels the urgency I felt. Nor did I feel fear, for there was no time for that, nor was this the place.

Another rifle boomed, a larger rifle, maybe a Sharps buffalo gun, and I cringed as the huge slug whapped past, sounding very close. Then suddenly I was there, where I had decided I must be. I squirmed through the boulders to see where the men were located and to decide what I must do to prepare.

Of the ten that I could count, only one was on a horse, and that would have to be Felix Friendlessman. He was much closer than the others, whom I could now see were some reinforcements I had never before seen, and the outlaws Silvertip and Blue John and—

Well, that dirty little sneak and liar! There was Doolin, big as life, after he'd promised he'd let me be, and it was him who was firing the big buffalo gun!

I grinned again, but it was more a gritting of my teeth than it was a smile. "Mr. Doolin," I muttered, "you come any closer, you'll run smack into a Soderberg with real fur on his brisket. I've come up mighty shy of patience in this last toss of the dice, and I'm ready to add up your points. Mr. Doolin, you can bank on that."

Yet still he came on, and so I looked away, at Friendlessman now, who was that much closer. I waited until he'd come through the dark green of the edge of the pines, and then I began to move back into a higher field of boulders. I picked my way carefully up the slope, glancing behind me, not wanting to stumble and lose time, yet not wanting to lose sight of Friendlessman either. Yet I caught only glimpses of the man, and I did not feel safe.

The slope was not steep where I climbed, and the boulders, huge monoliths of black stone, seemed almost uniformly placed, like an abandoned, petrified orchard. It was not a good place to stand with an ancient Spanish pike and face a man who had two Colts and all the time in the world in which to use them.

I moved back a little farther and came to an open place where no great rocks lay. It was spotted with patches of holly and cliffrose, but there was nothing to use for cover, not on the entire, gravelly, nearly one hundred feet of ground that stretched upward to the great stone cliffs above me.

Perhaps I could make it, but not straight up. It was now too steep, too open. I would have to angle across the slope and Friendlessman would have time to shoot me. Still, it was worth trying, and it was better than staying where I was. I would have to forget about Friendlessman and the others and concentrate on reaching the great bulging cliff. There I might escape—or I might not—but there I would most surely have led them away from Ida Mae and Caleb Rhoades.

I was in the open then, hobbling diagonally across the open space, my boots digging hard into the muddy talus of the slope. Almost at once I felt knotted pain in my wounded leg, that and the wetness of blood. But I kept going, not looking back and trying not to picture Felix Friendlessman closing in on me, or the others, farther back, taking aim with their rifles.

I cut through a patch of cliffrose, getting a better foothold and running as hard as I could with my club foot and wounded leg. But then I came suddenly onto a spine of smooth rock—it humped no more than two feet above the ground—and here I lost my footing and slipped to my hands and knees. I tried to get up and stumbled again, then I rolled over the side of the smooth rock surface and finally lunged to my feet.

I saw movement then, quick movement, off behind that smooth hump of rock, and instantly my breath caught. But it was only an animal, I was certain of it—probably a marmot. But I didn't have time to study it, for Friendlessman was coming still closer, and I needed desperately to hurry.

Anxiously my mind searched for a way out of the trap I was in, some great military strategy that Tacitus or Pliny or some other ancient had discovered and that would also serve me. But there was nothing in my mind, nothing but the growing understanding of what Friendlessman was going to do.

I was climbing again, less than twenty feet from the rubble at the foot of the cliff, when Friendlessman's voice finally reached me.

"Soderberg!"

I stopped, catching my breath and letting it out slowly before coming around. I knew I would never make the rubble, but perhaps now it wouldn't matter. Enough time had passed, and the old man and Ida Mae would surely be safe.

I watched Friendlessman walk out of the maze of boulders below; he had left his horse and now was afoot, facing me. His Colt pistols were holstered, but his hands hung close to them. He came on slowly, his face calm and his eyes not straying from my own.

"Why don't you show us where the gold is?" he asked as he advanced up the slope. "You've no chance against us, and if you'll cooperate, we will go easy on you."

He was not looking at the ground but was feeling his way along with each careful step, his dark eyes boring relentlessly into mine.

"You want to show us, don't you," he declared suddenly. "You want to, but you are stubborn as old man Rhoades, and you don't know how to change."

He was through the cliffrose now, still coming slowly along. "It will be easy, Soderberg," he called. "Drop that silly stick. Give me the word and I will call the men off. You perhaps noticed that we have added reinforcements? There will be many more, all of whom consider you to be their enemy. Your only hope of living is with me, and I will give the word as quickly as you agree to show me the mine."

I said nothing but stood silently, facing Felix Friendlessman and watching him move across the small field of muddy talus.

"Decide quickly, my young friend. Tell us of your own choice and easily, or refuse and tell us anyway as we slowly take your life." He seemed almost to be smiling. "Thinking of dying does tighten a man's nerves, doesn't it."

Friendlessman was ready, standing on his own ground, and for the first time I felt the fear of dying rise up within me. There was no way I could get to him, no way at all. Yet he could shoot and I would die a little at a time, and who knew what I would say as I suffered? How could I possibly keep from betraying the location of the sacred mine, especially when I was so powerless before him? Oh, if only I could stop him!

But no, I had no time, no chance.

Unless Friendlessman hesitated, or was thrown off guard.

My gaze went from the talus to the spine of slick stone where I had slipped. Again I thought I saw movement there, not much, but . . . pesky marmot. Didn't it understand there was great danger in this place?

Quickly I studied the spine of rock. If I could draw Friendlessman to that point, if I could startle him, jiggle him somehow, if I could throw him off balance only for an instant, then perhaps I could get to him with the pike. If I could do all that . . .

And the other men were into the orchard of boulders now, still climbing.

No—one thing at a time. Slowly I began again to back away.

Friendlessman shook his head. "Don't be foolish. You will never make it. Not ever."

I was still edging back, covering six, eight, almost ten feet before Friendlessman started forward again. I stopped, watched him come out of the talus and onto the spine of rock, watched him grope with one foot before stepping onto the smooth, rounded surface.

As Friendlessman's foot inched forward again, I stepped to the side, and with an underhanded fling I chucked the rock I still held, the rock that Caleb Rhoades had tossed back to me, the one that was so heavily laden with gold.

Friendlessman was with me, his right-hand Colt revolver out and swinging onto me, but the movement shifted his weight, and my rock, hitting him in the shoulder, threw him off balance. His boots slipped on the smooth stone, and even as he fired and fired again he was falling back, his free hand outstretched and clawing for stability.

Before me Friendlessman seemed suddenly suspended, and lifting the ancient pike I started forward, aware that he had caught his balance and that his Colt pistol was coming down once more upon me.

I saw that big gun dropping down in line with my body, and I knew that there I would die. With the late afternoon sun on my face and with the rocks of the mountain beneath me, I would die. It was not fair, for I did not deserve such an end when a woman like Ida Mae Sorenson waited for me. Yet Pa had told me that in this life there was no such thing as fairness. There was only ultimate, and eternal, justice.

Was I feeling sorry for myself? Yes, I think so. Yet I was also feeling sorry for Ida Mae and our children who would never be, who would never feel my love or live to enjoy life as I had. I was also feeling sorry that unfairness had become so rampant and uncontrolled, and suddenly that sorrowful feeling made me angry!

"Friendlessman," I shouted, "shoot! Do it now, but do it well, for I will be coming for you, and there's no stopping a man who knows he's in the right!"

Friendlessman hesitated, his dark eyes glaring into mine, and I lifted the ancient pike to the ready and took another step toward him. Surprised, he involuntarily took a step backward, and then his face set and—

Suddenly there was a slight hiss, and from the air a rope settled down around the body and poised arm of Felix Friendlessman. There was a quick jerk and he was falling. The pistol went off into the air and clattered away from his hand, and I found myself staring once again into the grinning face of my younger brother Ernest.

"You did it again, Hy," he said easily while I stood gaping. "You've just got to stop being so doggone predictable!"

I had started to grin myownself, for he had been the marmot I thought I had seen. Suddenly there was another explosion, and rock chips once more stung my face. I ducked down, heard the rattle of more rifle shots, wiped a streak of blood away from my cheek, and looked up in time to see one of the most amazing sights I had ever seen.

Down the slope those men had seen Friendlessman go down and had started to come to his aid. Suddenly there was rifle fire among them, and they held up, bewildered, as a giant of a man with a missing front tooth and a star on his chest rose up from behind a boulder directly before them.

Marshal Tinsdale, as he lived and breathed, direct from the Provo jail! I could hardly believe it! What was *he* doing there?

Three men suddenly ducked down into the pines, and I hadn't even had time to more than notice them when they hastily backed out of the timber again, their hands in the air, followed by three men on horses. The men held rifles upon them.

Those three riders looked awfully familiar. Criminently, I thought. They were my brothers, Lyman, Jim, and Johnny! Now where had they—

I heard another scuffling, and from the boulders emerged the outlaws Blue John and Alpha Rachel "Silvertip" Garrett. Silvertip was striding up the hill, grinning like he always did, and putting up no struggle at all. Blue John, on the other hand, was dragging his feet somewhat but was being helped along pretty regular by the boots and stove-lid hands of my black-suited father, Jons Soderberg.

"Hyrum," Pa called out, "are you and Ernest all right?"

"Yeah, Pa. We're fine."

"I expected that you would be. I told your mother and Polly that both of you had a knowing way and that they needn't worry about either of you."

"Mr. Bishop, sir," Silvertip said then, his voice warm and cheerful enough to light a candle from, "what you say is sure true. That Hyrum and the little one up there with the rope sneak around quieter'n tumblebugs falling off a buffalo chip. Why, twice they slicked our horses right out from under us, and with Blue John around that ain't exactly an easy thing to do. Yes sir, Mr. Bishop Soderberg, sir, you've a right to be proud. Them're *my* kind of boys!"

"Silvertip," Blue John suddenly growled, "you ain't nothing but a chuckleheaded nincompoop. It's no wonder your mother named you—"

He never did finish his insult, however, for the huge hand of the outlaw Silvertip reached out, balled Blue John's shirt, and lifted him strangling into the air.

"Blue John," Sivertip said easily while I and everyone else around me stared in amazement, "in promulgating your esoteric cogitations or articulating your superficial sentimentalities and amicable, philosophical, or psychological observations, let your extemporaneous descantings and unpremeditated expatiations have intelligibility and veracious vivacity. Shun double entendres, prurient jocosity, and pestiferous profanity, obscure or apparent. And above all else, Blue John, be polite to your friends!"

Carefully then the big man set the bug-eyed outlaw Blue John back upon the earth and attempted to straighten his shirt. Blue John stared, gurgled, reached for his pistol and realized that it had been taken from him, and gurgled again, and suddenly he tightened his fist to come at his companion. Instantaneously, the meat-cleaver slash of Alpha Rachel "Silvertip" Garrett's huge fist neatly clipped Blue John's jaw, and without another word the thin and rangy outlaw dropped to the earth.

"He's my friend," Silvertip mumbled apologetically to my pa, "but I've enjoyed about all of his compliments I can stand. His manners are somewhat scant, and I reckon I'm tired of waiting for 'em to show up. Still, the poor misbeguided fool needs someone, so I'd best be loyal and stick with him. Maybe I can learn him a thing or two."

Pa clapped the big man on the shoulder. "You will. As Hyrum would say, you have more lip than a muley cow. Anyone who can speak as you have will have no trouble reforming a poor, unconscious outlaw."

Silvertip instantly turned red and was back to his old self. "Ah," he mumbled, "it wasn't nothing. Most folks think I ain't too smart, but my mother and pap were educated, and they learned me a few things, even if I don't always show it."

"They taught you well, my son's friend," Pa said quietly, and Silvertip beamed like he'd just been handed the winner's roses at the Irish Sweepstakes. And coming to that, maybe he had, for a compliment from Pa was a rare and meaningful thing, and not lightly given.

"Pa!" I called out, suddenly realizing that Marshal Tinsdale was headed directly toward him. "Look out! It's that marshal from Provo!"

But Pa only looked up at me, grinned, and waited for the marshal to reach him. The two men glared at each other; then they suddenly smiled and shook hands, and I was still staring in bewilderment when I felt a hand upon my shoulder.

"Hy," Ernest asked, "are you sure you're all right? There's a sight of blood on your leg. I thought that would've healed by now."

"Not hardly," I answered, noticing for the first time that my younger half-brother was suddenly growing. "But it will now. Golly, am I glad to see you, Ern. I was afraid you'd not get through."

Ernest smiled brightly. "No trouble at all. I had me a little upscuddle with Loose-lip Lundstrum and his horse. Still, the horse was spirited, and last time I saw Loose-lip he was flying through the air with his legs flapping like a migrating bullfrog. Then, too, the telegraph operator at Soldier's Fort was some stubborn; he wouldn't send my message until I fetched old Chief Tabby along to encourage him. But finally he saw the light—"

"Chief Tabby? You saw him again?"

"Sure as lilacs smell sweet in spring I did. Me and Ingersol hunted his camp out. Fact is, he's the one who brought Pa and the rest of us here, showed us right where you'd be."

I stared at my little brother. He pointed behind me, I turned and looked, and there, standing quietly atop the rubble at the foot of the great cliff, were the ancient Chief Tabby and almost a dozen of his tribesmen.

"Ungh," the Chief grunted. "Hy-mum still strong, throwum money-rock far and well."

"Just luck," I declared modestly, knowing that it truly had been. "I don't—"

"Hy-mum have good heart. Tabby have good heart. Enn-nest have good heart. Tabby take Enn-nest as new son. Tabby giveum Hy-mum money-rock as gift. Takeum all the same takeum."

He stood still, in dignity, and the tall Ute brave with the scar down his face stepped forward and handed me the rock I had thrown at Felix Friendlessman. I looked closely into the man's eyes as he handed me the gold, for I knew who he was, but whatever I thought I'd see wasn't there. I saw only calmness—that, and a hard dignity that I knew I would never thoroughly understand.

"Thank you," I told the chief. "For as long as the sun shines upon these mountains, I and my family will treasure this great gift."

I don't know how much of what I said he understood, but old Chief Tabby bowed his head slightly. "It no considerable thing," he replied carefully. "Cover tracks over in your memory." Then he turned, was helped down from the rock, and was gone.

Suddenly there was a rattle of horses' hooves, and before I could hardly do more than turn around again, Ida Mae and Caleb Rhoades were there, and Ida Mae was once more in my arms.

"Ida Mae," Pa asked, and his voice was filled with surprise, "how did you get here?"

"I rode Pa's white mare up from Soldier's Fort."

"Alone?"

"Of course. I heard that Hyrum had been wounded, and I had to get here in a hurry."

"But—but—" I stuttered at Ida Mae, "I thought . . . Didn't you come here with my family?"

"I most certainly didn't. I didn't know anyone but your mother was coming, and I left her down at Soldier's Fort. You see, I knew *I* had to come, and so I did."

"Then who showed you the mi—"

Ida Mae quickly reached up and put her hand on my mouth. "Showed me what, Hyrum? Showed me you? That was easy. No one did, but somehow I was led right to where you'd be. I walked and climbed directly to your side. After all, that was my place, wasn't it?"

Well, what could a feller say to that? Nothing, for words at such a time aren't exactly needed. What is, however, is action, and a little of that I promptly initiated.

"Whew," Johnny said, grinning. "I'd admire, Hyrum, if you'd give me a few lessons, happen you ever take a break. I've been sparking Mattie Butts a little, and we *are* fixing to get married, but I can tell I am a babe in the woods when compared to your expertise."

"Me too," Jim grinned. "It's purely obvious that Hy's learned how honey draws more flies than vinegar when it comes to gathering women. I'll bet his verbal lather is some scented, too. Let's hear us a little of that sweet-talking syrup right now, little brother, and see how it increases what's already proceeding!"

"Now come on, fellers," Lyman put in, grinning from ear to ear, "can't you see how the poor boy is some busy. Kiss her a good one for me, Hy. That's the kind of lesson *I'd* like to see."

They all hooted. Pa and Marshal Tinsdale and his deputies and even the gentle outlaw Silvertip grinned, and both Ida Mae and I were getting redder'n maple leaves in October. This was going to have to stop, by thunder, or I—

"It plain to see boy knowum how," a deep voice grunted in agreement with my brothers, and I turned to find Zene Hill standing behind me. Good grief! I thought. What was this? A family reunion? Of course I knew it wasn't, but I can't hardly tell you how thrilled I was to see all of those folks there. Yes sir, friends and family are all the wealth a man ever needs in this life, and I surely had them in abundance.

"Yesum," Zene went on in his fake reservation talk, "it be plenty obvious. Lady, you be-um good squaw for boy. You tough likeum bottom of boot, tender likeum backfat of young steer." Zene rolled his eyes in obvious enjoyment of the fact that he was embarrassing poor Ida Mae and me plumb to death. "Yesum," he went on, "him heapum man, you heapum woman. Me betum in time make plenty heapum noisy kids."

I turned beet red and would maybe have slugged my sheep-herding partner had not other, more important things come to hand. Suddenly Felix Friendlessman stood there, glaring at Ida Mae and myself.

"Children," he snarled with derision. "Lucky, foolish children. Ida Mae, you and I had something fine between us, and with me you might have gone far. But now you choose to throw it all away on this . . . this *cripple!*"

Ida Mae turned white, but I stared straight at the man. "Don't you worry, Ida Mae," I said quietly, doing my best to control my temper. "Felix here thinks he's powerful evil, but that isn't so. Why, he isn't even a patch on a real bad man. He's just sort of petty, with a real mean streak in him."

"Bah," the man snorted, and then he spat. "Listen to my words, little girl, and remember. I will return when you have grown enough to become wise, and when I do, you will honor the promises you made me, promises sealed with the ring and with the kiss."

Well, I stared, thoroughly surprised. Friendlessman had fallen for Ida Mae, he truly had. Not that such an understanding thrilled me much, for it didn't. It only surprised me, is all.

I was about to come to Ida Mae's rescue, for I knew the man was trying to frighten her, to intimidate her, to punish her for turning against him. Therefore it can be clearly understood that I was just as surprised by Ida Mae's quick and ready response as I had been by Friendlessman's words, my family's timely appearance, and Silvertip's sudden verbosity. And believe you me, Ida Mae's response was quick and it was ready. That little woman needed help from no man alive. Right then I knew she was one to ride the river with, and again I determined one day to do it.

"Promises?" Ida Mae Sorenson snapped, drawing herself up stiffly and facing the tall man before her. "And kisses? Felix Ethelbert Friendlessman, I ought to have given you a kick instead of a kiss. And that ring of yours turned my finger green clear up to my elbow. I was lucky I didn't get the lockjaw from it! Promises indeed!"

"Why you rude and stubborn female jackass—"

"Female jackass? How could that be, you simpleton, you moron who claims to be educated? A female jackass is a jenny. A jackass is always a male. As well, some males are always jackasses. Especially you, Mr. Friendlessman, you misbegotten, half-baked excuse for a gentleman! Why, you . . . you're nothing but a festering pimple on the skin of time!"

Well, I grinned at Ida Mae's delightful way with words, but Felix Friendlessman fumed! "Miss Sorenson," he sputtered, "I've a mind to—"

"A mind?" Ida Mae snapped back, quicker'n scat. "Mr. Friendlessman, you've got no more mind than a mud coot. I've seen more brains in a lightning-struck sheep than you can claim. You have finally and truly lived up to your name, for you have no friends left in all the world. Why, I wouldn't look at you again if you were the last man in Sanpete Valley! And you might very well be, by the time you get out of jail.

"Hyrum," she then said as she spun to face me, "would you and your family be so good as to escort me off this mountain?"

I grinned and nodded, and as she and I turned away there was a loud cheer from my brothers—yes, and even from some of the others, if my ears hadn't mistaken me. Seemed like that little gal of mine was a real hand at winning friends.

Suddenly from down slope there was a flurry of movement, and I looked in time to see the little weasel Doolin scurrying down through the rocks, trying to escape. Without even thinking I shouted at him to stop, but of course he didn't.

Then without warning Silvertip reached out and took the old Spanish pike from my hand. Pulling back his arm, he heaved it quickly in Doolin's general direction. The pike arched through the air and slammed into a rock no closer than five feet from the fleeing little man, shattering itself to pieces. The throw was terrible, and poor Silvertip seemed embarrassed to have us see it. However, the results were what counted, and they were instantly evident.

It almost seemed as though poor Mr. Doolin had been shot. He screeched, grabbed his head with both arms, hollered and moaned, and finally dived headfirst into the rocks where he lay quivering and whining in fear.

I saw him do it, and so did the others. Virtually everyone sat up and took notice. The ability to act swiftly under fire never went unrecognized in a society of western men. That little thief could move! Such an instant sense of decision was an important asset in any frontier community, and I began to think maybe I had been wrong to order him away. His actions had to be saluted, and big Silvertip, who hated the name Alpha Rachel but manfully owned up to it anyway, supplied the verdict. "Feller's no ordinary coward," he said, and all of us there assembled, willing or otherwise, instantly agreed.

37

West Slope of Uintah Mountains—Utah Territory

Ida Mae and I and my pa and brothers had a fine ride down from the mountain to Soldier's Fort and my mother and the railroad, and I wouldn't have stopped there except that Zene had reminded me that he still needed a camp tender, and Ma and Pa had reminded me as well that the family still needed money. In spite of the temporary truce between Pa and Marshal Tinsdale, Pa would still have to stay in hiding, and our family funds would be mighty limited for some time to come.

Somewhere behind us rode Deputy Tinsdale, his posse, and all their prisoners, and believe me, he had several. Ahead of us by about fifty feet rode my pa and my four brothers and Zenos Hill, side by side through the deepening twilight, and I'll have to admit that watching them choked me up so I could hardly talk. Just knowing they had risked their own lives to come and help me made me feel prouder'n a banty rooster in the first light of morning. Why, it was—

"They're wonderful!" Ida Mae suddenly declared, somehow sensing what I was feeling.

"They are," I agreed. "Good, strong men, all of them."

"Your mother is wonderful, too."

Well, I looked over at Ida Mae and grinned. Looked like a little peace had been made in other quarters while I'd been gone. "There is no finer thing," I said quietly, "than to have good friends like you and Zene and to be part of such a fine and wonderful family as is mine. I hope the Lord above knows how thankful I am to be a small part of all of you."

"He does, Hyrum. I'm sure He does. That's why He continues to bless you so."

"Well," I said sincerely, "you must be right, for I can't imagine a man having any greater blessings than I do."

"How's your leg feeling?" Ida Mae asked.

"Not bad. One of Tinsdale's posse was a doctor, and he cleaned it up good. He says all I need now is rest and time."

"Are you coming home?"

"No, I reckon not, at least for now. My job's here, and I'd better see it through. That way, happen Zene doesn't work me to death, I'll have plenty of time to heal."

Ida Mae giggled, and for a time we rode in silence while the darkness gathered quickly around us. "It is passing strange," I finally declared, "that I have been in the midst of more gold than a man can even imagine and yet have chosen to walk away and leave it behind, thus ensuring that my pa and my family will remain poor and so must struggle."

"Yes it is," Ida Mae responded quietly.

I reached down into my saddlebag and pulled out the heavy, gold-laden rock that Tabby had given me. "How much do you reckon this is worth?" I asked.

"Your word and your honor," Ida Mae answered instantly, and she looked steadily at me as she spoke.

Well, that set me back some, and so carefully I put the rock away again. "You're right," I finally admitted. "And you know something else, Ida Mae? That's what all the rest of the gold in that mine is worth too. My word and my honor. I gave ol' Caleb Rhoades my word that I didn't want none—I mean any—of that sacred money rock, and I meant what I said! That mine can sit there until doomsday, and I won't ever go back again."

"I know you won't, Hyrum. That was why I stopped you from mentioning that you had even seen it. You and I must make a promise that we will never mention, for so long as we both shall live, that we were there. It would be too difficult for others if we did. I now make that promise. Do you?"

"Yes," I said quietly, "I promise, though I feel badly to think that the children won't know of it."

"Children?"

"Uh . . . I . . . well . . . uh . . ."

"Perhaps we could write it down," Ida Mae said sweetly, rescuing me, "and keep it hidden until after we are gone."

"Yeah," I agreed. "We could do that."

"I'm proud of you," Ida Mae said sincerely as she reached over and took my hand in hers.

Well, I was waxing somewhat proud myownself, and my courage was growing more powerful by the minute. Still, it wouldn't do to show it, so very humbly I said thank you.

"But what about us, Hyrum?" Ida Mae suddenly asked.

"Us?"

"Yes, us. After your mission, of course. What if *we* need a little money as we begin our family?"

Well, I started to color up some, but it didn't matter because it was full dark and Ida Mae couldn't see my embarrassment. Still, such tongue oil as she was spreading out set my heart to pounding.

"No matter," I declared. "I'll find some other way. I took an oath about that gold, and need it or not, I'll never remove an ounce of it from that mine."

Ida Mae smiled sweetly. "I'm glad that you won't, Hyrum. I'm also glad that Mr. Rhoades told me I didn't have to take that oath."

"What? But—"

"Remember this, Hyrum. What I have is for you and for me, for the children you mentioned, and never for anything but good. And if you ever tell anyone about it, I'll deny it forever!"

Mystified, I stared at her. Then she smiled mischievously and drew back the hem of her long skirt, and I saw, glinting out of the top of her high boot, something that looked an awful lot like the tip of an anciently smelted gold bar.

"Ida Mae!" I said, and then she stopped me once again with a finger on my lips. Quickly then she started to sing; I gulped, grinned at this little lady who was so full of surprises, and joined in the singing with all my heart. Of course, I'm a singer from way back, having sung before crowds of several hundred—sheep, that is. Pa and the others up front heard us and joined in too, and it was a powerful chorus that we made coming down off that mountain.

A dozen or more songs we sang, Church songs and otherwise, and I was happier than I could ever remember being. That's what being with Ida Mae did to me. Made me happier'n a sheepdog with no wolves around. Finally, however, we all grew quiet. Ida Mae and I rode stirrup to stirrup with our arms about each other, and from then on we left the singing up to the coyotes that had joined up with us out in the dark.

Besides being a whole lot better looking than I was, Ida Mae Sorenson surely did have a better voice than me.

So did Pa, Lyman, Ernest, and maybe even Jim.

For that matter, so did the coyotes.

Seven Days for Ruby

Seven Days for Ruby

Blaine M. Yorgason
Brenton G. Yorgason

Deseret Book Company
Salt Lake City, Utah

For Dick and Sharleen, and for Jim and Analee

Contents

Acknowledgments

We would like to acknowledge the invaluable help of Cora Beck Adamson and Stephen F. Beck, who recorded their histories as they unfolded.

Prologue

Saturday
October 1, 1910

The sun beat mercilessly against the concrete of the Los Angeles street, and the passersby walked faster, hoping to get more quickly into the coolness of their destinations. The street was not crowded, for it was Saturday. Neither was it empty. Yet the scattered pedestrians paid almost no attention to each other, all hurrying along on their own predetermined errands.

An automobile horn blared at an intersection, from down the street another answered, and two carriages passed around each other, the hooves of their teams clattering loudly against the pavement. A freight team dragged its creaking wagon slowly through the intersection, blocking the way of yet another motorcar. Overhead, a maze of telephone, telegraph, and electrical wires swung between poles, and the quiet buzzing from some of them added to the din of the street.

Fifty feet west of the intersection, a solitary man leaned against the front of a cafe, a copy of the *American Fork Citizen* folded neatly in his hand. His face and clothing were dark, and his white shirt showed more patches of dirt than of white. He was of indeterminate age, though his gray hair made him look more old than young. Between his teeth burned a large cigar, and every few seconds he puffed the red end aglow, expelling the smoke from the side of his mouth.

Suddenly the street was filled with the clatter of an engine, and seconds later a second man, riding an Indian motorcycle, pulled up to the curb across the street. He was dressed like the first and looked strangely similar. The difference was that he was younger, quite a bit younger.

For a long breath the second man leaned against his bike in front of the office of the *Los Angeles Times,* looking around. Then, as though he were ashamed of what he was about to do, he dropped his head and eyes. Next he lifted a bundle of newspapers from the front of the motorcycle and furtively carried them into the newspaper office, his eyes never once lifting from the sidewalk.

A moment later the man reappeared, climbed back on the motorcycle, glanced briefly in the direction of the man who still leaned against the cafe, and then roared off down the street.

For several minutes nothing else happened. Then, slowly, the remaining man looked up and read the sign that hung above him.

CHOICE FRUITS
CANDIES
CIGARETTES
HOT FRANKFURTERS
2¢ each

Satisfied that the sign had not changed since he had read it moments earlier, the man puffed again on his cigar, pushed away from the cafe wall, and limped slowly across the street. Then he pushed his way through the door of the newspaper offices, stopped, and looked around.

There were more people in the office than he had expected, several more. In fact, he had been led to believe that the office would be almost empty. It wasn't, and the street held more traffic than he had anticipated, too. But such things hardly mattered. Maybe, he thought, grinning, it would make the deal better than ever.

Casually he moved to the counter and saw that the clerk was busy. And so, as a waiting man might, he glanced at his feet. A stack of newspapers rested there, old papers, and he gingerly stooped down to leaf through them.

A long article caught his attention, and like a man deep in thought, he took the cigar from his mouth, held it between his fingers, and continued to read.

The ash built up. He subconsciously flicked it onto the floor, and as he brought the cigar back, the burning end touched a thick, black string that twisted out of the stack of paper at his feet. There the cigar held.

For an instant nothing happened, and the man glanced down. But with nerves of steel he held the cigar steady as he began again to read. Finally, with a sputter, the string or fuse caught fire.

Casually the man dropped the paper back onto the stack, where it covered the spitting fuse. Without hurry, then, he smiled at the young woman who was so busy behind the counter, nodded politely at a man who stood with her, and started for the door. A moment later he tipped his hat to an elderly woman who had come in, held the door open for a newsboy who seemed in a hurry to leave, and then passed outside.

Scant seconds afterward, with no warning, the stack of old papers, hollowed out and containing eight sticks of Du Pont Superior Brand dynamite, exploded in a ball of red and yellow flame. The fire rose to the thin ceiling and billowed on upward and outward, burning, consuming. The explosion blasted out windows a city block away, blew down walls in several adjoining buildings, killed twenty people who had the misfortune of being nearby, and, of course, stopped the presses.

And in the screaming melee that followed, no one saw the older man limping quietly away, a twisted smile of grim satisfaction on his face.

Day 1

Friday

October 21, 1910

Chapter 1

Ruby Soderberg Alder was fit to be tied. She had been up half the night and most of the morning waiting, and yet nothing had happened. Still, something was going to happen, she just knew it was. Not good, necessarily, nor bad—but *something*.

For the hundredth time she looked out the window, scanning her horizons, searching for something, anything . . .

It had been a beautiful October morning. Earlier the frost had blanketed everything, and then the sun had come up and the air had been crisp and bright and clear. Quickly the sun had melted the frost, and everything had been damp and clean-looking. It had been one of those mornings when nothing could have been more perfect than it already was.

Except that something unusual was going to happen, and Ruby knew it.

She had experienced that same feeling before, perhaps two dozen times in her seventy years of life. And not once had she ever been wrong. A few times it hadn't been quite so strong a feeling as she was having now, but always it had been *something*. And so she believed this feeling with all her heart.

The last time had been when her son had been called as bishop of their ward down in American Fork. She had known that blessed event was coming for two full days. Not precisely, of course, but something . . . something . . .

Another time had been when her milk cow had birthed a two-headed calf. She'd thought it a disaster until her nephew Hyrum Soderberg had sold it to a traveling gypsy show for twenty-five dollars. That money had come in handy, and so the something had turned out good. But good or bad, Ruby had known *something* was coming for almost an entire week before that calf was born.

Just like now, she thought as she moved the needle back on her new talking machine so that the music would start over. Something was going to happen, and she could hardly contain her anticipation.

Drying the last dish and putting it in the cupboard, she was dancing gaily to the music when through her kitchen window she saw the old man.

And instantly, she knew that the *something* she had expected was there.

Anxiously she watched the old man's steady approach, noting his limp, his slightly stooped shoulders, his tattered overalls, the shock of white hair that seemed to peek out from beneath the brim of his battered old hat. But mostly she watched his face, noticing that he looked neither to the right nor to the left but kept his gaze fixed upon the small house wherein she stood. Nor did he hurry. He just kept coming slowly forward, and Ruby felt her throat constrict as she watched him draw near.

The needle on the talking machine reached the end of the song, then scratched over and over as it continued to revolve, stopping only when the spring had finally wound down. And Ruby, watching the old man in the road, didn't even notice.

At last the man paused in front of her home and gazed around him. Carefully he looked up the road where it crossed the Highland or Mitchell Ditch, and then just as carefully he looked down to where the road dropped off the hill toward American Fork. In both directions the road was empty.

For a long moment then, while Ruby hardly dared to breathe, the man just stood there. But then, with a sudden lifting and resettling of his hat, he reached out, lifted the latch, and walked through Ruby Soderberg Alder's front gate.

Flustered and more than a little frightened, Ruby removed her apron and draped it carefully over the rack next to the damp dish towel. Moving quickly to the mirror, she patted down her hair, noticing as she did so that her fingers were trembling.

"Gray," she muttered to herself, "my hair's so gray. And look how I'm shaking. Law, but I must look old."

Taking a deep breath, Ruby smoothed her dress and was just turning toward the front door so that she could confront the old man, when she heard the sound of an ax striking wood in her backyard. Startled, she hesitated and then moved quickly through the kitchen and washroom and out the back door.

"Here, there, Mister," she called out bravely, "what do you think you're up to?"

Without acknowledging Ruby's presence or her question, the old man continued his swing, striking the wood and splitting it cleanly.

He picked the two pieces up, set them carefully on the small but growing stack, and straightened up, and only then did he turn and face the woman.

"Top of the mornin' to ye, ma'am," he drawled softly, removing his hat as he spoke. "The haythun frost is on the pumpkin, but faith, now, it's almighty purty, just the same."

Startled by the sound of the man's voice, Ruby actually had to force herself to smile and reply.

"It—it *is* beautiful," she stammered.

"Aye, lass, like you. Faith, but ye've been gettin' purtier ev'ry garjus day of yer life, I'm thinkin'."

"Now—now you stop that! You hear?"

"I hear."

"Good. Why—why are you chopping my wood?"

"Man's got to do something to earn his breakfast," the old man replied, his Irish accent gone. "That's one reason."

"Is there another?"

"There surely is, ma'am. I figured the sound of an ax would get you out here so that I—uh, into the sun, I mean."

"I don't understand," Ruby said quickly. "What does the sun have to with anything?"

"Holy Michael O'Murphy, ma'am, ye don't understand because ye haven't looked at yer'self. Shure and I was thinkin' that if I was to meet ye, it would only be fittin' to do so with the sun splashin' over yer beautiful hair. Faith, now, but yer the spittin' image of a Gibson girl."

"Ohhh," Ruby said, fussing with embarrassment, "get along with you and your glib-tongued blarney. I'm an old woman, and you know it."

"I know nothing of the sort. I meant every word I said. Why, if you was to look at yourself now like I am looking at you, it'd likely give you heart palpitations."

"I just *did* look," Ruby declared, patting her hair nervously. "Just before I came out. And I've got to admit, I palpitated alright. Only it surely wasn't because of my ravishing beauty. Besides that, those Gibson girls are all fictitious drawings, and you know it."

"Drawings they are," the old man agreed. "But you are surely the model from which Charles Dana Gibson derives his ideas and his inspiration."

Ruby giggled nervously about the man's foolish compliments. Yet she had the strangest feeling that he meant every silly word he said, and suddenly she was worried. Why would that be? Why would an old man, a vagabond, be speaking to her in such a manner? She didn't know, but just as surely it didn't matter. It couldn't matter.

"Well," she said glibly, deciding to turn the tables on the old man, "you're right. I *am* a Gibson girl, disguised as an old woman. Now, why in heaven's name did you want to meet *me?"*

For an instant the old man was silent, searching for words. Then, with a sudden wink, he grinned and said, "Holy Michael O'Murphy, ma'am. Your fame as a cook has spread far and wide. I just naturally had to see for myself if the legends were true."

Despite herself, Ruby giggled, a strange excitement and embarrassment burning the back of her neck.

"So you're hungry, are you?" she asked.

"Yes, ma'am," he said, suddenly coughing. "It's been most of three days since I've been on the outside of a square meal."

Ruby stared, hardly able to believe he had been so long without food. "Well," she finally declared, "you're not going to pad those ribs of yours standing there. The wash pan's on the bench here on the porch, the towel is clean, and I made the soap only a week past. Just take your time, and I'll see what I can throw together."

"Why, thank you, ma'am. I've been told you're an accommodating lady. But to be truthful, I didn't figure you'd pay me much mind, what with these whiskers and twice-patched overalls I'm wearing. Seems to me, me garjus lass, that there's a great deal more to yer beauty than what first meets the eye."

Acutely aware that she was enjoying the feeling the old man was giving her, Ruby hurriedly spoke: "I never did think whiskers and clothes should make a man."

For an instant the old man gazed steadily at her. "That's uncommon wisdom," he said slowly. "In Proverbs the good Lord declares such a doctrine, but most times us mortals fall shy of the mark when it comes to judging. To my way of thinking, a good woman like you—"

The old man was suddenly seized with another coughing spell, and Ruby was appalled at how weak he looked after it had passed.

"Now see here," she scolded, doing her best to cover her emotions. "You shouldn't talk so much."

The old man grinned. "Folks have always said I was somewhat windy. But about that meal . . ."

"For goodness sake," Ruby said, "listen to me running on. Talk about windy! Other than family, I haven't had a pair of man's boots under my table in nigh onto ten years, and I've most forgotten my manners. Seems to me it's about time I made some changes."

"Well, if there's space under your table and food on top, I'd be happy to help you. And I'll cut wood until it's paid for, too."

"You can cut wood after you've eaten," Ruby stated matter-of-factly. "Man shouldn't go to work on an empty stomach, especially one that's three days empty."

"Uh . . ." Ruby continued, her heart hammering loudly in her chest, "My name is Ruby Alder. And yo—yours?"

For a long moment the old man did not answer. He simply stood, his hands on the ax, gazing into Ruby's eyes. Behind him, in the shed, a chicken squawked in the triumph of a newly-laid egg; and in the corral, Ruby's old milk cow, Jezebel, lowed with the contentment of a new mouthful of cud.

For Ruby, the moment seemed strangely frozen in time, and the tiniest details of life around her became entire worlds of motion. The fly trying to get through the washroom window, Stephen Adam's matched team acting up out in the meadow, the water squirting out of the tap where the early morning ice still blocked the hose, and a dozen other things, all perfectly normal, except that she stood in the middle of them, somehow frozen in that instant of eternity.

"Name, ma'am?" the old man suddenly drawled, breaking the spell. "Faith and I've got me a name. Shure and I'm thinkin' it's been a spell since I used it much, but it's there just the same. Folks who know me call me John."

"And—and your last name, John?" Ruby questioned, doing her best to ignore the roaring that suddenly seemed to fill her ears.

She could see the old man standing there, but he seemed to be a long way off, and he was swaying from side to side, almost as if he were swinging. Yet Ruby knew that it wasn't him who was swinging. It was herself. She felt faint, the roaring in her ears was growing louder.

"Phips," the old man answered, as if from a great distance. "Phips, it is. John William Phips. From England by way of Ireland and the Civil War and a whole lot of lonely wandering since."

Ruby Alder, her temples pounding and her face flushed with emotions that she thought were long dead, gripped the porch post and turned quickly away. How could this be happening to her, she wondered? How was it possible that after all this time she could be feeling this way? Her heart was beating and her face was red as though she were a schoolgirl.

With a valiant effort, she pulled herself together and forced herself to think. He . . . John Phips was standing there waiting. He was hungry. And no matter how she was feeling, no matter how foolish or unreal it all seemed, this man who called himself John needed breakfast. That was where she needed to focus her attention. The rest, if indeed there was any, would surely work itself out in time.

"The—the wash pan is right here, John William Phips," she said, looking him square in the face. "I—I'll be waiting inside, and I'll have your breakfast ready whenever you are ready to eat it."

And with that, Ruby Soderberg Alder turned around and fled into the desperately needed safety of her kitchen.

Chapter 2

John Phips slowly pulled himself away from the table. He had just eaten more of Ruby's bacon and eggs and fried red potatoes than anyone else she had ever fed, and the way he had devoured the peach jam on her homemade biscuits made her think that he had never in his life seen such a thing as preserves.

Slyly she watched from the corner of her eye as he sat back and laced his rheumatic fingers together across his middle. Then he sighed with contentment, eased out one leg so that it would be more comfortable, and looked back at her.

Except for the kettle whistling on the stove and the ticking of the Regulator clock on the wall, the room was silent. And yet with the quiet, there was a strange and unusual peace, and Ruby wondered at it.

Hardly daring to look at her guest, she kept herself busy cleaning up the dishes that had already been washed once that morning. And John Phips did not seem able to keep his eyes off her, of which fact Ruby was painfully aware.

"Ruby, me darlin' lass," he said at last, breaking the long silence, "ye've done yerself proud. Legends are fine, but they don't come near the mark as far as yer fixins' are concerned."

"John Phips," she replied almost sternly, "get along with that blarney."

"No blarney, ma'am. Simple truth. You're a good cook."

"Thank you." Ruby was pleased, and her face showed it. She smoothed her apron with her hands.

"A woman should be a good cook."

Rising, John Phips limped to the back door and surveyed the yard and corrals.

Ruby looked out past him, trying to see her property from his perspective. Her place had been well built, and it showed. But so too did the years when no man had been about to keep things in repair. She had tried, and so had her son, William. But she wasn't up to such work, and her son had grown so busy with his own life that now he hardly had time to stop at all.

John Phips ran his fingers through his hair and returned to the chair by the table. He looked up at her and suddenly grinned.

"I'm a good cook myself," he said. "Had to be."

Startled by such a declaration from a man, Ruby looked at him. But he said no more, and so Ruby began, for the third time, to wipe the cabinet top.

"I—I knew a John Phips once," she said hesitantly. "Long ago."

"I know," the old man answered quietly.

"He's dead!"

For a long moment the old man stared at the table top. Finally he looked up, and his eyes bored into Ruby's.

"Are you sure?" he asked.

"Of course! I . . . the whole town had word, near fifty years ago. He's dead."

"Well, lass," the old man said with a grin, "stranger things have happened. I'm the man you knew, and thanks to your wonderful cooking, I'm not dead yet."

"You don't look like him," Ruby declared emphatically.

John Phips's smile grew wider. "You don't look much like the Ruby Soderberg *I* knew, either. You're prettier now, by far."

Ruby stared at the old man, her mind whirling. Was this the man she had known? But of course he wasn't! That was silly even to consider. That man was hardly even a memory, he was so long dead. And this man, well, he wanted something, and she had better be on her toes.

"What do you intend to do now?" she asked quietly.

Before the old man could reply, a horse came pounding into the yard. A saddle creaked, footsteps sounded on the front porch, and into the room burst a stout, middle-aged man of apparent means.

"Morning, Mother," he almost shouted. "Just passing by, and I wanted to make sure everything was all right.

"Well, hello there, sir," he continued, turning to John Phips. "I didn't know Mother had company."

"I . . . uh . . ." Ruby hesitated. "Willy, uh . . . this is Mr. Phips. John Phips. Mr. Phips, this is my son, William Alder."

Fumbling for his hat, the old man rose to his feet. "It's a pleasure, son. You do favor your mother."

"Uh . . . I suppose so," William responded, doing his best to understand the goings-on in his mother's kitchen. "Did you just come in on the train, sir?"

"Why . . . uh . . . yes, I did. I suppose I look like it too, don't I?"

"Well, I didn't mean it that way," William replied sheepishly. "It's . . . well, it's my job, sort of, keeping track of folks around here."

"What Willy means, Mr. Phips, is that he's the bishop of our ward."

"That's right, sir," William responded. "We're Mormons, of course, and small geographical areas are called wards. I guess I'm what you would call the pastor of our congregation. Fact is, we'll be meeting day after tomorrow morning at ten o'clock sharp. If you're still in town, you'd be welcome to join our worship service."

John and Ruby glanced at each other, and Ruby dropped her eyes.

"I'd be right proud to come," John Phips replied. "If I'm still in town, then count on me being there. I haven't partaken of the emblems of the Lord's Supper in some time, and it would be a pleasure to do so."

"Do you have a place to stay?" William asked.

"Uh . . . yes, he does," Ruby answered. "Yes, he does."

"Well, that's fine. Mother, I must be running along. Seems to be a bit of trouble at the newspaper office, and apparently I'm the only one who can take care of it. I'll chat with you after meeting on Sunday. It's been a pleasure to meet you, Mr. Phips. I hope to see you then, as well."

With a polite nod, Bishop William Alder turned and made his

way out the door. The sound of the departing horse echoed in the room, and for another long moment the clock and the teakettle made the only sounds.

"Willy, huh?" the old man mused. "Seems like a fine man. And a bishop to boot."

Turning, then, he gazed at Ruby, who began fidgeting with her apron.

"Willy is quite famous," she declared. "He writes political editorials, and they are printed in newspapers throughout the nation."

"Willy . . . Willy Alder . . . My goodness, is he *the* Will Alder?"

"One and the same," Ruby declared proudly.

"Does he own the newspaper here in town?"

"Oh, no. The *American Fork Citizen* is owned by William Loveless, from over in Payson. But Willy has his office next door, and as a favor to Loveless, Willy is acting as editor. And of course that means his editorials are first published here."

"You must be very proud."

"I am."

"Well, Ruby Alder, I'm reluctant to change the subject, but just where is it that I'm to spend the night?"

"I . . . uh . . . uh . . ."

"Don't ye worry yer purty little head about it, me wee lass. Ye've a fine barn out back, and if yer cow won't mind the haythun company, I'm thinkin' I'd be delighted to bunk there."

"The—the barn?" Ruby questioned, her voice betraying relief that she didn't understand at all. "Why, I—"

"Good," John Phips replied, grinning. "Then it's all settled. Thank you for that lovely repast, ma'am. I'll be along now. By night, if you'll be good enough to give me a hand at sharpening that ax, you'll have enough wood to last for some time."

"I'd be pleased to help," Ruby said quickly, surprised at the eagerness she felt.

And with that, John Phips arose and escorted Ruby Soderberg out of her door.

Chapter 3

John Phips held the ax lightly in his hands, his thumb expertly feeling the rough edge of the blade. "It's been a spell since this ax had a decent edge."

"I know," Ruby said with a sigh. "I've tried sharpening it, but I just can't do it by myself."

"You shouldn't even try."

"Willy told me he would do it, but he's so busy."

"He looks busy. Tell you what—I'll turn the grindstone if you'll hold the ax."

Ruby smiled. "I'll be glad to. To be honest, that ax has been driving me crazy."

The grindstone was a heavy, old-fashioned type and turned heavily. John Phips started the stone turning, and the rasping whine of steel against stone cut into the clear, still air of the morning. Stopping the grinder, he poured water into the funnel-shaped can that allowed drops to fall slowly on the turning stone.

"How long have you lived in Highland?" he asked as he started the wheel turning once again.

"Most of thirty years," Ruby answered as she worked to hold the blade in place. "My folks came into the Salt Lake Valley from Sweden back in '58 and settled in South Cottonwood. From there we went to Sanpete, and took up land in Moroni. I was living there when I—I married Mr. Alder. We were only there a short time before we came here, and I haven't budged since."

John stood up, stretched, and looked carefully around. "It's a good place," he said quietly. "Good stone house, adequate barn and corrals, even an anvil and forge and tools there in your shed. Do you still keep horses?"

"Not anymore," Ruby answered, smiling. "In fact, that forge hasn't been fired in at least ten years. Mr. Alder always insisted on shoeing his own horses, and from time to time he did a lot of blacksmithing for others."

John started the stone turning again, and quickly the ax showed an edge, carefully honed down.

He straightened, taking the ax from Ruby's hands. "What's that building yonder?"

"It was our granary."

"Mighty big doors for a granary."

Ruby brushed back her hair. "Yes, they are. I had those doors put on this past spring. Now the building is a garage."

"A garage? You mean . . ."

"That's right," Ruby declared proudly. "I own one of the five automobiles in Highland, a brand new 1910 Oldsmobile Special."

A grin spread slowly across the face of John Phips. "A horseless carriage, is it? And can you drive it, Ruby Alder?"

Ruby pulled herself up to her full stature. "Of course I can drive it," she declared. "I have even changed a tire, though a neighbor boy helped me some."

"I meant no disrespect," John said easily. "Knowing you as I think I do, I'd guess you would be a fine driver. In fact, I'm surprised you don't have another granary with a flying machine inside."

A dreamy look came over Ruby's face. "A flying machine," she said. "I've heard they're wonderful inventions. I hope one day I'll be able to see one."

"And fly in one too, no doubt."

"Oh, yes! In fact, I'd like to—"

Ruby, suddenly realizing that she was showing the giddy excitement of a young lady being courted, stopped in confusion.

"I—I'm sorry," she said. "I dream too much, and my son says that I talk too much about my dreams."

"He doesn't approve of dreams?"

"Not for women, I'm afraid. He didn't want me to purchase the Oldsmobile. He says that a woman, especially an *old* woman, has no business doing any sort of business at all. I told him stuff and nonsense, but it didn't change his thinking any.

"He says that when I drive my motor car, I have no dignity. And he hates even more to hear me talk about flying machines. I told him once that I thought they were the transportation of the future and that I wanted to live long enough to ride in one. He was terribly upset with me. Sometimes," and now Ruby giggled, "sometimes I worry that Willy is a bit of a stuffed shirt."

John smiled. "We all have to learn," he said. "I saw a flying machine once, and I think you're right. To see a man actually soaring through the air, not just gliding or ballooning but actually soaring with power and controls, why, it gave me goose bumps."

"You actually saw one *fly?*" Ruby asked breathlessly.

"I did. I was in Dayton, Ohio, last year, and saw both Wilbur and Orville Wright make flights at their Dayton homecoming celebration."

"What . . . was it like?"

"Oh," the old man said enthusiastically as he lifted his arm to explain, "it was one of the grandest sights of my life. Imagine an automobile that has left the road and is climbing up in the air—an automobile without any wheels, we will say, but with white wings instead, like a great huge bird. Well now, imagine this automobile with its wings spread twenty feet each way, coming right toward you with a tremendous flap and roar of its propellers, and you'll have something like what I saw."

Ruby looked dreamily into the distance. "Isn't it marvelous," she said, "to be living in a day when the good Lord has brought such wondrous things to pass?"

"That it is, Ruby, that it is."

For a moment there was a silence; and then, in a quiet voice, John Phips broke it.

"And as for dreaming, Ruby Alder, don't you ever stop. A man, *or a woman,* who can't dream, isn't worth a belch in a high wind."

Ruby giggled. "I declare, you must be a fan of Alice Roosevelt."

"That I am," John answered. "Alice *and* her father. President Roosevelt is a great man, and I love the spirit of his daughter. Furthermore, I've read Shaw, Ibsen, and Zola, and I agree with them and the others who hold that women are the equal of men, or at least ought to be. After the war I met a woman who'd been a spy for the Confederates, and it was said that she had no peers in that terrifying and normally male profession. I also heard that a woman helped the Wright brothers design or build their flying machine. I don't know if that's true, but I do know that Jesus Christ, the greatest exemplar of all, spent a great deal of his earthly ministry in the company of women. He even chastised one of them, Martha by name, for being impatient with another dreamer such as yourself—a woman named Mary.

"Now, Ruby Alder, I've raised a verbal wind again, and I've done it long enough. If you'll excuse me, I'll be about earning my breakfast and a little more besides."

John then went to work, and Ruby climbed her porch steps and entered her home. For the rest of the day, she watched from her window as the old man worked about her yard. She didn't go back outside, yet neither did she go far from her window. Instead, she drew up a chair and sat with her knitting, watching intently as he went about the tasks he had set for himself.

Taking the sharpened ax, he went to the woodpile, which was composed of several logs and two or three old stumps. His first swing split the log he had chosen, and for an hour he worked slowly but steadily, even methodically.

And as she watched, Ruby marveled. Despite his age, John Phips had an easy rhythm in his movements. He didn't work fast, but neither did he waste effort, and shortly he had cut through the largest of the logs. Then he cut through it again and again, and then he split those sections into kindling and firewood.

Ruby continued to marvel, but she was also filled with a sudden aching loneliness, a feeling she hadn't experienced in years. It was John Phips who caused that feeling, she knew that. And yet even with the knowing, she could not stop watching. His movements were so familiar, so ingrained into her thinking that she could hardly deal with her emotions.

Yet it was an old, gray-haired man who stood out there chopping wood, while the image in her mind was of a young man with dark hair and powerful, rippling muscles. But so much seemed the same—the way he rested occasionally on the ax handle, the way he lifted his hat and wiped his brow, the way he smiled when he spoke.

Might this man truly be John Phips? So much seemed to fit, and yet nothing really fit at all. The man she had known was dead, and this old man might just be using his name to . . . to . . . Well, *why* would he be using that name? And how could he seem so much like . . .

Angry with herself, Ruby walked to the water bucket and fetched herself a drink.

What is wrong with you? she asked herself. *Why does this old man cause your heart to pound and your breath to feel like it was caught in your throat? How on earth could you, an old woman of seventy years and one month, be feeling like a giddy schoolgirl?*

For nearly forty years she had been married, and for ten years since the death of her husband she had associated with the good men of her church and community, but almost never had she felt like this.

Moreover, and this was far worse, Ruby was certain that John Phips knew how she felt. Yet he did not look like a man who had had much to do with women. He was friendly enough, yes. But he was also remote, and—the woman in her told her this—he was lonely.

Yet he was a man who shielded his loneliness well. He covered it with his ready smile, his glib tongue, and, perhaps most of all, his wandering. Yet even that made her wonder. Had he never had a home? Had he never had a woman who could penetrate and ease his loneliness?

Or would the likenesses never end?

Finished with the wood, John sank the ax into one of the stumps so that it would not rust, and then while Ruby watched from behind her curtain, he walked into the shed.

Moments later she saw him at the rear of the barn, where recent rains had washed under the foundation timbers, gouging out a dangerous hole. This he filled with gravel from the ditch, tamped hard with the shovel handle. Then he found a large rock, which he rolled to where the runoff fell, positioning it so that the next rainfall would hit the rock and splash away from the barn where it would do no further damage.

Next Ruby watched as he mended the gate to the corral, stoking up the old forge and doing a bit of smithing to repair the hinges. And when that was finished, she stared in open-mouthed amazement as he heated her husband's branding iron and proceeded to rope and brand the rapidly maturing calf that her cow had given birth to the previous spring.

Was there nothing the man could not do? Would he never stop filling her with thoughts and emotions and memories that ought to have been long dead? Why had he come, and what sort of a spell was he weaving that she had so little ability—

"Ma'am?"

Spinning, Ruby was startled to see John standing in the doorway.

"Y-yes?"

"Didn't mean to startle you, but the sun's about to set, and I was wondering if I might have permission to quit for the day so's I could go into town and pick me up a shirt."

"Permission?" she asked blankly.

"Yes'm. I reckon as long as you're feeding and boarding me, I ought to clear my goings and comings with you."

"John Phips," she stormed, suddenly angry, "I am *not* your master!"

"No ma'am," he answered, grinning, "you aren't. But you are my employer, and I never worked for one more lovely. And your eyes flash when you get excited. Did you know that?"

Ruby, stretched beyond what any one woman could possibly endure in a single day, looked at the wrinkled, grinning face of the man who had caused her consternation, and then she did the only sensible thing she could have done. She clutched her hands at her sides, her arms stiff, her face rigid, and fervently uttered a single solitary order.

"Go!" she said as her eyes grew large and her brows furrowed. "Gooo!"

And John Phips, with a youthful smile still playing on his tired old face, went.

Day 2

Saturday

October 22, 1910

Chapter 4

"Ruby," John Phips said with a sigh as he pulled back from the table, "I have never in my life tasted finer pork chops."

Ruby blushed, thinking that it had been ten years since she had received such a compliment. "You're just saying that, John Phips." she said.

"Aye, lass. Of course I'm sayin' it. That doesn't make it any less true. Faith, and I'll tell you something else, me darlin'. That peach cobbler tasted like it was made in heaven and carried here by angels, just for me."

"Stuff and nonsense," Ruby argued, smiling coyly. "You probably talk like that with all the ladies."

"Nope," John replied, "I don't. Truth is, Ruby, there aren't any other lady friends. Never have been."

John Phips had been busy that day. Steadily, since breakfast, he had been painting, putting a white coat on the dilapidated picket fence around Ruby's home. And again, as she had throughout the entire day before, Ruby had watched, fascinated.

He had not worked fast, but he worked steadily, and she had been amazed at his progress. The painting of the fence was now complete, and he had some planking in place on some old sawbucks so that he could start on the trim of her home. He was remarkable, and she knew that if she fed him every meal for a month, she could not pay him for all he had accomplished.

Apparently he had learned much in his life, and he seemed able to do anything he set his hand to do. But to think that he had spent his life alone . . .

"Oh, John," she declared, "I don't mind if you speak of other women."

"I would speak of 'em if there'd been any. But there haven't. All my life, I've just been waiting for you."

For a moment Ruby looked into John's blue-gray eyes. And then, to hide the tears that were filling her own eyes, she arose and began clearing the dishes.

"My turn to wash," John abruptly declared, getting up and grabbing the apron from its nail.

"Now, you sit down, John Phips. This is woman's work, and after painting all that fence, you need to rest."

"Fiddlesticks," John said as he began ladling hot water into the pan. "You're the one who has worked hard today. I've just spent a few hours on the dumb end of a paintbrush, is all. Now, hand me those dishes and grab a towel. We'll have this job done in no time, and then I can hike down into American Fork before all the stores close."

"But you just went yesterday."

"I did. But it took me so long to get there that the stores were closed. I still need that new shirt."

"Well," Ruby declared, smiling, "I can take care of that. You crank up the Oldsmobile, and I'll have you down in town in a jiffy."

"Now, Ruby, you don't need to do that."

"John, for two days you have worked like a slave for me. Giving you a ride is the least I can do."

For a moment he said nothing, but at last he grinned. "Shure and ye've got yerself a deal, me garjus lass. Now hand me those dishes."

For a few minutes they worked in silence, and Ruby watched the man with the familiar name, looking for characteristics that might help her to know. He limped, and that was not the same. His hands were gnarled and a little twisted, but that would be age, as would the wrinkles in his face and his white hair. Those things she couldn't consider.

His eyes, as far as she could remember, were the same. He also had some very disturbing mannerisms, little traits that reminded her of the man she had known, briefly, so many years before. Then there was his Irish brogue and blarney. Those too had been traits of a very young John Phips.

There were other questions, many of them. Yet how could she possibly ask them all? She would seem so forward. She just could not bring herself to pry.

So was it him? She honestly didn't know. But deep inside, a strange little voice seemed to be telling her yes. And more and more, Ruby Alder was starting to believe that voice.

Thirty minutes after the dishes were done, Ruby pulled the long black Oldsmobile touring car to an abrupt and dusty stop outside the Jackson Gents' and Boys' Clothing Store on Main Street in American Fork. As Ruby pushed back the magneto, the car shuddered to a stop, and nimbly she climbed out.

"Come on," she said to the ashen-faced John Phips. "Let's go in and—John, is anything wrong?"

John opened his eyes. "I—I don't think so. Am I still alive?"

"Alive? Of course you're alive. What are you talking about?"

"I don't—I—Ruby, who on earth taught you to drive?"

"Nobody. I just figured it out by myself."

John sighed. "I thought so."

"Why do you ask?"

"Uh . . . Ruby, why don't *I* drive us home?"

"But John—"

"Ruby, it's only good manners. A gentleman *always* drives, and the lady sits and enjoys the tour."

"Really?" Ruby asked incredulously.

"Absolutely. And while I'm driving, watch me closely. I'm certain you can pick up a few pointers—things such as proper speed, how to stay on the road, how to slow for flocks of chickens and herds of cattle and gaggles of geese and folks' careless children. You know, the sorts of things that might damage your car should you run over them."

Ruby smiled. "John, of course you can drive. And I will watch. Willy won't teach me how to be a motorist, won't even get in the motorcar with me, and so I've been desperate for someone to teach me. Besides, Marshall Hamilton told me just the other week that I drove far too fast for the public good. I just don't know how to drive more slowly."

"I'll show you," John said.

"Good. And John, I'm so glad that you aren't one of those awful men who say terrible things about women drivers."

"Terrible things?" John asked, feeling suddenly uncomfortable.

"Yes, jokes and tales. Just last Sunday my grandaughter Allyson told me one. It goes, 'Papa, how can you tell that Mommy is a woman driver?' Answer: 'Because she's always running somebody down.'"

John did his best not to snicker. "That—that's not very funny, is it," he stated quickly.

"Not very. If they would just make rules instead of those cruel jokes and stories, I would live by them."

"Oh, they're trying, Ruby. Here and there, folks are trying to put a few rules in place. In Vermont it's illegal to drive an automobile unless somebody runs along out in front waving a red flag. That tends to slow folks down, though it might be rough on the flag-carrier, happen the driver gets careless. In Tennessee it's illegal to drive anywhere unless the motorist has posted a notice at least a week in advance, outlining his trip. A law such as that would surely promote planning ahead."

"How awful!" Ruby declared. "The next thing you know they'll be telling me I can only drive on one side of the road."

"Might at that," John agreed.

"Well," Ruby said as she untied her hat and unbuttoned her colorful duster that had only recently come by mail order from Saks and Company of New York City, "let's go in and get your shopping done. Joseph and William Jackson are good friends of mine. They'll fit you up with a suit in no time."

"Suit? Ruby, I came for a shirt. A shirt is all I can afford."

"I know that, John. But I owe you much more than a suit would cost. Besides, you need one."

"Why do I need a suit?"

"Well, for church tomorrow, silly. Besides, Monday they're laying the cornerstone for our new tabernacle here in American Fork, and I have been invited as one of the guests of honor. You will be escorting me, and so obviously you need a suit."

"Ruby, I don't know. I try not to get in public too often."

"John, don't be silly. Now take my arm and let's hurry. I also need to visit Manda and Ida Chipman's Millinery, and I am completely out of corn plasters and St. Jacob's Oil. Thomas Steele has been holding them for me in his drugstore all week, and we simply *must* pick them up."

"Does he sell sodas?"

"He does."

"Then let's be going, my sweet. I'm in the mood for a red raspberry soda. And I'll buy, if they aren't over a dime."

Ruby laughed, and together they entered the Jackson Gents' and Boys' Clothing Store. Neither of them saw the man who stood across the rutted street, gazing steadily off in the other direction.

Chapter 5

"Hello, Mother."

"Well, hello, Willy. This is a surprise."

Willy looked about his mother's neat home. "I was out here on the bench, so I thought I'd drop by. Can we talk?"

"Of course. Sit down there in Mr. Alder's horsehair rocker and tell me what is on your mind."

"Mother, when I say talk, I mean alone."

"All right."

"I mean, is that old man—"

"Mr. Phips."

"Yes, Mr. Phips. Might he walk in on us?"

"Oh, I doubt it. He's out getting an early start on digging the potatoes, and I imagine he'll be busy until dark."

"He does seem busy."

"Yes, Willy, he's marvelous! Have you seen all that he's done? And in only two days. I'm so thrilled."

"Yes," Willy replied, scowling, "he has kept himself occupied. Pretty nigh becoming indispensable, isn't he?"

"Well, I wouldn't go *that* far," Ruby answered slowly. "Still, I am so thankful for his help."

"Effie McPheeters told me that you bought him a suit and practically an entire wardrobe this afternoon."

"Effie told you *that?*" Ruby asked in surprise. "Well, that old busybody! I always said those telephone operators were nothing but gossips and busybodies. Do you know that every time I use that telephone I have to *ask* her to get off the line? Well, I do, and I think it's a disgrace! Why, I'm of a mind to—"

"Mother, it wasn't Effie's fault that she put through the call from Joe Jackson to his wife. It's her job, you know."

"It isn't her job to listen in!"

"She isn't the only one who's talking, Mother."

"Oh, pshaw, Willy. I'm seventy years old. What on earth are people going to say?"

"Plenty, Mother. In fact, two different women have already asked me what is going on out here."

"Have they really?" Ruby beamed. "Glory be, maybe we'll have a scandal. I haven't ever had a decent scandal, and I've often thought how much fun it would be, having folks all over town just wagging their tongues with juicy nonsense about me. My goodness, I would imagine—"

"Mother, for goodness sake, listen to yourself."

Ruby smiled. "You're right," she declared. "I am being silly, aren't I."

"I'd say so. Now I want to know if it is true. Did you buy that old man some clothing?"

Ruby glared at her son. "I did," she answered defiantly.

"May I ask why?"

"Do you need to ask? Look around you, Willy. That old man, as you insist on calling him, has worked his heart out for two solid days, and he shows no signs of stopping yet. I had to pay him some way, didn't I?"

"Mother, I told you that I was going to do those things."

"Yes, three years ago."

William Alder dropped his head and sighed. Then he looked back at the almost angry woman. "Mother, it isn't my fault my editorials became so popular, or that they called me to be bishop."

"Nor was it mine, Willy. And I wouldn't want it any other way. I'm thrilled to death with your success, and especially with your calling. But I must go on living, and things need to be kept up. Since you're so busy, John has been doing that for me. Now tell me, why are you so worried?"

William sighed. "Mother, I'm concerned for you. I've only been bishop for three months, and twice in that time I've had to deal with situations where vagabonds have taken advantage of innocent

Church members. Sister Lippencroft lost her entire life savings not thirty days ago to that fellow who was going to reroof her home."

"And you think John might be after my money?"

"I'd say the possibility is certainly there. Wouldn't you?"

"I would. I've even thought about it."

"Good," William said. "Then you'll send him on his way."

"No—no, Willy, I won't. At least not yet. John Phips hasn't asked for any money, and I've promised to feed him until he gets my place in order. That should be sometime by the middle of next week. Meanwhile, to be warned is to be prepared. I promise I'll be careful with him."

The bishop sat silently, rocking back and forth. His mother was an intelligent woman, and he knew it. Yet he felt a strange sense of worry, and he didn't know how to get at it. Idly he picked up his mother's new stereoscope and glanced at the double-imaged slide, an image of New York's growing skyline.

"Mother," he said quietly as he put the stereoscope back beside her talking machine and stack of record cylinders, "is there something going on that you aren't telling me?"

"Not telling you?"

"Yes, Mother. Not telling me. Do you know something about that old man that I don't know?"

"I—I—well, why do you ask?"

"Because you aren't acting like yourself."

"Is—is that all?"

"No, it isn't. Since yesterday I have learned some very strange things, and I *think* you are being set up to become my next 'Sister Lippencroft.' Let me tell you a little about that old man out there. He came into town on the 9:15 yesterday morning, asked directions from Luke Savage and Lowell Nelson at the depot, and then proceeded directly to the Highland Road. Ed Tucker gave him a ride in his wagon, and from where Ed let him off, he proceeded directly here. And on his way, he didn't stop off at one other place. Mother, that man was not looking for a good meal. He was looking for *you!*"

Ruby stood and walked nervously to her counter to rearrange the location of her new-fangled bread toaster, wondering what she should say. She knew that she could give Willy a little information, but nothing that was definite. And she wanted to do that, for she would have liked his help.

But on the other hand, she knew Willy Alder very well, and that knowledge made her want to protect the man called John Phips. Willy had a penchant for digging out facts no matter what the cost, for in certain things he was almost unbendable in his personality. Because of that, she was not at all ready to throw that dear old man, *whoever* he really was, to the wolf who wrote those nationally syndicated editorials.

"Willy," she finally said, laughing her son's charges off, "how you do carry on."

"Mother, I fear that old man is up to no good. I can see it in his eyes. He isn't telling you the truth."

"Very few do," she said quietly.

"That's correct, but it doesn't make it right. Would you mind if I talked to Mr. Phips?"

Ruby spun about in surprise. "Do you really want to?" she asked.

"Of course! You know me, Mother. I don't beat about very many bushes. I'll talk to him straight out, and if his answers are satisfactory, then I'll quit worrying. He can stay in town as long as he wants, and with my blessing."

"Very well," Ruby said as she walked to the door. "I'll call him in."

Moments later John Phips stood, battered hat in hand, in Ruby Alder's kitchen. "You wanted to see me?" he asked of the seated William Alder.

"I did. Have a seat."

"Thank you."

John pulled a chair out from the table and sat, while Ruby, sensing the old man's nervousness, remained standing by the counter.

"Frankly, Mr. Phips," William said quietly, "you worry me."

"How's that?"

"Because I've learned a few things about you, and those things give me concern. Why are you here? Or, why are you at my mother's home? Would you mind responding to those questions, Mr. Phips?"

Ruby watched as John sat silently, gazing at her son. Then, without answering, he turned his head and looked steadily at her, momentarily holding her gaze. She dropped her eyes.

John was asking her a question, she knew. But she did not know how to respond. How could she, when . . . when . . .

"Well?"

"What . . . what has your mother told you?"

"Frankly, she has told me very little, and you know that. You've told her practically nothing about yourself, so how could she?"

"Yes," John answered quietly, "I see that you are right."

"So, why are you here?"

"I . . . I was just sort of passing through. I had heard from Ruby's brother about her cooking, and I was hungry. So I thought, well, why not give it a try? I did, she was truly hospitable, and I've just been trying to help her out a little in return."

"That's it?"

"Yes," John answered slowly as he looked at Ruby, "I suppose that's it."

"You're a tramp, then? A vagabond?"

John smiled. "If you mean by that, a wanderer, then the answer is yes."

"Are you employed?"

"Most folks won't talk work with a man as old as I am."

William looked quickly at him. "Yes, I can see that, and I hadn't thought of it. But you do admit that you are broke?"

"No harm in admitting the truth, I suppose. I do have a couple of dollars, so technically—"

"Mr. Phips, if you plan on trying to get my mother's money, then you had better cancel such plans immediately."

"Bishop, I resent that deeply. I respect your mother more than you could ever imagine. When we part, our accounts with each other will be square."

"Willy," Ruby added, "I have told you that John has not done anything to take advantage—"

"Mother," William interrupted, "let me finish."

Turning back to John, he spoke again. "You spoke about when you leave. Will that be soon?"

John's eyes dropped. "I—I'm not certain. I need to . . . to . . . There are many factors . . ."

William sat back in triumph. "Come, Mr. Phips, be honest. Tell us exactly why you are here!"

Miserably John looked from Ruby to her son and back again. "I can't," he answered finally, his voice almost a whisper.

"Can't? Or *won't*."

"Doesn't much matter, does it?"

"Not at all," William responded. "Mother, I think that you've heard enough."

Ruby stood silently, her face reflecting her pain.

"Reckon I'll finish what I can of the potatoes," John declared as he rose slowly to his feet. "Then I'll be on my way."

Limping slowly, John crossed to the door, opened it, and stepped outside. There was silence then in the home, and finally William stirred uneasily.

"It's for the best, Mother. It truly is "

"All right, Willy," Ruby replied with great resignation. "Whatever you say. I just wish . . ."

"You wish what?"

"I just wish you could get to know him, Willy. I really do."

"Well, under different circumstances—"

"Willy, I can tell you about him, if you'd like. Please let me. I know a great deal, and I am certain you would want—"

But William Alder was looking at the watch he carried in his vest pocket, his mind already elsewhere. "Sorry, Mother, not today. I'm just relieved that he will be going, and you should feel the same way."

Ruby did her best to smile. "Thank you for coming, Willy. That was very sweet of you."

William Alder kissed his mother, and then, after taking a deep breath that indicated his own sense of satisfaction, he strode out the front door, mounted his horse, and was gone.

Ruby watched him for a moment, and then with a sigh she turned and walked to the talking machine. Carefully she wound it up, chose a cylinder from the rack, and put it in place. Then she eased back the spring-drive, setting the record to revolving. Lastly she lifted the needle and set it in the first groove, and while the scratchy strains of "In My Merry Oldsmobile" wafted through the room, she closed her eyes and tried to keep the tears from flowing.

Ruby Alder was worried but trying not to show it. But the worry was there, nevertheless.

Chapter 6

"Nine dollars? Ruby, that is shameful."

"John, stop worrying about it. If we hadn't been in such a hurry, I'd have ordered a tailor-made suit and paid ten dollars. Already you've earned much more than that."

"But Ruby, look at all this. Shoes, suspenders, a linen collar, two shirts, a pair of trousers, and woolen hose. And then on top of that, the suit. Why, you must have spent twenty or twenty-five dollars! I can't let you—"

"John, you've earned it."

"Twenty-five dollars in less than two days? Ruby, that's nonsense, and you know it."

"Well, if you finish digging my potatoes Monday after the meeting, then you surely will have earned it. Now stop fussing and finish that pie and ice cream."

John sighed and took another bite. "I can't do it, Ruby. I'll be leaving in a bit, and there won't be any more of *anything*."

"John, you don't need to leave."

"According to William, I do. He seemed pretty emphatic about it, too."

"He was. But after all, John Phips, this is *my* home."

"Ruby, did you tell him that we had—had known each other before?"

Slowly Ruby shook her head.

"Why didn't you?"

"I . . . I . . . John, I can't. I don't even know for certain."

"I thought that was it."

"Well, can you blame me? For fifty years a man is dead, and then a stranger walks up and announces that he is the dead man. Would *you* believe that? I need more time, I need—"

"This is wonderful pie, Ruby, me lass."

"Huckleberries. And stop changing the subject. I will not allow you to leave until . . . until . . ."

"And this ice cream is absolutely delicious. Better than any I ever found in Los Angeles when I was staying at the pigeon ranch."

"Joseph Elsmore makes—you *really* spent some time in Los Angeles?"

John quickly looked up. "Did I say that?"

"You did. And you told Willy that my brother had told you about my cooking. Do you really know Jons Soderberg?"

"I do," John replied quietly, "though that isn't his name there. James Y. Johnson, he calls himself. He's mighty proud of you, Ruby. Like I said, it was upon his recommendation that I came here."

"Yes, you did," Ruby stated flatly, not wanting to think the things her mind was telling her. "How is he?"

"Doing well. James's ranch has over a hundred thousand pigeons, I reckon, and the railroad has even built a spur to it for shipping and cash-paying tourists. He does appear to be prosperous."

"And?"

"And what?"

"How is *he?*"

"Ruby, I don't think—"

"John, I want to know!"

"Well," John said with resignation, "he still talks about being bishop and about his horse race from Fountain Green to Salt Lake. He even has that big old Belgian plug down there. Ingersol, I think its name is. The horse is mighty old now, but I doubt it will ever become glue. James thinks too much of it."

"Go on."

"Ruby," John replied with exasperation, "what do you want me to tell you?"

"About his family, John. Anything and everything. Are any of them there?"

"None of his wives. He's still in hiding, and none of them would go with him. I think that stint in prison about did him in. Then, when none of those women would hide with him after he got out on bail, well, he just up and left them behind. Probably wasn't smart, but he did it, and now it's too late to go back and do it all over again the right way.

"But his son Ernest has been with him some, and Johnny and Hyrum, too. Tell the truth, though, I think he's lonely."

"Oh, poor Jons."

"Yeah," John replied quietly, "loneliness is a hard thing, a hard and never-ending thing. At least it seems so. I used to wonder if I would ever . . ."

And then, with a shake of his head, John Phips turned to his companion and smiled.

"Do you have any further questions?"

Ruby stared, her heart pounding. "One," she said, her voice almost a whisper. "Would you roll up your sleeve and show me your left arm?"

John Phips stared silently. Painfully he stood and walked to the doorway, where he turned back and looked at Ruby. Slowly then, and with great care, he unbuttoned the cuff of his shirt. And then he began to roll it up.

Chapter 7

"Faith now, Ruby me lass, but why don't we take in the ayv'nin sunset together out on yer front porch swing."

Bashfully, Ruby giggled. Then the two of them cleared off the table and banked what was left of the ice cream inside the wooden icebox.

Later, as they sat together on the screen porch, John Phips spoke. "You do have a fine home here."

"I've enjoyed it."

"Mr. Alder must have been a good husband for you."

"He was, John. And though I was his polygamous wife, he did his best to take care of me and treat me with the same respect he showed his first wife. She and I were good friends, too, and she was a dear, dear woman. I think we got along so well because he was the sort of man he was."

"Well, the place shows that he was a good man."

Curiously Ruby looked at him. "How can you tell that? From my home, I mean."

"Oh, I can see more in a place than you might think. Over the years I've kicked around quite a bit, and a man learns. For instance, there has been a great deal of work done here, good solid work that a man ought to be proud of. That tells me that your husband took pride in what he built."

"He did, but tell me what you see that can tell you that."

John smiled and leaned back in the swing. "First is your home. If he built it, he knew his business. If he hired it done, then the craftsman did. The stone has been well cut and fitted carefully, and the house sits on the highest point of land on your place. Forty or fifty years ago, it would have been easy to defend your home from maurauding Indians. One good man with a rifle and enough food and water could hold it indefinitely."

"They had Indian troubles here for a time," Ruby declared. "Both the Walker and Blackhawk wars affected this area. Most folks could fort up in a hurry, and up in Alpine the Moyle family even built a stone tower to defend themselves. I don't recall hearing if it was ever used, but it was there—in fact, it still is."

John nodded. "I've seen a little Indian trouble myself from time to time."

Silence followed, not strained, but easy, and in it they both drifted off into memories, recalling a life now mostly past.

"What else do you like about the place?" Ruby asked, wanting to hear more of John Phips's voice.

"What else? Well, the corrals have been well built. They need work, but they're strong and should last for years to come. So should the shed, though its roof needs to be reshingled. Your garden was once a fine and well-watered piece of land, but the dams are mostly gone, and the ditches are grown in with weeds. Your well is deep, and the water is clear and cold, but I've never in my life heard such a squeaky pump. If you have any grease, I'll take care of that first thing Monday morning. So it's a fine place. It just needs the hand of a man who can make do."

Ruby didn't answer that, for she had no idea what to say. On one hand, John might have been saying that Willy ought to do more to help her out. One part of her thought so too, but the other part, the mother part, looked upon her son with patient tenderness and hoped that he wouldn't always be so busy.

On the other hand, John might have been making an offer, an offer of himself. But did she want that? It was an intriguing thought, but also unsettling. It had been forever since she had had a full-time man about, and she had grown quite used to her independence. Besides that, there were a lot of unanswered questions about the man who sat next to her on the swing, even if he was the man she used to know.

Still, John Phips had crept into her thoughts in a way that frightened her but also left her breathless with hope, and so she didn't know, she didn't know . . .

"Your boy, William, is quite a man."

Startled, Ruby felt the strangest let-down. John *was* talking about her son. The offering of himself was simply the foolish dream of an old lonely woman, a woman who ought to learn once and for all to obey her son and stop dreaming.

"He's never given me a bit of trouble," she declared almost defensively. "In fact, he's spent his whole life trying to make mine easier. Don't know what I would have done without him, especially these past ten years. To my motherly way of thinking, he's a mighty honorable and handsome man."

"Well, like I said, he does favor you, Ruby."

"In looks, maybe. I haven't ever been as good a person as he is. He's terribly busy, but good. Smart, too. I think he must have picked those traits up from his father."

"Now, don't think too harshly of yourself, Ruby. We're all different folks, and that's the way the good Lord made us to be. You raised him, and you did a fine job of it. That's why you can tell me honestly that he's such a good man."

"Yes, I suppose you're right. I just don't know what to do about him and you. I would never have thought that he . . . that he . . ." Ruby's voice drifted off, and for a moment there was silence.

"Well," John declared finally, "I could tell he was some displeased with me. He surely does want me to go."

"Oh, he'll come around, John."

"Perhaps. Are you going to tell him that you knew me once?"

"I—I—don't think I'd dare. Willy is an investigator of the first order, and I'm not at all certain that I want to know what he might find."

"That's a very honest answer, Ruby."

"Yes, I believe in honesty. Do you?"

John stared off into the evening. "I do," he said slowly. "Sometimes, though, a man gets himself into a position . . . But enough on that. I am John Phips, the man you knew so long ago. And I would like to find a way to tell William that bit of news."

"It will happen, John. All in good time, though."

"Well, the good bishop is getting a bit impatient."

Ruby tried to smile. "He's just not used to seeing me with a man, John. After all, Henry Alder has been dead almost ten years, and I'm just past seventy, myself."

"Holy Michael O'Murphy," John exclaimed, "I'd 'ave bet good money that you weren't a day over fifty-two."

"Johnny." Ruby giggled and felt very surprised that she had dared use such an informal name. "You're awful, do you know that?"

The man grinned, "I reckon I am. But you like it, don't you."

Ruby glowed anew and then closed her eyes, in heaven with her thoughts. It really was him. Goodness but that was something! She almost giggled, just thinking of it. It was all crazy, totally insane, but still there were her feelings and the mark on his arm, and now the old man had proved it beyond doubt. Besides, there was the warm and wonderful way that he made her feel . . .

The two aging people rocked in silence then, each warmed with the memories of the past two days, and neither wanting to say anything that would break the spell of what was taking place.

At last, piecing together a lot more courage than he knew he had, John reached up and scratched his neck. Then gradually he worked his hand back to his trousers, inched it closer to Ruby's hand, and then hesitantly pulled it back.

Ruby, suddenly aware of her companion's intentions, and aware too of the man's obvious inexperience, gently reached out and placed her hand over his trembling fingers.

For a moment John Phips's entire frame stiffened with fear. But then, as Ruby felt his muscles relax, she laid her head gently against his shoulder.

Off in the west, the sun slipped quietly down behind the mountains. Behind them, where the American Fork Canyon sliced through the northern reaches of Mount Timpanogos, the gold of the sunset climbed rapidly upward until only the highest peaks remained aglow. Then these peaks, too, grew dark; and in the deepening twilight John Phips carefully, fearfully, placed his arm around the shawl-covered shoulders of Ruby Alder.

"I'm glad you came here yesterday," the elderly woman said quietly, breaking the long silence.

"Reckon I am, too," John replied huskily.

The twilight deepened, and the silence grew with it. Ruby kept her eyes on the last of the lighted sky, and John Phips, watching her, wondered that anyone could be so beautiful.

"Are you a happy woman, Ruby?" he asked, almost in a whisper.

"Yes I am."

"And have you always been?"

"Oh, I've known sadness," Ruby countered thoughtfully. "But William and my husband have eased that with their goodness."

"I'm glad," John replied. "You deserve happiness."

Slowly, John Phips paused and took a deep breath. "Besides your son, William, do you have any other children?"

"Well, Botilda, Henry Alder's first wife, had thirteen, nine of whom are still living. I always felt that I was their mother, just as Botilda was."

"What—what about you?"

"No, Willy was my only child. And you, John?"

John Phips coughed. "Like I told you, Ruby—there's never been anyone in my life . . . until you."

"Oh, Johnny, you must have been so lonely."

"Well, I have been, from time to time. Still, a man gets along as best he can. A long time ago, almost in a different lifetime, I had a memory that caused a powerful load of loneliness. Strangely, that same memory, of you, has also kept me happy—until I found you yesterday."

"Willy thinks you're after my money," Ruby said with a girlish giggle.

"That's what he said. And maybe I am. Do you have much?"

"Oh, I have sufficient for my needs . . . and then just a little bit more. Henry took good care of me."

"Then you'd better be careful," John said with a grin. "If you judge me by the outfit I'm wearing, your son has every reason to worry."

Again there was silence—long and deep, but increasingly comfortable.

"What . . . what have you done in your life?" Ruby finally

asked. "I feel like I have known you forever, and yet I don't know anything about you."

"Well," John said with a sigh, "actually, there's nothing much to tell."

"Oh, there must be something, Johnny. I think that you're just being modest."

"No," he replied, "not really. There was my mission to the Eastern States. And then one night a band of Confederates raided a town where I was staying, and they hit the house where I was being boarded. I was wounded, and the next thing I knew I was in that Confederate prison camp. The bullet wound, here where the scar is on my head, made me forget things, and for a long time I even forgot who I was. But I already told you that."

"Well, after the war then, Johnny. What came next?"

"Oh, nothing—at least nothing much to tell about. I still couldn't remember much about myself, and I couldn't find anyone else who knew anything either. I thought I must have been a soldier, but I never could find any records with the war department. So for quite a spell I did odd jobs and just lived from day to day. Did some whaling, too—went around the Horn a couple of times. Matter of fact, I went clear to China once. That was a fine voyage, and the captain wasn't a bad man, either. Mostly though, I reckon I've just been drifting along, earning a dollar or two here and there, just waiting."

"Waiting?" the elderly woman asked, almost timidly.

"Yes," John whispered, quietly and peacefully. "Waiting to . . . to find myself. Once I did that, then I began waiting to find just the right woman."

"Oh, Johnny," Ruby replied, her voice quivering with emotion. "Have you . . . have you found her?"

Smiling into the increasing darkness, John Phips did not reply. Instead, he quietly and securely took Ruby's other shoulder, pulling her around to face him.

Then, in the quiet of the night, as the man and woman looked into each other's eyes, John leaned forward and kissed Ruby tenderly on the forehead. Then he held her tightly against him.

"I . . ." Ruby paused as she pulled away, searching for breath and for words all at once. "I . . . I think I love you, Johnny Phips."

"I surely do hope so, ma'am," he muttered, his voice low. "I reckon I love you, too. Fact is, I've loved you in my mind ever since I can remember. I just wish I could have found you sooner."

"I do too, Johnny. But I guess it just wasn't to be."

"No, I suppose not. But I'll tell you what, Ruby Alder. We'll have us a grand old time now that I *have* found you!"

Ruby giggled, and the two were snuggling together again in the cool of the October evening when a pot shattered at the side of the porch. That was followed by a gasp of fear, and then silence.

"Goodness!" Ruby exclaimed as she sat up.

"Sounded like a flower pot," John declared as he pulled himself to his feet. "I wonder—"

Ruby, also standing, suddenly put her finger over John's mouth. "Listen," she whispered.

Together the couple stood, and out in the darkness of Ruby's yard there was a whispered question and answering giggle. That was followed by running footsteps, and again John and Ruby were alone.

"Who was that?" John asked.

"It doesn't matter," Ruby answered quietly as she took John's arm in her hands. "Now, are we going to stand here all night, or do you have a little snuggled-up swinging left in you?"

In the darkness John smiled, and together the two sat back down to enjoy each other and the chilly October night.

Day 3

Sunday

October 23, 1910

Chapter 8

"Top o' the mornin', me beautiful lass."

Ruby, excited but instantly flustered, stood at the back door of her home, gazing upon the freshly shaved and Sunday-dressed John Phips. Without knowing that she did so, she nervously patted her hair and smoothed her dress.

"I . . . uh . . . Johnny, you look so very nice."

"Thank you," he answered simply. "So do you."

"That suit is very becoming on you."

John grinned. "Feels good, too. It's been quite a spell since I had Sunday-go-to-meeting clothes like these. Are you ready?"

"Let me get my shawl," Ruby smiled, "and I will be."

A little later, John pulled the Oldsmobile to a stop outside the meetinghouse in American Fork where Ruby's ward met. A few horses shied as the car clattered up beside them, but the sight and sound of automobiles was becoming common enough that most horses, and their drivers, were used to the commotion and did not go into full fright.

"My lady," John said gallantly as he helped Ruby to the ground, "may I escort you to your pew?"

"You certainly may, good sir," she replied with a flourish. And together the two entered the church and walked to their seats.

For a moment they sat in silence, listening to the organist's rendition of a hymn designed to keep the congregation in a reverant mood. John sat without moving, but his eyes were busy scanning every inch of the chapel, missing nothing, cataloging in his mind the whereabouts of the people, the doors, and so on.

"It truly has been a spell," he finally whispered.

"Since you went to church?" Ruby questioned in surprise.

"Yes. Especially in a regular church building. There was a branch in Los Angeles, but it was so far across town that I only got there once. I went with your brother James. Back in Ohio and down in Texas there were hardly any members at all, and only occasionally could I find a branch to meet with. This feels good, mighty good."

"What is he like, Johnny?"

"Your brother?"

"Uh-huh. Tell me about his spirit."

"Well, like I told you, I think it was about broken when his family wouldn't go to Los Angeles with him. He still doesn't understand that. And that's why he's never been back up to visit. What's more, I don't think he'll ever come back."

"Does he . . . is he still active in the Church?"

"Of course he is. He believes it with all his heart and supports it every way he can. The missionaries live with him at no cost to them, and he regularly holds meetings on the ranch for them and their investigators. In fact, one day he and I were standing on the corner when two missionaries called together a street meeting. They got it going and the one elder was just getting into his sermon when a few ruffians started to harrass him.

"James didn't take kindly to that, so he stepped to the front and invited any of those fellows to start their anti-socializing off with him.

"Now James is still big and powerful, and I've never known anyone who could beat him for sheer brute strength. A couple of those boys set at him, not really seeing clearly who it was they were dealing with. But it didn't take long for your brother to set the record straight."

"What did he do?"

"Oh, not much. He took hold of their necks with those stove-plate hands of his, lifted them into the air, and cracked their thick and unrepentant skulls together. Made quite an impression on them, too. They slept for a while after that, real peaceful-like; the others were quiet as could be, and each of the elders got off a real fine sermon. All in all, James was a terrific support to the Church that day. And active too, if you know what I mean."

Ruby smiled. "Jons is such a good man."

"Well, good morning, Mother."

Startled, Ruby looked up into the smiling face of her son.

"Good morning, Willy," she beamed. "Beautiful day, isn't it."

"It is at that. Unusual for this time of year. So you're still here, Mr. Phips."

"I am."

"Well, we welcome you to our meeting. I . . . uh . . .well, I might as well say it now as later. I learned in bishopric meeting this morning that a fellow was asking about you yesterday. Said he was from Los Angeles."

"Oh?" John asked casually. "Did he have a name?"

"I didn't hear it. Heard he was a small man, though, fiftyish or sixtyish. Looked official, too. Oh, and one other thing—he carried a detective's badge." William Alder smiled. "I thought you might want to know."

"Thank you," John Phips replied, nodding politely. "God bless you with your meeting."

William Alder stood still for an instant, uncertain. It looked to Ruby as if he had expected John to bolt, or at least to make some response other than what he had. When nothing else happened, however, he walked to the stand, and John and Ruby sat silently together.

"Johnny," Ruby finally whispered, "do you know what Willy is talking about?"

"Hard to say," John replied easily. "Fellows come and fellows go, they tell tales, and sometimes the truth isn't in them at all. I'd have to see the man myself to be certain. Might even be an old acquaintance."

"How would he know you were here?"

"Well, that's what detectives are good for, tracking people down. If he is who he claims he is, then that explains it."

Puzzled, Ruby looked at him. "How does what explain what?"

"It just does," John answered, smiling. "Now hush. The bishop's getting ready to start the meeting."

He was, and so Ruby, with dozens of questions spinning in her mind, turned to the front and did her best to focus her thoughts upon the Sabbath School meeting. And she did not see at all the man on the back pew whose eyes were carefully averted to the floor, but who knew exactly where she and John Phips were sitting.

Chapter 9

"Magneto's set," Ruby called.

"Good. I'll crank it up."

With several hard turns John cranked the engine of the Oldsmobile until the spark caught. Then, straightening slowly, he moved around and climbed behind the wheel.

"Do you feel all right?" Ruby asked.

"Fine. A touch of rheumatism is all. Must be a storm coming."

"Oh, that couldn't be. Look at this weather, John. It's lovely, far too lovely for a storm."

"It is beautiful," John responded as he swung the automobile out into the street. "No clouds, nothing but this warm south wind. If it weren't for my joints coming apart, I'd say I was wrong."

"Well, let's hope you are. I'm getting too old to enjoy winters anymore."

"Now stop that talk," John declared chidingly. "You're only as old as you think you are. And I'll tell you the truth, Ruby. You don't look any older to me than a fresh-picked mountain daisy."

Ruby smiled wanly. "Johnny, you do say the nicest things. I just wish my son would be a little more tolerant of you."

"Now Ruby, don't be too harsh on him. Willy is a good man who happens to be very worried about his mother and her welfare. You wouldn't want him to be unconcerned, would you?"

"No, I don't suppose I would."

"He's a fine man, Ruby, and you have every right to be proud of him. By the way, what are your plans for him and me?"

"Plans?"

"You know that he's going to push until I'm gone, don't you? He won't let up, Ruby, and you're the only one who can stop it."

"I know," she replied miserably, "and I . . . I just don't know how. I've tried. Oh, how I've tried, but I just can't do it. My hope is that it will just sort of work out."

"Mostly things do," John responded quietly. "If given time."

For a few moments John drove in silence, steering down Merchant Street past Shelly and Thornton General Merchandise, Roberts Brothers Drugs, E. H. Boley Meats and Groceries, and the Chipman Mercantile Company. At Main he turned east, and it was there that Ruby noticed his eyes fasten briefly upon a gray-haired man who seemed busy studying the new outfits behind the window of Studebaker Brothers Wagons, Carriages, Buggies, and Harnesses.

"Is that the man?" Ruby asked quietly. "The one Willy was talking about?"

"It could be. Say, what do you say we go for a drive?"

"A drive?"

"Certainly. On a beautiful day like this, a couple of old spooners ought to do a little sight-seeing. Normally I wouldn't use the Sabbath for such activities, but I don't know if you and I will ever have another Sunday together, and I'd like to make it memorable. What is there that we might see, do you think?"

"Johnny, I'll never understand you."

"Shure and ye will. Ye already do, me garjus wee lassie. Now, where should we go?"

"You already know the Highland Bench, so that isn't—"

"How many roads come off the bench, Ruby?"

"Roads? Well, the one we drove on this morning that crosses the Mitchell Ditch, and another over on the west side of the Bench by the Lehi Ditch. That one also comes into American Fork. Then there's the road up to Alpine, and a road that cuts across the dry farms and through Dry Canyon toward Salt Lake City. Then over by the mountain there's a road that goes into Pleasant Grove. It follows their ditch, too."

"How about up the canyon?"

"Yes, there's a road up there, a pretty good road, in fact."

"But that road is a dead end, isn't it?"

"I'm certain that it is, at least for automobiles. Why?"

"Well, I'm partial to canyons, always have been. But sometimes they're traps, you see."

"Johnny, what is going on?"

John grinned at the woman at his side. "It's a puzzle, isn't it."

"Johnny?"

"Ruby, I'd tell you if I could, but I don't even know all of it myself. Shall we go for a ride up the canyon?"

"Johnny, are you in trouble?"

John smiled thinly. "Ruby, I've lived with trouble of one sort or another for most of my seventy-two years. If I didn't have more, it would be a real surprise."

"What have you done?" Ruby then asked, her voice quiet.

"Done? Why, I've found me the loveliest woman in all the world, and I've fallen end over teakettle in love with her."

"And?"

"And? Isn't falling in love with you enough?"

Ruby finally laughed. "You're a hard man to get information from, Johnny Phips. Let's go for that ride up the canyon."

John beamed and, following Ruby's directions, drove the Oldsmobile into the mouth of American Fork Canyon.

"There has been a great deal of work done up here," John said as they drove up the rough and winding road.

"I'll say. This canyon has been in a turmoil since the first ore was discovered, back in 1870. There was a toll gate back there at the canyon mouth until just four years ago, with the revenue used to keep the road in repair. Teams passed through for fifty cents, buggies twenty-five cents, saddle horses a dime, and livestock five cents a head. I don't know that I ever heard the toll for automobiles."

"Likely they never had one pass through the gate," John declared.

"No, I don't imagine they did. That building over there is the power plant built by the Graff Brothers. There's a new one going in higher up, and both will supply power to us through the Utah County Power and Light Company."

"Is that a railroad bed?"

"It is, or was. Eric Adamson told me that back in 1870 the Miller

Mine was discovered on Miller Hill. The Aspinwall Company, which bought the mine, built this railroad in 1872 to haul supplies in and ore back out. The terminus was up the canyon at Deer Creek, though they intended to go higher. At first the cars were hauled up by locomotive, and then sent down the grade under power of gravity. During the last year or so of operation, the locomotive was sold and mules were used to haul the cars up the canyon. I never could determine which was the noisiest, mules or locomotive."

John smiled. "It must have been a profitable mine."

"It was, until 1878, I think. Then the ore ran out and the tracks were torn up. The old bed is still down in the river bottoms below my home."

"So this was a mining canyon."

"Was, and the way I hear tell, still is. Once there were even a couple of communities up here—Deer Creek and Forest City. Other than a boarding house and some charcoal kilns, I don't know what was at Deer Creek. Forest City, on the other hand, had about one hundred and fifty inhabitants. Mr. Alder frequently did business with the principal mines and sawmills in the area. It was a rough town, though, and he didn't usually let me visit there with him.

"There was an epidemic there, too. Several people died, including the three Birk children, whose parents ran the saloon. Because of the cemetary, the entire area has since become known as Grave Yard Flat."

For a time the only sound was the automobile grinding its way up the canyon. John drove, and Ruby relaxed, her memories of the canyon filling her mind.

"A few moments ago we passed Dance Hall Cave," she explained. "I went there once with Mr. Alder and had a grand time. But it was difficult to get to, and as a business enterprise it faded away."

"Is that the road up there?" John asked as he looked up the steep side of the mountain.

"Yes. That cut is called Van's Dugway. Sometime, years back, a fellow named VanHousen was hauling mail up here when he was killed by a snowslide. He was buried right here, and the dugway was named after him. A few years ago I heard that a flood washed out his coffin, and so he was taken out and reburied in the cemetery on Grave Yard Flat."

"Well, I hope this outfit of yours can make the climb. I drove one of Ford's new Model T's last year, and on grades like that, we had to drive in reverse."

"Why?"

"Well, it's the way Ford's gear ratio is set up. The doggone automobile has more power in reverse than it does going forward."

"I . . . I don't know about my Oldsmobile. I haven't ever driven it up here."

"Neither have I, Ruby lass. What say we give it a try?"

Smiling, Ruby nodded, and so John started the motorcar up the steep cut-bank.

"Johnny, don't get so close to the edge."

"Now, Ruby—"

"I mean it! I'll get out and walk if you—"

"Easy, woman. Easy does it. I won't go off, and coming back down, you can be on the inside and *I* will be the poor, frightened soul looking down into the awful void."

"Johnny, please . . ."

Inching upward, the Oldsmobile finally topped out above the dugway, and both John and Ruby breathed a sigh of relief.

"This is mighty pretty up here," John declared as he stopped the motorcar to let it cool.

"It is. And the air is so fresh that it feels like you can drink it. Why was that dugway so frightening to me, Johnny? I've never been frightened going up it in a wagon."

"Well, wagons go more slowly. Then too, wagons have teams pulling them or holding them back, and animals are notorious for taking care of their own good health. I think we've depended upon them a great deal more than we ever thought."

"And this motorcar has no animals in front."

"Exactly. All we have to trust is a machine, and machines break down with frightening frequency. I don't wonder that you feared, Ruby. I was a mite nervous, myself. By the way, where are we now?"

"I think this is called Dutchman's Flat. Up ahead are the terraces where Forest City was located. Off that way is Shaffer Fork, with all those kilns they used for making fuel for the smelter. On this other side is Mary Ellen Gulch. Up there is where the Sultana Smelter was located, and where Ed Hines still lives. He's been there most as long as the canyon, I think, and he never loses his dream about making his big strike. From what I hear, he's the one who keeps things concerning mining and rich ore stirred up."

"Must be a lonely life."

"Well, the story is that he had a girl in New York but couldn't afford to marry her. He came west, and years later when he went back for her, he found that she had given up on him and had become a nun. I heard he finally married and has a family, though I won't swear to it. There's also a story that during a terrible storm up here, his wife became so frightened that her hair turned white in a single night."

"Must have been quite a storm."

"They do get bad up here. One night Mr. Alder and I were in an electrical storm up in Mineral Basin that I would have sworn would kill us all. That it didn't, I still believe, was a miracle.

"Johnny, why do you keep looking behind us? Is that man following you?"

"I doubt it," John replied. "I've just been looking for . . . uh . . . what is all that mining up there called?"

Ruby looked at the old man, wondering why he was so secretive. He was a master at changing subjects, and she didn't want them changed. She wanted to know what was going on. Only . . .

"That's Miller Hill," she answered reluctantly, "where it all started back in 1870. Over there is the Blue Rock area, and this is . . . Well, that's funny. I can't remember what this is called. I know that there is ore all around us, though."

"What sort of ore do they mine here?"

"Well, gold, of course, and lead and silver and some zinc. Miller's Hill was so rich when they first started mining it that they used oxen to plow the ore right off the surface. Jacob Beck, one of my neighbors, was working the oxen one day, dragging timbers as I recall, when he was gored in his cheek. He still carries that terrible scar.

"Up there near the top of Miller's Hill is a solitary grave, and in that grave lies a wonderful man, George Tyng. Would you like to hear about him?"

"Faith an' I would. Any time I can hear yer garjus voice, Ruby lass, I enjoy it. Yez keep talking, and I'll keep listening."

Ruby giggled. "You know, you do that Irish accent very well, especially for an American. But you've surely gone and kissed the Blarney stone, so maybe, by right of blarney, you are a true Irishman."

"I mean every word I say, Ruby, and you know it. Now tell me about this Tyng fellow."

"All right," she smiled. "He came here in 1899 or 1900 and stopped at the Grant Hotel and livery stable. There he hired Christopher Beck, the owner of the hotel, to pack him up into either Mineral Basin or Miller Hill—he didn't seem to care which.

"Christopher agreed to pack him in for fifty dollars, and so they went. And on Miller Hill, the back side, actually, Tyng started mining immediately. By that fall, he had spent nearly $35,000 and had found no ore in his mine. Then, on the last day of operation, his foreman, Jack Howes, accidentally struck rich lead ore while picking out some rock. Thus Tyng's fortune was made."

"So what happened to him?"

"Johnny, he was a wonderful, generous man. I can't tell you how many people I know who have been helped financially by him. He bought great amounts of produce and dairy products from our local farmers for his miners, and he always paid a dollar more in wages than anyone else around. He was just grand.

"There is even a story that the Mormon Church needed a $5,000 donation. They sent a General Authority down to see him, and Tyng felt that the amount requested was a little steep, especially since he wasn't a Mormon. So the authority told him to go pray about it and ask the Lord if $5,000 was too steep and if it wasn't the Lord himself who wanted the money.

"Tyng prayed, came back to the General Authority the next day, and wrote out a check for $10,000. He said the Lord had told him that he should have been smart enough to listen to the General Authority in the first place. But since he hadn't been, the Lord was teaching him to listen better the next time."

"That's a great story, Ruby. Do you think it's true?"

"I think so. I've surely heard it often enough."

"Well, true or not, it's a great story. So what ever happened to Tyng?"

"Well, the winter of 1905-1906 was a terrible winter, with a great deal of snow. Tyng stayed up on the mountain running his mine, but one afternoon in January, a snowslide slammed into the building where he was working, killing him instantly. His will stated that he wanted to be buried up here on the mountain that he loved, and so there he is. And I don't think a more lovely place could be found. In fact, one day I picked twenty-two different kinds of wildflowers within ten feet or so of his grave."

John sat silently, his mind obviously somewhere else.

"Johnny?"

"I . . . I'm sorry. What did you say?"

"I said I once picked twenty-two kinds of wildflowers near his grave."

"Twenty-two," John replied almost absently. "That's a lot of flowers."

"It was," Ruby responded nervously. She knew John was troubled about something, but she didn't know how to get him to share it with her.

"A few years ago," she continued hesitantly, "Willy brought me back up here, and the ground had been so grazed by livestock that I hardly found any flowers. Now I hear that they don't permit grazing up here."

"So there's a lot of livestock up here?" John questioned, looking around.

"Oh yes. Kitty Nash, mother of Worthy Nash, first brought dairy cows up here back when the first mines were operating on Miller's Hill. Since then there have been thousands of head of cattle and sheep summered on these mountains. This is wonderful graze. I think that . . . Johnny, what on earth is wrong?"

"Wrong?" he asked, turning to look at her.

"Yes. You ask questions, but for the past few minutes your mind has been a thousand miles away. What is it?"

"It . . . it's nothing. I just . . ." John Phips looked at the woman by his side. "You know," he declared, changing the subject again, "I think it's time that we started back. You ready?"

Ruby nodded, so John turned the motorcar around, and for a time they rode in silence, working their way down to the downslope of Van's Dugway.

"Here we go again," John said, and with not a word from Ruby he started down the cut. It was not difficult, and John was enjoying the ride when he made a turn around a projecting cliff and suddenly looked through an opening in the trees.

"Now this is what I need," he exclaimed. "Just the stretch of road I have been looking for. Where does that canyon down there at the bottom of the dugway, the one running west, end up?"

"At Silver Lake," Ruby replied. "American Fork, Lehi, and Pleasant Grove recently dammed it, and they are still squabbling over water rights. Meanwhile, lowly Highland, directly in the mouth of the canyon, gets legally not a drop, and some folks, just to drink and water a few head of livestock, have even had to resort to stealing it."

"I thought Brigham Young told the Saints that water was not to be owned."

"He did. Trouble is, cities owning water is different from people owning it, and few cities can be classified as Saints. It has been a long and difficult battle, and it still isn't over. I'm one of the lucky ones, because Mr. Alder dug a well and we were fortunate enough to find plenty of good water. Many of my neighbors didn't fare so well."

"So the Saints fight over water," John mused. "Folks don't change much, do they. Here, it's water; in Ohio and Los Angeles, it's political and economic power; in Colorado, it's ore; in Texas and the Northwest, it's land; in . . ."

Suddenly John spun the wheel of the Oldsmobile and drove the car into a turnout on the steep grade of the road. Levering the gasoline down, he climbed out, stood for a minute while the dust settled, and stretched.

"Do you want to wait in the motorcar?" he asked.

"Where . . . where are you going?"

"Just up into those trees, so I can see the road down below."

"Is he . . . is he . . ."

"Ruby, I don't know. That's why I stopped. Why don't you wait in the car, and I'll be back in a moment or two."

So, while John climbed quickly onto the low, pine-covered ridge, Ruby sat in silence in the idling automobile. She was confused, but more than that, she was afraid. What was John Phips involved with? Why would he be showing such fear?

It reminded her vividly of the days and nights of fear during "the raid," when federal marshals were seeking Mormon polygamists and jailing them as fast as they could capture them. Her brother Jons had finally been caught, and that had been the night when a neighbor had sounded a warning and he had been forced to slip away into the darkness.

She had hated that, for she had loved the man dearly and hated to see him suffer. And now she was feeling all that agony again, for truly had she come to love John Phips, and just as truly did she fear for him.

"Ruby?"

Startled, Ruby spun about to see John standing beside the car, smiling.

"I didn't mean to frighten you," he said easily. "You looked like you were an awful long way off."

"I . . . I was. Johnny, please be honest with me. What is going on?"

John didn't answer. Instead, he got into the car, backed onto the road, and started down the canyon.

"Johnny—"

"Ruby lass, I'd tell you if I could."

"Johnny, this isn't fair."

"I know. It's just that . . . well, Ruby, it has something to do with all those years that I don't like to talk about, all those lonely years when I was dreaming of finding you. They weren't happy years, but still I had to live, to keep going. I did so by accepting various kinds of employment, and all this has to do with some work I did some time back."

"Work? Johnny, did you get on the wrong side of the law?"

"Would you believe me if I said no?"

"You know I would."

"Very well. No, I didn't."

"That's all?"

"It is for now. I just wish that . . . Uh, Ruby, is that creek up ahead the one you called Tibble Fork?"

"Yes," she answered hesitantly.

"Good. Now I know where I am. Can you drive home from Tibble Fork?"

"I . . . I suppose. But why, Johnny? What—"

"I need to walk."

"From *there?*"

"Yes ma'am. And that's all I can tell you, except this: Ruby Alder, I love you. And if I can do it, I'll be back later tonight."

"You . . .you love me?"

"I do."

"Promise you will come back, Johnny?"

"Of course."

"For . . . for me?"

"Well," he grinned, "partly. I don't want to miss that dedication tomorrow morning, either."

Pulling to a stop, John climbed out of the automobile. "Here," he said quietly, "now remember, you don't need to travel full throttle. Take it easy until you're out of the canyon. And Ruby, trust me, please."

"I do, Johnny. I just . . . Oh, please come back. I can't bear the thought of you going away."

But John Phips was already descending the side of the road, and Ruby knew that he had not heard her. And he was limping, limping badly. Once again Ruby cast her eyes at the sky.

Was a storm coming, as Johnny had predicted? Did those high, thin clouds mean something? Was that something else with which she had to contend? How could she do it, when there was so much more to be afraid of?

Afraid. How she despised that word! For so many years she had lived with fear, and now it was back again, clutching her innards in a terrible gripping knot, making her head pound while she watched the man she loved walk away from her.

But no, she wouldn't let it get to her. For Johnny she would be strong. She would go home and wait, and she would do all in her power to ease his life until this terrible thing, whatever it was, had passed.

"That's a promise," she shouted into the mountain fastness where John had disappeared. "John Phips, come back to me, for I will be waiting!"

And with a forced smile upon her face, Ruby Soderberg Alder started the automobile and lurched uneasily down the narrow mountain road back to town.

Chapter 10

"Mother, I swear it! Grandma let that old man *kiss* her last night right there on her porch. Ferd and I both saw her."

Allyson Alder stopped speaking, but her wide eyes spoke volumes.

"We've talked about it all day, Mother, and after seeing Grandma sitting so shamelessly with that old man at church today, we decided that we needed to tell you and Father what we saw."

Flora Alder stood still, looking from her seventeen-year-old daughter, Allyson, to her neighbor Ferdinand Burroughs, who at the moment was Allyson's steady beau. Then she looked back to her daughter.

There was no question about it. The two were serious about their accusation, and Flora didn't know what to do. In her mind she pictured her mother-in-law, and no matter how she twisted things around, she could not imagine Ruby kissing that old man. Yet Allyson had never deceived her, and the look on Ferdinand's open face told her that Allyson wasn't beginning a career in lying just yet. So that left things about as they appeared. Ruby Alder had allowed the old tramp who was staying in her barn to kiss her.

Flora thought of her husband, Willy, and wondered what he would do when he learned of his mother's indiscretion. Poor Willy. He was very conscious of his position, and this would cause him great discomfort. But even more, he was worried about his mother, for he had seen just such indiscretions destroy many others before her—lonely women who fell in love with men who were only after their money, and who ended up with broken hearts and empty bank accounts as the result of their misplaced love.

But why would Ruby fall in love with such a man? Flora cast about in her mind, and for the life of her she couldn't imagine an answer.

Senility?

No, hardly that. Ruby was somewhat feeble, but certainly that didn't apply to her mind.

Desire for romance?

Perhaps, but in the ten years since Henry Alder had died, there had been no sign of that, ever. And there *had* been opportunities for Ruby, plenty of them. Many times she had been approached by one or another of the lonely male citizens of the community, and always Ruby had rebuffed their amorous advances.

So why now?

Flora's thoughts were interrupted by the harsh ringing of the new telephone. She jumped a little just as she always did when it rang, and with a tight smile she walked to the wall.

"Hello," she shouted, holding the phone to her ear and straining to get her mouth near the too-high mouthpiece. "Oh, hello, Willy dear. What? You *what?* No . . . no I wasn't questioning you, I just can't hear . . . Oh, very well, that will be fine. Good-bye, darling."

Flora hesitated an instant after her husband had hung up, and then with a mischievous smile she spoke again into the speaker.

"And good-bye to you, Effie, my dear."

There was a gasp and a hurried click, and with a satisfied smile Flora placed the phone back in its cradle. Effie was a wonderful operator, but nosy, terribly nosy. Do her good to know she wasn't fooling anyone.

Turning away from the telephone, Flora walked back to Allyson and Ferdinand.

"Well?" Allyson asked.

"Well what?"

"Well, what are we going to do? Are you going to tell Father?"

Flora shook her head. "I don't know, but I don't think so—at least not just yet."

"Why not? Do you think he'll cut her off from the Church?"

"Either that or shoot her," Ferdinand said, speaking for the first time.

"Ferdinand," Allyson stormed, "what an awful thing to say!"

"Aw, I was only funning," Ferdinand mumbled. Then, with a lopsided look that might have been intended as a grin, he spoke again. "Speaking of utterly, Mother's cousin Tom has a cow who grins every time she walks through tall grass."

"What? Ferd, I declare, I don't—"

"Yup. She's *udderly* tickled to be there. Har de har har."

Allyson looked helplessly from Ferdinand to her mother. "I swear," she said. "He's got more awful jokes than any two people I ever knew."

Flora smiled. "I don't think it was awful. In fact, I think it was wonderful. Ferdinand, in his own sweet way, is trying to get us to laugh about this instead of treating it so seriously."

Surprised, Allyson looked back at Ferdinand. "Is that true?" she asked him.

"Yup," the boy declared, happy that this out had been so well articulated for him.

"Well, I declare. What a sweet thing to do."

Ferdinand grinned. "Yup. Smooching's supposed to be a laughing, fun-time, feel-good sort of thing. Was it me on that porch, I'd just as soon be left alone to enjoy myself, instead of being hauled off before some bishop."

"Even if that bishop was your son?" Flora asked curiously.

"If I had a son who was old enough to be a bishop, I'd certain sure be legal age to try smooching," Ferdinand declared. "Seems to me by the time someone's as old as Grandma Alder, she ought to be old enough to make up her own mind about what she feels up to doing. And she sure enough felt up to lettin' that tramp feller smooch her a good one. Most made me wish a certain girl was smooching me, seeing how good and fine that smooching looked to be."

"Ferdinand Burroughs!"

"Well it did, and I'll speak my mind about it, too. That one kiss you gave me last week made me wish for a whole lot more, but I can't seem to find the well."

"Well?"

"Yup, the wishin' well where I can throw in my fortune wishing for more of them kisses you promised me after that first one. Reckon I've about give up the search, though. I'm fixing to go join the French Foreign Legion like Pa's second cousin once removed, feller by the name of Martin T. Futzbusket. Like poor Cousin Martin, I'm fixin' to pine my life away with memories of your sweet lips brushing that one lonely time against mine. No sir, I don't blame Grandma Alder even a little. A person's got to enjoy what kissing they can, when they can. Seventeen or seventy, it makes no difference. You just never know when your smooching'll be cut off and your heart tossed out in the dust to wither up and blow away in the terrible winds of loneliness and sorrow while the one you love skips away without so much as a backward glance.

"Puts me in mind of Pa's uncle Zach, who had him a terrible spat with his wife, a mean little woman name of Zinnie. Zach was a big strapping man of one hundred sixty pounds when they had that spat, and for a whole year Zinnie wouldn't talk to him nor kiss him nor even admit that he was livin' with her. When asked about it, Zach would say, 'Treats me as though I am dead,' he'd say, and soon his weight began to drop like flies on a cold night, until there wasn't left of him no more'n enough to hold his shoes down to the floor. He died at about fifty pounds, killed on account of a woman who held back her simple, natural affectionate smoochin' from the man who loved her.

"No ma'am, smoochin' is terrible important for keepin' a body alive and well, and if I can't get any more smoochin' of my own, well, I'm awful pleased that Grandma Alder can."

Allyson, at that prolific speech, turned a bright red, Ferdinand glared at her defiantly, and Flora fought back the laughter that was struggling for release. Ferdinand Burroughs, she suddenly realized, was good for Allyson, who quite often got as uppity as her father, and who quite regularly looked down her nose at the boys who chased after her and tossed their hearts at her feet.

"I . . . I do declare!" Allyson fumed. "Ferdinand Burroughs, just you see if I ever—"

"Allyson," Flora Alder said, placing her hand upon her daughter's arm, "don't you be hasty. Ferd's right, you know. Grandma

Alder wouldn't be kissing that old man if she didn't want to."

"But Mother—"

"No, I mean it. Grandma Alder is a fine woman, and kissing is something very special to her. You can bet your best Sunday frock there is something behind this that we don't know about."

"Well, we'll know when Daddy finds out what Grandma is doing. He'll get the truth out of her."

"Allyson, I don't think your father should know about this just yet."

"But Mother, he's . . . he's her *son*. He ought to know! He can tell her to stop before—"

"What if she doesn't want to stop?" Ferdinand asked.

"Well of course she does! Why, kissing that old man is . . . is *lewd*."

"Then how come that kiss you gave me last week wasn't lewd?"

"It . . . it . . . I mean, I . . ."

"Allyson, your father is still at the ward meetinghouse. He won't be home for maybe another hour. Why don't you and Ferdinand go and see Grandma Alder, and—"

"What? I wouldn't go *anywhere* with this nincompoop."

"Nincompoop, am I? Who was it sneaked up to your grandma's porch when you saw them sitting there? Who was it knocked over that pot of geraniums and broke it in a million pieces? Allyson Alder, I may be a nincompoop, but I ain't a sneaky, clumsy one. Next time I take you anywhere, I'll crate you, just to protect the citizens of this fine community and their valuable property."

"Why, you big oaf. I'll have my father throw you out."

"Ha! He couldn't throw nothing but a fit."

"Says you, you skinny lummox. When Father gets through with you, it'll take fourteen doctors to fix all the things that'll be broke."

"That's broken, not broke," Ferdinand said easily.

"You're a fine one to be teaching grammar," Allyson stormed.

"Yep, massacrein' grammar's my specialty. Now come on. Put a smile on that cute little face of yours and let's go do what your mother told us to do."

Without waiting for an answer, Ferdinand Burroughs took a protesting but obviously willing Allyson Alder by the arm and led her out the door. Smiling, Flora watched them go, and she was just turning back into the parlor when the telephone jangled again, frightening her half out of her wits.

"Blasted new-fangled contraptions," she muttered as she strode toward the too-high wooden box. "They ought to put warning lights on them so they don't startle a body so badly. I do declare, this is worse than that automobile Grandma Alder bought last year—peskier, at least. Makes me wonder what will be coming next. Progress and Grandma Alder, it's all trouble with a capital T."

And with that she picked up the telephone and shouted, "Hello!"

Chapter 11

"Grandma, are you home?"

Starting at the voice of her granddaughter, Ruby looked up from the old teakwood box that held the photographs and letters that made up the treasures of her life.

"Grandma?"

"I'm in the parlor," Ruby called. "Come in, dearie."

Carefully Allyson made her way through the darkened doorway, Ferdinand following closely behind her. In the parlor she paused, and Ruby stood and turned on the single electric lamp.

"Hi, Grandma."

"Hello, Allyson. And is this Ferdinand Burroughs? My goodness but you have sprouted, young man."

"Yes, ma'am, so my ma says when she buys me new britches."

"Well, sit down, both of you, and tell me to what I owe this visit."

Allyson seated herself and squirmed a bit with her discomfort, and Ruby almost smiled at the young lady's transparency. Oh how long it seemed since she had been Allyson's age. Yet the memories of those golden years were fresh and brilliant, and she knew without even thinking about it that Allyson was concerned that Ferdinand had placed his arm behind her on the sofa.

"Ferd," she finally whispered. "Don't—"

"Now don't be nervous," Ferdinand responded. "Grandma Alder ain't like my great-aunt Amanda Minerva. No she ain't, not a bit."

"What? What on earth are you talking about?"

"I'm talking about Grandma Alder and my great-aunt Amanda."

"Ferd!"

"Well," the boy smiled, "I am. You don't need to be so nervous about Grandma Alder. With Aunt Amanda, me and my brother Frank always ran and hid when we seed her comin', 'cause she allus kisses a feller and wants him to pick her some berries or something. That's her long suit—berries. I don't reckon she'll be happy in paradise without they've got berries there. And Frank bets there'll be a great old scramblin' amongst the angels, too, to keep from getting kissed. She's a terror, Aunt Amanda is. I'm thankful your Grandma Alder ain't like that."

Allyson stared in disbelief at the sober young man seated next to her. She hadn't an idea in the world what he had been talking about, but already she had forgotten the arm on the sofa behind her, trying to understand.

"No . . . she isn't . . . I think . . . ," she murmured. "I mean, I . . ."

Ruby, quite aware of Ferdinand's ruse and enjoying his loquaciousness immensely, decided it was time to get to the heart of Allyson's errand.

"Well?" she asked again, intentionally not beating around any bushes. "A visit is somewhat unusual, isn't it?"

"Uh . . . yes, it is. But it is Sunday, and I . . . we thought it might be nice to . . . to . . . we just wanted to see how you were."

Allyson did her best to smile, and Ruby returned it instantly.

"Well, how sweet of you" she responded. "I am feeling just fine, though I do notice that I'm not so quick about some things as I once was."

"Quick?" Allyson asked blankly.

"Yes," Ruby smiled. "A year or two ago and I would have caught that prowler who broke my geranium pot. But I'm not so quick now, so I didn't even try to catch you."

With a startled expression, Allyson stared at her grandmother. "You knew?"

"Of course I knew. I heard you gasp when you broke it, I heard you whisper and giggle afterward, and I only know of one person alive who sounds just like you do."

"Ha," Ferdinand laughed, "I told you she would know."

"You did not."

"Did so, and you know it."

"Brother. Next thing you know, you'll be proclaiming yourself the next prophet of the Church."

Ferdinand grinned. "Funny thing you should mention that, Allyson. Once Grandpa Burroughs lost his false teeth, and Ma hauled me in and set me down and told me to trance. I did my best and had me a good snooze and then woke up sudden and says to them, wild-like, 'Seek ye within the well!' So they did it. But they didn't find the teeth. But only a week afterward, when Pa cleaned the cistern, there them teeth was. Grandpa Burroughs says, 'Well, anyhow, Ferd knowed they was in the damp,' he says. So you see, I did know, just like I knowed that Grandma Alder would hit on it being you that broke her pot."

Ruby laughed, and Allyson, finally caught in the mood, relaxed and giggled a little, herself.

"Ferd," she said, "I do declare. I never heard anybody go on like you do."

"Chin music," Ferdinand answered. "Pa says it warms the soul, and I reckon we all have souls that need a little warming."

"That's right," Ruby agreed. "We all need a little thawing out from time to time. Thank you, Ferd, for helping us. Now Allyson, I think you wanted to speak to me of Mr. Phips. Isn't that right?"

Shocked once again, Allyson could do little besides gape at her grandmother. "I . . . I . . . Well, I . . . we had hoped . . . uh . . ."

"Allyson," Ruby asked seriously, "what is troubling you?"

"That kiss!" Allyson finally declared. "Grandma, how could you do that? I mean, he's a tramp, and we . . . I saw you let him kiss you."

"You . . . you did?"

"I did!"

Slowly Ruby smiled. "Well then, I admit it."

"But . . . but . . ."

"Allyson, I love John Phips, and whether a person is seventeen or seventy, love feels about the same."

"You *love* him? That old man, I mean?"

"I do."

"But Grandma—"

"Allyson, may I take you and Ferdinand into my confidence?"

"I imagine so. I—"

"Now you must promise not to breathe a word of this—not until I tell you that it's all right."

"Sounds pretty deep and dark," Ferdinand observed.

"Well, deep, anyway. Johnny and I are old friends. We . . . we knew each other long ago."

"Grandma, why can't I tell this to Daddy?"

"Why?" Ruby said, confused. "Because . . . because . . . Well, because *I* have to be the one who tells him. And I'm just not ready to do that. I want—"

"Grandma, don't tell me any more. I'll have to tell Daddy, and I really don't want to."

"Yes," Ruby agreed instantly. "You're absolutely right. Doing that wouldn't be fair to either you or your father. Instead, let me simply ask you for your help."

"Both of us?" Allyson asked in surprise.

"Oh, my, yes."

"What would you want us to do?" Ferdinand asked.

"Help me to show Mr. Phips a good time. You see, for most of his life he has been alone. He has had no family, and from what little I can learn, few friends. I'd like to make a little of what time he has left, happy. Would you two be willing to help me?"

"He hasn't *any* family?" Allyson asked.

"None that he knows of."

"Oh, how sad."

"Yes, it is. And he's such a fine man, too. He was baptized when he was a child and even served a mission to the eastern United States."

"Then why . . . why is he a *tramp?*"

Ruby smiled wanly. "That is a sad question, Allyson, but I think it's because he has nowhere to go."

"So how did he come to you?"

"I . . . I'm not certain. I know he met my brother Jons down in Los Angeles and got to know him quite well. From what little I can learn, Jons sent him here."

"But why?"

"I think . . . I think Jons was simply trying to get two lonely people together. He did, too, thank goodness."

"You really do love him—Mr. Phips, I mean?"

"Yes I do, Allyson."

"Daddy is convinced that he's some sort of crook, you know."

"I know."

"Daddy also thinks he's after all your money."

"Well, Allyson," Ruby smiled, "there isn't much to get. But he isn't after my money. Neither is he a crook."

"Are you sure, Grandma?"

"Absolutely. He has assured me of that."

"He might be lying," Ferdinand declared quietly.

"Yes, he might. But he isn't, and I . . . I'm not at liberty to tell you why I feel this way. You'll simply have to trust both him and me about that."

"What about the detective that Daddy heard about?"

"Now," Ruby sighed, "that is a hard question. I really don't know. But I know Johnny, and I know that whatever is happening, he isn't at fault. Will you two help me to show him a good time?"

"Daddy might really fuss at us," Allyson stated.

"Yes, he might. But if you get to know Johnny a little better, then you'll be able to help your father come to know him too. I would suggest, for the time being, that we keep this idea between the three of us. Ferdinand, do you have some suggestions for fun things to do?"

"You bet! But I can't afford—"

"Don't worry about money. We'll spend all of mine, and then John Phips for sure won't be after it."

Both Allyson and Ferdinand laughed with her.

"Thank you both for coming to see me," Ruby declared as she rose to her feet. "I'll look forward to 'sparking' with you."

"Me too," Ferdinand agreed instantly. "The sooner and the oftener I can do a little sparkin' with Miss Alder here, the happier my poor, lonely, miserable soul will be."

"Oh, Ferd, how you do carry on!"

"Yes, I do. It runs in the family, too. Why, I recollect the time when Bige Peebles was working for Pa down in the store. Bige was a bad egg, I want you to know. Couldn't stop consuming nefarious spirits, he couldn't, and it affected him something awful. One night he slept out on the wooden sidewalk in front of the store, the sleep of the drunk, if you will, and Pa took and tacked all his clothes down all around. Then when Bige woke up the next morning and tried to get up and couldn't, it scared him 'most to death and he hollered, 'Help! I'm paralyzed.' 'Oh, no you ain't, Bige,' Pa says, 'but you was yesterday.'

"Yes ma'am, I do come from a long line of carriers-on."

The young couple left, holding hands, and Ruby watched them go. They were so carefree, so happy, so unafraid . . .

And with that, Ruby began, very softly, to cry.

Day 4

Monday

October 24, 1910

Chapter 12

The sun was bright in the hazy sky of another incredibly warm October day when Ruby heard the light tap on her kitchen door. Her breath caught, for the tap was not like Johnny Phips's knock. Yet it had to be him! It had to be. She could not bear the thoughts of him not being there.

Until late into the night, she had remained near the window, watching for some sign of movement within the barn. Yet not once had a light shown, not once had she seen the door open to admit Johnny to his sleeping quarters.

Alternately she had prayed, wept, and sat shrouded and silent with memories, thinking of Johnny in every way that she could, trying to understand what it was that he was involved in. She trusted him, implicitly. And yet Willy, who carried the mantle of her bishop, and who was such a conscientious news examiner, was so against him, and so she had to give consideration to that as well.

And what really did she know about the man called John Phips? Actually, little more than he had told her. His entire history might be one long fabrication, a lie gotten up for almost any reason. If it were, then no matter what was happening, she would be the victim.

But no! How could she be thinking these things? She knew Johnny Phips, and she knew that he would never harm her, never—

The tap came again at the door, and with a start, Ruby realized that she was indeed acting older. Quickly she stepped to the door and opened it. And there he stood, smiling and freshly-shaved and Sunday-suited again.

"Johnny!"

"Top of the mornin', me lovely wee lass. And how be yer spirits on this grand and auspicious day?"

"My goodness gracious," she exclaimed. "You're the cheerful one today."

"Ought to be. Yesterday was the Lord's day of rest, today's the day of the big dedication, and I have the glorious privilege of being with you throughout both. Are you ready to go?"

She was, and moments later the two were motoring south toward American Fork.

John drove in concentrated silence while Ruby sat stiffly beside him, wondering. Should she ask him about last night? Would he tell her if she did? She could probably ask, but just as likely she wouldn't get any answers. She had never known a man who could so easily evade sharing information about himself. Still, she ought to try, for she had a terrible feeling that somehow what Johnny was involved in concerned her.

"I hope we're on time, Ruby. If we aren't, then likely we won't get a seat."

"Oh, I must not have told you. I have a seat on the stand, and you've been invited to sit with me."

John stared. "You want me to—to sit on the *stand?*"

"Yes, I do. Right next to me."

"But Ruby, I don't think I should."

"No arguments or excuses, me handsome laddie-buck."

John looked over at Ruby, his eyebrow lifted in surprise at her own bit of Irish. Then he grinned, and a short while later Ruby escorted him to their place under the canvas canopy where the cornerstone dedication ceremony of the Alpine Stake Tabernacle would take place.

"President Chipman," she declared proudly, "I would like you to meet my dear friend, Brother John Phips. Johnny, this is President Stephen L. Chipman, our stake president."

"It's a pleasure, President," John responded nervously.

"It is, indeed," President Chipman declared. "Ruby is a fine woman and has done a great deal to hold the Church together out on the Highland Bench. We're honored to have her with us on the stand this morning. And any friend of hers is a friend of ours."

"Thank you," John declared. "This will be a lovely edifice."

"Yes, it will. We have allocated $80,000 for the construction, and of course that kind of money can pay for almost anything. As a stake, we're thrilled with what this building should do for our people. Excuse me, please, Brother Phips. I must greet these other folks. I do hope you'll enjoy your visit to our stake."

"Johnny," Ruby said then, turning to another man, "this is Brother Henry Moyle, our stake patriarch. He recently gave Allyson a most marvelous blessing."

"That was the Spirit's doing, Ruby, not mine. Will you be with us long, Brother . . . ah . . ."

"Oh, I'm sorry," Ruby apologized. "This is John Phips, Brother John Phips."

"It's a pleasure," John acknowledged, taking the man's hand in his own. "As to how long I will be with you, Brother Moyle, it's hard to say. I'd like to stay forever, but we'll just have to see how things work out."

"Yes, I see what you mean. I think. Have you and Ruby known each other long?"

"It seems like it. In fact, it seems almost like forever," John declared. "Ruby is a remarkable woman."

"That she is. She was a fine Relief Society president, too."

"Johnny," Ruby said as Brother Moyle was interrupted by another group of well-wishers, "I would like you to meet Sister Jemima Durrant. She is our stake Relief Society president. And this is Sister Annie Hindley and Sister Harriet Jacobs, her two counselors."

"Ladies," John said, bowing slightly, "it is a pleasure."

The women smiled and greeted him and seemed more than gracious. Yet Ruby felt that the sisters, and the brethren as well, were deeply curious about John Phips. And there were one or two who gave her looks that were openly unfriendly—even critical.

"You know," Jemima Durrant said with a smile, "you don't look anywhere near like the ogre I have been told you were."

"You were told I was an ogre?"

"Or monster or a thief or who knows what else. People always talk when a stranger moves in, especially if he does it as you did.

Anyway, I'm glad I've been able to meet you, John Phips. I am greatly reassured."

John nodded and watched the woman turn and go, and then for a moment he and Ruby stood together, greeting others on the stand and watching the crowd gather in the congregation before them. John was terribly nervous, Ruby knew, for he fidgeted constantly and did not seem his usual gracious self.

"Johnny," she finally asked, "what is it? What's going on?"

"Ruby, please. I just can't . . . Look, there's William."

Ruby turned and smiled at her son, who approached, then, and took his mother's hand.

"Good morning, Willy."

"Morning, Mother. I see that our Mr. Phips is still with us."

"Yes I am, Bishop," John answered boldly. "How are you today?"

"I am well, but somewhat surprised that you are yet here."

"That has surprised me as well," John replied.

"Well, I wonder about that, sir. It seems, from the pieces of the puzzle I have been given, that you are here for a definite reason, one that has little to do with my mother's cooking. You should be the last one to be surprised by your presence."

"And do you know that reason?" John asked, too quickly.

"No," William answered slowly, "but I am studying on it, and here and there, good friends are helping me. Shortly the puzzle will fit, and I will know you very well."

"It sounds as though you know what to look for."

"I do," William declared, smiling. "Frankly, for Mother's sake, I hope that you are not what you seem. Good day, sir. Good day, Mother."

Without a backward glance, Bishop William Alder strode off to mingle with other dignitaries, and John and Ruby stood silently, the strain between them almost a palpable thing.

"Ruby—"

"John, don't say anything, at least not now. Let's both simply do our best to enjoy the meeting."

"Fair enough. But I do want to speak with you later. I don't think I'm being fair to either you or William."

Ruby, looking at John's downcast eyes, felt a terrible sinking within her soul. What was he going to reveal? What awful calamity was he about to bring into her life? Was Willy correct? Did this man have evil intentions that would break her heart? Did he have a dark past that might destroy her? How could she know?

"Oh, that must be Elder Orson F. Whitney!"

"You know him?" Ruby questioned in surprise.

"No, but from what I've read, I feel as though I know him. I love his poetry, and his four-volume history of Utah is one of the most profound documents I have ever examined."

"You've read all four volumes?" Ruby asked.

"Most of them twice, Ruby. You see, when a man is alone, he has to fill his evenings in one way or another. I just always assumed that my growing, at least for the time being, would have to be in an area other than family life. I reckon maybe I didn't grow enough."

Ruby didn't answer, but she squeezed his hand and did her best to smile. Then quickly she took her seat while her heart ached with the fear of what she felt certain was coming.

The meeting was memorable, and the dedicatory prayer by Elder Whitney was filled with power and had much that to Ruby seemed prophetic.

Elder Whitney had just finished and returned to his seat when John Phips visibly stiffened in his seat beside her. His eyes were riveted upon an area of the congregation near the back, and Ruby could tell that something had definitely upset him.

"What is it, Johnny? Who—"

"Shhh," John whispered. "I think . . . I think . . . Oh, dear. This is going to embarrass you, Ruby, just as William told you it would. Please forgive me for what I am about to do, but I have no choice. I must deliver a message, and there is no other way."

"What? What are you—"

Without answering, John Phips rose to his feet, crossed in front of the astonished presiding officers, and leaned close to Elder Whitney's ear.

Dumbfounded, Ruby watched as Elder Whitney first listened closely and then nodded in response to John Phips's whispered message.

Turning to the pulpit then, John took a deep breath, smiled a disarming smile to the audience, and began to speak.

"Brothers and Sisters," he said, speaking more loudly than Ruby had thought possible, "'tis a beautiful and memorable morning, to be sure. When it was determined that I needed to take a moment of your time today, I was not given a subject. But I have noticed that I am shaking a little as I stand here, and so that shall be my text.

"For a moment, I would like to tell you the story of a young man who was sick of the palsy. The palsy, as you are all aware, is a terrible disease, a wasting scourge. And the palsy, as you know, is strongly hereditary. It had been in his family lo those many years. His father had been sick of the palsy, and his mother had been sick of the palsy. And, in fact, every member of his family had been sick of the palsy. Yes, my dear brothers and sisters, he had had it for years and years, and—*he was sick to death of the palsy*.

"Brothers and sisters, like that young man, I am sick to death of a palsy we all seem to be afflicted with—the trembling instability of our Christian love for each other. Why, the damage we do is the same as if we, this very day, *planted a bomb in the newspaper office and killed the editor*. Or *murdered him within the walls of his own home!* It would be the same thing.

"I feel to say to you that before such a thing be allowed to happen, I would *try to stop the culprits,* be they *a young man* or an *old,* from perpetrating the deed. Yes, and I would *guard both the editor's office and his home* in my efforts, while my associate should *follow them all the way to their hole*.

"Thank you, brothers and sisters, and may the good Lord prosper us that none will die of this terrible form of palsy. Amen."

In absolute silence, John Phips turned, shook Elder Whitney's hand, and then limped back to his seat, a worried look creasing his face.

"What . . ." Ruby whispered, "Johnny, what in—"

"Shhh," he whispered, "the choir is getting ready to sing the closing number."

"But—"

"Ruby, I'll explain later."

With that, John Phips folded his arms and watched with tense expression while the children's choir concluded the services.

Chapter 13

"Johnny," Ruby said while the buzzing of the surprised members of the congregation surrounded her, "I don't understand—"

"Ruby," John held up his hand, "I can't talk just yet. Can you get a ride home with someone else?"

"I think so, but—"

"May I borrow your automobile? Immediately?"

"Johnny—"

"Decide quickly, Ruby. I don't have an extra second to burn."

"You want to take my motorcar?"

"I *need* to. Right now. I'll be back."

"Oh no you don't, John Phips! If you go anywhere else, anywhere at all, it will be with me at your side. Last night took three hundred years or so to pass, and I won't be spending another evening like that, wondering if I've seen the last of you, wondering if you are all right."

"Ruby, this might be dangerous."

"Good. Then let's get started."

John looked at her, his expression guarded. Then he smiled, and Ruby knew that she had won. She didn't know exactly *what* she had won, but she had won something, and that in itself made her feel indescribably happy.

Almost running, the not-quite-so-young couple made their way off the stand. And Ruby heard, as she hurried behind John, the most amazing comments about "that older brother's *wonderful* testimony." She also saw, as she was pulled off through the crowd, the portly form of her son, Bishop William Alder, who was anxiously questioning a hopelessly puzzled Elder Orson F. Whitney.

"I don't know him," she heard the apostle declare quite loudly. "I tell you, Bishop, I never saw him before in my life. But it was an interesting sermon, don't you think?"

"Very interesting," William responded. "But you see, Elder Whitney, *I* am the editor in question, and that sounded very much like a threat."

Ruby saw her son, his face and voice reflecting his confusion and doubt, and then she and John were outside the canvas walls and running through hordes of buggies and wagons and milling teams, trying to get to her automobile.

"It's mighty crowded," John muttered as he ran.

"Is that good or bad?"

"Neither. Just crowded. I hope our hurrying in that Oldsmobile doesn't start all these teams to stampeding."

"Why do we need to be in such . . . such a hurry?" Ruby gasped.

"Because I can't afford to let them get ahead of me," John declared as he reached the automobile and hoisted Ruby aboard.

"Let who?"

"Later. Is the magneto set?"

"Uh-huh."

"Okay, here comes the crank."

Quickly John turned the automobile to life. And then, hurrying as best he could, he clambered up behind the steering wheel.

"Now where—Johnny! Look! There is that man we saw in front of Studebaker Brothers!"

"I know."

"Well, hurry, before he sees us!"

At exactly that instant the man looked over, gazing directly at Ruby and John.

"John," she whispered urgently, "he's looking."

And then, to her amazement, she saw John Phips look back at the man and signal to him with a head nod. Then John pulled the Oldsmobile out and into the dusty street and the hot October sun.

"Grandma?"

Turning, Ruby was surprised to see Allyson and Ferdinand running into the street behind them.

"Grandma, may Ferd and I have a ride?"

"I don't think—" Ruby started to say, when she was interrupted by John Phips.

"Is that your granddaughter?"

"Yes."

John slammed on the brakes. "Climb in," he called loudly. "But hurry!"

They did, and John started the automobile again.

For Ruby, the next half-hour was the most frustrating time she had ever spent in her long life. First they drove madly to the west, pulling off the street directly in front of William's office. Quickly John ordered Ruby and the others out of the car and directed Allyson and Ferdinand to stand together at the rear of the building near the eastern corner. Then he and Ruby stood together at the front.

He didn't speak, and after one or two attempts at speech herself, Ruby stopped talking also. Instead, she watched as the traffic from the Tabernacle rolled past, raising clouds of dust as various sorts of vehicles pulled off the paved main road onto the side streets.

Many people stopped to shop, but John seemed to pay attention to no particular person or group. He kept his eyes moving, and Ruby was certain that if an ant had crawled across the sidewalk, John would have noted it.

"Mother, what on earth are you doing here?"

"Oh, hello, Willy. Johnny and I were . . . were . . ."

"Waiting for me? I hope not. I'm still trying to digest that thinly veiled threat that Mr. Phips made, and I'm not at all certain that I could maintain my temper."

"Then we won't trouble you," Johnny declared easily.

"You already have," Willy scowled. "From this moment, Mr. Phips, I will pull every string I can pull to find out why you are here and to stop you from hurting my mother or any other individual in this community. Now good day to you."

William Alder walked through the doorway of his office, and John and Ruby stood silently as long moments drifted past. Finally, with a muttered "There they go," John took Ruby's hand and pulled her toward the Oldsmobile.

"Time to go?" Ferdinand called from behind the frame office.

"It is," John answered. "Let's hop to it."

Ferdinand and a bewildered Allyson ran to the motorcar and climbed aboard, and within moments the four were speeding north toward the hill and Allyson's home.

"Johnny, what on earth are we doing?"

"Protecting things, I hope."

In frustration, Ruby shook her head. "I don't understand, Johnny. I—"

"You don't need to understand right now, me lovely lass. Just trust me."

So Ruby tried, while the two in the back seat sat very quietly, trying to do the same. Suddenly a horseman came out of a side street and rode for a moment beside them, and Ruby was astounded to recognize the man who had been in the parking lot at the Tabernacle site.

"Johnny, it's him again! I—"

"Ruby, be still!"

Surprised at John's tone of voice, Ruby meekly obeyed. Then she watched in wonder as John and the other man made signs at each other with their fingers. That done, the man galloped on ahead, and with pounding heart Ruby watched him go.

"Is . . . is he the man who has been following you?"

"He's been around me, but not following me."

"He followed us up the canyon."

"Yes. We had to meet. That's where I went when I left you last evening."

"So you and he *are* working together. May I . . . may I ask who he is?"

"Certainly," John smiled. "His name is Frank Burns."

"The name means nothing to me."

"It shouldn't."

And Ruby, completely confused, grew still as John drove in silence toward the Highland Bench.

A horse hitched beside the road began to pitch and buck as they flew past, but another one, standing hip-shot a few yards farther along, merely switched its tail at bothersome flies and the noise. Then, as they reached the bottom of the hill, John pulled close up behind a buggy that Ruby recalled having seen near her son's office.

Without hesitation John squeezed the rubber bulb of the horn, pulled to one side of the road, and passed by the buggy. And he was grinning without mirth as the two men in the buggy came into view and then passed quickly behind them.

"That is a wonderful machine," he mumbled to a wondering but silent Ruby. "The speed comes in especially handy."

Without another word, John drove the remainder of the distance to William Alder's home, pulled off the road in front, and turned to a surprised Allyson.

"Young lady, your grandmother wishes a word with your mother."

Allyson cast a glance at Ruby, who nodded her agreement.

"Would you have her come out in the yard, please? Right now."

Allyson looked blankly at Ruby, who again nodded.

"Mother," she called loudly as she climbed down out of the motorcar and approached the screened front door of her home, "can you come out to see Grandma?"

They all waited a moment, and Ruby sensed that John was nervous. He had not looked behind him, but she knew he was aware of where the buggy was that they had passed. Looking back over her shoulder, she saw that it was coming up the hill slowly, and—

"Hi, Mother."

Flora Alder stepped quickly off the porch. "I was hoping that you'd drop by after the meeting. This must be Mr. Phips, about whom I've heard so much."

"Johnny, my daughter-in-law, Flora Alder."

"I'm pleasured, ma'am."

"As am I. Grandma, would you and Mr. Phips like to stay for lunch?"

"I . . ." Ruby responded, "I mean, I . . ."

"We'd love to do it, ma'am," Johnny answered. "Only today isn't a good day. Now we don't have much time, and I'm going to say a couple of things that won't make much sense. May I have the liberty to speak freely?"

Surprised, Flora nodded, looking carefully at her mother-in-law.

"Good. For the next thirty minutes or so, will you stay out here in your yard?"

"But Will's lunch . . ."

"Only about thirty minutes. Maybe less. Your husband won't be home before then, or at least I don't think he will. Could you and Ruby find something to do so that you will both be very visible?"

"We can weed what is left of the flowers," Flora replied quietly.

"Wonderful. Do that. Just stay outside and be very visible from the street.

"Now," he said, turning to Allyson and Ferdinand, "what do we do about you?"

"Us?" Ferdinand responded. "Why do you—"

"I know. Do the same thing that you did down at Mr. Alder's office. Go stand in the back and just visit together for a little while."

"Grandma, what is going on?"

"Allyson," Ruby entreated, "please do as Mr. Phips asks."

"Yeah, Allyson," Ferdinand concurred. "Let's go."

Holding hands, the young couple hurried toward the rear of the home, Ruby and Flora got busy with the flowers, and John unlatched and opened the side-hood of the Oldsmobile. Then he leaned in as though he were working on it. Seconds later the driver of the buggy pulled off the road about fifty yards away. There he and the man who rode with him sat, silently watching the house.

Ruby, observing them as well as she could without ever looking directly at them, was suddenly filled with an awful feeling—almost a feeling of evil. It was, she suddenly knew, going to be a long afternoon.

Chapter 14

"Johnny, are you certain that taking these youngsters with us is safe?"

"Should be," John muttered. "When they left, those boys in the buggy were mighty perplexed. Just when they thought they had things worked out, something came along that didn't add up."

"You mean us?"

"Exactly."

"And now we'll follow them?"

"Well, not quite. Frank has that job. We'll just sort of follow along behind."

"And that isn't dangerous?"

"Shouldn't be."

"Johnny, who *are* those men?"

"Couple of brothers called the McNamaras, Ruby. Mighty unsavory fellows."

Ruby stared ahead, perplexed. She felt so lonely, without information or understanding. If only John would be open with her!

"Johnny, did you threaten to blow up Willy's office?"

"Ruby me lass," John sighed, "I was sending out a message. That's all."

"When you shouted?"

"That's right."

"What about your hands?"

"Same thing, Ruby. A variation of Indian sign language. Frank and I worked it out years ago."

"It was he that you were signaling?"

"That's right."

"Why did we go to Willy's office? Or his home, for that matter?"

"You sound like Sergeant Mike Calahan."

"I . . . I do?"

"You do."

"I just want to know—"

John stopped her with a lifted hand. "Ruby, the McNamara brothers work for some evil people within the unions. They bomb places, like the Los Angeles Times offices, that are against union organization."

"And Willy is against union organization," Ruby breathed.

"Exactly."

"Then why don't you tell him?"

"I can't. Not yet. I intended to tell him at the outset, but somehow you and I sort of got in the way, and now he wouldn't listen to me if I did."

"I think you're right, Johnny," Ruby agreed.

"So there's no telling what William might do that would alert them, and it is very important that they not be alerted. They must be captured instead. That's why I have been so quiet about it."

"Well, why haven't they been captured already?" Ruby asked.

"We've tried, several times. We just haven't been able to find them where an arrest would not endanger other people. Nor have we been able to find their hole here in Utah. I hope that is what Frank accomplishes this afternoon."

"Are . . . are you police?"

"No," John replied quietly. "Sometimes, though, I help the police out a little. Now, where do we turn toward Pleasant Grove?"

"I . . . I . . ."

"Two blocks straight ahead," Ferdinand called from the back seat.

"Thanks," John responded. "By the way, son, what's your name?"

"Ferdinand. Ferdinand Burroughs. You'll be Mr. Phips."

"Call me John."

"All right, John, then you call me Ferd."

"Fair enough. And of course you'll be Allyson," John said then, smiling at the girl.

"I am, but I don't understand what is happening here. Is this . . . the getting together we were going to do?" Allyson asked hesitantly.

"Not that I know of," Ruby answered. "Still, we are together, so we might as well take advantage of the situation."

"Why, I do hate that," Allyson fumed, suddenly upset. "I'm hardly ready for that sort of day, and I only just this morning got this tear in my frock mended. If I get another one—"

"Let me see," Ferdinand said as he reached down and examined the mended tear. Then he rolled his eyes and sat back.

"Yep," he declared, "she's mended, all right, but like my pa's Uncle Filbert says of his wife Agnes's stitchery, I'd hate like thunder to reap as you sew."

There was a startled gasp and a solid slap as Allyson attempted to amputate Ferd's leg with her open palm, and Ferdinand howled in mock pain.

"You . . . you imposter!" Allyson stormed. "You should be butchered for a remark like that."

"Butchered?" Ferdinand asked, his eyes wide. "Funny you should mention that. Saturday morning last, Ma went to the butcher and give him a lathering. 'Just how do you explain these pieces of rubber in the meat you sold me?' she asks while the butcher cowers in mighty fear and tremblin'. 'Why,' the butcher says, doin' his best to sound brave in the face of such terrible adversity as my mother, 'I reckon it's just another instance of provin' that the autymobile is replacing the horse,' he says."

"Oh, Ferd!" Allyson began to storm. But then noticed that both Ruby and John were smiling widely, and slowly she started to smile herself. "That didn't really happen, did it?" she asked then. "I mean, your mother . . ."

"Mother," Ferdinand interrupted while John and Ruby laughed out loud, "why, she's a caution and an honest-to-goodness wonder. So's her mother before her, who is my grandmother, as I allow you'll agree when you hear. I like 'em. But Pa, he can't take Grandma for no more'n two hours in any six weeks, he can't. So April last, when Grandma comes to visit, Pa takes about all the vexation his constitution can stand up to. Of course, Grandma was awful cross, and she seemed set on staying most of forever, so Pa, he got desperate and put a wad of cotton in Grandma's ear trumpet so's she couldn't hear anything, and she thought she was going plumb deaf and left that very day for home to see her doctor. Pa, he's a caution too, as I allow you'll agree."

Now all the inhabitants of the Oldsmobile were laughing, and Ferdinand was enjoying himself so much that even he smiled, at least a little.

"And speaking of folks being a caution," he drawled as the automobile sped along, "my uncle Adoniram Huckstressor was a caution, too. He was a farmer and a hard-shell Baptist preacher. Once when Mother says, 'Uncle Ad is a power,' Pa says, 'Git out, you don't mean power, you mean pow-wow-er.' That made Mother pretty mad, I'll tell you, though Uncle Ad does filibuster considerable. He's close with a dollar, too, awful close. One time he went into a hardware store to get a tin cup, and after he'd looked careful at several, he says, 'How much is this one?' 'Nickel,' says the storekeeper. Then Uncle Ad says, 'I s'pose you make the usual reduction to the clergy?'"

All laughed harder than before, and Ferd went on.

"Tell you more about Uncle Ad," he said. "One time winter last he got awful mad at a church meetin' because things didn't go his way, and he stomped out yellin', 'My hands is clear! I wash my skirts of the whole matter, and I won't be back!' he says. Then, outside, he found he'd forgot his specs, and he had to sneak back in and get 'em, with everybody snickerin' up their sleeves. I reckon he felt purty cheap, he did.

"Uh . . . where we going, John?"

"Only for a ride, son. We're following that fellow on the horse. Sounds like quite a family you have there."

"Yep," Ferdinand stated. "Plumb crazy. Fact is, last time Grandma came to visit, Pa caught her out of her chair and down on her knees washin' and scrubbin' the floor. 'Mercy!' Pa exclaimed when he saw her. 'Have you gone off your rocker?' he asked. Reckon maybe all us Burroughs have.

"Why, I recollect the time—"

"John," Ruby interrupted, "I haven't seen—"

"They're somewhere up ahead," John responded quietly. "Are we in Pleasant Grove City yet?"

"Matter of fact, we did just enter the city limits."

"Must be something going on here," John mused. "Look at that crowd."

"I haven't the slightest idea what it might be."

"I hope that Frank's close enough," John continued. "If those two birds get into that crowd, they'll abandon that buggy sure as rain falls down. Faith, me garjus lass, and that'll be a haythun disaster."

Suddenly Johnny whipped the automobile around, neatly spilling Allyson into the lap and arms of the pleasantly surprised Ferdinand Burroughs.

"I. . . oh . . . I didn't mean . . ." Allyson stammered as she righted herself.

"Think nothing of it," Ferdinand grinned as he helped her, "for I will. Fact is, I won't be thinkin' of nothin' else."

Pulling off the road, Johnny climbed slowly to the ground. "Sorry to do this, folks, but I'll be back momentarily."

Ruby watched him walk away, his limp noticeable, his shoulders stooped.

"Mighty mysterious, ain't he?" Ferdinand declared.

"Mysterious?" Allyson questioned. "Haunted's a better word. I get the jitters just thinking about what might be going on."

"Jitters? Allyson, I've got me a cousin name of Alphie Jitters Montooth, and one day he says to me, 'Ferd,' he says, 'I won't never be sold down the river—'"

"Ferd, not now! For goodness sake, don't you *ever* run out of relatives?"

"Well, relatives are a relative thing, Allyson. For instance, Pa's got this great-great-uncle whose grandson's nephew's daughter was my kissin' cousin a year or so back at this family ruination we held. I knowed we was related, but she could lay a smooch on a feller quicker'n Mother slappin' my hands out of her cookie dough. She layed a few on me, long ones that like to curl a feller's toenails, and I most got addicted. Then the ruination ended, she went one way and I went another, and I like to have expired from lack of social nourishment. Standin' aside for you, she set up the best anatomical juxtaposition of two ollicular muscles in a state of semicontraction that I ever saw. So like I was saying, relatives is a purely relative thing."

Allyson rolled her eyes in dismay, and Ruby smiled at her. "First time," she said, "that I ever heard a fellow out-talk a girl with just plain jabbering."

"Oh," Ferdinand said, "she generally gets the upper hand, though I warn her she ought not do it too often. Ma's cousin Stella always got the upper hand, too. But she ended up like the Greek soldier name of Ajax, defyin' the lightning bolts of matrimony to the day she died—"

"Well, there comes Mr. Phips," Allyson declared, cutting Ferdinand off at the verbal pass. "He doesn't look very happy, either."

"Either that or he knows that he's lost his chances with Grandma Alder," muttered Ferdinand. "He's certain stuck on you, ma'am."

"Do you think so?" Ruby asked quickly.

"No doubt of it, no doubt at all. I've seen gents that were stuck before, but never one that was stuck quite so deep. Fact is, there was this fellow worked for Pa, name of Fester somethin'-or-other, and he had him a cute little girl name of Gertrude P. Pennybottom, and he says to Pa one day, he says . . ."

Ferdinand rambled on, but Ruby stopped listening, her attention focused on John Phips.

"Confound it!" John muttered as he climbed into the car.

"You mean . . ."

"I mean he lost them in that crowd. How could Frank have been so clumsy?"

"Now what?"

John Phips looked down into the gently inquiring face of Ruby Alder. "Now I don't know, Ruby. I reckon all that is left is to search them out and hope that we get lucky. Now let's get you home. I imagine that you've had enough chasing for one day."

"Or one lifetime. I just wish—"

Only John Phips wasn't listening. Instead, his mind was back on the men he had followed, and as Ruby listened, she heard him muttering under his breath.

"Dern!" he fumed. "Now what am I to do? Alder will be bombed, and I can't . . . I can't . . . Holy Michael O'Murphy, why does it have to be *him* who writes those editorials?"

"Johnny . . ."

John looked down at her, closed his mouth abruptly, and only then, as he started the Oldsmobile back onto the road, did Ruby become aware that, in the back sat, Ferdinand Burroughs was still telling his stories.

Day 5

Tuesday

October 25, 1910

Chapter 15

"Johnny," Ruby called from her back door, "there's a call for you on the telephone."

John, just finishing milking the cow, looked up in surprise.

"For me?" he said.

"Well, that's what Effie says."

Slowly John made his way out of the corral, his rheumatism slowing his walking. At the rear door he stamped the dirt from his shoes. And then, removing his hat, he stepped inside.

"There's surely a storm coming somewhere," he said as he eyed the wooden telephone box on the wall. "Who is it? Do you know?"

"Effie," Ruby called up into the mouthpiece, "who is it?"

For a moment she listened, and then she turned back to John. "Jake? Does that make any sense to you?"

John smiled. "Enough. I'll take it."

Reaching out, Ruby almost handed him the earpiece, but then she suddenly drew it back and turned back to the mouthpiece.

"Thank you, Effie. Mr. Phips is here, so would you please get off the line?"

There was an abrupt click, and with a smile of satisfaction, Ruby handed the earpiece to John.

"Yes?" he questioned, speaking quietly.

Ruby walked away as he spoke, but she could not help but see the concern that appeared on John's face. Something was troubling him, and Ruby was certain it was serious.

Oh, if only she could help! If there were only some way that she could ease the burden that John was carrying. But she could not imagine how she could.

"Bad news?" she asked when John replaced the earpiece, doing her best to push her constantly lingering doubts from her mind.

"No, not exactly. I'm just not certain what to do. I've spent since early this morning doing all I know how to do, to track those birds down and to protect William's office and his home. But I can't find them, Frank Burns can't find them, and neither one of us is effective at protecting Will Alder. I just wish he would listen so we could tell him what he's up against."

"Could you and Frank go in and see him?" Ruby asked.

"We might could. We've talked about it off and on all day, and we both made a mistake. We should have gone to him first off, before you and me and a whole lot of personal ancient history got all mixed up in it. Now the poor man is so caught up in worry about what I seem to be doing to you that he won't even consider listening to me."

"I don't think that little speech yesterday helped either," Ruby said sadly.

"No," John agreed. "That's another in a long line of my mistakes. I didn't think Frank Burns was watching me, so I had to verbally get his attention and send a message that way. It has worked for us before, at a couple of rallies, and so I thought it would work again. I never even considered that William might think it a threat. Ruby, I'm just getting too old for this sort of thing. I think maybe I'd best–"

The telephone jangled loudly, and both John and Ruby jumped as if they had been shot. John smiled sheepishly, and Ruby smiled back and then took the call.

While she spoke, John stood at the window, staring off into the distance. With half her mind Ruby continued to worry about him, and with the other half she did her best to listen to Allyson.

"Yes," she answered. "It might work, but I haven't . . . Are you *sure,* Allyson?"

Her granddaughter responded, and so with a smile and a promise, Ruby hung up.

"Ruby, I think I ought to leave," John said.

Startled, and with a terrible pain quickly expanding within her, Ruby stared at the old man.

"L-leave?"

"Yes. This has been wonderful, and you'll never know how

much it has meant to me. But things are not working out like I had thought, and I don't want to get you caught in anything that might bring you any more hurt and sorrow. You've had enough of that from me. Besides, this thing is getting out of hand, and I don't know if I have the strength or the intelligence to stop it. By leaving, I will make certain that you, at least, will be protected."

"That . . . that was a nice speech," Ruby declared quietly.

"Well, it was a sincere one."

"But misguided. Johnny, if you have been honest with me, then nothing that could happen, absolutely *nothing,* would cause me greater sorrow than your departure."

"Ruby—"

"Johnny, I mean it. I couldn't take being left alone—not *again*."

John Phips sighed deeply and then sat down in the old horsehair rocker, where he continued to stare off into the distance.

"Ruby, I really don't have a choice, especially now. I've got to leave you. But before I do, I think I owe you an explanation about these past few days. Like you said, I owe you a little honesty."

"Johnny, *please*. I don't think I can stand it."

Tears were welling up in Ruby's eyes, and John quickly looked away. Ruby didn't know if it was because he was unable to stand the sight of her foolishness, or if it was because he didn't want to see her hurting. So she tried to stop crying, but the harder she tried, the less able she was to do so.

"Ruby," John finally declared, "I can't help it! I'm only thinking of you. If I haven't been totally open with you, it was to protect you. The feelings I have expressed for you, however, are open and more honest than anything else I have said or done in my entire life. And that's why I must leave. I can't bear the thought of hurting you, of causing you more pain. Ruby, sweetheart, with all my heart I love you! That is why I must go."

"No, you *don't* love me, John Phips!" Ruby snapped through her tears. "Not if you leave! Men always use that old line as an excuse for getting out of . . . of their responsibilities!"

"Ruby, people could die. *You* could die."

"Johnny, I'm going to die anyway. I'm an old woman. My body aches just like yours does, and until you walked into my yard and started chopping my wood, I was anxious to get my dying done with. Now I don't want to die, unless I have you beside me, and then I'd like to put it off for another seventy-odd years. But I guarantee you this, John Phips—I'll die a lot sooner if you walk out that door than I will for any other reason."

"Ruby me lass, you don't understand."

"No, Johnny, *you* don't understand. I may not understand all of what is going on, but neither do I think it can be solved by your leaving. To me, what is important is that I want to be with you. Now please stop talking about going away."

John stopped trying to explain, and for several moments the two were quiet, John thinking and Ruby sniffing and drying her tears.

"That was Allyson on the telephone," she finally said softly. "She and Ferdinand have invited us on an outing tonight."

"An outing?" John replied absently, his thoughts obviously elsewhere.

"Yes, but I won't tell you about it unless you pay attention to me."

Slowly John's eyes focused and turned to Ruby. "You know," he said quietly while a smile grew upon his face, "I think you're *better* looking than those Gibson girls. I especially like your blue eyes—how you look at me from behind them."

Ruby blushed. "Oh, stuff and nonsense. Shows how much you know about anything. My eyes have cataracts, and I can hardly see you at all."

"You can't fool me," Johnny teased, grinning. "I know, O fainthearted one, that you have hardly been able to keep your eyes off me."

"I wish I could *really* see you," Ruby teased back. "It'd serve you right, having all your false hopes blasted so thoroughly and so quickly by my telling you what I could see. Now what about that outing?"

"What outing? I don't recollect—"

Ruby sighed. "John Phips, I *knew* you weren't listening. Now pay attention, for I won't say this again. Allyson and Ferdinand have invited us on an outing with them tonight, and I'd like to go."

"What . . . what do they have in mind?"

"Well, if you had had a day, we were thinking of going to Saltair."

"Isn't that a resort up on the Great Salt Lake?"

"It is. There are games to play and a roller-coaster that you wouldn't get me any nearer to than a hundred acres of poison ivy guarded by hornets. And, of course, folks go floating in the lake."

"Well, we can't go there, so what do you have in mind now?"

"Do you mean that you'll go?"

"Only if we can shut that Ferdinand kid's mouth for the evening."

Ruby laughed. "Maybe he's out of relatives."

"Not that boy. I've a hunch most of those relatives were born in the fertile but twisted valleys of his own warped brain."

"Johnny, that's awful!"

"So are his stories."

"But you laughed."

John grinned. "I know. Shows what an old fool I've grown to be. Ring 'em up on that telephone contraption, and let's get on with this grand tour."

Ruby picked up the telephone and took hold of the crank, and then she paused.

"Should I invite Willy and Flora?" she asked.

"Why not?" John grinned. "Flora seemed to like me, and given most of an evening, maybe I could convert Willy."

"Give him time, Johnny."

"That's easy to say when you have it, Ruby. Unfortunately I don't."

"Maybe you have more than you realize."

"And maybe we *all* have less."

Ruby sighed. "Well, you don't mind if I ask them, do you?"

"I surely don't. And by the way, me garjus wee lass, I really *do* like your eyes."

Chapter 16

Rarely had Ruby enjoyed an evening more. Willy and Flora didn't go, but John and Ferdinand and Allyson did, and the four of them had more fun than she could even imagine. They went for a ride, and as they rode they sang such favorites as "Come, Josephine, in My Flying Machine," "Bird in a Gilded Cage," "You're a Grand Old Flag," "My Wife's Gone to the Country, Hurrah! Hurrah!" and "Shine On, Harvest Moon," a song made famous by Nora Bayes and Jack Norworth.

Later in their ride they drove west toward Lehi across the dry farms, with Ruby explaining the history of the Orrin Porter Rockwell tavern site, located just north of Lehi; John telling a few whaling stories from his life at sea; and Ferdinand continually regaling the group with tales of his "pestiferous and nefarious" relatives.

"Oh, my hair!" Allyson gasped as a particularly heavy gust of wind slammed into the southbound automobile, tossing her hair even more than it had already been tossed.

"Hair?" Ferdinand asked, while both Ruby and John immediately began laughing. "Hair, you say? Well, folks, let me tell you about Mother's Uncle Tom's cousin, fellow name of Beezum Tweedie. He's a professor, teaches penmanship at some high-falutin' college school, and he knows Shakespeare better'n old Mahomet knew the Koran, or so Pa says. But ain't he a hairy one, though. Once him and a fellow name of Frank Mendenhall was doing Brutus and Cassius wrapped up in sheets in Liberty Hall up in Bozeman, and when Beezum says, 'Here is muh dagger and here muh naked breast!' Pa hollers out, 'Get a shave, Prof, so's you won't be a liar.' Well, it pretty nigh busted up the show."

"Should have just stabbed him in the back," Allyson giggled.

"Oh, my, no," Ferdinand declared, shaking his long, serious face. "That wouldn't have worked none either. Old Beezum had more hair on his back than he had in front. Pa always allowed Beezum was just some poor kidnapped ape that somebody'd hauled up from Africa and shaved a little off the face of.

"But faces? We got two in our family that are more than regular famous, if you know what I mean. The first belongs to Aunt Phoebe, who married up with Mother's brother Jed, who is an awful good singer and who used to travel with Doc Lighthall. He's handsome, too, I think; but Aunt Phoebe ain't very. Mother says she used to be awful pretty till after she got the rheumatism so bad, but Pa says he guesses she must of had it before ever he saw her.

"Pa says she went to a party one time down to Nephi with Uncle Jed, where they was givin' a prize to the one who could make the most homeliest face, and when she walked in the judge walked right over to her and give her the prize. Aunt Phoebe says, surprised-like, 'Why, I ain't even begun yet.'

"Aunt Phoebe sings too, but let me tell you, she's got a voice what's a terror to snakes and all forms of small rodents, and I don't want to talk about it, either.

"The second famous face belongs to the husband of Pa's sister Elviry, fellow by the name of Alvy Freemantle. Now there's a pair, Alvy and Elviry, but of the two, Alvy's got the hardest mug. He was a lieutenant of artil'ry with President Roosevelt during the last war, and he done real well. Pa says the reason why is 'cause of his looks. Pa says, 'Why, if I was a Cuban and seen that expression onto Alvy's mug and him a comin' at me, I wouldn't only hit the high places during my departure,' he says."

By then John and Ruby were holding their sides with the droll humor of the lanky youth named Ferdinand Burroughs. Allyson didn't see all the humor that her grandmother saw, but she smiled and laughed with them anyway, and more and more she was becoming impressed with her young neighbor.

"And speakin' of soldiers," Ferdinand continued, "there's Winfield Scott Zachary Taylor Peebles, Mother's cousin. He was named for two old heroes, Revolutionary War I think it was. Anyway, he could always think of the grandest and noblest things to say. Once when he was in the war, an officer got killed, and they put Cousin Win in his place, so that's how he got to be a corporal. First thing he says was, after whoever it was appointed him to his place, 'Boys,' he says, 'if I fall in this day's battle, march over muh dead corpse just as you would that of a common private!'"

"Humble," John declared.

"Absolutely."

"Especially for a private."

"Correct," Ferdinand continued unabated. "And just hearin' the word *private* reminds me of the twins, Abner and Freddie Spinks, who belong to the youngest daughter of Pa's oldest sister's first husband—"

"Say," Ruby interrupted, trying to stop the ubiquitous flow of verbiage splashing forth from behind her, "wish we were closer to Samuel Wagstaff's or George Jacklin's homes."

"Wh-why?" John asked through his laughter.

"They make molasses, and I could sure do with a molasses sandwich to feed poor Ferdinand. Only thing I can think of that would hold his mouth closed.

"Say, all of you," she declared then. "I've an idea. A year or so back the Ramsey Brothers remodeled the motion-picture house, and I haven't been inside since. Their equipment is good, or so I've been told, and they even have a player piano, so it never misses any notes. Should we see a motion picture?"

All agreed, and the next hour was spent watching the latest in cinematic adventure and romance in the Lyric Theatre. Once the picture ended, they walked north to the Apollo Hall, which had been operating since 1903. It had a spring floor, the first of its kind in the state, and was owned by Joseph J. Jackson, Thomas E. Steele, and associates.

There they danced until Ruby thought she would surely drop, and until John finally did.

"Can't do any more," John moaned as he led Ruby to the side and out into the darkened foyer. "I might have been young once, but the way my leg's carrying on, it's been a spell."

"Your leg," Ruby argued as she limped to the open door, "can still dance circles around mine. After tonight my varicose veins will have varicose veins on them."

"Those two inside don't seem bothered."

"Well, young love is blind to pain as well as to almost everything else."

For a time they sat in silence as Edison's marvelous talking machine ground out another dance inside. Then, as the sound died and Allyson and Ferd talked with the half-dozen other couples out on the floor, John spoke again.

"It's been a wonderful evening, Ruby. Thank you for sharing it with me."

"Johnny, the pleasure has been mine. You've been such a gentleman."

"Well, maybe I've learned a little in the last fifty years. Faith and I shure needed to."

"Johnny, forget that, will you?"

"I wish I could, Ruby me lass. I wasn't much of a man . . ."

"John Phips, you're a fine man, and I appreciate how you have treated me, more than you can know. Why, as simple a thing as that fifteen-minute break you gave me a little while ago did wonders for my tired old body."

John, his eyes again distant, did not respond, and Ruby felt herself wondering again, wondering.

"Maybe you and I can get a moment to sit down together with Willy," she suggested, trying to get him back. "If we go in together, certain of ourselves, maybe we can clear all this up."

"I . . . I don't know. I—"

Whuuuumph!

The muffled sound of the explosion was nowhere near so noticeable as the shaking of the dance hall, and for an instant everyone froze. Then, with a groan, John Phips limped hurriedly out the door and down the steps.

"Johnny, what is it?"

"Willy's office! Stay here."

"Willy!" Ruby cried as she ran after the rapidly limping John Phips, "not my son . . ."

"Confound it all," John was muttering as he hurried toward the small office where William Alder did his writing. "I *knew* I shouldn't have listened to them! If I'd just done what I felt . . . Oh, I hope he wasn't in there. Why did I pick tonight of all nights to go off acting like a little kid? Confound it all, if William was in that office . . ."

The office, when they arrived, was surrounded by people. Or at least what was left of the office was surrounded. A little fire still burned here and there, but the blast had been of sufficient force to literally dismantle all of the building but the foundation.

"Faith," John muttered. "The murderin' whelps must've used more blastin' powder than those Cuban lads lit off under Admiral Dewey."

"Willy?" Ruby cried. "Oh, Willy . . ."

"Ruby, honey, you stay here!" John ordered sternly, ignoring her pleas.

"But Johnny—"

"Please don't argue! I'll find out about Willy, and then I'll be right back. I promise."

"Johnny, please hurry. I must know about Willy."

Fighting the fear that filled her, Ruby stood with tear-streaked face, watching as John limped into the rapidly gathering crowd. Her mind whirled, and desperately she filled her mind with prayer, pleading both for Willy and for John Phips, praying that both of them would be all right.

"Well, Mother, are you satisfied?"

With a small scream of surprise, Ruby whirled to face her soot-covered son.

"Oh, Willy," she cried, "thank God you're all right!"

"I am, no thanks to that old man you've been harboring."

"You . . . you mean *Johnny?*"

"None other. Mother, I told you we'd all suffer if you didn't send him packing. Now he's done this, trying his best to murder me in the process."

"No, Willy! Johnny wouldn't—"

"Mother, you don't know that old man even a little. If he'd only been after your money it would have been bad enough. But this! Oh, why did I let you bamboozle me?"

"Where is he, Mrs. Alder?"

With tears now running freely, Ruby stared at Marshal Harvey Hamilton, who now stood beside her son.

"I . . . I don't know . . ."

"Mother, the man's a known criminal, and has been for years! Harvey here has information linking him to the Molly Maguires in Pennsylvania way back in 1877. He was in Telluride in 1902 when Arthur Collins was killed, and three years ago he was in Boise during the 'Big Bill' Haywood murder trial."

"Wh-what? I don't remember—"

"Sure you do. When Haywood was tried for assisting in the murder of former Idaho Governor Frank Steunenberg. That athiest lawyer Clarence Darrow got Haywood off on a technicality, but your John Phips was there just the same.

"Mother, he's a Wobblie and an anarchist, it is obvious that he works for the unions, and it's *more* than obvious what he has done to me."

"Do you know where Phips is, Mrs. Alder?"

"He . . . he went . . . to see if Willy had been . . . Oh, Willy, he didn't do it! I know he didn't!"

"Do you know where he was tonight?"

"Yes . . . yes I do. We went to the picture show and then to the Apollo Hall to dance. We were there when the explosion occurred!"

"Were you with him every minute?"

"Yes, I . . . I . . ."

"Mother, why do you hesitate?"

"I . . . uh . . ."

"He left for a few moments, didn't he!"

"Willy, when a man gets old, or a woman, too, for that matter, they must make rather frequent trips outside."

"How long was he gone?"

Ruby looked frantically at her son. "N-not long. When you're older, those things take longer, and—"

"That cinches it," Marshal Hamilton declared quietly. "Let's go get him."

And while Ruby Alder buried her face in her tired old hands and wept, William Alder and Harvey Hamilton turned and began forcing their way through the crowd surrounding the demolished office, seeking the arrest of one John Phips, "anarchist."

Day 6

Wednesday

October 26, 1910

Chapter 17

Silently the large old man sat on the bleachers, staring out into the moisture-shrouded Wednesday afternoon. The rain fell steadily upon Los Angeles and its environs; but there was little wind, and the man was sheltered by the high, sloping roof that covered the short grandstand, and so did not get wet.

Out in the field a few pigeons wheeled in the downpour, but most of the hundred thousand birds that made up the famous James Y. Johnson Pigeon Farm were in their coops, long rows of hundreds of stacked pens that bordered the feeding field.

In wonder, the man shook his head. He was amazed that so many pigeons could be gathered into one place *anywhere*. And their sole function, which to him was even more amazing, was the laying of eggs that would hatch out into squab, half-grown baby pigeons. Those, served plucked but uncleaned and steaming hot under glass, had become a delicacy and connoisseur's delight throughout the United States and Europe.

Then, too, he was amazed that the place had become such a tourist attraction. Postcards showing the ranch were sold throughout the West, he had read articles on it in journals published as far away as London, and the Union Pacific Railroad had even built a spur to the ranch in order to accommodate shipping and interested tourists.

The old man had never before been here himself, but somehow the thought of a hundred thousand pigeons wheeling overhead didn't excite him, and so he didn't think he ever would have visited the place. That is, he wouldn't have visited if it hadn't been for—

"Howdy."

Turning, the old man looked up into the eyes of an equally old and equally large gentleman, whose mustache was very similar to his own.

"Hello," he responded quietly.

"Mighty foul weather," the second man said as he sat down. "No pun intended, of course."

"Of course. Are pigeons fowl?"

"Well, they smell like it. I can't believe I own a whole farm of 'em. Mighty interesting seeing the unexpected directions a man's life takes."

For a moment the two sat in silence.

"I hear these storms travel all the way inland, clear to Utah," said the second man.

"Is that so?"

"Way I heard it, by tomorrow this one will be punchin' those Mormon folks pretty hard."

"Interesting. You're James Y. Johnson?"

"I am. And you're the legendary Wyatt Earp."

"Some days," the first old man grinned. "The rest of the time, it's too much trouble even to claim I'm related. From what I hear, you've had a similar problem."

The man called James Johnson turned. "You know?"

"Man keeps his ear to the ground, he learns a lot. For instance, I know you're real name's Soderberg, and I know the Feds once wanted you up in Utah. For all I know, maybe they still do. There are many reasons why a man keeps his name quiet."

"You're right."

The two sat silently then for several minutes, listening to the steady drumming of rain on the grandstand.

"Not much activity out there today," James Soderberg finally declared.

"There is if you're looking backward," Wyatt Earp responded quietly.

"Backward?"

"Uh-huh. Into the past."

"Ghosts, you mean?"

"Plenty of 'em."

Carefully then, Wyatt Earp pulled his watch out of his vest pocket, flipped open the cover, and checked the time. "It's funny," he said quietly, "how you and I have been thinking alike today. You spoke of unexpected twists in a man's life, and I've been sitting here thinking exactly the same."

"We do have them."

"That we do. I find it amazing that a few seconds in a seventy-year life-span will absolutely determine the road a man will follow for the rest of it. And those few seconds are no different than any others, so far as a man can see when he's coming up on them.

"See this watch? Two o'clock in the afternoon. Jim, I . . . Do you mind if I call you Jim?"

"Not a bit."

"Good. Twenty-nine years ago today, Jim, in 1881, at precisely this hour, my few life-determining seconds began. It was even on a Wednesday, just like today."

"Was that the famous gun battle at the OK Corral?"

"It sure was. Me, my brothers Morgan and Virgil, and Doc Holiday were involved. All of us had responsibility for keeping the law down in Tombstone. That day we went up against a bunch of outlaws, part of a band called the Clanton band. The ones we fought were Ike and Billy Clanton, Frank and Tom McLowry, and Billy Claiborne.

"Now, you have to remember, Jim, that the fight occurred in just a few short seconds. Still, the entire scene is burned into my mind as though with a branding iron. I'll never forget it as long as I live."

"I don't think I'd like a memory like that, Wyatt."

Wyatt Earp sat quietly, his face sober. "I don't like it either, Jim. I just don't know how to get rid of it. Whenever I close my eyes, I see men dying. I hear gunfire everywhere, I see faces filled with fear or hatred, and I can't get shut of the nightmare."

"Sounds like a regular war you fought."

"It was—a short, deadly little war. The way I've counted it, Jim, there were seventeen shots fired by each side. Three of the five rustlers died, and three of the four of us were wounded. It's still hard for me to believe, but I was the only one who stood up to the fire and came through unscathed.

"But the scars are there, nevertheless," Wyatt continued. "By Christmas of that year, many folks, at least those who read the Tombstone *Nugget,* thought *we* were the outlaws.

"If they'd read Clum's *Tombstone Epitaph,* they'd have read something else. I've memorized it, and I quote: 'The feeling among the best class of our citizens is that the marshal was entirely justifiable in his efforts to disarm these men, and that being fired upon they had to defend themselves, which they did most bravely.'

"Later on, Judge Wells Spicer held an inquest and examination on a murder complaint that had been filed by Ike and Sheriff Behan against Doc and me. Judge Spicer found not only Doc and me, but Virgil and Morgan as well, innocent of all charges.

"But unfortunately it didn't end there. Right after Christmas, Virgil was shot from ambush and maimed for life. Then in the spring, Morgan was murdered, and I suppose Doc and I went on a vendetta—Sheriff Behan and his crooked law machine in Cochise County just wouldn't help.

"Down in Tucson, I caught up with Frank Stilwell, who had helped kill my brother Morgan. After my shootout with Stilwell, Sheriff Behan tried to arrest me for *that* murder. But Behan had been crooked all along, and I paid no attention to the warrant.

"Not long after, I found Indian Charlie, whose real name was Florentine Cruz, and Curly Bill Brocius. They'd both been in on the shootings of Virgil and Morgan. It didn't take me long to give each of them a fatal dose of .44 slugs or Wells Fargo shotgun pellets.

"After that, Sheriff Behan organized his forces and drove Doc and me up into Colorado, and things have just been a continual round ever since. I've run saloons in Colorado, Coeur d'Alene, and El Paso. I even ran a saloon for a time in Nome, Alaska."

"So in all of that you never got wounded?"

"Nope, but I have been shot, though I'm embarrassed to tell you how."

"What did you do? Shoot yourself?"

"Just about. It was when I got careless in a card game up in Lake City, Colorado. I was accused of cheating, took exception to the charge, even though there was some justification for it, and ended up with a bullet in my arm. The other fellow came out way ahead on that deal."

"That must have been a bad day," James sympathized.

"Well, I have had better. But it taught me a good lesson, and I haven't dealt from the bottom of the deck since then."

"I heard you had a tangle with Clay Allison. You don't mind if I mention these altercations, do you? I've heard about them so often and for so long that it's plumb interesting hearing the facts from one who ought to know them."

"I don't mind. But as to facts, my memory's no better'n anybody else's. Still, I do remember Clay, and I did have a run-in with him—him, John Wesley Hardin, 'Rowdy' Joe Lowe, Sergeant King, and Mannen Clemments. This last bunch I met up with in Wichita. I never did have shoot-outs with them, though. Thumping them on the head with my log-barreled Buntline Special, coldcocking or buffaloing, it was called, has always been my style.

"That's how I took out Clay Allison, down in Dodge, right in front of the Long Branch Saloon. I thumped him when he tried to shoot me. Allison was a bonafide crazy killer. He used to ride naked in the streets shooting at folks, and one night he had a knife fight with a fellow in a new grave out on boot hill just to see which one would fill the grave. Clay didn't."

"Sounds like he wasn't much of a Christian."

Wyatt laughed. "He wasn't. But then, Christianity sort of took a back seat in those wild and woolly days. I've often wondered if I'd been a better man had I stayed where the frontier wasn't."

"Well, most of us have regrets, Wyatt. In a fit of anger I left my wives behind in Utah when the Feds put the heat on me for polygamy, and that was seventeen years ago. Now we've drifted so far apart that I don't know if I'll ever even see them again. It's been awful, and I've often wondered the same thing. What if I'd done it different?"

The two men sat silently then, each wrapped in his own thoughts, each consumed with the heavy burden of memories. Finally James spoke again.

"What are you doing now?" he asked quietly.

"Well, I've refereed a prize fight or two, I've looked for gold out in Tonopah, Nevada, and lately I've been guarding bullion for one of the banks here in Los Angeles. They pay me well, and the job's fairly easy. I'm also developing some real estate, and with one thing or another my third wife, Josephine, and I, seem to manage."

"You've had three wives?"

"Yep," Wyatt agreed. "But I've never had a whole passel of 'em all at one time. What's that like, if you don't mind my asking?"

"Oh, I don't mind. It's about like being penned up in the OK Corral for fifteen or twenty years straight, with seventeen shots a minute coming at you—and your own gun usually empty."

The two old men laughed and then grew quiet.

"I guess we all carry our own ghosts," Wyatt declared.

"That we do . . . that we do. Now, what did you want to meet me about?"

"Well," Wyatt responded quietly, "maybe nothing. But it might be something. And if it is, and I don't tell you, I'll be carrying a few more ghosts. That's why I'm here."

"I'm not certain I understand."

"Well, I'll explain. Years ago I worked a freight line from San Bernardino to Salt Lake City. I got to know you Mormons some and made a few friends, and I was always treated well. There was even a bishop once who stood up for me when I was in a bad fix, and he got me out of it. That means I owe him, and since he's long dead, I reckon I owe the Mormons in general. And whatever else is said of me, let it never be said that I have forgotten my friends.

"The other day, playing cards, I heard such a thing as might be of interest to some of your people. That's what I want to pass along."

"So, why did you come to *me?*" James asked.

"Jim, you're the only man I know in Los Angeles who is a for-sure Mormon. Besides, I heard you used to be a bishop, and that other man taught me that bishops can be trusted."

"I was a bishop, all right. As for my integrity, you can hear both sides of that issue. Depends on who you ask."

"As with most of us," Wyatt chuckled. "Anyway, I figure I can trust you. Do you want to take this information on?"

"Well, I'll see. What is it?"

"A crazy deal, if I ever heard one. You remember a couple of weeks or so ago when the *Times* office was bombed? Last night I heard that the fellows who did it are holed up in Utah—place called Pleasant Grove. They've got another job planned up there."

James, his mind whirling, stared at the elderly marshal.

"Do you . . . do you have any idea how important it is to me to receive this information?"

Surprised, Wyatt looked at him. "No. Do you mean personally?"

"I'll say! Wyatt, from what I can learn, those birds are nesting in Pleasant Grove until they can kill my nephew, a fellow by the name of Will Alder. That's their job."

"Will Alder is *your* nephew?"

"Has been since he was born," James countered. "Funny fellow. Stiff as a ramrod, but he is honest, and he does know his facts."

"I know," Wyatt mumbled. "I read his editorials."

"Wyatt, do you know exactly where those men are in Pleasant Grove?"

Quietly, Wyatt considered the question. "Matter of fact, Jim, I believe I do. At least I heard it. Now all I have to do is recollect it. They're holed up on a street name of . . . of *Locust,* in what's called the old Ed Platt home. It's rock, an older home, they say. And it faces the mountains. That's all I heard."

James breathed a sigh of relief. "Wyatt, I'm beholden. I've been worried about my nephew, and this information just might save his life. I'll send a telegram right away."

"Hope it helps, Jim. I've been mixed up in a little bloodletting in my day, but I don't hold with out-'n-out, indiscriminate murder. Bombs do just that, killing anybody nearby. Like I say, I don't hold with that at all."

"Neither do I. Want any squab, Wyatt? I feel like I owe you something."

"No . . . no thank you."

"Take some. I've even got some pies made up ready for cooking. Be happy to give you a dozen."

Wyatt grinned ruefully. "Jim, I've eaten a lot of things in my life, but somehow I just can't bring myself to eat uncleaned half-growed pigeons that are still wearing their feet."

The man called James Y. Johnson laughed easily. "Tell you the truth, Wyatt," he declared as he rose to his feet, "I don't blame you. I don't eat them either. I just throw out three tons of wheat a day, gather the pigeons in, take their babies, pop their necks, and ship them out. Then I smile all the way to the bank."

Both men laughed heartily, shook hands, and then together walked out into the increasingly intense October storm. And, at least from this visit, Wyatt Earp carried no further ghosts.

Chapter 18

When Ruby opened her door in response to the insistent knocking, she was shocked at the coolness of the air. For over a week the days had been glorious and warm. But now, with almost no warning at all, the temperatures had lowered so far that the men outside were wearing overcoats and their breath swirled away in frosty mist.

"H-hello, Marshal," she said, her voice catching in her throat.

"Mornin', Mrs. Alder. It's turned off mighty cold out here, hasn't it."

Silently Ruby nodded. She was frightened by the cold, but not for her. She was frightened for Johnny. What on earth would he do? He had no coat, no warm home to stay in . . .

"May we come in?" Marshal Hamilton asked.

"Of . . . of course."

The three men entered the warmth of Ruby's home, and she bade them be seated.

"Mrs. Alder," Marshal Hamilton said, "this is Marshal Bill Bromley, and of course you know George Cunningham, American Fork's city justice."

"How do you do, gentlemen."

"Mrs. Alder, we . . . uh . . . we have a warrant for the arrest of John Phips. If he's here, we'd like you to get him for us."

"A . . . a warrant? But on what charge?"

"Arson, Mrs. Alder. Arson and attempted murder."

Ruby's ears pounded with the sudden pressure that filled her head, and for a moment she thought she was going to faint. He hadn't done those things—she *knew* he hadn't! Why couldn't they see it? Why on earth did Willy—

"Did Willy sign the . . . the warrant?"

"The complaint, ma'am. He signed the complaint, and the judge issued the warrant. Is Mr. Phips here?"

"No . . . no he isn't."

"We have a search warrant as well, ma'am. In case it should appear that you are harboring him."

Suddenly Ruby was angry, and it showed in her eyes. "Are you questioning my integrity, Marshal Hamilton?"

"Well, ma'am, it is known that you are not a disinterested party. Mr. Alder, your son, told us to expect little cooperation from you; and so we came prepared for whatever we might find."

"Willy told you *that?*"

"Yes, ma'am. He did."

"That surprises me," Ruby mused. "I thought he knew me better . . . Gentlemen, my home is yours. Look as you will."

"It is known that he lodged in your barn, ma'am."

"Oh, by all means look there as well. In fact, look in the privy, the garage, the outbuildings; look where you will. I have told you that he's not here, and he isn't. I haven't seen him since the explosion last night."

"Thank you, Mrs. Alder. We'll take our look around and then be on our way."

Ruby nodded anxiously, the men began their search, and with hammering heart she sat in her parlor worrying. Where was Johnny Phips? It was getting terribly cold outside, the law was after him for charges that her own son had filed, and she was scared.

So far as she knew, Johnny didn't even have an overcoat. But maybe he wouldn't need one. Maybe he had caught a train and had gone out of town in the same manner he had come in. Perhaps even now he was nearing Los Angeles . . .

No! He wouldn't do that! He wouldn't leave without telling her that he was going. Johnny surely must know how she felt about him. He was a good man, likely even the best man she had ever known. Surely he wouldn't do such a thing to her. To think that was to deny—

"Ma'am?"

"Yes?" she started, turning to face the men.

"There's nothing here, ma'am. We're sorry to have troubled you, and we'll be on our way."

"Thank you."

"You're welcome. And ma'am, if you should happen to see him, we would appreciate a call."

"No, Marshal Hamilton," Ruby declared emphatically, "I won't call. To tell you I would, would be a lie, and I don't lie! John Phips is innocent, and I know it. If you and my well-meaning son would just listen to a few things, you'd know it too."

"Mrs. Alder," Marshal Hamilton said quietly, "with this warrant, it has gone some beyond my listening. You can tell me all you want, and it won't do either one of us any good. Now the issue is for a judge to decide. Please remember that, and remember all that you know, too. We'll catch the old man, and when we do, you will very likely be called upon to testify."

"What if Willy were to drop his complaint?"

"That'd change things some. Our office would still want to talk with John Phips, but only to question him. The only charge we might have would be a 'suspicion' charge."

Ruby sighed. "Very well. Thank you for coming."

"Thank you, ma'am. Have a nice day."

The three men walked out into the cold, and Ruby stood silently, watching them go. She felt so helpless, so old and foolish and inept. Where could Johnny have gone, and how could she possibly help him now that he had?

Turning away from the door, Ruby was startled to see a boy straining his bicycle up the hill, fighting the wind as he strove toward her house. Quickly she stepped out into the cold to see what he wanted.

"M-Mrs. Alder," he gasped as he reached her gate, "telegram here for you."

"Telegram?" Ruby echoed in surprise.

"Yes'm. Here it is."

"Do I owe you anything? I mean, I've never received a telegram before, and—"

"No, ma'am," the youth declared as he beat his hands together to get them warm again. "Not, that is, unless you want to."

Ruby smiled warmly. "Well, come inside then, and be quick about it."

The boy followed, and Ruby opened her purse and took out a silver dollar.

"Is this enough?"

The boy's mouth hung open for an instant, and then quickly he gulped and nodded. "Yes, ma'am, enough and a whole lot more besides. I only make two bits a day, so I don't think you ought to give me all this."

"Oh, stuff and nonsense!" Ruby declared sternly. "Take it and be gone with you."

The youth thanked her, took the dollar, and sprinted for his bike, his mind no doubt filled with visions of where he would invest his newly acquired wealth.

Ruby watched him go, closed the door, and looked at the telegram. Finally, with heart pounding, she tore it open, very carefully, and then she read:

JAKE STOP W EARP SAYS MCNAMARAS OLD ED PLATT HOME PLEASANT GROVE STOP LOCUST STREET FACES MOUNTAINS ROCK STOP BE CAREFUL STOP LOVE TO FAMILY STOP JAMES Y. JOHNSON

Ruby read the cursory telegram over and over. She was certain that she knew what it meant, but how would it help now? Jake had to be Johnny, for the man on the telephone a day or so before had used that name. That also meant that the McNamaras were located in Pleasant Grove. Only how could *she* capture them? How could this telegram from her younger brother possibly do any good? What could she possibly do?

No, not her, she realized. How could *Johnny* do anything about it? He was nowhere to be found. Or was he? Might he even now be out in the barn? Could he have sneaked in and hidden from the marshals?

Quickly taking up her shawl, Ruby hurried out the back door and ran to the barn.

"Johnny!" she called. "Johnny Phips, are you in here?"

There was no answer save for the wind and the soft lowing of her old milk cow.

"Johnny, if you are here, make yourself known to me this instant! I have news, and it's terribly important!"

She waited, her breath stilled in anticipation, her eyes peering into every corner of the old barn. "Johnny—"

"He ain't here, ma'am."

In surprise Ruby spun to face the sober-faced marshal she had met earlier. He held a rifle in his hand, and she could see that he was very serious.

"What . . . what are *you* doing here?"

"Guarding you, Mrs. Alder. That man's dangerous, and there's no telling what he might do to you if he should return. Now about that terribly important news you wanted to tell him . . ."

"It . . . it was nothing," Ruby stammered. "I wanted him to know that you folks were after him."

"And the telegram?"

"It was from my brother."

"May I see it?"

"I . . . I . . ."

"Ma'am."

Slowly Ruby handed the yellow document to the marshal, who scanned it quickly.

"Who's Jake?"

"It . . . it's a name he made up."

The marshal grinned. "Yeah, I call my sister Fred, too. I made it up when we were just kids. She doesn't mind, but no one else would understand. And who is W. Earp? The famous Wyatt, no doubt?"

And with that the marshal laughed with genuine mirth, almost doubling over at such a ludicrous thought.

"And the McNamaras?" he gasped, trying to be serious again.

"People he . . . he wants me to look up."

"He says to be careful. Must be boorish relatives, huh."

"I . . . I guess that's as good a way to put it as any. I'm sure that's why he told me to be careful."

"I know folks like that, myself—I'm related to more than a few of 'em. When you see 'em coming, you want to lock the door and go hide in the root cellar. These McNamara folks just get into town, did they?"

"I think last week."

"Well, Mrs. Alder, I wish you luck with 'em. And don't you worry none about this Phips fellow. We'll get him."

The deputy lifted his rifle and patted it. Ruby did her best to smile, and then she took the telegram and walked back to her home.

For a moment she stood inside the closed door, shivering and thinking. She was being guarded, not protected, and no matter what the marshal out there said, she knew the truth. Willy didn't trust her, and neither did any of the others. Nor, for a fact, did she blame them.

Slowly Ruby turned and walked back into her parlor, where she sat and took up the old teakwood box that contained the treasures of her youth. Slowly she went through them, letting her memories carry her into times past when things had seemed happier, sadder, easier, and more difficult.

Life, she thought ruefully, never seemed to change much. It was one long series of terrible crises, with lulls between them that were composed only of more crises that didn't seem so terrible. It was no wonder that the Lord had instructed his children to '*endure* to the end.' He surely hadn't said 'skip' or 'slide' or 'walk easily.' Life was an endurance test, pure and simple.

And while enduring, what was she going to do about John Phips? What *should* she do?

"Dear God in heaven," she prayed in desperation, "I've got troubles, real troubles, and I don't know where to turn. Johnny is innocent, I feel that he is, I know he . . .

"Lord, *is* Johnny innocent?"

Ruby waited then, as she had learned through her life to wait, exercising her faith by telling the Lord that she knew he could give her an answer, and that she wasn't budging until it came.

And so it did, a warm sweet feeling that filled her heart and mind with the peaceful understanding that Johnny *was* innocent.

"Thank you, Lord," she whispered, "for that answer. Now I have one more question. Will you protect him from my son Willy and those well-thinking men of the law who are seeking him?"

Again she paused to wait, and almost instantly the certainty was there again, a confirmation that John Phips would indeed be protected.

But being a practical woman, Ruby understood that the Lord usually performed his miracles through his children. Only who on earth could possibly . . .

In silence she stared at a photo in her lap, a very old photo of a young man seated with a young woman standing behind him. It was an often-looked-at-photo, yellowed with age, and with two names at the bottom. A man and a woman, stern-faced as in all old photographs, but obviously in love.

So, she thought, men and women frequently fell in love. And when they did, what was a woman's responsibility to that man? Especially what was her responsibility when the man that she loved had such troubles as John Phips was having?

And she loved John Phips—she knew that she did. Willy was right; it didn't make much sense. But it was true, and there was nothing she could do about it.

Now John Phips, the man she loved more than life itself, was in trouble, serious trouble. And *she* was the only one left who might be able to help him. But how *could* she help? Just how did a seventy-year-old, formerly polygamous widow go about finding a chance of survival for a seventy-two-year-old fugitive from justice, even a slim chance? Where could she turn? Who could she ask for help?

Not her family, for that was too much to expect. Not the Church, for the same reason. And not the law; that was out as well.

So if she could get no help in preventing a terrible miscarriage of justice, whom could she turn to?

The answer was obvious, and hopeless.

There was only Ruby Soderberg Alder left to help the lonely old man through his ordeal.

And who was there to help her?

Nobody. Not a solitary mortal soul.

Or was there?

Other than Johnny, she had but two people she felt she might trust in this situation. The first was her granddaughter, Allyson Alder, who might just as quickly go to her father as not. And she should, Ruby decided instantly. A young girl should never be torn away from her father. So Allyson was out.

And that left only the highly unusual and outspoken Ferdinand Burroughs, who acted as quirky when he had no reason to, as ever he did when he was in public. And who was just as likely to be spouting poetry in Latin or complaining about his irrascible family as he was to be listening to and helping Ruby Alder with her problems.

Still, the beset woman's mind grounded on the thought of that tall, scrawny, dour, pimple-faced youngster. For all his eccentricities and outlandish stories, Ferd was a good boy, and smart. If anybody could help her, he just might be the one.

White-faced, growing sicker inside with every passing minute, Ruby Alder closed her box of memories and stood. Then with measured step she walked to the wooden telephone on the wall.

"Effie," she shouted after she had rung through to central, "I want to talk to the Burroughs home—Ferdinand Burroughs. And Effie, this is a *private* conversation! Thank you."

Chapter 19

"Hello, Flora," Ruby said as she stood on the front porch of her son's home, shivering with cold. "Is Willy at home?"

"He is," Flora responded with a smile. "Come in out of the cold, Mother. Isn't that open automobile a terrible cold thing to drive in weather like this?"

"It is, and I will come in. It surely feels like a storm is coming."

"Hard to believe, after the weather we've been having. Sit down, and I'll get Will for you."

"Hi, Grandma."

"Hello, Allyson. How are you today?"

"Well, to tell the truth, I'm scared. Grandma, how could that nice old man try to murder Daddy?"

"He didn't, Allyson. You were with us all day, so you ought to know—"

"Grandma, I saw him leave the dance last night. He was gone a long time, too."

"Yes, he left, but not to . . . to bomb your father's office."

"But how do you *know* that?"

"Allyson, you know John Phips quite well now. Except for me and Ferdinand, you've spent more time with him than anybody else. Knowing of him like you do, do you think Johnny could ever do such a terrible thing?"

"Grandma, I don't know how to tell. I wouldn't have thought so, but Daddy says—"

"I say what?" William Alder asked as he strode into the room. "I say what, Allyson?"

"You . . . you say that John Phips's guilt is a lead-pipe cinch."

"That's true. It is. That thief's guilt has been written all over his face since the day he marched into town and maliciously swept Mother off her feet. I've warned you, too, haven't I, Mother."

"Yes, Willy, you warned me. Only—"

"Just Monday last, at the dedication, I confronted him and confounded him in his guilt. And oh, he took it hard, he did. Mumbled and stumbled and finally ended up threatening me in that silly speech. And he made a try, too, with that bomb. It's just a lucky thing I forgot and left my light on last night, making it look like I was there. Otherwise the old fool might have tried my home."

"Willy, please don't. You don't understand."

"I understand that he's gone," William declared, interrupting her. "I can't say that I'm sorry, except I do wish they could have apprehended him quickly. Now it appears that it will take a little longer."

"They're not going to catch him, Willy. He's innocent, and the Lord has promised me that Johnny will be protected."

"Innocent!" William stormed. "Good heavens, Mother, what is it going to *take?* First he comes into town and takes advantage of you—"

"Willy, that is a lie, and I won't stand for you speaking of him like that. You know better, for I have told you!"

"A lie? Come, Mother—"

"Very well, I see that you need to receive an accounting. In clothing and shoes, I gave John Phips, my hired hand, thirty-two dollars, none of which he asked for. In food, I imagine that I've spent no more that ten dollars more than I would have spent feeding just myself. In actual cash wages, I have not paid him one single dollar.

"Now Willy, suppose that Sister Trimble down here came to you and asked you to dig her potatoes. What would you do?"

"I'd assign her block teachers or the Aaronic priesthood—"

"No, Willy, you misunderstood. I mean you personally. How much would you charge her to dig her potatoes?"

"Mother, she couldn't afford me. My time is worth too much."

"Yes, you are probably right. It's also too valuable to spend on your mother. So who is there to dig my potatoes, or paint my fence or the trim on my home? Who is there, Willy, to chop my winter firewood? Who is there to repair the barn and the fences, to mend the well, to stop the erosion behind the barn, to sharpen the ax, to brand the calf, to milk the cow morning and night—"

"Mother, except for the milking, I will get at all those things."

"Yes, Willy, I know. In eternity, or after you are released from being bishop; and after you stop being famous, which I think is probably the same thing."

"Now, that isn't fair!"

"Maybe not, but it is true. Willy, John Phips, in this one short week, has accomplished every single one of these tasks that I have listed. You no longer need to worry about them. How much, in dollars and cents, would that week be worth to you?"

William stood silently, his mind unable to stop adding up the hours such a work-week might cost him. Ruby could see that she had him thinking, so rather than give him the opportunity to think of a lower figure, she continued.

"The answer, Willy, is considerably more than forty-two dollars, and you know it. Especially if you were to pay yourself to do the work. Now pay attention to your mother. *Never again will you accuse Mr. John Phips of taking advantage of a poor, defenseless widow-woman*. Do you hear me?"

William sighed. "Yes, Mother, I hear you. Now tell me how I can use that same illogical formula for deciding that the old man did me a favor when he bombed my office and tried to kill me."

"He didn't do it, Willy."

"Oh, Mother, he did so! All the evidence points to it. Other than that detective fellow who was looking for him, he's been the only stranger in town."

"But Willy—"

"Mother, with what we know of his past, and with his presence here verified, the circumstantial evidence is overwhelming. That old man bombed my office. What's more, he tried to kill me in it. That you are still defending the man who tried to murder your only son is so overwhelming to me that I cannot comprehend it.

"Mother, let me tell you a little about him. The Molly Maguires were a secret society, akin to the Gadianton Robbers in the Book of

Mormon, who robbed and murdered to get gain and to achieve their own selfish political labor goals. They had legitimate gripes, but they chose illegal means to achieve them. John Phips was a Molly Maguire."

"You don't know that."

"But I do. He was there the week they were wiped out, way back in 1877. It's a wonder that he wasn't hanged with the rest of them. Since then, every time a subversive labor group has surfaced in our country, your man has been there, right in the middle of that group. He was even in Los Angeles three weeks ago when Harrison Gray Otis's newspaper office was bombed. Of course you already know he was there, for that ne'er-do-well brother of yours sent him from there to here. Or at least so Phips claims.

"Mother, the *Times* is a powerful voice against organized labor. When Phips bombed it on October first, twenty people were killed. Did you hear that, Mother? Twenty!

"John Phips is a rabid animal who kills indiscriminately. He tried to kill me, and I will not rest until he is apprehended and brought to justice."

"Willy, I know that all you say is historically accurate, all except for Johnny. He didn't do those things. He couldn't! And especially he couldn't attempt to murder you. The Lord told me that he is innocent, and I know he is. With all my heart I feel it."

"Mother, you don't *know* he's innocent. You're responding emotionally, and emotions always cloud issues."

"Then why did the Lord give us emotions, Willy?"

"I don't know, Mother. I just—"

Ruby smiled. "There! *You don't know*. How thrilled I am to hear you admit that you still remember those words. You don't know. Isn't that a wonderful phrase, Willy? Even the Founding Fathers used it, and governed their writing of the Constitution by it."

"What?"

"Willy, none of us *know*, except as things are manifest to us by the power of the Spirit. You may be a bishop and therefore a judge in Israel, but you are not John Phips's bishop. Therefore, you have no right to be his judge and jury, nor will the Holy Ghost have informed you of his guilt. Therefore, until such time as a *legally* assigned judge and jury of his peers hear his case, *if* that is ever necessary, John Phips has the right to be presumed innocent. I grant him that right and would hope that the renowned Will Alder, champion of the rights of free men throughout the nation, would also grant it."

William Alder stood silently, and Ruby could see that he was wrestling mentally with her logic, trying to find a hole through which he could reach to turn it around. *You poor boy,* she thought. *Don't you know that you had to get your great gift for logic from somewhere? I may not be as skilled, but put my back to the wall, and you've got a real argument ahead of you, son. A real one.*

"Mother," William finally said, "all that you have postulated is true, and I have no argument with it. What I don't understand is this: There is, legitimately and legally, suspicion directed against the man in connection with the bombing of *my* office. That being the case, how can you so actively take his case as opposed to mine?"

Ruby took a deep breath, then sighed. "Are you sure that you want to know?"

"I do."

"Very well, sit down and I will tell you. I had hoped that if it ever came to this, that Johnny would be with me. But . . . It is a long story, Willy, and you must promise to be still until I finish—"

Ruby was interrupted by a loud knocking upon William Alder's front door. All waited, and seconds later Allyson spoke from the hallway.

"Daddy, it's the marshal."

William excused himself and strode into the foyer of his home, and Ruby, almost unconsciously, arose and followed.

"Yes, Harvey?"

"Will, we've got a lead. Someone saw a feller up the canyon, near Tibble Fork. Said it looked a lot like our man."

"Tibble Fork, huh. Now how would he know about the canyon, I wonder?"

"Daddy, I . . . I . . ."

"Yes, Allyson?"

Allyson turned nervously, looking at her father and then at Ruby. "I . . . uh . . ."

"Tell him, Allyson," Ruby said quietly. "He ought to know."

Allyson smiled thankfully at her grandmother and then hurriedly spoke to her father.

"Daddy, Grandma told Ferd and me that she rode up there with Johnny Phips last Sunday, showing him the sights."

William looked at his daughter, and then he turned to Ruby, who was still standing by the door to the parlor.

"Mother, is that true?"

"It is."

"Well, men, that's it. Let's get a posse together and get moving."

"But Willy, I wanted to tell you—"

"No, Mother, not now. There'll be plenty of time to talk when John Phips is behind bars."

"Willy, the day will come when you'll be sorry—"

But William cut her off, laughing. "Sorry, Mother? Sorry to be *alive?* The only thing I am sorry about is that I waited so long to get the law after him. Now, have Flora fix you some warm broth, and we'll continue our little talk when I return."

With that he took his overcoat and was gone. And Ruby, Flora, and Allyson stood silently in the cold of the open doorway, watching the men depart.

"I'm sorry, Mother," Flora declared gently. "I do wish that there was an easier way."

"I . . . I'm sorry, too," Allyson said as sudden tears streamed down her face. "Grandma, I feel so torn! I like Johnny, I love you, and I love Daddy. Was I wrong in telling him? What . . . what am I supposed to do?"

Ruby took the girl in her arms. "You did just right, sweetheart. A girl should always support her father. And Flora, you should always support your husband. That's the right thing to do. I can't even blame Willy for thinking as he does."

"But . . . but I *feel* so guilty," Allyson declared.

"Well, you shouldn't. You couldn't help it, either of you, for you simply don't understand. I'm not even certain that *I* understand everything. But one of these days, when things all come to light, please don't feel too badly about this, either of you."

"What? But Grandma, I don't know what you mean."

"I don't understand, either, Mother. Are you really certain of John Phips's innocence?"

"Positive. I know him, and I know he has been trying all week to protect my family, especially Willy. That's why he had you stand out in your yard on Monday. I think he was trying to frighten the men who did the bombing."

"But how would that frighten them?" Flora asked.

"I'm not certain, but at least they wouldn't dare come into your yard in open daylight and put a bomb under your home. If no one had been visible, they might have done just that."

"Yes," Flora agreed thoughtfully. "I see. I . . . But Mother, who *is* he, and why would he be trying to protect our family?"

"I . . . I can't tell you, Flora. I'm sorry. Willy should be told first, and then if he wishes—"

"Grandma, I really want to believe that Johnny is innocent. I really do."

"Of course you do. And you will, Allyson. I promise. *All* of my family will believe. Now I really must run. Good-bye, my darlings. I love both of you more than I can ever say."

"We love you too, Mother."

Ruby smiled. "I know. That's why I have the courage to go ahead. Bye."

"Bye, Grandma."

Ruby wrapped her shawl about her neck and walked outside to her automobile. There she set the magneto, cranked the car until it started, and then wearily climbed in.

So now the law knew about the canyon, she thought as she pulled out into the road. They knew, Ferdinand had not come back, and so there was only one thing left to do.

Pray.

Chapter 20

"Hi, G-Grandma Alder."

The wind was blowing terribly, there was a touch of sleet in the air, and Ruby Alder was cold. She was also relieved that Ferdinand had returned, and she could see that he was cold, too. Yet she was not through with the young man, not quite. He still had at least one more mission, though even he didn't know of it. But he was a smart boy; and she hoped, with the right questions, to inspire him to give the *right* answers.

She also hoped to keep him out on the porch for a moment or so longer, and so she purposely stood with the door partly closed, blocking his way.

"Ferdinand," she shouted so that her voice would carry above the wind, "what a nice surprise. You look terribly cold."

"I am!" Ferdinand shouted back. "It's freezing up that canyon, and it's even starting to snow."

"Up the canyon?" Ruby questioned in mock surprise, keeping the shivering and slightly confused Ferdinand on the porch. "What on earth were you doing up there?"

For an instant Ferdinand looked at her, his face registering his surprise. But Ruby flicked her eyes back and forth from the corner of the house, and suddenly Ferdinand grinned.

"Why was I up the canyon? Why, ma'am, that's a powerful long story. My Pa's Aunt Frieda and her husband, Long Tom Plunket, had a few cows up there, and Aunt Frieda she says to Long Tom—"

"Did you find them up there?" Ruby shouted.

"No, ma'am, I did not! Pa'll be mighty worried, too, for he was fixin' on gettin' one of their cows for our winter beef, and—"

"Did you see anybody else up there, Ferdinand?"

Again Ferdinand paused, confused. But Ruby nodded encouragingly, and the youth, understanding at least partly, slowly answered.

"Yes, yes I did."

"Oh, my goodness. Who on earth would be up there on a day like this?"

Again Ruby got a questioning look, and again she encouraged the young man to answer.

"Well," he said slowly, so that she could shut him off should he say something he shouldn't, "I met a feller up there, name of . . . of John Phips."

"John Phips!" Ruby shouted. "You mean the man who stayed out in my barn? Why, I thought he'd gone."

With that Ruby winked and lifted her hands slightly, as though she were a choir director encouraging her group to greater volume. Ferdinand understood perfectly and launched quite loudly into one of his 'accounts'.

"It was John Phips, all right! He was fixin' to leave, too. Up over the top, he said. Minds me of the time that Pa's uncle's wife's brother, fellow by the name of Zeus Taylor, tried to cross up there with a storm comin' in on him. Pa's uncle, he tried to warn Zeus out of it, but Zeus was a stubborn man, he was, and wouldn't talk out of it for nothing. Says he, 'I'm a'goin', and I'm a'goin' alone,' he says. And he went, too. Guess he figured since he was named after one of them Greek god fellers, he'd have extry power or something. Did pretty good, I'm told, though no one knew it till the next spring, when he was found about halfway down into Heber Valley, curled up under some mighty thin bushes, and deader'n last fall's leaves. I tried to tell ol' Phips that, but he was determined, and last I saw of him he was headin' up Tibble Fork like the devil hisself was on his trail. But it's snowing up there, ma'am, and I do worry. Fact is, I think maybe I ought to report it to the marshal."

"I agree, Ferdinand. Why don't you come in and use my telephone?"

Ruby smiled, Ferdinand entered, and seconds later they both heard the rapidly departing sound of hooves as the marshal headed for the canyon.

"Who's that?" Ferdinand asked as Ruby poured the shivering youth a cup of hot postum.

"One of our marshals. That was wonderful, Ferdinand. You did that just right."

"Well, ma'am, it was about the truth, if you know what I mean."

"Wh-what?"

"I found Johnny, ma'am, and he was fixin' to do exactly as I said outside. He told me he was beat and couldn't see any possible way out of it. Howsomever, I told him you had an urgent message to give him that might color his decision somewhat, and so he reconsidered. He was waverin' considerable anyway, what with thinkin' of you, but word of that there message turned him total. If he can work his way past that posse sweeping up the canyon, he'll be back to see you.

"If he doesn't get past them, well . . ."

"Ferdinand," Ruby declared as she took the boy's empty cup, "you've no idea how much I appreciate what you've done. I know that weather is miserable, and I know you've had quite a ride."

"Yes, ma'am, it was. Minds me of the time—"

"Ferd?"

Ferdinand Burroughs grinned. "All right, Grandma Alder. I'll close my yap. And I'll be home in case you and . . . well, in case you should need me again. And please call. Another couple of adventures like this and I won't never have to talk about my goofy relatives again. I can spend my days bragging upon myownself."

Ruby smiled, hugged the young man, and saw him to the door. Then, with her teakwood box in her lap, she sat and began once again to wait.

Chapter 21

The Regulator clock showed just after three in the afternoon when Ruby came suddenly awake. She had no idea what had awakened her, but the room was chilly, and so stiffly she rose to her feet to stoke the fire.

To her chagrin, however, the woodbox was empty. And so with a sigh Ruby took her shawl and walked outside to go to the woodpile. But on the porch she paused, almost reluctant to move into the face of the growing storm.

Tightening the shawl, however, she stepped to the edge of the porch and—

"Top of the afternoon to ye, Ruby lass. And what might ye be wantin' to fetch out here in this haythun storm? Faith, now, and the blessed mercury has dived so far down in the bulb that ye can't see it with a spyglass."

With a gasp of surprise, Ruby looked down to see the wrinkled, tired face of John Phips smiling up at her from the wash-bench upon which he was seated.

"J-Johnny?"

"At yer sarvice, me ravishin' beauty. Mercy, me lass, I take sober oath that yer gettin' purtier ev'ry garjus day of yer life!"

"Johnny, look at you! Just sitting in this storm, and without a coat, too. Get in the house this second, before you catch your death of cold!"

"Ah, it's a temper, is it? Faith, but I thought ye'd grown out of that weakness in yer soul—"

"Weakness? Listen, you fake Irish hypocrite . . ."

Johnny coughed. "Now there's the Ruby I've fallen in love with. You want wood, do you? Well, while you slept the sleep of the innocent, I've stacked your porch here with it. And if that isn't enough, I'll stack more until you won't be able to get out the door."

Standing slowly, John reached down and took up a few sticks of wood. Then, with a lopsided grin and a painful-looking limp, he followed Ruby into her cozy kitchen. There he proceeded to stoke up her stove.

"Well," he said when the fire was blazing and he had a hot drink in his hand, "the lad said you had urgent news."

"Sit down and drink your drink, and I'll tell you when you are finished. Good news can always wait, and bad news ought to."

Nodding, Johnny sat in the old horsehair rocker with his drink, and Ruby walked to her place of refuge at the sink, where she busied herself cleaning that which had already been cleaned.

Oh, her heart cried, *what are you going to do with this sick and tired old man called John Phips? It is hardly a trick at all, when he is away and out of sight, to shudder and tell yourself that he has no place in your life. Or even to see the way he looks at you, like no man has looked in more years than you care to remember, and be afraid of him. It is easy to say, when you have listened to your good and only son describe this man, that he is a deceiver and that you never want to see him again in your soft little life. It is easy to believe that he is a liar and a man who gives hurt, and that what is between the two of you isn't, nor ever was. It is easy, that is, when he is off and far away.*

But when he is sitting across a two-foot table from you in the toasty-warm lamplight of your cozy home, with nothing between you and the exciting look of him but fifty-some years of waiting and the low arm of an old horsehair rocker, it is quite another, confusingly passionate, matter.

Still, Ruby Soderberg Alder, where you don't know yourself, and where you certainly don't know the strange old man with the soft blue eyes and the easy, flattering tongue who is beguiling you, you do know right from wrong. John Phips, innocent or guilty, is a man wanted by the authorities in your beloved state of Utah. No decent woman, knowing what you know of his whereabouts, could move another mortal step with him along the unknown path he wills you to follow.

Only you love him! You poor, miserable fool, with all your heart you love him, and you know you will do all that he says—

"Well?" he asked quietly.

Without a word Ruby handed him the telegram, and then she stood trembling only slightly while he slowly read it.

"Ahhh," he breathed, "Imagine that! James and the famous Wyatt Earp. I'll bet those two had a lot to talk about."

"Johnny, the telegram!"

John grinned, coughing again as he spoke. "Yes, this could be important. I *knew* they were in Pleasant Grove. Even when we lost them, I felt it in my bones. The question is, are they still there now?"

"I . . . I don't know."

"I imagine the only way to find out is to go and see. Have you heard from Frank Burns?"

Ruby shook her head.

"Neither have I. But I don't think he'd leave town without getting word to me, so that means he must still be around."

"Do you know where he was staying, Johnny?"

"Yes. Down at the Grant Hotel. Would you mind ringing him up on the telephone for me?"

Without answering, Ruby walked to the telephone and rang central. "Effie," she called, "ring me the Grant Hotel. What? The storm? Very well. I said, *ring . . . me . . . the . . . Grant . . . Hotel!* Did you hear me? Good."

For a moment there was silence, and then Ruby shouted again, asking for the guest named Frank Burns.

"What?" she called. "When? Very well. When he returns— What? Oh . . . I . . . see! Then . . . give . . . him . . . this . . . message . . ."

And loudly and slowly, Ruby gave the information she had obtained from the telegram.

"Now what do we do?" she asked when she had rung off.

"I suppose *we* just stay put. *I* will go—"

"Oh no you don't, Mr. Phips. From now on, where you go, I go. That's final!"

"You really feel that way, Ruby?"

"I . . . I do."

John smiled. "Thank you, darling. So do I."

"You . . . you do?"

"I do. Up that canyon, thinking about going over the top and leaving you, I did a little thinking of my own. I decided, up there in the wind and the cold, that a person has to face up to himself sometime or other. You can go on being satisfied or ducking the issue only so long, and then there comes a time when you start asking yourself, not what you've done with your summer's wages, but with your whole life's earnings up to that point.

"The thing we have to realize is that it's never too late. I've known many people who have braced up and made something of themselves after they were forty or fifty or sixty, with nothing to show for the years before that but scars and the cluttering up of dead wishes. I don't know if it will work at seventy, but I'd like to give it a try.

"About the worst thing a person can do, Ruby, is to let a dream die. Long ago, when I wasn't much more than a youngster, I used to dream of having my own place, and of just how I'd handle it. I even found a girl, the perfect girl, and made her a part of my dream. Ruby, an idea like that, a dream, doesn't just lie fallow; it builds up and gathers background, trying to fit itself for realization. Even if nothing seems to happen, yet it does. Here and there you pick up an idea or a thought, you work for somebody else who does well or badly, you see a lot of different women and you compare them with the perfect one you've found, and thus you add to your little stock of information. And you do it mostly without thinking.

"You get to studying things out, thinking deeply, trying to understand why things didn't work out like you thought and even hoped they would. Every idea you have about that is like a seed; and like a seed, it germinates. Only you have to feed it and make it grow properly.

"You were surprised the other day when I told you that I had read Elder Whitney's works? Well, that's why I read them. I was feeding my ideas and understanding. My trouble was that after a lot of years of thinking, I'd sort of fallen into the rut of taking things as they came and moving on if I didn't like them. My idea of a place and family of my own was still there, I imagine, but it was mighty spindly, and growing weaker by the year.

"Ruby, people never get old until they start to forget their dreams. I've started growing old. Somebody once said that nature abhors a vacuum. Well, from all I've seen, I'd say that God abhors anything that doesn't produce. And me? Well, up in that canyon I decided that if I was going to give up one more time on that dream of a place of my own and that perfect woman to go with it, especially now that I knew where that perfect woman was, well, I'd ought to just give up and die instead.

"But Ruby, darling, I can't. My dream isn't dead. Until a few days ago it had been lying there, starving for lack of hope. But then your brother sent me flyin' this way, I saw you on that back porch, and suddenly it was alive and well. If you'll have me, I'll spend whatever amounts to the rest of my life, doing my best to protect you and to make you happy."

"Oh, Johnny . . ." Ruby sighed, her eyes moist with love and . . . and the belonging she had so long sought for. And she knew at that moment, with that certain knowledge that is occasionally planted in the hearts of women, that no matter what happened, no matter what turned out to be his history, she would stand beside John Phips forever. And she would do so happily, with no regrets.

Only, and she hated herself for thinking this, could she really believe what he was saying?

"Now don't you say a thing," Johnny was saying. "You think about it, and if we can lay our hands on those McNamara boys and get them shipped back to Los Angeles with Frank, then you can tell me."

"But I already know—"

John stopped her with his hand on her lips. "Not now. Do you think Ferdinand can help us again?"

Ruby nodded and rang him up, and shortly the three, bundled heavily, were sliding and spinning through the icy mud toward Pleasant Grove, Utah.

Chapter 22

The capture of the McNamara brothers, when it came, was surprisingly easy. Because John was known to the two, he and Ruby hid behind some outbuildings and sent Ferdinand to the front door.

Loudly he knocked, again and again. Ruby had almost decided that they had missed the murderers when suddenly the door opened and a dark-visaged man stood there.

"Good afternoon," Ferdinand declared joyfully. "Sir, my name is Ferdinand Burroughs, Ferd for short, and I am earning my way through school selling the handiest little kitchen gadget you have ever seen in your life. It is good for peeling fruit—"

"Not interested," the man growled as he started to shut the door.

"Not interested? But sir, you have no idea—"

"I said—"

"Yes, but did you know that this wonderful little tool will unlock even the most puzzling lock? It will, I tell you. It will even decode the combination of the strongest safe, so in case you lock yourself out of a safe, you can take this little tool—"

"It'll unlock safes?" the man asked, his interest sparked.

"Oh, my goodness, yes! The Jiffy Kitchen Joy Tool—that's what it's called, by the way—will even crack bank safes, though of course you wouldn't be interested in that. But I have a cousin, Bartholomew James, he is called, direct descendant of the notorious Jesse James, I believe he is, who this very month told me, he says, 'Ferd, I'm a wealthy man,' he says. I say, 'Wealthy? But Bart, last I heard you was poor as a church mouse.' And he says, 'I was, but you sold me that handy little Jiffy Kitchen Joy Tool,' he says, 'and now some banks will be somewhat poorer but I'll never have need of money again', he says. Mister, I was some startled, for of course you've read of the same string of bank robberies that I've read of, and speaking of robberies, Pa's aunt Pernicious Humdrum bought one of these little Jiffy Kitchen Joy Tools, and let me tell you, she turned herself into a whiz at perpetratin' the most gosh-awful home burglaries . . ."

Ferd went on, while the poor man who listened was made a slack-jawed captive in his own doorway.

"Ruby," John whispered as he led her around to the back door, "I swear, that kid'll out-talk the bishop at his own funeral. I think he'll die of old age long before ever he runs down!"

Ruby only had time to smile before John pushed her against the side of the rock house and told her to stay put. Then, producing a small revolver from somewhere inside his coat, he quietly opened the door and passed inside.

Little more than a minute or so later he reappeared, two handcuffed brothers grumbling before his unwavering pistol. He was thanking Ferdinand for his help when a team loomed out of the gathering twilight, and the man Ruby had seen several times before jumped down and hurried toward them.

"Good work, Johnny," the man called Frank Burns declared as he gazed at the men in cuffs. "I'd have thought they'd be gone."

"We would have," the obviously older of the two snarled, "if this idiot hadn't met some handsome little fillie at that church meeting we went to the other day. 'One more night,' he says. 'One more night . . .'"

"Aw, that wasn't nothin'," the younger one growled. "You was the one got suckered into that Jiffy Kitchen Joy Tool setup!"

"So'd you, you lummox! You was standin' right behind me with both your big ears bugled out, takin' that safe-crackin' nonsense right in. Besides, did you have a listen at this kid? I ain't never met a man with so much axle-grease on the hinges of his jawbones. Kid, where'd you learn to throw verbal lather like that?"

"Well, I . . . that is . . . my pa . . . Say, fellers, speakin' of lather, my pa has a nephew name of Wilbur Peebles that grows facial hair faster'n lizards scoot across hot rocks. And when he shaves, which is about every hour on the hour, why, talk about lather . . ."

Ferdinand continued relating his story to his truly captive audience, and Frank Burns turned to John Phips.

"John, I've got the train holding for us, so we'd best be hurrying. I'll get these fellers loaded while you're saying your goodbyes."

"Frank, put them in the wagon, let Ferd hold the team, and come back for a minute. We need to make a little medicine."

"Are you sure the kid can do that?"

John Phips grinned. "I'll say. Besides a never-stopping mouth, that kid's got more guts than you could stick in a six-hundred-pound steer with a snow shovel. He'll hold 'em good."

"All right, John. I'll be back directly."

Frank Burns did as he was requested, and soon he was back beside the quietly standing couple.

"Well?"

"I won't be going back with you," John said quietly.

"What's that?"

"Frank, I've been waiting all my life to . . . ah . . . to find Ruby here, and now that I finally have, I'm not running off from her, ever."

"Johnny, are you sure?"

"Sure as an old man can be."

"What'll you do about the law?"

"Take you to the police station in American Fork and let you announce that these boys have been arrested for the bombings. Then I figure the heat will be off, and I can tell Ruby's son, William, as well as the local constabulary, the entire story."

"Johnny," Frank Burns said quietly, "I can't do it. Not today, anyway. If I do I'll miss the train, and we'll all be held until tomorrow. That'll completely eliminate the element of surprise, and you know how badly I need that. These birds are only a small part of an illegal scheme that stretches all the way from the northwest, down to the south, and clear back to New York. Before I can make very many announcements to local police, I've got to get after the big boys. Even with this boost, I have at least a year's worth of investigation ahead of me. If I took the time to clear you before I got to Los Angeles, it might jeopardize the whole investigation. Can you hold out until I get back to L.A.?"

John looked down at Ruby. "Can you stand being associated with such a nefarious criminal as myself, even temporarily?"

"I can," Ruby said, gazing admiringly into John's eyes.

"I'll hold out, Frank."

"Good. For a day or so, you'll have to content yourself with being a true, unsung hero. I'm sure you understand."

Quietly Johnny nodded.

"Thanks, Johnny. I'm sorry you must take the brunt of all this."

"Yeah, me, too."

"I'm sorry as well that you won't be with us any longer. John, you're the best that ever was!"

"That's my gift for being average," John said with a smile.

"Well, you're a mighty unique average, old son."

"Thanks. Good luck, Frank."

"Same to you, John. And you too, ma'am. I think you're right, John. She does have the most beautiful of Gibson girl eyes."

Frank winked and then walked silently back to the wagon. "Ferdinand," he said, "could you drive to the station while I keep an eye on these birds? Then you can take the wagon back to the livery. Be happy to pay you, too."

"Be glad to, mister. I've got me a cousin I've been wantin' to elucidate upon, and this seems like a twenty-four carat heaven-sent opportunity. She goes by the name of Abigail Chilene—"

"Mister," the younger of the two anarchists whined, "shut this kid up, will you please?"

"Yeah," the older one agreed heartily. "If he ain't going to sell us one of those Kitchen Joy Tool things, then I don't want to hear no more blabber. This kid's yap is more lethal than the big earthquake out in San Francisco. Shut it up, please!"

"It can't be done," John said, walking up. "I've tried."

"It's *got* to be done," the dark-visaged, younger man, whimpered. "I just can't take it—"

"Can't take it?" Ferdinand postulated thoughtfully as though he had heard nothing of the arguments concerning him. "Spence Abercombe, first cousin to Pa's uncle George Peebles, once said those very words. 'I can't take it no more,' he says, an then he upped and took leave of—"

"You sure you won't change your mind?" Frank asked as he did his best to ignore the incessant verbosity coming from the young man who sat beside him.

"No thanks," John replied, grinning. "They're yours, now, and so's Ferd. Enjoy 'em all."

"I'll try. I'm just glad the kid's not going all the way to Los Angeles."

"Yeah, I'll bet you are. I've decided ol' Ferd there could talk the scab off the world's biggest blister."

Frank Burns grinned. "Or the hide off a full-grown cow. Do you reckon he gargles with that axle-grease these birds spoke of?"

"Likely. Was I you, I'd haul him all the way to Los Angeles, anyway. Stick him in the same berth with these two anarchists, and it'd be pure torture. Ten to one they'd break before the train got to Nephi. Good way to get information, wouldn't you think?"

"I would at that. Only since I'd have to be with 'em, I'd go just as nuts as they would. Besides, it'd be extremely cruel and inhumane treatment. Nope, even murderers I couldn't do that to.

"Be seein' you, John. Good day, ma'am."

"Luck, Frank."

"Be careful, Frank," Ruby chorused. "And good luck with your . . . project."

And so in the growing darkness of the evening storm, John Phips and Ruby Alder stood while the wagon creaked off down the slight hill. Then, arm-in-arm, they turned and made their way to the snow-dusted Oldsmobile, and within minutes they were made invisible with the darkness of the storm and the evening settling around them.

Chapter 23

"The saints be praised, me garjus Ruby lass, but 'tis nothin' but the pure luck o' the Irish and one flannel-mouthed, scrawny kid who kissed the Blarney stone, that I ain't arguin' with the divil this same minute."

John was driving the Oldsmobile, and though there was already more than two inches of snow on the ground, the automobile handled it well and moved steadily up the hill onto the Highland Bench.

"You . . . you were really going?"

"I couldn't see any other way. I'd missed the McNamara brothers, and I could see that my staying would do nothing but make life more and more miserable for you. Your son doesn't like me at all, and you don't exactly know what to do with me. For your sake, it seemed best to head over the mountain and be gone. Of course, I didn't know this storm would be hitting so hard."

"Johnny, you don't understand, do you. I love you, you silly old Irish-talking Englishman. Without you, my life would be meaningless. With you beside me, I can face about anything."

"Even Willy?"

"Especially Willy. Johnny, as soon as he understands, he'll be the best friend you ever had."

"Yes, but will he ever understand?"

"I don't even know that I do," Ruby stated quietly.

"Shure and it's a simple tale, lass. Ye can hear it an' ye want to, if yer not minded of boredom."

Ruby laughed. "I'm not, Johnny. Let's hear it."

"All right. In a nutshell, Frank Burns and I have been friends for years and years. I happened to be working in Pennsylvania when the Molly Maguires got so strong, and Frank contacted me. He was working for the government, and he asked me to go underground for him. I did, and learned a great deal about organized labor and the men who wish to see it enforced.

"Ruby, the workers have a great many grievances, and organizing is one way to solve them. Unfortunately, some of the men who lead these movements are seeking wealth and power, not the good of the men they are supposed to represent. They resort to murder, bombing, arson, kidnapping, and other such bullying tactics, using force and fear not only to win their goals, but to force the common workers to stand behind them."

"Joseph Smith," Ruby said softly, "was certainly right when he declared that it was the nature and disposition of almost all men, as soon as they got a little authority, to begin to exercise improper dominion over the lives of others."

"That he was, Ruby. That he was. Anyway, after Pennsylvania there were other trouble spots, and Frank and I were always in the middle of them, working with another man named McParlan. McParlan is now head of the Pinkertons, over in Denver; Frank founded Burns Detective Agency and works in the open, and because I am such an ordinary-appearing fellow, I have always been able to go underground and get into the very middle of the unrest. That way I've been able to tell who were the legitimate workers with honest complaints, and who were the 'Big Bill Haywoods' of the trouble, the men who were festering it for their own selfish gain."

"So you *were* all those places that Willy said you were?"

"Well, I don't know what places he told you, but over the years I've certainly been here and there. There's a lot going on right now, too. Frank and I have evidence of political corruption in San Francisco, kickback schemes in the railroad industry, land frauds in the Northwest, embezzling schemes in some of the nations's most powerful banks, racial strife, white slavery right under the noses of the administrators of the newly passed Mann Act, and on and on. Ruby, it is all tied together, too. Sure those McNamara brothers bombed Willy's office and the *Los Angeles Times,* but who did they work for? *Who is behind all this?"*

Slowly Ruby shook her head.

"I don't know either, Ruby, but I can tell you that McParlan has picked up a couple of hot leads, which he passed on to us, and Frank Burns won't rest until he has unraveled the entire ugly mess. Our hope is that the McNamara brothers will open a few doors, letting us into their organization even further than I have been able to get."

"But won't they . . . those men who are behind all this, try to stop you? I mean, *all* who oppose them?"

"Of course they'll try. That's why Willy's office was bombed. Beyond that, they'll hire fancy lawyers like Clarence Darrow out of Chicago. He got Heywood off on a technicality up in Boise, and you can bet he'll be the one who represents the McNamara brothers. That's why Frank Burns needs to move fast. Only with mountains of absolute evidence will we be able to stop this chain of satanic corruption that seems to be sweeping the nation."

"And what . . . what about you, Johnny?"

"Me?" Johnny laughed quietly. "Ruby me lass, tonight yer Johnny lad has retired from the firm. From now on, all I want to do is chop yer wood and pester ye to death with the fixin' of yer fine and fancy meals."

"Johnny, are you *sure?*"

For a moment John was silent, and the only sound was the automobile moving through the new and still-falling snow.

"Ruby, like I told you earlier, I'm an old man, for I've let my dreams nearly die. But they aren't dead, and I've known that since the day your brother James first told me that you . . . well, that I might enjoy seeing you. Ruby me darlin', fer such time as I have left of this mortal probation, until the garjus sound of harps calls me home, I'd like to enjoy the pleasure of yer company and do me haythun best to make ye a happy woman."

"Then we'll have to start by convincing Willy of who you are."

"Can you do that, Ruby?"

"I think so. I can show him some things, and with what you and I have to tell him—"

"Faith, me garjus Ruby lass," Johnny interrupted, his eyes straining forward through the falling snow, "but it looks to Missus Phips's boy Johnny as though we've got the divil's own problem upon us now."

"What? But—"

"Ah, now, Ruby, and that crowd at your home makes things look blacker than an anarchist's heart!"

"My goodness! What on earth can it be?"

"The posse, lass, every spittin' one of 'em."

"But . . . but . . . Oh, Johnny, they're here for *you!*"

"Shure and I'm thinkin' you're right," John breathed.

"What will we do?"

"Well, Ruby my sweet, if they take me, I'll be fixed for a spell. There'll be no proof of my innocence forthcoming, not for at least a few days. You heard what Frank Burns had to say, and I don't blame him at all. Nor can I give out that information myself. What he has yet to do is too important.

"Captured, then, I'll likely spend some time in jail. And if Darrow does his usual work and the McNamaras go free, I just might swing for the murders of those folks in Los Angeles. The last's unlikely, but then a man never knows. And that's the bold truth of it, lass."

Slowly John braked the Oldsmobile to a stop, Ruby's home still a quarter of a mile away.

"What do you think?" he asked quietly.

"I think . . . I think it isn't fair," Ruby cried, tears starting in her eyes.

"Yer right, me sweet lass. 'Tis sad tidings, for shure."

"Johnny," Ruby suddenly declared, her voice firm with conviction even as her eyes dripped silent tears, "it will work out! Willy will learn who you really are. I'll convince him, and then everything will be fine. We'll be able to live here together. And as I have been happy, at least your last years will be happy ones. Johnny, I promise that you'll never be lonely again."

"And if it doesn't work out?" John asked wryly.

"Then we'll go away together."

"You'd . . . you'd leave with me, Ruby?"

"In a minute, Johnny. I mean it. You and I belong together, and I will stay with you forever."

John Phips sat silently, listening to the idling engine and the whistling of the wind. His eyes were wet, and Ruby wondered as he wiped at them with his gnarled old hands. She had never seen him weep, and she suddenly knew, as she watched him, that his heart had at last been given to her.

"Ruby, darling," he said then as he wiped his eyes a final time, "let's go meet the boys."

"No, Johnny, don't. The law in these parts has been a mighty uncertain thing, and I'm not convinced at all that it has changed. You wait out here. Hide somewhere, and I'll go in alone."

John Phips looked at the elderly woman at his side. "You're sure?" he asked.

"Very."

"All right, you go talk to them. Get rid of the posse, and maybe when you and Willy are alone, you'll be able to tell him. With all my heart I hope that you can, for I've never wanted anything so badly as I want this."

"I'll do it, Johnny. But . . . but what will I say to get rid of all those men? They will surely ask if I have seen you."

"That they will," John replied as he climbed out of the automobile. "And when they do, tell them that the last you saw of me, I was heading for Los Angeles. That should get rid of the marshals and their men."

"But I can't lie."

"Goodbye, Ruby me darlin'. Faith and it'll be a long walk, I'm a thinkin'. And only a fool would be tryin' it, too. Any sane man alive would be holed up in a nice warm barn on a night like this. But it's likely off to Los Angeles with the likes of me."

With a wink and a smile John turned and started walking southward into the falling snow, toward the distant city of Los Angeles, and Ruby, her heart in her throat, watched him go. Then, resolutely, she slid under the steering wheel and started the Oldsmobile to moving again. She was going to convince Willy of John Phips's innocence. Either that, or she and John Phips would go where no one would accuse them. The decision would be a simple one to make, and the next few minutes would determine it.

Day 7

Thursday

October 27, 1910

Chapter 24

"Johnny?"

"It . . . it's me," the old man whispered as he huddled outside Ruby's darkened door. "C-can I come in?"

Quickly Ruby opened her door, and with a painful groan, John arose and slipped silently inside.

"Are there still men out there?" Ruby asked as she closed and bolted the door.

"They left, finally," John replied as he drew the rocker toward the stove and sat down. "I g-guess it got too cold. I know it did for me."

"Oh, Johnny," Ruby moaned as she lighted the old lantern, "what in the world are we going to do?"

She turned then, and instantly wished that she hadn't, for John saw her tears and struggled back to his feet.

"Ruby, what is it?"

"Johnny, sit back down and let me fix you something warm to drink."

"All . . . all right. Are the windows covered?"

"Yes. And that's why I lighted the lantern. The light is too faint to be seen through my blinds."

Ruby then busied herself pouring milk into a pan and heating it, while John Phips sat silently beside her, trying to ease the cold out of his trembling body.

"Here," she said softly as she handed him a steaming glass, "this should help."

John took it, drank a little, sighed heavily, and gave Ruby a wink to show his gratitude. Ruby smiled in response and then turned slowly away.

"I reckon they wouldn't listen to you?" John asked then, his voice almost a whisper.

"No," Ruby replied, and with the word out, her tears started again. "Johnny," she cried as she buried her face in her hands, "doesn't it *ever* get any easier? Isn't the pain ever going to stop?"

"Brother Wells said it would," John answered as he stood again and came to her. "You remember that, don't you?"

"I . . . I remember."

"It will stop, Ruby me darlin' lass."

"Well, I wish it would hurry! I have waited so long."

"Even William wouldn't listen?" John asked then, changing the subject.

"No, he wouldn't. I've never seen him like this, Johnny. He loves people. He always has. But his mind is so set against you that I can't even talk to him. He isn't loud or angry. He's just . . . just, well, determined."

"If he wasn't a determined man, Ruby, he'd never have been able to accomplish all he has in his life."

"You . . . you always stick up for him, Johnny."

"Well, he's a good man. I could hardly do otherwise."

Carefully Ruby looked up into John Phips's eyes. "You know, don't you," she said quietly, her voice trembling a little. "About him and—"

"Yes," John responded as he turned back to his chair. "I know."

"How long have you known?"

"I don't know, Ruby. Maybe always. I guess, when you get right down to it, that was why I came from Los Angeles."

"It . . . it wasn't me?"

"No, not at first."

Ruby's gaze dropped to the floor. "S-somehow I understood that, Johnny. All along I knew that I'd had little or nothing to do with your coming."

"Ruby me darlin', I had no hope that you'd even talk to me. No hope at all. When you did, and when I sensed all those feelings between us, well, I don't recall ever being so happy. But I've certainly failed in protecting William. And so the greatest gain of my life has also become my greatest loss. It has surely been a mixed-up week, Ruby lass."

"So what do we do now, Johnny Phips?" Ruby asked, drying more tears from her face.

"Do? Well, we've a choice, you and I. We can stay here and take our chances with the law and your family; we can separate again and hope to meet in eternity; or we can go elsewhere and spend what life we have left, together."

"Do you have a preference, Johnny?"

John Phips grinned. "Aye, me garjus one, but it's the divil's own choice, too. Me heart says to grab ye and go, but me tired old head says it'd be cruel to take ye away from yer family, haythun son or no. To give ye the quickest and most peace, my head tells me that I'd better slip out that door yon and be gone with myself."

"That certainly seems most reasonable," Ruby agreed quietly. "Could you do it?"

"Faith, but ye've a black-hearted tongue, Ruby lass. What sort of haythun question is that?"

"A hopeful one. Johnny, could you walk out that door now and be forever gone?"

"No, Ruby," John answered quietly, "I couldn't."

Ruby smiled. "I'm glad to hear that, me sweet laddie-buck."

Surprised, John Phips looked up into Ruby's moist and glowing eyes.

"Johnny, I do not want to leave my family, for I love them more than I love life itself. But I feel the same about you. My family is grown—they have their own lives to live, and so do you and I."

"So whatever we do, then, we do together?"

"Absolutely!"

"Well, I still think that the best choice is to stay and trust the exigency of the law."

"No, Johnny, I don't think so. My heart is weak, and I couldn't stand the fear I'd feel by seeing you arrested and carted off to jail, even if it was only for a few days."

"But Ruby, that's hardly any time at all."

"Perhaps not, but you forget that I have lived through scenes of the most terrible miscarriages of justice. I watched my brother Jons's life destroyed because of wicked laws and officers who had no choice but to obey those laws. I saw poor Jons arrested and jailed for no reason other than that he was trying to live his religion, and I saw him rot in that jail for almost half a year before a hearing finally allowed him out on bail, giving him a chance to escape to California and the anonymity of being James Y. Johnson.

"I watched my own Henry Alder flee my home in the middle of the night, time after terrifying time, and me never knowing from one day to the next if I would ever see the poor man again. No, my dear Johnny Phips, that is not a choice for me. That is a clear decision. I will not stand by while you are jailed because you have done your best to prevent a terrible crime.

"Besides . . ." she concluded, her voice drifting off.

"Besides what?"

"Johnny, I simply *can't tell* Willy. I can't bear such pain!"

For a long moment John watched Ruby as she wept, and she knew that he was suffering every bit as deeply as she herself. They both hurt, they had both suffered for so long. But would it never end? Would it never stop?

Finally, John Phips dropped his gaze toward the floor.

"And so?" he asked softly.

"And so the choice that is left to us, Johnny, is to leave."

"Now?"

"Right now! This very night."

"It's mighty cold out there, Ruby."

"Well, it *has* stopped snowing, so likely the storm has passed. But storm or not, cold or not, that is my decision. Johnny Phips, I intend to spend the rest of my life at your side."

John Phips sighed. "Faith, Ruby me lass, but ye are a determined one. It's no wonder that William is the same. The poor lad had no choice in his life, no choice at all."

"I know that." Ruby smiled through her drying tears. "I've always known that. But neither, I think, do any of us; at least if we want to serve the Lord and live righteous lives. For fifty years I've tried to do that, Johnny, and I've a feeling that the Lord is about to reward me for it."

"Well, if this old man who sits at your stove is the reward, Ruby me lass, then ye've been sadly short-changed."

Ruby giggled like a little girl. "Likely," she agreed. "But it's too late to change my mind. I want to write Willy a note, and then I'll be ready."

John looked up. "Say, do you think I should write him a message, too?"

"Johnny, I think that would be wonderful."

"Well, lass, fetch us each a pen and paper, and let's be after it before the night grows any later."

And smiling, Ruby hastened to comply.

Chapter 25

The pre-dawn night was cold and still when John rose from his writing and walked to Ruby's side.

"It looks cold out there," he said quietly. "Real cold."

"It does," Ruby agreed, "but the wind has stopped, and the snow, so I think the storm is over. These October storms look just awful, though they never have any teeth in them. Are you ready, Johnny?"

"The two valises are in the back seat of the Oldsmobile. Doesn't take a man like me very long to pack."

Ruby laughed. "I don't need much, either. I have my letter written to Willy. We can pack these quilts around us for warmth, and that should do it."

"Did you make these yourself?" John asked, admiring the fine stitching in the quilts.

"I did."

"You do beautiful work, Ruby. I've never seen better, especially this yellow star quilt. They look real warm, too."

"Thank you."

"Ruby . . . I don't know whether to leave my note to Willy or not."

"Why not?" Ruby asked, puzzled.

"I don't know. I just have a funny feeling about it. I think I'll take it along and mail it when we get to—"

"Don't say it, sweetheart. The walls have ears, you know."

John laughed. "All right, I won't. But I think I'll mail it from there."

The clock struck five, and in the light from the solitary lantern, John and Ruby looked at each other.

"Are you sure you want to do this?" John asked quietly.

"More sure than I could ever say, Johnny. There isn't any other way left for us."

"I suppose you're right. I just wish you didn't have to leave your home and family."

"You forget, sweetheart. *You're* my family now."

"Yeah, I do forget. Well, me fair and garjus darlin', bundle up and let's get after it."

Blowing out the lantern and opening the door, they both gasped at the savage bite of the cold air. For an instant they hesitated on the back porch, wondering. But then, because each understood that a decision had been made, even long ago, and that there were no choices left to them, the couple took the quilts and Ruby's treasured teakwood box and made their way out to the automobile.

"Sure wish we had a team and wagon," John growled as he worked at the crank. "If this contraption breaks down or gets stuck in the snow, we'll be in serious trouble. I don't know the first thing about fixing it."

"Where's your faith, Johnny? We just need to pray ourselves across the dry farms to the railroad and everything will be fine. It's less than five miles. We'll get there without any trouble at all."

"I shurely hope so, me darlin'. Faith and I do."

Once the automobile was started, which because of the cold took several minutes, Ruby bundled up with her sweetheart. Then she watched with a feeling of trepidation as the darkened outline of her home receded into the darkness behind them.

The snow had fallen to the depth of six inches, with small drifts here and there that were much deeper. By the time the laboring Oldsmobile Special had inched its way westward, down into and then up out of the bottom of the deep wash known as Dry Creek and onto the gently rolling land that stretched westward to the railroad, John and Ruby knew they were in for a battle.

The road was difficult because of the snow, almost impossible, and John was straining every inch of the way just to keep the automobile on the road.

"Ruby me love," he muttered as he fought the vibrating steering wheel, "this is a bad trail, rougher than a polygamist's beard. And to tell you the truth, I'm worried."

"So am I, Johnny. But the Oldsmobile is doing fine, and that climb out of Dry Creek Wash is the worst part of the journey. We're already on top of it, so maybe things will be all right."

"I hope so, me darlin'. I just have a bad feeling. I'm not strong like I once was, and my leg is so game I can hardly use it."

"Stuff and nonsense, honey. You do just fine. You're just worried about me because I've become such a weak old sister."

"Well, I am at that. But Ruby, that sky looks bad. If the storm starts in again, we're likely to be in severe trouble."

"It won't, Johnny. These fall storms always pass quickly. We'll be fine. Three more miles and we'll be at the railroad, and then the elements can rage and conspire against us all they want. We'll be on our way to a land where the sun always shines, and where people in love never quarrel."

"I admire your optimism, Ruby. I surely do."

But as much as optimism usually counts in the lives of good people, on that day it came up to bat and went down swinging in the lives of Ruby Alder and John William Phips. Optimism was a strike-out all the way.

Forty minutes after they had left home, and less than a mile out of Dry Creek Wash and onto the dry farms, John Phips's worst fears were borne out. Blind and black and suffocating as the inside of a hard-tied gunnysack, the gale raged down off the top of Windy Ridge. All landmarks were lost within minutes, all human instincts confused and useless shortly thereafter. It was a ground-blizzard such as neither of the two had ever seen.

In spite of the unbelievable conditions, John managed to keep the open-topped Oldsmobile moving for another ten minutes. But then the sturdy automobile slammed into a six-foot drift that had been all but invisible until the moment of impact. And from that moment on, the motorcar went no further.

Within minutes, the engine compartment filled with drifting snow. Then the inside of the automobile began filling, and in her heart Ruby felt a terrible, sinking feeling of doom.

"Ruby, me darlin'," Johnny shouted into the wind, "we've got troubles, you and I."

"What . . . what are we going to do?"

"I don't know. Let's get down on the lee of this motorcar, get under these blankets, and make a decision. One thing's for certain—this outfit isn't going anywhere very soon."

Quickly the two climbed under the meager shelter of the motorcar, where the engine still radiated a little heat. Then they pulled their quilts in after them, wrapped themselves together, and did their best to protect each other from the cruelty of the wind.

But, as though conditions were not already bad enough, the elements became worse, unleashing their fury with unparalleled vengeance.

The winds struck with the nerve-shredding suddenness of a hysterical woman's scream, and then they didn't let up. Thirty seconds after the first shriek, the wind was shaking the open Oldsmobile like a winter-starved bear shakes a spring shoat by the neck.

For three straight hours John and Ruby huddled together, while outside the quilts there was nothing but wild, strangling wind. Then, about nine o'clock in the morning, with the two old people still welded by common insomnia beneath the motorcar in their darkened, quilt cocoon, the snow began again.

"W-well, *Wasiya* is h-howling today," John stammered through chattering teeth.

"W-Wasiya?" Ruby asked as she pressed her shaking body against the old man's frail form.

"S-Sioux winter giant, honey. The Indian b-blizzard god. Ruby, we're in trouble, and we're in trouble deep. It's light out, the storm is getting worse instead of better, and I don't see any alternative but to walk for it. Otherwise we'll never be found."

"No, J-Johnny. We're b-better off s-staying here. I heard Jacob Beck tell the s-story of one morning finding a strange mound of s-snow in the road near his home. Upon investigation he found a f-family who had been caught in one of these s-storms. They had turned their wagon upside down and had c-crawled under it, and for an entire night had weathered the b-blizzard. After he fed them a hearty breakfast they were f-fit as f-fiddles and went their way."

"Ruby, we c-can't turn your Oldsmobile upside down."

"M-maybe not, but we surely can't go out in that."

"Not *we,* Ruby. Me."

"No, sir, John Phips. You w-walk and I'll be right in your tracks. We're in this together; we'll g-get out of it together."

In spite of their predicament, John grinned. "You'll d-do, Ruby lass. You'll do."

For an hour longer the two huddled together, praying and hoping that something would change. But if it did, it was only the degree of cold and misery they were feeling. That truly became worse. Finally, obviously unable to bear the thoughts of doing nothing any longer, John shook the quilts and struggled out of them.

"S-so we're going?" Ruby asked.

"I think we'd better, Ruby. Otherwise we'll f-freeze right here. You ready?"

"Ready as I-I'll ever be."

Working the rest of the way out from beneath the storm-battered automobile, John stood up against the tearing wind and helped Ruby to her feet.

"I'll bet it's ten below, by holy Michal O'Murphy!" John shouted into the gale. "Shure, and it's the divil's own beauty of a drop for but the fourth week in October!"

"With the wind, it's likely c-colder than that," Ruby agreed, shouting hoarsely. "Which way sh-should we go?"

"Only one way *to* go, Ruby, We go back."

"But Johnny, they'll catch you! They'll c-catch you, sure."

"And we'll both be alive."

"I won't be, Johnny. If you're t-taken away from me again, I'll die."

"What are ye sayin', lass?"

"I'm s-saying the railroad's to the west, our freedom's to the west, and th-that's the way we've got to g-go. Besides, we're a lot closer to that railroad depot than we are to my home."

For a long moment John stood silently while the wind tore at him and the snow pelted his wrinkled face.

"Ye always were a stubborn one, lass," he finally declared. "But

I can see that ye're likely right, as well. If that's your wish, Ruby girl, then to the r-railroad we'll go."

Wrapping themselves in the snow-covered quilts, the two travelers broke their way through the giant snow drift that had stopped the Oldsmobile. And then they pushed westward against the fury of the storm. John took nothing with him but the woman he loved; but beneath her blanket, Ruby clutched her precious teakwood box of treasures.

For the better part of an hour they staggered forward, falling, rising, falling again. Their worn-out bodies, working feverishly, ached with the dull throb of bruised and battered muscle and bone. Yet somehow they were able, again and again, to get their hands under them and push themselves to their feet.

John, his one eye closed by the battering he had taken, and his other a mere slit for the same reason, pulled Ruby along, his exposed hand literally frozen to her blanket. His other hand, the one he felt and pawed his way forward with, was swollen out of shape and beaten so badly by the packed snow that it resembled an animal's withered claw.

Often the two stopped and gasped for breath, and yet just as often they pushed forward once more, the will to live strong within them.

Finally coming to the edge of a high, hard-packed drift, the two dragged themselves to the top. But then Ruby's legs gave way and she fell back, her chin hitting the ground so heavily that a thousand lights exploded in her brain. After a minute, however, she tried to climb the drift again, this time digging her fingers into the grainy snow and pulling herself upward.

Doing so took all the strength she had, and on the top of the drift she lay exhausted, her eyes almost shut, her ears barely able to hear Johnny's whispered words of encouragement.

"Johnny," she cried suddenly, "I-I'm going blind."

"So am I, R-Ruby me darlin'. It's the wind and the cold."

"Can . . . can you see anything at all?" she gasped.

"I can't. I'm blind as a weanling cave bat, Ruby. Worse, I don't know if these old legs can go much further."

"But we've . . . we've got to keep going, Johnny."

"I know, sweetheart. I know. Only . . . I can't see!"

The pure panic of John's blindness set him wild, then, and Ruby watched in amazement as John, growling with anger, dug at his eyes, scooped up fresh snow and scrubbed them out, beat them crazily with the heel of his knotted fists. But nothing happened. Not a glimmer broke through. Not a shadow or shape nor a sound of movement showed anywhere about him. It was true! He could not see!

But the terrible realization acted quickly as its own sedative, and within seconds John was sitting quietly again, holding tightly to Ruby's hand, thinking.

"Ruby," he spoke quietly, "th-this blindness isn't permanent. I had a puppy once that got k-kicked by a horse. It stumbled around for a week, blind as could be, before its sight came back. Then I heard about an Oglala Sioux brave who got lost in a blizzard. For f-five days he was lost, and when the camp found him he was walking in empty circles five hundred yards away, out of his head and stone-blind. Three days and he was good as new."

"So th-there's hope?"

"Not hardly; not unless we f-find some shelter. The way I see it, we've got less than that in hours, Ruby lass. The storm's too bad, and we've way too f-far to go. It looks bleak, mighty bleak."

Numbly Ruby absorbed what John had said. And he was right. She knew it, and she knew too that the only shelter between them and the railroad was in the lee of such drifts as the one behind which they crouched.

The cold of the snow and wind seeped into their very bones, and they sat huddled together, shaking uncontrollably. A drop of blood fell from John's nose, congealing instantly as a crimson spot on the snow. In John's blindness, however, he did not see it, and so Ruby didn't say anything.

Struggling desperately, John finally got his hands under him, growled at his own weakness, and then began to crawl. Ruby did her best to follow, and the two went perhaps a dozen feet before they collapsed again, almost simultaneously, into the white and blinding snow.

"R-Ruby," John gasped, working his body around toward the

woman whose very life depended on his own. "Ruby, me garjus d-darlin', our only hope is to hole up and pray. I'm down and dead as a swallowed mouse in a horned owl's belly, and I can go no further. Lass, I'm thinking yer not much . . . better off."

"Johnny, I c-can still crawl. See, I—"

And then Ruby cried out in pain.

"What is it, Ruby? *What is it?*"

"My . . . my leg, Johnny. I . . . I can't use it. For years it's been giving me fits, and n-now when I need it most, it's gone. Oh, Johnny . . ."

"W-well," he chattered as he settled back into the snow, "faith and we're shure a c-couple of stove-up old fogies, ain't we?"

Ruby, her lips cracked and bleeding, did her best to smile in return. "We are, Johnny. W-we surely are."

In silence, John gently pushed Ruby down into the snow beside him, and then he began to scoop snow up around her.

"Wh-what are you doing?"

"We'll hole up right here, Ruby. We've no ch-choice, so we'll hole up and pray. The good Lord is bound to send somebody along."

"But we'll f-freeze."

"Then like you said, we'll do it together. Here, you put my coat on, and we'll wrap ourselves around with both of these blankets. If I can get on top of you so that we can k-keep each other warm, why, we'll be fine."

Without protesting, Ruby accepted the instructions and burrowed deeper into the lee side of the drift. John, struggling out of his coat, wrapped it around her. Then he pulled the blankets over them both, tucked them under as best he could, and in their darkness snuggled up against her.

"I-I've been wanting to do th-this for an awful long time," he muttered.

"W-why didn't you s-say so?"

"Bashful, I reckon. Always h-have been."

"I don't c-care much for bashful fellows."

"Faith, and now I remember."

"Y-you do not."

"Do so. B-best of all, I recollect the night we first kissed, after that p-picnic down on Cedar Hill. It was you kissed me; d-do you remember?"

"I kissed you?" Ruby questioned. "Why, what an impertinant soul you are, Johnny Phips. D-don't you ever change?"

"There! You so m-much as admitted it. I'm glad you finally did. It'll be good for your soul."

The two lay silently then, each of their minds playing with things long past, as their bodies welcomed the warmth of each other.

"Well, me darlin'," John finally said, "you'll get used to my bashfulness, I promise. Given eternity, you're bound to."

There was another silence then beneath the quilts, a long silence broken only by the screeching of the wind and the ragged breathing of the elderly couple.

"J-Johnny, are . . . are you afraid to die?"

The silence lengthened, and Ruby wondered if John Phips had heard. Finally, however, he answered, his voice deep and rasping, and sounding very far away.

"Afraid, me lass? No . . . not anymore. Not now that I have found you and your love again."

"Does that really make a . . . a difference?"

"More than I c-can say. But still, long ago the Lord and I became friends, and many is the day when I have ached to end this mortal hour and greet him face-to-face. If today's to be the day for it, then I am content."

"That . . . that's w-wonderful, Johnny. I f-feel the same. Long ago I stopped carrying my burdens in my heart. But I've wondered, for so very long, when Brother Wells's promise would be fulfilled."

"You remember it too?"

"It . . . it's the only thing I *do* remember, Johnny. Do you realize that we've had another week together, just as he promised?"

"Well, the man *was* a prophet."

"Do . . . do you think that the end of this week signals the end of our lives, Johnny?"

"I don't know. Brother Wells never said that."

"But it might be that our deaths mark the final fulfillment of that promise."

John Phips was silent for a moment. Finally, with a twisted grin, he spoke.

"Should that be the case, Ruby me lass, your dreams of flying will come true. And you won't need a flying machine, either."

"Only if I go up, Johnny. What if I go down? What if I haven't . . . haven't fully repented?"

"You have, Ruby. We both have. And should we cross over that old river between this life and the next, me darlin', I can't imagine anyone I'd rather make the journey with."

"Oh, Johnny. Do you . . . really mean that?"

"All my life I've wanted to say those words. I th-thank God that I have found you, and that I can say them n-now."

"But . . . but what about all the th-things we were going to do?"

"Ah, Ruby, me lass. We'll do them. W-we have all of eternity stretching before us. You know, the only thing that has ever really mattered to me, in all my years of living, is that I find my way back to you. Now, at long and eternity-deep last, that for which I have sought and hungered above all else has been g-granted me. I have f-found the woman with whom I will share the brilliant fires and faraway nights of eternity, and . . . and with whom I will listen in the celestial springtime to the wild cry of the warm south wind as it sings to us the eternal song of love."

"K-kiss me, Johnny," Ruby whispered faintly. "Please hold me t-tight and kiss me."

And so, wrapped tightly in the arms of each other's eternal love, John Phips and Ruby Alder, together again at last, kissed each other . . . hello.

Epilogue

The afternoon sun streamed warmly through the window, and dust particles drifted aimlessly in and out of the shafts of light, dancing separately, lonely. The Regulator clock beat a steady cadence for the dust dance, and it was joined by the rapid dripping of water, muted through the thick walls of the home. The snow was melting fast, and by morning it would be gone, leaving miles of mud as the only testament of the snow's passing.

Will Alder sat silently in his mother's old horsehair rocker, aware of the dust and the sun and the clock and the dripping water, but moved by none of it. His wife, Flora, sat across from him, crocheting quietly, and Allyson was in the parlor, reading.

In his hand, Will held a hastily written note, penned by his mother, and though he had read it many times, he still could not understand. Yet even now, it dominated his thoughts.

What had possessed her? Why would a perfectly sensible woman go hightailing it off into a blizzard with a man like John Phips? It made no sense to him, and until it did, he wasn't about to let go of it.

And John Phips. Imagine that old man being an undercover detective. The wire from Burns Detective Agency had come early that morning, and Will still had a difficult time grasping its contents. Why, all along that old man had been trying to protect him. In spite of how badly he, Will Alder, had treated him, John Phips had gone quitely about his business, and in the end he had used his mother and even that screwy Ferdinand Burroughs to apprehend the anarchists.

To say that he felt silly would have been an understatement; to say that he felt terrible, now that they had found his mother and the old man, would have been even worse. Good grief! Why did men persist in making such fools of themselves? Why—

Footsteps in the doorway made him look up, and as the doctor came into the kitchen, Will rose to his feet.

"Well," the doctor said as he washed his hands, "I've done what I could. Now it's prayer time."

"Doc, will she . . . Is she . . ."

"Oh, your mother's fine, Will. By giving her his coat and snuggling down on top of her, that old man saved her life."

"I know, and I can hardly comprehend it. But after all, he dragged her out there—"

"Ruby wasn't dragged," Flora stated quietly, "and you know it, Will. Remember that letter, and the wire this morning. She went of her own free will, and she wanted to go."

"But *why,* Flora? Detective or not, I don't understand why she was so attracted to that man!"

"I don't know why either. But he was likable, and she had known him from a long time back. Maybe they were once in love."

"Mother and John Phips? Flora, that is preposterous. If it were so, I'd surely have heard about it."

"Maybe not," Allyson declared as she walked into the room. "I've had a couple of beaus that I won't ever tell *anybody* about."

"Allyson—"

"Well, I have! And just because Grandma is seventy and I'm not, doesn't change anything. She told me herself that age doesn't change how we feel about such things. I'll bet she and Johnny were sweethearts a long time ago, and—"

"Allyson," Will said quietly, "I don't think you should pursue that line of thought. We have no way of knowing anyway, and—"

"Why don't you ask her?" the doctor asked from the hallway.

Will Alder's head snapped up. "Ask her? You mean . . ."

The doctor grinned. "That's right. She's awake. But Will, she's weak, so don't talk for long."

"Willy?" Ruby gasped faintly as Will hurried in and sat down beside her on her bed. "Willy, is . . . is that you?"

"Mother," he cried. "It's me. *Yes!* And Flora and Allyson, too."

"Oh, Willy, take c-care of Johnny . . . He has been k-keeping me warm, and—"

"We know, Mother. And he's . . . he's being taken care of."

"Oh, thank the . . . the good Lord. He is s-such a good man."

"Here," the doctor interrupted. "Drink this, Mrs. Alder."

Straining, Ruby did her best to swallow the warm liquid.

"Mother," William asked as he took her frail and trembling hand into his own. "Where were you going? What—"

"Willy," she suddenly cried, her voice filled with understanding, "he's dead, isn't he."

"Mother, I don't think—"

"Willy . . . *tell me!*"

"No, Mother," William answered in the stillness of the storm-deadened October afternoon. "He isn't. But he's in a mighty bad way. He's in the other bedroom, and the doctor is doing all he can for him."

"Oh, Johnny!" Ruby wailed, turning away from her son. "N-not now! You c-can't leave me, not after all these years."

"Mother, you don't know how lucky we were to find you. Talk about a miracle! Another twenty or thirty minutes, and . . . and . . .

"Mother, *why* did you do this?"

"You d-don't know, do you Willy. I . . . I've tried to tell you a dozen times, and at least a thousand times I was . . . afraid to."

"Tell me what, Mother? I always listen to you. I always do."

With fumbling, bandaged fingers, Ruby pulled open the lid of her teakwood box of treasures, a box that Will had placed beside her on the bed when she had been carried in. Carefully, then, she took out the photograph that lay at the very top.

"Will, this is a photograph of your father and me on the . . . the day we were . . . married."

"But . . . but that isn't Father."

"But it is, Willy. It *is!* We were sealed by Brother Daniel H. Wells in the Endowment House in . . . in Salt Lake City. The date was March 23, 1862."

"You mean—"

"Yes, Willy. John William Phips, the man who saved my life

this morning, is . . . is the man in the photograph. You see, he signed each of our names at the bottom. John and Ruby Phips. He . . . he is your *father,* my dear. H-he is the man whose name you were given."

"That man is my *father?*" William asked incredulously. "But . . . but why didn't you *tell* me, Mother?"

"Oh, Willy, how can I say it? I . . . I . . ."

"Never mind, Mother. Don't say anything now. Just rest, and we will—"

"No, Willy," Ruby insisted energetically. "I can't rest. Not . . . not yet! I must tell you, so . . . so that you will understand. Johnny and I were . . . we went to be sealed to each other . . . *unworthily!* We knew we shouldn't do that, only . . . only we were so afraid and so . . . ashamed.

"But that night, after we had been sealed, we talked all night . . . and in the morning we sought out Brother Wells and told him of . . . of our unworthiness.

"Willy, we should have gone to our bishop and *not* to Salt Lake City and the Endowment House, just like folks come to you now when they need to repent. But travel was so hard, and we had already made the tragic mistake of going all the way to Salt Lake City and getting married unworthily. So, because we could not live with what we had done, Brother Wells, who was serving as second counselor to President Young, told us we could work out our repentance through him."

Bishop William Alder sat stunned, his mind reeling with the import of what he was hearing.

"So you were *married* to Phips?" he declared. "And besides, you . . . you . . ."

"Brother Wells did not . . . chastise us, Willy," Ruby continued, interrrupting her son. "Instead, he sent us out . . . and he went . . . before the Lord. A little later he called us back and commended us on our desire to . . . to come true before God and gain a measure of integrity. And . . . and then he gave Johnny his mission call."

"But how could he do that? Such a thing is not right."

"I know, Willy. It does seem contrary to the way things are done nowadays, sending a man on a mission before he has been cleansed by a time of sorrow and repentance. But Brother Wells was a prophet, and he had the right to speak for the Lord. He told us that this was the best thing we could do, at least in *our* case. Johnny's mission was to carry messages east and then to do as the brethren there directed him.

"I cried," Ruby continued, her voice more quiet. "But Brother Wells explained that it was . . . the Lord's will that we be given a week together and then be separated for a time so that both Johnny and I could learn about laws, and about . . . service. We had been terribly selfish when we had both known better, and a separation was the best way for Johnny and me to learn how to think of others. Brother Wells told us it was the price we had to pay.

"But he promised us that if we would both be t-true and faithful, that when our repentance had been completed and the Lord had forgiven us, we could forgive ourselves and each other, and then we would be reunited forever, with our eternal sealing still intact. He even said that someday we would . . . have another week together, if we were both worthy."

Ruby grimaced then, as her eyes closed, a tear working itself down her cheek. Will found himself aching with loneliness and with understanding, for he was certain that if he had known—

"Five more days we had together," Ruby continued, her eyes again opening. "Five of the happiest . . . and saddest days in my entire life. It was on the last of those five days, my dear son, that you . . . that you came into . . . being. Somehow I knew the exact moment when it happened, and I was not wrong."

"But . . . but Mother, I . . ."

Ruby, holding her weak and shaking hand up against her son's arm, stopped him, and then she continued, her voice strangely not quivering.

"Johnny left on his mission, Willy, and oh how I wept. And then, just six weeks later, and after receiving only three letters from him, he vanished. I learned from him only this past week that he had been wounded and mistakenly taken prisoner by the Confederacy. But back then, I didn't have any idea what had happened to him.

"When . . . when he never returned, Mr. Alder approached me.

He knew I was with child, and he and his first wife offered me a home. More importantly . . . he offered to be . . . your father. By then, of course, word had come back that Johnny had been killed, and I was almost past the grief of it. From what Brother Wells had told us, I was . . . certain that Johnny's death must have been the Lord's will, part of the price we had to pay, and the fulfillment of Brother Wells's prophecy.

"Thinking of your approaching birth," she concluded, smiling weakly up into her son's eyes, "I accepted Mr. Alder's offer. Both of us, Willy, thought it best that you look upon him as your real father. Besides, I . . . I was *so* ashamed! And that's . . . that's why you were never told."

"But when I was grown, Mother? Why not then?"

"I . . . I don't know. Somehow it never seemed quite time. I was always going to tell you, but I was worried for Mr. Alder's feelings, and I *knew* how . . . how disappointed you would be in me.

"But Johnny Phips, your *f-father,* loved you, Willy. More than life itself, he loved you. And he was so proud of all you have become. In . . . in his coat is a letter he penned for you last night. We were going to mail it . . . later. I think . . . I think you will enjoy it."

Without reply, William Alder stood and walked to the other bedroom. There he reached into John Phips's coat and retrieved the folded letter. This he brought back to Ruby's room and carefully read, and then read again.

"Oh, Mother," he cried, his tears suddenly released from where they had been held for so very long. "Until today I . . . I didn't *know*. I didn't *understand.*"

"He knew that, Willy, and that is why—"

"Ruby, me lass?"

Spinning, William was shocked to see John Phips leaning against the doorjamb, his face looking rough and haggard.

"Mr. Phips—"

"Faith, lad, but ye look like ye have seen a ghost."

"Mr. Phips, Mother just told me. I didn't know, and—"

"Johnny," Ruby cried as she pulled off her quilts and staggered to his side. "Johnny William Phips, you get back in bed this instant!"

"In bed? But lass, I thought ye wanted to fly. Hadn't we ought to be about finding us one of those new-fangled flying machines?"

"This is no time to be funning us, Johnny Phips. Now back in bed with yer haythun soul! I won't have you—"

"Oh, yes ye will, me garjus, darlin' lass. Ye'll have me forever, I'm thinkin'."

"Yes, yes, of course," Ruby whispered as she drew within his arms.

"And you, Bishop? If you'll have me—"

"Us," Ruby corrected quickly.

"That's right. If William will have *us*—"

"Have you?" Will Alder declared as he dropped John's letter and strode toward them. "Have you? Just let me get my arms around both of you, and you'll know the answer to that. I'm famous for my bear hugs, and if one of them isn't large enough to encompass a mother *and* a father, then my name isn't Will Alder Phips."

And with that, Ruby's boy Willy took his parents in his arms and squeezed, while his wife and daughter stood beaming, ready to join in.

And thus Ruby's seven days, as they had been promised by a prophet of God some fifty years before, were again, happily and fruitfully, fulfilled.

Historical Note

While the preceding story is fictional, and is based at least in part upon a dream Brent had in the spring of 1986, much of what was written is actual history.

American Fork and Highland, Utah, were as they are described. The businesses were owned and operated by the people named in the story. Civic and Church leaders, with the exception of the fictitious Bishop Alder, served as stated. The Alpine Stake Tabernacle cornerstone was dedicated October 24, 1910, by Elder Orson F. Whitney. Telephone and power lines were strung throughout the city between 1888 and 1889. Water rights from the creek that issued from American Fork Canyon—rights divided between American Fork, Pleasant Grove, Lehi, and the latecomer, Highland City—were still being settled in 1910 by armed sheriff's posses, and in 1905 a franchise was granted to B. Mahler to operate an interurban railroad through the streets of American Fork City, though it was never built.

American Fork Canyon was the scene of virtually all the activity that Ruby related to John. Mines gave forth precious metals from 1870 onward, lumber was an important industry from even before that time, and grazing followed soon after. The cities of Deer Creek and Forest City flourished; and Grave Yard Flat, the building terraces, and the charcoal kilns at Forest City are still visible today.

George Tyng struck it rich in Miller Hill, and the story of his encounter with the General Authority is, at the very least, commonly known folklore.

The railroad out of the canyon ran daily for six years, carrying supplies and tourists into the canyon, and ore and tourists back out.

Today, over a hundred years after it was abandoned, the old railroad bed still crops up in places, and even forms a hill in Blaine's front yard.

On the national scene, Theodore Roosevelt was president of the United States, the Gibson girls drawn by Charles Dana Gibson were the models that all American girls tried to emulate, automobiles were available, and flying machines were just coming into their own. The offices of the *Los Angeles Times,* which opposed organized labor, were bombed October 1, 1910. The McNamara brothers were eventually arrested for the bombing, though the book's description of the Utah episode of their career is fictitious. Attorney Clarence Darrow did defend the brothers, and he would have gotten them off had it not been for the extensive investigative work of Detective Burns, founder of Burns Detective Agency. Because of the evidence Burns compiled in secret, the McNamara brothers, in the middle of their trial, confessed, and were sentenced accordingly. Burns went on to become, in 1921, head of the Federal Bureau of Investigation.

James Y. Johnson, the pigeon rancher in Los Angeles, was the authors' great-grandfather. At the time of this story, he was actually in Los Angeles running the huge pigeon ranch and going under his "Johnson" alias to avoid prosecution for polygamy. Wyatt Earp was also in Los Angeles at the time, and all details of his famous gunfight at the OK Corral, including time and date, are accurate according to the most current research.

Even the storm described in the story is historically correct, though it did not happen in 1910. According to meteorologist Mark Eubank of Weatherbank, Inc., in Salt Lake City, the storm swept out of the Gulf of Alaska and into Utah the week of October 23, 1984, dumping twenty-three inches of snow in various Utah County locations, including the Highland Bench, during one twenty-four-hour period.